THE HARD DRUG CHRONICLES

COCAINE
SPEED
HEROIN

THE HARD DRUG CHRONICLES

THE COCAINE CHRONICLES | EDITED BY GARY PHILLIPS & JERVEY TERVALON
THE SPEED CHRONICLES | EDITED BY JOSEPH MATTSON
THE HEROINE CHRONICLES | EDITED BY JERRY STAHL

NO EXIT PRESS

First published in the UK in 2013 by No Exit Press,
an imprint of Oldcastle Books Ltd, PO Box 394,
Harpenden, Herts, AL5 1XJ, UK
noexit.co.uk
© NO EXIT PRESS
© *A Hard Drugs Tale* by Howard Marks

Originally published in the USA by Akashic Books as;
The Cocaine Chronicles Edited by Gary Phillips & Jervey Tervalon, 2005, 2011
The Speed Chronicles Edited by Joseph Mattson, 2011
The Heroin Chronicles Edited by Jerry Stahl, 2013

The Cocaine Chronicles, *The Speed Chronicles* and *The Heroin Chronicles* are available as
seperate ebooks in the UK

A CIP catalogue record for this book is available from the British Library.

This is a work of fiction. Names, characters, places, and incidents either are the product
of the author's imagination or are used fictitiously, and any resemblance to actual persons,
living or dead, businesses, companies, events or locales is entirely coincidental.

ISBN 978-1-84344-192-2
2 4 6 8 10 9 7 5 3 1

Printed and bound by CPI Group (UK) Ltd, Croydon, CR0 4YY
For more information about Crime Fiction go to @crimetimeuk

CONTENTS

AND BY WAY OF INTRODUCTION

A HARD DRUGS TALE

A NEW STORY BY HOWARD MARKS

HOWARD MARKS was born in 1945 in Kenfig Hill, a small Welsh coal-mining village near Bridgend, Howard Marks attended Oxford University where he earned a degree in nuclear physics and post graduate qualifications in history and philosophy of science.

Described by the *Daily Mail* as 'the most sophisticated drugs baron of all time', Howard Marks was recruited by MI6, and has been connected with the Mafia, the IRA, and the CIA.

Busted in 1988 by the American Drug Enforcement Administration and sentenced to twenty-five years at America's toughest federal penitentiary; Terre Haute, Indiana. He was released on parole in 1995 after serving seven years.

In 1996 he released his autobiography, *Mr Nice*, which remains an international best seller in several languages.

It was a typical night at eighty year old Tadcu Taliesin's terraced house. In the living room, Tadcu was smoking a pipe of Mango Haze and drinking Horlicks. Bernie and Gwyn, Tadcu's grandson, were attempting to identify some white powder, a friend's gift, which they hoped was cocaine. They snorted some. The music was blasting, distorting from the speakers positioned on the floor. Gwyn and Bernie sat about, smoked, ranted, and waited for the drug to hit. An hour passed. Boredom and frustration set in.

'This was supposed to be strong,' said Gwyn, the taller, better looking one of the two, 'I say we do the rest, I'm just not getting anything.'

Conversation was not happening either. Bernie's mouth betrayed him. He tried talking, but all that came out was the same strange slurping noise. His mouth and surrounding facial area was numb. Teeth grinded and his head started to buzz like someone had just shoved a vibrator up his nose.

The music sounded drunk, and then it stopped. The sudden realisation of such abrupt silence shook them, and a case of the screaming shits propelled Bernie into the toilet. He looked into the bowl and gazed at what he interpreted as his lower digestive system. Everywhere was splattered with blood, and he had an incredibly empty feeling where his arsehole used to be. He stared down more intently at a landscape that could appear only on a Mott the Hoople album cover. He pulled the chain and walked out, disgusted.

'No! I don't want that. Is this all I get after all these years of loyalty, fucking Mott the Hoople album covers? This is definitely not cocaine. Let's call it a night, Gwyn. Your Tadcu's fallen asleep. We would have been better off sniffing his fucking Horlicks.'

Gwyn Jones and Bernie Jones were not related, but they were almost precisely the same age, came from the same South Wales mining village, and had known each other since birth. The lads shared a love of fine Indie music, high purity cocaine, and women well out of their league. Gwyn had attended Cardiff University, earning himself a respectable degree in chemistry. He was bright but a little naïve about several matters. Bernie had been to Carmarthen Art College. He was a good artist and graphic designer, a little mutated by his vast intake of narcotics, but good nevertheless. However, he had an unrealistically high opinion of his own abilities in other areas and no sense of his own limitations, which were considerable. Neither of them had ever even tried to put their different talents to any conventional use: they worked as 'ticket men,' delivery boys for the Bridgend area's local crime boss, David 'Dai Sly' Davies. The local economy, generally, as in so many other South Wales valley communities, was based upon drugs, benefit scams, and backstreet webcam porn operations.

Dai Sly owned Gomorrah, the local massage parlour, often the only place open in the area. A gigantic, garish red and blue neon sign flashed on and off outside, and the road was constantly filled with parked, relatively new, saloon cars. An S/M dungeon, which Dai Sly hired out for pornographic movie shoots, filled the basement and was presided over by rubber-clad 'Evil Bethan', the local dominatrix. At least three times a week, the Jones Boys went to Gomorrah, and picked up supplies of cocaine, speed, and other drugs to deliver to Dai's local associates. Invariably, the Jones boys cheated Dai Sly by cutting the cocaine, selling it sideways to their mates, and using it to lever shags from local girls with easy reputations. The Joneses' sole visible redeeming feature was to supply Tadcu Taliesin with free marijuana to relieve his arthritis and glaucoma. But even that good deed was double-edged: the boys used Tadcu's terraced house as a stash and an ideal safe location to adulterate the cocaine while the old man delivered lengthy stoned narratives about his younger days. As far as the boys were concerned, marijuana was for the people, and cocaine was for milking the rich.

Feedback to Dai Sly on the quality of his cocaine was far from good. His wholesale supplier always provided high purity, and although Dai Sly would step on it a bit, he did so conscientiously, diluting it with a small percentage of acceptable adulterants such as benzocaine, lignocaine, and phenacetin always mixed in the same precise proportions. Dai Sly reached the inescapable conclusion that the Jones boys were at it. He decided to have them tailed.

Gwyn, with his dwindling knowledge of chemistry, almost always did the cutting, but one hot summer evening in 2003 when he was concentrating on a sexual adventure, he left both the tasks of giving Tadcu his weed and of cutting the cocaine in Bernie's hands. It was a foolish decision. Bernie used the wrong agent, a type of bicarbonate powder that began foaming on contact with moisture, and he was far too stoned to realise what he'd done: he was concentrating on Tadcu Taliesin's tale of when he was a member of the South Wales Miners Federation group of soldiers, the largest contingent within the British Battalion of the International Brigades in the Spanish Civil War. The story involved Tadcu's saving of a leading Andalucian family member from a Republican death squad. Bernie was much taken by the story but thought the grandfather was describing a new Xbox game.

'That's a new one, like is it?' asked Bernie when the tale

drew to a close.

'No boy, that all actually happened, as God is my judge,' answered Tadcu.

'I look forward to watching it on DVD,' said Bernie, switching his understanding to thinking he'd been hearing a description of a war film.

Later the same evening, the boys began their rounds, making drops of the bicarbonated gear to a series of local characters. Gwyn and Bernie, like all cocaine dealers, were invariably late but executed their transactions obviously and quickly, which was often the best way. They were done in less than 30-seconds. As usual, they got distracted at a girl's basement flat and began partying, aided considerably by the girl's kind offer of dabs of MDMA. Bernie danced while the music seemed good, if you can call what he did dancing: his arse stuck out, and he jigged from one rubbery leg to the other, making fists in random directions, resembling a Hitler youth with St Vitus' dance.

As Bernie left the flat's toilet for what he remembered as the last time that night, something snapped inside: the feeling when, even before he had finished doing it, he already knew that was the line he had just crossed over. And now it was only going to get worse. No matter how hard he tried to salvage the night, each action would just makes things worse. And no amount of class-A drugs would drag him from the brink of total destruction.

Bernie was right. Stumbling up the steps out of the basement, unable to walk or even open a car door, he and Gwyn attempted to clamber into a car that looked like it hadn't seen an MOT certificate for five years. Both boys were jumped on by Dai Sly's enforcers and taken back to the S/M dungeon. Dai Sly took back the cocaine, not realising it had already been cut.

'I'll fucking teach you not to bosh my gear and fuck up my

reputation. You'll never deal in the Bridgend area ever again. Just disappear to some other shithole, you understand me? But to help you on your way to find a new career, I'll make you into movie stars. Every wanker in the valleys will soon be watching you.'

The boys were tied up on the racks, and Evil Bethan got to work on them. Dai Sly, filming each stroke of the whip with his video camera, took a hit from the gear. The dodgy cutting agent reacted with moisture, and he began foaming profusely from his nose. Seeing him panting and down on all fours, Evil Bethan turned her attentions to Dai Sly.

'Want some as well, do you Dai? It will be my pleasure, yet again.'

She began using him as her bitch.

'Stop it, Bethan,' cried Gwyn, 'Can't you see Dai's having an epileptic fit? And cut us loose for Christ's sake!'

Grabbing the video camera containing the tape of Evil Bethan whipping the three of them, the boys made it outside, only to find out their earlier customers were already out on the streets, their noses foaming from the dodgy gear, and searching for the boys. They were all wandering about like a scene from Night of the Living Dead. After a long chase, the boys finally made good their escape out of the South Wales valleys down to Plymouth and took the next morning's 24 hour ferry to Santander. Diazepam enabled them to sleep through the entire journey. Then they hitch-hiked to Andalucía.

After buying a second hand tent and other basic essentials, Gwyn and Bernie stopped to lay low at an extremely cheap camp site near the Bay of Gibraltar. They pitched the tent, took the rest of their diazepam, and slept like babies.

The next morning, why the place was so cheap and why there were so few other campers about soon became apparent.

The site was in the middle of a hunting trail used by trigger-happy local villagers and their dogs. Alongside was a truck stop with big rigs pulling in and out, and the drivers tended to use the camp site as a large open-air toilet. One of the rigs was loaded with ten foot high figures of Diego Maradona but didn't seem to be going anywhere. Pitched next to the lads was Pedro, a deadbeat wino. He told them about rumours of a big cat at large in the surrounding hills. Apparently several wild animals had escaped from a nearby private zoo and had begun breeding in the wild. Dead chickens and sheep had been found in the area. He advised them not to wander about after dark.

Gwyn and Bernie began getting paranoid and hearing shrieks of wild animals, even though it was only midday. Their misery was made worse by the presence a short distance down the hill of Dutch John. With his large Winnebago and state-of-the-art barbecue, Dutch John was the daddy of the site, and his pitch was a magnet for attractive young girls. Bernie, against Gwyn's advice, went down to chance his luck, while Gwyn stayed guarding the tent. One of the girls briefly toyed with Bernie for her amusement and then spiked his drink. Bernie passed out. While he was asleep, the Dutch crew took off his clothes and left him out in a nearby field. He awoke naked to find a spaniel-like dog licking his face. He chased it off and made his dazed way back up the hill, the dog following at a distance. It was a scrawny stray, abandoned, presumably, by the hunters from the village. Gwyn was highly sceptical of Bernie's story and utterly convinced that Bernie had simply drugged himself unconscious, too selfish to bring back any of the drugs he had clearly taken to share. It wouldn't have been the first time.

While the boys were cooking their bangers and beans in the early evening, the dog returned, clearly hoping to be fed. They chased the dog off, but after a few minutes the dog came back with a yellow waterproof sealed packet. Bernie tore it open.

'Gwyn, it's coke, a bag full. There's got to be half a kilo here. Top quality stuff by the looks of it.'

Bernie racked up a couple of lines, the boys immediately lost their appetites, and the stray dog was allowed to stay for dinner.

A line of cocaine, both lads thought, wasn't really a line at all, it was just the start of a line, a much longer line. Have a snort, wait a bit, come up to an exhilarating place, and feel the optimism. Twenty minutes later, start plateauing, pure pleasure, total control. Then the feelings would start to dissolve. Before coming down, have another snort. Gwyn and Bernie were getting better at timing it so that the plateaus all joined up seamlessly. A snorted line was just the beginning: the real line was several feet long, stretching out from the first one at regular intervals, with its own rhythm. Just let it go to work, and it would last several hours. Then have a break from it.

As night was beginning to fall, Gwyn and Bernie tried to work out where the cocaine had come from. They pushed the yellow bag under the stray dog's nose, and followed it down to the mouth of a cave near the shore. Dutch John was there with a couple of the guys from the Winnebago carrying the same ten foot high figures of Diego Maradona that the boys had seen earlier out from the cave and lying them down on the beach. The men were walking a dog - a similar breed to their own stray - around the figures, allowing it to sniff them. Then they moved the figures up towards the rig. Their own dog yelped with excitement, tore off to join in the sniffing, and started running around the figures, barking furiously, Gwyn and Bernie reasoned they were too close to danger and decided to make a run for it. They lay low behind some gorse bushes for about an hour and then returned to the camp site.

When they arrived, Pedro told them that some men had just

come looking for them and had been searching through their tent. Most of their newly purchased kit, as well as other possessions, had been vandalised or nicked, including the video camera containing the tape of their and Dai Sly's shame. Manifesting admirable stoicism, they concentrated on not arguing with the universe and racked up an array of lines of cocaine.

At the truck stop the next morning, the Guardia Civil turned up. Dutch John and his crew were there looking tense. The stray dog had also joined the throng. As it approached the rig it began sniffing around the figures of Maradona and barking furiously. The boys watched as the police dogs sniffed in the same places and uncovered several of the same yellow waterproof packets from inside the hollow figures. Dutch John and his crew were handcuffed and bundled away protesting their innocence. Gwyn and Bernie crept unobtrusively back to their pitch. Pedro emerged from behind the bushes and joined them. He explained he had been watching events for a while. The figures of Maradona were part of a promotional campaign run by a European-wide supermarket chain and were made locally. Dutch John had stashed cocaine in the figures without the drivers' knowledge and de-stashed them when they reached Northern Europe. He had paid Pedro to spread the story about the big cat to keep campers away from the cave.

Gwyn and Bernie went into their tent, ostensibly to make an inventory of what had been stolen the day before, but actually to snort a few more lines. They could hear Pedro trying to befriend their dog so went outside and cornered him. Pedro explained he had a business opportunity for them involving the stray - a dog with a good nose was a valuable asset in the smuggling community. He pointed out how Dutch John's dog had not detected the smell while theirs had.

Pedro pointed to someone lying out on the terrace of a large beach villa nearby and explained that only a year ago that character, Tariq, was living rough on the beach like they were, but now he was a powerful operator. One morning he had looked out of his tent and had seen bales floating ashore: bales full of finest Moroccan hashish jettisoned, presumably, by a Zodiac about to be busted in the Gibraltar Straits by the Spanish authorities. Pedro explained the rules of the game: if any of the Zodiacs or other small power boats doing runs got spotted by the Spanish coast guards, they would have to dump their loads in the sea before they were allowed to return to Gibraltar waters. Gwyn's interest perked up, and he began to ask Pedro some sensible questions. Pedro said that on average every month at least two hundred kilos were discovered by beachcombers on the beaches from Tarifa to San Pedro de Alcantara. It was just a question of being in the right place at the right time.

Pedro went off to have some lunch and secure his tent, while Gwyn and Bernie took some more cocaine in theirs.

Gwyn and Bernie each consumed approximately the same daily quantity of cocaine. They shared many of the same reactions to the drug, but there were differences. The main effects on Gwyn were fourfold: it made him think he was shagging whatever female he was chatting to, rather than merely talking about himself, it made him want more cocaine, it made him realize how cheap everything else was, and it encouraged him to talk endlessly about new hair-brained, dangerous scams in meticulous detail. Bernie, on the other hand, was continually convinced cocaine could provide his entire being with instanta-⁜-neous happiness on a scale he had never dreamed of. Accordingly, the need for any event whatsoever dis-appeared and, with it, the need for expending great amounts of work, time, and energy to bring it about. Cocaine produced immediately in him a feeling of physical happiness psychically independent of all external events and deadened any feelings that might have aroused what psychologists called inhibition. Bernie became absolutely reckless, bounding with health, bubbling with high spirits, and incapable of worrying about anything. He would think dirty perverted thoughts, which invariably got him nowhere as a result of erectile dysfunction – the single major downside of the drug as far as he was concerned.

Pedro's information on the benefits of methodical beachcombing had triggered off possibilities of a new scam in Gwyn's mind.

'Bernie, what we should do is somehow get a pair of strong night-sight binoculars and a radio scanner and go up to the top of the Rock, where those baboons, chimps, or whatever the fuck they are live, and camp there. Remember Pedro said that's where the lookouts were in radio contact with Zodiacs. We could hack into the radio frequencies and follow the patterns of the crossings. Then we could work out the optimum interception points and the sheltered coves that are suitable for shallow water off-loading from the boats. The dog will be able to sniff out the drugs from the rubbish.'

'That's a banging idea, Gwyn. Shall we have another line?'

Gwyn went to work immediately and spent the next few hours studying the tide tables and weather forecasts that were posted along the sea shore. Then, they rented a Zodiac and did a few dummy runs, working out how long it took loads of different weights to come ashore, and at what points they came ashore. But by nightfall, the results were disappointing. All they came across were crates of old condoms, a boatload of sub-Saharan Africans and more of the hollow Diego Maradona figures, all empty. The lads were tired and had an early night. As a result of the cocaine they had consumed and the theft of their sleeping bags, their sleep was painfully short and massively uncomfortable.

The next day, Pedro took the lads and the dog to Tariq's villa nearby. The place had seen better days but was still grand and impressive. Gwyn's attention was caught by a girl languishing at the poolside. Pedro introduced the lads to Tariq, a tall Turkish heap of rippling muscle, and introduced the girl as his girlfriend Ilka. She was sleek, sophisticated, clearly trouble, and appeared to have an eye for Gwyn. Pedro explained the dog's virtues to Tariq, who set up some basic tests for the dog in the cellars. The dog passed them all easily. Tariq then offered to put the boys up and help them train the dog in return for half the profits from its hiring fees. The lads, eager for both money and an improvement in accommodation, quickly agreed. Earnest training began immediately. Reward techniques were used, and the dog was taught to sniff through various plastics and synthetic materials. He was trained in different conditions and temperatures and given the call name, Rhodri.

Later the next day Tariq took Gwyn, Bernie, and Rhodri to do their first job at a hashish stashing facility in the hills near Algeciras, run by a Moroccan firm from Ketama, the source of most of Morocco's hashish. Large quantities had been packed in an amateur fashion and run across the straits. The firm were now professionally re-packaging the load into thick plastic bags, which they smothered in industrial grease and re-packaged again in slightly larger plastic bags. Finally, they washed the entire re-packaged load in detergent and stored them in cabin trunks. Several dogs were also there, sniffing their hearts out, but Rhodri easily proved to be the most efficient. Tariq was delighted and paid the boys over 1,000 Euros.

With money in their pockets and at least a quarter of a kilo of the cocaine discovered by Rhodri still unused, the boys were able to kick back a bit. They went down to the local video shop.

Bernie looked for the film that he thought Gwyn's grandfather was describing about the local man saved from the Republican Death squad. The owner, Paco, a local boy, listened carefully. He seemed to recognise the story but not the film. Paco took them into a back room where a porn pirating operation was in progress. Various online sites were linked to plasma screens. Suddenly the film of Dai Sly's shame came on. It had been uploaded and had somehow spread virally. Some sleazy meth heads were jerking off to it. They wanted to know if the boys, whom they instantly recognised, had any more similar material. Gwyn and Bernie said they would see what they could do. Gwyn quickly changed the subject back to his grandfather's heroic Spanish Civil War activities and explained to Paco it was not a film but the truth. Paco seemed immediately impressed by the historical connection of the grandfather with a powerful local family and stated this would have had to be the Gomez family, of which he was a member. The lads spent the entire evening drinking endless cups of coffee, averaging six cups an hour. During the whole evening neither of them pissed, resulting in bodies full of excess fluid that needed to be dumped somewhere, and quickly. The result was not good: a half-hour constant relay to the primitive toilet at the back of the video shop. Both felt like they had vomited their body weights in warm coffee by the time the sun set over the rooftops and let in the darkness.

Gwyn and Bernie were feeling very much at home when they woke up in Tariq's villa the next morning. Whenever Tariq's back was turned, Ilka would come on to Gwyn. At first, fear of Tariq's wrath encouraged him to resist, slightly, but he soon succumbed. Bernie found a video camera in the villa and would surreptitiously film Gwyn and Ilka's sexual antics with the thought of perhaps selling the results to Paco. Bernie had already managed to set fire to the sofa with a Zippo lighter whilst loading a bong. Thinking he had snapped shut the lid, he laid the lighter on the sofa. There it burned for several minutes until he noticed the flames lapping his leg. Things were getting very slack. Just before lunch, Tariq took the boys and Rhodri out to their second assignment, a warehouse facility in the hills nearby where a crew of Ukrainian chemists was employed. Tariq left them there. Gwyn and Bernie were treated as experts in smell-proofing, and they played along as best they could. But on the side, they started sampling the training stashes and getting seriously stoned. They watched customs training films of state-of the-art sniffing technology provided by the chemists, and were put to work with the staff training pigs, rats, and bees. By the evening of the same day, the animals got loose and things went badly wrong. The boys scarpered and hitchhiked back to the villa. Tariq was away.

Their only trusted visitor was Paco the video man, and the Jones boys confided in him about Rhodri's unique sniffing abilities and the problems they would be likely to face when Tariq discovered what had happened at the Ukrainian chemists' establishment. Paco was sympathetic and insisted they come to see the village where Gwyn's grandfather saw action and saved the life of one of the local and very powerful Gomez family. No one would mess with the Gomez family. There would be nothing to fear from Tariq or Ukrainian terrorists. The boys agreed. Paco took them in his car to a large hacienda in the hills. It was empty. The family, apparently, was visiting friends for lunch, but Paco knew how to enter and showed them round. Paco explained that the honour code dictated the family must give him protection, which would be automatically extended to his friends, Gwyn and Bernie. But Gwyn sensed something wasn't right. There were obvious signs in the house that the Gomez family fought for Franco in the Civil War, while his grandfather had fought on the

Republican side. It was a trap. He realised Paco had been setting them up ever since he saw them in the porn film and, once he got wind of Rhodri's potential, he moved into top gear. The family connection had been fabricated in order to gain their trust. Gwyn didn't let on he had smelt a rat – always best to keep one's cards close to the chest.

Paco dropped the lads back at the villa and bid goodbye. Rhodri was dancing around barking. The dog had something to show them and led them to a blanket of plastic bales lying in the shallow water of a nearby cove. When they pulled them out of the sea, they could scarcely believe their eyes; it was a stash of more than 10 kilos of cocaine. They took it up to the villa, thoroughly tested the product, hid it, and decided to take Rhodri back to the area to see if there was any more. Within minutes of their arrival, they began to notice men methodically searching the coast around the cove, closing in on their position.

Gwyn insisted they immediately return to the villa and stayed there without venturing out from it for as long as possible. Gwyn further insisted they start selling the cocaine but only in small amounts through reliable proxies, such as Pedro. The trouble was they didn't know anyone else, and it was not long before Pedro and a series of small time dealer associates of his started turning up and asking for credit. Gwyn became increasingly paranoid and thought he saw some of the men from the beach through one of the villa's windows. Gwyn decided the safest move was to make the villa look as if it was uninhabited while they hid out in a couple of the rooms, didn't answer the door, and kept up surveillance on the neighbouring land.

As they started caning their way through the coke, Gwyn's paranoia increased, mainly due to Bernie saying he was seeing hallucinations of various animals. Soon, Gwyn saw wild animals from the woods, sniffer bees, pigs and rats closing in on him from every direction. The noise of a motorbike pulling up outside the villa distracted Gwyn from his zoological torture, and he rushed to the lookout window. Outside, Ilka was revving up her Honda. Gwyn ran out. To his astonishment, Bernie was sitting on the pillion seat. The Honda sped off. Gwyn tore off after them, but they were quickly out of sight. Breathless, Gwyn staggered back to the villa. There was no sign of the stash of cocaine. Gwyn realised too late that Bernie had been playing dumb all along. Gwyn walked out of the villa and stood alone on the hillside, definitely a poorer but possibly a wiser man. He wondered how Bernie could have done that. His first friend, his bosom pal, his brother in all but blood. He trusted him completely. They had done everything together for the first time: smoked under age, drank under age, vomited pure alcohol, lost their virginity to Evil Bethan, suffered whiteys smoking super-skunk, snorted cocaine until their eyes bled, sniffed ketamine until dissociation, dabbed MDMA, lost it on mushrooms, passed out chasing the smack dragon, reinvented themselves on LSD, broken the law for financial reward, and looked after Tadcu. Back to back they had stood in schoolyard brawls and scrapped until unconscious, prepared to defend each other until death. All gone for the sake of some Turkish pussy (mind, she was fit) and some bags of white powder (worth about £200,000). Where was all that unity, faith, loyalty, trust, and camaraderie? Had it all been bullshit? Gwyn could never go back to Wales. Dai Sly wouldn't have it. He would have to leave Spain, now, too. It wouldn't take long for Tariq to track him down. What about the Ukrainian chemists? They looked nasty. Life had never been so bad and empty.

Gwyn tapped his pockets – an iPhone, a bunch of keys, a few Euros, a packet of tobacco, and a very small bag of cocaine he had forgotten about. Dipping a key into and out of the bag, he snorted the lot and walked towards the sea.

He could resume the beachcombing, he thought. He'd find some more washed up bags of drugs, for sure. Pedro would be a useful assistant in this. And Paco was still on side. Gwyn could carry on playing him along and not let on he knew his family were a bunch of fascists. Maybe Tadcu would like a few days on the Costa del Sol. He'd hardly spent any of his old age pension.

Gwyn noticed a dog following him. It wasn't Rhodri, but it was a similar type of stray. It stayed with him as the full moon came up over the straits. Life was good and full of promise.

End

THE
COCAINE
CHRONICLES

EDITED BY **GARY PHILLIPS & JERVEY TERVALON**

The Cocaine Chronicles is also available as an ebook:

www.amzn.to/16kltVq (Kindle)
www.bit.ly/16klybI (epub)

For all our brothers and sisters who now only get high on life

CONTENTS

Cocaine made me feel like a new man. And he wanted some too.
—Richard Pryor

I went right home and I went to bed
I stuck that lovin' .44 beneath my head
Got up next mornin' and I grabbed that gun
Took a shot of cocaine and away I run.
—Johnny Cash

But consider! . . . Count the cost! Your brain may, as you say,
be roused and excited, but it is a pathological and morbid process
which involves increased tissue-change and may at least leave a
permanent weakness. You know, too, what a black reaction comes
upon you. Surely the game is hardly worth the candle. Why
should you, for a mere passing pleasure, risk the loss of those great
powers with which you have been endowed? Remember that I
speak not only as one comrade to another but as a medical man to
one for whose constitution he is to some extent answerable.
—Dr. John Watson to his friend Sherlock Holmes
in *Sign of the Four* by Arthur Conan Doyle

Ibarionex R. Perello

JERVEY TERVALON & GARY PHILLIPS

introduction
by gary phillips & jervey tervalon

So, Jervey, how about it? Did you ever partake?

No, G, I've never smoked cocaine, never hit the pipe, didn't tempt me in the least, because I had been inoculated against it with a healthy dose of junior high school ass-kicking. I assumed the pusherman would just as soon poison me as get me high. It never occurred to me that it would be a way to live, but it's always fascinated me, how folks fall into it, plunge headlong into the depths of human tragedy through the pursuit of the pipe. I've written about murderous crack addicts, about dope fiends, the true zombies of the streets *because.*

If you lived through the '80s anywhere near an urban core, you'd have to be stone-cold stupid not to notice them. And you'd have to be dull-witted not to know that these drug zombies were fictionally interesting and shouldn't be consigned to the lower rungs of pulp fiction or ghetto literature. Certainly cocaine has had a long-lasting appeal in popular culture, from Cab Calloway's "Minnie the Moocher" to Public Enemy's "Night of the Living Baseheads." But it's not just about popular appeal, it's also about an inclusive literary landscape.

What about you, G?

For me, blow serves as two clear demarcations in my life. The first was the summer of '73, when I was home from my first year of college at San Francisco State. That summer there were sartorial ripples in the ghetto culture caused by the film *Superfly*. That flick laid down some serious iconographic shit in the brains of my friends from high school like crack would grip fools in the years to come. Cats were stylin' in long quilted coats, wide-brim hats, and flared slacks. Everybody was sporting ornamental coke spoons around their necks when they hit the club, trying to keep their balance in those silly-ass platform shoes while rapping to a fox in fake leather thigh-high boots and a velvet mini.

I didn't sport a coat like the anti-hero drug dealer Priest in *Superfly*, with a style and attitude that would influence other movies and TV shows like *Starsky and Hutch* and *Baretta*— Antonio Fargas as Huggie Bear in the former, and Michael D. Roberts as Rooster in the latter. But I do remember going to a hat store on Manchester and purchasing a gray gangster brim and wearing that bad boy to parties, driving my dad's yellow '65 Galaxie 500 with the black Landau top and blasting Curtis Mayfield's too-cold *Superfly* sounds and Isaac Hayes's "Theme from Shaft" on the 8-track. There was a lot of weed at those parties but I don't recall much blow—though there was a lot of talk about somebody knew a dude who knows a dude and we can get some—but sure as hell, if there was some getting, nobody offered me any that summer. This was before crack became synonymous with the inner city, and powder the suburbs.

Drugs are class-driven like everything else, and stories about crack cocaine aren't for the mainstream readers of fiction; not the polite subject for drug literature or its crasser little brother, *heroin fiction*. Lithium is cool, antidepressants are too, but don't mention crack or freebase . . . those low-class drugs for self-medication.

Which brings me to the second incursion of coke into my life, Jervey. This was a few years later when I met this older woman—I mean, she was in her thirties and I was in my twenties—and we started going around together. She introduced me to the wonders of the toot. Now, given my wife might be reading this, or my teenage kids, I shall eschew graphic reportage of intimate encounters enhanced by the 'caine. But as Hendrix would say, I did, indeed, kiss the sky.

≈

As to how this book came about, we'd been invited to the *Los Angeles Times* Festival of Books to participate on a panel commemorating the tenth anniversary of the Los Angeles riots of 1992.

Jervey had edited *Geography of Rage*, a collection of essays about the civil unrest published in 2002, and Gary had a piece in it.

Later we talked about how weird it was that with all the anthologies, from the erotic to the criminal, we hadn't come across any inspired by cocaine, the scourge of our times. We both thought it would be a good idea, but good ideas get lost with bad ones.

So we met a few weeks after the panel, kicked the idea around some more, and came up with an outline, but didn't get too far beyond that. We went our separate ways assuming it wouldn't get done.

Then along came Akashic Books publisher Johnny Temple, who, fresh from the success of *Brooklyn Noir*, an ambitious collection of crime-fiction stories, asked us about the cocaine idea months after we'd mentioned it to him in passing. Soon the concept was cranking, and not long after we began inviting submissions, excellent stories started blowing in.

The stories we ultimately selected for this collection reflect what interests us as observers of the human condition in its various physical and psychological permutations. The four sections of the book are used as a rough breakdown of the effects cocaine has on the participants in a given story, no matter what side of the tracks it occurs on—though some relate tales of those who actually *cross* those tracks in their hunt for the flake, the rock . . . or in their attempt to escape its grip.

Here are some samples:

Detrice Jones's powerful vignette of a young girl living with addicted parents who spend their days trying to gank their daughter's lunch money; National Book Award–nominee Susan Straight's hard-ass story of an aging crackwhore; Jerry Stahl's absurd, ribald portrayal of a debased coke fiend; and Bill Moody's low notes about the nature of caring and waste. There's also Bob Ward's tale of love gone strange, Nina Revoyr's harrowing piece revealing how things do not always go better with coke, and Laura Lippman's hilariously twisted slice of the underbelly.

These are some of the scary charms found in *The Cocaine Chronicles*. We hope you find value in them.

Every contributor to this anthology stepped up and delivered. We are very grateful to each of them for coming through on relatively short notice and relatively minimal pay. They were truly inspired by the subject matter.

For as the late, great superfreak Rick James once said, *"Cocaine, it's a hell of a drug!"*

PART I
TOUCHED BY DEATH

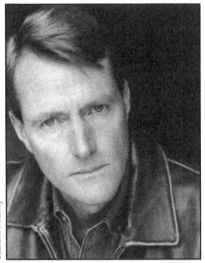

Blanche Mackey

LEE CHILD worked as a television director, union organizer, law student, and theater technician before being fired and going on the dole, at which point he hatched a harebrained scheme to write a best-selling novel, thus saving his family from ruin. *Killing Floor* went on to win worldwide acclaim. The hero of his series, Jack Reacher, besides being fictional, is a kind-hearted soul who allows Child lots of spare time for reading, listening to music, and the Yankees. Visit him online at www.leechild.com.

ten keys
by lee child

Mostly shit happens, but sometimes things fall in your lap, not often, but enough times to drop a rock on despair. But you can't start in with thoughts of redemption. That would be inappropriate. Such events are not about you. Things fall in your lap not because you're good, but because other people are bad. And stupid.

This guy walked into a bar—which sounds like the start of a joke, which was what it was, really, in every way. The bar was a no-name dive with a peeled-paint door and no sign outside. As such, it was familiar to me and the guy and people like us. I was already inside, at a table I had used before. I saw the guy come in. I knew him in the sense that I had seen him around a few times and therefore he knew me, too, because as long as we assume a certain amount of reciprocity in the universe, he had seen me around the exact same number of times. I see him, he sees me. We weren't friends. I didn't know his name. Which I wouldn't expect to. A guy like that, any name he gives you is sure to be bullshit. And certainly any name I would have given him would have been bullshit. So what were we to each other? Vague acquaintances, I guess. Both close enough and distant enough that given the trouble he was in, I was the sort of guy he was ready to talk to. Like two Americans trapped in a foreign airport. You assume an intimacy that isn't really there, and it makes it easier to spill your guts. You say things you wouldn't say in normal circumstances. This guy certainly did. He sat down at my table and started in on a whole long story. Not immediately, of course. I had to prompt him.

I asked, "You okay?"

He didn't reply. I didn't press. It was like starting a car that had been parked for a month. You don't just hammer the key. You give it time to settle, so you don't flood the carburetor or whatever cars have now. You're patient. In my line of work, patience is a big virtue.

I asked, "You want a drink?"

"Heineken," the guy said.

Right away I knew he was distracted. A guy like that, you offer him a drink, he should ask for something expensive and amber in a squat glass. Not a beer. He wasn't thinking. He wasn't calculating. But I was.

An old girl in a short skirt brought two bottles of beer, one for him and one for me. He picked his up and took a long pull and set it back down, and I saw him feel the first complex shift of our new social dynamic. I had bought him a drink, so he owed me conversation. He had accepted charity, so he owed himself a chance to re-up his status. I saw him rehearse his opening statement, which was going to tell me what a hell of a big player he was.

"It never gets any easier," he said.

He was a white guy, thin, maybe thirty-five years old, a little squinty, the product of too many generations of inbred hardscrabble hill people, his DNA baked down to nothing more than the essential components, arms, legs, eyes, mouth. He was an atom, adequate, but entirely interchangeable with ten thousand just like him.

"Tell me about it," I said, ruefully, like I understood his struggle.

"A man takes a chance," he said. "Tries to get ahead.

Sometimes it works, sometimes it don't."

I said nothing.

"I started out muling," he said. "Way back. You know that?"

I nodded. No surprise. We were four miles from I-95, and everyone started out muling, hauling keys of coke up from Miami or Jax, all the way north to New York and Boston. Anyone with a plausible face and an inconspicuous automobile started out muling, a single key in the trunk the first time, then two, then five, then ten. Trust was earned and success was rewarded, especially if you could make the length of the New Jersey Turnpike unmolested. The Jersey State Troopers were the big bottleneck back then.

"Clean and clear every time," the guy said. "No trouble, ever."

"So you moved up," I said.

"Selling," he said.

I nodded again. It was the logical next step. He would have been told to take his plausible face and his inconspicuous automobile deep into certain destination neighborhoods and meet with certain local distributors directly. The chain would have become one link shorter. Fewer hands on the product, fewer hands on the cash, more speed, more velocity, a better vector, less uncertainty.

"Who for?" I asked.

"The Martinez brothers."

"I'm impressed," I said, and he brightened a little.

"I got to where I was dealing ten keys pure at a time," he said.

My beer was getting warm, but I drank a little anyway. I knew what was coming next.

"I was hauling the coke north and the money south," he said.

I said nothing.

"You ever seen that much cash?" he asked. "I mean, really *seen* it?"

"No," I said.

"You can barely even lift it. You could get a hernia, a box like that."

I said nothing.

"I was doing two trips a week," he said. "I was never off the road. I wore grooves in the pavement. And there were dozens of us."

"Altogether a lot of cash," I said, because he needed me to open the door to the next revelation. He needed me to understand. He needed my permission to proceed.

"Like a river," he said.

I said nothing.

"Well, hell," he said. "There was so much it meant nothing to them. How could it? They were drowning in it."

"A man takes a chance," I said.

The guy didn't reply. Not at first. I held up two fingers to the old girl in the short skirt and watched her put two new bottles of Heineken on a cork tray.

"I took some of it," the guy said.

The old girl gave us our new bottles and took our old ones away. I said *four imports* to myself, so I could check my tab at the end of the night. Everyone's a rip-off artist now.

"How much of it did you take?" I asked the guy.

"Well, all of it. All of what they get for ten keys."

"And how much was that?"

"A million bucks. In cash."

"Okay," I said, enthusiastically, deferentially, like, *Wow, you're the man*.

"And I kept the product, too," he said.

I just stared at him.

"From Boston," he said. "Dudes up there are paranoid. They keep the cash and the coke in separate places. And the city's all dug up. The way the roads are laid out now it's easier to get paid first and deliver second. They trusted me to do that, after a time."

"But this time you picked up the cash and disappeared before you delivered the product."

He nodded.

"Sweet," I said.

"I told the Martinez boys I got robbed."

"Did they believe you?"

"Maybe not," he said.

"Problem," I said.

"But I don't see why," he said. "Not really. Like, how much cash have you got in your pocket, right now?"

"Two hundred and change," I said. "I was just at the ATM."

"So how would you feel if you dropped a penny and it rolled down the storm drain? A single lousy cent?"

"I wouldn't really give a shit," I said.

"Exactly. This is like a guy with two hundred in his pocket who loses a penny under the sofa cushion. How uptight is anyone going to be?"

"With these guys, it's not about the money," I said.

"I know," he said.

We went quiet and drank our beers. Mine felt gassy against my teeth. I don't know how his felt to him. He probably wasn't tasting it at all.

"They've got this other guy," he said. "Dude called Octavian. He's their investigator. And their enforcer. He's going to come for me."

"People get robbed," I said. "Shit happens."

"Octavian is supposed to be real scary. I've heard bad things."

"You were robbed. What can he do?"

"He can make sure I'm telling the truth, is what he can do. I've heard he has a way of asking questions that makes you want to answer."

"You stand firm, he can't get blood out of a rock."

"They showed me a guy in a wheelchair. Story was that Octavian had him walking on his knees up and down a gravel patch for a week. Walking on the beach, he calls it. The pain is supposed to be terrible. And the guy got gangrene afterward, lost his legs."

"Who is this Octavian guy?"

"I've never seen him."

"Is he another Colombian?"

"I don't know."

"Didn't the guy in the wheelchair say?"

"He had no tongue. Story is Octavian cut it out."

"You need a plan," I said.

"He could walk in here right now. And I wouldn't know."

"So you need a plan fast."

"I could go to L.A."

"Could you?"

"Not really," the guy said. "Octavian would find me. I don't want to be looking over my shoulder the whole rest of my life."

I paused. Took a breath.

"People get robbed, right?" I said.

"It happens," he said. "It's not unknown."

"So you could pin it on the Boston people. Start a war up there. Take the heat off yourself. You could come out of this like an innocent victim. The first casualty. Nearly a hero."

"If I can convince this guy Octavian."

"There are ways."

"Like what?"

"Just convince yourself first. You were the victim here. If you really believe it, in your mind, this guy Octavian will believe it, too. Like acting a part."

"It won't go easy."

"A million bucks is worth the trouble. Two million, assuming you're going to sell the ten keys."

"I don't know."

"Just stick to a script. You know nothing. It was the Boston guys. Whoever he is, Octavian's job is to get results, not to waste his time down a blind alley. You stand firm, and he'll tell the Martinez boys you're clean and they'll move on."

"Maybe."

"Just learn a story and stick to it. *Be* it. Method acting, like that fat guy who died."

"Marlon Brando?"

"That's the one. Do like him. You'll be okay."

"Maybe."

"But Octavian will search your crib."

"That's for damn sure," the guy said. "He'll tear it apart."

"So the stuff can't be there."

"It *isn't* there."

"That's good," I said, and then I lapsed into silence.

"What?" he asked.

"Where is it?" I asked.

"I'm not going to tell you," he said.

"That's okay," I said. "I don't want to know. Why the hell would I? But the thing is, you can't afford to know either."

"How can I not know?"

"That's the exact problem," I said. "This guy Octavian's going to see it in your eyes. He's going to see you *knowing*. He's going to be beating up on you or whatever and he needs to see a blankness in your eyes. Like you don't have a clue. That's what he needs to see. But he isn't going to see that."

"What's he going to see?"

"He's going to see you holding out and thinking, *Hey, tomorrow this will be over and I'll be back at my cabin or my storage locker or wherever and then I'll be okay*. He's going to *know.*"

"So what should I do?"

I finished the last of my beer. Warm and flat. I considered ordering two more but I didn't. I figured we were near the end. I figured I didn't need any more of an investment.

"Maybe you should go to L.A.," I said.

"No," he said.

"So you should let me hold the stuff for you. Then you genuinely won't know where it is. You're going to need that edge."

"I'd be nuts. Why should I trust you?"

"You shouldn't. You don't have to."

"You could disappear with my two million."

"I could, but I won't. Because if I did, you'd call Octavian and tell him that a face just came back to you. You'd describe me, and then your problem would become my problem. And if Octavian is as bad as you say, that's a problem I don't want."

"You better believe it."

"I do believe it."

"Where would I find you afterward?"

"Right here," I said. "You know I use this place. You've seen me in here before."

"Method acting," he said.

"You can't betray what you don't know," I said.

He went quiet for a long time. I sat still and thought about putting one million dollars in cash and ten keys of uncut cocaine in the trunk of my car.

"Okay," he said.

"There would be a fee," I said, to be plausible.

"How much?" he asked.

"Fifty grand," I said.

He smiled.

"Okay," he said again.

"Like a penny under the sofa cushion," I said.

"You got that right."

"We're all winners."

The bar door opened and a guy walked in on a blast of warm air. Hispanic, small and wide, big hands, an ugly scar high on his cheek.

"You know him?" my new best friend asked.

"Never saw him before," I said.

The new guy walked to the bar and sat on a stool.

"We should do this thing right now," my new best friend said.

Sometimes, things just fall in your lap.

"Where's the stuff?" I asked.

"In an old trailer in the woods," he said.

"Is it big?" I asked. "I'm new to this."

"Ten kilos is twenty-two pounds," the guy said. "About the same for the money. Two duffles, is all."

"So let's go," I said.

I drove him in my car west and then south, and he directed me down a fire road and onto a dirt track that led to a clearing. I guessed once it had been neat, but now it was overgrown with all kinds of stuff and it stank of animal piss and the trailer had degenerated from a viable vacation home to a rotted hulk. It was all covered with mold and mildew and the windows were dark with organic scum. He wrestled with the door and went inside. I opened the trunk lid and waited. He came back out with a duffle in each hand. Carried them over to me.

"Which is which?" I asked.

He squatted down and unzipped them. One had bricks of used money, the other had bricks of dense white powder packed hard and smooth under clear plastic wrap.

"Okay," I said.

He stood up again and heaved the bags into the trunk, and I stepped to the side and shot him twice in the head. Birds rose up from everywhere and cawed and cackled and settled back into the branches. I put the gun back in my pocket and took out my cell phone. Dialed a number.

"Yes?" the Martinez brothers asked together. They always used the speakerphone. They were too afraid of each other's betrayal to allow private calls.

"This is Octavian," I said. "I'm through here. I got the money back and I took care of the guy."

"Already?"

"I got lucky," I said. "It fell in my lap."

"What about the ten keys?"

"In the wind," I said. "Long gone."

Jim Burger

LAURA LIPPMAN is a *New York Times* best-selling writer who has published sixteen novels and a collection of short stories; she also edited *Baltimore Noir,* part of the award-winning Akashic Noir Series. She lives in Baltimore and New Orleans.

the crack cocaine diet
(or: how to lose a lot of weight and change your life in just one weekend)
by laura lippman

had just broken up with Brandon and Molly had just broken up with Keith, so we needed new dresses to go to this party where we knew they were going to be. But before we could buy the dresses, we needed to lose weight because we had to look fabulous, kiss-my-ass-fuck-you fabulous. Kiss-my-ass-fuck-you-and-your-dick-is-really-tiny fabulous. Because, after all, Brandon and Keith were going to be at this party, and if we couldn't get new boyfriends in less than eight days, we could at least go down a dress size and look so good that Brandon and Keith and everybody else in the immediate vicinity would wonder how they ever let us go. I mean, yes, technically, *they* broke up with *us*, but we had been thinking about it, weighing the pros and cons. (Pro: They spent money on us. Con: They were childish. Pro: We had them. Con: Tiny dicks, see above.) See, we were being methodical and they were just all impulsive, the way guys are. That would be another con—poor impulse control. Me, I never do anything without thinking it through very carefully. Anyway, I'm not sure what went down with Molly and Keith, but Brandon said if he wanted to be nagged all the time, he'd move back in with his mother, and I said, "Well, given that she still does your laundry and makes you food, it's not as if you really moved out," and that was that. No big loss.

Still, we had to look so great that other guys would be

punching our exes in the arms and saying, "What, are you crazy?" Everything is about spin, even dating. It's always better to be the dumper instead of the dumpee, and if you have to be the loser, then you need to find a way to be superior. And that was going to take about seven pounds for me, as many as ten for Molly, who doesn't have my discipline and had been doing some serious break-up eating for the past three weeks. She went face down in the Ding Dongs, danced with the Devil Dogs, became a Ho Ho ho. As for myself, I'm a salty girl, and I admit I had the Pringles Light can upended in my mouth for a couple of days.

So anyway, Molly said Atkins and I said not fast enough, and then I said a fast-fast and Molly said she saw little lights in front of her eyes the last time she tried to go no food, and she said cabbage soup and I said it gives me gas, and then she said pills and I said all the doctors we knew were too tight with their 'scrips, even her dentist boss since she stopped blowing him. Finally, Molly had a good idea and said: "Cocaine!"

This merited consideration. Molly and I had never done more than a little recreational coke, always provided by boyfriends who were trying to impress us, but even my short-term experience indicated it would probably do the trick. The tiniest bit revved you up for hours and you raced around and around, and it wasn't that you weren't hungry, more like you had never even heard of food; it was just some quaint custom from the olden days, like square dancing.

"Okay," I said. "Only, where do we get it?" After all, we're girls, *girly* girls. I had been drinking and smoking pot since I was sixteen, but I certainly didn't buy it. That's what boyfriends were for. Pro: Brandon bought my drinks, and if you don't have to lay out cash for alcohol, you can buy a lot more shoes.

Molly thought hard, and Molly thinking was like a fat guy running—there was a lot of visible effort.

"Well, like, the city."

"But where in the city?"

"On, like, a corner."

"Right, Molly. I watch HBO, too. But I mean, what corner? It's not like they list them in that crap Weekender Guide in the paper—movies, music, clubs, where to buy drugs."

So Molly asked a guy who asked a guy who talked to a guy, and it turned out there was a place just inside the city line, not too far from the interstate. Easy on, easy off, then easy off again. Get it? After a quick consultation on what to wear—jeans and T-shirts and sandals, although I changed into running shoes after I saw the condition of my pedicure—we were off. Very hush-hush because, as I explained to Molly, that was part of the adventure. I phoned my mom and said I was going for a run. Molly told her mom she was going into the city to shop for a dress.

The friend of Molly's friend's friend had given us directions to what turned out to be an apartment complex, which was kind of disappointing. I mean, we were expecting row houses, slumping picturesquely next to each other, but this was just a dirtier, more run-down version of where we lived—little clusters of two-story town houses built around an interior courtyard. We drove around and around and around, trying to seem very savvy and willing, and it looked like any apartment complex on a hot July afternoon. Finally, on our third turn around the complex, a guy ambled over to the car.

"What you want?"

"What you got?" I asked, which I thought was pretty good. I mean, I sounded casual but kind of hip, and if he turned out to be a cop, I hadn't implicated myself. See, *I* was always thinking, unlike some people I could name.

"Got American Idol and Survivor. The first one will make you sing so pretty that Simon will be speechless. The second one will make you feel as if you've got immunity for life."

"O-*kay*." Molly reached over me with a fistful of bills, but the guy backed away from the car.

"Pay the guy up there. Then someone will bring you your package."

"Shouldn't you give us the, um, stuff first and then get paid?"

The guy gave Molly the kind of look that a schoolteacher gives you when you say something exceptionally stupid. We drove up to the next guy, gave him forty dollars, then drove to a spot he pointed out to wait.

"It's like McDonald's!" Molly said. "Drive-through!"

"Shit, don't say McDonald's. I haven't eaten all day. I would kill for a Big Mac."

"Have you ever had the Big N' Tasty? It totally rocks."

"What is it?"

"It's a cheeseburger, but with, like, a special sauce."

"Like a Big Mac."

"Only the sauce is different."

"I liked the fries better when they made them in beef fat."

A third boy—it's okay to say boy, because he was, like, thirteen, so I'm not being racist or anything—handed us a package, and we drove away. But Molly immediately pulled into a convenience store parking lot. It wasn't a real convenience store, though, not a 7-Eleven or a Royal Farm.

"What are you doing?"

"Pre-diet binge," Molly said. "If I'm not going to eat for the next week, I want to enjoy myself now."

I had planned to be pure starting that morning, but it sounded like a good idea. I did a little math. An ounce of Pringles has, like, 120 calories, so I could eat an entire can and not gain even half a pound, and a half pound doesn't even register on a scale, so it wouldn't count. Molly bought a pound of Peanut M&Ms, and let me tell you, the girl was not overachieving. I'd seen her eat that much on many an occasion. Molly has big appetites. We had a picnic right there in the parking lot, washing down our food with diet cream soda. Then Molly began to open our "package."

"Not here!" I warned her, looking around.

"What if it's no good? What if they cut it with, like, something, so it's weak?"

Molly was beginning to piss me off a little, but maybe it was just all the salt, which was making my fingers swell and my head pound a little. "How are you going to know if it's any good?"

"You put it on your gums." She opened the package. It didn't look quite right. It was more off-white than I remembered, not as finely cut. But Molly dove right in, licking her finger, sticking it in, and then spreading it around her gum line.

"Shit," she said. "I don't feel a thing."

"Well, you don't feel it right away."

"No, they, like, totally robbed us. It's bullshit. I'm going back."

"Molly, I don't think they do exchanges. It's not like Nordstrom, where you can con them into taking the shoes back even after you wore them once. You stuck your wet finger in it."

"We were ripped off. They think just because we're white suburban girls they can sell us this weak-ass shit." She was beginning to sound more and more like someone on HBO, although I'd have to say the effect was closer to *Ali G* than *Sopranos*. "I'm going to demand a refund."

This was my first inkling that things might go a little wrong.

So Molly went storming back to the parking lot and found our guy, and she began bitching and moaning, but he didn't seem that upset. He seemed kind of, I don't know, amused by her. He let her rant and rave, just nodding his head, and when she finally ran out of steam, he said, "Honey, darling, you bought heroin. Not cocaine. That's why you didn't get a jolt. It's not supposed to jolt you. It's supposed to slow you down, not that it seems to be doing that, either."

Molly had worked up so much outrage that she still saw herself as the wronged party. "Well, how was I supposed to know that?"

"Because we sell cocaine by vial color. Red tops, blue tops, yellow tops. I just had you girls figured for heroin girls. You looked like you knew your way around, got tired of OxyContin, wanted the real thing."

Molly preened a little, as if she had been complimented. It's interesting about Molly. Objectively, I'm prettier, but she has always done better with guys. I think it's because she has this kind of sexy vibe, by which I mean she manages to communicate that she'll pretty much do anyone.

"Two pretty girls like you, just this once, I'll make an exception. You go hand that package back to my man Gordy, and he'll give you some nice blue tops."

We did, and he did, but this time Molly made a big show of driving only a few feet away and inspecting our purchase, holding the blue-capped vial up to the light.

"It's, like, rock candy."

It did look like a piece of rock candy, which made me think of the divinity my grandmother used to make, which made me think of all the other treats from childhood that I couldn't imagine eating now—Pixy Stix and Now and Laters and Mary Janes and Dots and Black Crows and Necco Wafers and those pastel buttons that came on sheets of wax paper. Chocolate never did it for me, but I loved sugary treats when I was young.

And now Molly was out of the car and on her feet, steaming toward our guy, who looked around, very nervous, as if this five-foot-five, size-ten dental hygienist—size-eight when she's being good—could do some serious damage. And I wanted to say, "Dude, don't worry! All she can do is scrape your gums until they bleed." (I go to Molly's dentist and Molly cleans my teeth, and she is seriously rough. I think she gets a little kick out of it, truthfully.)

"What the fuck is this?" she yelled, getting all gangster on his ass—I think I'm saying that right—holding the vial up to the guy's face, while he looked around nervously. Finally, he grabbed her wrist and said: "Look, just shut up or you're going to bring some serious trouble to bear. You smoke it. I'll show you how . . . Don't you know anything? Trust me, you'll like it."

Molly motioned to me and I got out of the car, although a little reluctantly. It was, like, you know, that scene in *Star Wars* where the little red eyes are watching from the caves and suddenly those weird sand people just up and attack. I'm not being racist, just saying we were outsiders and I definitely had a feeling all sorts of eyes were on us, taking note.

"We'll go to my place," the guy said, all super suave, like he was some international man of mystery inviting us to see his etchings.

"A shooting gallery?" Molly squealed, all excited. "Ohmigod!"

He seemed a little offended. "I don't let dope fiends in my house."

He led us to one of the town houses, and I don't know what I expected, but certainly not some place with doilies and old overstuffed furniture and pictures of Jesus and some black guy on the wall. (Dr. Martin Luther King, Jr., I figured out later, but I was really distracted at the time, and thought it was the guy's dad or something.) But the most surprising thing was this little old lady sitting in the middle of the sofa, hands folded in her lap. She had a short, all-white Afro, and wore a pink T-shirt and flowery ski pants, which bagged on her stick-thin legs. Ski pants. I hadn't seen them in, like, forever.

"Antone?" she said. "Did you come to fix my lunch?"

"In a minute, Grandma. I have guests."

"Are they nice people, Antone?"

"Very nice people," he said, winking at us, and it was only then that I realized the old lady was blind. You see, her eyes weren't milky or odd in any way, they were brown and clear, as if she was staring right at us. You had to look closely to realize that she couldn't really see, that the gaze, steady as it was, didn't focus on anything.

Antone went to the kitchen, an alcove off the dining room, and fixed a tray with a sandwich, some potato chips, a glass of soda, and an array of medications. How could you not like a guy like that? So sweet, with broad shoulders and close-cropped hair like his granny's, only dark. Then, very quietly, with another wink, he showed us how to smoke.

"Antone, are you smoking in here? You know I don't approve of tobacco."

"Just clove cigarettes, Grandma. Clove never hurt anybody."

He helped each of us with the pipe, getting closer than was strictly necessary. He smelled like clove, like clove and ginger and cinnamon. Antone the spice cookie. When he took the pipe from Molly's mouth, he replaced it with his lips. I didn't really want him to kiss me, but I'm so much prettier than Molly. Not to mention thinner. But then, I hear black guys like girls with big behinds, and Molly certainly qualified. You could put a can of beer on her ass and have her walk around the room and it wouldn't fall off. Not being catty, just telling the literal truth. I did it once, at a party, when I was bored, and then Molly swished around with a can of Bud Light on her ass, showing off, like she was proud to have so much baggage.

Weird, but I was hungrier than ever after smoking, which was so not the point. I mean, I wasn't hungry in my stomach, I was hungry in my mouth. And what I wanted, more than anything in the world, were those potato chips on the blind lady's tray. They were Utz Salt 'n Vinegar; I had seen Antone take them out of the green-and-yellow bag. I looooooooooooooooooooooooooooooo oove Utz Salt 'n Vinegar, but they don't come in a light version, so I almost never let myself have any. So I snagged one, just one, quiet as a cat. But, like they say, you can't eat just one. Okay, so they say that about Lays, but it's even more true about Utz, in my personal opinion. I kept stealing them, one at a time.

"Antone? Are you taking food off my tray?"

I looked to Antone for backup, but Molly's tongue was so far in his mouth that she might have been flossing him. When he finally managed to detach himself, he said: "Um, Grandma? I'm going to take a little lie-down."

"What about your guests?"

"They're going," he said, walking over to the door with a heavy tread and closing it.

"It's time for *Judge Judy!*" his granny said, which made me wonder, because how does a blind person know what time it is? Antone used the remote control to turn on the television. It was a black-and-white, total Smithsonian. After all, she was blind, so I guess it didn't matter.

Next thing I knew, I was alone in the room with the blind woman, who was fixated on *Judge Judy* as if she was going to be tested on the outcome, and I was eyeing her potato chips, while Antone and Molly started making the kind of noises that you make when you're trying so hard not to make noise that you can't help making noise.

"Antone?" the old lady called out. "Is the dishwasher running? Because I think a piece of cutlery might have gotten caught in the machinery."

I was so knocked out that she knew the word "cutlery." How cool is that?

But I couldn't answer, of course. I wasn't supposed to be there.

"It's—okay—Granny," Antone grunted from the other room. "It's—all—going—to—be—*Jesus Christ*—okay."

The noises started up again. Granny was right. It did sound like a piece of cutlery caught in the dishwasher. But then it stopped—Antone's breathing, the mattress springs, Molly's little muffled grunts—they just stopped, and they didn't stop naturally, if you know what I mean. I'm not trying to be cruel, but Molly's a bit of a slut, and I've listened to her have sex more times than I can count, and I know how it ends, even when she's faking it, even when she has to be quiet, and it just didn't sound like the usual Molly finish at all. Antone yelped, but she was silent as a grave.

"Antone, what are you doing?" his granny asked. Antone didn't answer. Several minutes went by, and then there was a hoarse whisper from the bedroom.

"Um, Kelley? Could you come here a minute?"

"What was that?" his granny asked.

I used the remote to turn up the volume on *Judge Judy*. "DO I LOOK STUPID TO YOU?" the judge was yelling. "REMEMBER THAT PRETTY FADES BUT STUPID IS FOREVER. I ASKED IF YOU HAD IT IN WRITING, I DON'T WANT TO HEAR ALL THIS FOLDEROL ABOUT ORAL AGREEMENTS."

When I went into the bedroom, Molly was under Antone, and I remember thinking—I was a little high, remember—that he made her look really thin because he covered up her torso, and Molly does have good legs and decent arms. He had a handsome back, too, broad and muscled, and a great ass. Brandon had no ass (con), but he had nice legs (pro).

It took me a moment to notice that he had a pair of scissors stuck in the middle of his beautiful back.

"I told him no," Molly whispered, although the volume on the television was so loud that the entire apartment was practically reverberating. "No means no."

There was a lot of blood, I noticed. A lot.

"I didn't hear you," I said. "I mean, I didn't hear you say any *words*."

"I mouthed it. He told me to keep silent because his grandmother is here. Still, I mouthed it. 'No.' 'No.'" She made this incredibly unattractive fish mouth to show me.

"Is he dead?"

"I mean, I was totally up for giving him a blow job, especially after he said he'd give me a little extra, but he was, like, uncircumcised. I just couldn't, Kelley, I couldn't. I've never been with a guy like that. I offered him a hand job instead, but he got totally peeved and tried to force me."

The story wasn't tracking. High as I was, I could see there were some holes. *How did you get naked?* I wanted to ask. *Why didn't you shout? If Grandma knew you were here, Antone wouldn't have dared misbehaved.* He had clearly been more scared of Granny than he was into Molly.

"This is the stash house," Molly said. "Antone showed me."

"What?"

"The drugs. They're here. All of it. We could just help ourselves. I mean, he's a rapist, Kelley. He's a criminal. He sells drugs to people. Help me, Kelley. Get him off me."

But when I rolled him off, I saw there was a condom. Molly saw it, too.

"We should, like, so get rid of that. It would only complicate things. When I saw he was going to rape me, I told him he should at least be courteous."

I nodded, as if agreeing. I flushed the condom down the toilet, helped Molly clean the blood off her, and then used my purse to pack up what we could find, as she was carrying this little bitty Kate Spade knockoff that wasn't much good for anything. We found some cash, too, about $2,000, and helped ourselves to that, on the rationale that it would be more suspicious if we didn't. On the way out, I shook a few more potato chips on Granny's plate.

"Antone?" she said. "Are you going out again?"

Molly grunted low, and that seemed to appease Granny. We walked out slowly, as if we had all the time in the world, but again I had that feeling of a thousand pairs of eyes on us. We were in some serious trouble. There would have to be some sort of retribution for what we had done. What Molly had done. All I did was steal a few potato chips.

"Take Quarry Road home instead of the interstate," I told Molly.

"Why?" she asked. "It takes so much longer."

"But we know it, know all the ins and outs. If someone follows us, we can give them the slip."

About two miles from home, I told her I had to pee so bad that I couldn't wait and asked her to stand watch for me, a longtime practice with us. We were at that point, high above the old limestone quarry, where we had parked a thousand times as teenagers. A place where Molly had never said "No" to my knowledge.

"Finished?" she asked, when I emerged from behind the screen of trees.

"Almost," I said, pushing her hard, sending her tumbling over the precipice. She wouldn't be the first kid in our class to break her neck at the highest point on Quarry Road. My high school boyfriend did, in fact, right after we broke up. It was a horrible accident. I didn't eat for weeks and got down to a size four. Everyone felt bad for me— breaking up with Eddie only to have him commit suicide that way.

There didn't seem to be any reason for me to explain that Eddie was the one who wanted to break up. Unnecessary information.

I crossed the hillside to the highway, a distance of about a mile, then jogged the rest of the way. After all, as my mother would be the first to tell you, I went for a run that afternoon, while Molly was off shopping, according to her mom. I assumed the police would tie Antone's dead body to Molly's murder, and figure it for a revenge killing, but I was giving the cops too much credit. Antone rated a paragraph in the morning paper. Molly, who turned out to be pregnant, although not even she knew it—probably wouldn't even have known who the father was—is still on the front page all these weeks later. (The fact that they didn't find her for three days heightened the interest, I guess. I mean, she was just an overweight dental hygienist from the suburbs—and a bit of a slut, as I told you. But the media got all excited about it.) The general consensus seems to be that Keith did it, and I don't see any reason to let him off the hook, not yet. He's an asshole. Plus, almost no one in this state gets the death penalty.

Meanwhile, he's telling people just how many men Molly had sex with in the past month, including Brandon, and police are still trying to figure out who had sex with her right before she died. (That's why you're supposed to get the condom on as early as possible, girls. Penises *drip*. Just fyi.) I pretended to be shocked, but I already knew about Brandon, having seen Molly's car outside his apartment when I cruised his place at two a.m. a few nights after Brandon told me he wanted to see other people. My ex-boyfriend and my best friend, running around behind my back. Everyone feels so bad for me, but I'm being brave, although I eat so little that I'm down to a size two. I just bought a Versace dress and Manolos for a date this weekend with my new boyfriend, Robert. I've never spent so much money on an outfit before. But then, I've never had $2,000 in cash to spend as I please.

KEN BRUEN is the author of twenty-nine books. Three novels in his Jack Taylor mystery series have been adapted into films for television. The films based on his novels *London Boulevard* and *Blitz* debuted in theaters in 2011. Bruen recently received his second PhD, in Breton linguistics, and he currently lives in Tangiers. He has one daughter.

white irish
by ken bruen

Man, I'm between that fuckin' rock and the proverbial hard place. Hurtin'?

Whoa . . . so bad.

My septum's burned out. Kiddin', I ain't. There's a small mountain of snow on the table. Soon as the bleed stops, I'm burying myself in there, just tunneling in. The blood ran into my mouth about an hour ago, and fuck, made the mistake of checking in the mirror.

Nearly had a coronary. A dude staring back, blood all down his chin, splattered on the white T-shirt, the treasured Guns n' Roses one, heard a whimper of . . .

Terror.

Horror.

Anguish.

A heartbeat till I realized I was the one doing the whimpering.

How surprising is that?

The Sig Sauer is by the stash, ready to kick ass. Say it loud, Lock 'n' fuckin' load. Is it an echo here, or does that come back as *rock 'n' roll*?

I'm losing it.

Yeah, yeah, like I don't fuckin' know? Gimme a break, I know.

All right?

Earth to muthahfuckah, HELLO . . . I am, like . . . receiving this.

The devil's in the details. My mom used to say that. God bless her Irish heart. And I sing, *"If you ever go across the sea to Ireland . . . It may be at the closing of your day . . ."*

Got that right.

A Galway girl, she got lost in the nightmare of the American Dream and never got home again. If she could see me now.

Buried her three years ago, buried her cheap. I was short on the green, no pun intended. A pine box, 300 bucks was the most I could hustle. I still owe 150 on it.

A cold morning in February, we put her in the colder ground.

Huge crowd and a lone piper playing "Carrickfergus."

I wish . . . There was me, Me and Bobby McGee.

Sure.

One gravedigger, a sullen fuck, and me, walking point. For the ceremony, a half-assed preacher. Him I found in a bar, out of it on shots of dollar whiskey and Shiner.

Bought him a bottle of Maker's Mark to perform the rites.

Perform he did and fast, as he wasn't getting the Mark till the deal was done.

Galloped through the dying words. "Man, full of misery, has but a short time."

Like that.

Even the gravedigger gaped at the rapidity, the words, tripping, spilling over each other.

"Ashes to ashes."

I was thinking David Bowie. The first pound of clay was shoveled, and I went, "Wait up."

Didn't have a rose to throw, so what the hell, took my wedding band, a claddagh, bounced it off the lid, the gold glinting against the dirt.

Caught the greed in the digger's eyes and let him see mine— the message: *"Don't even think about it."*

I get back down that way, he's wearing the ring, he's meat.

My current situation, fuck, it just, like, got the hell away from me, one of those heists, should have been a piece of cake.

Cake with shredded glass.

Take down a Mex named Raoul. A medium mover of high-grade powder. Me and Jimmy, my jail buddy, my main man.

Simple score, simple plan. Go in roaring, put the Sig in Raoul's face, take the coke, the cash, and *sayonara* sucker.

No frills.

Went to hell in a bucket.

Raoul had backup. Two moonlighting Angels. We never thought to check the rear, where the hogs were parked. Jimmy had sworn Raoul would be alone, save for some trailer trash named Lori.

And so it had seemed.

We blazed in, I bitch-slapped Raoul, Jimmy hit Lori on the upside of her skull—then the bikers came out of the back room. Carrying. Sawed-offs.

The smoke finally cleared and I was in Custer's Last Stand. Everyone else was splattered on the floor, across the carpet, against the walls. Improved the shitty décor no end, gave that splash of color.

Jimmy was slumped against a sofa, his entrails hanging out. I went, "You stupid fuck, you never mentioned Angels. This is way bigger than us."

The coke, too, more than he'd known. I needed two sacks to haul it out of there, and a bin liner for the cash.

Shot Jimmy in the face. Did him a favor. Gut shot? You're fucked.

So, bikers, cops, and some stone-cold suppliers from way south of Tijuana on my tail. I covered my tracks pretty good, I think, only made a few pit stops. A bad moment when I saw a dude give me the hard look, but I'm fairly sure I shook him.

I'm holed up in the Houston airport Marriott. Who's gonna look there?

Checked in two days ago, leastways I figure it. Living on room service and the marching powder, thinking I'd have one hit, but it kinda sneaks up on you and you're doing a whole stream without realizing. Got me a bad dose of the jitters, real bad.

The first day, if that's the day it was, I was nervous as a rat, pacing the room, taking hits offa the coke, chugging from the Jack D. Had made the pit stop for essentials, loaded up on hooch and a carton of Luckies, oh, and on impulse, a Zippo—had a logo if not the edge.

Yankees, World Champions, 1999. Like that.

Made me smile, a good year for the roses. The year I almost made first base. McKennit, met her in a bar, I'd been drinking Lone Star, nothing heavy, and building a buzz, almost mellow. Hadn't even noticed her.

Me and the ladies, not a whole lot of history there, leastways none of it good.

She'd leaned over, asked, "Got a light?"

Sure. Got a boner, too.

Bought her a drink, figuring, a fox like she was, gotta be a working girl. I could go a couple of bills, have me a time.

I was wrong, she wasn't a hooker.

Things got better, I took her home and, hell, I didn't make a move, hung back, kissed her on the cheek, and she asked, "So, Jake, wanna go on, like, a . . . date?"

Two months it lasted. Had me some fun, almost citizen shit, even bought her flowers and, oh god, Hershey's Kisses, yeah, like, how lame is that?

Got me laid.

I'd a cushy number going, a neat line in credit card scams,

pulling down some medium change. I was on the verge . . . fuck . . . I dunno. Asking her something. Telling her I'd like to set us up a place . . . Jesus, what was I thinking?

We were sitting in a flash joint, finishing plates of linguini, sipping a decent Chianti, her knee brushing mine.

I can still see how she looked, the candle throwing a soft blush on her cheek, her eyes brown, wide, and soft.

Before I could get my rap going, the layout, the proposal, two bulls charged in, hauled me out of the chair, slammed me across the table, the wine spilling into her lap.

The cuffs on my wrists, then pulling me upright, the first going, "Game's up, wise guy, you're toast."

The second leered at her, spittle at the corner of his mouth, asked, "The fuck a looker like you doing with this loser?"

And her body shaking, she stammered, "There must be some mistake."

The bulls laughing, one went, "Nickle-and-dime con man, penny-ante shit, never worked a day in his goddamn life, he's going down, honey, hard. You wanna spread your legs, baby, least get some return."

They weren't kidding about the hard bit. I got two years on that deal, fuckin' credit cards. They call it white-collar crime, meaning they do not like you to fuck with their money.

Did the max, the whole jolt. Never saw McKennit again, used my one phone call to try and reach her, heard, "This number is no longer in use."

Sent a letter, got *"Return to sender."* Like the bloody song.

So, so fuck her.

The two years, in maximum-security penitentiary, trying to sidestep the gangs, the Crips, the neo-militia, the Brothers, the Mexs—motherfuckahs, would put a shiv in you for two bits or a pack of Camels.

How I met Jimmy. Hooked up the first week, walking the yard, my hands in the pockets of the light denim jacket, a north-easterly howling across the stone, freezing my nuts off.

Wasn't one of those movie deals. He didn't, like, save me from the white supremacists or prevent some buck from turning me out.

Slow burn.

A favor here, a nod there, a gathering of little moves, till we had the buddy system cooking.

Guy could make me laugh, and on the block there wasn't a whole lot of . . . what's the word I want . . . heard it on *Regis* . . . or *Leno* . . . yeah, *frivolity*.

He got early release, and when I finally got out, he was waiting in a Pinto, some speed, a six of Miller (ice cold), and a wedge, said, "Some walking 'round bills."

A buddy. Am I right or am I right? We had one album in the joint, belonged to Jimmy, Patti Smith's *Horses*. Fuck, goes back thirty years. How old is that?

Thing is, I flat out loved it, still do. The reason why, in this tomb hotel room, I have the new one, *Trampin.*

Fuckin' blinder.

Dunno is it cos Jimmy's dead, or the whole screwed-up mess, but the goddamn songs speak to me.

You're on the zillionth floor of the airport Marriott, with the sole view being the runways, planes moving 24/7, you better have something talk to you. I'm chugging Jack D., singing along to "Mother Rose."

And is this weird or what, I sound like Roy Orbison. My mom, when she wasn't whining along to Irish rebel ballads, would play Roy endlessly.

Man, I don't know politics from Shinola, but Radio Baghdad, hearing that, watching CNN and the body count, I'm weeping like a baby. Like what? Some kind of loser?

Loser? Me?

Hey, shithead, look in the corner, see that hill of coke, the bag of Franklins? Who's losing?

My mom, her wish was to get back to Ireland, walk the streets of Galway, have oysters near the Spanish Arch, do a last jig in the Quays, but money, yeah, never put it together. So I'm, like, gonna make the pilgrimage for her—why I'm at the airport, got the documents, ticket, the whole nine.

Only worry is the beer isn't cold there. How weird is that? But hey, I'll drink Jameson. A few of those suckers, I might dance a jig my own self.

I rang a guy to offload the coke. Can't really bring that shit to Ireland, and I'm worried he might sell me out, but we've done business before so had to tell him where I'm at, thinking maybe that was stupid, but I wasn't focusing real hard when I dropped the dime.

Gotta get my shit together.

So I jump in the shower, blasting in the scald position, and I freeze. A knock at the door.

The Sig is where?

Think, fuck.

Another knock. Louder. Insistent.

And I'm stumbling outta the shower, hit my knee against the sink, that mother hurts, hobble to the bed, grab the Sig from under the pillow, shout, "With you in a sec."

Slide the rack, my voice coming out croaked, sounding like, "Wiv y'all." Texas, right?

I look through the peephole, and it's the maid, fuckin' room service. I shout, "I'm good, *muchas gracias.*"

Hear, *"De nada."*

And the trolley moving on, oil those goddamn wheels. My body is leaking sweat, rivulets down my chest, back, thinking, *Gotta . . . get . . . straight.*

Rest of the day is purple haze, must have ordered some food as I came to on the floor. It's dark, the only light coming from the runway, throwing an off/on flicker across the wall.

Half a turkey hero is on the floor, close to my mouth, smothered in mayo. The Sig is in my right hand and, yeah, my nose is pumping blood again.

The carpet is, like, fucked.

I have clothes on, 501's, and, naturally, a white T with the bloodstained logo.

Redemption Road.

Almost illegible, it's stuck to my chest.

I get to my feet, stagger a bit, so do a quick hit of the snow to straighten out, no biggie. I'm sitting on the bed, waiting for the rush, the phone rings, I pick up, figuring reception.

A voice goes, "You're dead, sucker."

Things to do in Houston when you're dead.

I slam it down, hurting the palm of my hand.

I'm waiting. Let 'em come. I'm, like, ready . . . ready-ish. I'd play Patti but I'm listening to every sound, for every sound . . . a 747 about to take off . . .

Wonder where that's bound?

Kurt Hegre

DONNELL ALEXANDER is a multimedia documentarian whose work has appeared in *McSweeney's, ESPN The Magazine,* and on National Public Radio. The Ohio native's best-known work is the short film *Dock Ellis & the LSD No-No.* Among his other works are the essay "Cool Like Me: Are Black People Cooler than White People?", the 2008 tell-all *Rollin' with Dre* (with Bruce Williams), and the memoir *Ghetto Celebrity.* He can be followed on Twitter @DonnyShell and lives in Los Angeles.

beneficent diversions
from the crackdkins diet
by donnell alexander

She was the most accomplished person in Jerome's life. Something central to her, he could not trust. Down and out, Jerome couldn't fathom the chasm between Elaine's refined lust and his own hunger.

His lover held a doctorate in sociology and an undergrad minor in statistics. Daughter of a minor painter mom and a documentary editor old boy, the woman's sense of applied visual art was not something he could argue with—even as an artist, one of almost feral ambition.

That animal appetite would ultimately win out, Elaine told him time and again. It would save him from the insinuating downward tug. "Follow *that* urge," she said, "and you'll be free in no time . . . It will feel like nothing."

Usually she had just swallowed his semen, and before that demanded "baptism of the throat"—her words. Then she forecast. Elaine also offered her most explicit descriptions of the fashion in which he would recover.

She would wipe her chin clean of—again, her words—the "gravy," his silver, silky gravy.

And next she'd rise and take Jerome by the shoulders, tap his chin up so that their eyes met, and swiftly paint a picture with words, numbers, and theory. Taken as a whole, they said, "It's going to be all right. I swear it will be all right."

* * *

He hardly ever ate because Jerome was on what he called the Crackdkins Diet. The habit had brought about an effortless— necessary, frankly—yet undesired weight loss. For Jerome's first date with Elaine—downtown, off Ludlow Street—he forced himself to consume four pieces of sushi.

Although they were hardly acquainted, Elaine at that time seemed peculiarly invested in his becoming nourished. "I really get off on turning people on to new things," she said, voicing an urgency not often associated with high-end Eastern cuisine. "Don't you find it sexy when someone enjoys an experience you introduce them to?"

It had become difficult for Jerome to bask in the reflection of another's pleasure. His joys were now too dualistic, illumination and malevolence twinned. By the time of this dinner, he had taken two or three casual acquaintances into the Tenderloin's remaining unoccupied buildings for smoking and communion. Recalling those scenes while sitting in this Lower East Side restaurant made him lick his lips.

Jerome thought of hits taken 3,000 miles away.

Those friends were like Elaine—good, adventurous souls looking for the next vivid sensation. Jerome knew the address of every cool rockhouse in SF, Oakland, and Richmond, but he was never clear on how solidly his buddies had stepped into their tango with the rock. For sure, he saw them afterward in the workplace and at openings and award ceremonies. There were no references to crack-fueled rocket rides with tenements for launch pads and homeless junkies as audience. Bic lanterns bright, not spotlight. Jerome's casual acquaintances kept it quiet.

The blind date, promising as she was, turned into a reminder. As would Elaine, these slumming kids from Generation X had tongued their lips upon swallowing, and he now saw those other lips thin and almost begging, all but squirming now that the caressing was through.

She said, "It's like when your photographs are published, I'd imagine. Do you ever happen upon readers glimpsing them? Does it turn you on?"

"I almost never see people see my pictures. They're at home in their pajamas, drinking coffee. Or taking a poop. Generally, it's a gloss, the way they look. People are mad busy. They pass through the horror. I can't get there, to the turn-on, so much."

Jerome picked over his California roll. Mashed into wasabi, the food lost its artfulness and seemed a bit primordial. The Japanese eatery disguised its elegance aurally, through a soundtrack of outer-borough hip-hop and obscure European soul tracks. The DJ, tucked away in anteroom shadows, wore his knit, brimmed Triple Five Soul cap low on his brow and played fewer than ninety seconds of each song.

Cool scene, Jerome thought, but nobody's gonna face death. And in that, this place struck him as deprived.

The last time he had been drug-free was in Fallujah.

That San Diego soldier, the one who had dropped 150 pounds between enlisting and being sent out, died horribly.

Jerome had seen viscera before. He had even seen that of other youngsters eager to strike up friendships with a black war photographer. Insides out, yes, he'd seen that, but Jerome hadn't seen the insides of someone with such exquisite back story.

Josephine Six-Pack has got to witness Dude.

And he began clicking away—auto-drive, auto-focus— at the boy's boots and his gear. From a variety of angles Jerome photographed an iPod clutched in the SoCal corpse's stiff, newly thin, chalky fingers. Wedged as it was between belt buckle and sand, the iPod would make subscribers wonder what the boy was listening to when death hit. A candid shot might make them ponder the concerns of his parents back home.

This documentarian of deadly conflict thought, *They will be so trippin' on the train.*

And Jerome felt kinda high.

He resented that his favorite rhetorical device for preparing for war no longer provided.

The freaks come out at night . . .
The freaks come out at niiight . . .

Because they attacked during the day now. And they were not freaks. These were not the coca-crazed rebels and U.S.-worshipping zealots he'd gotten used to in Central American insurgencies. In this war, they were the faithful. They prayed all the time. Or they blindly followed scripture favored by that other land, the one whose bounty earned its minions' trust.

They came out during the brightest times. Bombing in a fashion that appeared on the surface to be indiscriminate, the locals calculated with the personal specificity of a high-level computer-code creator. Yet their rationale unearthed the truth in terror, robbing light of meaning and upsetting Jerome's metaphor.

On a return flight to Berlin, surfing the Web via wireless modem, he grasped exactly how untethered his worldview had become. A pop-up for an international restaurant had tweaked Jerome's sensibility. He'd pushed away a prefab meal he'd pushed away 500 times before. This time he pushed away the food with feeling.

And the faithful came out all day. Maiming their own. They invoked the name of Allah and the other God, and they grabbed hold of their weapons and refused to let go.

* * *

While on a brief break from his legal theater of pain, Jerome had dallied with the girl who got excited by sharing what turned her on. He had bracketed the episode by ingesting rock cocaine in San Francisco. Next thing, the most real place on earth was where Jerome set. He huddled with Air Force officers, saw some death, took some pictures. And now the shooter was on his way to the Baghdad airport.

That reporter he hung with, the Aussie who had ended his career in the States by announcing that the war in Iraq wasn't going so well, was done and so was Jerome. This was his shortest fling yet. He caught a ride with an American newspaper columnist and a documentary photographer he knew only from textbooks and lore.

The reporter talked nonstop about the American mission. The iconic shooter stared impassively into the sand.

Five miles outside town a shell hit, about 150 yards off the bumpy path that passed for a road. The writer insisted the car be diverted.

No one argued, so the Jordanian hired to drive took the next left he could find.

The explosions only got closer. And louder.

The car stopped completely just outside Baghdad. The gunshots started, bullets arriving from every angle, first strafing the top of their Hummer, then piercing its metal and glass. Jerome took cover, pulling his flak jacket over his head. He dug himself as deep as he could into the space between the driver's side backseat and the floor.

When an acidic explosion blew apart the passenger side, Jerome was surprised to see the documentary photographer still moving, albeit slowly and with more than a little pain. The man's arm had nothing beyond its wrist. No more bullets hit the vehicle.

Careening slightly, the Hummer ambled off the road in low gear.

A degree of same-old, same-old cut in on Jerome's reaction to the sight of both that writer's destroyed body and the utter health of their driver. The Jordanian gestured to the roadside man in a skullcap who dropped his Russian rifle and fled. Jerome rose and rammed the length of his telephoto lens into the Jordanian's ear. As the Hummer commenced to spinning, he again buried himself in the space beneath his seat.

Jerome was on the roof, then back on the seat, and back on the floor. His door turned to the floor. His backseat partner fell onto Jerome, drenching him with blood, touching him with gore.

As minutes passed, both photographers became soaked in the absolute desert quiet.

Jerome tied a tourniquet on his photographic hero. He called his agency's Baghdad bureau, then picked up a camera and climbed out.

As he captured images of the blown-apart reporter in front of the vehicle, Jerome thought of Elaine. This new thing needed no introduction, even where the afterlife holds so much sway. Death can be a kind of baptism. The reporter's back story, familiar enough to Jerome, seemed canned and uninteresting. He'd tell it easily enough. But for the folks back home and in Europe and even here, the hit wouldn't be much stronger than the name that accompanied the man's newspaper column. No one would be turned on.

And that was fine for once. Not every hit could be truly killer. In fact, each hit seemed to be diminishing in its potency.

Jerome looked at his stoic comrade and, just past him, spotted sandwiches—hints of turkey, cheese, and wheat— sticking out of the man's Nikon bag.

Lactose-intolerant or not, Jerome wanted—nay, needed—to consume what he saw.

"Can I have some of that?"

His colleague reached with a limb that could not perform the task. He laughed and began to cry and Jerome documented every emotion.

When he finally got hold of the sandwich, Jerome devoured it in half a dozen bites. Perhaps the worst thing about the Crackdkins Diet is that it only satisfies its adherents' appetites for destruction. And what he really wanted was life.

PART II

FIENDING

Photo courtesy of UC Riverside

SUSAN STRAIGHT is the author of seven novels, including *Highwire Moon* and *A Million Nightingales*. Her latest, *Take One Candle Light a Room*, began with "Poinciana" and the story "The Golden Gopher," which originally appeared in *Los Angeles Noir*. She has published stories and essays in *Zoetrope All-Story*, *Harper's*, *The Believer*, the *New York Times*, and elsewhere. She was born in Riverside, California, where she lives with her family.

poinciana
by susan straight

Why you waste your money here?" she asked Sisia. The smell of the chemicals at the nail salon went through Glorette's eyes and into her brain. Passed right through the tears and the eyeballs. *Through the irises*, she thought.

"Not a waste," Lynn Win said, moving around Sisia's hand like a hummingbird checking flowers. Like the hummingbird that came to the hibiscus in front of Western Motel. Mrs. Tajinder Patel's hibiscus. "Only to you," Lynn Win said.

"Please." Glorette walked into the doorway to breathe and looked at the cars roaming past the strip mall. Every strip mall in Rio Seco, in California, in the world, probably, was like this. Nail salon, pizza place, video store, doughnut shop, liquor store, Launderland, and taqueria. All the smells hovering in their own doorways, like the owners did in the early morning and late at night, waiting.

Like she and Sisia hovered in their own route: Sundown first, Launderland in winter when it was cold in the alley, taqueria when the cops cruised by. All the standing and waiting between jobs. They were just jobs. Like clean the counter at the taqueria. Take out the trash. Uncrate the liquor. Wash the sheets. All up and down the street. Lean against the chain-link fence, against the bus stop but you can't sit on the bench, shove your shoulder into the cinder-block wall outside Launderland and sleep for a minute, if the fog settled in like a quilt, like the opposite of an electric blanket, and cooled off the night.

The nail polish vapors stung her eyes. Why you couldn't get high off these fumes? So convenient. 7-Eleven was a convenience store. Easy. She could sit here and close her eyes, and Lynn Win would paint her like a statue and the vapors would rise up into her mouth and nose and make the inside of her forehead turn to snow. She would pay Lynn Win. Instead of paying for the rock to turn into fumes.

The plant to a powder to a chunk the size of a cocklebur in your hand. Then it turned red and glowed, like a rat's eye in the palm tree when you looked up just as headlights caught the pupils. Did rats have pupils?

Then you breathed in. And behind your eyes, it was like someone took a Wite-Out pen and erased everything. Your whole head turned into a milk shake. Sweet and grainy and sliding down the back of your skull.

Look at all these nail salons. She turned the pages of the advertisements in Vietnamese, the flyer on the coffee table. Massage pedicure chairs. Swirling water. The women with perfect eyebrows and lips and hair. Every other name Nguyen.

Linh Nguyen. She remembered what Lynn Win had said when she changed her name: "Win like money I get."

Glorette breathed again at the open salon door. "Sisia. Please. Tell me you ever heard a man say, 'Girl, I love those nails. That color perfect with your clothes. The decals are fresh.'"

"Shut up, Glorette. You just cheap."

Lynn Win glanced up at her and frowned, her perfect Vietnamese face sheened with makeup, her eyes encircled by a wash of pale green, her lips pink as watermelon Jell-O. On the left side of her neck was a scar. A healed gash that must have gaped, against tight neck skin.

No one had loose neck skin until forty. *She must be about thirty-five*, Glorette thought. *Just like us.*

Sisia had a scar on her neck, too, a keloid caterpillar, shiny as satin. Curling iron. Fifteen. They'd been getting ready for some high school dance. Back when Sisia still hot-combed her hair and then curled it back like Farrah Fawcett and Jayne Kennedy. Hell.

What did the DJ play at that dance? Cameo? She'd have to ask Chess when she saw him next time. Funkadelic?

The hot air at the door mixed with the cold air and nail polish fog.

No scars. She had never done anything with her hair other than wash it, comb in some Luster Pink or coconut oil, and let it hang loose in long, black ripples. Back then. Now she wore it in a high bun every night, unless a man requested that she unpin it.

Now this new woman cruising Palm in the brown van had poked her finger into the bun a few nights ago and then pulled. "Man, I know that shit ain't real," the woman had said, her voice New York like rappers in a video, her words all pushed up to the front of her lips. People from New York kept their words there, just at their teeth, never deep in their throats like Louisiana people. Like her mother and father.

Then the new woman had said, "I-on't-even-care you think you the shit around here. Just cause you light. Cause you got all that hair. Anybody get hair. Bald man get hair he want to. You need to move your ass off this block. Cause I'm parked here."

She couldn't have been more than twenty, twenty-two. Short, thick-thighed in her miniskirt, her hair in marcelled waves close to her forehead. Her words moved behind her lips and her lips moved like a camel's, while her eyes stayed still.

"Sound like she said she some pork," Sisia said, hands on her hips.

Glorette just shrugged and looked back over her shoulder at the woman near her van. That's where she worked the men. She had a CD player in there and some silk sheets, she said. And her man stood in the doorway of the liquor store for a long time, talking with Chess and Casper and the others who were just biding their time.

"I ain't no crack ho," the girl called, and Sisia laughed.

"I ain't either," she said. "I'm somethin else."

"This ain't the eighties." The girl shot them the finger.

"And I ain't Donna Summer."

Glorette watched Sisia move her head on her neck like a turtle and stalk away, and she followed.

Glorette thought, *1980? Was I fifteen?*

Damn.

Gil Scott-Heron said the "Revolution Will Not Be Televised," brother. You will not be able to turn on or tune out. But they did. That's what Sere always said. Brothers tuned out. *Green Acres* and *Beverly Hillbillies* will not be so important, Gil Scott-Heron said—but they were. The revolution will not be televised, brothers, the revolution will be live.

One night Glorette had run into Marie-Therese at Rite Aid. Marie-Therese used to be with Chess, back then when they were girls in the darkness of the club called Romeo's. 1981? Only two clubs in Rio Seco back then—Romeo's for jazz and funk, and Oscar's Place for nasty old blues and knife fights and homebrew.

That was where she met Sere. A brother with a flute. Didn't nobody in Rio Seco have a flute.

Gil Scott-Heron's band had a flute. Yusuf Lateef had a flute. War had a flute. Herbie Mann had a flute. Sere had loved that Mann song—"Push Push." She could still remember it. Sere's band was called Dakar. His last name.

Called himself Sere Dakar.

Where the hell was Sere playing his damn flute now? For

Jay-Z or 50 Cent? For Ludacris? What else did this girl from New York always have blastin out her CD player when she was waiting?

Nobody said *hey, brotha*. Nobody but the old ones. Her age. Chess and Octavious and them. That Sidney, the one ran into her at Sundown. He used to work at the hospital. Chess and them said he burned the body parts after the doctors cut them off. Said he burned up Mr. Archuleta's leg, and Glorette always wondered how heavy that piece of meat would have been. She ran her shoulders up under her ears with the shivers. Piece. *Give me a lil piece, sugar. Just a lil piece.* What the hell was that? What they wanted wasn't no size. You couldn't give anybody just a lil bit of anything.

Sisia handed the money to Lynn Win. Sisia's skin was so thin over her facial bones that her temples looked stretched from the tight cornrows.

They had been smoking for so long. Chess gave her the pipe first but then he got done with it. He said he didn't need it.

He had his weed and Olde English.

How was the skin distributed over the bones? How did her buttocks stay in the right place? When did men decide they wanted buttocks and cheekbones and hair instead of something else? Like a big nose or huge forehead or belly? Some caveman picked.

Sisia stood up with her nails purple as grape juice and rings winking. But could a woman kill someone with her nails? Because this new woman from New York looked like she wanted to kill Glorette.

The man stopped in his old Camaro. Moved his chin to tell her *come on*. Glorette knew he wanted head. That's all. He parked in the lot behind the taqueria. Five minutes. A little piece of her lip and her tooth banged on his zipper when he jerked around.

Her piece. Twenty dollars. She walked back toward Launderland where Jazen and his boys kept their stash in a dryer.

The rock was so small. Not even a piece. A BB. A spider egg. A grasshopper eye. But not perfectly round. Jagged-edged.

A white freckle, she thought, and started laughing, waiting for the screen like a windshield in front of her eyes when she breathed in hard. Like someone had soaped up her brain. Store was closed.

Headphones. Al B. Sure—"Nite and Day." Switch—"I Call Your Name." All those sweet-voiced men from when she was first walking out here. Not jazz. Jazz was Sere. "Poinciana." "April in Paris." And funk. Mandrill and Soul Makossa and Roy Ayers.

But somebody always stole the headphones. And she wanted Victor to have headphones, and they kept stealing his, too. So he slept in them, with a chair against his bedroom door. She tried to make sure only Chess or someone she knew came home with her, but sometimes Sisia begged to let her use the couch or the floor with a man and then sometimes he stole.

Her son Victor knew everything about music.

"New York rappers, man, I have to listen real careful to understand," he always said. "Oakland and L.A. are easy. St. Louis is crazy—I mean, they mess with the actual words."

Victor analyzed everything. Sometimes Glorette stared at his forehead while he was talking, at the place where his shorn hair met his temples. He kept it cut very short, and the hairline curved like a cove on a map. She had been to a cove once. To the ocean. With Victor's father. Sere.

He'd seen her in the club. He thought she was twenty. He got her address. He'd borrowed a car, pulled up in front of her father's house and leaned his chin on the crook of his elbow like a little kid. A little boy with an arm turtleneck. He told her, "I'm fixin to see this place California's supposed to be. What they all talk about in Detroit."

"What you think you gon see?" Glorette had watched the freeway signs above them, the white dots like big pearls in the headlights.

"Remember Stevie singing 'Livin for the City'? Skyscrapers and everythang. I'ma see waves and sand and everythang. Surfers."

"At night?"

"They probably surf at night." He'd turned to her in the passenger seat. That car belonged to Chess. It was a Nova and someone had spilled Olde English in the backseat and the smell rose from the carpet sharp like cane syrup. "It's an hour to the ocean and you never been there?"

Glorette had shrugged. She had felt her shoulders go up and down, felt her collarbone in the halter top graze the cloth. He had left a love bruise on her collarbone. He'd said her bones made her look like a Fulani queen. "I bet them sorry brothas call you a Nubian or Egyptian. Cause they don't know the specifics. Huh?"

She'd touched cheekbone and collarbone and the point of her chin. But after all that it was the soft part they wanted.

No bones.

Sere took out the Cameo cassette from the old stereo and slid in an unmarked one. "Poinciana," he said. Piano hush-hush and cymbals. Like rain on a porch roof and swirling water.

"It's an hour I ain't never had free," she said.

Then, after they'd driven to the ocean and sat in the car looking at the blackness that was one with the horizon, a cold purple-blue blackness like charcoal, with the waves the only sound and then a splash of white in a long line as if someone were washing bleach clothes in too much detergent, Sere turned to her and he only wanted the same things as the rest of them.

* * *

Why have buttocks? What good were they? And hair? If Glorette's great-great-whoever had been Fulani and had gotten with some Frenchman in Louisiana, why all this hair down her back? How was that supposed to keep her warm? Hair was fur. Nails were claws. Sisia was ready to kill some damn lion now that they were done with Lynn Win's place. Glorette had gotten high off the fumes anyway, waiting for Sisia's toenails to dry. Who the hell was she gon kill with them toenails? Lynn Win's mother sat in front of the spa chair waiting for the next pedicure. The mother looked old but probably wasn't. She wore knit pants like an old woman, and her hair was in a bun on her head. Black hair with gray threads shot through like moss.

All the blood moving through the pieces of their bodies. When she woke up at noon or so, the already-hot light streaming through the blinds like X-rays on her legs where she lay on the couch, she would see the tops of her feet smooth and golden, her toes dirty from the walking, but her skin still sleeping.

Sometimes Sisia spent the eighteen dollars on a pedicure so she could sit down for an hour, she said.

But Glorette didn't want decals on her toes. She saved twenty dollars a day for Victor. For CDs and ramen.

The store was open. She went to the older mall with the Rite Aid and auto parts store. The lipsticks stacked in the bin like firewood. Hair color boxes always started with blond. Blond as dental floss and then about thirty more yellows. Saffron and Sunflower. Gingercake and Nutmeg. Black always last. Midnight.

Black hair ain't nothin you could eat.

There were flowering plants in front of the drugstore. Her father always shook his head and said, "Anybody buy plant when they buy cough syrup don't grow nothin. Put that tomato in the ground and throw water on it and wonder why it die, *oui*."

She walked past the window of the auto parts store. When she was with Chess, she'd wander the aisles touching the oil filters like paper queen's collars and fan belts like rubber bands for a giant's ponytail. Chess fixed cars all day and loved her all night. But he had to love Marie-Therese and Niecy, too, and she told him, "Only me," and he shrugged and said, "Only always too small. Only one dollar. Only one rib. See? I ain't livin only."

She saw the boxes and boxes of fuel filters near the window. Same size as hair color. A lil piece. Only a lil piece.

Ramen was ten for a dollar. Beef.

Now, when she looked at her hands on the counter, they were smooth and gold. She slid the dollar across. But by midnight, when she sat in the taqueria just before it closed, she would study her hands, the veins jagged like blue lightning. Her feet—it looked like someone had inserted flattened branches of coral under her skin. The skin so thin by midnight, at hands and feet and throat and eyelids.

She imagined she was swimming down the sidewalk. The pepper trees in the vacant lot after the strip mall, where the old men used to play dominoes on orange crates, where the city had put a chain-link fence, trying to keep "undesirables" from loitering. She didn't loiter. The streetlights shone through the pepper branches. She was under the ocean. Sere had brought a flashlight that night they went to the ocean, and he'd found tidal pools where the water only swayed in the depressions of the rocks, and the flashlight beam showed her a forest of seaweed and snails clinging to the leaves—were they leaves, underwater? stems?—and the whole world under the surface swayed.

Like now, when the evening wind moved the whole street. The pepper branches swayed delicate and all at once, the palm fronds rustled and glinted above her, and the tumbleweeds along the fence trembled like anemones.

She'd gotten a book, a child's book, after that night at the ocean and learned the names of every animal in the tidal pool. She had waited a year for him to take her back there, but he disappeared when she was eight months pregnant, veins like fishnet stockings all stretched out along her sides.

She swam along the sidewalk now, wondering where Sisia had gone, waiting to see who was looking for her. Maybe Chess. Maybe the brown van, with New York City in the back pissed at Glorette because she'd shrugged and said in front of the woman, "Ain't hot to me. Long as my hair up and my soda cold."

"Pop."

"What?"

"You mean pop."

"I'ma pop you," Sisia came up behind the woman and said. "Don't nobody care if you from New York or New Mexico. Time for you to step. Don't nobody want to get in no nasty van. Fleas and lice and shit."

The woman spat a cloud onto the sidewalk near Sisia's sandals. "Then why I had five already tonight? Make more in one night than you make all week. This the way in New York. Mens want some convenience. And it's the shit up in there. I got incense and candles and curtains. So you take your raggedy country ass back to the alley." But all this time she was looking at Glorette. "And your high yella giraffe, too."

The custodian at the junior high said, "Just a lil minute, now. Just stand still. I ain't even gon touch you. But it ain't my fault. Look at you. The Lord intended you for love. Look at you. Hold still. See. See. Lord. See."

The mop was damp like a fresh-washed wig at the back of

her neck. "Pretend that's me." He stood close enough that she smelled Hai Karate, and then the bleach smell of what left his body and he caught in a rag.

"See." His voice was high and tight. His white name tag was small as a Chiclet when she crossed her eyes and didn't focus at all.

She wanted some chicharrones. Explosions of fat and chile on her molars.

When she turned down Palm to head toward Sundown, seeing Chess and two other men, thinking the chicharrones would give her enough time to let Chess see the backs of her thighs and her shoulder blades, her miniskirt and halter top better than what New York had, better than curtains or candles, it was like her thoughts brought the brown van cruising down Palm slowly, stopping at the liquor store. The woman got out and folded her arms, cocked her head to the side, the tails of her bandanna like a parrot's long feathers curling around her neck.

Glorette turned down the alley and headed toward the taqueria instead.

"Look here," the custodian said. Mr. Charles. But he was not old. His fade was not gray at the edges. "Look here." He held out money rolled tight as a cigarette. "I ain't gon bother you no more."

The five dollar bill was a twig in her sock all day.

She sat at the table in the taqueria for a few minutes, feeling the blood move and growl in her feet. No socks. Sandals. Heels. The money not in her cleavage. No money yet tonight. When she got money she put it inside the thick hair at the back of her head, just before the bun.

Chess would give her money. But most of the men just slid a rock into her palm.

The custodian didn't have to touch her after that. He didn't give her money ever again. He watched her walk in the hallway, and she knew he went into his broom closet and stood there and saw her when he moved his hands. Free. A lil piece. He stood facing the mop. The string hair. Then he was gone.

They were all gone.

At the taqueria, the woman behind the counter watched her, waiting patiently. Her mop was already wet. It stood up behind her, at the back door. Her night was almost over. The carne asada was dry and stringy in the warming pan.

Just a lil piece of meat. And a warm tortilla.

She still had the bag of ramen but Victor would be asleep now. He was seventeen. He was about to graduate. He stayed up late studying and fell asleep on the couch, even though he knew she might bring someone home if she had to. The only one who always insisted on coming to her apartment was Chess. He liked to sit on the couch and drink a beer and pretend they were married. She knew it. He would watch TV like that was all he came for, laughing at Steve Harvey, like this living room was TV, too, and there were sleeping kids in the bedrooms and a wife.

"Look at your feet," he would say, like she'd been working at 7-Eleven all day. Convenience. "You should get your feet done like Sisia. Look like they hurt. And get your toes did. Ain't that how y'all say? 'I done got my toes *did*.'"

Glorette smiled.

Victor was afraid of fingernails. He'd cried when he was little when Sisia came over and Glorette didn't know why. Sisia wasn't pretty. She was dark and her cheeks were pitted like that bread. Pumpernickel. What the hell kind of name was that for a bread?

Sisia was a brick house, though. She liked to say it. A real mamma-jamma—36-24-36 back in the day. More like 36-30-36 now, but still Glorette heard men say, "Close your eyes, man, and open your hands, and you got something there, with that woman."

But it was the fingernails that Victor cried about. Long and squared-off and winking with gems or even a ring through the nail. Lynn Win had to bore a hole through the tip and hang the jeweled ring.

Claws. For animals.

But now only women were supposed to fight with them. You could scratch a man's face, but then he'd probably kill you. You could scratch his back—some men wanted you to dig nails into their backs, like you were out of control, and that made them lose it, their whole spines would arch and tremble. But some men, if you dug your nails experimentally into the wider part below their shoulder blades, the cobra hood of muscle, just frowned and elbowed your hands off. "Don't mark me up and shit," they'd say, and then Glorette knew they had a wife or woman at home.

But Glorette just used her regular nails. Her claws. The ones God gave her. The ones Victor said were designed different from apes and chimps, and different from cats and dogs. "I don't think we ever dug," he'd say. "Not like badgers or rabbits. And we didn't need the fingernails to hold onto food or anything. So it must be just for fighting, but we didn't have teeth like the cats or dogs to bite something on the neck and kill it.

"I think they're just leftover. From something else."

Sere had a vein on his temple, from his hairline toward his left eyebrow, like twine sewn under his skin. When he played his flute or drums, the vein rose up but didn't throb. It wasn't red or blue under his brown skin, not like the white baby Glorette had seen once at the store whose skin was so pale that blue veins moved along its head and temples like freeways.

But Victor's temples were smooth and straight, though he thought all the time, read and wrote and did math problems and studied for graduation tests and played music and didn't just listen but wrote down all these bands' names and dates and song titles. He asked her once, "This one, the one you like so much. 'Poinciana.' What is it?"

She thought for a long time. "A flower? I don't know."

One crystal of salt from a cracker on her tongue. The cracker exploding like hard-baked snowflakes and pieces of rock salt on her molars. Then a white sludge she could work at while they walked.

She had to have saltines when she was pregnant with Victor.

Sisia's aunt used to eat starch. White chunks of Argo. Only one she wanted. That box with the woman holding corn. Indian woman. Corn turned into knobs of snow that squeaked in the teeth. *Like new sneakers on a basketball court*, Chess used to say when they were young.

The corn husks were green skin when they peeled off. The kernels milky white when pierced by a fingernail. How did that turn to starch?

The leaves of the coca wherever those Indians grew it. And how the hell did it turn to little chunks of white? Baby powder cornstarch flakes of Wite-Out powdered sugar, not crystals, not cane sugar and molasses, like her mother would only use, like Louisiana. They cut the cane and crushed it in the mill, her mother said. Mules going round and round. Then the juice had to boil and boil and boil and finally sugar crystals formed. Diamonds of sweet. Diamonds of salt. On the tongue. But this chunk—which she picked up out the empty dryer drum while Jazen watched, her twenty in his pocket—she couldn't eat.

It had to turn to gray smoke inside her mouth, her throat, her lungs. Insubstantial. Inconvenience. The convenience store. Controlled substance. Possession of a controlled substance, but if you smoke it or swallow it if they pull up, you ain't in possession. It's possessin you. Ha. Sisia laughing. Chess laughing. Come on. Let's go home.

He liked to pretend her couch was home.

Swear he would ask her to make grits. The tiny white sand of corn. Not crystals. Not chunks.

Call it cush-cush back home, her mother used to say.

Victor had eaten grits at his grandmére's house and loved to call it that. Cush-cush.

Victor was sleeping now. His math book open on his chest. Sere's brain. My brain? He had the third highest grades in the whole damn school. His ramen was in her hand. The plastic bag handles were rolled into pearls by now.

She walked down the alley behind the taqueria, more for the smell of the put-away beef than anything else. Ain't no charge for smelling. She paused beside a shopping cart parked against the chain-link fence. The slats of vinyl worked through the fence. Sideways world. She smoked her last rock in a pipe the man had given her. Pipe made of an old air-freshener tube blown larger with a torch.

The chunk was yellow and porous. Small as aquarium rocks. The fish in the pet store went in and out of the ceramic castle. Her head was pounding. Maybe he gave her some bad coca. A bad leaf.

Someone was behind her. Sisia. Sisia was ready to quit for the night. Glorette was tired now. She had Victor's ramen in her hand.

She heard a voice kept up all behind front teeth. "Old crackhead bitch," the voice said. "See if that hair real now. One a them fake falls. Drink yo damn soda? You ain't gon pop nobody now."

Not Sisia.

Fingers dug into her braid, at the base of her skull, and pulled hard enough to launch Glorette backwards, and then the silver handle of the shopping cart was beside her eyes, and the girl was tying her hair to the handle.

"Real enough," the girl said. "But this ain't the eighties. You ain't Beyoncé. You some old J.Lo and shit. You finished."

She was still behind Glorette. Her footsteps went backward. Was she gone?

Glorette couldn't untie her hair. Her hands shook. She was bent too far. Spine. So far backward that she could only look up at the streetlight just above. She felt pain sharp like a rat biting her heart. Teeth in her chest. A bad leaf? *I tasted salt.* A crystal. The teeth bit into her chest again. Just a muscle. Victor says just a muscle like your thigh. *Flex.* She closed her eyes but the streetlight was brighter than the moon. Yellow sulfur. The sun. Like staring into the sun until you were blind, until the thudding of your heart burst into your brain and someone slid chalk sideways into perforated stripes across your vision until you couldn't see anything.

Andrew Brown

JAMES BROWN is the author of several novels, along with the memoirs *The Los Angeles Diaries* and *This River*. He has received the Nelson Algren Award in Fiction and a National Endowment for the Arts Fellowship. His work has appeared in *GQ*, the *New York Times Magazine*, the *Los Angeles Times Magazine*, and *Ploughshares*. Brown teaches in the MFA program at California State University, San Bernardino.

the screenwriter
by james brown

The Las Palmas Behavioral Modification Center is located on the outskirts of Palm Desert, not far from its more famous counterpart, the Betty Ford Clinic, in the neighboring community of Rancho Mirage. Both cities are renowned for their spectacular eighteen-hole golf courses, plush landscapes, and million-dollar retirement homes. But water is not natural to this otherwise barren land, and without it everything but the indigenous snakes and lizards would shrivel up and die. In the summer months temperatures reach 110, often higher, and in the winter come the powerful winds that darken the sky with clouds of dust and debris. Life here stops where the water ends, and it's that borderline, on the cusp of survival and devastation, that strikes me as exactly the right place for the alcoholic and addict who spends his days constantly navigating between the two.

From Los Angeles, depending on traffic, it's a good two hours or more before you escape the congestion of the San Bernardino Freeway and turn onto the less traveled Highway 111. From here it's a narrow two-lane blacktop that cuts through Palm Springs and Rancho Mirage and takes you still deeper into the desert. The land is flat and dry and the distant mountains are steep and rocky. A few miles past the city of Palm Desert, you turn off the highway and onto another stretch of blacktop that twists and bends and leads you, finally, to the Las Palmas

Behavioral Modification Center.

It's a sprawling, Santa Fe–style structure made of stucco and adobe and painted white. Outside the main doors is a rock garden with cacti and desert flowers and a small waterfall. At first glance it looks like it might be one of those trendy, out-of-the-way desert spas for people in the know, a quaint hideaway for L.A.'s hippest, but as you come closer, when you step through those front doors, you recognize it for what it is: a hospital for the mentally unstable and those wrestling with their own self-destruction by way of alcohol and drugs. The latter group comprise the majority of its patients, though many of us fit neatly into both categories. Directly after my release from St. Mary's Hospital in North Hollywood, where I was treated for second-degree burns on both arms and a host of contusions from head to toe, I take up residence at the Las Palmas BMC.

I arrive in the late morning, accompanied by my best friend, Tim O'Neill, who's taken it upon himself to drive me here. It is also at his urging that I choose this rehab over dozens of more local ones. According to Tim, it has a high success rate with its patients and an excellent reputation within the film community for its discreetness.

Unlike the Betty Ford Clinic, there are no photographers lurking behind the bushes, no *National Enquirer*, no news cameras. Even executive-level alcoholics and addicts can pass unnoticed through its doors and return clean and sober with no one the wiser for it. Why my friend thinks I need protecting, however, I have no idea. My place on the totem pole of movie making is just a notch above the caterer in the last of the rolling credits. And it's not like my drinking or using is or has been any secret for quite some time now.

"This is the best thing for you," he says, as we climb out of his car. He drives a Mercedes SUV, exactly like my ex-wife's, only a different color. "Like it or not," he adds, "this is your home for the next twenty-eight days. Don't get any bright ideas and try to bolt."

Given that it's in the middle of the desert, I assure him that I won't be going anywhere in the foreseeable future, particularly in my present condition. It's been nearly two days since my last drink, and I'm beginning to feel really sick. I'm beginning to sweat. "Clean up your act," he says, "and as soon as you're out of here, I know I can get you some work. A lot of people still believe in you." I know what kind of work he means, the kind I used to turn down. TV dramas. Cop shows. Sitcoms. Of course now I'd be grateful to get it. As for Tim's mention of those who still believe in me, he's talking about my meteoric rise to the higher echelons of screenwriting, followed by my equally meteoric descent years later when the drugs and alcohol took ahold of me. Tim, on the other hand, is a screenwriter turned TV producer, and he's at the top of his form by any measure. He slaps me lightly on the back. I can see the concern on his face.

"Are you okay?" he asks. "You're not looking so good."

"I'm all right," I say.

"C'mon, let's get you inside."

As with any hospital, the amount of admitting paperwork is staggering, and the Las Palmas BMC is no exception. Had I been in better health, the process may not have seemed so overwhelming, but soon after Tim leaves I feel the shakes coming on. I'm a real trooper, however, and instead of asking the head counselor if we could postpone these admission procedures until I can at least hold a pen steady enough to sign my name, I push forward. I follow the man down a long, wide hallway to his office where I take a seat across from him at his desk. He's around my age with thick glasses and a bushy mustache, and while I sit there, sweating, I wonder what he thinks of me. I wonder if to him I'm just another casualty in that long procession of drunks and addicts who pass through his life, few probably ever staying sober for any real length of time. It has to be frustrating, and I wonder if he cares anymore. I wonder if it even matters. He glances down at my arms, which are both wrapped in white gauze from the burns I suffered in the accident.

"What happened?"

"I burned myself."

"How'd you do that?"

"It's a long story," I tell him.

Reaching into one of the drawers, he takes out some sort of form, or questionnaire, and lays it flat on his desk.

"I have to ask you some questions," he says, "and I need for you to be completely truthful. How long has it been since your last drink?"

"About two days."

"How much, on average, would you say you've been drinking?"

"About a quart a day."

"Of hard liquor?"

"Vodka usually. Sometimes bourbon."

The mere mention of liquor triggers my thirst. I want a drink, I want it now, and I want it badly. My hands are shaking, so I hide them in my lap.

"What about other drugs?"

"Like what?"

"Let's start with heroin. Do you use it? Have you ever used it?"

"I've done it a few times," I tell him. "But not in the last few years."

"Intravenously?"

Needle users always look the worst, and it's a bum rap because it's the most cost-efficient and expeditious way to get it into your system, offering the biggest bang for your buck. But I leave that part out, not wanting him to get the wrong impression.

"Sometimes. Yes."

"How old were you when you first started?"

"Heroin? I was fourteen. Drinking? I'd say ten or eleven."

"What about cocaine?"

"I've used lots of it. Too much."

"How much is that?"

"When I'm bingeing, I'd say three or four grams a day."

"And how often do you binge?"

I shrug.

"I don't really keep count," I say. "Maybe a couple times a month."

As we talk he is taking notes and checking off boxes on the form. He has on a sport coat and a red-and-white–striped tie that he likes to tug on now and again between questions. I'm starting to feel nauseated. I wipe sweat from my brow with the back of my hand.

"How long is this going to take?" I ask.

He smiles. "What's the hurry?"

But he knows damn well.

"I need something to steady my nerves."

"That'll be up to the doctor," he says. "Tell me, when was the last time you used cocaine?"

"On Christmas Eve."

"Any methamphetamines?"

"Only when I can't get coke."

"But you use them?"

"Yes."

At first, when he started asking these questions, he struck me as nonjudgmental. But as the process continues, and I admit to more abuse, he appears to grow irritated. He looks at me and takes a deep breath.

"Let's try another approach," he says, "and see if we can't save us both a little time. What drugs, Mr. Lewis, haven't you abused?"

I have to think about this for a while.

"Ecstasy," I say. "I've never tried that but I've pretty much done everything else, from Percodan, OxyContin, and quaaludes to LSD. Marijuana, I don't like, never have. To cut to the quick, my problems are with booze, coke, and speed. I've been using them all since I was a kid, but it didn't really get out of control until around my late thirties."

Again he smiles. That smug, knowing one. I'm quickly coming to dislike this guy.

"Or so you think," he says. "Alcoholics and addicts almost always cross the line into addiction years before they're ever aware of it. I'm betting you're no different." Then out of the blue he asks, "Do you have thoughts of suicide?"

I'm caught off guard.

"What?"

"Do you ever think about killing yourself?"

It's my firm belief that anyone of any intelligence has at some dark point in life seriously weighed the pros and cons of checking out early. But I also know that if I'm honest, I'll be treated as a threat to myself and they'll throw me into the lockdown psych unit. Which means I won't be going anywhere until the shrinks say I'm psychologically fit. That could be a whole lot longer than the typical twenty-eight days of rehab.

"No," I lie.

"Never?"

A wave of nausea passes over me.

"I think I'm going to be sick," I say. "Where's your bathroom?"

Inside of an hour I'm in the throes of full-fledged withdrawal and the formalities of the check-in procedures are temporarily placed on hold. I'm escorted directly to the staff doctor where it's determined that I'm in the first stages of delirium tremens. The nurse gives me a healthy dose of Valium, and because my blood pressure has rocketed off the charts, I'm also administered an additional shot of Clonidine, a powerful antihypertensive, to further reduce the possibility of stroke.

The combined effect of these drugs knock me out, and when I wake, when the drugs have worn off, I start to panic. My heart beats fast, and I'm still sweating. I'm still shaking and sick to my stomach. The room is dark, and for a minute or so I'm completely disoriented, not knowing where I am or what's happening to me. I sit up. I look around. The door is slightly ajar and a wedge of light falls across another bed in the room. Someone's in it, curled up in the fetal position, and I can hear his labored breathing. He's shivering under the sheet, like you do when you have a bad fever, and every now and then he moans. I lie back in bed and stare at the ceiling, knowing full well now where I am. I think of my daughter. I think of my ex-wife, and I ask myself, what's wrong with me? How come I can't straighten up? What have I done to my family? What have I done to myself?

I've hit a real bottom.

I've hit a brand-new record low.

It's around this time that a nurse slips into the room pushing a cart. She turns on the light on the nightstand between our two beds and gently places her hand on the shoulder of the curled-up figure.

"Eddie," she says, "how you doing?"

"Not so great."

"It's time for your medication," she says.

He has to sit up now, and when he does I see that he's just a kid, probably no older than my daughter, and he's drenched in sweat.

"What happened to you?" she asks me.

"I burned myself."

"How'd you do that?"

"It's a long story," I say.

I swallow the pills with the water and she takes the cups from me and leaves. Maybe fifteen, twenty minutes later, just before I go under, I hear Eddie in the next bed. "This is fucked up," he says under his breath. "I ain't never doing that shit again." Then it sweeps over me, whatever it is in the pills she gave me, and I'm down for the count again.

For both of us it goes on like this for the better part of two days, our sweating and shaking, passing in and out of consciousness. It's a rebellion of the body crying out for the drug it's been trained to need. The heart pounds. The head throbs. You can't hold down food, and every nerve ending is on fire. Except to use the toilet, neither of us has the strength to get out of bed, let alone leave the room. The detox process is exhausting, and when the tempest finally subsides, and I believe I can speak truthfully for Eddie as well, we're overcome with relief and gratitude.

After that we sleep.

And it's a wonderful, deep sleep.

When I finally wake up, I look over at Eddie in the next bed and find him staring at me. It's night, and the light on the stand between us is turned on. I feel immensely better, though the term *better*, in this case, is relative; even slight improvement, given where I started out, is a major breakthrough. I tell myself that this is it.

That I will change.

There will be no more drinking. No powders. No pills. No potions. From this day on I will make my first earnest, and hopefully last, attempt to put it all behind me, finally and forever.

Eddie asks the running question of the week. "What happened to your arms?"

"I burned them."

"How'd you do that?"

"It's a long story," I say.

"I got time," he says.

He's propped up on one elbow and I notice his arm, the left one. It's black and blue at the bend from sticking it with needles. Though I already know the answer, I turn Eddie's question back on him.

"What happened to your arm?"

"Heroin," he says, but he pronounces it "hair-ron," as they do in the ghetto. I also detect a trace of pride in his voice, one typical of the heroin addict, especially the younger ones. It's the mother of drugs, and in the hierarchy of addiction there's a certain romance, a certain prestige factor, in being strung out on smack. A few years ago his attitude wouldn't have bothered me, but now I see myself in this kid, on the fast track to destruction, and that mind-set troubles me.

He nods at me. "What're you kicking, man?"

"Booze and coke."

"I like coke, too."

Again he's a little too enthusiastic with volunteering this information.

"I'm starving," he says. "Want to get something to eat? The cafeteria's closed but the lounge stays open all night."

Until now I hadn't thought about it, but I'm famished, too. I rise slowly from the bed, still unsteady on my feet. I'm wearing a T-shirt and a pair of sweatpants. Eddie has on the same. In the closet I find my tennis shoes. I put them on and together we emerge from our dimly lit room and into the brightly lit lounge, a little broken maybe, a little shell-shocked for the experience, but nonetheless alive.

In the days to come Eddie and I will be subjected to a grueling schedule designed to get and keep us clean and sober. Breakfast is served at seven a.m. followed by an hour-long group therapy meeting. After that it's a drug and alcohol–education class, which satisfies one of the state requirements for those who've lost driver's licenses on DUI charges, myself included. Then it's off to individual counseling. Then comes lunch. An hour later we have a study session with the *Big Book* of Alcoholics Anonymous, copies of which all patients receive on their first day. We break again for dinner and afterward we endure a lecture on the damaging physiological and psychological effects of alcohol and dope on our bodies and minds. And every other night, Sundays included, we attend either an A.A. or N.A. (Narcotics Anonymous) meeting held here at the hospital but open to the community. I switch off between the two, since I've earned lifelong memberships in both, though I feel more at home with your run-of-the-mill alcoholic. Eddie switches off, too, mainly just to hang with me.

Tonight, after dinner, we flip a coin: heads it's A.A., tails N.A., and it comes up heads. The meeting is held in the rec room at the far end of the hospital, and Eddie and I get there early to help set up the tables and chairs, make coffee, and put out the A.A. literature. The leader of the meeting is one of our head counselors. His name is Dale Weiss but he's better known among the staff and patients as Tradition Dale for his strict and unwavering allegiance to the principles of Alcoholics Anonymous. One glance at his face and you know he spent the better part of his fifty-odd years drinking hard and heavy before he ever sobered up. He has the telltale bulbous nose, and across it runs a thin spiderlike pattern of broken blood vessels. In his heyday, I'm sure the whites of his eyes were bloodshot and yellowed with jaundice, but now they're clear as ice, and that's how he looks at you. An intense stare, eye to eye, until you glance away.

"How many days you got, Lenny?" he asks.

"I think about twelve."

"You think or you know?"

"I know."

"You need an exact date," he says. "You need to keep an accurate count. I have 3,672 days, and God willing, tomorrow it'll be 3,673."

Tradition Dale is big on God, which has always been a stumbling block for me. Though I'm no atheist, I'm not exactly a churchgoer either, and I have a tough time embracing the religious aspects of A.A. The disciples say I need a Higher Power and that this Higher Power can be anything I want it to be, the options ranging from a doorknob to the group itself. "Fake it," they say, "till you make it." But I have trouble with that line of reasoning, too. It's like lying to yourself until you're convinced the lie is true.

People begin shuffling in five minutes before the meeting is supposed to start. It's a small group, maybe fifteen or so, about half of them patients at the BMC, the others visitors from the surrounding communities. Eddie and I've arranged the foldout chairs in a circle, and Tradition Dale takes a seat at the head of it. He passes around three laminated placards, one with the Twelve Traditions of A.A., another taken from Chapter Five in the *Big Book* called "How It Works," and a third with "The Promises," which is all about the important, life-affirming benefits of sobriety. The first two are read aloud as a kind of preamble before the sharing of stories begins. "The Promises" is saved for the end, so as to put a spin of optimism to even the darkest of meetings.

And they can get pretty dark.

One of the greatest realizations to come from A.A., at least for myself, is learning that there are plenty of others out there just as messed up and troubled as me. Some more so. It's no consolation but it does give me an odd sense of belonging in a world that by and large considers people like me weak-willed, moral degenerates. After the preambles are read, Tradition Dale calls on one of the group to share. In this case it's a young woman with a bony, angular forehead and sunken cheeks. A borderline anorexic. I'd say she's in her late twenties, and she looks scared. She looks emotionally fragile, as if any second she could burst into tears. I've seen her in other meetings, but she's not a patient here.

"I'm Gloria," she says, "and I'm a grateful alcoholic. I'm glad I've been asked to share because I'm going through hell right now. It's been a year since Charlie died, and I know they say it's supposed to get easier with time, but for me it only gets worse." She pauses. She looks around the group. "I don't think I'll ever be the same. He was always happy to see me when I came home, always there to cheer me up when I was feeling blue. You couldn't ask for a better companion. We went everywhere together. Did everything together. Now he's gone and I still can't believe it. Last night I woke up thinking he was in bed with me again, but when I reached over to touch him there was no one there. The sheets were cold." Again she pauses, this time to stare down at the floor. Her pain seems genuine, and I find myself feeling for her. "My friends," she says, "tell me to look on the bright side—that we had twelve wonderful years together. And no one can ever take that away from us. I've been thinking about getting another puppy, but it wouldn't be fair to Charlie. I mean, it's just not right, especially so soon."

Eddie is sitting next to me. He leans over and whispers in my ear. "Has she been talking about a dog?"

I shrug. "I guess so."

I don't like to think of myself as a cruel or insensitive man. Certainly you can deeply love a pet. At the same time, however, it strikes me that this woman has issues independent of alcohol and drugs and that maybe she'd be better off sharing her feelings with a good psychiatrist.

If addiction has one redeeming value it's that it does not discriminate, crossing all ethnic, economic, and social barriers. In this group of BMC patients, we have a doctor who used to prescribe his own morphine sulfate, a paramedic who couldn't keep his hands out of the med kit, a housewife strung out on wine and antianxiety pills, and a Beverly Hills building contractor hooked on OxyContin. Then there's my pal, Eddie Salinas, a sixteen-year-old heroin addict, and a thirty-something-year-old crackhead who hails from the friendly city of Compton, home to the notorious Crips and their beloved brethren, the Bloods. He has prison tats covering both arms, and on his neck, in fancy script, is the name *LaKesha*. Dale asks him to talk next.

"I'm Ronnie," he says, "and I'm a dope fiend and a drunk. My father was a dope fiend and a drunk. My mother was a dope fiend and a drunk. Both my brothers are dope fiends and drunks. Getting wasted is a way of life." This guy doesn't so much talk as shout, and he can't seem to sit still in his seat. I've heard him share before and I like his passion. I like that he's a little over the top, since the rest of us are usually more subdued. "Normal, for me, is being fucked up. Normal, for me, is getting sick on Thunderbird wine. Normal, for me, is spending every cent I make on rock. Can't pay the rent, no problem. Just do another rock. Electric company turns off the power, no problem. Just do another rock.

And when the money's gone, and the dopeman don't answer the door to you, you do what you got to do. Pimp your wife. Pimp your daughter. Rob some punk, split open his motherfucking head. Ain't nothing stop me from getting the rock till the police send my sorry black ass back to prison where it belongs. Who all here would go that far?" He looks around the group, trying to register his effect on us. He wants to shock. He wants, I think, to show us that his addiction is somehow stronger and more real than ours because it comes from the streets. "That's the monkey," he says. "That's the jones. Let me tell you all something, and then I'll shut up. When I get out of here, first thing I'll do is fire up that crack pipe. And you know what? Listen now," he says, "because this is the kicker. It won't be because I want to. I mean, I know rock's bad. I know it takes me back to prison. Every time. But I'll do it anyway. I'll do it because of one thing. Because," he says, "it's who I am."

On that hopeful note, Tradition Dale calls on the doctor to speak, the morphine addict, who confesses to having intercourse with his female patients after he's knocked them out with a potent anesthetic. After that it's the building contractor from Beverly Hills whose foray into addiction started with a minor back injury and a generous prescription for OxyContin, a synthetic narcotic similar to heroin. Others in the group share, too, but these are the highlights of the meeting, and when the hour is up everyone rises from their seat. We form a big circle. We all hold hands and recite what's called the "Serenity Prayer": *God grant me the Serenity to accept the things I cannot change, the Courage to change the things I can, and the Wisdom to know the difference.* This is followed by individual outbursts of various A.A. clichés:

"Keep coming back."

"It works if you work it."

"And it won't, if you don't."

Communality has never come easily to me. By nature I'm a cynic, and in my book any public display of camaraderie is automatically suspect. I'll accept as truth man's darker nature far more readily than I will his goodheartedness, what little there is. Still I know I'm in exactly the right place. Still I know I belong here, that I'm no different or better than anyone in the group, and when I leave the meeting that evening I somehow feel uplifted. I feel, somehow, that I'm making progress.

On the way back to our room I stop at the pay phone across from the nurses' station and tell Eddie to go on, that I'll catch up. We're not supposed to use it after eight p.m., and it's well past that, a few minutes before ten, but the nurses' station is closed for the night and the hallways are empty. I dig into the pocket of my sweatpants and come up with a handful of change. I haven't spoken with Alex and Nina for a couple of weeks now, and I want to hear my daughter's voice. I want to let them both know I'm making real headway. That I'm pulling it together this time. I deposit the coins. I dial the number.

Alex answers, and she sounds groggy.

"Did I wake you?" I say.

"No, I'm just lying here on the couch watching the news."

I want to ask if she's alone but I know better. It's none of my business anymore, and the last thing I want to do is get her started.

"How's Nina?"

"Fine," she says.

"Can I talk to her?"

"She's not here."

"Where is she?"

"Out with her friends."

"But it's a school night," I say. "It's almost ten o'clock."

Alex laughs, a scoff. "This from her father in rehab. C'mon," she says, "give me a break. Since when did you start caring about your daughter?"

"I never stopped."

"Get off it, Lenny. I'm the only parent here. While you were off getting fucked up, who do you think raised that little girl?"

I have no answer for her, none that doesn't shame me, but it doesn't mean I ever stopped loving Nina. And for that matter, Alex, too.

"Anyway," she says, "let's change the subject before I lose my temper. My lawyer's been trying to get ahold of you but they have some stupid policy there about only friends and family and they won't put his calls through."

"What's he want now?"

"He wants to make an offer."

"You mean *he* wants to make an offer," I say, "or *you* want to make an offer? On what? What for? Just get to the point."

There's a long pause, and when she speaks again her voice is dead calm and businesslike. "I'll let him fill you in on the details," she says, "but basically we've agreed not to press charges if you'll sign over your half of the equity in the house. The way I see it, we're doing you a tremendous favor. Seriously, you're looking at attempted murder, or at the very least attempted manslaughter."

"For Christ's sake, it was an accident."

"That's your version."

"You know I'd never try to hurt you or Nina."

"Save it for the judge. I'm sure he'll agree that plowing your pickup truck through the house was just an innocent mistake."

At that she hangs up.

For a while I stand there in the empty hallway, listening to the hum of the receiver, wondering why it is that we can't ever talk civilly. Why it is that we always end up arguing? At what point did we surrender our marriage? At what point did I cross the line from recreational use and social drinking into addiction, where I needed a drink, a line, a pill, anything just to make it through another day? What began as fun, or escape, had somehow turned deadly serious through the years. And in the end it wasn't so much about getting high as numbing myself to the guilt and shame that accompanies a lifetime of abuse.

I return the receiver to its cradle and head back to my room. There I find Eddie lying belly down on his bed, writing in a notebook under the dim light of the table lamp.

He looks up at me as I come in. "Have you started your letter yet?"

"I will tomorrow," I say.

"It's due tomorrow," he says. "You'd better get on it. That counselor is a real bitch."

Eddie is referring to our group-therapy leader whose approach to sobriety involves belittling his patients, dismantling the self, or the ego, so that he can supposedly reconstruct it for us from scratch. His assignment calls for us to write a detailed letter of apology to the one person who we believe suffered the most from our drinking and drugging. We're asked to make a list of all the times we let that person down, how we hurt and humiliated them, and we're not allowed to make excuses for ourselves. No rationalizations. No justifications. We're to take full responsibility for our actions, and when we're done with the letter, instead of sending it, we're supposed to share it with the group and then destroy it.

For me, that one person would have to be my ex-wife, though Nina runs a close second. For Eddie, it's his deceased mother, the only person, he says, he ever truly loved. In my case, the wrongdoings go back further than I can possibly recall, but at the top of that list are the many nights I didn't call or come home. These are followed by the needless arguments and turbulent mood swings. Then come all the promises I made to quit and never kept, not to mention the thousands and thousands of wasted dollars I put up my nose or drank away at some bar. All this and more I put into that letter, writing deep into the night, long after Eddie's fallen asleep. It comes out to thirty-two handwritten pages—or that's where I stop anyway. Toward the early morning hours my eyes grow heavy and I drop off.

I don't put much stock into the importance of dreams. I don't believe much in symbols or hidden, subconscious meanings. In fact, I rarely ever remember my dreams. But this one is different. It's the kind that seems so real that when you wake up, for those first few seconds, you're absolutely certain it happened. That you were there. That you *are* there. In it I'm sitting at the edge of a dock looking out over the ocean, and beside me is a bottle of vodka. I know I'm not supposed to drink it. I know if I do I'll erase all the progress I've made. That it'll trigger the craving. And once the craving is on, I'll be off and running—next stop, the dopeman's house. But I pick up the bottle anyway. I uncap it. I raise it to my lips and drink, and I can taste it, I can feel it going down, the actual burning sensation in the back of my throat. This is where I wake up, flooded with guilt for having drank again, and then relieved, suddenly, when I realize it's only a dream.

Now the room is just beginning to grow light. Outside the sun is rising, and I roll out of bed. I go to the bathroom and douse my face with water. What happens next is totally out of character for me, but I get down on my knees in front of the sink. I place my hands together. I close my eyes.

Part of me feels silly.

Part of me wants to believe. In what, in whom, I have no idea. And the funny thing is, for me, it doesn't really matter. It is after all the act, not the message, that ultimately gives form to prayer.

Frank Delia

JERRY STAHL has written six books, including the memoir *Permanent Midnight* and the novels *I, Fatty* and *Pain Killers*. His nonfiction and journalism have appeared in *Details*, *The Believer*, the *New York Times*, and a variety of other places. *Hemingway & Gellhorn*, written by Stahl, premieres on HBO in 2012, and he is currently working on *The Thin Man* with Johnny Depp.

twilight of the stooges
by jerry stahl

S o it's 1980-something. I'm nowhere.

Suzy, this older white lady I buy cocaine from, tells me she'll give me a free gram if I help her do some.

I say, "Sure, why not?"

She says, "Exactly." Then, before my eyes, she gets on her hands and knees on the cat pee–marinated shag carpet. She raises the salmon nightie she lives in, exposing a pair of sixty-three-year-old, weirdly hot, baby-smooth ass cheeks, which she introduces as Heckel and Jeckel's albino cousins. Jiggling her cheeks the way body builders will jiggle their pecs, left-right-left, she makes them talk to each other.

"Heckel likes to get spanked. Bad little crow!"

"Jeckel, you're such a freak."

After fifteen minutes, or maybe a day, Suzy pretends to get annoyed with her chatty buttocks. She tells them to shut up. As I zone in and out, grinning like I haven't seen Miss Chatty Cheeks 5,000 times already, I am simultaneously wondering how long I can go without asking/begging/stealing another hit, and obsessing on the name of the guy who did Topo Gigio on *Ed Sullivan*.

By the time I write this, I am acutely aware of how old remembering The Ed Sullivan Show *makes me. Tennessee Williams routinely shaved a year off his age. When people caught him he'd explain that he didn't count the year he worked in a shoe store. I sometimes think the same could be done with drug years. They don't count. Though probably they count more. Like dog years. My liver, in point of fact, is well over a hundred. It sometimes forgets its own name and will doubtless be placed in a rest home by the time you read this.*

Suzy's TV is always on with the sound off. After a while you begin to think the rays soak into your head and over the blood brain barrier with the rest of the shit you're putting in there. Suzy resembles Miss Hathaway, Mr. Drysdale's horsy secretary on *The Beverly Hillbillies*—if Miss Hathaway had been locked in a dark room and force-fed Kents, cocaine, and gin for twenty-seven years, while bathed in color Sony light.

She reaches back and hands me a straw, a regular sweetheart. "Okay, soldier, pack some in there."

"In the straw?"

"In my *ass*. Jesus! How dumb are you? Put some powder in the straw, put the straw in my ass, and blow."

"I've done worse for less," I say with a shrug, trying to convey an emotion I do not even remotely feel. In fact, there is actual screaming in my head, a voice that sounds alarmingly like Jimmy Swaggart. (More TV-adjacent damage; I might as well be in the box, getting transmissions directly into my pineal gland.) I am never not awake Sunday morning at four, when Jimmy comes on in my neck of the world.

Am I nervous or am I happy?
Why are you staring?
Fuck, HELICOPTERS!

Right before I angle toward the target, I start to feel chiggers under my skin, and I fight the urge to scratch myself bloody digging them out. This is when I hear Jimmy Swaggart start speaking directly to me: "Hey, loser! You're about to blow drugs into the anus of a woman old enough to be your mother. You know what Jesus says about that?"

Happily, I am so cocaine-depleted I instantly forget that I'm aurally hallucinating, and that I itch. You don't know you're having a white-out until you come out of it. I just kind of *blink to*. I remember that I'm trying to keep my thumb pressed on one end of the straw while I slip the other end in Suzy's pink O without spilling any coke. (Her sphincter, for reasons I can't fathom, makes me think of a dog toy.) I hold my breath, mouth poised by the business end of the tube, the length of a *TV Guide* away from the bull's eye. I have a weird pain in my spleen. Though I'm not sure where my spleen is. I just know it's unhealthy. And I should go to a dentist, too. I can only chew with the left rear corner of my mouth.

"When I say do it, *do* it!" Suzy says, and launches into some kind of Kundalini fire-breathing that expands and puckers her chosen coke portal. For one bad moment I am eyeball to eyeball with a jowly, Ray Harryhausen Cyclops, who won't stop leering at me. Then I avert my gaze and take in the pictures of Suzy's dead B-celebrity husband on the wall. The Teddy Shrine . . . *That's better.* Suzy met her late husband when she was a call girl. (Many of her clients were half-washed-up New York stage actors.) In a career lull, Teddy appeared in a number of *Three Stooges* vehicles. But not, as Suzy would interject when she repeated the story—which she did *no more than ten times a night*—"the good *Three Stooges* . . ." Teddy made his Stooge ascendance in the heyday of Joe DeRita, the Curly-replacement nobody liked. "Twilight of the Stooges," Suzy would sigh. "People even liked Shemp better than they liked DeRita."

Suzy worked a finite loop of peripheral celebrity anecdotes . . .

Bennett Cerf liked to be dressed like a baby and have his diaper changed . . . Broderick Crawford liked to give girls pony rides. Goober from *Andy Griffith* was hung like a roll of silver dollars but had a dime-size hole burned in his septum. She also claimed that her apartment on Ivar, a cottage cheese–ceilinged studio a short stagger up from Franklin, used to belong to Nathanael West. I can still see her tearing up, missing a dear friend: "The midget from *Day of the Locust* died the same day John Lennon was shot."

I spent more time with Suzy than my own wife, which is a whole other story. After a certain point, junkies are rarely missed when they're not home. (If they happen to have a home—as opposed to a place they still have keys to, from which they can steal small appliances.)

A half-second before I think she is ready to blast off, Suzy abruptly turns around and chuckles. "I ever tell you how much Larry Fine loved his blow? The man was a hedonist . . . How do you think his hair got that way? He wanted to be the white Cab Calloway but it never worked out."

Luckily I don't spill anything. Did I mention the white-outs? I did, didn't I? Why am I telling this story? It's not even a story. It's just, like, a snippet from a loop. Like Suzy's bottom-feeding monologues. I don't have memories. I just have nerves that still hurt in my brain. Shooting coke does that. Even more than smoking it, when you fixed you could just wipe the inside of your skull clean as porcelain. Coke was about toilets and toilets were shiny white. Especially at four a.m. with the lights on and the bathroom door locked. Sometimes the blood in your head would crash over your eyeballs and you'd just go blind for a while, but you wouldn't notice till you could see again—when you came back and realized you were standing there, knuckles buckling, one hand propped on the wall, the other compulsively flushing and re-flushing the toilet, for the whoosh that could make you come.

* * *

I've done okay since getting off all of it—the dope and the cocaine— but I still think, much as the smack destroyed my liver, the coke shorted my synapses. All systems will be firing and then, next thing I know, I'll blink into vision again and realize I've gone blank. It's not so much as if the power's been diminished, it's as if the power just suddenly . . . goes out. Can we feel anything as sharply as the absence of a specific feeling?

What the fuck does that mean?

What was I just talking about?

Never mind. It's not coming back.

When I think about getting high, what I remember, viscerally, is not the dope rush—those faded years before I stopped the dope—I remember the coke hitting, that fork-in-the-heart jolt, like you dipped your toe in a puddle and tongue-kissed a toaster.

Before the needle was halfway down, you could see God's eyes roll back in His head.

So I twitch back and there's this gaping Eberhard Faber eraser-colored hole, two hummocky cheeks yanked open, scarlet chipped fingernails against baby skin.

"Hey, Whitey Ford, throw the dart through the hula hoop, dammit! What's the puzzle!?"

So (first time's always the hardest) with no further ado, I stick the straw into Suzy's ass, careful not to inhale, and blow the Pixy Stix's worth of flake into her alimentary canal, or whatever it is, and watch the teeny mouth shut tight around its deposit.

Suzy squirms. "Unggghh-uhhhh . . . Oh God . . . NNNNNNGGGGGG!"

Then she twists her head around, glassy-eyed. *"I'm a regular*

Venus flytrap!"

That's when I realize I left the straw in her. I look everywhere but it's gone. Sucked right up with the blow. Should I tell her? Would she get mad when she found out? What if she cut me off? Or was there some kind of ass-acid that could eat a straw to pulp—so she'd never know?

Suzy mistakes my panic and paralysis for awe. "Impressive, right?" Smacking herself on the flank, she adds, "I used to smuggle guns for the Panthers in there. There's a man named Jackson who could tell you some stories, if he was in a position to tell anybody anything."

Then she giggles, doing a little wiggly thing with her bottom. "A lot of guys paid a lot of money to be where you are right now! Now blow some more, Daddy. Blow! Blow! Blow!"

I reload from a Musso & Franks ashtray full of powder and go in for Round Two. Her capacious anus quivers like some blind baby bird. And this time (with a fresh straw) I close my eyes, unload the blow, then quickly get up and weave into the bathroom to shake up a shot. I should put some dope in but can't find it—and can't wait—and before I have the needle out I'm on the floor, doing the floppy-fish. It takes everything I have to slap a chunk of tar on tin foil and take a puff to stop the convulsion. I make it back out to the living room. (Blinds always pulled, no day or night, like a one-woman keno lounge.) I never saw Suzy get off her couch to pee. I never saw her eat. I never saw her do anything but cocaine, generally up her nose—or, on special occasions, the odd ass-blow.

Suzy didn't geeze, she thought it was low class. She left the freebasing to her roommate, Sidney, a shut-in who could generally be found in his room, sniffing a pillow between hits. Sidney hadn't left his room, Suzy liked to say, since *The Rockford Files* was new. His claim to fame was playing drums behind Lenny Bruce at a Detroit strip club.

I didn't have any money, so I would keep Suzy company. I never had to be anywhere.

Suzy is still talking when I come back from the bathroom. She never stopped talking. It was not quite white noise. Suzy's clients were a talk show host, a couple of soap stars, a slew of jingle musicians, one name actor who required oz's mailed to him on the set, and my favorite, a TV evangelist famous for his high-rise hair and his multi-hour rants from a cowhide chair in Pasadena.

"I know what you're thinking."

Suzy's voice is jagged with pleasure. Her nose so permanently blown out she sounds like she's just unplugged her iron lung. "You're thinking, 'Suzy musta stole the ass-blow move from Stevie Nicks.' Well, you're wrong, baby. It's apocryphal. Stevie Nicks kept a guy on the payroll whose only job was to blow coke up her ass. Well, not his only job. His other job was to make sure she didn't stop for KFC on the way back from a concert. She'd put a broken nail file to her throat if the driver didn't stop for a half-dozen nine-piece boxes. She was a chicken hoover, if you know what I mean."

"I know what you mean."

"I know you know," Suzy says, lowering her nightie, squirming with pleasure as she eases her behind back on the couch.

"Did I ever tell you about the time Larry got Shemp drunk and they put a hooker's eye out in Canter's?"

Only 5,000 times.

"I never heard that one."

"Here, have some more."

Years go by.

Celeste Wesson

ROBERT WARD is the author of nine novels, including *Four Kinds of Rain*, which was nominated for the Hammett Award in 2006; *Red Baker*, which won the PEN Center USA Literary Award for Fiction; and, most recently, *The Best, Bad Dream*. Ward has published fiction and journalism in *Esquire*, *GQ*, the *Village Voice*, *Sport*, *Rolling Stone*, and *New Times*. For television he has written and produced *Hill Street Blues* and *Miami Vice*. He is the father of four boys and lives in Los Angeles with his wife, radio producer Celeste Wesson, and his son, Robert Wesson Ward.

chemistry
by robert ward

This is the story of how I, hardheaded and some might say hard-hearted, Roger Deakens, actually learned something about the highly touted, but seldom seen, spiritual side of life and found my own true love.

My little tale begins in a bar, The Lion's Head, my favorite old haunt, the great hang for journalists, novelists, village politicos, and the occasional famous actor from the Theatre In The Round, which was just down the street, on the other side of Sheridan Square.

The dark, friendly dive where I met Nicole.

She was trim-hipped, with shining black shoulder-length hair, and she stood between the service station and the last seat at the bar, my usual spot.

I slid onto my stool and was immediately attracted by her perfume. Subtle, classy, a fog of desire. She had a long, sensitive, fine-boned face, and small pearl earrings. She wore a dark tweed business suit that accentuated her tight, athletic body. I ordered my usual, Scotch and soda, from Tommyboy, the 300-pound Yeats-quoting bartender, and tried to remember if I'd ever seen her in the Head before. I thought not, but there had been more than a few nights over the past six months when I couldn't emember much of anything at all. No, I figured, she must be a new girl, probably worked in one of the office buildings nearby, perhaps one of the restaurants that had been springing back up after a few rough seasons.

She sipped a glass of white wine, not looking at me at all, which was fine. I had plenty of time. That was my edge with women. I could wait them out. A lot of guys come on to every girl with the same kind of game-show-host jokes and fast riffs, but that's not me. I've learned through hard-won experience that when you're trolling for love, you've got to be "riff-specific." Tailor each and every riff to the particular girl in question. That's how you get them to fall in love with you, which after all is the ultimate goal. Or at least it was my goal. I never felt that it was satisfying to merely get them to undress, to open their beautiful legs. No, I wanted them to want me, to need me, to love me. I'm talking about the hurting kind of love, where they'd beg to see me the next day and the next and the next. They wanted to be my girl.

But I didn't want a girl. Not that way. Love wasn't my thing, not back then. Not that I didn't care about them. I did, like another man might care about a vintage car. I was a young man, the field was ripe, and I had become a connoisseur of hearts. Okay, technically speaking, I broke their hearts. But, come on, they loved it. Well, at least some of them did. Or else why would they keep coming back?

In those happy days, I liked to think of myself as an artist, an artist of seduction. An overblown, self-regarding epithet, to be sure, but I did have a more than modest talent for love. What were my talents? Well, first off, I could size up any woman within the first two minutes. *Oh, what do we have here? Short, spiky hair, glasses, Levi's . . . must be the intellectual type.* The way to proceed here is to drop some little thing about a lady poet. I'm not talking about Sylvia Plath, for God's sake. Even a frigging football lineman can quote something from Plath. She's just another pop suicide now. No, with this kind of "sensitive rebel type" you have to mention a woman poet only women revere. Like, drop a nice line from, say, Mary Oliver. That's the kind of poet close to a bright woman's heart, the kind she's sure that no man would even know about. Oh yeah, you lay a little Mary Oliver on her and she starts thinking, *Wow, this guy isn't bad looking and he's so sensitive, as well. Maybe, just maybe, he's the man of my dreams.* Yeah, that's the thing. You want to be her dream lover, you have to pay consummate attention to the details.

But details aren't the only thing. Oh no . . . You have to appear to be a fun guy, as well. Sensitive plus fun. If you're too sensitive, after all, you might just as well be some kind of pushover. No, you have to show you're a little dangerous, but fun-dangerous, not deadly dangerous. And what better way to show this than to have your ready vial of pure white cocaine with you.

Ah, with the coke plus the riff-specific sensitivity, you were just too good to be true. (Which pretty much sums up what I was . . . way too good to be true, ever.)

Anyway, after a few laserlike riffs, which honed in on something the woman couldn't see coming, and a few spoonfuls of the requisite powders, well, she was pretty much all yours.

Man, I know it sounds cold but it wasn't . . . not really. It was fun, sharp, predator-and-victim fun. And what's more fun than that?

Not to mention the fact that I got something else out of it. I mean, besides the obvious things. Can you guess?

Nah, you're not smart enough.

Reverie. That's right, reverie. Of the two or three hundred girls I bedded with my artistic approach, I could remember about half of them in stunning detail. I mean, every lick of their tongues, the curve of their thighs, the way they looked in naked profile. I could see them down on all fours; I could see them on their backs, their legs open. I could see them up against the wall, their asses out, their long legs spread, begging for it again.

Yes, I could replay my conquests any time, night or day. At my little pad, there was no need for television. I had my own movie theater, Roger's Memory Lane, and in every frame I was the star. And some beautiful, fantastic creature I'd picked up was my costar.

And, I might add, I was very picky. I didn't exert all this energy or attention on just anyone. No, the girl had to have a certain quality, and she needed to present a specific technical problem for me. A challenge, if you will.

Now take this girl . . . the one in question, Nicole. There was something special about her, not just her great dark looks. At first I wasn't sure what it was . . . so I waited, watched.

Then I began to see. There was a sigh after she sipped her wine. The way she wearily shifted her weight from one great-looking leg to the other. She was beautiful, but above all, she was tired. Right away, I guessed she'd been through something tough. That told me how to tailor my opening gambit. What she needed was a little coke and sympathy. Well, reverse that. Sympathy first, then coke.

Fortunately I had a ready supply of both. Sympathy, in New York City, perhaps more than in any other place, is essential to seduction. For making women fall in love with you, sympathy is a basic ingredient . . . like, say, bread or water to a starving man. The city is so full of truly creepy guys that most women spend half their time frightened, wary, bummed out. If you don't have a fine reservoir of feigned sympathy, you really have no shot. And as for the chemical side of the equation, I'd just purchased a gram or so of coke from my local dealer, a guy named Wease, who stood at his post at the south end of the bar. The Wease, as his customers called him, sold decent, cheap blow. Granted, sometimes it might have a little crank in it—the kind that made you grit your teeth for about fourteen hours—but basically it was good, reliable stuff. And the nice thing is, if you got greedy and snorted all the shit up, all you had to do was hustle down to the other end of the bar, and there he was, ready with another handy little packet to enrich your emotional life.

Yeah, I thought, looking at the surreal sheen of her black hair, *this promises to be a very exciting night.*

"Roger Deakens," I said, smiling in my most understanding way.

"Nicole," she said, smiling in a sad way. "Nicole Draper."

A great name, a great-looking girl. Classy, with that touch of sadness. I felt my heart begin to beat.

"You okay?" I said, using my soft, caring voice and doing "concern" with my eyebrows.

"Is it that obvious?" she said.

"You just look a little down," I said. "Hard day?"

"Hard week," she said. "Our stock is down and my boss is going nuts. Not to mention that he's hitting on me every chance he gets."

"Oh man, I hate that," I said, trying out my PC chops. "And let me guess, you go over his head, complain, and you're gone."

She smiled and nodded her head. I saw her nostrils flare a little. God, she was a good-looking woman. And those lovely, small breasts, obviously all her own.

"You got it," she said. "But I don't want to bum you out."

"You're not," I said. I shook my head and sighed.

"What?" she said.

"Oh, it's just I wonder sometimes . . . when two people meet in a bar, why there's all this pressure to be witty and happy."

I could see a certain measure of relief spread across her lovely face.

"That's true," she said. "Which is why I never come to bars."

"So how come you're here tonight?" I said, doing my good-guy, smiley-face thing. (A cross between, say, rakish Mel Gibson in *Lethal Weapon* and country-boy innocent Ron Howard playing Opie.)

"Meeting my boss," she said.

"But I thought you just said . . ."

"I did. But he wants to get together with me to 'discuss certain problems in our mission statement.'"

"Oh," I said. "I get it. And while he's explaining these deep problems, he's playing footsies with you under the table."

"Exactly," she said. "Only it's more than footsies. He actually groped me during a presentation last week."

"Jesus," I said. "What an asshole."

"Yeah," Nicole said, smiling, "but he's the top asshole. Nothing I can do. Short of quit and bring in the lawyers, and you know where that gets you."

I sighed and took a sip of my drink. What a bummer. We'd established a real connection, I mean, even a kind of rapport, and now her jerkazoid boss was coming and she'd have to leave. I excused myself and went into the men's room, which was just opposite the bar.

Once I'd locked the battered old door, I put the toilet cover down, had a sit, took out my little vial of coke, and dipped in the spoon. The white flakes were big, chalky, and when I snorted them up, I was pleased to find they didn't burn the lining off the inside of my nostrils. Indeed, this stuff actually *was* coke and not some weird Wease combination of Mannitol and greaser speed. Within a few seconds I felt that ebullient lift in my head and the racing of my heart. Ah, that was good, truly good, and if I could just add the fair, elegant Nicole to the mix . . . Images of delight flashed through my head: Nicole lying in bed in front of me with her garter belt on, her legs open, on her knees, her lovely lips parted. Ah, but what of the boss? How could we rid ourselves of the boss?

I got up from the toilet, checked the mirror to see if I had any telltale white residue under my nose, and headed back to the bar.

She was still standing there, but she was no longer alone. Looming next to her was a hulking guy with a $200 haircut and a tan Burberry coat, the kind that would have cost me a month's pay. Obviously, the boss had arrived, and before I could walk the three or four feet to the bar, he'd edged even closer to her and put his arm on her back, moving it up and down in a familiar way.

Perhaps it was the drugs that made me do it, perhaps the challenge, but before I could think the thing through, I found myself opening my arms and stepping to Nicole's left.

"Nicole," I said. "I can't believe it."

She turned and looked at me. Stunned. The boss, a big, dark guy with thick eyebrows and a broad bear's nose, was shocked and, better yet, annoyed.

"I was just over at your office and they told me you might be here."

She hesitated for about a nanosecond, then went along with my performance.

"Terry," she said, winging it and throwing herself into my arms.

The combo of her fabulous little breasts pushing into my chest and my cocaine high filled me with a kind of soaring inspiration.

"It's so great to see you, baby," I said.

I kissed her on the cheek, and after beaming at her like Mister Sun himself, I looked up at the boss, who stood looming, glowering, totally usurped.

I pretended not to notice the scowl on his broad, thick-lipped face.

"Hi," I said. "Terry Andrews. I'm Nicole's fiancé. Just in for the night from Chicago."

"Fiancé?" he said, his head jerking like I'd backhanded him in the mouth. "Nicole, you never mentioned that you were engaged."

She smiled and looked at him with big, innocent eyes.

"You never asked, Ronnie," she said.

"But I assumed that . . ."

She ignored him, put her arm around me, and beamed into my face.

"Terry, this is my boss, Ron Baines."

"Hey, Ron," I said. "Great to meet you."

I flashed my hand, but he pulled away from me like I had a fungus on my fingers.

"Yeah, well, you're from Chicago, how come you're here?" he said, blurting out the words with a barely disguised hostility.

"I had a few days off between meetings, so I got the first plane out this afternoon. Man, I miss my baby. She's a real great girl, huh, Ron?"

"Right," Ron said, gritting his teeth and quickly tossing back his vodka. "One in a million. You staying long?"

"Not that long," I said. "Just long enough to get married."

There was a long silence after that. Finally, Nicole spoke up. "Oh, Terry, you're serious?"

"Why not?" I said. "That is, if Ron will give you the morning off. I bet he will, too. You're a married man, aren't you, Ron?"

"Well, yeah, technically," he said, biting his lower lip.

"Oh, separated?" I asked.

"Not yet. I mean, practically."

"Oh, you don't want to do that, Ron," Nicole said. "What about the kids?"

"Yeah, the kids," I said. "You have to consider them. How many do you have, Ron?"

"Three," Ron replied, sounding as though he'd announced that nuclear war had just commenced in New Jersey.

"That's great," I said. "Well, Ron, I hate to take this little girl away from you, but it's kind of a big night for us. I'm sure you understand."

"Yeah, well . . . yeah, right," was all he could come up with. He looked down at Nicole's finger. "How come you don't have a rock on your hand?"

"Tomorrow, Ronnie," I said. "We take care of all that tomorrow. Well, we have to run, pal. I just want to say what a pleasure it's been to meet you. Great to know my baby is in such good hands . . . professionally speaking, of course. Take care."

I looked up at Tommyboy, who gave me a smile from the side of his mouth, as I put my arm around Nicole and hurried her out of the Head. When I looked back, Ronnie-baby was hanging over the bar like a dead sentinel. It couldn't have been sweeter.

Out on cold, dark Christopher Street we laughed and hugged one another.

"That was wonderful," she said. "How the hell did you come up with that?"

"Inspiration, my dear," I said. "The source of which is your beautiful face, your stunning eyes, your raven-black hair."

She looked at me and actually blushed.

"You're wonderful," she said.

"We're both wonderful," I said.

Then we kissed, one of those long, passionate public kisses, the kind that makes love a spectacle. The kind that draws attention from everyone on the street, and the kind I always loved for exactly that reason.

And yet, this time, this time something happened. You know

all that heart talk—I mean, how one kiss can make you lose your heart, your heart skipping beats, zing went the strings of my heart—all that kind of pop crap, the likes of which I had never felt before? Well, this time, God help me, something happened. Kissing those lips, feeling her breasts press into my chest, I not only wanted her sexually, I wanted, God help me, to take care of her, too. Oh God, what was happening to me? I wanted to cherish her. I was gone, wasted, down the blue drain of love.

I literally pulled myself away from her. This wasn't happening. Not to me, Roger Deakens, adopted son of Alfie.

It was the coke . . . had to be the coke . . . *Yeah*, that's what it was, the cocaine. What the hell had the Wease put in that shit? Maybe some kind of goddamned love potion? Yeah, that was it. That had to be it. He was jealous, very, very jealous of me and all my success with women. He'd even said so on more than one occasion. I remembered the night we'd both been hustling this blonde from Iowa, Susan something, a real looker, and he'd really wanted her, felt, he told me later, something really strong for her, and I'd just whisked her away doing my riff-specific Kansas corn-fed routine. Yeah, I'd aww-shucked her right into bed. And he was pissed because he knew that I didn't give a damn if I ever saw her again. That really pissed him off. He'd even said he'd get even with me someday, and this must have been that day. He'd put some kind of goddamned erotic love potion in the coke, but even as I entertained these thoughts, I knew it wasn't so. Nah, that was bullshit. That was crap I was telling myself so I wouldn't feel this horrible and yet so unbearably wonderful feeling of losing control, of slipping away . . .

Oh God, what had happened to me? As we walked toward Seventh Avenue I had my arm around her and I felt, really felt, that if I lost Nicole I was doomed, that I would do anything for her love, that if I didn't have her and keep her, my life would be nothing but the proverbial empty shell.

And then we were waiting for a cab, and she hugged me and said, "God, I want you inside me. I want your cock in me so bad."

And I heard myself groaning with lust, with a need that was worse than any lowly junkie's H-jones.

And she said, "My place. Let's go to my place. I'm just two blocks away on Barrow and Hudson."

"Right," I said. "Right. Let's go. I've got some coke with me."

"Fabulous," she said. "I love coke."

And then we were running across Seventh, stopping every two or three feet to kiss, to grope one another, and I knew that it was all over. Impossible as it sounded, I was finished, dead, totally whacked on love. By the end of this very night, I knew without a shadow of a doubt, I would ask this complete stranger to be my wife.

"Oh God, I can't stand it," she said, as I groped her in the elevator at 72 Barrow Street.

"Baby, baby, baby," I said, knowing it was a hopeless cliché but not caring anymore. Originality, it occurred to me, doesn't matter when you're in love. Neither does being riff-specific.

We scrambled out of the elevator on the fifth floor. I put my hand up her dress and felt her unbelievably tight ass, as she opened the door, moaning.

Then we were inside. I can't describe the place . . . only her lips, her hair, her arms around me, my hands under her blouse, the incredible tautness of her nipples.

"Nicole, Nicole, Nicole," I repeated like an idiot.

"Roger, Roger, Roger," she refrained. I'd always hated my name but now it sounded like pure sex.

I kissed her hard, harder, my tongue found her throat. We

staggered across the room as I pulled up her dress and put my hand into her throbbing, wet cunt. It was literally pulsating with pleasure and she screamed when I put my middle finger up her asshole.

She fell back against the wall, and I pressed my hard cock into her. A picture fell down. Crashed to the floor. I laughed wildly. This was real sex, not one of my carefully orchestrated little games. And I loved every second of it. And yet it was terrifying, for I felt wildly out of control.

I took off her suit top and started in on her blouse but she pulled away, panting.

"I need to see you naked first."

"Really?"

"Yes, believe me, it'll be worth it. I need to see your hard cock, baby."

I felt suddenly frightened. I was used to giving the orders. But now . . . God, I only wanted to please her.

I stood back, unbuttoned and slowly unzipped my pants. Smiling, I let my pants drop to the floor as I started kicking off my $300 shoes.

She smiled back as she saw my cock, and I knew she was mine. All mine, my lovely Nicole. Oh man, I loved her. I did . . . I wanted her. I needed her. I would fuck her until she screamed, begged for more, then screamed again, again, again . . . Or maybe, maybe this time it would be me doing the screaming and begging. I no longer cared.

"Do you like it?" I said, looking down at my hard member.

"Yes," she said. "Oh yes, I do."

"Me too," said a voice from behind me. "That's a real winner, for sure."

I turned, breathless, and to my horror saw the boss, Ron Baines, coming through the unlocked front door. There was a .38

in his right hand. "What the fuck are you doing here?" I yelled.

He didn't say a word, but ran right at me, raised the gun, and smashed the butt into my skull.

I felt a hot flash pass through me as I fell into a very undignified heap on the floor.

Blood rolled down my nose, over my lips. I was drowsy and my head pulsated with pain, but I was still conscious. I looked up at Nicole, my Nicole, for some kind of help, if only moral support.

But she didn't look like Nicole anymore. She was staring down at me as if I were a bug under a microscope.

"Get his hands," Baines said.

She reached down, and I weakly pushed her away. That was another mistake because Baines whacked me again with the gun butt, and this time I fell on my back, barely conscious. Blood ran down my neck and collar. They tied my hands behind me with some kind of cord that cut into my wrists, nearly cutting off my circulation.

Lying there in my own blood, I felt like an old dog whose body was covered in tumors.

"Now I could gag you, but we have to talk to you first. You scream at all, you get this." He reached in his pocket and pulled out an old-fashioned push-button knife. He hit the button and I was staring at a saw-toothed eight-inch blade.

"I won't scream," I said.

"Good. By the way, you were really excellent back there at the bar," Baines said. "The whole fiancé bit was a real good improv. You're fine, for an amateur."

"Look," I said, "I have a hundred bucks in my pocket. Just take it."

They looked at one another and laughed.

"He thinks we want money," Baines said.

Nicole reached down and held up my chin. "Look at this picture," she said.

I looked at the snapshot she thrust at me. A young blond woman with a nice face, a cheerleader's freshness, but with slightly big teeth. The photo looked to be several years old. The woman seemed vaguely familiar.

"I don't know her," I said.

"You fucking liar," Nicole replied. "She met you in that same bar two years ago. Her name was Gail. Gail Harden."

I tried but I couldn't quite recall her. Still, there was something—that overbite.

"You remember her, don't you?"

"No," I said. "There's some mistake. I never knew her."

She kicked me in the ribs with her high heels. I groaned, shook my head.

"You were all she could talk about. Roger, the ad genius. Roger, who made love to her for five weeks. Roger and she were going to get married."

"Married? No. No way I ever told her that."

"Then you do admit you knew her."

Now I remembered. Two years ago. I had just gotten back from the Hamptons and wasn't quite ready to give up my good times. She was sitting in the Head one evening, just before it got dark, dressed in this pretty little flower-print gown. She just looked so young and summery. The perfect way for me to launch back into work.

"Okay," I said. "We went out for a few weeks. Three, maybe four times, but that was it. And I never promised her anything . . ."

"Bullshit, you gave her coke, right?"

"Maybe."

Now it was Ronnie's turn to kick me in the ribs. I groaned

and thought I could feel my organs leaking blood.

"Okay, I did. So what? Everybody does a little toot or two. C'mon. It wasn't like it was her first time."

"No, but it was the first time she'd fallen in love. Then you dumped her. She called you over and over, begged you just to call her back, to be her friend."

"That's not how it works," I said. "When it's over, it's over. I didn't want to lead her on. I never promised her anything. You bring her here and ask her in front of me. You'll see."

"That would be kind of hard," Nicole said. "My sister went home to Minnesota and hung herself. She left these poems all about you."

She dumped a book that looked like a journal in front of me. It fell open and I saw poems written in colored inks. The kind a junior high school girl might have written.

"No, that's a lie," I said.

She stuck another picture on the floor. A police photograph of Gail hanging from an attic beam. She had on that same summery floral dress. She had long, beautiful legs, like her sister's. Suddenly, I didn't know why, I began to pray, "Oh God, God, God . . . You can't blame that on me. She must have been unstable to begin with, right? She must have been crazy."

"She loved you. You turned her onto drugs, made her crazy for you, then you dumped her. You murdered her, as surely as if you'd kicked over the chair she stood on."

"Who are you, her brother?" I said, crying.

"No, I'm Nicole's husband, asshole. We planned this for a long time. We were going to invite you out to dinner with us . . . but you turned the tables on us. But it doesn't matter. You can just as well drink your dessert right here."

He pulled two small vials out of his big Burberry coat. One red, the other blue.

"See these?" he said. "One works like battery acid. The other will just make you violently ill, but you might survive. We're going to give you a chance. Drink either one, then wait five minutes. You'll know. They're both bad, but the poison makes you start to bleed from your ears, nose, and asshole. The other one will only destroy most of your intestines."

"Bullshit. You're nuts. I'm not drinking either one of them," I said.

"If you don't," Nicole said, "we'll knock you unconscious and pour the one with the poison down your throat."

Up until that point I'd been scared but somehow numbed by the whole thing. I mean, there was an air of unreality to the whole strange affair thanks to the coke, but it was rapidly wearing off.

"Which one will it be, Rog?" Baines said. "The red bottle or the blue?" He put them close to my lips; that's when I began to scream.

"Help me! Help, they're killing me!"

"Wrong answer," he said, slamming the gun butt down on my head.

I came awake in a white room, my stomach burning, my throat scorched by fire. I tried to talk but it felt as though someone had used a flamethrower on me. Then I tried to move my arms, to signal somebody for help, but I was strapped to a gurney, like a madman. That made sense because I *was* a madman, a madman burning alive from the inside out.

I thrashed my bashed-in head from side to side, looking for help, making dying-bird noises.

Suddenly, the white curtain flew back and there was a tall woman who looked like a doctor peering down at me through thick glasses. Behind her was . . . Wease. My coke dealer.

"Weease," I croaked.

"Keep calm, Mr. Deakens," the doctor said.

"Gonna . . . Gonnaa . . . die," I croaked. "Poisoned."

Wease moved forward.

"No," he said. "They pumped your stomach. You're gonna make it, Rog."

"Besides," the doctor said, "whatever you drank wasn't poison. It was a habanero pepper drink. It only feels like it's going to kill you."

I fell back on the gurney and shut my eyes.

"What the fuck you drink that stuff for?" Wease said.

"Made me," I croaked.

"Who?"

"Don't know. People . . . met at the Head."

Every word felt like someone poking barbed wire into my throat.

"Oh, the chick at the end of the bar and the big guy in the coat?"

I nodded, a bilious stream of liquid fire coming up my throat and nose.

"The police are going to want to talk to you, Mr. Deakens," the doctor said. "And you too, sir."

She glanced at Wease, who furtively looked away from her into the hall.

"Hey, I was just in the 'hood and heard a scream," he said. "I don't need to talk to any cops."

Before she could say another word, Wease was out the door. Guess he wanted to get rid of his stash before the Village cops came.

I started to give a little laugh, but the pepper drink came up inside me again, and I fell back, gagging, choking, and generally sounding like a guy with throat cancer.

The doctor put a needle in my arm, and right before I fell asleep I thought of the damnedest thing. Not the way they'd tricked me, not the way they'd beaten and humiliated me, but instead I thought of Nicole's kiss. The softness of it, the perfection of her flesh. How I was sure, so sure, I loved her. How even now, after all this had happened, I wanted to kiss her again. Absurd as it was, it was almost a happy memory, and I'd have been content to go out with it, but right before I lost consciousness I saw the sister, Gail Harden, hanging from the rafters, and I wanted to die. *Just let me go to sleep, God, and never wake me up again.*

I was weak as a kitten when they let me out of St. Vincent's the next day. Two detectives, Barrett and Strong, came to see me, and I managed to whisper the whole damned story to them. About halfway through I broke down and said, "Maybe it would have been better if they had finished me off." Strong, a big guy, with a mobile, sympathetic face, put his big hand on my shoulder and shook his head.

"You can't think that way," he said. "Girl kills herself, could be a ton of factors."

"Yeah, but I was the main one," I said.

The two cops looked at each other.

"You got your house key?" Barrett said.

I fished into my pants. It was gone.

"Maybe we better take you on home," Strong said. "Let's call for the wheelchair."

We were a block away from my place at 77th and West End when I saw a lamp and clothes, my clothes, spread all over the street. Mostly underwear and mismatched socks, a few old paperbacks, a pile of CDs.

I followed the cops to my third-floor walk-up and saw the front door lying there, half torn off its hinges. Inside, it looked like a hurricane had swept through the place. My Eames chair was smashed, "Murderer" was written all over my paintings. The silverware was gone, the lava lamp I'd kept around for laughs, smashed. Books, records, CDs, all smashed into a thousand pieces.

In the bedroom, a strong box I kept far back in the closet was gone. Which meant so was $10,000. Somehow I didn't mind.

"They got you good," Strong said.

"We're gonna dust this place," Barrett said.

"Fine," I said. "That's great."

I picked up an overturned chair and sat down in the midst of all the debris. It was like I was the emperor of some Third World country that had suffered a coup d'état.

During the next few hours, more police came . . .

The cops made calls on their cell phones. Pleasant technicians came and did their work, just like on television. People were sympathetic in my building, but there were no witnesses.

I went to the precinct and ran through mug shots until my eyes were red, but found no one who looked like either of them.

In the coming days I felt strangely disassociated, out of my body. And then that phase ended and I began to feel a monster depression, as though I had a thousand pounds of fat hanging off my frame.

I dreamed constantly of Gail Harden. It was as though the photograph had come to life. I saw her doing a lot of coke, getting wired out of her mind, then stepping on a chair, putting the noose around her neck . . . and then swinging to and fro, while outside the snow fell silently over Minnesota.

Night after night the same images. And every time I saw her I fell deeper and deeper into the snow outside her house. I was caught in a snowdrift and my blood and bones turned to ice.

I tried to forget it, her, I tried to forget Nicole's kiss—the first kiss I'd ever been really struck by . . . Zing went the strings . . . of the murderer's heart.

But it was no use. I felt the kiss on my lips, and saw the vials of poison in front of me, one blue, one red.

I'd always thought I was strong, very strong. But I knew now I was weak, nobody could be weaker than me.

I made it down to the Head and spent 500 bucks on coke, thinking that it was the only thing that would pull me out of it.

Every day I snorted the shit just to get out of bed. Every afternoon, every evening, and every night.

But the images of Gail Harden wouldn't go away. If anything, the coke made them stronger.

I lay in bed at night, my nose running, my head pounding, listening to Billie Holiday on an old CD. That's when I started to hear it in the kitchen. A sound, like a chair being moved. I leapt from my bed, made it out there, but I was too late. She had hidden. In the closet, in the pantry, in my filthy little toilet. I couldn't see her, but that didn't matter, I knew she was there. Gail Harden was coming back.

How I wished it was Nicole.

At some point Barrett and Strong caught up to me. I was walking down West End, going nowhere, when they pulled up in their Cavalier and beckoned me to get in.

I did as they said. Nowadays, I did as anyone said.

"How you doing?" Barrett asked.

"I'm Mister Wonderful," I said.

They looked at one another and smiled.

"Well, maybe you'll be doing better when you look at this," Barrett said.

He handed me the photograph of Gail Harden. Hanging around. Still dead.

"Yeah, what of it?"

"It's a fake," Strong said. "Well done, but a fake. Been Photoshopped."

"Really?"

"Yeah, really. What's more, there's no record of any Gail Harden committing suicide in Minnesota during the past three years. The whole thing was a hoax."

"Take a close look at the photo."

I did.

"What do you see?"

"I still see Gail Harden hanging . . . very dead."

"No, you see Nicole Harden hanging there. Wearing a blond wig."

"No," I said. "I slept with Gail Harden and I'd know . . ."

"That's right," Barrett said. "You remember anything about her?"

"She had a very . . . shy kiss."

"She coulda faked that," Strong said. "What about her body? Any distinguishing marks?"

I thought for a second, then: "A cat. She had a cat face tattooed on the inside of her left thigh."

"Right, and what about Nicole? She have one, too?"

"I don't know 'cause she made me take my clothes off first."

The two detectives looked at one another and smiled.

"Of course she did. She didn't want you to see her naked. They couldn't have pulled the 'dead sister' act on you if you had seen the cat on her thigh."

I stared down at my feet. There was so much I wanted to tell them, but they wouldn't have listened.

Finally, I looked up.

"But why?" I said. "Why did they go to all that trouble?"

They looked at one another and shrugged.

"A game," Strong said. "Basically, the two of them are con artists, set up lonely guys, steal all their money. But these two, when they pick out a mark, they like to make it a little more dramatic. Like it's a movie. Or reality TV. It's no fun unless the vic really suffers. You know what I mean?"

"Yeah," I said. "I know, all right. I know just what you mean."

"Yeah," Barrett said. "You know the show they had on a few years back where the guy thinks he's an action hero in a movie but everybody else knows he's a schmuck? That kind of thing. No offense intended."

I laughed at that, and felt small, the incredible shrinking schmuck.

"We're getting more bizarre crimes than ever these days," Strong said. "It's not enough to rob and beat a guy, you gotta fuck with his mind, too. Everybody wants to direct."

"Oh," I said, realizing how lame it sounded.

"So make sure you change your locks and watch out for strange women wearing wigs," Barrett said.

"You bet," I replied. "Thanks for coming by."

"Bet that's a load off your mind," Strong said.

"Yeah, it sure is."

"You want a ride somewhere?" Strong asked.

"No thanks. I'll walk."

I climbed out of their car, gave a little wave goodbye, and headed down the block. They made a U-turn and cruised up West End.

I had only walked about two blocks when I started laughing. They were good guys, if a little rude. They'd probably seen the desperation on my face, noticed that in the past week I'd lost so much weight that my pants fell down on my hips, like I was some cholo wannabe. They could tell by the hollow look in my eyes. They knew how to read the signs. That was their job.

So they'd cooked up that story about how Gail Harden was really Nicole, how Ron and Nicole were just fucking with me because they were evil gamesmen. How it was all an offshoot of reality TV. But in the end, nobody was really hurt.

Hey, no harm, no foul, right?

But I knew better. They'd have to do a lot better than that.

Gail Harden was dead, all right. How did I know? Because she was living there in my apartment. Of course she was. Only it might not have been Gail. It might have been Nicole. Gail, Nicole . . . one or the other was hanging over the pipes.

I know. I know. You think I've gone nuts, that I'm unsettled by what happened to me, but I say you're wrong.

And how do I know?

Well, I found her that very same night, hanging from the pipes in my kitchen, turning north, south, east, and west, and all the time, whispering, *"When will you admit it, Rog? When will you finally admit you love me?"*

I cut her down, washed her face, cleaned her rotting flesh. But it was no good, she got up in the night and tied herself back up there. She was a real Johnny-one-note. The same lame riff over and over again. Whispered and all noose raspy.

"When will you admit it, Rog? When will you finally admit you love me?"

"When you can kiss like your sister," I said.

But she didn't laugh.

It took me three days to finally get it. She was right, dead right, if you will. I was living in denial. She was my own true love. My only true one. Gail or Nicole. Nicole or Gail. Didn't really matter how you named it.

Thursday, I cut her down for the last time and told her the words she died to hear.

"I love you, baby. How can I not love the woman that died for me?"

Now, when it gets dark, we sit there in my kitchen,

drinking white wine, snorting Wease's good white powder until our noses bleed. I tell her not to worry, not to fret, because at last I've learned how love chooses you, not the other way around. You think you're in control, but oh baby, that's the greatest illusion of all. So I tell her I love her . . . Gail, that is. Or is it Nicole?

Sometimes her ghastly face changes and I just can't tell.

But whatever, whoever, these days I'm straight and true.

No more fucking around for this guy.

When I go to work now I speak only when spoken to. When I have my lunch, I eat alone. When the workday's done, I stop to see the Wease and come right home.

And trust me, I stay there until it's cutting time. Then my girl and I kiss, hug, drink our wine, and do a little blow.

You wouldn't believe the things she says, the worlds she knows.

And at last, when black night looms over the unreal city, we cling to one another just like all the other desperate, wired lovers, in my warm and blood-red bed.

PART III
THE CORRUPTION

Guy Dill

KERRY E. WEST, a thirty-seven-year veteran welder from the motorcycle, aircraft, and architectural iron industries, is very active working with metal sculptors in Venice, California, building public and private works. He has been a writing tutor for over six years at the University Writing Center at California State University, Los Angeles. His other work has been featured in Los Angeles City College's 1998 and 1999 *Citadel*; California State University, Los Angles' 2007, 2008, and 2009 Significations Conferences; and the 2008 Society of Composers' Student National Conference. He is currently writing a series of Vietnamese boat people stories.

shame
by kerry e. west

Nicole!" Lorna shrieked at her twelve-year-old daughter. "Get in there and feed the babies." This was actually more about getting the kid out of the room than anything else. Nicole wordlessly tromped into the bedroom knowing quite well what we were up to.

Lorna whipped out the mirror and razor. Uncle Jeff pulled out the crank. I watched with impatient fervor. The three of us were like slobbering dogs, intent on a single-minded endeavor: a good, harsh toot up our sniffers. And any thoughts of what may have been wandering through the mind of the young girl in the other room were obliterated by this urgent social priority. Hey! Whadda-you-want? We were addicts. We just needed the kid *out* of the room so we could guiltlessly burn out our nasal canals—as if Lorna really gave a shit anyway.

"Where's the key, Mom?" came Nicole's raised voice from within the bedroom; it was a voice with nuances that often seemed matured years beyond what should have been normal for a twelve-year-old. The voice was unemotional and businesslike; she stolidly had the household routines down. It always impressed me how reserved Nicole remained around her mom, but then in her mom's absence she would instantly revert to her independent, playful, but far from naïve self.

"You don't need the key. Get them food *now*, and keep it quiet!" Lorna hollered back; she had a scowl on her face with tension lines wrinkling the corners of her eyes. Lorna, with the character natural to a screaming banshee, gave a daunting performance of stern parental control, and Nicole, and her two-year-old and three-year-old sisters, usually obeyed.

Lorna turned back to the main issue at hand and began to chop. She paused a second to brush back a long, light-reddish lock that had annoyingly fallen forward from behind her ear and into her face. She continued: *chopchopchopchopchopchopchop* . . . for a *long* time. Actually, it was only for about half a minute but, eager as I was, it seemed an eternity. She drew out some lines. I remember looking at her pale-skinned, freckled face, the matching flesh on her big-boned arms, and I remember thinking what a large girl she was. Oh . . . I don't mean corpulent; I mean hefty and muscular. She certainly had no beauty to speak of, and I possessed no sexual desire for her. She'd'uv probably kicked my ass if I'd tried anything anyway. Lorna proceeded to nostrilize the glittering powder and passed the mirror to Jeff.

Now, the family's Uncle Jeff was a precious find. He was a pleasant guy. He was cultivated. He was the most delightful druggie you could ever hope to know—should you wish or *need* to know one. His tamed soul made him an incessantly jolly man, content to live out life with a fresh blast every ten minutes. Very unselfish guy, too, and I don't mean this just because it was *his* stash we were doing up in the living room. He just liked sharing in good company; this, regardless of the enhancement to supply-and-demand that was bound to result. Jeff was a lofty six-foot-two, plump, and he supported a tarnished-silver, longhaired Genghis Khan moustache that flowed around and down the sides of his mouth. And his nose was large and red with a straw stuck up it.

He finished and passed the mirror to me. *Finally.* The line was smaller than I had hoped for.

"Say, Lorna? Did you get your check yet?" I asked conversationally as I bent over the mirror, inhaling, then releasing a sound wave apposite of relief, "Ahhh." I was hoping she'd be able to pay her part of the bills, or at least some of her part—I'd been having enough trouble with "unpredictable" utility disconnections. I had been renting my guesthouse to her. It was not really a large enough dwelling for her family, but they managed. Lorna slept on the living room couch, and the girls used the only other available room as a bedroom. What had become a real problem, though, was that Lorna never used any of her welfare check for rent or utilities. Never. She always got over on me somehow. It wasn't until years later that I was able to understand how she suckered me into accepting them as tenants in the first place.

She answered with an arrogant grin, "No. But I'll let you know when I do."

As usual, this predictable answer caused my anger to flare up for a second. I thus found it necessary to promptly establish some priorities and said to her, "Cool. Can I have another line?"

So there it was. It was a situation that was more costly for me than if I'd lived alone on the property, a situation superseded by the delicious incentive that their Uncle Jeff was a darn good connection, one I didn't want to lose.

Anyway, good . . . we did another round. When my turn came, I snorted *hard* so as to lay down a thick and speedy blanket over those vast reaches of my nasal canals that may have yet remained untainted—this time, *Wow*! Satisfaction guaranteed, let-me-tell-you. Graciously, I then excused myself to go out into the yard to give my van one of its meticulously scheduled oil changes.

Minutes later—lying out there under my van—the shit *really* kicked in. My teeth clenched and ground against themselves. My periphery narrowed; my concentration pinpointed heavily on the task at hand. And then my heightened ambition sensed all the cruddy grease clods encrusting the van's underside. Sidetracked now, I grabbed the first purposeful utensil within reach—a screwdriver—and began arduously scraping away all the caked-on deposits from the bottom of the engine. This single-minded contagion spread and I started on the frame. Next would be the transmission. So there I was an hour and a half later, still frenziedly preparing for an oil change, when Nicole and her baby sisters came barreling out through the side door of their bedroom. Uh-oh! They looked to be on a mission.

The girls, all blondes looking nothing alike, were pretty much a riotous bunch. Whenever those three erupted into the yard, the three-year-old, little curly haired Autumn, would break into a full and flashing smile the moment she'd see me, gleefully calling, "Kee-ee. Hi, Kee-ee." That seemed to be the extent of her vocabulary, to which I'd be required to reply, "Hi, Autumn." She'd return with, "Hi, Kee-ee." To which I'd again reply, and so on and so on, until I was the one to give in to this contest.

Then, in her usual waddling fashion, followed the youngest: scraggly haired Jessica. Jessica, always with a variety of purplish sores on her face and arms, never uttered a word. Two years old and she still wasn't able to talk at all. Well, she'd come stumbling out the door with her giant, wide-open eyes, taking in the whole yard, giggling frantically, and acting like a million Christmas gifts were now hers to ransack. She always seemed infatuated with the world, always tagging along behind Autumn, emulating her every move.

And finally, of course, there was the preordained babysitter, Nicole. Nicole could be a handful of monkey business if she wanted to be. But during "business" hours she had an absolute yet incredibly compassionate ability to keep her sisters in check. When Nicole spoke, the little ones would listen acutely, earnestly falling in before her like her own private little army, an integrated machine tuned to her every command. It always seemed to me that the two younger ones might have thought *she* was their mother, as well.

Now Nicole, despite all the responsibility that her mother

would lay upon her, naturally needed her own diversions and wouldn't hesitate to seize any opportunity that allowed her to sway from everyday procedure. Such it is that she would offer to assist in *my* chores whether I needed help or not. I think this finagling may have been a perfect excuse for legitimately disobeying her mother: "But he needed help, Mom," she'd always plead, all the time knowing I was too soft to favor a contradiction.

Anyway, the three girls inevitably found my prone body hiding under the van. And Nicole leaned over to offer her assistance but I turned her down. I mean, after all, an oil change is a one-man job, isn't it? So Nicole let her sisters help instead. And *boy*, did they help. Autumn came over to one side to distract me, "Kee-ee. Hi, Kee-ee." Jessica stole a socket wrench from behind me and ran. Shoot! Now I had to get out from under and chase down the tool. Meanwhile, Autumn was left wide open to take off with the filter wrench. Here things got tricky. Since Autumn had a head start before I'd returned from tracking J essica—and you can bet she went in the opposite direction—this gave Jessica all the time in the world to take her pick of the rest of my tools while I was off stalking Autumn. Apparently, all this was quite entertaining for Nicole, for she simply sat quietly on a bench giving me sweet, wide grins as I darted hither and thither.

You know? I'd almost swear under oath that since the two younger ones were so verbally limited, they all used telepathy to gang up on me. Can you not help but love such shenanigans? The ultimate joy of this world should be nothing larger than kids having a real ball.

Later that night there came an aggravated banging on my door. I answered in irritation, becoming delighted as soon as I saw whom it was. "Hi, Jeff! Come in. *Come in*."

He entered looking more than a little concerned and told me

straight out, "Lorna just got popped after she came over to cop some shit."

"Oh, man! What a hassle. How she gonna get out?"

Jeff, already motioning for a mirror, replied, "Not a problem, I bet. They're probably going to let her out on O.R. in the morning. Right now, man, I need to check on the kids." His mind spaced for a second, then he began crushing the small rock he'd pulled out and asked, "Know how to change a diaper?"

I looked at him dumbfounded. I didn't *even* want to touch that one. And I think neither did he, judging from his expression. So, with that startling revelation in mind, we both saw the highly fitting rationale in reinforcing the stamina of our polluted bloodstreams. We did so and dispatched the mirror.

As we walked over to the guesthouse, we consoled each other with the fact that we could always ask Nicole to do the diaper thing if need be. When we neared the door, Jeff called to Nicole to open it. She did; she had a cheery grin and let us in. An Olsen twins video was on the television.

Jeff spoke despondently to his niece: "Nikki . . . your mom's in jail."

"I know," she said brightly. "She called and told me." Nicole was definitely not upset. She almost seemed exuberant. Perhaps the evening was running more smoothly for her without her mother's interventions. Either that or Nicole had simply lit up to the fact that her Uncle Jeff had arrived. She utterly adored her Uncle Jeff. He was much like a father figure for her, yet she never gave him reason to reprimand her. He was stern but kindly, and perhaps devoted more time to Nicole than did anyone else. Lorna, on the other hand, couldn't, for she was a very busy woman; busy tweakin' around the clock just as most the rest of us were.

"Nikki, did you eat dinner? Did your sisters get fed yet?"

"Yes, Uncle Jeff."

"Where are they?"

"They're in their beds."

Then Jeff turned to me, an unsure gaze in his eyes, and said, "I'd better check on them," and I followed him while Nicole indifferently went back to sit in front of the television.

We passed through a doorway draped over with a heavy woolen blanket, and I realized I hadn't been in this room for quite some time. As we drew back the blanket, an appalling odor woofed out to slap us startlingly in the face. It was very dark in there, too dark to see. Jeff felt around for a light switch, found one, and snapped it on. The two of us, blinking vacantly as our eyes adjusted, froze for an instant, horrified as the sight before us materialized. We both quickly glanced to check each other's reaction, reactions that were meaningless in light of what we were looking at. We again peered back into a room neither of us had seen since the day Lorna moved the kids into it.

The room was a shambles of microbe-ridden rubbish heaps. Stuffed animals and rumpled clothes were strewn everywhere, with the majority of them heaped in a pile on the floor of the doorless closet. Under this bedlam lay a mishmash of kitchen knives, a hammer, a shower head, waterlogged toilet paper, paper clips, the closet door, you name it. The room's only decoration was another heavy, brown blanket nailed over the solitary window and feces-smeared walls. In one corner on the floor was a rancid pile of loaded diaper bundles. Out of the corner of my eye those bundles appeared to spasm when we first turned on the light, but it was just the cockroaches trying to take cover. There were only two pieces of furniture: a playpen and a small crib. I saw no bed for Nicole.

Autumn sat on her rump in the playpen, grinning and staring at us but saying not a word, not even a single "Kee-ee." With her were a couple of mangled toys, a pillow, and a dirtied dinner plate. Her hands, mouth, and blouse were mottled with food. There was no way for her to stand erect—covering the top of the playpen, secured in place with padlocked motorcycle chains, was a section of wrought-iron fence.

Jessica was asleep in the crib, which had a thick-corded fishnet draped over its top; it was pulled taut down the sides and tied off underneath. Movement was limited. For Jessica, sleep was likely a blessing. Her restriction didn't seem as severe as the playpen situation until Jeff pointed to the soiled colorings of the sheetless mattress; it seethed with soggy patches of some weird dark and moldlike growth. I only then began to relate the sores Jessica always bore to the meaning of "crib rot."

Suddenly, Jeff directed a blaring roar at the other room, which startled me and woke up Jessica: "*Nicole!*" He paused to swallow for control and then continued angrily, "What have you done here? Unlock this playpen *now*."

And I heard the meek reply from the other room, "I can't. Mom has the key."

We stood there a moment . . . bewildered, to say the least.

It was then that a large assortment of envelopes partially covered by a ragged jacket and several tiny socks strangely summoned my attention. I moved sulkily over to them and apathetically brushed aside the jacket with my foot. The items seemed vaguely familiar. I stooped down for a closer look. Behold! What did I find but . . . *my mail*? Here were the unopened phone and power bills that I had sworn to the utility companies—after several disconnections—I never received. And I began to see the logic: If I didn't get the bills, Lorna couldn't be held for what she owed. I cursed out loud, already raging beyond forethought for the younger presence in the room.

I looked to Jeff for support but he looked both nauseated and in a struggle to control his rage. The little ones thought we were there to play; they were thrilled. From the other room I heard Nicole stifle a sob.

How do you reckon a course of action when you are so caught up in your own concerns—and your own *habits*—that you are unable to perceive the full weight of a very serious problem? And open confrontation of this very problem could certainly threaten the frequent drug trafficking so conveniently wrought through my tenant's door. In that moment, it seemed there were only two available options: Avoid making waves with a charade of ignorance, or take all-out aggressive action despite the consequences.

I am ashamed to say I chose inaction.

After I had taken a bolt cutter to Autumn's chains, I retired to the main house and Jeff remained with the kids for the night. I really, really needed something to lift my spirits, yet there was to be no consolation in subsequent toots. Nor did I have the high and faithful expectations I usually did at the sight of Jeff, when, around midnight, he snuck over to use the phone. Strangely, he too did not feel reassured that supplemental blasts would fortify our moods. Fortunately, he had his glass pipe handy so we could smoke some hits instead; smoking crank gives a completely different, more brain-deadening effect.

"The fuckin' phone's been turned off again," I complained in response to his request—in those days neither of us had cell phones.

"Listen. I *gotta* go make a call. Can you keep an ear out till I get back?" And he left, trailing a ribbon of bluish smoke behind him. At the time, I merely figured he had personal business to tend to. All the same, the chore was no big deal for me as long as it didn't entail reentering the guesthouse again. Even should one of the girls have awakened, I trusted that Nicole would be far more qualified than myself at handling any quandaries. Fortunately, all remained peaceful.

Jeff returned, bid me goodnight, and I passed out. And I never saw the girls again.

* * *

Late the next morning I awoke to deadening silence. Something seemed wrong, for silence is not natural where children do dwell. Kinda freaky! A sense of dread spread over me along with a terrible urge to run out there and see what was going on—I immediately broke into my own stash so I could load in a waker-upper. Ouch! . . . Nothing burns like *that* first thing in the morning.

As I stepped through my back door, I could already see the guesthouse door was slightly ajar. I advanced and rapped on it. There was no answer. "Hello . . . *hello*!" I called. No answer. I slowly pushed the door open the rest of the way and was not surprised to find no one there. Circumstances being what they were, I did not think it tactless to proceed. The girls' door to the yard was also fully open. It felt strange; it *was* strange. All seemed the same as I last saw it except that the bathroom lacked amenities. No toothpaste, no hairbrushes, no girls, no Jeff, no note. Silence.

I tried phoning Jeff several times that day, got tired of running out to phone booths, and finally drove by his house, only to harvest the same result. Damn! I realized I should have stocked up while he was around. It meant I'd just have to go over to Pacoima and settle for some lower-grade shit.

Four days later there came a banging at my door. I answered in a downcast temperament, becoming delighted as soon as I saw whom it was. "Hi, Jeff! Come in. *Come in*." Needless to say, we went through our traditional formality before commencing with the idle chatter.

That done, I chattered, "What happened?"

Turns out that the phone call Jeff had gone to make was directed to some cousins of the girls' father—Daddy himself being in prison—who'd leapt into action, swooping down from the mountains where they lived to scoop up the girls and spirit them away.

As their uncle explained, they'd secretly had this in the works a long time. They'd already pulled the legal papers and were just waiting for their chance. It had all been expected. Meanwhile, it was *not* Lorna's first drug offense, which hung her up a week before they rescinded the bail and let her out on O.R. The courts, though, quickly made provisions that, until she proved herself under a year of random drug testing, Lorna was banned from all communication with her kids and from the welfare benefits connected to them. Matter of fact, the only person *not* banned from visiting the girls was Uncle Jeff.

"They live on a ten-acre ranch with horses and miniature goats and pigs. Both cousins have jobs and are financially supplemented by their church, and the church has already filled the girls' closets with new clothes." Jeff continued, "By the way, I want to trade some shit for that old gas-driven lawnmower of yours. We're gonna build Nicole a minibike so she can ride it around the ranch."

I was *ecstatic* and demanded exclusive rights to the oil change.

One evening three months later, I went over to Jeff's to party. He'd already been smoking heavily and I was making a commendable effort to catch up. He piped in, "Hey! I have something for you," and nonchalantly leaned back in his chair to reach for a small photograph on the shelf behind him. He handed it to me. It showed a helmeted Nicole racing madly down a dirt road on her minibike, chased by a rip-roaring golden retriever that was in turn being pursued by a screaming little lunatic named Autumn. Aside and closer in the foreground was Jessica. She had a tiny piglet cradled gently in her arms whence upon she gazed protectively.

I beamed approvingly at the photo. Looking up, but not really caring, I asked in afterthought, "So what's Lorna been up to?"

Jeff screwed up his lips and looked me straight and stonily in the eyes. "She's pregnant again."

Anne Fishbein

DEBORAH VANKIN is a staff writer at the *Los Angeles Times*, where she covers arts and culture, entertainment, and nightlife. She has been a staff editor-writer at *LA Weekly* and *Variety*, and her work has also appeared in the *New York Times*, among many other places. She is the author of the graphic novel *Poseurs*, a "party noir" that follows three teenagers who get sucked into the seemingly glamorous world of L.A. nightlife.

viki, flash, and the pied-piper of shoebies
by deborah vankin

I lost my virginity three times—each occasion marked by the presence of coke. The first time, a medical procedure, came at the hands of Viki, our family doctor and my mom's best friend. They'd met the night my mother, brother, and I moved into a low-rent high-rise on a downtown Pittsburgh side street. My mom was out of cigarettes that night and Viki, who lived in the neighboring apartment, bought Kool Menthol Lights by the carton. It was the early eighties; single mothers bonded over things like that back then.

Viki was a former teen beauty queen, now in her early forties, who wasn't submitting gracefully to the aging process. "Huh? Huh? Does this look cute or *what?!*" she'd say, fingering her jaw-length, silky blond bob in our hallway entrance mirror when she arrived for weeknight happy hours. A gimlet, straight up. Viki was five-foot-nine and disproportionately leggy in tight Sassoon jeans—the dark blue kind, with script across the back pocket—and for emphasis, she'd jerk her bony hips to the right, then swivel a half step to the left, before slowly, cautiously, backing away from the mirror as if she were having separation anxiety parting with her reflection. "Nice, huh? Fifty bucks it cost me to go blond." Then she'd break into this unnerving, too-wide smile.

This was our family doctor. And when I turned thirteen—"a woman now, *officially*," my mom bragged to whomever at the supermarket would listen—I was not only bat mitzvahed in a tailored lavender pantsuit that matched the one in my mom's closet, but I was sent off to Viki for my first "Women's Wellness Exam."

I walked. Living in East Liberty, a busy commercial district, we hardly ever used the crappy silver Pinto except, from time to time, to lug groceries. And Viki's office was just a few blocks away. Aside from a cluster of elaborately framed degrees and academic awards hovering above the reception desk, Viki's practice was sparse, disturbingly devoid of activity. She'd converted the basement of a small-frame Victorian into a medical office and had just one employee, an obese Latvian woman named Odessa, who had a lisp and the most pronounced dimples I'd ever seen—as if someone had gone into her fleshy cheeks with a needle and thread and stitched a tight little notch into each one. Odessa had no medical training nor a valid work visa; but she was a friend of a friend and she needed the cash. Plus, Viki looked thinner and cuter by comparison—the real reason, I suspected, that she kept Odessa around.

While the cramped examining rooms in the back were strictly medical-looking, with lots of chrome, crinkly white paper, and cold tile flooring, the waiting area had clearly once been a child's bedroom—and still could be, if you ignored the assorted cholesterol and AIDS-awareness brochures on the windowsill. There were giant rainbow-colored butterflies sponge-painted across the upper crown molding and the nubby blue carpet featured a hopscotch pattern. "Fun, huh?" Viki had boasted when she opened for business. But really, she'd simply exhausted her divorce settlement and had no money left to replace it with beige plush.

As I waited for my appointment, it occurred to me that I'd never run into any other people at Viki's. Who *were* her other patients? If you didn't know exactly how much it had cost Viki to go blond, or that she habitually put crushed ice in white wine to keep it cold, or that she sometimes did coke ("just to stay awake, like for finals during med school"), would you take her seriously, like a real doctor? Would you depend on her to keep you well?

Thirty minutes I'd been sitting there when, finally, Odessa whirled herself around in the deluxe office chair that she'd insisted upon from the catalogue, and marched back to nudge Viki. There was some indiscernible quarreling, then stomping around, followed by the clank and clatter of steel instruments dropping. Then: "Damn, where *is* it?" Clank. "Fuck." To which the response was a sort of sharp, singsongy outburst that, even in Russian, had the ring of condemnation. Odessa was laying into Viki for *something*. Then: quiet. A somewhat unsettling stillness took hold of the place, followed by a soft chopping, as if Viki were back there mincing herbs.

When Viki emerged, striding into the room confidently as if her white lab coat were a brand-new designer jacket she'd just scored on sale, her eyes were wide and her pupils dilated. I suppose on some level I knew she wasn't amped up on caffeine. Lots of my mom's friends did coke; it was always around at parties, along with crackers and a fragrant hunk of cheese.

"I'll be with you in just a . . ." Viki ducked below the reception desk, then popped back up with a stack of mail, distracted, flipping through a book of coupons. "You know, it's just been crazy-busy today."

I nodded empathetically, as if I weren't the only patient there.

"Odessa" she said, "has someone been calling and hanging up? It happened to me twice this morning. Twice. Like it was deliberate." She tossed the mail aside and thumbed through her messages. "Okay, let's get a look at you. Why don't you get undressed."

As I slipped into the green paper gown, I could hear Viki outside the door, still going at it: "But are we still getting that *static* on the line, like someone's listening?"

Viki checked my weight. "One-twenty, nice," she smirked. "Bet you look cute in a bathing suit." From her tone, I could tell this wasn't a straight-up compliment; it almost sounded like a challenge. Then my height: "Tall for your age. I'm tall, it's sexy, you'll see." Another one of those sassy, crooked smiles. "And *I* still got it, right?" Again, the tone was clear: This wasn't a question. Viki laughed, then sniffed brusquely, as if warding off a cold. "Allergies."

"You know, when I was your age I had lots of boyfriends. My mom had to keep a schedule on the fridge just to keep track." She checked my nascent breasts for lumps. "So, do you have a boyfriend?"

"No, not really."

"But you've obviously fooled around, right?"

"Um . . ."

"Come on, I'm not that out of touch. Do you think you might, you know . . . soon? *You know* . . ."

She slipped on a pair of plastic gloves. Then the womanly part of the exam.

"All looks good. Do you want me to go ahead and clip your hymen?"

"What?"

"You know, so when it comes time, it won't be complicated. Really, it's no big deal."

"Um . . ."

"It'll be easier, believe me. That's what I did when I was your age."

I couldn't think of any excuse not to. It seemed to make sense. I mean, I trusted Viki; she lived next door. So I shut my eyes and, for some reason, I thought of butterflies.

Afterwards, as I was dressing, Viki locked herself away in

the bathroom for quite some time. Again, the mincing of herbs followed by another allergy attack. Viki did this occasionally, and I knew better than to wait around for a proper goodbye.

On the way home, aside from the swatch of cotton gauze in my underpants, I didn't feel any different—just lighter, as if I'd lost or left something behind. I thought about the day Viki had alluded to, that moment in the future when I'd appreciate this practical maneuvering and reap the benefits for real. And I wondered if it was true what the girls at school said about the girls who, *you know*: Did I walk differently now?

The second time I lost my virginity, I was on a college road trip along the Susquehanna River with a frat boy named Flash. Sophomore year. Flash was short and stocky and regardless of how hot and muggy the Pennsylvania weather, he'd always wear those itchy wool camping socks—gray with red trim—scrunched way down around his ankles. From his just-blossoming beer belly, one could imagine Flash, twenty years forward, kicking back in a cream pleather armchair from Sam's Club while taking in the last quarter of a pivotal football game. But Flash had a great smile—hence, the nickname—and he always had coke.

Perhaps now, years later, Flash is a grizzled newspaper man writing obituaries or ad copy in a dusty corner cubicle (he wasn't dumb), because Flash liked words. He had an affinity for rattling off synonyms, especially for the names of drugs—proof, he no doubt believed, that he was "in the know." Flash was the "goodies buyer," he bragged, for a fraternity we'd dubbed the House of Skull. Flash was "suburban street" long before hip-hop had become popular.

"Blow, snow, flake, toot, marching powder," he rattled off as we flew over the potholes of the bumpy, gravel-coated driveway. "Rock and roll!" he wailed. Then he leapt out of his 1987 red Jeep Wrangler Laredo, proudly, protectively tapped the side pocket of his khaki shorts, and shot me an expectant, conspiratorial grin. It was almost charming. His parents' cabin had been empty for months and when I emerged from the master bathroom a few minutes later—which was fusty and moldy-smelling, with a little pile of polished river rocks resting in a dish on the sink—Flash was already cutting lines with a razor from his Dopp Kit. The one I'd planned on shaving my legs with on the off chance we went water-skiing.

Our backpacks were still lying in the hallway, but the stereo was already blasting: Billy Idol. Priorities. I noted the plethora of frosted pink in the decor, collapsed beside Flash on the living room couch, and set my feet on the edge of the glass coffee table. "Don't rock the boat," Flash whined, and he pushed my legs aside. "You'll spill." He was fully absorbed in divvying our supply and didn't even look up when I leaned forward in a stringy bikini top. I ran my finger across the glass surface, collected a trace of powder, and sucked it off, smearing it over my gums with my tongue. Numb. I appreciated numb in all its varying forms— even if that meant spiritually.

"Dance for me," Flash said, finally breaking his concentration.

He knew it was a long shot. I never danced. I avoided parties because I had trouble saying no when some seemingly well-meaning boy walked up to me and asked, guilelessly, "Care to dance?" Like it was a 1940s USO event and we'd be doing the jitterbug. Or the opposite: an unthinking and drunken tug of the wrist to get me up from my bar stool. There were exceptions: nights at crowded frat parties when the wood dance floor, warped from years of spilled beer, filled to mosh pit capacity, and I could fall into the throng of people, letting it rough and tumble me until I was adequately flushed, covered with sweat, and no longer cared. But for the most part I preferred private parties, like this one.

"No. *You* dance. For *me*," I teased Flash.

"Come on, babe. I'm not kidding. I'm doin' all the work here."

I leaned back and let my head drop off the back of the couch, contemplating the sparkly cottage-cheese ceiling. Flash (all proud and regal looking, presenting me with his supine palm) passed me his World Philosophy textbook, which had six meaty lines carefully arranged on the cover, as if he were the butler serving a tray of champagne.

I eyed them appreciatively. "I'm still not gonna dance," I said.

Flash rolled his eyes and we took turns sucking up the good stuff until the coke was long gone and my sinuses started to burn. For the rest of the evening, we subsisted on scraps of leftover snack food from the trip up—beef jerky, cheese curls, and warm Mountain Dew—and since we could no longer sit still, we resorted to a somewhat frenetic and disjointed version of charades. We alternated positions in the front of the room, performing wildly animated renditions of song titles and TV shows, while the viewer basically ignored the game from the couch, eventually looking up and saying something like: "I give up."

"Lucille Ball, stupid. *I Love Lucy*. Duh!"

To mellow us out, we did chilled Jell-O shots off one another's bellies until the sky lightened up and I came to realize that Flash's parents' cabin was a riverfront property.

"Come have almost-sex with me," Flash pleaded, slapping the empty spot next to him on the oriental rug. There was a big difference back then, it's worth pointing out, between "sex" and "almost-sex." A girl could have engaged in "everything but," been promiscuous enough to make even Madonna proud, but still, no matter how skilled she was at giving head, crossing that last frontier was a big deal. It was "reserved" for someone special.

I settled in next to Flash and he kissed the side of my neck with his parched, sun-cracked lips before gnawing gently on my ear. "Bump, charlie, nose candy," he whispered. "She, her, lady flake . . ."

That's pretty much the last thing I remember from that night—Flash's warm breath on my earlobe, the litany of coke nicknames, and his itchy socks against my ankles as the ceiling fan whipped around, creating dark, elongated triangles that cut, repeatedly, across our strung-out faces.

The next morning, I woke up naked but for a wide-brimmed sombrero adorned, all the way around, with little bells—the kind you typically find on cats' collars. I've no idea where the straw hat came from or why I'd woken up wearing it; but it jingled with ear-splitting clarity as I made my way down the hall to the bathroom, the lumpy comforter draped around my bare shoulders and dragging behind me. When I flipped up the toilet seat, there, in the bowl, was Flash's limp and waterlogged social security card floating around and around and around in the now blueish water. His runny, blurred signature was still legible: *Ronald P. Anson.*

Ronald. His real name was Ronald.

Roughly a year after my rendezvous with Flash, my family moved from Pittsburgh to Philly so that my mom could take a "real job, with benefits" at Temple University. She was a clerk in the admissions office but hell-bent on the idea that if she held the job long enough, she'd somehow get smarter by osmosis. During this time we vacationed in Brigantine, a sleepy South

Jersey island nearly as populated with dive bars and drug dealers as it was with washed-up sand crabs and tall, grassy weeds. There was never enough money for designer-brand clothes or frivolous food items or the slicker-looking school supplies, but somehow my mom had managed the mortgage on a small beach bungalow. She went in on it with Viki, and they alternated weekends.

Situated just across the bay from Atlantic City, Brigantine was a bedroom community for casino workers. Each evening, card dealers and cocktail waitresses, hotel maids, bartenders, and lounge singers made the trek over the bridge onto the glittering Vegas "mini-me" strip. Here, barely out of earshot of gagging slot machines spitting up coins, is where I lost my virginity for the third time, the one I count as "official." I was nineteen, not yet aware of what had really happened with Flash, and still holding out for "that special someone." It's what goes on record in the annals of "important girl moments" in my mind because a) it involved another person, and b) I remembered it.

I was on coke quite literally that night—a makeshift bed of flattened cola boxes laid out discretely by a bank of sand dunes on the beach. The little nook, sandwiched between a spindly wood fence and a ten-foot-high mound of sand flecked with bits of jagged shell, was a landmark of sorts—couples tramped there after dark for some privacy—but it never received a deserved nickname, like "makeout point."

Sean was a bartender at the Big Brown Bar, or "B-cubed" as we called it, a local dive with a jukebox that leaned toward reggae and soul, and a shabby back porch that emptied onto the beach. We'd met in a darts tournament. As I stared down the bull's-eye, nibbling the inside of my cheek to harness my concentration, I caught Sean ogling. I reminded him of an old girlfriend, he told me later. I had the same pouty mouth.

What I came to notice about Sean, once he sparked my interest and I'd gone back, repeatedly, to B-cubed, was his erratic temperament. One night he'd be charged up and tending bar as if it were an extreme sport, all but tossing bottles in the air like Tom Cruise in *Cocktail*. The next, he'd be sulky and sullen, quickly irritated. But like so many of the girls who padded behind him, I sat there night after night—ingesting ridiculous amounts of greasy fried mushrooms and teaching myself to blow smoke rings from bummed Camel Lights—until he remembered my name. His mood swings would come to make sense. Sean made an okay living mixing drinks, but his rent came from coke.

B-cubed sported a somewhat uninspired nautical theme, with lots of dark wood and hanging, knotted rope. From the porthole above the toilet in the bathroom, one could see Atlantic City in the distance, a toy, snow-globe skyline glittering against the sooty sky, its fuzzy reflection calling attention to itself in the murky water below. Brigantine was to A.C. what Brooklyn had been to Manhattan in the 1970s: a place you aspire to leave. But Sean never got Saturday Night Fever. Sean took pride in hardly ever leaving the island. The last time he embarked from the fourteen-mile stretch of gravel and sand had been nine months earlier, to have a tooth pulled. Sean detested Atlantic City. "It's a playground for shoebies," he'd say.

"Shoebies," that's what they called the summering crowd. Because shoebies wore their weathered, strappy leather sandals, flip-flops from the five-and-dime, beat-up Converse All Stars onto the beach; then, after the methodical ritual of spreading out oversize towels, setting down coolers, and muttering some form of "ah, smell that fresh air," the flock of shoebies would enter into a flurry of buckle-and-shoe-strap-releasing and the subsequent, near-choreographed wriggling of newly emancipated toes. The locals, they didn't mind hot sand on their feet. The locals went barefoot.

We were shoebies of the worst variety. We actually owned a house on the island. And B-cubed was situated, a little too conveniently, on the corner of our street, so that you had to walk past its rowdy entrance—which reeked of sweat, salt water, and coconut-scented tanning lotion—after every stint on the beach. The bar was popular not because it was any good, but because the owners were generous to underage drinkers and it was, simply, the nearest toilet around if you weren't the type to pee in the ocean.

Sean was in an especially spry mood the night we hooked up, full of jerky, happy movements and short bursts of laughter, all white teeth and lanky, toned limbs, lips so fleshy and red it was as if he'd just soaked them in a Dixie cup of Kool-Aid. I was sitting at the bar with several other shoebie girls from the city who had equally weighty crushes on Sean, facing the open door, when a yellow Camaro with a wheezy muffler pulled up and Sean slipped out. I recognized the driver from Island Pizza. He was still in uniform. Through the doorframe I could make out a slice of activity: Sean leaning a little too deeply into the driver's window, laughing nervously and glancing periodically over his shoulder. There was the quick, surreptitious exchange of cash accompanied by another cautionary glance in either direction, then a handshake and "See ya later, man. Yep."

Back inside, Sean was leaning against a pinball machine thumbing through a wad of bills, when the Camaro screeched to a halt and did a 360. He stuffed the cash in his pocket and headed back out, a nothing-to-hide lilt in his step, walking straight into the car's headlights—too overtly confident to be anything but scared shitless. The Island Pizza guys were rankled over something and, illogically, as their voices rose they bumped up the volume on their tinny car stereo.

Finally: "Can you turn that goddamned thing off?" Sean said.

"Fer Christ's sake."

I couldn't make out what, exactly, the Island Pizza guys were accusing him of. But Sean's voice was fairly audible.

"No way, man, I work here. Weigh it out in the back of the car."

More protesting from within the Camaro.

"Nuh-uh, there's nowhere private here, I've got customers, I'm on the clock."

Perhaps I craved adventure, and this was my late-teen, melodramatic way of claiming it; or maybe it was the beer, which was finally kicking in; or possibly the confidence induced from finally having perfected the smoke rings. Who knows? But I strode outside and rammed up against Sean, as if I'd known him since we were kids. "You need a place to go?" I said. "Because my house is right there, the little yellow one on the corner."

That was the pinnacle of the drama, however. The Island Pizza guys, Sean's "clients," as he referred to them, had been mistaken about his cheating them. And to smooth over the discrepancy, they offered us each a line before finally cranking their car radio back up and rumbling off down the street. Sean and I walked back to the bar, but when we got there, he led me past B-cubed and onto the beach. "It's late, they don't need me anymore tonight," he said. "Come on."

As we reclined on the sand, I mistook the gnawing in my stomach, the butterflies, for some premature version of love. "You're so cool, you know that?" Sean said. "Thanks for doing that. Really, really cool. Yeah." He stretched out the "yeah," a Jersey thing. "Yeehhh." Then he held my face and stared into my eyes as if they weren't mine, in a way that was far too familiar, too loaded with intimacy, for the short time we'd known one another. "Yeah, you're all right." And then we did it; simple as that.

Later, as we lay in each other's arms, the cardboard cola boxes under our bare backs, Sean turned onto his side and kissed my eyelids gently. He traced the bow of my upper lip with his index finger—over and over again—and, just before nodding off to sleep, he silently mouthed what appeared to be *"Trina."* Which, even under the muted rumble and crash of ocean waves, isn't remotely close to my name.

I spent the next morning tanning with a school friend, Amy, who'd driven up to spend labor day weekend "with you!" she'd said. But she was a casual classmate, the type of friend who rotates in and out of your life according to the semester schedule; and I suspected she was really after a good browning of the neck and shoulders before classes started up the next week. I didn't particularly enjoy sunbathing; but the night out with Sean had been significant enough that only a grossly girlish activity— gossiping while baking baby-oil-slicked bodies on those silver foils, say—would do.

As I filled her in on the night before, our tangerine wine coolers nearly the exact shade of our toenails, Amy went from puzzled to agitated to flat out rude: "I don't get it. Why would you lie to me?"

"What do you mean?"

"You know I don't care how many people you've slept with. So why say Sean was your first?"

"I have no idea what you're talking about."

"I know about Flash. We have Mid East History together. He told me all about your road trip."

"But we didn't sleep together. I mean, we *slept*, but that was pretty much it."

"That's not how he tells it."

We went back and forth like this for a while, then Amy

peeled the now warm and wilted cucumber slices from her eyelids and tossed them into the sand. She stood up and dusted off her roasted shins and calves. "Whatever," she said.

I sat on the beach alone for quite some time after that, wringing my brain for details about that night along the Susquehanna River; but all I remembered with any clarity was the careening coke binge and my last moments with Flash before, apparently, passing out.

Flash could have been lying, of course. *Amy* could have been lying, though I don't see why. She'd only recently taken a liking to Sean and she wasn't even a shoebie, not officially. But there was no way to know for sure after what had happened in Viki's office so many years earlier. No proof, in other words. So I wrote off the first time as unfortunate, the second time as a sloppy mistake, and I trudged back to join Amy inside the Big Brown Bar. It was Friday and still warm outside and, well, *the first time*—that was worth a round of shots.

After I returned to college for my senior year, Sean did a stint at the Jersey State Penitentiary for dealing. And when Viki was carted off to rehab that fall by her newly appointed fiancé— a "sea captain," he called himself, but really he just operated one of those boats that carried tourists across the bay—we sold the beach house because my mom couldn't keep up the payments. Flash, who knows what happened to him; but he was well-equipped with a large vocabulary, at least. And except for a few lines off the back of a navy three-ring binder on the way to a concert that year, I didn't bother much with coke anymore. I preferred beer and pot and mineral water with a spritz of lime. But one thing was certain: I walked differently now. I held my head up high and walked like a lady.

I had to. You know, consider the alternative.

NINA REVOYR was born in Japan and raised in Tokyo, Wisconsin, and Los Angeles. Her four novels include *Southland*, an Edgar Award finalist, winner of the Lambda Literary Award, and a *Los Angeles Times* "Best Book" of 2003; and *The Age of Dreaming*, a finalist for a 2008 *Los Angeles Times* Book Prize. Her latest novel, *Wingshooters*, was an IndieBound "Indie Next" selection and one of *O, The Oprah Magazine's* "Books to Watch For." Nina is vice president of a nonprofit children's service organization and has taught at a number of colleges. She lives in Los Angeles with her partner.

golden pacific
by nina revoyr

t all got harder when my mother left, three weeks ago now. That's when Chester started saying he needed somebody to drive around with, and there's no one left to go with but me. He's got a big car, would *have* to be to fit him in it; his belly's like a sack of potatoes stuffed under his shirt. When we came out to L.A. ten weeks ago, my mother looked at him once and said, "Don't ever go near him." My mother understood about men.

He grabbed me one day with a grubby hand, slid his fingers down my shoulder, said I looked older than I am, thirteen. Close up, he smelled like old tobacco and sweat. I pulled loose and stayed away, but now my mother is gone. I sit next to him while he puffs his cigarettes and watch the smoke curl toward the ceiling, looks almost pretty till the car fills up. He laughs when he sees my eyes tear from the smoke, me bent over to cradle my cough.

Every day at lunchtime we drive down to the school. All the kids come outside at 12:15, and we go so he can watch the little girls. Chester parks the car on the street right next to the schoolyard, under a row of big trees with leafy fingers hanging down. He's like an old animal washed up on the beach, brown and wheezing. The little kids don't see the fat man and the girl watching from the car in the shade. They're only five or six years old, same age my sister was. They look so shiny and pretty, chasing each other and laughing, in shorts and white T-shirts or bright blouses. Sometimes they fall and start crying and then the older girl runs over and scoops them up. She's got almond eyes and gold-brown skin, royal-looking, a Mexican girl. Chester doesn't notice her, though. He keeps his eyes on the small ones. His breath changes when they squat on the sizzling pavement, bony bottoms pressing tight against their shorts.

We left D.C. in June, right after school got out. My mother said too much was happening and she had to get away. She said the weather was bad for thinking. D.C. summers so sticky and hot they sweat the soul right out of you. It didn't matter that we left because she had no steady job, worked off and on, a lot of places wouldn't hire her because of her crumpled hand. Then a man she knew said he was driving out west to California, so we packed two bags and went with him. She had a friend in L.A. who said we could stay with her, but when we got here and called, the friend was gone. So we were stuck in L.A. with twenty-six dollars, the man who drove us on his way to San Francisco. All the clothes except the ones on our backs stolen out of the car in Oklahoma. Most of the money gone after two plates of greasy chicken and a night at the Golden Pacific Motel. We were right downtown, you could see City Hall. This place was supposed to be a motel, but it looked more like a bunch of boards standing up with some paint slapped on to hold them together. So old the whole building shook when they ran the washing machine downstairs. My mother's eyes sad the whole time she talked to the shriveled old man at the counter, said she'd never take me into a place like this except she couldn't do any better just now. Piss stains on the outside wall and dirty air that pressed like fog against the window. Inside our room there was a Bible under a chair leg where the end got broken off, grooves in the wall behind the headboard so deep I could lay two fingers in them. There was a freeway outside the window, and it was loud in the room, like the sound came in and got trapped there, bounced and bounced off all the walls.

It was the next morning we met Chester. We walked into the coffee shop down the street for breakfast, and he looked up from the counter, said he knew the Lord was looking out for him when He sent two such beautiful ladies his way. He was wide awake and cheerful, as if he thought he was somewhere else. My mother smiled like something hurt her, quick-shuffled me into a booth. Chester got up, stretched wide, sleeves slipping down his arms, and slid into the booth right next to her. He said he had no particular plans that day and wouldn't we like to go for a ride. L.A. was dangerous, he said, could eat people alive, especially those who didn't know their way around. I don't know how he figured out we were new. There were big rips in the fake red leather seats and I poked my fingers in them as he talked. My mother looked away from him, held her bad hand in her good one; it was dried up, shrunken, a bit darker than the rest of her. She kept saying we were busy, but anybody could see she was just putting him off, and Chester smiled at her the way she smiled at me when she knew I was lying. Chester's fingers are like splotchy brown sausages, and he has big liquid eyes. His forehead and upper lip are always wet, too, and when he walked ahead of us toward the door that day, I saw the sweat spread like disease across his back.

He paid for our room that night, twenty dollars. My mother didn't like the neighborhood—men hovered in doorways, caked in their own dirt, talking to themselves in low, lurching voices. Boys slid down the sidewalk, watery-eyed and wary, stopping to palm money for packets pulled from their big pockets, or to follow nervous men into cars or motels. We walked around the block once and saw shells of buildings with boards for windows, covered with graffiti, food, a few speckles of blood, the sticky yellow-brown patterns of piss. My mother hated the motel, but Chester had paid for it, and there was nowhere else to sleep except the beach. I would've gone—I like palm trees and water, the salty smell of the ocean—but my mother wouldn't have it, said no child of hers was going to sleep outside like a beggar. So every day for a week Chester drove us around the city, and every night he paid for our room. He took us to Hollywood, Venice Beach, the San Fernando Valley, and told us stories about what he'd seen there. He bought us burgers and burritos, poured beer into an empty Coke can so he could drink as we drove. He didn't tell us about himself—he had no job that I could see, and I didn't know where he got his money. My mother wouldn't talk much on these drives, not unless he asked her something, but Chester didn't seem to notice or care.

When we were alone in the room at night, my mother shut the window against the noise of the freeway and made plans. She said she was going to start looking for a job, something easy where she didn't have to use her hand much. She said she was going to get us an apartment, and me into school, and enough money together to buy us both some new clothes and pay Chester back. We prayed every night, and sat and looked at the picture of my sister Tammy she'd set up on the dresser. Tammy was always happy. Mother said that when she was born and the doctor slapped her, she opened her eyes and laughed. When she was older, she chattered and cuddled, took her Raggedy Ann doll everywhere; even strangers had to smile when they saw her. She was skinny; I could feel her bones poke my legs when she sat on my lap. Those nights in our room, my mother didn't want to talk about Tammy. I guess she had enough to think about with me, and I could tell she was worried. I stayed thin no matter what I ate, which wasn't much, because I couldn't eat in front of other people without feeling my stomach shove the food back up my throat. I had to scoot around a corner to eat the burgers Chester bought, and chase my mother out of the room to eat my dinner.

It was all right, though, until one night I went downstairs after eating a chicken sandwich to tell my mother she could come back inside. She was sitting in Chester's big tan car, and it was facing the other way, and the windows were rolled all the way down. It was sunset, the sky was hazy and brown, and I heard Chester talking in that big ripe voice of his, still cheerful but something else now too, and he was telling my mother that he wasn't the social services department, that he expected something in return for all his kindness. He said she'd better reconsider what she was saying because if he stopped paying for that room, she and I would be out on the street. But if she was smart and did like he told her, then he'd give her something special, something to take her troubles away and make her feel better. And as I stood there I heard an unfamiliar sound, and it took me awhile to realize it was the sound of my mother crying. I didn't recognize it because I'd never heard it before, not when we'd left D.C., not even when Tammy died. I stood there a second, but then my mother saw me in the rearview mirror, and she straightened up in her seat and stopped crying so quick I wasn't even sure I'd really heard it. Then she said something to Chester and opened the door, calling me over. She told me to wait in the car with the door locked until she came back out and got me, and then she hugged me, hard, the heel of her crumpled hand pressed tight against my ear. Then she and Chester went into our room and shut the door.

There's not more than fifty kids at the school Chester drives us to, which is a few miles away from the motel, in Culver City. I thought there were so few because it was summer, and the only kids who go to summer school in D.C. are the ones who have to. These kids get twenty minutes to eat their lunch, at picnic tables where the green paint is chipping so bad there's white spots big as quarters. Then another half hour to play before they go back inside. I wish my mother was here to see them, but it's probably better that she's not. Every time she saw a little kid on our drive across the country, she pressed her lips together and all the lines in her face got deeper. The kids in the schoolyard make me feel better, though—they all seem so young to me, only babies, still happy. But it's the older girl I keep my eyes on. Every once in a while she looks down for a second when she thinks that no one's watching, and I think how alone she seems, even with all those kids. Then she looks up again, and smiles at whoever's near her. Sometimes after they eat she takes the kids to the park right next to the school, lets them play on the slide and the swings. She pushes them gently, their small, sneakered feet tracing the arc of their swing; she laughs when they come squealing down the slide. After a while a bunch of boys show up, Mexican boys, thin nets over their hair, bright white T-shirts under plaid work shirts with the sleeves rolled up, and baggy tan pants buckled high. They look about the girl's age, or a little younger. Sometimes, when they scratch their arms and their shirts flap open, you can catch a glimpse of black metal. The girl's hands flash left and right as she touches the kids, gathers them in, takes them back to the school in a hurry. The boys are real respectful, though. They nod to the girl as she passes and don't start talking until the kids are all gone. Then they sit on the swings and rusting merry-go-round, laughter lifting from their circle like smoke.

One day the girl walks the kids past the car. She leans toward the window and asks if I have the time. I'm so surprised it takes me awhile to answer. Then she tells me her name, Yvonne, and asks mine. Right before she turns away she smiles, and that white smile flashing out of her gold-brown face is like a birthday gift, a burst of bright flowers. Her hair is clean and shiny, reflecting the sun; it twists and flows like smooth black water.

After that I start getting out of the car. As soon as the kids come pouring from the building for lunch, I get out, shut the door, and walk over to the metal fence. Chester doesn't seem to mind—he's maybe fifteen feet behind me, can hear everything that goes on, anyway. Yvonne comes to meet me, half an eye still on the kids. "I'm going to college soon."

"When?" I ask.

"Next month." She's real excited, as if she were getting married or something. It's a quiet kind of excitement, though, more in her eyes than in her voice, like she doesn't quite believe that it's true. She says the college is about five miles away, but the bus trip takes an hour—she'll take the commuter line that goes down Venice Boulevard.

"I just graduated in June," she says. "I'm the first one in my family to go to college." I can tell she's real proud. I am, too, although I don't know why. A gust of wind comes along and shakes the fence, makes a sound like twenty people rattling chains all at once. The fence is maybe eight feet high, diagonal squares set spinning on their corners, three strands of barbed wire across the top. I glance up at the barbed wire and then back to Yvonne, who's smiling.

"So what are you doing here?" she asks. I tell her my mother and I just came out from the east a few weeks ago, and I'm not doing much of anything because school hasn't started yet. "My mother went away for a while, but she'll be back soon," I say.

"Don't you get bored?"

"No, I'm kinda busy."

"Who's that man?" she asks quietly, gesturing toward Chester.

I pause. "Just a man."

Then a little girl comes running over and hugs Yvonne around her legs. Yvonne leans forward to face her, and I think of how bright her red blouse looks against the gray concrete, the dead grass, the dry summer.

"Hi," I say to the little girl, but she says nothing, and those big round eyes fix on me from out of that chocolate-brown face.

"You look pretty today, Carla," says Yvonne, but the girl doesn't answer her either; she makes a strange, low noise, almost like she's in pain, although I can see she's smiling. Then she scrambles toward something chalked onto the pavement. It's on a slope, facing away, and it looks like a curving bell shape, with a half-circle on one side and two straight, branchlike parts on the other.

"What's that?" I ask.

"It's a Mary," Yvonne says. "Mother of God."

I stand on my tiptoes, peer down the slope, see the vague shape of a person, the thin legs and covered head. "Who drew it?"

"I did. I draw one every day. There's a whole bunch more on the other side of the schoolyard, and one by the park, and one over there on the sidewalk."

I look where she's pointing, to the right of me, and sure enough there's one on the sidewalk, right next to the car. "Why do you draw Marys?" I ask.

"I don't know," she says. "I've always drawn them."

The little girl squatting next to the Mary sticks her finger in her mouth and then rubs it against the chalk, smearing part of the outline. I don't tell Yvonne that her Mary reminds me of the police drawings I'd seen sometimes on the streets of D.C. I think of Chester in the car behind me and don't want to go back; when I do he'll be sitting there with his pants shoved down around his thighs. Yvonne turns toward the little girl, who stands up and runs back over to the other kids. She keeps looking at the drawing, even after the girl has left. We both stand there staring at the Mary, not saying anything, as if it might peel off the ground and fly away.

At first the only man my mother took into the room was Chester. Then there were others, until I had to wait for hours at a time in Chester's car, or in the coffee shop with the torn red vinyl seats. The owner of the coffee shop, Pedro, gave me hot dogs and grilled cheese sandwiches. I'd go around back to eat them, watch the cars speed by on the freeway forty or fifty yards away, and wonder where all those people were going. My mother still drove around with Chester and me in the morning, but she got quieter and quieter, and hardly said a word to either of us.

Then one day in the coffee shop, when she wouldn't even look up at Pedro when he brought her scrambled eggs, Chester leaned over the table and said real low, "I keep telling you, woman. I got something that'll make you feel better." My mother sighed and looked past him and said, "Okay." They sent me upstairs and went someplace else; I just waited and watched an hour pass by on the clock. When my mother came back to our room, her eyes were red and she was jumpy like a nervous animal. She moved from the bed to the chair to the bed again; she couldn't seem to keep herself still. She kept saying that she was thirsty, but when I gave her some water, her hand shook so bad she couldn't hold the glass.

After that it seemed like she was always off with Chester somewhere, asking him for something. Even when she was with me she didn't seem like herself; her hair was stringy and dull, and she was starting to lose weight. She didn't seem to sleep much, but she never got tired; I'd wake up and find her mumbling to herself. Then one day when I was changing the sheets, which I did every afternoon, I found a little plastic sandwich bag like the kind I used to take for lunch, with some clear, jagged pebbles inside. My mother grabbed it from my hands and started yelling at me, eyes wild. I was scared, but then she stopped, came and put her arms around me. "I'm so sorry, baby," she kept saying, and I could hear the tears in her voice. "I'm so sorry. I never meant for this to happen." She pulled away and put her head down, bad hand laying in her lap like a dead bird, and for a second she looked like she did the day we heard about Tammy. Then she got herself together and left. I don't know where she went, maybe to tell Chester to leave us alone, maybe off someplace by herself. When she came back, though, her eye was swollen and there was dried blood around her mouth. She went straight to the bathroom and shut the door. She wouldn't let me help her. That night one of the men who'd been coming around picked her up and didn't bring her back till the next morning. She'd never spent the night outside the motel before, but after that she did it three more times. Two weeks later she drove off with a man about seven o'clock, his car blending in with all the traffic on the freeway. That was the last I saw of her.

I waited a couple of days, thinking the man just wanted her for longer than usual. Chester was pissed, said the man had cheated him, left with his woman and his best shit, too. He raged around, kicking his car tires and yelling at me like I'd stolen her. But he paid for my room and kept buying me food. The third night, though, he grabbed my elbow and shoved me into the room, said that debts left by the parent had to be collected from the child. He threw me down on the bed, pressed one fat arm across my chest, and yanked my shorts down with the other, popped the buttons. What I remember is his lips against mine, his tongue a slimy fish in my mouth, his skin so moist and rancid it was like I was drowning in his sweat. Pain so sharp between my legs I thought he'd stuck a knife inside me. The sound of the bed banging against the wall and the bunched-up sheet like white flowers in his fist. It was like he was hammering me down into something, making me disappear. His eyes were half-closed and he made high crying sounds like an animal having the life squeezed out of it.

After that there were others, some the same ones who had come for my mother. Chester told me I had to earn my room and board, kept my pockets stuffed with condoms, held clean cloths against me after as I bled and bled. He bought me new clothes, tight things it embarrassed me to wear. He sits in the parking lot or the coffee shop now and waits, talks to the men and gets their money when they're through. They don't leave, though, he won't let them leave, until I tell him they didn't hit me, and that they put on the condom I offered. They're all different, those men—some never say a word to me, some use language my mother would have covered my ears against, some talk to me awhile, before and after. Some bring a flask or bottle into the room, some the little plastic bags that Chester sells them. Most of them drive nice cars and dress in suits, sneaking over from their downtown offices on their lunch breaks. Two of them are lawyers, one works in a bank, another does something in movies. Sometimes they're young, no bristle of beard against my cheek, but most of them are older than Chester.

When I'm with them I try to listen to the sounds of the freeway, or to count, and not think about my mother, or what she would do if she knew what was happening. I look away when they take out their mirrors or their little glass pipes, and as soon as they leave, I run to the shower and scrub myself all over until it hurts. It doesn't matter, though. The dirt's under my skin, and I can't seem to get it off me. The bed smells like the men, and me, and I don't want to sleep there; I curl up at night on the floor. Chester started buying me more food to fatten me up—spaghetti and bread and milk shakes—but it doesn't work, I can't keep it down anymore, even when I eat alone. I think of running away, but if my mother comes back she wouldn't be able to find me. So I stay.

Once a week Chester takes me somewhere nice, the movies or the mall or the beach. He buys me things—a radio, a small stuffed pig to sleep with. One time he even took out a pipe and asked if I wanted something to make me feel better. But I just shook my head no, because I saw what that did; I knew what it could do to me. Chester tries to get me to talk, but I don't say much, and I never laugh at his stupid jokes. Sometimes when we're driving around, I look out the window and start to cry, and he looks over at me between sips of his Coke-can beer. "Why you so sad?" he asks. "I take good care of you, don't I? Shit, at least you ain't out on the streets."

At 12:10 we pull up beside the schoolyard. I get out of the car to wait the five minutes till the kids come out, hoping Yvonne will be with them. She doesn't disappoint me. She steps out the door and smiles so wide I can see her teeth all the way across the schoolyard. As she comes toward me, I notice for the first time how she always walks a little awkwardly, faltering now and then, like her body's a borrowed car she isn't sure how to handle.

"Hi," she says, "I missed you yesterday."

"I was sick," I say. That isn't true. I was in the motel room with the banker.

"Are you feeling better?"

"Yeah."

"Want a candy bar?" She takes a Mars bar out of her pocket and sticks it through the fence. I take it. There are no Marys on the concrete today, but two on the side of the building. They're bigger than Yvonne, but nothing's in them, they're just outlines—cold, white, untouchable. "Aren't those clothes a little old for you?" she asks. She looks at me kind of sideways, then she glances toward the car.

"They're all I got," I say, and I start to tell her that Chester picked them out for me, but don't.

She looks over at the car again. "Listen," she says softly, "do you need some food? Some clothes? Cos I've got a whole bunch of stuff at home I could—"

"No thanks," I say, and I look quickly behind me. Chester's watching us now, his forehead wrinkled, his hands wrapped tight around the wheel.

Yvonne looks like she's about to say something else but then three little boys run up to her. They're cute, smiling and huffing, and they only come up to her waist. One of them makes a high, weird, wavering noise, and another answers him the same way; they sound like whales talking underwater. The first one holds his arms out toward Yvonne, asking to be picked up.

"Hey, handsome," Yvonne says, and then, "You're a little old for this, Miguel," but she picks him up anyway. She turns to me again, and the two boys on either side of her tug at the legs of her shorts.

"Hi, guys," I say. They all keep staring at Yvonne and don't say anything. I look at her. "Hey, how come the kids never answer when I talk to them?" I ask.

Yvonne looks at me like she's surprised at the question. "Don't you know?" she says, smiling. "They're deaf."

It's the mornings I think most about my sister. The picture my mother brought is still in the room, and when the men come in, I turn it face down on the dresser. Early mornings I have time, though, and I sit and look at it awhile. It was taken two years ago, when Tammy was three. She's laughing in it and looking off at something above the camera, and I remember the day it was taken, a Saturday, and that we all went out for ice cream after. When the picture was made and framed, we showed it to Tammy. She'd never seen a picture of herself before and she didn't believe it was her.

What happened was that Tammy came down with something, maybe pneumonia, no one ever knew for sure. She got a real high fever and my mother pressed ice bags to her head, put her in a tub full of cold water, but nothing brought her temperature down. My mother had no insurance, and we couldn't afford a doctor. Three days after she took sick, Tammy died. My mother went a little crazy after that, shaking Tammy like she could shake her alive, my sister's head flopping forward like that Raggedy Ann's. It was a few days later that we up and left for L.A.

One Friday we get to the school a little late. The kids have eaten already, and a bunch of them are climbing on the jungle gym. Yvonne stands next to them, laughing out loud and talking although she knows they can't hear. I look at the way the sun shines off her hair, the way she stands so straight and proud, and I think of how lucky she is, how she has everything, or at least she can someday. I get out of the car and go to the fence, and when she sees me, she starts to walk over.

"I brought you a candy bar," I say, and I have, a Milky Way that one of the lawyers gave me. But when I reach into my pocket, I pull a condom out, too, and the blue square of foil flutters down my leg and lands in front of my feet.

Yvonne sees it and her eyes get wide. "Is that yours?" she asks.

I keep my head down, not able to look at her, and I want to say I'm sorry. I can't seem to hold my face together, and I feel the tears begin to come. "Not exactly. I mean . . ." I move my shoulders a bit, half-nod in the direction of Chester. She doesn't say anything, and I finally bring myself to glance at her. She looks like she can't believe it, but like she *has* to believe it, and then she steps up close to the fence.

"Why don't you come in here?" she says. "Let me call someone. Go around to the front of the building and come in."

Just then I hear the car door slam, and Chester yells, "Hey!"

I turn and look at him; he saw the condom fall, or maybe he heard Yvonne. He starts to walk over, glaring at me, hands open like he's ready to catch something.

"Come on, come in the school," Yvonne urges quietly, but I can't move, I feel stuck, and Chester's getting closer. When he's right behind me, I stick my fingers through the squares of the fence.

"Hey, girl, let's go!" Chester says, but I tighten my grip, and then I feel him grab the back of my shirt, pull so hard it starts to tear.

"Stop it, leave her alone!" Yvonne says, but Chester just ignores her, and starts pounding my fingers, hard metal cutting into my flesh.

Yvonne reaches out with both her hands and touches my fingers, hooked down to the second knuckle through the squares; it's the warmest touch I've felt in weeks, and I want to close my eyes and fall into it. But Chester's yanking at my shoulders now and I think, *I hate this man, I hate him*, and I think, *Please let me squeeze through these squares so I can be safe with Yvonne*. And I think how nice it would be to play in the schoolyard with the kids, who are finally looking over at us now, but my fingers are getting tired and the metal starts to hurt and he's pulling even harder and I let go.

Chester falls backward with the weight of me, but then he gets his balance again. He goes up to the fence and punches out at Yvonne, slams his fist against the metal so hard I see the blood on his hand when he pulls away. He drags me to the car, and I look back at Yvonne, her foot on the head of a Mary and her fingers looped through the fence where my hands just were. Chester throws me into the front seat and then shoves himself in after me, screeches away from the curb. He raises his hand, and I expect to feel it any second, but although his fist is clenched, he doesn't hit me. "*Goddamnit*, girl," he says, "we're never going back there."

And as he puts his hand back on the wheel and cuts hard around a corner, I look at him and say, "Where's my mother?"

"I don't *know!*" he yells, swerving into the middle lane, and then, again, softer, "I don't know."

I turn from him and look out the window, toward downtown, toward D.C., and I know that she's not coming back. Chester keeps driving, breathing heavy, and I don't say anything. But when we stop at a red light, I open the door and jump out of the car.

"Hey!" Chester yells, but I'm running already, toward the sidewalk, where I'll turn right, go down the block. I hear him get out and start after me, hear the honks of the people stuck behind his car. I'm on the sidewalk now, on Venice, heading west toward the school and Yvonne. Chester's not far behind; he's faster than

I thought. We pass a taco place, a liquor store, a place that sells car radios. Chester's breathing hard, and every second or two I hear another scrap of his shouts: "Get . . . back here . . . girl! You . . . can't . . . get away!" And maybe he's right—my lungs hurt and I'm tired; maybe he'll catch up with me and take me back to the motel and it'll all start over again. But right now, this second, the wind is cool and the sky is clear; right now, I've left him behind me and I'm free.

Florence Hernandez-Ramos

MANUEL RAMOS has authored seven novels including *The Ballad of Rocky Ruiz*, a finalist for the Edgar Award, and a noir private eye novel, *Moony's Road to Hell*. He is a cofounder of and weekly contributor to La Bloga, an Internet magazine devoted to Latino literature, culture, news, and opinion. Recent publications include "The Skull of Pancho Villa" in the anthology *Hit List: The Best of Latino Mystery*; and "Fence Busters" in the award-winning anthology *A Dozen on Denver*. His latest novel, *King of the Chicanos*, was published in 2010.

sentimental value
by manuel ramos

1988

The Sunday insert, tucked in among the comics and grocery coupons, had a three-page, color baseball article. *Latin American Ball Players. Latin Stars of the National Pastime. The Latin American Connection.* Latin?

Plenty of hype about the current crop of players. Sure, they were good. Who wouldn't want Canseco, or Valenzuela? And some of them born in the States. But they couldn't even be bat boys for Cepeda, Aparicio, Marichal, or Zorro-Zoilo Versalles, MVP that year it all changed for Ray. He had read about these players when he was growing up, had kept their cardboard images in a box with his glove. They were the men who inspired the skinny, quiet Raymond López.

He had been fast. Fifty stolen bases his senior year, good hands, a better bat. Ah, but his arm. ¡A toda madre! A cannon that made him famous, a starter for four years at North High, and a City League All-Star right fielder. That arm generated a couple of calls from bald short guys in plaid sport coats who said they were scouts. Talk about characters! Smoking their smelly cigars, going on about the big leagues like Ray was the next bonus baby and it was right around the corner.

"Just sign this contract and we'll hook you up in the Instructional League, buy your momma a house one of these days, boy. A little extra in it (*and for you, too, Mr. Scout, as long as you got my name on a piece of paper that locks me in forever, but if, just if, mind you, if I don't cut it, phfft! So long, boy!*). We'll even cover your bus ticket to spring training."

Mamá wanted Ray to continue with school, a community college, and that was fine with the scouts, but they couldn't provide any help.

"Let's see how you do against stiffer competition, boy, then we can talk about financial assistance."

And the scouts shook their heads, flicked the ashes off their cigars, and walked away, muttering about the waste of time, late for the next Latin or black or farm kid with the strong arm, fast legs, quick bat.

Clemente. Had to be included. Roberto Clemente. Nice picture, good-looking guy, for a P.R. First Latin in the Hall of Fame. Exactly 3,000 hits. Lifetime .317. Played in fourteen World Series games and hit in every one. The long throw to Sanguillén at home, right on the money, and *you're out!* Yeah, yeah, everyone knew about the New Year's Eve mercy mission, the horrible plane crash, and the special election to the Hall of Fame. So what? Ray knew what was really important about Clemente.

No mention, this time, of how they all hated him. Even Ray understood that and he was just a kid during that 1960 season when the writers bypassed "Bob" for MVP and gave it to Groat. Clemente had to wait six years, and by then Ray had forgotten about a baseball career.

The usual quote not included.

"The Latin player doesn't get the recognition he deserves. Neither does the Negro unless he does something really spectacular."

Not that kind of feature.

Ray trimmed the pages of the article, carefully applied glue to the edges, and gently centered them in a scrapbook. He waited for the glue to dry, took one last look at Clemente, then returned the scrapbook to the makeshift shelf where it sat with a dozen other scrapbooks. He threw the rest of the paper in the trash. It was time for Christina and he had to get ready. He pushed himself into the bathroom and began the ordeal of cleaning his body.

The hot towel felt good on his arms and chest. Of course, he couldn't feel it on his legs, what was left of them. Only three weeks since her last visit and he was horny as a teenage kid. Business had been good, thank God. Pumping his sax for the tourists down in LoDo might not sound like a real gig, but he made enough to pay the rent on his dump, eat a couple times a day, and every once in a while buy a bottle of Old Crow, or something close.

He anticipated her touch, her mouth, the feel of her breasts in his hands, the sounds she made when he worked his Chicano magic on her. God, he was hot already. Think of something else, man, don't get too worked up or Christina won't have anything to do.

Lefty Gomez, half-Spanish, half-Irish. Ray couldn't believe it when he read about Lefty in the *Baseball Almanac*. He assumed that the great Yankee pitcher, winner of the first All-Star Game, was a Chicano from California (he wouldn't have been Chicano, of course—what would they have called him back then?), but there it was, half-Spanish, half-Irish. A cover? Apparently not. "El Gomez," "Goofy." Colorful nicknames for a colorful personality, everyone said. One of the greatest, but Ray still felt disappointment because Lefty wasn't raza.

Ray had a way with baseball. He knew from the day he picked up a bat and hit his father's first toss back at the old man and knocked him on his butt. Ray, Sr. shouted, "Wise ass," and threw him some smoke. Ray swung and missed, but he stood his ground and the old man got this gleam in his eyes and a smile about a mile wide, and then he tried a curve and damn if little Ray didn't drill it in the direction of first base. Ray, Sr. couldn't spend a lot of time with little Ray, working at night, on the weekends, or on the road, doing anything to hustle a buck, but when he had a few hours they gathered the mitts and balls and bats he had scrounged from second-hand stores and junk dealers, and father and son played ball.

Ray slipped on his cleanest shirt. Christina liked him to be fresh and neat, she demanded it, and at fifty bucks a shot he thought he should try to maintain some standards. She was his last luxury, his only extravagance.

Why would the old man, a wetback orphan with a wife and three of his own kids before he was twenty years old, on the edge of big-city desperation, pick up on American baseball? It could be something as simple as playing the game in an overgrown field somewhere on the outskirts of Durango, Mexico. Sneaking in to watch winter ball. Sal Maglie and those other gabacho players who told the Major Leagues to get screwed, for a couple of years anyway, and then crossed the border to keep in shape, make their fortunes, until they realized where their bread really was buttered. Or it could be—he never let on—that the old man understood the more complex things in life, like the fact that his kids were definitely not Mexicans, and although they carried tags like Chicano or cholo or pachuco, they were American, even if he wasn't, just not quite as American as the snot-nosed, blond-haired children who wanted to play with little Ray, and what could be more American than baseball?

Nah. The old man just liked to play ball.

He rushed to the door when he heard the knock. Christina waited for him, smiling.

"Ray, how've you been? We got to get together more often, baby. I kind of missed you."

Christina earned her money. She bent over and planted a kiss on Ray's lips that almost raised him out of the chair, a crane lifting steel girders. She tongued him, rubbed his back, brought him back to life—miracle worker, Christina!—then eased up.

"How about a drink, Ray? I got some time."

Ray poured the last two shots from his bottle, then pulled two beers from the fridge and twisted off the tops with an easy flick. His meaty arms and thick wrists looked as if they could swing a forty-ounce bat with the precision of Ernie Banks.

"How's your boy, Christina? Haven't seen little Julián for months. Must be big, eh?"

"Jules, Ray. His name's Jules. He ain't no Spanish kid. He's a terror. Can't keep up with him. He's got all this energy, the terrible twos."

She swallowed the shot in one gulp and sipped the beer.

Ray could see the tiredness around her eyes, but he didn't check her out too closely. She was sensitive about her looks. Ray thought she was fine. She liked to show her legs. She wore tight skirts with slits up the side, or skirts so short that Ray knew before they had a date that she had a rose tattooed on her thigh. Ray told her often that she would be surprised how good she would look and feel if she laid off the coke. She needed it, she would answer with a grunt. Her line of work required something to get over, something to take off the edge.

In any event, she was getting old, she said, especially for what she did, and the extra dose of "fire in the blood" kept her on her feet—and her back.

But damn, Ray was already in his forties, what the hell can you do about getting old? Did Ray, Sr. get old, was he even alive, did he ever think about playing catch with little Ray?

"Bring him by, Christina. I'll show him my scrapbooks, teach him how to play ball."

"Oh, Ray. He's too little. He'll tear up your books. Maybe when he's older. You guys can play catch or something. Or teach him how to play some music."

Sure, Christina, whatever.

She stretched a line of powder on his wobbly table and snorted it quicker than Ray could get it together to object.

"*Oh yeah,*" she whispered.

Her eyes glazed and a faint reddish tint crept up her jaw line. She breathed deeply for a few minutes, then she shook her head and gave Ray one of the smiles that filled his dreams. She walked around the room, stepping out of pieces of clothing, and Ray watched in silence. He loved it when she stripped for him. Lacy black things with hooks and straps hung on her skin, jiggling when she moved slowly toward him. The rose sat like a bruise on her leg, warm and swollen, ready for his caress. She stood at the edge of his desk, turned away from him so that he could watch her wiggle her ass.

"Ray, you never showed me this. Wha's it?"

She held a baseball in her hands.

"Uh, Christina, be careful. My old man got me that. Here, give it to me."

And although he didn't want to ruin the mood, he rolled to her with a little too much speed, a little too much urgency in his response, and snatched the ball from her hand.

"Is jus' a ball, ain't it?" Her words slipped out half-formed. She wasn't wiggling anymore.

Ray relented. He handed it back to Christina.

"All right. But be careful. See, there it is, Roberto Clemente's autograph. The old man got it for me one time when he worked in L.A. Clemente signed it before a game with the Dodgers. He's dead, you know."

"Your old man?"

"Clemente. Plane crash. The ball's worth a lot of money. But it's about the only thing I got from my old man, so it's kind of special to me."

Christina returned the ball to its space on Ray's desk.

"You kept it all these years? How old's it?"

"Early sixties. I was a kid. Actually, I lost it, didn't know what the hell happened to it. But when my mother died, I came back from 'Nam for the funeral, and there it was in a box with her rosaries, pictures, and mantillas. She didn't have much. For some reason she kept this old ball."

Christina watched him drift away. His scarred face saddened, his body slumped in the wheelchair. She took his head in her hands and held him against her, smoothed the strands of wispy hair, and helped Ray in the only way she knew.

Clyde tried to stay calm. But handling his habit was not an experience that lent itself to calmness. And making the money by breaking into houses, apartments, and an occasional second-hand store, the kind that should not have alarms, only added to the tension. No wonder he always felt tired—except when he was riding the blow, of course. Then he could do anything, anytime, anywhere. Make love to the most beautiful woman. Pull off the most outrageous heist in thief history. Kick ass. Be the man.

Ripping off old Ray's sax didn't exactly fall into the historical category. Stealing the cripple's instrument, Ray's source of income, probably ranked as outrageous, pitiful but outrageous.

He tried to explain to Linda but she didn't get it.

"I can get twenty, thirty bucks for the sax. Ray keeps it in good shape. Take me five minutes to get it, maybe. His lock's gotta be a joke. And what can Ray do about it if I get in his crib and yank the sax? Not a damn thing. Nothin'."

Linda arched her eyebrows.

"But crap, Clyde. It's Ray. He don't harm no one. He's a little weird, but who around here ain't? And you know him, man. He knows you, too. What if he sees you? What if he turns you in to the cops? You ready for that?"

Clyde knew there was one thing he definitely was not ready for, and that was another lockup. He refused to consider the possibility.

"No way there's any risk. Ray drinks himself to sleep every night. Calls the juice his Oblivion Express. I heard him talkin' about it one day when he was on the corner playing for handouts, explainin' to that Jesus Saves preacher why he can't get up early for the coffee and doughnuts and sermon at the center. Goes out like a match in the wind. And in his chair, you think he's goin' to pull any hero stuff? Come on, it's a setup. Made for Clyde the Glide, smoothest second-story pro on the West Side."

Linda shook her head but she knew it was hopeless. And maybe Clyde could scrape enough together for a line or two, if he did an all-nighter and hit at least a half-dozen places. Ray's sax by itself wouldn't pay for a taste, much less a good time. It was stupid but it was Clyde's lifestyle, so to speak. To each his own.

Ray slept curled in a ball in his chair, clutching the saxophone he dreamed was his rifle. The street below his room shook with the noise from buses and taxis, ambulances screaming their warnings to the dealers, pimps, and winos prowling Ray's neighborhood. He slept through it all. He prowled, too, but the thick jungle that surrounded him held more terror than the actors in the midnight street scene could conjure up in their wildest drug-induced fantasies. He moaned and twisted his blanket into a sweaty, crumpled rag, but he slept.

The door creaked and Ray's eyes jerked open. For a horrible, ridiculous second, slant-eyed killers hovered around him, poked at him with their weapons, and Ray whimpered. The door eased shut and a shadow moved around the room. Streetlights bounced off the gleam of a knife blade.

"Get the hell out of here!"

Before the guy could react, Ray wheeled into the back of the intruder and knocked him over.

"What the . . . !"

The knife flew across the room. Clyde crawled on the floor, looking for the weapon, trying to regain the advantage. Ray ran over groping hands. A feeble scream mixed with the loud crunch of fractured bone. The thief struggled to his feet, turned around in circles, lost in the darkness, defenseless against the crip he thought would be easy. Ray moved smoothly, effortlessly. His strong, solid fingers grabbed the first thing they touched and flung it at the man. Dazed, Clyde stumbled out the door and collapsed at the top of the stairs.

Ray's neighbors flicked on their lights, threw open their doors, some with guns in their hands, and kicked the intruder sniveling on the stained, muddy carpet.

Ray wheeled to the hallway and picked up his baseball. The ink had been smeared by the impact on the burglar's greasy skin.

He held the ball with his viselike grip and carefully, slowly, used a Sharpie to fill in the words *Roberto Clemente* over the smudge.

Someone nudged his shoulder.

"Better get that door fixed, Ray. I walked right in. You okay?"

"Yeah, Art. Guess I still got my throwing arm. I think I know that guy. You recognize him?"

"No way. Dirty creeps around here. About time one of them got it. You really clobbered him. What the hell you hit him with?"

"This ball. Check it out. My old man gave it to me, about the only thing I got from him. It's worth some money, but it means more to me, it's kind of special. Sentimental value and all that."

Rich Alderete

DETRICE JONES was born and raised in San Francisco. She graduated from the University of California, Los Angeles, with a degree in African American studies. As a student Detrice worked as Managing Editor of *NOMMO*, UCLA's African people's student-run news magazine. The story in this volume is her first published work and is based on her own life experience. Jones is currently living and writing in Los Angeles.

just surviving another day
by detrice jones

There was a knock at my door. Then a jingle and he was in. Cheap-ass lock. I looked at the clock and it was 3:36 a.m. He turned on the light and began his search. I watched him, hoping he wouldn't find it.

"Let me get that money and I'll pay you back in the morning," he said.

"No. I need it for lunch."

"I'll give it back to you in the morning."

Yeah right. How was he going to do that? If he didn't have any money now, he wouldn't have any in the morning. He came over and searched near me and around the bed. It wasn't next to me. I learned quickly that it was one of the first places they looked. They had just given me the money no longer than six hours ago. I guess they had smoked up the little cash they already had. Which meant if he found the money, I wouldn't have any for tomorrow or the next couple of weeks when somebody got paid again. He found it in the little chest on my dresser.

"I'll give it back to you in the morning," he said as he left the room and turned off my light, as if I would be going to sleep anytime soon. I lay there and worried about food and eating for tomorrow. I had to get hunger off my mind. When I finally fell asleep, it seemed like it had been two minutes before the alarm clock went off. I hit the snooze and went back to sleep. This repeated five times. I finally woke up an hour later. I knew even if I missed first period, I would have to make it to my next class because we had a quiz that I couldn't make up.

After I got dressed, I looked for my dad. Like always he was nowhere to be found. My mom was in the kitchen. She pressed her blackened fingers on the stove looking for crumbs, little rocks or anything that was round and white. I made some toast so I wouldn't starve for the whole day. I didn't say a word as I tried my best to maneuver around her.

"Where Ronnie at? I gotta go to school."

"He'll be back soon."

Denial. I knew better. I took my time to eat and looked for some loose money around the house. I found fifty cents in the big couch. Beatrice saw that and had a slightly jealous look in her eyes. What the hell could she smoke with fifty cents? I went outside to see if I could find my dad, Ronnie. He was in the driver's seat of our van. At that moment I wished I wouldn't have talked so much in drivers ed, stopped procrastinating, and got my license sooner.

"You gotta get to school?" he asked in a mumbled, half-sleep voice, without turning his head at all.

"Yeah, I'm late, but I gotta go to second period, at least."

"I'ma have to give you that money this afternoon," he said, still looking straight ahead like he was unable to move his neck in either direction.

He drove like I was Miss Daisy. It took at least thirty minutes to get there when it should only take fifteen. I went to the attendance lady to get a tardy note. She knew my name, homeroom number, and grade by heart. Sometimes she would already have my note ready for me when I got there. I was there in time for the quiz I didn't study for. Nobody could convince me that I got anything less than an A, though.

During our nutrition break, I bought a Snickers from the student store. I was . . . kinda hungry.

"How was Mr. Springsted's quiz?" my friend Jessica asked.

"Pretty easy. Make sure you know about the Great Depression. Dates, how it affected minorities, shit like that."

"You think you did good?"

"I don't know, maybe a B. Hopefully. I didn't study."

"You said the same thing last time and got an A."

"I was lucky. Hey, you got some money I could borrow?" She looked at me and hesitated. She was going to say no. I could see it in her eyes. She must have been thinking about the money I already owed her.

"I'll give it back, I promise. I left my money at home today. I'll pay you back with all the other money I owe you."

"I only got a dollar to spare," she said while handing me the money.

"That's cool. Thanks. I'll pay you back tomorrow," I said, knowing she would forget. She always did until I asked her for some more. The bell rang. "I gotta go to class, you know how Mr. Gordon is about people being late."

"Yeah."

"I'll see you at lunch."

"All right."

"Good luck on that quiz," I had to yell at her down the hall.

"Thanks."

Mr. Gordon was known for not letting people in the class if they were tardy. You would have to wait in the hallway with all the other late people and not make too much noise. He would be madder if we made noise in the hallway when he was ready to let us in. He would ask us why we were late, then give us a lecture on why we shouldn't be late. Then, of course, there was the embarrassing walk back into class with the whole room watching. Later in the year I would learn to stay by the room during break. For now I had to damn near run to the class all the way on the other side of the tiny elementary school that they turned into a high school and packed us in like sardines.

Lunch took too long to get here. I always got hungrier when I thought that I might not be able to eat for the rest of the day, and a dollar wasn't gonna cut it. When I got through the crowded hallways to the place where my friends usually ate, they were almost done.

"How the fuck y'all get y'all food so early in that long-ass lunch line?"

They all laughed. They were something like little girls when I cursed. Coming from families with more money than mine, they were sensitive about that stuff. So cussing was always the fastest and easiest way to make them laugh.

"Why you always cuss so much?" April said.

"'Cause I can."

"Does your mom know you curse like that?" Erin asked, wiping cream cheese off her fingers.

"I cuss in front of her."

"She does," Keyona said.

"You bad," Erin said.

"Y'all didn't answer my question. How did y'all get y'all food so early?"

"We got out of art class early," Erin said.

"One of y'all got some money I can borrow?"

"You ain't got no money?" Keyona asked.

Obviously, I almost said with attitude. Why would I ask them for money if I had some? "I left my money at home." They were silent. "If each one of y'all give me a dollar, I will be able to eat." Still, nothing. "I'll pay y'all back tomorrow."

April gave me a wrinkled dollar out of her tight jeans.

Erin gave me four of the six shiny new quarters she had.

Keyona, reluctant to give me anything, asked, "Are you going to pay me back tomorrow?"

"I will."

She turned to her purse so no one else could see and pulled out a crisp dollar bill.

"Thanks, you guys. I'll give it back," I said, not knowing if I could live up to that promise. I would definitely have to repay Keyona tomorrow. I went to the lunch line and saw Jasmine and Jessica—the Big Ballers, even though they wouldn't admit it. They had the best cars in school. I would trade shoes with them any day. I had already asked Jessica for some money earlier. I had to figure out a way to ask Jasmine for some money without Jessica getting mad.

"Jasmine, can I borrow some money?"

"I just gave you some money earlier."

"A dollar? I can't eat with a dollar."

Jasmine pulled out five dollars and handed them to me.

"Thanks, I'll pay—"

"Don't worry about it. You don't have to."

"You sure?"

"Yeah. It's all good."

Good. I could pay back cheap-ass Keyona and eat tomorrow, and my parents wouldn't know that I had some money.

After school I went to basketball practice. If I didn't eat lunch today, I probably would have passed out.

"Point guards lead from the front." My coach yelled at me because I was the last to finish the suicides. I hated being a point guard because I was lazy. My coach was right, though. I was the leader and shouldn't be last. We had to do three sets of suicides today because two people were late and one person on the team couldn't come. We ran most of the time during practice. It was more like a track team than anything because our coach was not a basketball coach. So we ran, rarely ran plays out of his store-bought playbook, and almost never scrimmaged.

Basketball was my form of meditation. I got a chance to clear my mind and focus strictly on the game. I didn't have the energy or time to think about the bad things that were going on in my life. I didn't think about school, stupid high school boys, or my home life. I didn't have to think about being scared to get a drink of water in the middle of the night because my dad might be in his paranoid state and try to stab me, his own daughter, because he thought I was trying to get him. I didn't have to think about my mom taking back the lunch money she gave me because they spent the rest of hers. I didn't have to think about my little brothers and sister who might not be safe.

After practice Erin got picked up, while April, Keyona, and I caught the bus. I knew I didn't want to go home this early.

"April, can I go to your house?"

"I don't care," she replied.

At April's house I would be able to eat real home-cooked food instead of Top Ramen. When I got there, I had to wait for her to eat before I did. I couldn't just raid the fridge like I wanted to. We ate baked chicken, fried okra, and rice. I always waited until the last possible moment to go home, sometimes missing the last bus and spending the night over there. I didn't want to go home, not tonight.

"April, your friend can't spend the night again," I heard her mother whisper to her through the paper-thin walls. I made sure I made the bus that night. I guess I wore out my welcome. Instead of saying *Welcome*, it says *Well . . .* I guess you can *come*.

It was piercing cold high in the mountains where April lived. The always gloomy and foggy city didn't help either. April, fortunately for her, was immune to the cold. The bus was fifteen minutes late, and I didn't get home until 1:30 a.m.

My mom seemed like she hadn't moved since morning.

Still trying to pick up rocks. My dad, on the other hand, was in motion. Slow motion. He had his favorite knife in his hand, creeping around the house like a scared zombie. There was no use in talking to either of them. I had a little money so I would be able to survive another day. I took a shower and tried to hide the money somewhere no one would look. I had to find a good hiding place through trial and error. This time I simply kept it in my pocket and buried my pants deep in my dirty clothes bin. I went to sleep without even thinking about homework. I had more important things to worry about. It was 2:15 a.m. and I went to sleep as soon as my body touched the bed.

There was a knock at the door. Then a jingle and she was in. I gotta fix that door! I looked at the clock and it was 4:58. She turned on the light and began searching. Why did my mom have to come in tonight? I knew she wouldn't be afraid of a teenage girl's dirty clothes bin.

"You got some money?" she asked while searching me, the bed, and the mattress.

"NO! Ronnie took my lunch money yesterday."

"He did?"

"I didn't even get to eat," I whined, trying to make her feel bad. After ten minutes of searching, she gave up, only glancing at my dirty clothes. With her brain in this state, she wouldn't be able to remember what I had on today. She turned off the light, as if I would be going to sleep anytime soon, and closed the door.

I would survive another day.

PART IV
GANGSTERS & MONSTERS

Bob Buck

EMORY HOLMES II is a Los Angeles–based writer and journalist. He has reported on crime, schools, and the arts for the *San Francisco Chronicle*, the *Los Angeles Times*, the *L.A. Sentinel*, the *L.A. Daily News*, the *Amsterdam News*, *Los Angeles Magazine*, *Essence*, *CODE*, the *R&B Report*, *Written By* magazine, *American Legacy*, *The Root*, the *New York Times* wire service, and other publications. His crime fiction has appeared in *The Best American Mystery Stories 2006* and *Los Angeles Noir*. Holmes is presently completing *The Good Cop*, a novel of race and murder in L.A. County.

a.k.a. moises rockafella
by emory holmes II

I.

You said I could have water. I want some water," Fat Tommy
said again.

"You can have water, Moises, after you tell us how it went
down. That's our deal," Vargas reminded him.

Fat Tommy didn't understand. He wanted some water. Why
these other questions? Why this Moises shit? He wasn't goddamn
Moises anymore. That shit was dead; done. Why didn't these pigs
believe him? He felt so sorry for himself. None of it was his fault.
It was the Colombians and that goddamn Pemberton. He was the
bad guy. If they want their devil, there he is. But don't expect Fat
Tommy to commit suicide and snitch. That shit was dead.

Fat Tommy was having a really bad day. His big shoulders
slumped. His money was gone. His business was gone. His high
was gone. And the cops weren't buying his story. He laid his arms
tenderly across his knees. He tried to sleep, but the cops kept
butting in. He narrowed his eyes in the harsh light and squinted
down at his arms. Still, he had to admit . . . he certainly was well
dressed.

"Don't give those white folks no excuses, Tommy," his wife
Bea had advised. "We ain't gonna get kilt over this asshole."

Bea had borrowed her mother's credit card and bought him
two brand-new, white, long-sleeved business shirts from Sears for
his interrogations and, regrettably, for the trial. That was such a

sweet thing for Bea to do. Buy him new shirts that the cops would like. He loved his Queen Bea—she had been his sweetheart since grade school, way back when he was skinny and pretty. Bea was sexy, street-smart, and loyal to him. After he'd knocked her up, twice, he had started to hang with her, help her with his sons, and had grown to love her.

Gradually, she had encouraged him to develop his unique sartorial style: his dazzling jheri curl (forty bucks a pop at Hellacious Cuts on Crenshaw); his multiple ropes of gold, bedecked with dangling golden razors, crucifixes, naked chicks, powerfists, and coke spoons; his rainbow collection of jogging suits and fourteen pairs of top-of-the-line Air Jordans (and a pair of vintage Connies for layin' around the pad). He had restricted himself to only five or six affairs after they got married. The affairs were mostly "strawberries"—amateur ho's who turned tricks for dope.

Getting your johnson swabbed by a 'hood rat for a couple of crumbs of low-grade rock—not even a nickel's worth—wasn't like being unfaithful, he figured. It was medicinal; therapeutic; a salutary necessity—more like a business expense. Like buying aspirin or getting a massage on a high-stress job. But that was all past—the whores, the dealing, the violence, the stress. He had resolutely turned his back on "thug life" six months ago, when he realized that a brother, even an old-time G like him, was vulnerable to jail time or a hit—after he had experienced the deadly grotesqueries in which Pemberton was capable of entangling him.

So, hours after that goddamn murder, months before he knew the cops were on to him, he'd flushed the bulk of his street stash down the toilet—1,800 bindles—and thrown away most of his thug-life paraphernalia, even his jack-off books, *Players* and *Hustlers* mostly, and his cherished *Big Black Titty* magazines, and faithfully (except when the Lakers were on TV, or

Fear Factor, or *The Sopranos*) got down on his knees and read the Bible with Bea and promised to her on his daddy's life, and on his *granddaddy's* soul even, he wasn't going to disappoint her anymore. No more druggin', no more whores, no more hangin' out. No more street. Swear to Jesus . . .

"White folks like white stuff," Bea had explained that morning before he surrendered himself. They were in the bedroom of their new Woodland Hills bungalow, and Bea was standing behind him on her tiptoes and pressing her breasts against his back as they faced the dresser mirror. "They like white houses, white picket fences, white bread, and white shirts," she added grimly, peeking over his shoulder to admire her husband and herself in the mirror.

They both looked so sad, so pitiful and wronged, Bea thought. And all because of that shit-for-brains Pemberton. Fat Tommy thought so, too. Recalling those poignant scenes on that morning, he remembered that they'd both cried a little bit, standing there perusing their innocent, sad, sexy selves in the mirror. Little Bea had slipped from view for a moment as she helped Tommy struggle out of his nightshirt and unfastened for the final time the nine golden ropes of braid that festooned his massive neck, and then his diamond earring. Bea tearfully placed them in a shopping bag of things they would have to hock. She slid the voluminous dress-shirtsleeves over his backswept arms. Then her beautiful, manicured hands appeared, fluttering along his shoulders, smoothing out the wrinkles in his new shirt.

When Bea was satisfied with her effort, she slipped around in front of him and unloosed his lucky nose ring, letting him view her voluptuous little self in the lace teddy he'd bought her for Mother's Day, but which she had seldom worn. Then, while he was ogling her melons, she seized his right pinky finger, whose stylish claw he had allowed to flourish there as a scoop for sampling virgin powder on the fly and which he had rakishly polished jet black, and before he could stop her, she deftly clipped it off. Fat Tommy shrieked like a waif.

"It's better this way, Tommy," Bea assured him. She carefully placed the shorn talon in a plastic baggie. It resembled a shiny black roach; but for Fat Tommy, it was like witnessing the burial of a child.

"I'm keeping this for good luck," she told him, and stowed it in the change purse of her Gucci bag. She patted his lumpy belly, which protruded out of the break in the shirt like a fifty-pound sack of muffins. Then Bea buttoned the shirt and put on the new hand-painted tie with Martin Luther King, Jr.'s image on it that she'd had a Cuban chick she met in rehab make specially for Tommy. She cupped his big pumpkin head in her hands. She had paid her little sister Karesha fifteen bucks to touch up his jheri curl. The handsome thick mane of oily black locks cascaded sensuously, if greasily, down his forehead and neck.

"Try to stay where it's cool, so the jheri curl juice don't drip on your brand-new shirt, baby," Bea said in a sweetly admonishing tone.

"This new ProSoft Sport Curl Gel don't drip like that cheap shit, baby," Fat Tommy explained. "It's deluxe. I gave your sister two more dollars so she would use the top-drawer shit. I want to make a good impression."

"I know you do, baby. But you're gonna have a hard time keeping it up in the joint . . . I don't think you—"

Her husband had stopped listening and Bea stared once more into his eyes. Fat Tommy was such a big baby. Standing there he reminded her of a favorite holy card she'd cherished those two years she went to St. Sebastian's Catholic school before she met him. St. Sebastian, sad and pitiful, mortally wounded, innocent and wronged, pierced with arrows. She kissed him lightly on his shirt front and pushed him backward onto the edge of the bed.

"Pull yourself together, Tommy. I've got to go drop off the kids," she said.

Fat Tommy was still crying, sitting dejectedly on the side of the bed, long after she had dressed and gone out to drop their boys at her sister's new hideout in Topanga Canyon.

2.

It was still dark when Bea went out. The sun soon poked up. She hardly even noticed. She sped along the freeways and the awakening Valley skies unfurled before her in desolate, pink banners of light. She raced over the back roads, hurtling through space along the crests of the canyons. Again and again she skidded in a cloud of dust against the shoulders of the abyss. Again and again she slowed down a moment, then, thinking better of it, sped back up. She couldn't stop looking at her boys, couldn't stop cursing Pemberton under her breath and sadly reflecting on how that asshole had put them all up to their eyeballs in shit. The boys woke up during the forty-minute drive over to Karesha's, with Bea vainly scanning the radio the whole time for news of Pemberton's arrest.

Bea's mother was looking out the window of her sister's place when she drove up. Her mother would drive the boys up to Santa Barbara and they would take a cross-country bus to Texas that night. The three women and the two infant boys cried until Bea's mother drove off in Karesha's pink Lexus, fleeing in plain sight, with Little Tommy and baby Kobe waving bye-bye from their car seats.

After their mother and the boys were safely away, Bea's little sister Karesha, a cold, deadly customer in most circumstances, confided to her that she was a little nervous about the possibility of her own capture or the jailing and execution of her notorious former squeeze, Cut Pemberton, and what it all could mean for her Hollywood plans, and for her high-toned, social-climbing crew.

"You heard from him?" Bea asked, as she backed out the dirt driveway of Karesha's rented, brush-covered hideaway.

"I hear the Colombians got him. The cops don't know much about him yet. I'm sure he wants to keep it that way. Anyway, I trashed the cell phone," Karesha said quietly. "But if that sick motherfucker come 'round here I'm gonna send him to Jesus." She lifted her T-shirt and showed Bea the pearl-handled .22 Pemberton had bought her as an engagement gift. It was stuffed in the waistband of her jeans.

When Bea arrived back home, the neighbors were out, watering their lawns, pretending they didn't know Fat Tommy was a prime suspect in a vicious murder.

"How do, Miss O'Rourke?" Pearl Stenis, the boldest of her nosy neighbors, greeted her.

"I'm blessed, Mrs. Stenis," Bea said flatly.

She pulled into the garage and closed the door. She gathered herself a moment before she got out. She turned on all the lights in the garage and found a flashlight, and took a good twenty minutes making sure the Mercedes was clean of diapers and weapons and works and blow and any incriminating evidence.

When she was done, she poked her head into the house and called, "We're late, Tommy. I'll be in the car. Come on, baby. We got to be on time." She waited in the car and honked the horn a half-dozen times but had to come back inside. She found Fat Tommy back in bed, fully dressed, sobbing, with the covers pulled over his head.

"Where the hell was you at, baby?" Fat Tommy complained. "I thought Cut got you."

"That niggah better be layin' low," Bea said. "These

Hollywood cops would love to catch a fuck-up like that and Rodney-King his ass to death for the savage shit he done."

"I was there, too, baby. Remember, I was there, too," Fat Tommy murmured.

"Don't say that, Tommy! Don't say that no more," Bea demanded. "Put that craziness out your mind. You wasn't there. You don't know nothin'. You don't know nobody."

"It just ain't fair."

"Listen here, Tommy," Bea said sternly. "You don't deserve this beef. You don't know nothin'. You didn't see nothin'. You got a wife and family to protect. It was that goddamn Cut that fount Simpson. You didn't even know he was a cop. It was all Cut's idea. We wouldn't be mixed up in none of this if Cut hadn't . . ."

Fat Tommy began sobbing again. After a few minutes, he confessed that he had raided the emergency stash in the bathroom and had done a couple of lines to calm his nerves. He suggested that they do what was left. There was only a half-bindle anyway. He never did crack, the high felt like a suicide jump. Crack was for kids; toxic, cheap-ass shit meant to sell, not do. Fat Tommy was old school—White Girl all the way. Powder, he believed, was classier, mellower than rock cocaine.

Bea retrieved the emergency bindle out of the bottom of a box of sanitary napkins. There was only a portion of an eight ball left from the half-pound Fat Tommy liked to keep around the pad for Lakers games and birthdays and other special occasions. Bea used her mother's Sears card to line out six hefty tracks of the white powder on the dresser top. Rolling their last hundred-dollar bill into a straw, the couple snorted quickly, sucking the lines of blow into their flared nostrils like shotgun blasts fired straight to the back of their brains.

Quickly, the drug began to take effect: it eased its frigid tendrils down the back lanes of their breathing passages, deadening the superior nasal concha, the frontal and sphenoid sinuses, creeping along their soft palates like a snotty glacier before it slid down the interiors of their throats, chilling the lingual nerves and flowing over the rough, bitter fields of papilla at the back of their tongues and ascending, like a stream of artic ghosts, up through their pituitary glands, their spinal walls and veins, and into the uppermost regions of their brains. The pupils of their dark brown eyes became dilated and sparkling.

"Damn, that's good shit," Fat Tommy said, feeling the cold drip of the snow, liquefied and suffused with snot, glazing the commodious interiors of his head and throat.

Fat Tommy shut his eyes tight. The darkness inside his mind began to fill with amorphous, floating colors. His big body seemed to be shapeless and floating, too. He looked down at the drifts of sugary dust remaining on the dresser. Almost 400 bucks worth of Girl—gone in six vigorous snorts. As Fat Tommy admired the smeared patterns of residue on the dresser top, Bea leaned down and broadly licked the last thin traces of powder. Then she swept her lovely manicured forefinger across the dresser top, along the trail of spittle her tongue had left, sopping up the final mists of blow. She lightly dabbed this viscous salve on her teeth and gums. Normally Tommy prided himself on licking up the leftovers before Bea got to them, but he was immobilized with grief. And, too, the coke was Chilean, cream of the Andes, 90 percent pure.

"You right, baby?" Bea asked, staring at him with her pretty eyes.

"Baby, I'm froze from my nose to my toes," Fat Tommy told his boo.

Bea blinked hard and looked up at her husband. "Your slip is showin', baby," she said, noting a half moon of white powder around the deep alar grooves of Fat Tommy's right nostril. She pointed to his reflection in the mirror. Tommy pinched his nostrils closed, shut his eyes, and took a sharp snort. The lumps of powder were swept from the grooves in his face, shooting brilliantly past his nasal vestibules and septum in white-hot pellets of snot. His heart began to race. Neither of them said a word for a few minutes. They closed their eyes and surrendered to the high. When Fat Tommy finally opened his eyes, Bea was staring at him with a beatific look on her face.

"You look nice," Bea said. "Innocent . . . Don't let 'em punk you, Tommy. Just wear the shit outta this shirt and tie. Dr. King'll bring you through. All business. You know how to talk to white folks. Don't go in there like no G . . . talking all bad and shit, like you're that goddamn Cut. That's what they want. Give them your A game and you'll be all right. Remember: You wasn't there. You didn't see nothing. You don't know nobody. *We ain't gonna get kilt over some asshole.*"

Fat Tommy got in the car, gripping his Bible, sobbing and praying and assuring Bea and the Lord he loved them. Between his sobs he promised her he would savor her instructions and repeat them like a mantra: Don't say nothing that's gonna get us kilt *over some asshole.* She reminded him that his stupid-ass Uncle Bunny had done a nickel at Folsom on a break-in after Bunny talked too much. So—don't talk too much. Don't do nothing that will make you look guilty. They got nothing. That was the bottom line, Bea reminded Fat Tommy. They agreed if he was cool and smooth he had a chance to ease his way out of the beef with short time.

3.

The cops were nice to him at first; they said he was a stand-up guy for turning himself in and helping out with the investigation. They had interviewed him all day. Fat Tommy said he didn't "need no lawyer." He wasn't guilty. The cops didn't seem to be concerned about his coke business so much as they wanted to know what he knew about the recent murder of the undercover cop—Simpson—right in the middle of the projects on Fat Tommy's home turf, La Caja. Fat Tommy assured him he didn't "have no 'turf' no more, not in La Caja, not nowhere." Moreover, he certainly didn't know anything about a cop killing.

"We know you ain't no killer, Moises," Vargas told him a few minutes into the interrogation. "But you grew up in La Caja, where this murder went down. We figure you might know something. Point us to the bad guys. We know you're in bed with the Colombians. They're all over La Caja these days. One of them called you by name, Moises. He's quite fond of you. Says you're a big shot. You're looking at some serious time if you don't play ball. Play along and help us catch this killer . . . you'll be all right . . ."

Vargas offered him a jumbo cup of lemonade and four jelly doughnuts. His high had long ago been blown and he couldn't believe how hungry and thirsty he'd gotten. Vargas said that the pretty cop who had processed him that morning had asked to make the lemonade especially for him.

Fat Tommy said, "That was sure nice of her."

"Yeah. Officer Ospina is a sweetie. Drink up. That's the last of it . . . We need to get started," Vargas said, and smiled at him.

Braddock took the empty cup, crushed it, and banked it into the wastebasket in the back of the interrogation room.

"Great shot," Fat Tommy said. "Three-pointer."

Braddock and Vargas said nothing. Braddock walked to a chair somewhere behind him and Vargas turned on a tape recorder and intoned: "This is Detective Manny Vargas of the Homicide Detail, Criminal Investigation Division of the Van Nuys Police Department. I am joined with Detective Will

Dockery and DEA Special Agent Roland Braddock. This is a tape-recorded interview of Thomas Martin O'Rourke, a.k.a. Fat Tommy O'Rourke, a.k.a. Tommy Martin, a.k.a. Pretty Tommy Banes, a.k.a. Sugar-T Banes, a.k.a. Slo Jerry-T, a.k.a. Big Jerry Jay, a.k.a. T-Moose, a.k.a. Moises Rockafella . . ."

"Uh, my name ain't Moises," Fat Tommy protested, interrupting as politely as he could. "Some bad people started calling me that. But I don't let nobody call me that no more." He tried his sexiest grin.

Vargas looked at him blankly and continued: "This is a homicide investigation under police report number A-55503. Today's date is March 28, 2005, and the time is now 13:49 hours. Could you state your name once more for the record?"

"I'm Thomas Martin O'Rourke."

"Address?"

Tommy gave them his parents' address. That's where he got his mail now.

"How old are you?"

"Thirty-four, officer," Fat Tommy said.

"Employed?"

"I was assistant manager at the Swing Shop . . ."

"Was?"

"I got laid off."

"When was that?"

"1992."

Dockery and Braddock rolled their eyes, then Vargas said, "What were you doing after you got . . . laid off?"

Fat Tommy fingered his Martin Luther King, Jr. tie. "Odd jobs, here and there . . ."

"What kind of odd jobs?"

"Church stuff."

"Church stuff?"

Fat Tommy sat up straight in his chair. "I'm a Christian, sir. And I try to help in the Lord's work whenever—"

"You get that fancy Mercedes doing this church work?"

"Naw." Fat Tommy laughed out loud.

"The street tells us you're a big-time coke man—that true, Moises? You a big-time coke dealer, Moises?"

"Oh no, sir. Not no more. All that shit is dead . . . I mean, all that stuff is dead . . . I don't do no drugs no more. I don't sling coke no more. I got a wife and family . . ."

"You high now?"

"What was that?"

"You under the influence of drugs or alcohol at this time?"

"No. Oh Jesus, no." Fat Tommy wished to Christ he was.

4.

He couldn't make the cops believe him. They wouldn't give him any more lemonade, even though the girl cop said she made it specially for him. They wouldn't give him any more doughnuts—they said they were all out. Cops out of doughnuts! Now they wouldn't even give him water—and he was dry as shit. That Chilean coke had sucked all the good spit out of his mouth. The cops kept hammering away at his story. He shut his eyes. He was only pretending to listen, nodding yes, yes, goddamnit, yes, or gazing up at them with a mournful, wounded look in his eyes.

Their sharp questions droned on unintelligibly like the buzzing of wasps attacking just above his head. Then . . . the cops seemed to go quiet for a moment. Bea's admonitions echoed in his head and gradually, without realizing it, Fat Tommy allowed a luxuriant smile to creep across the corners of his mouth. Still smiling, he opened his eyes into a narrow slit and gazed down at his handsome shirtsleeves, admiring the shiny contours, like little snow-covered mountains really, that the polyester fabric traced along his thick, short arms as they lay across his knees.

Christ, he loved this shirt!

"Somethin' I said funny, Fatboy? Somethin' funny?" Braddock yelled, momentarily breaking through his reverie.

Fat Tommy jumped a little, snapped his eyes tight a moment, then slowly opened the slits again and looked back down at his arms. Braddock continued mocking him. Fat Tommy burrowed himself deeper into his thoughts. He looked at his arms and knees. They were such good arms—good, kind arms; and great knees—great, great knees. He stared down at his hands and knees lovingly as the cops droned on. He decided, with a hot, white tear leaking out of a crack in his right eye, finally, that he loved his knees as much as he loved his dick or his ass—better, probably, now that he had found the Lord again. His regard for his ass and dick now seemed so misguided, so . . . heathen. And these knees were much more representative of him—innocent, God-fearing, above reproach.

They had taken him all over—all over L.A., the Valley, even to Oak Town once on a church picnic. There was plenty of water there, beer and red pop and lemonade and swine barbeque, too. He was thin then, and pretty. Just a baby boy— so innocent, such a good young brother. The picnic was on the Oakland Bay, and they'd all rode the bus up there, singing gospel songs the whole way. There must have been a hundred buses, the entire California Youth Baptist Convention, someone said. And it was his knees that helped him get through it: basketball, softball, the three-legged race with pretty Althea Jackson. They were nine years old. Those were some of the best times in his life. And he was such a good guy, a regular brother, everyone said so, and now this lunatic murder and this fucked-up Pemberton, that devil, poking his bloody self like a shitty nightmare in the midst of all his plans.

Fat Tommy ached at beholding all these tender scenes—Bea, the picnic, the tears—all the images like flashing detritus in a river streaming across his upturned hands, it was just too much. He closed his eyes, but the river of images burst inside them, flooding the darkness in his head even more vividly than before: his first day at Teddy Roosevelt Junior High; the time he and Bea won third place at the La Caja Boys & Girls Club Teen Dance-Off; and his best pal . . . not that goddamn Pemberton . . . but Trey-Boy, Trey-Boy Middleton (*rest his soul*). That was his best friend. It was cool Trey-Boy who befriended him when everyone treated him like a jerk, and it was Trey-Boy who'd taken pity on him and helped him pimp up his lifestyle.

It was Trey-Boy. Not a murderer. A hip brother. True blue. Trey-Boy showed him how to affect a gangster's scowl, and helped him adopt a slow, hulking walk that could frighten just about anyone he encountered on the street. He'd showed him how to smoke a cigarette, load a gat, roll a blunt, cop pussy, weed, and blow. He had even showed him how to shoot up once. And Trey-Boy never got mad, even when that faggot Stick Jenkins bumped him on purpose and made him spill a good portion of the spoon of heroin he had carefully prepared. Trey-Boy had pimp-slapped the faggot—he called him "my sissy," and Stick had just smiled like a bitch and turned red as a yella niggah could get—and everyone laughed.

He remembered how Trey-Boy had cooked up what was left of the little amber drops they could scrape from the toilet seat and floor and showed him how to tie-off and find the vein and shoot the junk, even if he only got a little wacked—it was wacked enough to know he wouldn't do that anymore. It wasn't fun at all. He couldn't stop puking. It felt like now—in this hot room with no water, under this white light. But he wasn't no goddamn junkie. None of that puking and nodding and drooling shit was for him. He was strictly weed and blow, strictly weed and blow. He wasn't no goddamn junkie. Let them try to pin that on him. They'd come up zero. Just like this murder. He wasn't there; he didn't do it. He didn't see nobody; he didn't know nobody.

Trey-Boy had given him his favorite street moniker—Fat Tommy. When Trey-Boy said it, it didn't feel like a put-down. It was a term of war and affection. He was a lumpy 370 pounds but he didn't feel fat when Trey-Boy called him Fat Tommy—he felt big, as in big man, big trouble, big fun—there's a difference, really, when you think about it. A street handle like Fat Tommy made him feel like one of the hoods in *The Sopranos*—his favorite show. He'd made a small fortune with that name—not like he made with Cut Pemberton, when the margins and risks got scary and huge, and the fuckin' Colombians got involved, and people feared him and only knew him by the name Pemberton hung on him, Moises—Moises Rockafella, the King of Rock Cocaine. He didn't make big cake like that with Trey-Boy—but at least he didn't have to worry about a murder beef, and the living was decent.

Such a wave of woe swept over Fat Tommy as he contemplated all this that, softly, he began to weep. His whole bright life was passing before his sad eyes: there were pinwheels of light; a series of birthdays; his stint as a fabulous dancer; his wife, Bea, again; his kids—Little Tommy and infant Kobe—cuties! He didn't deserve this. And there was his old job as assistant manager at the Swing Shop—twelve years ago now—all those great records: Tupac, NWA, Biggie, KRS-ONE, Salt-N-Pepa, shit, even Marvin Gaye. He knew them like the lines in these hands that now stared up at him, glazed and dotted with sweat. All the bright scenes of his life seemed to be fading, all of them diminishing like faces in a fog. Even the fabulous good shit that was coming, close on the horizon—that seemed to be diminishing, too. If only he could get a glass of water, or maybe some lemonade.

5.

"I'm dryin' out inside," Fat Tommy pleaded, lifting his head slightly. He couldn't see Vargas, but could hear his footfalls pacing back and forth somewhere behind him. He closed his eyes a moment and tried to catch a wink.

"Steady, sweetheart. Steady. Just a few more questions and you're home free," Vargas said.

Tommy waited for the next question with the same despairing apprehension with which he had endured all the last. An hour earlier Vargas had turned the lights on so bright that when Fat Tommy looked up the next moment, he beheld not a pea-green interrogation room with a trio of sad-sack cops trying to sweat him for a cop murder he didn't commit—the whole room seemed to him as a single white spotlight, a moon's eyeball inspecting him on a disc of light. At many points during the long, arduous interrogation, the men drew in so close on the hulking gangster that the tips of all four men's shoes seemed to be touching. Now when Fat Tommy squinted into the light, it didn't even seem like light anymore but a kind of shiny darkness. And he felt as though he were falling through the brightness like a brother pitched off a hundred-story building.

Vargas switched the lights back to a single hot light again. The trembling darkness in the distance beyond the spotlight seemed like measureless liquid midnight.

"I need some lemonade!" Fat Tommy screamed. The voice startled him. It did not seem like his own, but rather like the voice of a child or woman screaming from the bottom of a well.

Vargas turned off the tape recorder. Dockery and Braddock pushed their chairs back from the cone of white light that made Fat Tommy look like a Vegas lounge fly sobbing under a microscope. The scraping of their chairs was like an utterance of disgust, and they meant it to be that. It sent shivers up their own backs, and shot a great hot thunderbolt of fear down the spine of Fat Tommy O'Rourke. Vargas cut a rebuking glance at Dockery and Braddock.

"It's late," Vargas said, looking around for a clock. They had started this session just before two p.m.

Braddock pulled out his watch bob. To view the dial, he swept his hand through the cone of light that seemed to enclose Fat Tommy in a brilliant Tinker Bell glow, and the watch flashed like a little arc of buttery neon framed in white.

"Almost six a.m. Sixteen goddamn hours and not a peep from this shithead," Braddock said. He smacked the back of Fat Tommy's chair. Tommy shivered briefly and settled deeper into his sob.

Dockery felt around in his pant leg for his pack of butts and stood up. "Just a little longer, sport, and you can get back to beatin' off in yer cell."

"Yeah, beatin' off in yer cell . . ." Braddock repeated.

"I need a piss break," Fat Tommy said as politely as he could, then added with a smile, "and a big glass of lemonade."

"Good idea, asshole. Think I'll go drain the lizard," Dockery said, and looked at Vargas. Vargas nodded and Braddock and Dockery went out.

Fat Tommy sobbed on. He was still crying when Braddock and Dockery came back in laughing. They both held huge cups of lemonade and they were eating fresh Krispy Kreme doughnuts. Braddock tossed a half-eaten doughnut in the trash.

"I'm starvin', officer. I'm sleepy. I don't know about no murder," Fat Tommy tried again. He shut his eyes tight.

"Pale-ass pussy," Braddock muttered. "Yer gonna fry for this. Why don't ya quit yer lying?"

Fat Tommy closed his eyes and took a breath and asked once

again, "Please, officer, can I have some water or some lemonade?"

"It's *detective*," Dockery said.

"Listen here, detective," Tommy assented, his big voice gravely and frail, "I don't deserve this beef. I don't know nothin'. I didn't see nothin'. I got a wife and family. I ain't no liar. Cut was the one who fount Simpson . . . He told us he was a snitch. Not no cop. It was all his idea. We wouldn't be mixed up in none of this if Cut hadn't—"

The room went dead quiet.

Fat Tommy eased his eyes open and strained to hear the shuffling of the cops' shoes behind him, but could only hear his own heart beating, *thu-thump, thu-thump*.

Then Dockery said, "Cut? You never mentioned any Cut."

Fat Tommy could feel the life draining from his chest. He began to hyperventilate and for the first time he could feel the jheri curl gel-deluxe begin to drip against his collar. "You said I could have water. I need some water," he pleaded.

"You can have water, Moises, after you tell us how it went down," Braddock growled from somewhere behind him.

"Tell us about this Cut," Vargas continued, piling on. "He got a last name?"

Fat Tommy felt his mouth moving. He couldn't make it stop. "Cut . . . um . . . Cut Pemberton . . . I think."

"And?"

He tried to think of innocent words. He tried to stall and think of what Bea would want him to say. "I didn't know him that good," he finally said.

"Go on," Vargas prodded. "What's he look like?"

Tommy tried to think of other faces, but all he could see before him was that goddamn Cut. "Gots a cut cross his ear, go straight cross his lip, like he's wearing a veil on one side of his face."

"Yes . . . ?"

"Said he got it in a fight with a cracker when he was in the Marines. But I heard he got it in prison—" He held his breath and tried to stop his voice from speaking again. He couldn't believe what it was saying, betraying him, snitching on him.

"Okay . . . go on."

Tommy's mouth burst open again: "He can talk Spanish."

"Go on," Dockery said. "Cut . . ."

Tommy's whole body seemed to slump. Special Agent Braddock smacked his chair hard and Tommy sat bolt upright. "Well, Cut was the onliest one that did it."

"Go on."

"Cut was one of them red, freckly niggahs from Georgia."

"Yes."

No one spoke for a moment, then Fat Tommy's voice said, "Spotted like a African cat. I didn't even know him good . . ."

"Um-hum."

"Wore plaits standing all over his head."

"Plaits? Really?"

Tears were streaming down his cheeks, but Fat Tommy grinned. "My Bea used to call him BuckBeet, 'cause he looked like a red pickaninny. That used to piss him off, 'cause of Buckwheat, you know?"

"Yes . . . Cut . . ."

"Yeah, Cut. First I knew of him . . . two years ago . . .when I was staying on Glen Oaks off Paxton . . . Him and Karesha — my wife's sister—and my Uncle Bunny banged on my duplex at 'bout two in the morning looking for some crack."

"You mean Bunny Hobart—the second-story man?" Dockery broke in again. The detectives had two tape recorders going now, but Dockery never trusted electronic equipment and was transcribing everything Fat Tommy said on a yellow legal pad.

"Yeah, that be him," Fat Tommy said. He slumped back in the hard metal chair, trembling as he recalled the scene. "He knew Cut from the joint. Cut had just got out and was chillin' with Karesha. He was already dressin' like a Crip, all blue, talkin' shit. I could tell he was trouble. He used to strong-arm young Gs and take their stuff."

"And Bunny told him you were the big-time coke man," Braddock said. It was not a question.

"I was gettin' out of the business. I was gettin' out," Fat Tommy explained. "It was Cut that fucked up all my plans. He wanted to impress the big-time talent . . . I was only stayin' in till he could get on his feets."

"What big-time talent?"

"Colombians, La Caja Crips . . . It was them goddamn Colombians that tolt Cut about Simpson," Tommy confessed. "Cut came up with the idea of settin' the guy up. He tolt us he was a snitch—not no cop! I tried to talk him out of it; I tried to reason with him . . ."

"A regular Dr. Phil," Braddock said.

"Yes, sir," Fat Tommy replied quietly. His heart was sputtering like an old Volkswagen.

"Catch your breath, son," Vargas said. "Get our boy King Moises some lemonade, will ya, Dockery?"

Dockery went out and Fat Tommy flopped his big grease-spangled head down into his hands. From the top of his jheri curl to the soles of his size-16 Air Jordans, everything about him was huge, extroverted, and showy. Now, he sat hulking in the metal chair, trying in vain to make himself smaller, hoping that the willful diminishment of his great size would in turn reduce in the minds of the cops the appalling grandeur of his recent crimes. He sat there in his bright white tent of a shirt with his Martin Luther King, Jr. tie strung tight around his bulging neck like a painted garrote.

His mind went blank, then black, then pale gray. Far above the dull cacophony of the cops grinding away at his statement, Fat Tommy O'Rourke—a.k.a. Moises Rockafella, La Caja's King of Rock Cocaine—could hear a plaintive, high-pitched wail, a shrill, sad voice, strangely resembling his own. He prayed to Christ it was someone else.

Teresa Moody

BILL MOODY is the author of seven novels and a dozen short stories, and hosts a weekly jazz show on KSVY-FM. A working jazz musician for over forty years, Moody has toured and recorded with Jon Hendricks, Maynard Ferguson, and Earl "Fatha" Hines, among others, and continues to perform in the Bay Area. His latest novel, *Fade to Blue*, was published in 2011.

camaro blue
by bill moody

Hello? Yes, I want to report a stolen car. Robert Ware. Oh, for Christ's sake. Okay, okay. I don't know when. Last night sometime, I guess."

Bobby Ware tried to calm down. He gave his address and license number and continued to answer questions. "It's a blue 1989 Chevy Camaro Sport." He listened to the other questions and lit a cigarette.

"It was in front of my house. Oh yeah, there was a horn too. What? No, not the car horn. A tenor saxophone in a gig bag. What? Oh, a soft leather case. Yeah, that's right. Okay, thanks."

Bobby hung up the phone and sat for a minute, smoking, thinking. "Fuck," he said out loud. "Fuck, fuck, fuck!" Finally got his dream car and some asshole stole it. *Man, I gotta move,* he thought. *Too much shit in this neighborhood.*

He got up, paced around. Barefoot, cut-off jeans, sandals, and a Charlie Parker T-shirt, his daytime uniform, trying to think who he could borrow a horn from for the gig tonight.

He was working in a quartet at a club on Ventura, backing a singer who was trying to convince everybody she was the next Billie Holiday, but she wasn't fooling anyone. But hey, a gig was a gig. Three nights a week for three months now, so he couldn't really complain.

He replayed last night in his mind. He'd come home, tired and anxious to get in the house, and totally spaced, leaving his tenor in the car. That wasn't like him or any horn player, but too late now. He sat down and turned on the TV, hoping he wasn't going to see his Camaro in one of those car chases the city had become famous for.

When Lisa got home, he was still sitting in front of the TV, watching the news, but there were no stolen car reports and no news from the police.

"Hi, baby," Lisa said. She was carrying a bag from the Lotus Blossom Chinese takeout. "You hungry?" She set the bag down on the kitchen table and walked over to Bobby.

She was in her Century City law-office outfit—skirt, blouse, half heels, her hair pulled back in a ponytail. She sat on the arm of Bobby's chair and kissed him lightly on the lips, then let herself slip over the arm onto his lap.

"What's the matter?"

"Somebody stole my car."

"Oh, baby, and you just had it serviced and waxed."

"Tell me. But it gets worse."

"What?"

"My horn was in the car."

"Oh no, did you report it?"

Bobby pushed her off him. "Of course I fucking reported it."

Lisa held up her hands. "Okay, okay."

Bobby sighed. "I'm sorry, babe, but you know what the chances are of getting back a stolen car in L.A.?" Especially that car. Bobby had read somewhere that Camaros, even older ones, were popular among car thieves. By now it was probably stripped clean at a chop shop, and somebody was trying to figure out how to put the saxophone together.

For as long as he could remember—at least since high school—Bobby had wanted a Camaro. He could never afford a new one, and good used ones were hard to come by. Then one afternoon, driving back from the store, he'd found this one parked on a side street with a "For Sale" sign in the window. A blue Camaro Sport. One owner, all the service records, and the car looked like it had hardly been driven more than to the store. Now it was gone.

He took Lisa's Toyota to the gig, after dredging up a tenor from a former student who wasn't sure he wanted to pursue jazz anymore. Bobby had helped him pick out the horn so it was a good one, but it wasn't Bobby's old Zoot Sims model he'd bought from a guy on the street in New York.

After the second set, he was standing in the parking lot behind Gino's with the bass player, a tall thin guy who played good and didn't care anything about singers. They watched a tan Ford Taurus pull in, and two guys in rumpled suits got out and came over.

The bass player cupped the joint in his hand and started walking toward the club. "Cops, man."

"Are you Robert Ware?" the older of the two asked Bobby. The younger one watched the bass player walk away.

"Yeah. Is this about my car?" Bobby was wary. They didn't usually send detectives out for stolen cars.

"I'm afraid so," the older cop said, casually showing Bobby his ID. He looked at Bobby for what seemed like a long time. "We found traces of cocaine in your car, Mr. Ware."

"No, that's not mine," Bobby said. "I'm not into coke."

The younger cop nodded, smiling knowingly at Bobby.

"No, seriously, man. Coke is not my thing." He held up his cigarette. "This is it for me."

The older cop took out a small notebook and flipped through some pages. "Do you know a Raymond Morales? Hispanic male, twenty-nine years old."

"No."

"You didn't let him borrow your car?"

"Borrow my car . . . What are you talking about? I don't loan my car to anyone. Ask my girlfriend."

"We did. She told us where to find you."

They all turned and looked as the side door opened and the bass player peeked out. "Hey, man, we're on."

"Listen," Bobby said, "can you guys wait a bit? We have the last set to do and then we can talk."

The two cops looked at each other and shrugged. The older one said, pointing across the street, "We'll be at Denny's."

"Cool," Bobby said. "You did find the car, right?"

The younger cop looked at him and smiled again. "Oh yeah."

Bobby found them in a back booth drinking coffee and eating pie. He sat his horn on the floor, slid in next to the younger cop, and ordered coffee.

"So? What's the deal on my car? When can I get it back? Was there much damage?"

The two cops glanced at each other. "There was some damage," the younger one said.

"Oh fuck," Bobby said, loudly enough that a couple in the next booth turned and looked. "I knew it. Totaled, stripped, or what?"

"Bullet holes," the younger cop said.

"What?"

"Mr. Ware," the older cop began, "your car was involved in a high-speed chase early this morning. Raymond Morales was driving. He apparently ran out of gas. He emerged from your car with a weapon and fired on the pursuing officers. They returned fire and Mr. Morales was shot at the scene."

"Jesus," Bobby said. He sat stunned, not knowing what to say.

"The driver's side door has holes, the window was shattered, and there were several bullets lodged in the seat."

"Is he . . . ?"

Both cops nodded.

"I'm sorry," Bobby said, wondering about Raymond Morales.

"It happens," the younger cop said.

"Your girlfriend said you reported there was a saxophone in the car?"

"Yeah, that's right."

"We didn't find it."

Bobby looked at both of them. "What do you mean, you didn't find it?"

"Wasn't in the car," the younger one said.

They talked some more without giving up much information about the incident or when he could get his car back. The older cop gave Bobby his card and said they'd be in touch. They left Bobby to finish his coffee and think about Raymond Morales.

Two days later Bobby got a call from the older cop. Lloyd Foster, Bobby remembered from the business card. "We're done," Foster said. "You can pick up your car tomorrow morning."

"Anything new?" Bobby asked.

"Like what?" When Bobby couldn't think of what to ask, Foster said, "See you in the morning."

Bobby was prepared for the worst when he arrived at the impound garage. Foster and the younger cop were waiting for him. Bobby was surprised to see the car mostly intact. The entire driver's side window was gone. The techs had cleaned it out, Foster told him. When he opened the door, he saw the small round holes in the seats where the bullets had lodged.

There were dark spots on the seat—blood stains that hadn't

been entirely erased—and there was a strange smell Bobby couldn't place. He looked at the two cops.

Foster shrugged. "Techs use all kinds of compounds, liquids to secure evidence. It'll go away eventually."

Bobby walked around the car. On the passenger door there were some minor dents and paint scrapings from when Morales had sideswiped a car or a telephone pole or something else in his attempt to get away.

"Why didn't he just, you know, give up, instead of trying to shoot it out?"

The two cops exchanged glances and shrugged.

They handed him some papers to sign to release the car and gave him copies. Then they watched him get in the car and adjust the seat. Morales must have been short—the seat was closer to the wheel than Bobby kept it. He nodded at them, backed the car out of the garage, and drove off. In the rearview mirror, he caught them watching him till he turned the corner.

He pulled into the first gas station and filled up. He used the Yellow Pages to find a glass repair shop and jotted down the address of two not far away. Ed's Auto Glass was the first.

"We can do it while you wait," the man at the desk said. "What happened? Somebody try to break into your car?"

"Something like that," Bobby said. "It was stolen."

"Wow, and you got it back. Lucky," he said, sliding a clipboard across the counter so Bobby could initial the estimate form. "Give me an hour."

Bobby went for a walk, bought a Coke at a convenience store, and smoked, thinking about Raymond Morales dying in his car. He pictured the car, out of gas, skidding to a stop, Morales throwing the door open, hiding behind it, firing at the cops, the glass shattering, bullets embedding in the seat, and then falling backwards as a bullet struck him in the chest. He couldn't get the vision out of his mind. All for some cocaine. How much? What was it worth? His life?

He got home before Lisa and examined the car's interior inch by inch, not knowing what he was looking for but unable to let it go. He felt under both seats, up in the springs, in the channel the seat slid back and forth on. He even lay under it with a flashlight, knowing the cops had already done this but not trusting their thoroughness.

He opened the hatch, raised the flap where the spare tire was kept, took the tire out and felt around the compartment, shined the flash everywhere, but it was no go. The car was clean.

The only evidence of the incident were the holes in the seat and the dark stain. Raymond Morales's blood.

"Hey, you got it back," Lisa said, getting out of her car. Bobby hadn't even heard her drive up.

"Yeah." He shut the hatch and locked it, as Lisa walked all around the car.

"Looks okay," she said.

He nodded and shrugged at her look. "No horn." He opened the driver's side door and showed her the bullet holes in the seat, the dark stain.

She just stared. "Jesus, kind of spooky, isn't it?"

Bobby got on Lisa's computer and went to the *Los Angeles Times* website to check on obituaries. He skimmed through starting with the date after his car was stolen and found it five days after:

Raymond Morales, 1974–2004. Beloved son of Angela Morales. Survivors include his sister Gabriela. A memorial service will be held Wednesday, May 15 at . . .

Bobby jotted down the date and time and glared at the

photo of Raymond Morales, obviously taken a few years before his death. It was almost like a high school yearbook photo. Just a nice looking kid, three years younger than Bobby. He told himself he was only going out of curiosity, maybe to see if someone had any information about the horn, but he knew it was more than that.

He drove into Inglewood Park Cemetery and found the site easily. There were at least thirty or more tricked-out lowrider cars and a single limo parked along the curb. A plain tan sedan Bobby recognized as Foster's car was also there.

Bobby parked as close as he could and got out. A ways in on the lawn, among the hundreds of tombstones, he saw the small crowd gathered around the grave site. Foster and the younger cop were standing behind the fringe of mourners. Foster turned as Bobby walked up.

"Interesting," he said to Bobby. His younger partner turned and smiled.

"What are you guys doing here?" Bobby asked.

"Routine," Foster said. "We know Morales ran with some of these dudes. We're just compiling some information." Foster looked at him. "What about you? Car spooking you?" This made the other cop smile again.

Several of the young guys turned and glared at Bobby and the two cops. They were all slicked-back hair, ponytails, sunglasses, sharply creased chinos, and black shirts. A couple started moving toward them but were held back by others. Bobby moved away to stand alone.

At the center of the gathering, two women sat by the casket as the priest finished. Bobby guessed they were the mother and sister. The younger woman raised her eyes briefly and looked at Bobby, then touched her mother's hand.

Bobby turned to look back at the cops as they walked

toward their car. He took a deep breath and wondered if this was such a good idea. As the service ended and started to break up, the young guys walked past, stared at him curiously with hate in their eyes, and went to their cars. Soon the loud sound of souped-up engines and glass-pack mufflers filled the air.

Bobby stood still, hands clasped in front of him, not sure what to do next, when Raymond Morales's mother and sister walked by. The sister looked at Bobby strangely as her mother stopped and also looked at Bobby.

"You were a friend of my son's?" she asked, studying his face.

"Well, no, not really," Bobby said, surprised that she spoke to him. "I, ah . . ."

"High school," the sister said. "Taft High School. I know you. Bobby Ware."

"Yes," Bobby said, taken aback.

"I'm Gabriela." She smiled briefly. "You played a saxophone solo at the school assembly. I was a freshman when you were a senior."

Bobby let his mind travel back ten years. He'd been in the marching band and the jazz ensemble, and he had played at the senior assembly. "Well, yes. I didn't think anybody remembered that."

"Come, Gabby," Raymond's mother said, starting toward the car, already losing interest in Bobby.

Gabriela followed her mother, then stopped and turned. "That was your saxophone, your car, wasn't it?"

Bobby stood mute, realizing she knew everything, watching her dig in her purse for a pen and a slip of paper. She scribbled quickly and pressed the paper in his hand. "Call me," she said. Then was gone.

Bobby waited for the mourners to clear out. He saw one group of three guys pause at his car and stare, then look over at him, before they got in a black Chevrolet and drove off.

* * *

The next morning Bobby dialed the number. "Barnes and Noble," a voice said. "How can I help you?"

Bobby thought it had been a home number she'd given him but quickly realized she wouldn't have done that.

"Can I speak to Gabriela Morales, please?"

"Let me see if she's in," the voice said.

Bobby was suddenly listening to canned music as he was put on hold. It sounded like Dave Koz or David Sanborn, one of those R & B saxes, vamping relentlessly over the same tired chords.

"Hello?"

"Miss Morales? This is Bobby Ware."

"I guess you want to talk to me."

"Well, if it's not convenient I can . . ."

"I have a lunch break at 12:30. There's a coffee place here in the store. We can meet there. This is the big one, on Ventura Boulevard."

"Yeah, okay, that would be fine," Bobby said.

After a pause she said, "This is strange."

"Yes it is."

He got there early and took a cup of coffee to an outside table so he could smoke. Gabriela appeared a few minutes later.

"Oh, there you are," she said. She was dressed in dark slacks and a white blouse with a plastic B&N name tag pinned to her blouse. Her hair was raven black and framed her face. *Very pretty*, Bobby thought as he stood up.

She put her hand on his shoulder. "No, don't get up. I'm just going to grab a sandwich. I'll be right back."

She came back quickly and sat opposite Bobby with a sandwich on a plate and a bottle of water. "Sorry," she said. "I'm on till 6. If I don't eat now, well . . ."

"No problem," Bobby said.

She took small bites of the sandwich and studied him. "You don't remember my brother at all, do you?"

"No," Bobby said. "I'm sorry . . . about what happened."

She nodded and looked down. "He had a lot of problems and it's not so uncommon. Raymond was lost a long time ago," she said, finishing her sandwich. Gabriela looked at Bobby's cigarettes on the table. "Can I have one of those?"

"Sure," Bobby said, offering her one. He lit it for her and watched her take a deep drag and cough a little.

"Wow, it's been awhile. I quit about a year ago."

"Yeah, I've quit a couple of times myself."

"I had quite a crush on you," she said, "after I saw you play at the assembly. I used to see you in the halls, by your locker, and I started going to the games to see you in the marching band."

"That was a long time ago." Bobby looked away, thinking of the early morning practices, the drilling, the music.

"You still play, right?"

"Yes, I'm working a gig not far from here on weekends."

"That's good. You were talented." She paused. "I remember Raymond wanting to be in the band but it wasn't cool, you know that macho shit, so he never pursued it. Maybe if he had he would . . ." Her voice trailed off.

"Look," Bobby said, "I don't want to bother you, I just, I don't know, it's been bothering me. I just had to—"

"See who Raymond was?"

"Yeah, I guess. Since I got the car back, I keep having these visions."

"And there's the horn."

"Well, yes, that too."

She nodded. "I have it in my car. Raymond came home that day, said he'd borrowed the car from a friend. I knew he was lying, but he brought the horn in the house, didn't want anything to happen to it."

"You're kidding."

"No, I think he still thought about playing." She stubbed out her cigarette and glanced at her watch. "I've got to get back to work. C'mon."

He followed her to the parking lot. She opened the trunk of her car. Bobby looked inside and saw the case. He flipped the latches and lifted the lid, and it was like seeing an old friend. He shut the case and took it out of the trunk.

"Thanks, thank you very much."

"Where's your car?"

Bobby hesitated. "Oh, a couple of rows over but you probably need to go and—"

"I want to see it."

They walked over to his car. Bobby unlocked the door and put his horn in the back.

"Do you mind?" She looked inside.

"No."

Bobby watched her run her hand over the seat, her finger tracing the bullet holes. Bobby shivered. She stepped back, her eyes moist now. "It's kind of closure or something," she said. "Thank you."

"I understand."

She managed a smile. "Well, I guess that's it."

"Would you like to come hear me play?" he blurted.

She smiled. "I don't know if that would be such a good idea."

Bobby nodded. "Sure, I understand."

She looked away, then back at him. "But hey, why not. High school crush makes good." She had a beautiful smile and she gave it all to Bobby.

Bobby gave her the address of Gino's and they shook hands.

She pressed her hand in his. "Thank you," she said, then turned and walked back to the bookstore.

On the way home, Bobby drove by a deserted warehouse with a huge fenced-in parking area. He slowed, then pulled in the open driveway and drove around to the back of the building. He sat for a moment, the car idling, then slammed his foot on the gas pedal. The car shot ahead. He got up to fifty, then hit the brakes and turned the wheel hard. He threw open the door, stood up, crouched down, stood up again, then threw himself back on the seat, trying to feel the bullet that killed Raymond Morales.

Eyes closed, leaning back, Bobby circled behind the singer on "Lover Man," looking for his openings yet not getting in her way. She finished her chorus and Bobby shuffled toward the microphone and played what he could till the bridge. He stepped aside and saw Gabriela Morales at a table to his left.

She was leaning forward, her chin resting on her hand, gazing at him with what he guessed was memory. Trying to remember that high school assembly? They finished the set with "Just Friends," and Bobby scorched the small audience with two choruses that got him a phony smile from the singer that said, *Hey, I'm the star, remember?*

He sat his horn on its stand and walked over to Gabriela's table. "So, you made it," he said.

She smiled. "You're much better now than in high school."

"Come outside with me," he said. "I need a cigarette."

"Me too." She picked up her purse and put a napkin over her glass.

They walked up Ventura Boulevard a ways, not talking much, just getting used to each other. Finally, they stopped and she turned to look at him.

"So where do you think this is going?" she asked. Her eyes were so dark and deep.

He moved in closer and kissed her lightly on the lips. She didn't resist, and when he pulled back, she opened her eyes and looked at him again. "That's what I wanted in high school."

"And now?"

She looked away. "What is this? You want to fuck the kid sister of the guy who was killed in your car?"

"What? No, I—"

She waved her hand in front of her as if she was shooing something away. "I'm sorry. I don't know where that came from. Really, I'm sorry. I don't know why I came. It's just, I don't know, a connection with Raymond. Does that sound crazy?"

"No," he said. "I think that's why I came to the service. I wanted to see what your brother was about, what his family was about. I don't know if I can keep the car now."

They turned and started walking back toward Gino's. "Raymond was a gangbanger, a cocaine dealer, and he lost. He got in over his head and couldn't get out, except the way he did. I loved my brother but he gave my mother endless grief and worry. End of story."

"And you?"

"This isn't a good way to start. There must be a girlfriend somewhere, right?"

Bobby nodded. "I live with someone. Two years now."

"Are you in love with her? Are you going to marry her?"

"I don't know," Bobby said. "I thought so."

"I'm not going to be your girlfriend on the side." A glimmer of fire in her eyes now.

"I know," Bobby said.

She got quiet again, but her hand slipped into his. "We're both here for the same reason," she said.

Bobby knew immediately what she meant. They had both been touched by death and they were connected by it in a way only the two of them could understand.

"It's maybe the one good thing Raymond did," Gabriela said.

"Yes," Bobby said. "Maybe it is."

Ibarionex R. Perello

JERVEY TERVALON was born in New Orleans and raised in Los Angeles. He is the author of five books including *Understand This*, for which he won the Quality Paperback Book Club's New Voice's Award. Currently, he is the executive director of Literature for Life, an educational advocacy organization, and creative director of the Pasadena LitFest. Tervalon's lastet novel is *Serving Monster*.

serving monster
by jervey tervalon

The interview for the position of personal chef for Monster Stiles was going to be at the Trump Plaza at this overblown, over-hyped restaurant that only idiots thought anything of.

Bridget, Asha's girlfriend, was a thin blonde who wore a short skirt, even as the first flurries of snow fell from the gray sky.

"I hate New Jersey," I said.

Bridget laughed. I didn't mean for it to be funny.

"So, you had that cute restaurant in the Village?"

I smiled. "I don't know about it being so cute."

"I loved that place," she said.

"I did too, but not enough."

"Really? How so?"

"When I think about it, maybe I didn't care for it."

Bridget nervously tapped a fork against her water glass.

"Gibson is a fantastic cook," Asha said. She glanced at me and probably could tell I was near tears.

"What happened?" Bridget asked.

I shrugged, and Asha took over. She leaned over and began to whisper to Bridget. Asha wore this loose-fitting, burnished-gold tunic. Her dark skin and hair looked even richer against the paleness of Bridget's skin and hair. As Asha whispered, whatever resistance Bridget had toward me faded. Bridget was totally smitten with Asha and when Asha took her hand, she was transported.

I was almost embarrassed to see how much she was taken with Asha.

"Listen," Bridget said, loud enough for me to hear, "I'll tell you the bottom line. We have a hard time getting quality people up on the mountain."

"Why is that?" I asked.

"It's a tough job, the type of job for a particular person who wants to be in a beautiful place and needs privacy. It's very private there."

"You mean isolated?"

"I call it very private. You can call it what you like."

"Isolated. I don't mind isolation. I don't mind it at all."

"Do you know who Lamont Stiles is?"

I shook my head.

"You've heard of Monster Stiles?" Bridget asked.

"The singer?"

"Yeah. He doesn't do much of that anymore. He's more of a producer with three acts at the top of the charts. Everything he touches is bling; his clothing line made millions last year and this year it's expected to double in sales."

"When you say bling, you mean . . . ?"

"Priceless. You had to have heard of that expression."

"Yeah, but I never used it."

She looked at me like she had already made up her mind.

"So, Mr. Stiles needs a chef?" I asked.

"He prefers to be called Monster. He fancies himself the monster of music, of cutting-edge fashion, of life."

"Monster, it is."

Bridget laughed. "I like how direct you are." Then her face hardened. We were going to get down to it. "You need to understand how this works. If you repeat this to anyone, I'll get fired and you'll get sued."

I laughed. "Listen, I'm on parole. If I don't jump through hoops I go to jail."

She nodded and smiled at me after Asha patted her hand.

"This might be hard to believe, but many people aren't comfortable on the mountain. It takes a special person, someone who really enjoys quiet and their own company. The perfect candidate for this job loves nature, because that's where you are, in the clouds. It's God's most beautiful, pristine country. That's what Monster loves about it, he's above it all, but people get lonely for their families, for life outside of the *Lair*. Plus, well, Monster is demanding. He says that about himself."

"How so?"

Bridget sucked her teeth. "You haven't heard all that rubbish about him?"

"No, I really don't keep up with the music scene."

"He made all those bubble-gum pop songs. You got to wonder about people like that," Asha muttered. "And he had that pet koala hanging around his neck."

"He's gotten rid of the koala, that was a big mistake," Bridget said, with perfect seriousness.

"I'm not sure about this. What do people say about him? Is there any truth to it?"

Bridget laughed. "I'm not going to go into it. People say all kinds of things about him. You'd think he bathes in the blood of little boys. That kind of *National Enquirer* bullshit."

"What do you think of him?"

"Well, it's hard to explain," she said softly, as though she were wary of being overheard. "Monster isn't really someone I see a lot of. He is a great employer in that he's very generous. But mostly he's on the road or holed up in the *Lair*. It's really his encampment, the inner grounds of his mansion and the gardens where most staff aren't allowed. I think that's how those horrible stories of Monster get out. Disgruntled former employees spread rumors when they really don't know what goes on in the *Lair*. Anyway, if you're really interested, I'll fly you out to interview. Asha can come with you. I'll show you Solvang and there's this wonderful little Danish bakery. You'll love the pastries."

"I'm not sure of what he wants. Will I be his personal chef or will I be running the kitchen for everyone there?"

"You know, I couldn't tell you at this point. With Monster you go with the flow. He'll fill in the blanks, he always does."

Bridget shrugged and put her head on Asha's shoulder.

Business was done for the evening.

Asha wore something beautiful. She told me the name, but I immediately forgot. A Jabari? Whatever it was I liked it—a kind of purple pantsuit with fringe around the waist and cuffs. Bridget was in black again, straight leather, suitable for nightlife in the big city but fucking silly on a brilliant day in beautiful Solvang. Bridget was just as schoolgirl giddy to have Asha near as I remembered.

"You are too wedded to that job," I heard Bridget say.

Asha shrugged. "You know, I trained to be a social worker. It's what I wanted to do, and I'm happy with my life," she said to Bridget. It was the same thing she said to me when I asked why she was so content to run a halfway house. I guess Asha was sincere in what she said to people; I admired that, and how rare it was.

At the Dutch bakery that Bridget was so high on, I lingered over stale strudel while the girls stepped outside to admire bachelor buttons and Mexican primrose growing along the road. They held hands, and I saw Bridget lean toward Asha to sneak a kiss. I hoped this Bridget knew what kind of woman she had in Asha, a human being of the first order. But maybe that was too much to hope for. I didn't get a good feeling from Bridget. She probably thought Asha was hot and exotic, the domestic equivalent of an incendiary foreign affair without the bother of having a passport renewed. Maybe I was jealous, but I knew I was right about this Bridget and her bitch nature.

I was supposed to be put up somewhere spectacular, a woodsy resort over in the hills with an amazing restaurant and a wonderful chef I was supposed to know. Bridget mentioned more than a half-dozen times just how excited she was to take us to this slice of paradise. However, something happened to the reservation, or the charge card, and plans had changed.

As we drove downhill, back to the valley, I thought we'd all be staying at Andersen's Split Pea Soup and Hotel—she mentioned that it was campy and fun—but Bridget obviously couldn't wait to drop me off. Even so, she took the time to remind me that Monster liked prospective employees to be an hour early for interviews, expected her to be two hours early, and with unctuous sincerity she mentioned again just how important it was to make a good impression. Oh yes, he'd be there, he wouldn't speak and I wasn't to speak to him, but he'd be highly involved in the process.

Flow.

Monster could flow in any moment and seal the deal, but I couldn't expect that.

Of course, I'd have an in, but really, it was up to me to seize the initiative.

Dragging Asha behind her, Bridget turned her rental around and roared back to the Santa Ynez Inn. Seemed Bridget made sure the Inn had one room available.

I had a bowl of very salty green soup and ate all the crackers in the cracker holder. I thought of ordering a beer, then I wanted a gin and tonic, then decided just a couple of hits off a crack pipe would do the trick. I had another bowl of very salty green soup and found the room Bridget had reserved for me.

I turned on the televison and flipped around. I watched rap videos for a while until it became painful, all that booty shaking and me not having gotten laid in almost a year.

I couldn't help fantasizing about being a third wheel between Asha and Bridget—maybe they would suddenly want to experiment and include me. Yeah, I couldn't sustain that fantasy, too improbable even for a hopeless optimist.

The next morning I got out of bed at 5:00, so nervous about how the day would go that I went for a walk, even though a fog had rolled in, concealing Andersen's Split Pea Soup and Hotel to the point that it was difficult to know what direction to go in. I was lost almost immediately and had to get directions from the surfer dude behind the counter at the 7-Eleven. Then I remembered I needed new razors and shaving cream.

I meandered a bit, eventually finding my way back to the hotel and my room to shave my head with the precision of an anxious man with nothing else to do.

Instinct.

It was obvious what Monster thought of himself. Look at how hard he worked to eradicate the last vestiges of identifiable color from his life and skin.

I wouldn't let him hold that over me. Lack of melanin never held me back; actually, it was a kick, a key to acceptance that never had to be explained. Never deny it, but why let them form the question? Don't make them question their own generosity, don't make them consider the intangibles. What does it mean to hire a black man? Is it the opposite of hiring a white man? The same?

Don't ask and I won't tell you.

I don't know.

I know this, that Monster bolts up from night terrors, chest heaving as he rushes to the mirror to see if that bleach/chemical peel/skin brightener bled off, shed, absorbed away, or simply vanished.

Bet he lives in mortal fear of a stray BB, the living nightmare of the paralyzing threat of a nappy head.

Cool.

Even if he has a nigger detector, he'll never see me coming.

I don't pass, I slip by on the strength of the fact that I can. Maybe it's self-loathing, but I never had the energy for too much of that.

I am what I am—the son of two African-American parents who were light enough to pass as white if they cared to. They didn't because they were proud of who they were and embraced their African-Americanness.

Monster, though, doesn't pass. He thunders by, shouting to the world, "See me! I'm not like them, I'm you!"

He hides in plain sight, and I guess I do, too. Race explains nothing about his insanity, or my blundering into acceptance and not wanting to rock the boat.

Probably, in that sense, we're brothers under the skin.

Bridget showed up two hours late, a woman in desperate need of a toilet, but without a bit of an apology other than a curt, "Monster rescheduled a few hours," before she hauled ass to the bathroom.

"Where's Asha?" I asked, after she returned. I needed to see a friendly face, and Bridget's wasn't it.

"Sleeping in. She needs it," Bridget said, with a hint of a leer, and I disliked her even more. It still ain't polite to hit it and strut. As much as I admired and liked Asha, I couldn't understand her taste in women.

Bridget sped to the 101 and headed east, back toward Santa Barbara. Another stunningly beautiful day. From the freeway, I could see the Pacific lurking behind the hammock of hills, and when we started to climb and banked west, I saw surfers, black stick figures on breaking waves.

Then Bridget turned east and we headed into the Santa Ynez Valley.

At an access road Bridget drove for another twenty minutes or so, until a craftsman bungalow came into view. Near the bungalow was an impressive gate, maybe ten feet high, blocking a well-maintained road.

A man in a gray uniform with a cap like that of a highway patrolman from the forties leaned into the window and took a look at me, then he thrust a clipboard into my hands. On the clipboard was a document which went on for four pages. I hadn't gotten through the first page before Bridget tapped me on the shoulder.

"It's a release. You can't interview without signing it."

"Give me a minute. I like to read before I sign."

She sighed, and watched with narrowed eyes as I hastily flipped through the document.

"Done? Good. Now sign."

I signed, and handed the clipboard back to the security guard.

Bridget burned rubber on the way out, as though she had to make up for lost time, though I thought we were early.

About a mile later she stopped at another bungalow with two very busy men sorting through packages stacked in the driveway. Bridget waved to them and headed inside and pointed to an oversize chair by a window. I sat down as she flipped through more paperwork. The interior of the bungalow resembled the layout of a nicely appointed law office. I remembered wanting to buy those heavy brass lamps with the hand-blown, leaded glass for the restaurant, but I had given up when I couldn't get a reasonable price.

"Wait here. The head of security will be by in a few minutes to begin the interview. Then, afterward, maybe Monster will be ready to ask you a few questions."

A door opened. A tall man entered dressed in the uniform that all these guys sported, as though they could change your oil, carry your luggage, or arrest you. All of them were trim, tall, and white; did Monster hire every washed-out Mormon FBI agent he could find?

Bridget handed him a ream of paper, and then he walked over to me with his hand out and paused, squinting as though he recognized me and wasn't happy about it.

"Mr. Gibson, my name is Timothy Steele. I run security here at the *Lair*. I wonder if you could clarify a few things."

"Sure, I'll do my best."

"You were arrested for attempting to buy a controlled substance. Is that correct?"

"Yes."

"What was the controlled substance?"

"Heroin, to smoke. Usually it was cocaine, but the time I was arrested it was heroin."

He paused for a moment and thumbed through the documentation on the clipboard, then returned his unblinking attention to me.

"You don't have any prior arrests?"

"Nope. I've lived a pretty straight life, other than my recent drug experience. I've received the best treatment and diversion-therapy possible, and I've been clean for a year."

"That's good to hear, but you should know that we do an ongoing security check on all employees. If at some point we discover that you concealed any aspect of your personal history, no matter the relevance, you will be terminated immediately."

I paused for a moment, wanting very much to tell him to fuck himself, that I didn't need this fucking job. However, I did need it. I needed to get back to a life that wasn't embarrassing. Oh yeah, I needed this job in the worst way.

I allowed myself to hope, a threadbare hope I kept in a sock drawer in the hidden closet in the backroom of my confidence, a sad little hope that I could resurrect my career, that I wouldn't fuck up, that I wouldn't make my life a slow suicide. I'd finally shake that fear that I was out to do myself in, that I couldn't trust myself.

I couldn't afford to tell anybody to fuck off, except for maybe myself.

"I told you everything, except for when I got drunk as an undergraduate and wore this coed's panties on my head home. I guess that could be considered a crime."

Mr. Security gave me a look, a look of disdain, of mild disgust. Then, like the sun breaking through the clouds, he smiled.

"I don't think I'll need to make note of that."

That seemed to lighten the ultra-serious moment.

"Good," I said, and stood to leave.

"One more thing," he said.

He handed me a paper bag. I looked inside and saw a plastic cup with a lid.

"We need a urine sample. If you're offered the job, you'll be subject to a random weekly drug test."

My pride sloughed off like a skin I didn't need. I dutifully took the paper bag and went into the restroom.

I was in luck. Someone had pinned the sports page above the urinal, the Giants were on a winning streak. Quite a few of the workers at the *Lair* must have to submit to this weekly ritual.

Sheepishly, I came out of the restroom holding the brown bag at arm's length. With a solemn nod, Security took it from me, then he ushered me to another door that led to another room. Inside, Bridget sat behind a very large desk, phone to ear, listening with strained concentration.

"Yes, he just came in. Do you want me to put him on?"

She gestured for me to sit down, her eyes flaring as though she'd toss a book at my head if I delayed for a second.

"Use the speakerphone."

I nodded, confused as to whom I was talking and why.

"Hello?"

I heard raspy breathing. I grinned at how silly this felt.

"This is Monster."

His voice didn't have that ethereal quality I'd heard on those interviews on VH1. He sounded grounded, even a little hard.

"It's an honor to talk with you," I said.

"What's your name again?"

"William Gibson."

"Right, you're the cat who owned the restaurant in New York. You lost it because of drugs."

"Yeah, that's about it."

"It would be cool if we could hire you."

"I would like that very much," I said, wondering what would stop him if he wanted to hire me. Did he need to check with his mother?

"But I need to ask you a question and you need to answer me honestly. Can you do that?"

"Yes, I can do that."

"Good."

I waited for him to ask the question, but he went back to that raspy breathing, as though he had a problem with his sinuses.

"Don'tassumeyoucanplayme."

He blurted it out so fast, at first I couldn't make out what he said.

"Could you repeat that?"

"Do you think you can play me?"

"What?"

"You know what I'm saying."

"I'm not sure what you mean."

Monster paused as though he were ready to drop the bomb on me.

"You gonna play me? That's what I want to know."

"I pride myself on my professionalism. I don't take it lightly."

"I'm not talking about that."

I wanted to ask what was he talking about, but I assumed that wouldn't get me hired.

"I'm a very loyal employee. That's how I've always been. It's second nature to me."

"It's more than loyalty."

"I'm not sure I understand."

"Then that means you're not down. I only hire down cats."

I was beyond confused.

"I'll ask you once more. Are you gonna play me?"

"I don't intend to play you."

Another pause and more raspy breathing.

"I'm supposed to believe you? I think you're lying. Tell me this, are you experienced?"

"What?"

"Are you experienced? Don't bullshit, answer me!"

"Do you mean like in a Jimi Hendrix way?"

"Yeah, exactly. That's exactly what I'm saying. You've got to be down for me."

My stomach sank. If he thought I was going to be getting loaded with him after dinner, that wasn't where my head was at.

"I think I understand," I replied.

"Understand what?"

"What you said about being down."

"Being down? What did I say about that?"

Now *my* breathing was raspy. Was he high? He had to be high. Only people who were fucked up out of their minds, but who thought they were under control, talked like that.

"Long as you down for me, it's all true. You know what I'm saying?" he said, excitedly.

"Yeah," I said, nodding, even though I knew he couldn't see me, unless he had a hidden camera. That, I wouldn't put past him.

"Are you gonna poison me?" he blurted, surprising the hell out of me. Of all the crazy-assed things I've been asked in my life, this surprised me into stupid silence.

"I've never poisoned anyone," I said, with conviction.

More raspy breathing.

"You're not gonna put anything sick into my food?"

"Sick?"

"Yeah."

"I can't say you'll love everything I'll cook, but I can guarantee I'll never poison you or put anything sick into your food."

"Hah, you funny. I'll get back to you."

The speakerphone went silent.

Bridget looked at me with suspicion.

"Did you have any idea what you were saying?"

I nodded without conviction.

"Monster likes people to be straight with him."

"I was being straight. What, I didn't sound straight?"

Bridget snorted. "I don't think you knew what you were saying. You were willing to say anything to get him to hire you."

If it wasn't for Asha I'm sure Bridget would have crossed me off her list. I don't have a problem with that, except for the fact that I did need this job, though it had became obvious that it must be hell to fill if I had gotten to the interview stage.

"I don't see what the problem is. We seemed to have hit it off."

"First of all, that wasn't Monster."

"Huh? Who was it?"

"Monster's assistant."

"Assistant? He sounds like a thug high on something."

"Well, he *is* Thug. He calls himself Thug. That's his name as far as you're concerned."

I felt tricked. It wasn't right and Bridget needed to know how I felt.

"Bridget, you know I need this job, but obviously you don't feel good about me applying for it. Am I wasting my time?"

Bridget looked surprised, like I had just come out of left field with that. She couldn't look me in the eye.

"Is it Asha? You promised her something and now you don't want to deliver?"

Bridget ran her hands through her hair, still avoiding my eyes.

"You might want this job, I know you need it, but once you get out there, it's different. I'm always looking for employees. It's a fucking strain. The lawyers, God, I talk to so many lawyers."

"That's big of you, trying to spare me some grief."

Finally, our eyes met. She looked like a woman who'd had enough.

"I've got my share of problems. I'll admit that. You're right. Asha really wants this for you."

"You don't think I'm capable?"

She shook her head. "It's not that at all. I don't want to have to answer to Asha when it's over."

"What do you mean, when it's over, and what do you have to answer to Asha about?"

"I might be a little jealous about how much she likes you, but it's not all jealousy. I just don't want her blaming me when everything goes to hell."

I stood up to leave. I was through with this shit.

"I finished that diversion program with no problems. You know that."

"Oh, this isn't about you. It's about Monster, and it's about why I want to quit this job. I don't want be responsible for the shit that happens."

"Quit this job? I don't get you at all! You bring me in, then decide I'm not right for the position, and now you tell me you're gonna quit."

"Don't get so pissed off. If I get the call that he wants to offer you the job, I'm not going to disagree. I'm not that kind of bitch. I'm just being up front. You need to know what you're getting into."

"What are you talking about? What am I getting into?"

"You'll see. You'll have to see how this place works. You'll know soon enough if you've got the stomach for it."

The phone rang and she snatched it up with a crisp, "Bridget here."

I walked outside before hearing the verdict; would I live or die? Was I hired or was I flying back to the halfway house to finish probation? But at that moment I just wanted to be outside, feeling the sun on my skin, whatever the hell would happen.

Silence, solitude, and breathable air, that's all I wanted, not exactly a miracle, but I guess this nightmare of a job is what I deserved.

I'm the cook; what goes on beyond the locked door of this

bungalow is not my concern. I turn up music, keep lights burning all through the night.

Safe.

No one cares about the cook, that's what I count on. I keep the door locked and I try not to leave, not anymore, after dark.

Cold.

This bungalow is torture, even in the spring. No matter how many logs I toss into the barely functional woodstove, heat slips through the walls like the mice when I turn on the light. I came with few clothes—two white tunics, a couple of thick sweaters, jeans, and T-shirts. I wear both sweaters to bed, all the socks I can fit on. Coldest I've ever been is spring in the mountains of Santa Ynez. Some nights I can't bring myself to get out of bed to use the toilet, just grit my teeth and endure until I can't stand it.

You'd think somebody as rich as Monster would insulate these bungalows, might have some idea that his employees are suffering. Even so, I should have been better prepared, should have known, paid more attention to what I was getting myself into. A man of Monster's stature probably spends his time plotting world conquest, opening a Planet Monster in Bali or something fantastic, not worrying about the frigid temperature of an employee's bungalow. Maybe that's why the last chef quit, fingers so numb she couldn't dice.

Another glass of a Santa Ynez Cabernet Sauvignon and I'm still feeling the cold, though it's not as sharp. I told myself I was through with twelve-step anything, I can't feel good about getting wasted. Numb is good and warm, but numb turns sour, numb gets you arrested, numb gets you a judge deciding what's best for you, and I can't stand to live through another diversion program. I pour the rest of the wine down the drain. I swore to myself that I would get high on life only and leave killing myself a little each day alone.

I know these extensive, meandering grounds well, but on a moonless night it's almost impossible to stay on the trail. A step in the wrong direction and you're in the middle of scrub brush and blood thorns that rib all sides of Monster's estate. Easily enough you can end up blindly wandering in the wilderness among coyotes, black bears, mountain lions, whatever.

See.

You must walk away from the light into the darkness.

The other direction isn't an option. The closer you get to the big house the more likely the lights will go on, blinding lights that'll make you feel like a frog ready to be scooped into a sack. Then you'll hear the sound of the heavy steps of Security as they converge, shouting commands. It's been worse after some nameless stalker managed, after repeated attempts, to sneak into Monster's *Lair* on some psychotic mission. Someone, maybe even Monster, came up with the *Lair* as the name for this place. Heard it's trademarked, and he's going to use it for his next CD, whenever he gets that done. Clever, I guess, but I don't know. Supposedly, he's been having a hell of a time, the music won't flow at Monster's *Lair*. Maybe it's the name, it's not conducive to creativity. Try telling someone you live and work at Monster's *Lair* and they laugh. *With that lunatic? How is that? What kind of craziness goes on there?*

I can't answer.

They never did catch the trespasser, supposedly a loser from Monster's past who's plagued him since long before he built this playland. I used to enjoy my nightly walks, but that was before enhanced lighting and the dogs. Security lets them run the grounds to get the lay of the land.

Once, I saw Monster walking alone in the middle of a pack of trained attack dogs like he was fucking Saint Francis of

Assisi. Security trailed behind him, skulking near the bushes, maintaining that illusion of privacy he demands. The dogs smelled me, and though I was trying to back away from the encounter, too late, they charged forward, frothing and kicking sod.

Monster looked for a moment like he had no idea of who I was, the man he hired to cook for him and his family. I raised my walking stick to bash a dog before the others mauled me, but an impulse of self-preservation kicked in and I shouted my name just as the dogs charged.

"It's me, Gibson! The cook!"

Security shouted something in German, and the dogs stopped in mid-stride.

I heard Monster's voice, high and nasal, a near whine: "Oh, you scared me."

"Sorry," I said, and hurried on in the opposite direction. I caught a glimpse of him in the moonlight—bundled in a parka, though that night the temperature was mild, walking with hands clasped behind his back, serenely in thought. Security caught up and escorted me back to my bungalow, which was more and more a jail cell and less the attractive perk of a rent-free cottage in the beautiful Santa Ynez mountains, the selling point to compensate for a modest salary. Security looked me in the eye and told me to watch it, don't forget who pays the bills.

"Monster does," I said, nodding to show, even if Security wasn't buying it, that I was a team player. It didn't go well. He looked for a second as though I might be jerking his chain, then turned to go, but not before jotting down something in a small gray notebook. I'm sure some notation scheduling another background check.

I didn't mind.

When you work for someone with great wealth you learn

quickly that you really do serve them.

You learn to be blind, deaf, and dumb, if that's what they need.

Monster needs all that.

Sometimes I see things that don't add up, that make me nervous.

I wanted isolation, but not like this.

The night sky has too many stars; the moon hangs like a gaudy lantern illuminating a path to my bungalow.

I've never felt so alone.

I know what goes on there, behind those hedges, those walls, gates, and sensors.

He's a monster and every day I serve him.

I'm not inclined toward depression, upbeat and all that is how folks describe me, but that was because of the drugs.

Married, living on the Lower East Side in a nice co-op, part owner of Euro Pane, a restaurant with witty angular (the publicist came up with that), Puglia-inspired cuisine that people wanted to spend good hard cash on, you'd think I'd be more than happy, but in truth it was too much for me. Maybe I couldn't stand prosperity, and with things going so well I knew my luck couldn't continue on the upside, something would give and I'd find myself flat on my face. Instead of waiting, I went for it, leaped for the pipe and returned to a long-dormant cocaine habit. If I needed to make an excuse, more so to myself than anyone else, I could offer that the restaurant was overwhelming, and I needed relief from the day-to-day, week-to-week, month-to-month, relentless grind, the kind where you wake yourself with the sound of your teeth grinding. The kind of stress that makes a man long for a hit off a crack pipe.

Ten years ago when I indulged in smoking a little cocaine, I handled it, but now was different. Then it was about staying up to dawn, for the second day, clubbing until I was sick of the whole idea of clubbing. Working and playing, trying to have everything, and it worked until I couldn't stand living like that. I gave it up, put down the pipe and cocaine easily. Proved to myself that cocaine didn't have me by the balls. Suddenly I noticed I had so much more money in my bank account, and I met Elena, fell in love, and that was that. It really was a good thing, and I handled it smoothly so smoothly I had it in the back of my mind that I could do it again. It wouldn't be no thing. But, I guess, shit has a way of catching up with you after a while. My addiction was like a cancer cell, dormant, kicking it until the conditions were right. Probably, the truth is I don't have the same discipline or constitution. I'm not that young man who could do that, keep it going, burning myself out in every direction. Soon enough I lost the restaurant to my partner, and my wife found my fucked-up, vulgar habit reason enough to leave me. I don't blame her. She didn't marry a fiend, I became one, it just took time for me to discover it, my inclination toward self-immolation. I call it that, the suicidal impulse to consume yourself with a Bic lighter. I'd see myself burned out, gone, a neat pile of ashes, but that's more acceptable to my imagination than the vision of myself as a pathetic, cracked-lip panhandler, a martyr to the pipe.

Maybe I wanted to fail, see how far I could fall.

Far and hard.

Lucifer had nothing on me.

Being broke is like having a bloody mouth and loose teeth and there's not a thing you can do about it, except stand it.

How does that song go?

"A knife, a fork, a bottle, and a cork—that's the way we spell New York . . . I got cocaine running around my brain."

Something like that, but I'm not judging.

I thought I could master my high. I wish I had the courage to have stayed in the city for everyone to see me living in a halfway house, trying to reassemble the remaining shards of self-respect.

What if I ran into her, Elena, my wife?

It's wrong to say that, we're more divorced than married, but far as I'm concerned she still is. Funny how memory works. When you don't fill it with anything new, it replays what maybe you don't want replayed.

My mind replays Elena.

Short, with hair like the blackest ink, strong legs and ass, a delicate face, almost Japanese, like a geisha in a Ukiyo-e print.

Passionate about love and making money and everything else.

Passionate about hating me.

I still love her, though it's hopeless to think she'll ever love me again. I want her back more than the restaurant, a reputation, everything, but it will never happen, not in this life and not the next.

Left with nothing, other than to lie in bed and think about what I've done, hurt the woman I love and lost her, didn't consider the consequences back then, didn't have bouts of guilt, didn't consider anything. It was about me, about what's good for the head. You know, the head. A selfish bitch, that's the truth about me. About me, that's all it ever was, my love was a fraud, my professionalism a joke, my self-respect, delusion.

And I'll never get it back; you'd think I'd find the courage to do something dramatic, maybe kill myself or find God. No, I indulged in self-pity, waiting to be saved from myself.

Elena partied hard, but you know, it didn't get to her. She did it all—heroin, coke, ecstasy—but when she was through with it, she was through. Maybe it was yoga or the StairMaster, but mostly it was because Elena wanted a baby, and she's that type of person, so directed and focused that she didn't stop to think that the rest of the world, and by that I mean me, might not be able to live the way she managed to. It took forever for her to see that I had a weakness. Never raised an eyebrow when, after a sharing a few lines, I excused myself to go to the bathroom to do a few more. She even laughed when she saw me fumbling to put everything away, hastily brushing white powder from my face, more evidence of my lack of control.

It was funny in a way. She should have noticed that I was craving, fiending, whatever you want to call it. I had started my downward journey, my decline—in it to win it, a new life consisting of one long, sustained need to stay high.

My recollection of conversations with Elena replay themselves, and I listen to myself ruin my marriage.

"We're four months behind on the mortgage?" Elena asked.

"No, I don't think it's that far along. Maybe two months," I replied.

"What happened to the money? We'll lose the apartment."

"Things got away from me. I'm sure we can put something together to work this out."

"What are the chances of that happening?"

I shrugged. I didn't want to lie to her.

"Do you know what you're doing to us, the fact that you can't control yourself? Why don't you admit it, stop being in denial."

She looked at me with smoldering, black eyes.

"You need professional help."

"I don't have that kind of problem."

"You're forcing me—no, you're giving me no choice but to leave you."

"Come on," I said. "We'll work this out."

This time she laughed bitterly.

"Sure we will," she said, but we both knew that was a lie.

After that she moved in with a friend and refused to talk to me, but that particular humiliation didn't sting much because later that week in court I pled guilty and was sentenced to nine months in a minimum-security prison.

In some sense I was content to be going, having done enough damage to my self-esteem that I wanted to crawl away into a corner and wait for the room to stop spinning. And when it did, I woke up to the humiliation of getting processed, prepped, and more to go to the place to do my time. My only regret is that I wasn't high during that humiliation.

The days inside prison weren't totally unpleasant. They had a good enough library, and I spent time lifting weights for the first time in my life. That's it, I thought, do positive things for myself while incarcerated and avoid being raped, but in a minimum-security prison, the only thing I had to worry about was getting athlete's foot in the shower.

I had hoped to hear from Elena at some point, but after months had passed, I began to wonder if I would.

When I was released and moved to the halfway house, she wrote and said she would be coming to visit so I could sign the papers.

Divorce papers.

I tried not to allow those words to rise to the surface. I waited with far too much hope on that moment when she'd appear at the door of the halfway house to be shown inside by one of the workers, who would sign her in and bring me out to sit across from her on the worn couch. Me, smiling stupidly, thinking, feverishly hoping, that her seeing me again would jar something loose and she'd want to forget about the divorce. It was what it was, paperwork.

She wore all black, tight wool skirt and a sweater that looked good on her, but she kept her arms crossed, probably remembering how much I liked her small breasts.

I don't think she ever smiled. Talked to me about some issues, bankruptcy, insurance policy. Nothing I was interested in. I was interested in her, but that was dead.

I was dead to her.

She took it personally, like I had rejected her for cocaine, but it wasn't like that.

How did she ask it?

"How could you be so fucking stupid? Getting yourself arrested buying crack on the subway?"

I shrugged. I guess if it was the first time, she might have been able to excuse it, but it wasn't.

To this day I don't know how stupid I am. I don't think I've plumbed the depths of my stupidity, and when I do, I plan to get back to her. I'll have charts and graphs, a PowerPoint demonstration.

I ruined my life, I know that, last thing I wanted to do was betray her, but I was good at that, too, excelled at it, even.

Asha, the woman who ran the halfway house, realized I could cook South Asian. Being Gujarati she was surprised that I made a better bhindi, spiced okra, than her mother. She discovered that I could stay in seclusion in a sweltering kitchen cooking up meals for the dozen or so losers that lived at the halfway house. I labored away in silent grief, working with old vegetables, day-old bread, not much meat, which pleased Asha because she didn't like the smell, some chicken, beans, lots of beans. I came up with meal after meal through backbreaking efficiency and invention. When I wasn't cooking, I cleaned. I scoured that kitchen, boiled water, added cupfuls of caustic soap, cleaned the filthy ceiling, cleaned everything. Made it spotless, and kept it that way as long as I was there, my six months climbing out of the black hole of my life.

Cooking and cleaning and not thinking was a meditative balm. I hated when thoughts would slither in on their own and have their way with me. Grief caught me slipping, I needed to see her. Thought of leaving, blowing the whole thing off, my contract with the halfway house staff, to make a run to see her, force her to listen to me.

I'd go to prison, and I had sense enough to know I didn't want that. Maybe I might have tried, maybe prison would have been worth it, if I got her to listen to me, but in reality I had no words left to beg with.

I was out of prayers and I was sick of lighting candles to the saint of hopeless causes.

She was gone, maybe here, probably some other city.

"It's for the best," my caseworker said, when I confessed why I wouldn't talk in therapy.

"It's not about the drugs. It's about losing my wife."

"Drugs are why you lost her. You drove her away."

I cried then, in front of that fool. I stopped talking to him after that. Before, I felt like maybe he was okay.

I was wrong.

Up until that moment, I didn't want to do cocaine again. I really was through with it.

Then the cravings started.

I knew she wasn't coming back, but that fiction kept me alive. Kept me thinking it was the drug. The drug did me, and not me the drug.

He ruined that conceit, better than therapy ever could.

Trying to avoid contact with my fellow losers at the halfway house, I took to mincing garlic like garlic would keep everyone at bay, like they were all vampires. I guess we are, vampires that suck smoke instead of blood. It worked, everyone kept their distance, except for Asha. I was her reclamation project and she tried to draw me out. I accepted her good attentions, but I didn't want to be drawn out or in, or anywhere. I wanted to stay lost. Alone would be good, but I couldn't expect that. I had to get with the twelve-step program, show requisite progress to get these people out of my life. Still, Asha was pleasant and charming, with big luminous eyes that were easy to look into. Good thing she didn't go for men, because our friendship would have been much more complicated. Finally, I explained a little about myself, and so when she came into the kitchen with this look on her face, I knew I had probably said too much.

"What's wrong?"

"You. I read about you."

"What? That I'm a fuck-up? You already knew that."

She shook her head.

"Yeah, I made a mess of what most people think was a promising career."

"Don't you miss that life? Running that restaurant, cooking?"

"I don't know. I guess I do."

"My girlfriend works for this famous entertainer. She says he needs a chef."

I raised an eyebrow, in spite of myself.

"I wouldn't get past the interview," I said.

"She's crazy about me and listens to what I have to say. If you're interested, you'd have a shot."

"I'll think about it," I replied, without a hint of enthusiasm. I wondered why she wanted to go out of her way for me, she was smart enough to know I truly was a fuck-up. It had to be her nature, trusting and giving, and maybe a bit naïve, coupled with being smart about people and hard-nosed about the everyday affairs of running the halfway house. I guess that's what you need in order to be in her line of work, skills that contradict each other. Strange how a woman, young and attractive, would choose social work; running a halfway house must be like hanging around unflushed toilets all day, when she could choose so many more attractive occupations. Maybe she wanted to be a Hindu Mother Teresa, and if she could drag me back to respectability, she'd be one giant step closer to sainthood.

Sometimes I think I hear him calling, a sibilant whisper from a satin-lined oak coffin hidden below the sub-basement in a tomb so cold he'd be able to see his rancid breath if he actually had breath. "Living food, that's what I'm feeling," he says.

Because he's feeling it, I'm feeling it, and that's why I'm drinking that Santa Ynez red, and I'm liking it more than I should.

Backsliding.

No more of this drinking after work, getting silly, having flights of fancy that do me no good.

I've still got to deal with living food, no matter how silly it is to consider cooking without fire an earth-shaking invention. Really, you'd think most reasonable people would agree that cooking is a good thing, a good invention, and we should feel good about it. Maybe Monster remembered something about predigestion in high school biology and it confused and disgusted him. Probably, though, it's the influence of a gastronomic guru who put him on the road to bliss through the chewing of fresh bark. Who am I to stand in the way of his path to enlightenment?

Monster is a freak, a freakish freak, maybe a child-molesting freak, but he's not a creature-feature villain, no matter how much red wine might insinuate that.

No.

He's a self-invented American, freakishly fascinating in his attempt at reinvention, and because of it, his self-invention, his desire to live like something out of a cautionary tale of how outrageously famous people go wrong, makes him unique, unique as crazy wealth and an addiction to television can make you. I bet as a kid he rushed home to watch *Dark Shadows* with a chaser of *The Brady Bunch*, which explains some of it—the blond children running around like chickens shooed about by giddy parents. Really, it's not Monster or the kids I wonder about, it's the parents. What must they be like? What do they want for themselves, for their children?

Monster bait.

I'm sure they have lawyers on speed dial, ready and waiting for something actionable. Maybe that's Monster's real value: pulling back the curtain on the banality of human perversity. Give somebody like him enough money and power and what gets revealed?

He's fucking crazy, but it's okay.

Everyone here knows it. It's common knowledge living up here on the mountain. When will the townspeople realize what's up and break out the torches and pitchforks and march on Monster's *Lair*? Isn't it inevitable?

I have another glass of wine and try to return my attention to the task at hand—planning Monster's meals for the week. I figured when I first saw him that the last thing he would be concerned with is eating, figuring him as a man who lived on meth and Twinkies and maybe Diet Coke, because these folks bathe themselves in Diet Coke. For a man over six feet, he must weight 120 pounds, and that's if he hasn't evacuated his bowels.

Considering what he wants to eat, he'd be better served by

hiring a botanist than a personal chef.

Living food isn't something a cook makes. No, give a kid mud, wheat, water, and whatever, and let him go at it.

But I'm a professional, and if that's want Monster is into this week, I'll give it to him straight, with a sprig of fresh rosemary on that sunbaked gluten ravioli.

Breakfast: Oatmeal with coconut milk and raisins.

Snack: Cracked-barley porridge with fresh strawberries.

Lunch: Vegan, sunbaked pizza with three kinds of tomato and Mexican salt from Oaxaca.

Snack: Fresh greens in a lemon sauce.

Dinner: Veggie sushi.

Snack: Unsweetened cider.

That's what my life is now; feeding Monster shit he calls food.

If I had more integrity, if I had that kind of character, I'd get my ass off of the mountain, face the consequences, and preserve my dignity.

Fuck yes. The first step on the road to recovery is to know yourself. I'd best start whipping up some sun-baked potato pancakes for Monster's snack, or find a crack pipe; maybe both if I know me, and I do.

GARY PHILLIPS is the editor of the best-selling *Orange County Noir*; and coeditor of *Send My Love and a Molotov Cocktail*. He has published two crime graphic novels, *Angeltown: The Nate Hollis Investigations* and *Cowboys*. He smokes cigars now and then, contemplating the strangeness of it all. For more information, visit www.gdphillips.com.

disco zombies
by gary phillips

Wild Willie stumbled backward, knocking against the rickety kitchen table, sending the two plastic bricks of coke somersaulting to the floor.

"Goddammit, Spree, pay up." Wild Willie wrenched hard to get the six-shooter free from the other man's grasp.

"Fuck that, Willie!" Spree Holmes blared. "I did." He had both of his hands clamped around Wild Willie's gun hand, his fingers tugging on the barrel of the revolver, even as Willie beat the shit out of his arm with his free fist. "You fuckin' reneged, man," he added, gritting his teeth.

Holmes sprung from a tiptoe position so as to maximize his weight bearing down on the heavier but flabbier Wild Willie. It worked, and the two went over and down onto the worn linoleum. They slid against one of the lower cabinets, busting off its handle.

"Shit!" McMillan hollered from the doorway, ducking and diving beneath the wind of the Samurai sword Crider swung at the top of his thinning hair. McMillan flopped onto his stomach in his vintage Hawaiian shirt atop the ratty shag carpet. But for once he wasn't worried about keeping his clothes neat. He twisted around onto his back, kicking and flailing his legs like an angry turtle, just as Crider chopped at him with the blade. A piece of the heel of McMillan's two-tone shoe was sliced off and he instinctively shut his eyes as if he'd been gored in the heart.

"Ugh," Holmes grunted after Wild Willie yanked the gun free. He'd been partially straddling him but flung himself sideways as the other man righted the piece. Desperate, Holmes reached out and latched onto anything he could off the counter. With brutal force he slammed alongside Willie's head a glass container used with a blender. Its impact caused Willie's shot to be misdirected and singe past Holmes's head—but not into it.

"Motherfucker," Wild Willie swore. A thick piece of glass was embedded in the meaty part above his eyebrow, and he had no choice but to grab for it to relieve the pain. As he did so, Holmes shoved the heel of his hand into the shard, driving it deeper. Willie's legs twitched in agony as he tore off another blast at Holmes's chest.

In the dining room McMillan keenly registered the shot but was concentrating on throwing a porcelain statuette of a trumpet player he'd plucked off a shelf with as much shoulder as he could put behind it.

"You throw like a little girl," the silver-toothed Crider taunted. A cut had opened up on his face as a result of the miniature musician hitting him. He was on one side of a round dining room table and McMillan opposite. Crider held his gleaming sword in both hands, the bulk of it poised over the table.

"Which you want to lose, man? Hand or ear?" Crider made a quick back-and-forth with the steel, letting it whistle in the stifling air of the little house.

"You ain't man enough to take me without your chop suey prop," McMillan said, inching to his left.

"Come on, I'll make it nice and clean and fast." Crider made a vicious swipe that caused McMillan to tense but not be so stupid as to start running and get the back of his neck severed.

Holmes and Wild Willie tumbled out of the kitchen, entangled. When Willie had shot at him the second time, Holmes was in the process of lowering his upper frame, and as the bullet funneled into the bone of his shoulder blade, his momentum carried him forward and he'd rammed into Wild Willie's chest, stunning him. Battling tears and doing what he could to ignore the stars exploding behind his corneas, Spree Holmes had pressed the fight, knowing if he let up, the next shot from that old Colt would blow his guts out.

Instinctively, Crider bounded over to the wrestling forms to give his homeboy Willie a hand. He turned to refocus on McMillan, who was now pushing the dining room table toward him. Crider dodged to one side but McMillan followed his movement and upended the table onto the swordsman's feet.

"Bastard!" Crider yelped. He got his left foot free but the right, in its snakeskin boot, wasn't so easily extricated. McMillan held onto the edge of the table and lifted it up quickly and then brought it down again on the right's instep. Crider gritted his teeth and wielded the blade toward McMillan's hand. The other man lunged out of the way and the sword sliced into the table's rim and held fast.

McMillan laughed and, putting effort behind it, shoved the table, sending Crider into a wall as he attempted to free his weapon. "I got your girl," McMillan said, and plowed a fist into the opposing man's nose as the sword came loose.

At that same moment, Holmes and Wild Willie were digging into each other's faces with their fingers. Holmes's thumb was gouging into the corner of Willie's mouth. The latter shifted and bit down on that thumb like it was fresh steak.

"That ain't gonna help you, Willie," Holmes said, leveraging forward and causing Willie's head to rattle against the doorjamb. Willie reached for the six-shooter, which was now lying on the kitchen floor, but Holmes wasn't about to allow that to happen. Holmes took hold of what material he could of Wild Willie's T-shirt and, jerking him up, head-butted him, opening the gash wider over Willie's eye.

"Ke-rist!" Wild Willie screamed, and tried to scurry away. Holmes was on his feet and stomped on the escaping man's side like he was a bothersome cockroach. He then pressed the barrel of the gun onto Willie's thigh and shot him.

"That ought to slow you down," Holmes said over Willie's whimpering.

Behind him Crider had his sword but was keeling over from a rocking blow delivered via the dining room chair hefted by McMillan. The chair was rusted metal tubing and a torn leatherette-covered seat, but it served McMillan well as a shield. Like a lion tamer from an old Saturday morning serial, he had it up and was using it to fend off the blows from Crider's sword.

"Put it the fuck down," Holmes ordered.

Crider and McMillan both turned and stared. McMillan then grinned broadly, stroking his goatee with his long-nailed hand. "Shoot him," he said.

The Colt in Holmes's hand didn't waver, even though the burning in his shoulder intensified.

Crider made a guttural sound and pivoted toward Holmes. The sword was at his side, the blade pointing outward— a Mississippi Samurai in pointy-toed cowboy boots and worn Lee jeans.

"I'm not fuckin' around, Crider."

"Smoke his ass," McMillan repeated. He still held onto the chair.

Crider cocked his head to the side, waiting and wondering. He grasped the sword by two hands on its hilt.

"Get the shit," Holmes said.

"On it." McMillan scooted into the kitchen, not letting go of the chair until he was in the other room. Wild Willie was curled into a fetal position and moaned softly, his leg leaking profusely.

"Something broke?" McMillan teased cruelly, as he scooped

up the two keys of flake. "Or is it indigestion from trying to cheat us, you cheap fuck?" Spittle dotted McMillan's graying goatee. "Huh, Willie, that it?" He leaned over, feigning like he was listening for a response.

"You . . ." the man on the floor began.

"You what, you fuckin' Shylock." McMillan planted his two-tone Nunn Bush shoe in Willie's stomach, making him wince and gurgle crimson. "You gonna try and play us, man? After the business we done together, making your own thirty-percent-state-disability-retard-self phatter than you deserve to be?"

Holmes called from the dining room: "Come on, let's hit the road!"

"Yeah, yeah. Can't have no more fun." He kicked Willie in the ribs, a bone giving way. As McMillan started to walk out, Wild Willie suddenly gyrated his body and reached for the exiting man's legs. McMillan reacted but still got tangled up as Willie continued to paw at him, and he fell forward.

Holmes knew better than to be distracted by his partner going timber. The problem was McMillan whirligigged his arms to stay upright, causing Holmes to reposition himself, and Crider took his opening.

There was a flash of silver and the sword swiped downward at McMillan's tilting head. "Oh, fuck me," the goateed man exclaimed and put a hand to the side of his head.

Crider turned on the balls of his feet, bringing the sword level like a batter going for a sliding pitch. Holmes cranked off a round even as he peddled backward to ward off being hacked. The shot blasted into the swordsman's forearm and he dropped his weapon.

McMillan was on his knees, his eyes saucers from fear. "Finish him, shit, finish him, Spree."

"We're done here," the calmer Holmes declared, already

heading toward the front door. He carried the Samurai sword, the peacemaker tucked into the hollow of his back. Redness soaked into his shirt and blood dripped onto the carpet.

"You sure?" McMillan stared at Crider, who was crumpled into one of the other chairs where the dining room table had been. He was holding his useless arm by his opposite hand. The .44 slug had entered at such an angle that it exited through his elbow, shattering the joint.

"What's he going to do," Holmes said derisively, "call the cops?"

"Still . . ." McMillan ventured.

"I gotta get patched up. And I'm hungry and I'm hurting." It occurred to him that the money they'd brought wasn't in his hand. No sense leaving it now, it wasn't like there weren't going to be hard feelings between him and Wild Willie.

He found the small gym bag beside the couch and tucked it under his arm like a football. With that, Holmes made for the front door, not particularly concerned with whether a nosy neighbor or the local law was on the other side. It was getting on toward dusk and he wanted to be out on the highway, away from Wild Willie, Crider, and this shitty town of Greenwood.

"You think this is over, Holmes? You know it's not."

McMillan pointed at Crider. "Shut up."

"Scared, McMillan? Scared I'm going to put my red magic on you?" Crider said, his sunken eyes swallowed up as if his face were caving in on itself.

"I told you to keep your mouth shut." McMillan smacked the wounded man with the plastic Circle K shopping bag he'd placed the coke bricks in. This upended Crider and he crashed to the floor, wailing as he landed on his exposed bone.

McMillan laughed and couldn't resist standing over the hurting man. "You know, Crider, I never did cotton to you."

Holmes called from the vicinity of the front door: "Stop fucking around!" McMillan grinned at him and looked back at Crider. A burst of a sparkling brown cloud engulfed his face.

"Hey," McMillan said, hitting Crider hard, twice in rapid succession, as he lay on the floor. Crider went limp but still wasn't unconscious.

McMillan put his angry face close to the still man. "Why don't I just shoot you?"

"I'm leaving, Mill." Holmes stepped through the door and into the coming darkness.

In the car, plowing across the gravel of the driveway and onto the residential street, each assessed the other's damage.

"How deep is it?" McMillan looked but didn't touch the wound atop Holmes's shoulder blade.

"I can feel the bullet grind when I move my arm." Despite this, Holmes was at the wheel. He glanced sideways. "How about that chunk Crider took off?"

McMillan blinked and felt along the top, or what had been the top, of his right ear. "Ain't that some shit? I got so excited I forgot that motherfucker chopped this off." He leaned so he could see his lobe in the rearview mirror as he gingerly fingered the flesh. "Can it be sewn back on?"

"Sure, want me to turn around so you can get the piece?"

McMillan gave him a lopsided look. "Shit," he finally said. "So where to, drive across the border to Arkansas? I used to know a cat there in Little Rock who can help us out." McMillan was reaching into his back pocket for his cell phone.

"Too far, and even though we ain't gushing out, I don't want to go that long without attention."

McMillan nodded, understanding his meaning. "You just lookin' to get your dick wet."

"Ain't you? We just scored enough coke that once it's

broken down to crack in the 'hood, it will keep us in dead prezs for months."

McMillan indicated the trunk where their cash kept company with the snow. "And the discount we got it at. I still can't believe after we'd already agreed to the price beforehand that Wild Willie tried to jack it up once we got there. What the fuck, huh?"

"Exactly," Holmes said, heading toward Highway 49. "Probably some static from his supplier. But that's his worry, not ours."

McMillan clucked his tongue. "Man didn't want to listen." He sneezed and coughed. "Goddamn ju-ju powder Crider blew on me. What was that about, huh?" He plucked at his nose.

Holmes tried to shrug but his shoulder was already stiffening. "Some kind of Indian thing, I guess."

McMillan looked blank.

"He's part Choctaw," Holmes illuminated. "Crider was always into hoodoo shit, casting spells and chanting and all that to protect him when we were about to do a job."

"You two used to run together?"

"Yeah," Holmes said, but didn't elaborate. He gave a number to McMillan and the other man handed the phone over when the line connected.

"Uh-huh," Holmes said, after saying hi and listening for a bit. "I know I have some nerve, Janey, but I'm hurtin', baby, and I need a safe port in the storm." He didn't dare look over at McMillan or he'd start laughing at how thick he was slathering it on and screw it up for sure. "Baby, I know, but I promise you we'll make it worth your effort."

He listened some more as Jane Corso chewed him out, but he could tell she was softening. What they had once was too strong and too real for either of them to pretend otherwise—and being able to help her with car and utility payments was certainly an added incentive. She was a practical woman, after all.

"And, uh, if it's not too much bother, maybe you could ask what's-her-face, you know, the one with the green flamingo, to help you out."

McMillan brightened and considered just where Corso's friend had that flamingo tattooed.

"Okay," Holmes said, after another minute or so of negotiating. He hung up. And even though his shoulder was starting to burn worse, he winked broadly. "We're set, man."

"Righteous." McMillan settled back, wondering how much reconstructive surgery would cost.

In less than an hour and a half the two reached Jane Corso's modest frame house, inherited from her grandmother, in Clarksdale, not too far from the Sunflower River. It was in a dead-end lush with overgrown shrubs and set down the slope from a small hill. Its location along an unpaved street gave it a semi-rural feel; the nearest house was half a block away.

Corso and her friend with the tattoo, Ella Fernandez, worked at the Diamond Stud Casino over in Tunica. Corso was a dealer and Fernandez a waitress.

"Like old damn times," Corso said, working the probe in Holmes's exposed shoulder area. She'd numbed the wound as best she could using a paste made from some of the coke and Lidoderm, a medicine for cold sores, she found in the medicine cabinet. Holmes sat rigid and gripped the sides of the chair's seat, grinding his teeth.

"You know, I—"

"Hush, Spree," she said, a suggestion of a smile on her face. She kneaded her bottom lip with her teeth while she dug for the slug fragments in him.

It wasn't merely nostalgia or a longing to see her that had brought Holmes to her abode. Jane Corso had been a nursing student at one point—before acquiring a taste for the nose candy and shady men like her current patient. "Ah," she said, removing the probe with part of the bullet. She held the tweezers to the light, examining her find.

"If you could finish up before I pee on myself, doc, I'd appreciate it," Holmes said, sweat moistening his face and chest.

Corso's sometimes pale green eyes lightened with mirth. "Best be cool or I'll really put you under and do a Lorena Bobbitt on you."

"You tell him, girl," Ella Fernandez encouraged. While Corso was in street clothes, Fernandez wore her casino uniform, given her shift had ended after the men had arrived. A short cowgirl skirt barely covered her ample rear and was complemented by a fringed leather vest with a revealing scoop. She and McMillan were sitting on the couch and he was regaling her about his real and exaggerated criminal exploits. They rested against an Afghan comforter spread against the back of the couch.

Fernandez had already snorted up three lines of blow from the glass-topped coffee table. There was a current *TV Guide*, a discount-store 1.75-liter bottle of Jack Daniel's, a few plastic cups, a pack of Kools, and a Zippo on the coffee table, as well. Corso had heated the ends of her tool with the lighter.

More digging and more discomfort and Corso extracted the remaining piece from Holmes. She stitched the gash closed. After that, she handed a grateful Holmes a plastic cup with a dose of Jack Daniel's sloshing in it. McMillan's bloody ear had also been stitched and taped.

"You always gotta do it the hard way, don't you, Spree?" She rubbed the side of his close-cropped graying hair.

He grinned thinly at her. "Bust my balls, why don't you?"

"I intend to." She took his hand and led him toward her bedroom. On the couch, McMillan was busy licking coke from around one of Fernandez's bare nipples. The green flamingo tattoo on the topside of her breast filled his vision.

Near 2:00 in the morning, Holmes and Corso lay awake in each other's arms.

"You heading for New York or L.A.?" Corso put a leg over his.

"L.A."

"Give that heartless city another go, huh?"

He didn't answer right away. "That's where we were going to make it," he finally allowed.

"We almost did, Spree. We sure gave it a good run then."

He pulled her tighter to him and kissed her, lost in what could have been. They soon started to doze off.

"Funny that song would be running through my head," Corso muttered, her head on his chest.

"'I Love the Night Life,'" Holmes remarked. "Alicia Bridges."

"How'd—" she began.

"You're not dreaming it," Holmes said, "I hear it, too."

Suddenly there was a loud blast of wood splintering and the crash of the front door being ripped from its hinges.

"Spree!" McMillan yelled over Fernandez's scream from the front room.

Holmes and Corso had already scooted out of bed. He quickly slipped on his boxers. She tossed the six-shooter to him, which had been resting on the night stand next to a rolled-up dollar bill. He tore into the living room, assuming that somehow muscle sent by Crider and Wild Willie had found them. There was no way he could have anticipated what was waiting for him.

"The fuck?" he breathed.

"Do something, Spree," McMillan pleaded. He was naked and pinned against the wall. Fernandez was clad in her panties and lying half off the couch on her back, her eyelids fluttering. A bruise welled on her jaw.

Holmes extended the gun and shot at one of the things that

had invaded the home. The bullet punctured the creature's eye socket, and that should have dropped any man, but as Holmes was rapidly grasping, these were not normal beings.

"Zombies," Corso gasped from behind Holmes.

The one with its hand around McMillan's throat was dressed in tattered clothing of an unmistakable vintage. He had on a dirt-stained silk shirt with billowing sleeves, once-tight bell-bottom slacks, a belt with a huge lettered buckle, and platform shoes. The other creature was wearing what had formerly been a white suit with a matching vest and a blue super-fly collar-point shirt, open and exposing a bony chest crawling with blind earthworms. This one had a raft of gold—now moldy green—chains and medallions draped around its neck, and the remnants of a puffy Afro full of leaves and twigs. He held onto the two bricks of coke.

The feculent odor rising from the two zombies was overpowering and caused Corso to gag. Holmes was more concerned about his dope. Medallion zombie had turned toward the door and Holmes shot him in the knee. The bone popped and the creature stumbled as if it had stepped into a pothole. Holmes ran forward but bell-bottom zombie hurled McMillan, and he had to prone out to avoid being struck.

"Thanks for breaking my fall," McMillan groaned, after colliding with the now broken TV set.

"They're taking our powder!" Holmes yelled, launching himself and tackling the bell-bottomed one. The monster made a guttural sound and hit him so hard behind his neck that Holmes was knocked to the floor, dazed.

"Coke," Afro zombie growled to his buddy.

"Ughh," the other one said, smiling. Dung and beetles spilled out of his maw.

The two shambled out the hole they'd made ripping off the door. Afro zombie walked lopsided due to its decimated kneecap.

"Spree, Spree, get up." Corso shook him.

Holmes rose to a knee like a fighter taking an eight.

"Come on," Corso said, heading out in pajama bottoms, her pump shotgun cradled in her arms. That was the other thing that Holmes liked about her—she always had his back in a scrap.

The two zombies were moving up the hill behind her house and Holmes and Corson went after them, joined by a limping McMillan who'd tied the comforter around his waist.

"Wait a minute," Holmes said to Corso, who was taking aim with the scatter gun. "Bad enough we've been shooting off pistols, but we're not that isolated around here. You start using that sumabitch, somebody's bound to call the law. We've got to follow them."

"To where?" she asked.

"Where they can snort up the shit." He trotted after the pair, clad only in his boxers. The two creatures were nearing the top of the rise.

"Greedy motherfuckin' zombies!" McMillan exclaimed. He looked around and spied a rock about the size of his fist. He picked it up and threw it, hitting the bell-bottom zombie in the back.

The thing turned around, growling and flailing his arms. He charged at them and Holmes grabbed the shotgun out of Corso's hand, swinging the stock at the thing's head. This knocked loose some gray, dry flesh, but it kept coming. Holmes made to swing again and the creature caught the weapon and snatched it out of his hands. He broke it apart by banging it against a thick tree trunk. As this transpired, Afro zombie made it over the top and disappeared.

"Get the coke," Holmes directed McMillan. "We'll take care of this undead shithead."

"Don't have to tell me twice." McMillan went wide when the zombie lunged for him, but as its muscles were atrophied and its joints long since dried out, it couldn't move with the attenuation and speed of a live person. McMillan got past and went up.

Holmes shot the zombie again and it turned toward him, snarling at the continuing irritation of Holmes putting bullets into it. "I need an axe or something to cut the head off or burn it," Holmes said.

"I'm with you, Spree," Corso declared.

They exchanged a quick, meaningful look, then the thing was upon them, clawing and snapping its jaw. Holmes was down on his back and he drove a fist into the creature's rib cage. Some of the brittle bones cracked, but it was taking all of Holmes's effort to keep the monster from biting into his head. He had both hands pressed under what was left of the zombie's clacking jaw, the rancid breath making his eyes water. The stitches on his wound ripped and he pumped red from atop his shoulder blade.

"Get off!" Corso screamed, jumping on the zombie's back and pummeling him.

"*Coke*," the creature intoned. It reached around and pulled Corso off by her hair and flung her away. It got its bony hands around Holmes's neck and squeezed, causing him to gag. The zombie's jaws opened and unhinged, and the thing bent down to eat the man's face off.

"Hey, shit-breath!" Ella Fernandez hollered. She brought the Jack Daniel's bottle down on its head. The thick glass broke apart, causing a dent in the side of the creature's skull. The alcohol spilled over its upper body.

"I got something for you, dead bitch," Fernandez avowed as the zombie started for her. She lit the Zippo and threw it on him, catching his head on fire. The zombie wailed and stomped about.

"I guess it doesn't like fire," Holmes observed in his grass-smeared Fruit of the Looms. The zombie was running around in a circle, screaming. It bumped into a tree and knocked itself down. But it didn't have enough presence of mind—or enough of a brain left—to roll and put out its now totally aflame body. It got back up and screamed some more as it clomped around, continuing to burn.

Corso helped Holmes to his feet. "Or it's the way he died," she said.

Fernandez breathed deeply, her heavy breasts rising and falling, the flamingo contracting and expanding. She was still only dressed in her panties.

"Good work, Ella," Holmes told her. He then asked Corso, "What do you mean?"

She started to run up the hill without answering. "We better get up there."

"The ya-yo," Holmes remembered, as he and Fernandez also took off. At the top it was a regular zombie jamboree. There were eight more of them that had crawled out of their graves, all dressed in disco regalia.

A female zombie milled about in what was left of a miniskirt. She wore torn fishnet stockings over charred legs, and a stretch velour top hugged a worm-infested chest. Another was clad in a spangle-studded safari suit and a broad-brimmed pimp hat. Part of his entrails hung from a gap in his silk shirt. Yet another was in hot pants, thigh-high platform boots, and her angel-sleeve blouse was being ripped off by another zombie in a poncho, gaucho pants, and dingo boots.

The zombies were growling and snarling and tearing at each other to get to the cocaine.

"Holy shit." Holmes held his head, ignoring his freshly opened wound, and marched around in total befuddlement. "What the fuck?"

Corso gulped. "They're the ones who were killed in the fire."

"What are you talking about, Janey?" Fernandez asked.

"New Year's Eve, 1980."

The miniskirted zombie had pulled the arm off the one in the gaucho pants and was beating him with it. "*Coke, coke,*" she repeated, as she drove the other one to the ground.

"Some local talent built a club down here, inspired by Donna Summer, Studio 54, you know, all that," Corso said.

Holmes stopped pacing. "There used to be a disco here?"

"Yeah. It was called, and this would prove to be ironic, the Disco Inferno. From what I understand, it was a popular place from 1976, when it started, to the night it burned down."

"The Bicentennial till the death of disco," Holmes gasped. Not a religious sort, he nonetheless sent a prayer up that the sky would rain gas and the Lord would then add a few lightning bolts to set the zombies ablaze.

Fernandez said, "You must have been a kid then."

"She was old enough," Holmes grinned wanly, grabbing some foliage to light with the recovered Zippo. He had to save his score.

"I'd already run off, wound up in L.A. Got involved with a creep that strung me out and pimped me out to this porn fuck. Even better that I was underage." Despite the humidity, she wrapped her arms around herself. "That's when I met Spree. The man in the white Charger—with a four on the floor."

Holmes gazed at her through the small fire he'd started with his crummy torch. "It was your ass that mesmerized me." With that, he ran into the thatch of zombies, but they were fevered and ignored his pathetic flame as they tore and ate into each other. He found McMillan on the ground, shivering.

"Aghhh," he grimaced when Holmes tugged on him. "Fucking freaks broke my arm." He got up, staring. "We're fucked."

The zombie in the thigh-high boots had jumped on the back of another who wore a torn gold-lamé cape. The cape man had gotten ahold of one of the bricks, or what had been the brick. He dipped his face into the powder, snorting madly like Pacino in *Scarface*. Thigh-high ripped the top of his head off and bit into his pulsing brain. She gobbled up pieces of the matter. The two stumbled about in stoned nirvana.

Holmes's flame petered out. "This ain't right," he lamented. "We gotta save our shit."

"Forget it, Spree," Corso advised, joining him. "These monsters will tear you apart if you get between them and their coke."

"It's not theirs!" he cried.

"It is now," Corso declared.

"'Fraid she's right," McMillan agreed, holding his busted arm. "Crider's spell or mojo or whatever the hell it was has us whupped good."

One of the zombies teetered on its feet, snow powdering its decomposed face. It ran into a tree and started to bang its head against the trunk so fiercely that it broke its face open. It continued hitting its head against the tree, smearing gore over the bark.

"Shit," Holmes swore. "Shit." He stomped about in frustration.

The zombies fought and scratched and snorted and mutilated each other until body parts were littered among the overgrown grass. Even legless zombies crawled their torsos over to any patch of flake on the ground to snort. The moon shone pregnant and brilliantly yellow against the warm night air.

Watching this, the four were soon witness to the actions of the last two zombies left standing. One was the creature with the nasty Afro and the other the ghastly one in the miniskirt. They each pulled on the end of a piece of plastic—a clump of the white stuff clung to the material. They stood among the battered and deformed heads, smashed eyeballs, torn-out tongues, broken teeth, severed fingers, cracked mood rings, ankh and cross ornaments, and knit caps of the walking disco dead.

Several of the disconnected heads mumbled, *"Coke, coke,"* over and over again, as a few of the mutilated hands crept across the ground in search of any fine white crystals left.

Meanwhile, miniskirt had an arm around Afro zombie's neck and was gnawing on his ear as he ignored her and snorted his treasure of blow. He then turned and bit into her face and the two bearhugged each other and rolled down the opposite side of the hill to a tributary of the river. Their bodies broke against a cropping of rocks, yet they continued to claw and rend each other.

Holmes wanted to cry. Corso consoled him as the four trudged back to the house. Each step along the way, all except Holmes grew slowly elated and pumped, having survived a vicious zombie attack.

"Come on, baby," Corso told a brooding Holmes back at the house. "I got something that will make you forget all about those funky zombies." And they made loud, rough love that left them both satisfied and weak, as was the same for McMillan and Fernandez. Fortunately for McMillan, his arm was merely wrenched, and he was able to use both hands to further explore the woman's body.

In the morning they ate well and Holmes and McMillan talked over other sources for some blow, given they still had their cash. Corso had declined any money.

"I'll call you."

"Liar."

"No," Holmes said, as they stood outside her house in the morning. "We connected again."

She kissed him.

Holmes and McMillan had started for their car when they spotted Wild Willie shambling from around a corner of the house. That he was dead was obvious from the hyperextended eyes, gray flesh, and festering leg with flies buzzing around it.

He sprayed bullets from his AK, all the while grunting, *"Coke, coke, give me my coke back,"* as the Tramps could be heard singing, *"Burn that mutha down,"* from their song, "Disco Inferno."

THE
SPEED
CHRONICLES

EDITED BY **JOSEPH MATTSON**

The Speed Chronicles is also available as an ebook:

www.amzn.to/19X3zfE (Kindle)
www.bit.ly/16fOre8 (epub)

*This book is dedicated to the liver—
the vital organ and the daring spirit*

CONTENTS

It shines in Paradise. It burns in Hell.
—Gaston Bachelard, *The Psychoanalysis of Fire*

I started hearing whispers from the people in the bedspread and in the window glass, and though I was a little embarrassed at first, I answered them, thinking, why deny anything?
—William S. Burroughs, Jr., *Speed*

The Bible never said anything about amphetamines.
—"Fast" Eddie Felson in *The Color of Money*

introduction
some gods, some panthers
by joseph mattson

Because some gods made work, ennui, depression, deadlines, and pain, and some gods (perhaps the selfsame mothers) made adventure, rapture, elation, creativity, and orgasm—and especially because some gods made dopamine—some gods made speed. The answer to some deserts is some jungles. While some panthers skulk breathily to rest after the hunt, some panthers hide out in the bush mad to live, licking their chops along with their wounds, transforming lovely day into lustful night, and they do speed.

Speed: the most demonized—and misunderstood—drug in the land. Deprived of the ingrained romantic mysticism of the opiate or the cosmopolitan chic of cocaine or the commonplace tolerance of marijuana, there is no sympathy for this devil. Yet speed—amphetamines (Dexedrine, Benzedrine, Adderall) and especially methamphetamine[*]; crystal, crank, ice, chickenscratch, Nazi dope, OBLIVION marching powder, the *go fast*—is the most American of drugs: twice the productivity at half the cost, and equal opportunity for all. It *feels* so good and *hurts* so bad. From its dueling roots of pharmacological miracle

[*] Though MDMA/Ecstasy is chemically part of the amphetamine family, it has a singular place in the world and deserves a collection of its own (the forthcoming *The Ecstasy Chronicles*) and is not covered in the following stories. Conversely, Provigil (modafinil), while not structurally a part of the amphetamine family, is included for its eerily similar functionality to pharmaceutical amphetamines—new speed that works in part like old speed, and neoteric enough to find a home here.

cure and Californian biker gang scourge to contemporary Ivy League campuses and high school chem labs, punk rock clubs to the military industrial complex, suburban households to tin-can ghettos, it crosses all ethnicities, genders, and geographies—from immigrants and heartlanders punching double factory shifts to clandestine border warlords undermining the DEA, doctors to bomber pilots, prostitutes to housewives, T-girls to teenagers, Academy Award–nominated actors to the poorest Indian on the rez—making it not only the most essentially American narcotic, but the most deceivingly sundry literary matter.

Some shoot for angst-curing kicks, some snort for sad endurance, some for explosive joyrides into the unknown, because no matter how delicious dying young might seem, they want to live forever.

The subject of speed is so innately intimidating yet so undeniably present that it begs to be written about. It is no secret that the drug has historically tuned up the lives of writers, including Jack Kerouac, Susan Sontag, Philip K. Dick, and scores more. Too rarely, though, has it been written of, and as California and the West, the Pacific Northwest, and now the Midwest, the South, and the East Coast toss for the crown of Speed Capital, U.S.A., its jolt to the bones of the American landscape continues to peak as it creeps onward into the farthest nooks of our physiography and consciousness. Wherever there is either something *or* nothing to do—wherever there is need for more gasoline on the fire—there is speed.

The majority of you, dear readers, have likely seen before-and-after anti-meth photo campaigns and have been at least brushed if not inundated with depictions of the horrors of the Crystal Death, but speed, like all sources of addiction, whether any of the brethren narcotics or food, sex, consumerism, and otherwise, is initially a wellspring for bliss. There are *reasons* people are willing to put the residue of acetone, lithium batteries, the red phosphorus of match heads, and other inorganic and toxic compounds the liver is not sure what to do with into their bodies: *It feels good. You get results.* The ancient longing to inhabit supernatural powers and kiss the orbits of gods is realized. The panther becomes superpanther with the rifle of a medicine cabinet. Anything is possible (giving credence to the old slogan, *Speed Kills*—rarely is ingesting speed a mortal wound; respectively, more people die or equally damage themselves from the feral, madcap things they do *on* speed than from the toxicity of the drug itself—except, of course, the lifers). Yes, it gets ugly, so ugly. But before your sex organs revert to embryonic acorns and your teeth fall out and feasting on your malnutrition are insects for your eyes only, it's a rush of pure euphoria and a seeming godsend to surmount all of life's daily tribulations.

Some panthers' antiphon to some gods' will.

Because speed is first and foremost an amplifier, the sparking ebullience and potential wretchedness it projects are possibilities already seeded in the human order, just waiting for the right drop of dew and hit of sunshine to come along and juice it up.

The fourteen stories in this book reflect not only both ends of the dichotomy above, but, more crucially, the abstractions within and between. Merely demonizing the drug would be the same crime as simply celebrating it. Condemning it outright and defending all recreational use are equal failures against illuminating the drug's complexity. The panther worships the god in a kaleidoscopic mayhem of alchemical felicity, and in real sorrow too. Though you'll find exultation and condemnation interwoven, these are no stereotypical tales of tweakers—the element of crime and the bleary-eyed zombies that have gone too far are here right alongside heart-wrenching narratives of everyday people, good intentions gone terribly awry, the skewed American Dream going up in flames, and even some accounts of unexpected joy. Juxtaposed with circumstances inherent to the drug (trying to score, the sheer velocity of uptake, the agony of withdrawal, death, etc.) are nuances often elusive but central to speed's mores: camaraderie, compassion, and charm.

Together with Scott Phillips's tale of Frank Sinatra's mummified penis as leverage in a surreptitious bulk cold medicine deal and Kenji Jasper's meth murder-run by way of Capitol Hill, you'll find Megan Abbott's benevolent doctor injecting fast relief into disenchanted townsfolk and Jess Walter's bumbling brothers-in-arms too innocuous for high crime. With Jerry Stahl's no-punches-pulled, I mean *the* de facto nightmare scenarios through amphetamine hell, and my own rendering of Hollywood psychosis (the district in Los Angeles and, in part, its Tinseltown abstract) gone to fanatics and sacrificial death-dogs, you'll find William T. Vollmann's empathetic transsexual portrait of meth as vitamin supplement and Beth Lisick's suburban housewife's giddy eagerness for validity and subsequent triumph. There's James Franco's metafictional take on the cautionary tale and Rose Bunch's story of Ozark yard wars together with Tao Lin's disaffected New York City hipsters quietly pandering for significance and Natalie Diaz's haunting embrace of a sibling addict; Sherman Alexie's meth-induced war dancer razing everything in his path, and James Greer's investigation of the existential magical realism inherent in eliminating sleep from one's diet.

I thank the authors—gods some, panthers some, and titans all—for their incredible contributions. The dream roster has come to fruition, and I remain ever humbled and appreciative of their interest, generosity, trust, and guts to tango with the beast.

Because some gods have ridden the rails, some panthers rail the ride, 'scripts and spoons and straws raised like torches to Rome. Let us now go unto stories of them and those whose lives they touch—let's go fast.

Joseph Mattson
Los Angeles
September 2011

PART I

MADNESS

NATALIE DIAZ was born and raised in the Fort Mojave Indian Village in Needles, California. She is Mojave and Pima. After playing professional basketball in Europe and Asia, she completed her MFA degree at Old Dominion University. She lives in Mohave Valley, Arizona, and directs a language revitalization program, working to document the few remaining Elder Mojave speakers. Her poetry and fiction has been published in the *Iowa Review*, *Bellingham Review*, *Prairie Schooner*, *Crab Orchard Review*, *Narrative*, *North American Review*, *Nimrod*, and others. Her first poetry book is forthcoming from Copper Canyon Press.

how to go to dinner with a brother on drugs
by natalie diaz

f he is wearing knives for eyes, if he has dressed for a Day of the Dead parade—three-piece skeleton suit, cummerbund of ribs—his pelvic girdle will look like a Halloween mask.

"The bones," he'll complain, make him itch. "Each ulna a tickle." His mandible might tingle.

He cannot stop scratching, so suggest that he change, but not because he itches—do it for the scratching. Do it for the bones.

"Okay, okay," he'll give in, "I'll change." He will return to his room, and as he climbs each stair, his back will be something else—one shoulder blade a failed wing, the other a silver shovel. He has not eaten in months. He will never change.

Still, you are happy he didn't come down with a headdress of green quetzal feathers, iridescent plumes dancing like an emerald blaze from his forehead, and a jaguar-pelt loincloth littered with mouth-shaped rosettes—because this beautiful drug usually dresses him up like a greed god, and tonight you are not in the mood to have your heart ripped out. Like the bloody-finger trick your father constructed for you and your brothers and sisters every Halloween—cut a hole in a small cardboard jewelry gift box, hold it in the palm of your hand, stick your middle finger up through the hole, pack gauze inside the box around your middle finger, cover the gauze and your finger in ketchup, shake a handful of dirt onto your finger, and then hold it up, your bloody-ketchup finger, to every person you see, explaining that you found it out in the road—it has gotten old, having your heart ripped out, being opened up that way.

He comes back down, this time dressed as a Judas effigy. "I know, I know," he'll joke, "It's not Easter. So what?"

Be straight with him. Tell him the truth. Tell him, "Judas had a rope around his neck."

When he asks if an old lamp cord will do, just shrug. He will go back upstairs, and you will be there, close enough to the door to leave, but you will not. You will wait, unsure of what you are waiting for. While you wait, go to the living room of your parents' home-turned-misery-museum. Explore the perpetual exhibits—"Someone Is Tapping My Phone," "*Como Deshacer a Tus Padres*," "*Mon Frère*"—ten, twenty, forty dismantled phones displayed on the dining table, red and blue wires snaking in and out, glinting snarls of copper, yellow computer chips, soft sheets of numbered rubber buttons, small magnets, jagged, ruptured shafts of lithium batteries, shells of Ataris, radios, and television sets cracked open like dark nuts, innards heaped across the floor. And by far the most beautiful, "Why Dad Can't Find the Lightbulbs"—a hundred glowing white bells of gutted lightbulbs, each rocking in a semicircle on the counter beneath your mom's hanging philodendron.

Your parents' home will look like an Al Qaeda yard sale. It will look like a bomb factory, which might give you hope, but you ought to know better than to hope. You are not so lucky—there is no fuse for you to find. For you and your family, there will be no quick ticket to Getaway Kingdom.

Think, all of this glorious mess could have been yours—not long ago, your brother lived with you. What was it you called it? "One last shot," a three-quarter-court heave, a buzzer-beater to win something of him back. But who were you kidding? You took him into your home with no naïve hopes of saving him, but instead to ease the guilt of never having tried.

He spent every evening in your bathroom with a turquoise BernzOmatic handheld propane torch, a meth-made Merlin mixing magic, chanting, "I will show you fear in a handful of dust," then shape-shifting into lions and tigers and bears and pacing your balcony, licking the air at your neighbors' wives and teenage daughters, fighting with the Hare in the Moon, conquering the night with his blue flame, and plotting to steal your truck keys, which you kept under your pillow.

Finally, you worked up the nerve to ask him to leave. He took his propane torch and left you with a Glad trash bag of filthy clothes and a meth pipe clanking in the dryer. Two weeks after that, God told him to do several things that got him arrested.

But since he is fresh-released from prison and living in your parents' home, you will be there to take him to dinner—because he is your brother, because you heard he was cleaning up. Mostly because you think you can handle dinner, a thing with a clear beginning and end, a specified amount of time, a ritual that everyone knows, even your brother. Sit down. Eat. Get up. Go home. You are optimistic about this well-now-that's-done-and-I'm-glad-it's-over kind of night.

If your brother doesn't come back down right away, if he takes his time, remember how long it took for the Minotaur to escape the labyrinth, and go to the sliding-glass window looking out onto the backyard. This is the exhibit whose fee is always too high, the reason you do not come to this place: your parents.

Your father will be out there, on the other side of the glass, wearing his *luchador* mask. He is *El Santo*. His face is pale. His face is bone white. His eyes are hollow teardrops. His mouth is a dark "Oh." He has worn it for years, still surprised by his life.

Do not even think of unmasking your father. That mask is the only fight he has left in him. He is all out of *planchas* and *topes.* He has no more *huracanranas* to give. Besides, *si tuvieras una máscara*, you would wear it.

Your father, *El Santo*, will pile mesquite logs into a pyre. Your mother will be out there too—wearing her sad dress made of flames—practicing lying on top of the pyre.

"It needs to be higher," she'll complain, "I've earned it."

See the single tower of hyacinth she clutches to her breast as she whispers to the violet petals, *"Ai, ai,* don't cry. *No hay mal que dure cien años."* But the hyacinth will already have gone to ash, and knowing she is talking to herself, your throat will sting.

Your father will answer her as always, "Oh," which means he is imagining himself jumping over a top rope, out of the ring, running off, his silver-masked head cutting the night like a butcher knife.

Do not bother pounding against the glass. They will not look up. They know they cannot answer your questions.

Your brother will eventually make his way down to the front door. The lamp cord knotted at his neck should do the trick, so head to the restaurant.

In the truck, avoid looking at your brother dressed as a Judas effigy, but do not forget that a single match could devour him like a neon tooth, canopying him in a bright tent of pain—press the truck lighter into the socket.

The route will take you by a destroyed field—only months before, that earth was an explosion of cotton hulls—your headlights will slice across what remains of the wasted land, illuminating bleached clods of dirt and leftover cotton snagged here and there on a few wrecked stalks. The only despair greater than this field will be sitting next to you in the truck—his eyes are dark but loud and electric, like a cloud of locusts conducting a symphony of teeth. Meth—his singing siren, his jealous jinni conjuring up sandstorms within him, his harpy harem—has sucked the beauty from his face. He is a Cheshire Cat. His new face all jaw, all smile and bite.

Look at your brother. He is Borges's bestiary. He is a zoo of imaginary beings.

When he turns on the radio, "Fire" or "Manic Depression" will boom out. He will be your personal Jimi Hendrix. No, he will be your personal Geronimo playing air drums for Jimi Hendrix—large brown hands swooping and fluttering in rhythm against the dashboard like bats trapped in the cab of your truck, black hair whipping in the open window, tangling at the ends and sticking to the corners of his wide-open mouth shiny as a freshly dug hole, wet teeth flashing in the rearview mirror as he bobs his head to the beat.

Sigh. He is not Geronimo. Geronimo held out much longer. Your brother has clearly given up.

The sun is bound to lose its grip on the horizon, and when it does, the sky will burn red. It will be something you understand.

Search the road for something dead—to remind you that he is still alive, that you are ungrateful—a skunk whose head is matted to the faded asphalt, intestines ballooning from a quick strip of black and white like a strange carmine bloom.

"This is what it's like," you'll say aloud, "to be splayed open," but you will mean, *This is what it's like to rest.*

He will not hear you over the war party circling his skull—horses, hooves, drums, and whooping. *"Ai, ai, ai."* He will smell the skunk and say, "Smells like *carne asada*."

Your brother's jaw will become a third passenger in your truck—it will flex in the wind, resetting and rehinging, opening and closing against his will. It will occur to you that your brother is a beat-down, dubbed Bruce Lee—his words do not match his mouth, which is moving faster and faster. He is the fastest brother alive.

The next thing you'll know, you and your brother will be on Han's island, trapped in a steel chamber—being there with him, being there together, in that impossible cage, makes you root for him, makes you understand that you could lose him at any moment, so you love him.

When you were ten, your brother took you to the powwow down the street. He held your hand as you walked up to the open tailgates of the pickup-truck vendors and bought you and him each a pair of black wooden nunchucks with gold and green dragons up the sides. Bruce Lee was his hero. Back then, your brother was *Fists of Fury*. He was *Enter the Dragon*. He was *Game of Death I* and *II*. But back then was a long time ago. Now is now, and now you are here with a brother faster than Bruce Lee. Bruce Lee is dead. In a way, so is your brother. But you cannot forget how hard he practiced that summer. How he took his shirt off and acted out each scene in front of the bathroom mirror—touching his imaginary bloody lip with his fingertips, then tasting that imaginary blood, and making that "Wahhhh" Bruce Lee face as he swung his nunchucks over and under his shoulders. Remember the welts across his lower back and ribs? Remember how he cried when he hit himself in the chin?

Admit it—that was another brother. This brother is not Bruce Lee. This brother is Han. He is Han's steel chamber. Keep an eye on him—be prepared if he unscrews a metal hand at the wrist and replaces it with a metal bear claw. It would not shock you. He has done worse things. Face it. You are not here with him. You are here because of him. Do not be ashamed when it crosses your mind that you could end him quickly with a one-inch punch.

Your brother's lips are ruined. There is a sore in the right corner of his mouth. His teeth hurt, he says, his "dead mountain of carious teeth that cannot spit."

At the stop light, he will force you to look into his mouth. You hate his mouth. It is Švankmajer's rabbit hole—a bucket you've tripped over and fallen into for the last ten years. One of his teeth is cracked. He will want to go to the IHS dentist. "My teeth are falling out," he'll say, handing you a pointy incisor, telling you to put it under your pillow with your truck keys. When he says, "Make a wish," you will.

When you open your eyes, the light will be green, and he will still be there in front of you. His tooth will end up in the ashtray.

On the way there, he will wave to all the disheveled people walking along and across the roads—an itchy parade of twisting arms and legs pushing ratty strollers with big-headed, alien-eyed babies dangling rotten milk bottles over the stroller sides, a marching band of cheap cigarettes and dirty men and women disguised as an Exodus of rough-skinned Joshua trees, whose grinning mouths erupt in clouds of brown yucca moths that tick and splatter against your windshield.

Take a deep breath. You will be there soon.

Pull into the restaurant parking lot. Your brother will not want to wear his shoes inside. "Judas was barefoot," he will tell you.

"Judas wore sandals," you answer.

"No, Jesus wore sandals," he'll argue.

Not in that moment, but later, you will manage to laugh at the idea of arguing with a meth-head dressed like a Judas effigy about Jesus wearing sandals.

Night will be full-blown by the time you enter the restaurant— stars showing through like shotgun spread. Search your torso for a wound, a brother-shaped bullet hole pulsing like a Jesus side wound beneath your shirt. Even if you don't find it, remember that there are larger injuries than your own—your optimistic siblings, all white-haired and doubled over their beds, lost in great waves of prayer, sloshing in the belly of a dark whale named Monstruo, for this man who is half—wooden boy half-jackass.

Your brother will still itch when you are seated at your table. He will rake his fork against his skin. If you look closely, you will see that his skin is a desert—half a red racer is writhing in the middle of the long road of his forearm, a migration of tarantulas moves like a shadow across his sunken cheek.

Slide your fork and knife from the table. Hold them in your lap.

He will set his hands on the table—two mutts sleeping near the salsa, twitching with dreams of undressing cats.

He will lick his shattered lips at the waitress every time she walks by. He will tell you, then her, that he can taste her. If you are lucky, she will ignore him.

Pretend not to hear what he says. Also, ignore the cock crowing inside him, but if he notices that you notice, "Don't worry," he'll assure you, "the dogs will get it."

"Which dogs?" you have to ask.

Your brother will point out the window at two dogs humping in an empty lot across the way—slick pink tongues rolling and unrolling, hips jerking and trembling. Go ahead. Look closer, then clarify to your brother, "Those are not dogs. Those are *chupacabras*."

"*Chupacabras* are not real," he'll tell you, "brothers are."

The reflection in your empty plate will speak: "Your brother is on drugs. You are at a dinner that neither of you can eat."

Consider your brother. He is dressed as a Judas effigy admiring a pair of fuck-sick *chupacabras*—one dragging the other across the parking lot.

The waitress will come to take your order. Your brother will ask for a beer. You will pour your thirty pieces of silver onto the table and ask, "What can I get for this?"

SHERMAN ALEXIE is the best-selling author of *War Dances,* winner of the PEN/Faulkner Award for Fiction. He is also the author of *Reservation Blues, Indian Killer, The Toughest Indian in the World, Ten Little Indians, Flight, The Lone Ranger and Tonto Fistfight in Heaven, The Business of Fancydancing,* and *The Absolutely True Diary of a Part-Time Indian,* winner of the National Book Award for Young People's Literature. Also a filmmaker, stand-up comic, and public speaker, Alexie lives in Seattle, WA, with his wife and two sons.

war cry
by sherman alexie

Forget crack, my cousin said, meth is the new war dancer.

World champion, he said.

Grand Entry, he said.

Five bucks, he said, give me five bucks and I'll give you enough meth to put you on a Vision Quest.

For a half-assed Indian, he sure talked full-on spiritual. He was a born-again Indian. At the age of twenty-five, he war danced for the first time. Around the same day he started dealing drugs.

I'm traditional, he said.

Rule is: whenever an Indian says he's traditional, you know that Indian is full of shit.

But not long after my cousin started dancing, the powwow committee chose him as Head Man Dancer. Meaning: he was charming and popular. Powwow is like high school, except with more feathers and beads.

He took drugs too, so he was doomed. But what Indian isn't doomed? Anyway, the speed made him dance for hours. Little fucker did somersaults. I've seen maybe three somersaulting war dancers in my own life.

You war dance that good, you become a rock star. You get groupies. The Indian women will line up to braid your hair.

No, I don't wear rubbers, he said, I want to be God and repopulate the world in my image. I wondered, since every Indian boy either looks like a girl or like a chicken with a big belly and skinny legs, how he could tell which kids were his.

Anyway, he was all sexed-up from the cradle.

He used to go to Assembly of God, but when he was fifteen, he made a pass at the preacher's wife. Grabbed her tit and said, I'll save you.

Preacher man beat the shit out of him, then packed up, and left the rez forever. I felt sorry for the wife, but was happy the preacher man was gone.

I didn't like him teaching us how to speak in tongues.

Anyway, after speed came the crack and it took hold of my cousin and made him jitter and shake the dust. Earthquake— his Indian name should have been changed to Earthquake. Saddest thing: powwow regalia looks great on a too-skinny Indian man.

Then came the meth.

Indian Health Service had already taken his top row of teeth and the meth took the bottom row.

Use your drug money to buy some false teeth, I said.

I was teasing him, but he went out and bought some new choppers. Even put a gold tooth in front like some kind of gangster rapper wannabe. He led a gang full of reservation-Indians-who-listened-to-hard-core-rap-so-much-they-pretended-to-be-inner-city-black. Shit, we got fake Bloods fake-fighting fake Crips. But they aren't brave or crazy enough to shoot at one another with real guns. No, they mostly yell out car windows. Fuckers are drive-by cursing.

I heard some fake gangsters have taken to throwing government commodity food at one another.

Yeah, my cousin, deadly with a can of cling peaches.

And this might have gone on forever if he'd only dealt drugs on the rez and only to Indians. But he crossed the border and found customers in the white farm towns that circled us.

Started hooking up the Future Farmers of America.

And then he started fucking the farmers' daughters.

So they busted him for possession, intent to sell, and statutory rape. Deserved whatever punishment was coming his way.

Hey, cousin, he said to me when I visited him in jail, they're trying to frame me.

You're guilty, I said, you did all of it, and if the cops ever ask me, I'll tell them everything I know about your badness.

He was mad at first. Talked about betrayal. But then he softened and cried.

You're the only one, he said, who loves me enough to tell the truth.

But I knew he was just manipulating me. Putting the Jedi shaman mind tricks on me. I wouldn't fall for that shit.

I do love you, I said, but I don't love you enough to save you.

As the trial was cooking, some tribal members showed up at the courthouse to demonstrate. Screaming and chanting about racism. They weren't exactly wrong. Plenty of Indians have gone to jail for no good reason. But plenty more have gone to jail for the exact right reasons.

It didn't help that I knew half of those protesters were my cousin's best customers.

But I felt sorry for the protesters who believed in what they were doing. Who were good-hearted people looking to change the system. Thing is: you start fighting for every Indian, you end up having to defend the terrible ones too.

That's what being tribal can do to you. It traps you in the teepee with murderers and rapists and drug dealers. It seems everywhere you turn, some felon-in-buckskin elbows you in the rib cage.

Anyway, after a few days of trial and testimony, when things were looking way bad for my cousin, he plea-bargained his way to a ten-year prison sentence.

Maybe out in six with good behavior. Yeah, like my cousin was capable of good behavior.

Something crazy: my cousin's name is Junior Polatkin, Jr. Yes, he was named for his late father, who was Junior Polatkin, Sr. Yeah, Junior is not their nicknames; Junior is their real names. So anyway, my cousin Junior Junior was heading to Walla Walla State Penitentiary.

Junior Junior at Walla Walla.

Even he thought that was funny.

But he was terrified too.

You're right to be scared, I said, so just find all the Indians and they'll keep you safe.

But what did I know? The only thing I knew about prison was what I saw on HBO, A&E, and MSNBC documentaries.

Halfway through his first day in the big house, my cousin got into a fight with the big boss Indian.

Why'd Junior fight him?

Because he was a white man, Junior said, as fucking pale as snow.

And he had blue eyes, Junior said.

My cousin wasn't smart enough to know about recessive genes and all, but he was still speaking some truth.

Anyway, it had to be shocking to get into prison, looking for group protection, and you find out your leader is a mostly white Indian boy.

I tried to explain, my cousin said, that I was just punching the white guy in him.

Like an exorcism, I said when he called me collect from the prison pay phone. I think jail is the only place where you can find pay phones anymore.

Yeah, Junior Junior said, I was trying to get the white out of him.

But here's the saddest thing: my cousin's late mother was white. A blond and blue-eyed Caucasian beauty. Yeah, my cousin is half-white. He just won the genetic lottery when he got the black hair and brown eyes. His late brother had the light skin and pale eyes. We used to call them Sunrise and Sundown.

Anyway, my cousin lost his tribal protection pretty damn quick, and halfway through his second day in prison, he was gang-raped by black guys. And halfway through his third day, those black dudes sold Junior Junior to an Aryan dude for a carton of cigarettes.

Two hundred cigarettes for the purchase of my cousin's body and soul.

It's cruel to say, but that doesn't seem near enough. If it's going to happen to you, it should cost a lot more, right?

But what do I know about prison economics? Maybe that was a good price. Well, I guess I was hoping it was a good price. Meaning: I was mourning the shit out of my cousin's spiritual death.

Here's the thing: my cousin was pretty. He had the long black hair and the skinny legs and ass. It didn't take much to make him look womanly. Just some mascara, lipstick, and prison pants cut into ragged cutoffs.

Suddenly, I'm Miss Indian U.S.A., he said.

I'm not gay, he said.

It's not about being gay, I said, it's about crazy guys trying to hurt you as much as possible.

Jesus, he said, all these years since Columbus landed and now he's finally decided to fuck me in the ass.

Yeah, we could laugh about it. What else were we going to do? If you sing the first note of a death song while you're in prison, you'll soon be singing the whole damn song every damn day.

For the next three years, I drove down to Walla Walla to visit

Junior once or twice a month. Then it became every few months. Then I stopped driving at all. I accepted his collect calls for the first five years or so, then either he stopped calling or I stopped taking his calls. Then he disappeared from my life.

Some things just happen. Some things don't.

My cousin served his full ten-year sentence, was released on a Monday, and had to hitchhike all the way back to our reservation.

He just showed up at the tribal café as I was eating an overcooked hamburger and greasy fries. Sat right down in the chair opposite me and smiled his bright white smile. New false teeth. Looks like he got one good thing out of prison.

Hey cousin, he said, all casual, like he'd been having dinner with me every day for the last decade.

So I said, trying to sound as casual, are you really free or did you break out?

I decided to bring my talents back to the rez, he said.

It was a hot summer day, but Junior Junior was wearing long sleeves to cover his track marks. Meaning: survival is an addiction too.

So pretty quickly we started back up our friendship. You could call us cousin-brothers or cousin–best friends. Either works. Both work. He never mentioned my absence from his prison life and I wasn't about to bring it up.

He got a job working forestry. Was pretty easy. There was nobody on the rez interested in punishing the already punished.

It's a good job, he said, I drive all the deep woods on the rez and mark trees that I think should be cut down.

Thing is, he said, we never cut down any trees, so my job is really just driving through the most beautiful place in the world while carrying a box full of spray paint.

He fell in love too, with Jeri, a white woman who worked as a nurse at the Indian Health Service Clinic. She was round and red-faced, but funny and cute and all tender in the heart, and everybody on the rez liked her. So it felt like a slice of redemption pie.

She listens to me, Junior Junior said, you know how hard that is to find?

Yeah, I said, but do you listen to her?

Junior shrugged his shoulders. Meaning: Of course I don't listen to her. I've had to keep my mouth shut for ten years. It's my turn to talk.

And talk he did.

He told me everything about how he sexed her up. Half of me wanted to hear the stories and half of me wanted to close my ears. But I didn't feel like I could stop him, either. I felt so guilty that I'd abandoned him in prison. I felt like I owed him a little bit of patience and grace.

But it was so awful sometimes. He was already sex-drunk when he went into prison, and being treated as a fuck-slave for ten years turned him into something worse. I don't have a name for it, but he talked about sex like he talked about speed and meth and crack and heroin.

She's my pusher, he said about Jeri, and her drug is her love.

Except he didn't say "love." He used another word that I can't say aloud. He reduced Jeri all the way down to the sacred parts of her anatomy. And those parts stop being sacred when you talk such blasphemy about them.

Maybe he didn't fall in love, I thought. Maybe he's time-traveling her back to prison with him.

But I also wondered what Jeri was doing with him. From the outside, she looked solid and real, like a soft dam on the river, but I guess she was a flood of shit inside. Meaning: if enough men hurt you when you're a child, you'll seek out hurtful men when you become an adult.

Talk about a Vision Quest. Jeri's spirit animal was a cannibal coyote.

Things went on like this for a couple years. He started punching her in the stomach; she hid those bruises and punched him into black eyes that he carried around like war paint.

Fucking Romeo and Juliet, my cousin said.

Yeah, like he'd ever read the book or watched any of those movies for more than ten minutes.

Then, one day, Jeri disappeared.

Rumor had it she went into one of those battered women programs. Rumor also had it she was hiding in Spokane. Which, if true, was pretty stupid. How can you hide in the City of Spokane from a Spokane Indian?

He found her in a 7-Eleven in the Indian part of town.

Yeah, as scared as she was, she was still hiding among Indians. Yeah, we're addictive. You have to be careful around us because we'll teach you how to cry epic tears and you'll never want to stop.

Anyway, you might think he wanted to kill her. Or break some bones. But no, he was crazy in a whole different way. In the aisle of that 7-Eleven, he dropped to his knees and asked for her hand in marriage.

Really.

He proclaimed it just like that too.

May I have your hand in marriage? he said to her.

So they got married; I was the best man.

In the parking lot after the ceremony, Junior and Jeri smoked meth with a bunch of toothless wonders.

Fucking zombies walking everywhere on the rez.

Monster movie all the time.

A thousand years from now, archaeologists are going to be mystified by all the toothless skulls they find buried in the ancient reservation mud.

There was no honeymoon. What rez Indian can afford such a thing? They did spend a night in the tribal casino. That's free for any Indian newlyweds. Mighty generous, I guess, letting tribal members sleep free in the casino they're supposed to own.

They moved into a trailer house down near Tshimakain Creek and they got all happy and safe for maybe six months.

Then one night, after she wouldn't have sex with him, he punched her so hard that he knocked out her front teeth.

That was it for her.

She left him and lived on the rez in plain sight. All proud for leaving, she mocked him by carrying her freedom around like her own kind of war paint. And I loved her for it.

Stand up, woman, I thought, stand up and kick the shit out of your demons.

Junior seemed to accept it okay. I should've known better, but he talked a good line of shit.

Like the poet wrote, he said, nothing gold can stay.

Robert Frost! My cousin was quoting Robert Frost! I guess he truly earned that GED he got in prison.

Late at night, when I'm trying to sleep, I think of all the ways things could have gone. How things could have been better. But in reality, there's only one way it went.

Jeri fell in love with the white dude we called Dr. Scalpel, though he went by Dr. Bob. He was the half-assed general practitioner who also worked at the Indian clinic and was just counting the days until he paid off his scholarship and could flee the rez. In the meantime, he'd found a warm body to keep him warm through the too-many-damn-Indians night.

Everybody deserves love. Well, most everybody deserves love. And Jeri certainly needed some brightness, but Dr. Bob was all dark and bitter and accelerated. He punched her in the face on their third date.

Ten minutes after we heard the news, Junior and I were speeding toward Dr. Bob's house located right next to the rez border down near the Spokane River. Yeah, he had to live on the rez, but he'd only live fifteen feet past the border.

I'm going to fuck him up, Junior said, you can't be hitting my woman.

I just rode along and never brought up the fact that Junior had hit his woman plenty of times. Yeah, I was riding shotgun for a woman-beating man looking to get revenge on another woman-beating man.

I should have been stronger. I should have been stronger. Meaning: I was kicking my face punched by my shame.

I kept thinking: Junior went to prison. He was a victim. And I ignored him. I let him suffer alone. So maybe it's okay if I let him punch Dr. Bob a few times. Maybe a little bit of violence will prevent a whole lot of violence.

But it doesn't work that way. Nowhere in human history has a small act of violence prevented larger acts from happening.

Small pain gets infected and causes big pain.

All the while he was driving, Junior was snorting whatever he could find within arm's reach. I think he snorted up some spilled sugar and salt. Any powder was good. So he was amped, he was all feedback and static, when we arrived at Dr. Bob's door.

Junior raced ahead of me and rhino-charged into the house. And once inside, he pulled a pistol from somewhere and whipped Dr. Bob across the face.

A fucking .45!

I'd seen tons of hunting rifles on the rez, but I'd never seen a pistol.

Junior whipped Dr. Bob maybe five times across the face and then kicked him in the balls and threw him against the wall. And Dr. Bob, the so-called healer, slid all injured and bloody to the floor.

You do not fuck with my possessions, Junior said to Bob.

There it was. The real reason for all of this. It was hatred and revenge, not love. Maybe at that point, all Junior could see was that Aryan who'd raped him a thousand times. Maybe Junior could only see the white lightning of colonialism. I don't mean to get so intellectual, but I'm trying to explain it to you. I'm trying to explain myself to myself.

I watched Junior lean over and slap Dr. Bob three or four times.

He's had enough, I said, let's get out of here.

Junior stood and laughed.

Yeah, he said, this fucker will never hit another woman again.

We walked toward the door together. I thought it was over. But Junior turned back, pressed that pistol against Bob's forehead, and pulled the trigger.

I will never forget how that head exploded.

It was like a comet smashing through a planet.

I couldn't move. It was the worst thing I'd ever seen. But then Junior did something worse. He flipped over the doctor's body, pulled down his pants and underwear, and shoved that pistol into Bob's ass.

Even then, I knew there was some battered train track stretching between Junior's torture in prison and this violation of Bob's body.

No more, I said, no more.

Junior stared at me with such hatred, such pain, that I thought he might kill me too. But then that moment of rage passed and Junior's eyes filled with something worse: logic.

We have to get rid of the body, he said.

I shook my head. At least I think I shook my head.

You owe me, he said.

That was it. I couldn't deny him. I helped him clean up the

blood and bone and brain, and wrap Dr. Bob in a blanket, and throw him into the trunk of the car.

I know where to dump him, Junior said.

So we drove deep into the forest, to the end of a dirt road that had started, centuries ago, as a game trail. Then we carried Bob's body through the deep woods toward a slow canyon that Junior had discovered during his tree-painting job.

Nobody will ever find the body, he said.

As we trudged along, mosquitoes and flies, attracted by the blood, swarmed us. I must have gotten bit a hundred times or more. Soon enough, Junior and I were bleeding onto Bob's body.

Blood for blood. Blood with blood.

After a few hours of dragging that body through the wilderness, we reached Junior's canyon. It was maybe ten feet across and choked with brush and small trees.

He's going to get caught up on the branches, I said.

Jesus, I thought, now I'm terrified of my own logic.

Just throw him real hard, Junior said.

So we somehow found the strength to lift Dr. Bob above our heads and we hurled him into the canyon. His body crashed through the green and came to rest, unseen, somewhere below.

Maybe you want to say a few words, Junior said.

Don't be so fucking cruel, I said, we've done something awful here.

Junior laughed again.

As we trudged back toward the car, Junior started talking childhood memories. I don't want to bore you with the details but here's the meaning: He and I, as babies, had slept in the same crib, and we'd lost our virginities on the same night within five feet of each other, and now we had killed together, so we were more than cousins, more than best friends, and more than brothers. We were the same person.

Of course, I kept reminding myself that I didn't touch Dr. Bob. I didn't pistol whip him or punch him or slap him. And I certainly didn't shoot him.

But I was still guilty. I knew that. Though I couldn't figure out exactly what I was guilty of.

When we made it back to the car, Junior stopped and stared up at the stars newly arrived in the sky.

You're going to keep quiet about this, he said.

I stared at the pistol in his hand. He saw me staring at the pistol in his hand. I knew he was deciding whether to kill me or not. And I guess his love for me, or whatever it was that he called love, won him over. He turned and threw the gun as far as he could into the dark.

We drove back down that dirt road in silence. As he dropped me at my house, he cried a little, his first sign of weakness, and hugged me.

You owe me, he said again.

After he drove away, I climbed on the roof of my house. I don't know why I did that. It seemed like the right thing to do. Folks would later call me Snoopy, and I would laugh with them, but at the time it seemed like such an utterly serious act.

I suppose, even if it became funny later, that it was the ultimate serious act.

I needed to be in a place where I had never been before to think about the grotesquely new thing that had happened, and what I needed to do about it.

I don't know when I fell asleep, but I woke, cold and wet, the next morning, climbed off the roof, and went to the tribal police. A couple hours after I told them the story, the Feds showed up. And a few hours after that, I led them all to Dr. Bob's body.

Later that night, as the police lay siege to his trailer house, Junior shot himself in the head.

No way I'm going back to prison, he said.

I wasn't charged with any crime. I could have been, I suppose, and maybe should have been. But I guess I'd done the right thing, or maybe something close enough to the right thing.

And Jeri? She left the rez, of course. I hear she's working on another rez down south. I pray that she never falls in love again. I'm not blaming her for what happened. I just think she's better off alone. Who isn't better off alone?

I didn't go to Junior's funeral. I figured somebody might shoot me if I did. Most everybody thought I was evil for turning against Junior. Meaning: I was the bad guy because I betrayed another Indian.

And yes, it's true that I betrayed Junior. But if betrayal can be righteous, then I believe I was righteous. But who knows except God?

Anyway, in honor of Junior, I started war dancing. I had to buy my regalia from a Sioux Indian who didn't give a shit about my troubles, but that was okay. I think the Sioux make the best outfits anyway.

So I danced. Well, I practiced dancing first in front of a mirror. I'd put a powwow CD in my computer and I'd stumble in circles around my living room. After a few months of this, I got enough grace and courage to make my public debut.

It was a minor powwow in the high school gym. Just another social event during a boring early December.

At first, nobody recognized me. I'd war-painted my whole face black. I wanted to look like a villain, I guess.

Anyway, as I danced, a few women recognized me and started talking to everybody around them. Soon enough, the whole powwow knew it was me swinging my feathers. A few folks jeered and threw curses my way. But most just watched me. I felt the aboriginal heat of their eyes. And I started crying. I'd like to think that I was weeping for my lost cousin, but I think I was weeping for my whole tribe.

Francis Delia

JERRY STAHL is the author of six books, including the memoir *Permanent Midnight* (made into a movie with Ben Stiller and Owen Wilson) and the novels *I, Fatty* and *Pain Killers*. Formerly "culture" columnist for *Details*, Stahl's fiction and journalism has appeared in *Esquire*, the *New York Times*, and *The Believer*, among other places. Most recently, he wrote *Hemingway & Gellhorn*, starring Clive Owen and Nicole Kidman, for HBO. Currently, he is completing a novel, *Jumping from the H*, and working on a remake of *The Thin Man* with Johnny Depp.

bad
by jerry stahl

THE RUSH! THE TERROR! The acrid stink of your sweat soaking through furniture three blocks away! Speaking of stink—what *is* that? Did somebody piss under your arms? Is that possible? Could they have pissed in your armpits three weeks ago, and you just now noticed? Like, say, when you get in a cab, and the seat's wet after a pack of frat boys beer-up too hard and leave Bud puddles. Hop inside and—QUESTION: *why does your God hate you?*—you hear the splat when you hit the seat. But—ANSWER: *because you're a tweaker!*—you don't know you're full wet-ass till you squish out of the cab. ("People never call the police until it's wet-ass time." Al Pacino, *Sea of Love*.) Speed keeps you so clammy you can't feel damp. Just one of the many advantages!

Fucking alcoholics! Where's the dignity? Remember that dancer—Lola? Lurleen? Patricia?—with the misspelled devil ink on her neck. *HAIL SATIN!* "It's not a mistake, it's a statement!" It *was* Lurleen. She had some kind of jailhouse harelip that slurred her words to the left. "You ass-maggot, you think I'm a fucking *creatine?*" Upscale. After eleven vodka tonics you'd see day-workers hand her five sweaty dollar bills to lift her skirt and geeze in her labia, which weirdly resembled a gorilla ear. You'd seen one once, in a French Quarter voodoo store. It was supposed to bring its owner lifelong protection and success. From the moment the Sisters of Marie Laveau Gift Shop door hissed shut behind you,

you knew you should have bought the thing. Everything would have been different. Why are you such an asshole?

Are you crying?

Want to talk about how Lurleen (Darla? No, *Zelda*) would boot the vag-needle, let it stand up and quiver by itself, then grand finale with a Heimlich-like shudder and pass out forehead-first on the bar with the rig sticking out between her legs? The pink tip made it weirdly like a little dog's organ, aroused. (You suffer compulsive thoughts—sometimes just images—that you do not want to think, but cannot stop thinking. This is one of them.) Sometimes she'd wet herself. Who wouldn't? *"Five more bucks!"* she'd croak when she came to and saw her condition. (Remember when mysterious Chasids began to speak to you out of the ceiling? A rabbi would just appear: you'd realize you were staring at him, and that he was talking. You'd think, maybe he was *always* there. And it took THIS MUCH crystal to see him. The sad old shtetl eyes followed you from the TV as he spoke. Vaguely reassuring, vaguely menacing.) *Does your life ever feel like a continuum of one aberration, misreflected in a series of cracked rearview mirrors?* You'd think: misreflected? How lame. Then you'd rethink. He's right! Every speed-freak car you ever twitched in did have a crack in the rearview. (You once drove across the state of Utah, steering the wheel from the passenger side when the 300-pound Cherokee who picked you up hitchhiking snorted something that gave him a heart attack going ninety-five on an empty interstate. You couldn't move him, so you just steered until his husk of an Impala ran out of gas on I-15, outside of Bountiful.) All the tweak-mobiles had cracked rearview mirrors. How does that even happen *once? And how does Rabbi Bowlstein know?*

You don't even want to talk about this, but here you are, talking about it. *Keep babbling, Chatty Speed Guy. People are really into it. You're crushing them.* Sartre knew what hell was—and it wasn't other people. That's a mistranslation. His translator had the twitches from *le meth* and spilled *vin rouge* on the words *dans ta tete*. THE OTHER PEOPLE WERE IN YOUR HEAD. If you were on speed, you'd know what he knew: speed means being your own audience for the running commentary of death. Or worse than death. More of *this*. What you're feeling right now.

CRASHING 2: WHAT'S *THAT* LIKE? Remember how you felt the first time you couldn't get it up? The scalding rage. The way Cheeto-dry Cindy Carmunuci looked at you when you stopped trying to cram your sixteen-year-old shame-handle into her. Look at you. Twenty years later, the episode still has you assuming the Cringe Position. You raised your sweaty face, your eyes met hers, and she looked at you like you were some kind of a cripple. A *sex-gimp*. Crashing is that feeling. That kind of fun— some version of—nonstop. From the minute you wake up. (If you sleep, which you don't. You're not an amateur.) If you died and the coroner knew what he was doing, your cause of death would read: *Extreme Awareness*. Every conversation was toe-curling in real time, and worse when you relived it later, which you did, without surcease, even when you were having *another* conversation. There was the babbling in your head, the babbling from the person in front of you, and then all the Other Random Voices. You ceased to think. You only obsess.

WHAT PEOPLE WHO WERE NEVER ADDICTED DON'T UNDERSTAND. You did not do this shit for pleasure. You did it for relief. (Plus the voices. Did you mention them?

How you'd miss them when they were not around?) *But when it was working and you felt good and you were really smooook, when every cell in the universe was humming to you, in the key of happy hell, and you were humming with them—when that shit was going on, and you felt abso-fucking-lutely tingly-tits optimistic . . . it was . . . it was . . . it was . . . Shoot enough and the world whooshed to quiet, and you were content just to sit, maybe drool a little, calm as a hyperactive toddler after his first lick of a Ritalin lollipop. When that happened, you never thought: "I am only this optimistic and one-with-the-cosmos because I'm on amphetamines." When a drug works, you don't feel like you're on a drug. You're just focused and vaguely orgasmic. Body and brain in stunning sync, running full-throttle. One cunthair from complete loss of control, but perfectperfectperfect.*

WHAT A GOOD DRUG DOES. *Is make you believe perfection is what you are going to feel forever. Then take it away . . . Throw you out of the cushioned fun-car onto a rocky shoulder. Shrink your 900-page thoughts back to garble. De–Dorian Gray your brain. Which makes you go from want to need. ("Maybe things weren't moving fast, or maybe things were moving too fast. I don't even remember anymore. I had it made. And I woke up. One morning. I looked down. And fell off my life." Paul Newman, WUSA. Screenplay by Robert Stone.) This is what's making crashing so . . . uncomfortable. So disappointing. So—ARE YOU STILL TALKING?* Remember the fake punk in Berlin who bit off his finger?

Be honest, Sparkle-pony, how's your life going? Really? Have you looked in the mirror lately? No, really looked. Good for you. Hold onto that magic.

(Of course you have ADHD. It's not like there's not a medical reason to stand in a puddle and stick your finger in a socket.) You were talking about—what was her name? Not Lurleen, now that you think of it, it was something showbiz . . . Dee-Lay! Dee-Lilah! Dee-Neero, maybe? One of Dee-Neero's through-the-pantie shots ended up abscessing—giving her what she called "cauliflower vagina." "That's pretty good," you said. And she said she had a degree in English, but they didn't pay her to talk about Chaucer with her thong pulled sideways. Which—it made sense at the time—led to her splashing the customers way before the "Squirt Craze." Which you found out about thanks to the social elixir that was quality trailer-park methamphetamine. Which—are you going to do this all fucking night? Speed never made you smarter. It just let you be what you already were longer. It turbocharged stupid. (The weird thing about Dee, you just remembered, was that she wanted to have a stroke. *"Like, if I can shut off my whole left brain, it'd be just fucking BLISS."*) Her sometime boyfriend Donnie, who might have also been her brother, but said he was her agent, spent five hours explaining how he actually thought up the "Squirt" concept in your dealer's doublewide; a model so spectacularly lush it had a hot tub. Donnie was one of those Valley porn guys who had gone into "lawn care." Strictly legit. But still. Drunk, with some crank flecks in his *Magnum, P.I.* crumb-catcher, he'd go all misty-eyed. Sigh right at you over the tub-scum frothing his chin. You weren't supposed to get into hot tubs on amphetamines. Guys got heart attacks. So Donnie told you. A little too enthusiastically. "Time it well, you go right to the edge, kiss a coronary on the mouth . . ." Then, wrapped in a beach towel, he'd pull out his wallet and unfold a yellowed issue of the long defunct *L.A. Reader.* (He did this more than once, pretty much nightly.) Once he unfolded and smoothed it, he'd let you see the picture of him, the cover story, young and smiling, wearing the same hair as Harry Reems, posed in a Hawaiian shirt with his arm around what may or not may not have been an underage Tahitian woman. In the photo her red nails were visible, fingers wrapped up to the mouth blowjob-style around a swirly-glassed green bottle of old-fashioned Squirt soda pop. The headline's in BOLD LETTERS over his Reems hair: *NOT YOUR FATHER'S SQUIRT*. Under the soft drink, in smaller print, the kicker: *Is it marketing if my new wife does it?* Below that—and you remember, because you knew the guy whose uncle laid out the cover, a total crankaholic whose aorta was going to pop on a bus in three years—below that, in the so-small-only-speedfreaks-would-notice thought balloon superimposed over the Belle of the South Pacific: *Would you believe it, my little Roxy can write her name on the ceiling!* (There is a world of secret messages when you're really hitting the pep pills. Reality is a crossword puzzle you can solve in your head—until you forget what words are.)

It's like you're outside and it's ten in the morning, and the sun is just scorching the rubber T-shirt you never saw before in your life. Which you realize after you've been peeling it off for half a day is actually your skin. You take a deep breath, groan out a rush that makes your fingernails itch, and suddenly dialogue that explains everything is projected in the sky. The letters remind you of your father's eyes, except you don't feel the seething. *This is what this means*, the letters say. *That is what that means.* Did you mention how sometimes your eyes bleed? You could write a book about bleeding eyeballs. *The more that wants more wants more, and the more that can't do anymore wants more too.* One day you wake up and you're letting your appetite sign your checks. You know that feeling? What was my name again?

IN THE DE-SPEED WING

DAY ONE. You write a poem with doorbell and cerebellum appearing in the same sentence thirty-six times. They give you something for the shakes and put an ice cube in your mouth, which cracks badly at the corners. Your blood appears to be plaid.

DAY TWO. A counselor later to become famous in a rehab reality show keeps asking you in group what "your deal" is. After the fifth time, when he's standing right over you, you finally start to answer and he laughs and yells in your face from two inches away. *"Bullshit!"* It's not your fault there are secret webs between things; that with enough amphetamine in your system, you see DEEP AND MEANINGFUL PATTERNS among seemingly random phenomena. How it all CONNECTS. After that you think—*So what?*

You are tired of not being a centipede. You just want a patch of dirt, somewhere you do not have to keep pretending to know how to be human.

DAY THREE. Circle the date, you're well enough for restraints! A Kush-breath orderly straps you chest-and-ankles over the gurney blanket, then wheels you down the hall. He leans in, like he wants to smell you, so close you know if you inhale you're going to test positive for something. Maybe THC, maybe chlamydia. He kind of smile-whispers: *"The first word in boundaries is bound!"* His voice is half hard-core speedfreak, half twink Widmark, psycho-giggly Tommy Udo pushing an old wheelchair lady down the stairs. (Most people only have one half. Once you realize that, life is not necessarily easier, but it's explainable.) *They put fluorescent lights in the elevator to make you epileptic, then cure you with expensive stimulants.*

DAY FOUR. You see the albino. He had some kind of paint-thinner-methedrine incident in his mother's carnival. Grabbing men and women's palms on the midway, reading them and weeping: *You don't fucking want to know!* You can't remember if he's the one who hung himself or became regional vice president of Nabisco South America.

Once you start trying to control your feelings, you have already lost control. Shame is like a rush in the wrong direction. Are you saying you've never wanted to obliterate the history of your own mind? There was a rumor: the guy who really burned down the L.A. downtown library on April 29, 1986 was a peckerhead tweaker trying to fry Jews and Mexicans out of his brainpan. But that was then.

This is now: You climb Everest, then you do laundry for the rest of your life. (The first time you go to a laundromat, without speed, you hate that the spinning laundry is boring . . . It used to explain the universe. That's how you knew you were really off speed. You had no fucking clue about the universe, except that it made you self-conscious. Speed and laundromats. Because sometimes you just have to do something. And washing clothes is always the right thing to . . .)

Describe "the burden of nonstop awareness." Why? Just go look at the lights at Rite-Aid at four in the morning, when it's just you and the eighty-year-old security man watching a hunched-up guy with shades and a leg brace screw the top off his Robitussin DM, guzzle half a bottle like it's Thunderbird, then smack his lips and take off his sunglasses. Eyes that peeled back don't come without a lot of speed-work. You recognize each other like Masons. The pharmacist, whose nametag says Bairj Donabedian, *stares at you and picks up a telephone. When did life get this good?*

ALL FUCKED OUT AND STILL AWAKE. Why is everything you remember bad? Now it comes back to you. What was her name? The ex-lawyer who dragged her little boy to the motel. Gave the kid an already-colored-in Yogi Bear coloring book? Even after the boy'd gone through half the book, he still had this hopeful look on his face before he turned every page. You were all in this motel room with a dozen other versions of you. All white guys. All waiting. But you couldn't help notice this kid. Every time he turned a page on that coloring book, he had his crayon in the air, ready to go. And every time, he was just *shattered* when he saw that it was already colored on. *Have you ever seen a five-year-old age?*

You were just there to cop. But you saw anyway. Each filled-in Yogi and Boo-Boo killed the kid a little more . . . Watching this, even your cells hated themselves . . . (Just because you give somebody something for the first time doesn't make you responsible if what you give them destroys their entire life. Does it?) Carmine—that was her name. *Why do you do this to yourself?* Carmine gave the child to the grinning simp in the cowboy hat. And what did you do? (You could have said something. You didn't. If you were staring straight at a pedophile—and there had to be at least a *chance*—if you *were*, you had other priorities. But still . . .) There's right behavior. And behavior that's right on methamphetamine. You did your job! You took advantage—of *empathy!* You glared at the little boy's mother—if Carmine really was his mother, and not his pimp! You registered the youngster's wince when Smiling Cowboy Man plopped a hand on his hunched-up, scared-shitless little-boy shoulders. But while you glowered at the woman who handed him to strangers, as if she were somehow morally reprehensible, what did you do? You stole. You wet-fingered a wedge of fresh meth off the motel desk like you practiced with a speed-thief trainer. You glowered at Carmine while you stole her drugs. It was a kind of morality. Was it stealing if they didn't know you did it? How much of your mental activity is spent worrying what other people can see? Is it pathology? Or is it Memorex?

OBLIVION HAS NO NARRATIVE. Just because there's no plot does not mean the story can't get worse.

After questionable man and boy left, Carmine (Britt), who must have been triple-jointed, brazenly lifted a bare dirt-crusted foot up to her nose *unassisted*. She sniffed a filthy toe—as if, you thought, to see if you were a dirty-toe man—then hissed at you. *"Don't give me that look. Dewey happens to be Dewey Junior's daddy! And don't think I don't know what you are, neither. God made a lower place in hell for lowlife drug thieves than kiddie diddlers."*

Is it normal to keep remembering horrible things? It's not your fault they keep happening. Remember? That tweaked-out voice low as the hell pit he was describing. "It's in the Bible." Did you dream the evangelist? Or is he in the walls? This is a question you didn't used to ask yourself. *"Ladies and gentlemen, I want you all to look in your heart, ask yourself this question. Is your life nothing more than a history of saying yes to the wrong things?"* Can zombies be sad?

THE ESKIMO WITH HOOKS FOR HANDS LOOKED UNFAMILIAR, BUT HE SAID HE WAS A VET. He was shooting up Penny, who you couldn't remember meeting, in the neck. While you watched, her jugular wriggled like a worm in cookie dough, cracking the makeup she used to cover up vein-puff. "It's important," she said, while the shooter dabbed her off, "I'm a nurse. People can see our necks." The story doesn't track. But speed stories never track. They only make sense if you're on speed. (This is a test.) At what point did the Inuit show up with the vial of liquid meth? "What you staring at?" The big-faced musher was eyeballing you, clicking his hooks. You screamed, *"Get the fuck out of here!"* and he backed away. Was he laughing? Maybe he didn't leave. Impossible to tell what was going on; everything three-day-up echoey. Maybe the Eskimo just went in the bathroom. Maybe they were married. Maybe she brought him white assholes to kill after she fucked them in front of him. Maybe she killed them after *he* fucked them. Shit. Why does all your energy go into panic? Except for everything you knew about her, Penny seemed almost normal. Like a cheerleader who slept outside.

NOT EVERYBODY KNOWS YOU CAN BLACK OUT ON SPEED. You can be unconscious and chatty at the same time. Flip back from a clammy sense-memory of Mommy-flesh to an IHOP booth beside a plus-size ironic shemale busy not eating her Belgian waffles. Miss Waffle is still talking when you rematerialize, when your star falls from the night sky over Methlehem. To reenter the earth's BO. Boring Orbit. *"What was that movie? They Shoot Horses, Don't They? Well, screw the ponies! I shoot the same go-fast that made Hitler, Sartre, Lucille Ball, and Philip K. Dick complete geniuses!"* Plus-size Tranny-pants cannot stop talking. Mouth moving in a face dead as the papier-mâché Belgian waffles in the IHOP display case. *"Listen up, 'kay? I don't mind payin' for the party, but you gotta at least look interested! My husband had a thing where he'd drop Black Beauties and touch himself. He wouldn't eat dinner. That was the tell. I'd peep him cracking open ten black capsules on rice puddin' and gulpin' it down. Then he'd put his hands on me, rough, all over, like he wanted to pull out my organs and dunk them in coffee. Oooooooooooooh! It was goddamn heaven."* You stay fake-interested. Long enough to burn through what's left of a crappy eight ball wedged between the honey bear and the teapot. Nobody at IHOP gives a shit. It's IHOP. It's five after fucked-up o'clock in the morning. Just as you get up, Miss Waffles blurts, *"You can't hide, I can read your mind in nine languages."*

You are eye level with a case of textbook meth-lips. So dry each syllable launches a tiny bursting pillow of speed feathers, which drift down to the Bondo-like untouched whipped cream below. *"Know why sexual relations on speed are so twisted?"* She makes a here-comes-the-funny face. *"Sexual relations! Listen to me! I stay up for a day and a half and suddenly I'm NPR!"* She lets out a pained giggle. (It's a meth tic—the pain giggle. All emotions are a shade of suffering, once you're beyond the ecstatic.)

When there's nothing else, you can love people just from knowing they suffer too. It hits right and you feel that vast, inchoate empathy. *How would you describe yourself at such "peak" moments. "Crippled and happy about it." But there you go, bragging!*

It's different when you do it with somebody else. Like when your hefty transgender friend says, "I think I hear a lump in my breast. Is that possible?" You nod with Real Concern, edging slowly backward away from the booth. Stimulants stimulate everybody: even the people near you. Beehived IHOP waiters just know, and they stay out of the way. (It's IHOP.) When she yells, you feel the eyes of family diners. "Thief!" Waffles warbles. "Thief. There he goes! *Thief!*" You keep your head down. The screams follow you. "You think if you keep moving backward, you can make your life unhappen? Smell yourself!"

(The shit helps you feel nothing. But not nothing enough.)

IN THE OLD DAYS, YOU HAD A SPONGE TEST. When the floor got spongy, you knew. You'd gone too far. Time to come back! Swallow a Valium. Swallow nine. Drink some mouthwash. You need *something.* By the time you hit Sponge Mode, reality feels fraught and menacing. (Could be two days up, could be twelve.) Regardless. Your life is reduced to walking the yard in a maximum-security bouncy house. Your heart hurts. You catch yourself talking out loud, explaining deranged sensations to strangers in the street. "My motel room hates me."

CAJANK! There is a girl in your room who won't stop screaming. Candy? Kembra? Cathy? Caroline? . . . *Crickle?* When you walk in she stops screaming and gets solicitous. Which is scarier than screaming. She could be twenty-three or forty. "Are you shivering, mister, or is that a convulsion?"

Kimberly! That was her name. The one with the diapers. You didn't dream this. You were geezing this evil-smelling grit you bought from a plumber in Bakersfield. Bathtub crank with a Drano after-drip. Kimberly says she bought special diapers with holes in them. Fuck-me diapers. Remember? Oooh, I wore my Sex Depends. Just for you!

This, you realized later, was *another* lie. Kimberly! Speedfreaks always lie. The diapers weren't REALLY called Sex Depends. She slit the crotch with a razor. Then she used felt-tip pens, magic markers to color faces on the diapers. Fifty-three tiny faces. (Look, there's Ringo! There's Abraham Lincoln. There's Helen Keller! There's you!) It took her days. Gink-work. That's how she made them. She had lots of razors 'cause she was also a cutter. Of course. Little Girl Cutters grow up to be Big Girl Speedfreaks.

Right, right, right, right, right, right, right. Doctors gave her Adderall for the cutting. Why wouldn't they? Adderall helped her focus on the H she was slicing in her forehead. H? *Stands for HELL, douche-lame!* And, right in front of you, she starts cutting her thighs. Sees you looking. Then explains. Amped-up and serene. "Cutting's better than picking. Last Christmas I picked a hole in my cheek you could put your finger through!"

God, she is screaming right in your face. Can bad breath give you cancer?

"In New Orleans," she tells you huskily, "you put the crystal in your eye. They call it Les Yeux-Yeux. Cajuns call it Cajank." She also said her mother used to eat her father's ball-hair. Every morning, after he shaved, Papa would snip at his scrotum beard. And when he was done, her mother would make her come into the bathroom and help her gather up the tiny hairs. She'd put them in a glass of water, swirl it a little, then drink up. Clarence Thomas style. "Mama say no woman will want Daddy when she's got his pubes in her belly. Mama knew things." Now it sounds weird. But then—with the light on the white walls shimmering the blood sloshing off the top of your skull, it made tremendous sense. It made you sob. (You had to keep reminding yourself to breathe; every moment felt either really right or really wrong.) Miss New Orleans told you the only reason she did speed was that her mother made her take "zese leetle capsools" so she could see better when they searched for Daddy-hair. Mama gave the little girl Dexedrine, just like little Judy Garland got. She'd spend the day studying every square inch of bathroom floor instead of going to school. When she found a curl she'd yelp and Mommy would give her a smooch. She covered her eyes as she told the story. She hugged her knees. Then the tears would come and she'd need something. What are mommies for?

STOP THINKING ABOUT DISEASE. That's how you get one. It's so fucking hard to breathe. Speedfreaks get sick. Not you. You're not one of them. You're different. You're never going to get a disease. Even though you've been up for . . . a while. You're not one of them. You're different. You still brush your teeth. (Manually now, since you took your Waterpik apart.) You floss. You even urinated. Maybe two days ago.

Your heartbeat could set off car alarms. How many days? What do insects feel when they fuck? Max Jacobson gave injections to Truman Capote, Tennessee Williams, Eddie Fisher, Mother Teresa, and JFK, who was so reliant on Dr. Max—a.k.a. Feelgood—he flew him to summits, like the B1 in Austria. With Khrushchev. Jack wanted to stay sharp.

Dr. J had amphetamine getaways for VIPs in his splash-pad on East 53rd. He made tapes. Wouldn't you? After three days, everybody's a pervaloid. There's Tennessee, wearing Mother Teresa's surprisingly plush, high-rise undergarments. "If I wore these, they'd call *me* mother!"

YOUR GRANDFATHER HAD A SCANDAL INVOLVING INHALERS. He got caught soaking Benzedrine cotton inhalers in coffee and drinking it with the other degenerates in Times Square. Before he moved back to Cleveland, missing his teeth, Gramps had his pocket picked by Herbert Huncke, also high on Bennies. Each time you share this, which you forget that you made up, you bust your buttons. But all your stories are from long ago. Even the true ones.

You are normal. It's the speed that made you a freak.

PART II
MACHINATION

Tex LeBeauf

SCOTT PHILLIPS is the author of six
novels, including *The Ice Harvest*
and, most recently, *The Adjustment*
(Counterpoint) and *Nocturne* (les
Éditions la Branche). He lives in St.
Louis, MO.

labiodental fricative
by scott phillips

torie

So you want to know something weird about Jerry?" I ask. Glen stops licking for a second and I immediately regret it. "Huh?"

"Get your face back down there, big boy." He starts up again, not the best head I've ever had but better than Jerry anyway. Better than none. "He has a tooth fetish."

He stops licking again and starts laughing.

"Get back to it," I tell him, "I'm just about ready." We're in the backseat of Glen's Lexus, which is pretty fucking sweet, even if he is living in it. When he first told me he was driving one I thought he was full of shit, because he looked like a guy who lived in a dumpster or maybe just a grove of trees down by the river. Or beneath an underpass or in a refrigerator box.

And while I can hardly believe I'm letting him go down on me like this, I also can't believe he's doing it so enthusiastically, because to be perfectly honest, I left Jerry's in kind of a rush this morning and I don't know exactly what it's like down there, but I'm experiencing that not-so-fresh feeling, if you know what I mean. I get the feeling he just wants to fuck me so bad he's willing to go through a lot for it, which is kind of romantic when you think of it, and he knows perfectly well why I'm doing it: because I know he's holding and right now Jerry isn't and inside Glen was hinting that he had a lead on a whole bunch of it and that was why he was trying to sell Jerry that penis back at the bar.

I'm getting tired of listening to the little animal noises he's making, like he thinks there's something sexy about being gone down on by a big old slobbery bear, and anyway I'm never going to come so I make some reasonably convincing orgasm noises and pull him up and in, and thank Christ it only takes him about fifteen seconds to come, which is when it occurs to me that I should have made him wear a condom and probably a dental dam too, because Christ only knows what a guy like him has swimming around on his tongue.

So anyway, he's pulling his pants back up, at which point I become aware of a pretty gamy odor that I realize is coming from his crotch, and I have to hold my breath until he gets buckled back up again, and even then it lingers like foreign cheese in the back of the Lexus, which has real leather seats, probably standard equipment, and he says, "What was that about a fetish?"

"Tooth fetish. I'm a dental hygienist."

"I thought you managed Furry's."

"I do. I *used to be* a hygienist, is what I should have said, and the first time Jerry met me he said what a beautiful big mouth I had, and I almost hit him because I'm sensitive about the size of my teeth, but I could see he was totally serious so I took it as sweet instead of, you know, insulting. So how'd you get hold of Dean Martin's penis anyway?"

jerry

The first time I saw Torie I was a lost cause. Big, round eyes, incisors prominent enough that her lips are slightly parted when her face is at rest, like she's just about to say something. Thick, wavy black hair, a long, aquiline nose, and perfect olive skin. I knew right then I'd follow her anywhere. Which is how Torie ended up managing the bar instead of cleaning other people's less attractive teeth, and living in my condo instead of at home with her husband and three kids. As well as snorting me out of house and home, which is a hard thing for me to complain about since I was the one got her started on crank when we first started partying together.

She used to come in with her friends and fellow hygienists after work. A couple of times when she stayed late, long after the other girls went home, we had deep discussions about life—hers, mostly—and its attendant disappointments—again, mainly hers. One night her husband came by to get her, and he made it clear that he didn't consider this the kind of place where a decent Christian wife and mother ought to be spending her evenings.

But the band was playing, and she'd been dancing and having a good time, and she had no intention of leaving. We had the Jake Hornor Blues Band playing every second Friday and Saturday of the month back then, best draw I ever had, and this was the third time I'd let her sample a little bit of what Larry the dishwasher had been selling me (and a good portion of my staff and clientele) for the last couple years. When hubby grabbed her upper arm on the dance floor to drag her out to her car, she swung at him with the other fist and the whole thing ended up with Kurt—that's the husband—eighty-sixed and thinking he was lucky I didn't bring the cops in on his ass. (I make it a rule never to call the cops unless we've been robbed, but he didn't know that.)

She lost her hygienist job a couple of months after, over chronic lateness and absenteeism. I hired her on as a waitress, and when she turned out not to have that in her, I just made her a manager and let her earn a living being hot.

And then a year and a half had gone by, and I'd gotten into the business of distribution myself, with Larry the dishwasher promoted to ID checker/procurer, and Torie had gotten herself seriously skinny. She was never a big girl, but by the time my old buddy Glen came in after two or three years' absence, she was getting, to these old eyes, a wee bit cadaverous.

Apart from his eyes being so bulbous, red, and wet, Glen might himself have passed for a corpse of a couple weeks' standing as he leaned on the bar and lectured me about how badly the place had gone downhill since the last time he was in. "Who you got playing this weekend?" he asked. "Heard Hornor won't play here anymore; says you stiffed him."

"He's a fucking liar. I won't book him anymore—he showed up drunk three times in a row and I fired his ass." This was true, though he played just fine when he was drunk. I had stiffed him twice, though I still had every intention of paying him what I owed. "Got the Jimmie Kralik Trio coming in."

"Fuck that, those guys couldn't draw a crowd to a public hanging," Glen said. He couldn't quit looking at Torie, who in turn was pretending he wasn't there.

Watching someone else ogle your girl ought to make you see her afresh, it seems to me, maybe renew your ardor, but whatever Glen was seeing wasn't there for me anymore. All I saw right then was how sunken her cheeks were looking, how stringy and lank her hair had gotten (she was way past due for a perm), how she didn't braid it up anymore. That beautiful olive complexion was veering toward the greenish and she was breaking out with zits that I had to keep pointing out because she didn't notice them herself. I'd been thinking about scaring up a little weed in hopes of getting her appetite up, maybe just enough to keep the weight she had on if not gain some of it back. Right about then I wouldn't have minded that husband of hers showing up and taking her back to the house and kids, which he'd quit trying to do about six months after she bailed on the whole failing enterprise.

"Got a business proposition for you," Glen said. He was a lawyer, or had been at any rate, and he'd presented me with opportunities in the past that hadn't turned out too badly, as well as a few others I knew enough to steer clear of. This was the first time I'd seen him since he'd headed up to Portland, Oregon, to help his brother run a rehabilitation facility for the blind and speechless or some such charity scam.

Torie snorted and turned away. I could understand, seeing Glen the way he looked now and never having experienced Glen the prosperous attorney: glad-hander Glen, buyer of rounds, purveyor of free legal advice to the indigent, ladies' man, bon vivant. This Glen looked like he could use a hot meal and a good night's sleep somewhere besides the backseat of his car. I poured him a shot and slid it in front of him; since he hadn't asked for one I assumed he didn't have the money to pay for it.

"On me," I said. "Welcome home."

"Much appreciated." He slammed it and set the glass back down on the table, then extracted from his inside jacket pocket a cardboard box. "Behold," he said, opening it to reveal what looked like a piece of beef jerky resting on a bed of cotton.

"Nice," I said.

"You know what I have here?"

"Looks like a dried-up turd," Torie said, her voice now raspy as any grizzled barfly's.

"Ladies and gentlemen," Glen announced in what I imagine was a weak echo of his erstwhile courtroom vocal style, "for your amusement and edification, the johnson of the Chairman of the Board."

"His what, now?"

"This is the mummified penis of Mr. Francis Albert Sinatra."

torie

I'm starting to get nervous because I'm all of a sudden conscious of the parking lot lights shining into the back of the Lexus.

"Jesus, who'd want to buy Dean Martin's cock?"

"Frank Sinatra's, get it straight."

"Whatever," I shrug, thinking it's no wonder Glen's not married, he hasn't said anything sweet to me since he came, the kind of things a lady likes to hear after intercourse, like *You have really pretty lashes* or *Your hair smells terrific* or *God, your boobs look good in the moonlight,* things like that. Anyway, I press the matter, thinking it has something to do with the meth. "Okay, Sinatra's junk, then, where'd you get it?"

"Guy sold it to me in the bar of a Mexican restaurant in Palm Desert. Said they'd had to disinter him for some kind of maintenance—the concrete seal was broken on the vault or some such thing—and while he was above ground they were storing the remains inside the mortuary. So this guy broke Frank's dick off and kept it for a couple years as a lucky charm."

"Huh."

"And as a lucky charm it didn't do him much good, because when I met him he was really hurting for some crank and I happened to be holding, so I traded him, and afterward it occurs to me that this might be worth some change. And when I hit town today, just by coincidence, I run into my old friend Chuck who wants to know do I know anybody who's got five hundred dollars, 'cause he's got himself several cases of store-brand cold medicine that just fell off a loading dock."

I don't believe there's any such thing as a coincidence and I tell him that I think Frank Sinatra's leaky vault and Chuck's case of cold medicine and Glen's and my meeting and Jerry being out of crank all coming together at once are a plan of the cosmos, which is the kind of thing I never would have said a few years ago but which I truly believe now, having experienced too many weird juxtapositions of reality over the last couple of years to take any of these signs and wonders for granted.

"Does that mean you've got five hundred?" he asks.

The truth is, I have about seventy-five bucks in my checking, because I have to pay child support, if you can believe that, to my ex-husband Kurt, who has an $80,000-a-year job in franchise relations at Pizza Hut, while I'm making $23,000 and change working for my cheapskate boyfriend, which Kurt knows perfectly well and so does his lawyer and so does the judge, but they're all about making me pay for being a runaway mom. Believe me, if the situation was reversed there'd be divorced dads support groups all over the case, but believe me too when I say nobody likes a runaway mom, especially when the youngest one wasn't even talking yet when I left and Kurt has trained her to call me Torie instead of Mommy, and Kurt's new wife Perfect Stacia gets called Mommy. Stacia who totally had her sights set on Kurt way, way before I split, who was licking her chops like a Doberman eyeing a three-legged kitten when she heard I'd blown. Like I give a shit anyway.

"We could get it," I tell him.

glen

My first thought was: kill Jerry and make it look like a stickup, take the money and the woman both. Jerry's always treated me like a schmuck, even when I've helped him out of a couple of legal scrapes, including one serious count of selling liquor to a minor. That one was no walk in the park, and all he did when it was over was piss and moan about the bribe money he'd had to lay out. And then there was the question of Frank Sinatra's desiccated organ. I was tweaking when I got hold of it, and I'd been tweaking ever since, and Jerry's dismissive attitude slammed home the obvious fact that I had no way to prove whose junk I was carrying, short of calling up Frank Jr. and asking for a DNA sample. The fantasy mountain of pure crystal and pussy and cash created by the tectonic activity of my overstimulated cerebral cortex collapsed instantaneously into a crevasse of despair and cheap-ass street meth. I had hit the wall, and just as I was running out of crank.

Yeah, I could have killed Jerry with no compunctions.

chuck

It is easy enough, I suppose, to underestimate the intelligence of a man who sells pot next to a dumpster behind the Choose'n'Save, especially for someone like Glen, who thinks himself a sharpy in the vein of a Hugh Hefner or a Warren Beatty or a Gary Hart. You know the kind I mean. When he sees a woman that pleases his eye he sets that eye on her until his filthy ends are met, then he loses interest in that particular lady who no doubt is or was the most precious flower of another. He did this to my own precious flower six years ago, when my girlfriend Gretchen was facing a charge of possession with intent to distribute.

Marijuana. *Cannabis sativa.* I was a slave to it as much as to her at that time; the fact that she had an ounce and a half of it on her person upon her arrest was strictly due to my own baleful influence. Enter, in the outward guise of savior, my friend (I thought) Glen, hotshot attorney and drinking buddy, occasional purchaser of my wares. He worked the case without recompense, for which I was grateful.

Then, six months later, Gretchen and I were going at it hammer and tongs over her little dachshund Tami's tendency to shit in my loafers—I did hate that awful farting bitch something fierce—when she pulled out the big rhetorical guns and announced that yes, in fact, Glen had charged a fee, and that it had involved her mouth and his organs of regeneration. I threw her and Tami out. Ever since I have been waiting for the moment (never really believing it would come) when I might pay Glen back for his perfidy.

torie

Jerry keeps a couple of grand in cash taped to the underside of his sock drawer, which is stupid. Right? Isn't that stupid? That's the kind of guy Jerry is. Smart and stupid both, sometimes in the same sentence.

glen

The woman was a mess and she smelled like chicken soup and swamp water, but she was the first human female in close to a year who'd consented to lay with me free of charge and I wasn't about to fuck that up, especially when she looked ready to fly the coop on Jerry. It cost me the last of my meager stash to get her out to the Lexus, where I explained to her about the five hundred dollars and the cold medicine. She didn't have it, she told me, and she pointed out that if we borrowed the money from Jerry unawares we wouldn't owe anything, either in terms of cash or product.

"I like the way you think," I told her, although what I saw in her was less thought than a kind of low animal cunning, a hillbilly slyness that made the betrayal of her boss and lover as natural and uncomplicated as switching brands of toothpaste.

We were driving out on Hydraulic headed for a supermarket. It was closed at that hour but the security guard let Chuck do some business out behind the dumpsters in return for modest monetary and pharmaceutical compensation. I'd known Chuck for twenty years, and despite a reckless and fearless way of doing business, he'd never been in any major trouble. A lack of guile and considerable personal charm had gotten him out of many a scrape, and a lack of ambition had kept him out of the bigger leagues where he probably would have gotten himself killed.

The female was talking about teeth, a subject she probably should have avoided. First of all, hers were huge and starting to get meth gray, despite her claims that she still brushed and flossed thrice daily. Second, nobody wants to hear about that kind of shit from a dental hygienist even when they're a captive audience in the chair, let alone when they've got an ongoing criminal enterprise they're trying to concentrate on.

"You ever hear of meth mouth?" I asked her, hoping she'd get the picture and shut the fuck up. No such luck. She went into lecture mode, expounding at length about her personal theory that meth mouth was a result of tweakers neglecting their flossing because they were too distracted by the getting and consuming of their drug of choice and not because of the drug's unorthodox chemical manufacturing process itself.

"Look at me," she said. "I've been doing this for like a year or more and my teeth are as beautiful and straight as they've ever been."

I agreed, but just because I thought I might want more access to her person later.

"So where are we going to sell this cold medicine once we get it?" she asked.

I had an idea, I told her, a friend of a friend up in Topeka went by the name of Crumdog, sergeant-at-arms for a bikers' organization.

"So how come this Chuck guy wants to sell it to you?" she asked. "Wouldn't he make better money selling it to some cook? Doesn't he know anybody?"

"You sure do ask a lot of questions," I said, trying not to sound like I was thinking about backhanding her.

jerry

God, I hated seeing what had become of Glen. I ignored the maybe-penis in the box and glanced back at Torie, who was still looking down her nose at him.

"So what happened to the home for the blind and deaf?"

"Well, my brother had some licensing issues with the state of Oregon, we never quite got it open, and then my girlfriend kicked me out. Blah blah blah, long story short, I'm back here. But I still got the Lexus."

"That's good."

"So how much for Frank's pecker?"

"Nothing, Glen."

"Nothing? For a relic that's seen the insides of Ava Gardner and Mia Farrow both?"

Just then Matt Sweeney walked in. He used to be a doctor, so I waved him over for a quick look. "That a human penis, Matt?"

He stuck out his lower lip and took the box from Glen. "Hard to say. Could be. You'd have to show a pathologist."

"How much, man?" Glen was whining now.

"Nothing. Even if that is a human penis, it's not Sinatra's."

"Prove it!" Glen shouted.

"Calm down now, pal," I said. "What makes you think it's worth anything, anyway, even if it is Ol' Blue Eyes' John Thomas?"

I could see his fantasy beginning to implode inside his skull. "You could charge money to see it. They auctioned Napoleon's off for big bucks."

"There's no proof. You'd have to show provenance. A chain of custody. Where'd you get it, anyway?"

chuck

When I ran into him at the Brass Candle, trying to get someone to buy him a drink without actually lowering himself to asking for one, Glen looked like a cat had done its business in his mouth. There was a slight pleasure in the recognition that I was now doing better than he, so I bought him a beer and a shot and he asked me how was Gretchen. It was the half-hidden leer I perceived that made my pity, such as it was, evaporate.

"Last I heard she was in jail for soliciting."

Did I enjoy the look of shock on his sagging face? I did for a moment, until I realized that there was no guilt in it, that he bore no sense of his own responsibility in this tragic matter. Though I am long out of the narcotics trade, it was plain Glen wasn't, and seeing my long-awaited shot at comeuppance, I asked him if he knew anyone who wanted in on a score.

His eyes narrowed as if he was already trying to figure out how to screw me out of the score I was generously letting him in on. "Might be I'd be interested," he said.

"For five hundred I can get five cases of store-brand pseudoephedrine," I said.

"I got something right here on my person worth a fuckload more than five hundred, and I'd trade you outright." He reached into the inside pocket of his coat, and I put my hand on his arm, shaking my head no.

"Cash only," I told him, which got him real quiet.

"You going to be out behind the Choose'n'Save dumpster tonight?" he asked.

"Fuck yeah, every night," I said, reverting to an exaggerated version of my former manner of speaking. In catching up with him I had deliberately skipped the uplifting "can-do" parts of my redemption story: the associate's degree in English, the pretty happy marriage to Bonnie—who is a nurse's aide and disapproves of any and all illicit drug use—and especially the assistant manager job at the very same Choose'n'Save behind which I once dealt dope.

torie

As soon as we got the money we went over to Larry the dishwasher's house and scored, then we headed out toward the supermarket where Glen's friend would be waiting with the cold meds. In the heady rush of new love Glen and I both maybe overdid the snorting, but God, it felt good. I'd packed my bag with all the clothes and jewelry I thought I'd need in my future life as Mrs. Glen Frobe.

Did I feel bad about taking Jerry's $2,565? Nope. The gun in his night table? A little, because what if someone broke in and there was Jerry scrambling for the weapon in the drawer and it's not there and he gets killed and his last thoughts are, *That conniving thieving bitch took my fucking piece and I loved her more than anything I ever loved, goddamnit,* while the intruders, bikers as I'm imagining them, cut off his slim-as-a-pea-shoot pecker and do all manner of horrid things to him in an orgy of speed-fueled sadism that lasts until one of the bikers, I'm imagining his name is Seth or something else biblical—I know: Esau!—says something like, "Shit, man, this is one dead motherfucker," and they go rooting around looking for whatever they can scavenge since Jerry never has much dope lying around the house and the money taped under the drawer is gone, another thing Jerry probably would be cursing me for, even as he reflects that he's never loved anybody like he loved me, with my prominent overbite and my twenty minutes of Kegels every day.

jerry

Soon as I saw something going on between Torie and Glen I sensed a golden opportunity, because Glen is a guy who can't say no to a piece of ass and Torie will do anything to get high, and when she made an excuse to leave five minutes after he headed out the door I had that magic feeling, like I might, just might, have a shot at getting rid of her for keeps. And for fucking his old friend's girl it would serve Glen right to get stuck with the bitch for a few years.

chuck

So I went out to the store, and after pretending to make some revisions in that week's work schedule (a job that strictly speaking should fall to Walt, my superior, who on the pretext of giving me valuable management experience via delegation has been weaning himself off just about all his own responsibilities over the last couple of years), I stepped onto the loading dock out back and removed from their hiding places five empty, flattened Choos-a-Fed cartons I'd been saving for a while. What kind of a man hides at his workplace empty cardboard cases of Choos-a-Fed, you may wonder? The answer lies in my abandonment some years ago of the drug life. I never, though I was so urged at the time, joined a twelve-step recovery program. Had I joined such a program I would not have encountered Glen in a bar, since participants are honor-bound, as I understand it, to shake off their other addictions as well. Had I joined such a program I would not have spent these last years stewing over Gretchen's fate and plotting different kinds of revenge on Glen. I'll bet I have twenty or thirty such scenarios, of varying degrees of complexity and practicality and lethality.

And now an opportunity had arisen, and I filled each case with what I figured the weight of the Choos-a-Fed would have been, and then I sealed it up carefully enough that it looked brand new and unopened, a level of craft that was probably unnecessary, because he was tweaking like the very dickens when I saw him at the Brass Candle. I loaded the empty cases into the bed of my truck and sat and waited out back by the dumpster.

torie

So I'm thinking maybe it's time to get out of the hospitality business altogether, once we've made this score up in Topeka, and cut way back on my crank habit before it turns into an addiction. Also thinking what beautiful babies Glen and I could make, and what a contribution I could make to society after getting my hygienist's license back.

glen

We're driving north on the turnpike and I am feeling pretty damned fine. This Crumdog will certainly, upon hearing who our mutual friends are, take the Choos-a-Fed off our hands for three, maybe four times what we would have paid poor old Chuck for it. As far as Chuck goes, the cops aren't going to spend much time on the shooting of a well-known low-level pot dealer tossed into a dumpster behind a supermarket. Not the cops I used to know.

As I listen to the female prattling on about our future of domestic bliss, I wonder about leaving her with the bikers. She needs more crank than I can afford to provide, and where I'm going I won't want a woman attached to me at the hip. The turnpike snakes through the Flint Hills, and up around Matfield Green I swear I can feel Frank Sinatra's penis start to vibrate in my pocket out of something not unlike joy.

Kenji Jasper

KENJI JASPER is the author of four novels, including *Dark*, a *Washington Post* and *New York Times* best seller, and *Snow*. He is also coeditor of *Beats, Rhymes and Life*, a collection of critical essays on hip-hop culture. His writings have appeared in *Newsweek*, the *Village Voice*, *Essence*, and on National Public Radio. His latest release is *Inter-Course: Moments in Love, Sex and Food*. A native of Washington, D.C., he currently lives in Los Angeles.

osito
by kenji jasper

Man, you know shit is fucked up when we comin' way the fuck out here," Gary said between puffs. He'd rolled the blunt with a Phillies, which meant it wouldn't last long. I'd told him that there were better brands, but he insisted. "This what I started with. So I'ma stick with these shits till I ain't have lungs no more."

I was never a fan of working high. Hell, I didn't even touch weed or anything else. For me it was all about control, all about making mind and body one whenever needed. But Gary was the one who'd got us the job. So Gary was calling the shots. That's how it was and how it is still, at least in theory. Execution, however, was a completely different matter. At least he wasn't smokin' meth.

"This is where the money is," I said.

Gary's country-fried English made me self-conscious about the way I pronounced my syllables so clearly, a lesson from my father about living in the "other" world, the one where people wore shirts and ties and worried about their balance sheets and annual reviews. All I wanted was a cubicle with my name on it. All I wanted was a quiet place to do my job. Too bad I wasn't any good at it.

"What the fuck does that shit even do?" Gary asked, the blunt already at half.

We'd boosted the car from the Dunn Loring station lot, a white Beamer wagon with factory rims. An '01 or '02 most likely.

But I couldn't be sure in the dark. We were headed to someplace called Osito, about an hour outside of Baltimore. Rico told us it would be like palming a Snickers from a checkout.

My name is Nsilo. Don't ask me where it comes from. I got it from my pops. Any explanation is as gone as he is. He took a .38 slug to the chest on a dance floor six months home from the first Gulf War. All he was trying to do was break up a fight. But when the line on the screen went flat, it was my mama who ended up broken.

Rico had a cousin in Osito, the only child of the only black family in the whole town. This cousin had a father who was on the road most days driving eighteen-wheelers. The mother was the secretary at the all-white Pentecostal church. I could smell the sellout all over them.

"I mean, why in the fuck would you wanna be up and runnin' around all the time?" The roach that remained of the blunt was practically burning his fingers. But he kept pulling from it, even though he was at the wheel a long way from home.

Gary had memorized the directions after a thirty-second read back at the house. A heavy-hitter with a photographic memory is a beautiful thing. As long as you can control him, that is. I'm middle management, which means that I'm the one who takes the dog for his nightly walks.

Much like rap, the crack business ain't what it was twenty years ago. Back in the day, you couldn't walk down a street in the neighborhood without somebody trying to hire you to work one of their corners. But Rockefeller and the Patriot Act and rap changed all of that. That's why Rico got into meth. There's still plenty of money to be made in that game.

So Rico's family of sellouts sold him the location to the biggest meth lab in the county, five trailers in a park of twelve cooking crank like a twenty-four-hour convenience store. We were being sent to make a pickup, one we weren't paying for. There was a bit of other business too. But I was supposed to handle that personally.

When the summer had started I was 100 percent certain that I was headed for the straight and narrow. Meechie had gotten shot outside The Crab House on Georgia Avenue over some broad with more stretch marks than a bag of rubber bands. Our fathers were brothers. My pops had at least made it back from the war. Meechie's had stepped on a land mine. And that was that.

Meechie was the only dude in the world who always had my back. I mean, even when I used to hoop back in high school, he'd be in the bleachers right above the bench, ready to pounce on anybody stupid enough to start a fight with me in it. I was good. But he was better. The game wasn't going to be the same without him.

I had done all right in school. And there was a lady at my church who worked on Capitol Hill. They were short on minorities in the Congressional Page Program. It didn't pay much but she said it was a way into working for the government. I was so fucked up over Meechie being gone that I actually thought it might be for me.

I was used to taking orders and making deliveries. I'd done it all my life. So taking the blue line to Capitol South for the same seemed like a walk in the park. White people were easier to manage than crackheads. Give 'em a smile. Make a joke they understand and you turn into their main boy in a flash. It's even easier when you know how to get 'em what they want. They assigned me to someone named Guy Medscar. He was an assistant to somebody's assistant. But his cousin was a big deal over at the Capitol, a senator I think.

Medscar was one of those dudes who got married out of

high school to a girl who didn't fuck him anymore. He had the four kids, the twin Beamers, the vacation house, all of that. But I could tell that it was more like a life sentence than a week in the Bahamas. My first lesson on the job was that the life everybody wants in the 'hood is a pain in the ass to somebody in the 'burbs.

Then he asked me one day, in a whisper, "You know where I can get some"—his fingers coming to together like they were holding an imaginary pipe—"meth?"

While I had a PhD in crack cocaine, meth wasn't big in my part of town. The way he asked was so funny to me that I thought he was making it up. Meth was for trailer park hillbillies and the fags in Dupont Circle. I might not have known much about it, but I knew where to get it. I knew where to get anything that wasn't nuclear or came with propellers.

"How much you want?" I asked him. His eyes lit up like the Washington Monument after six.

"How much can I get?" he asked.

It seemed simple enough. I went to see the guy sitting on Rico's stash out by Iverson Mall. I brought him a dub that Friday and he gave me a hundred dollars, five times what it was worth. That next Monday he asked me for an eighth. Every three days he'd page me after hours. The code after the number would say how much he wanted.

I hadn't been there two months before I was buying ounces to cover Medscar's orders. Then his boys got in on it. It got to the point where people in the building showed up at his office like it was mine. Since I didn't use (I didn't even drink), the money was all profit.

It really did seem like a foolproof situation. Then the fools got involved.

"So what we supposed to do once we get there?"

"We supposed to holler at this dude named Jeremiah," I explained. "That's all I know."

"You think they gonna have any food up in this jawnt? I ain't had shit since dem wings and fries I had for lunch."

Jeremiah was a prophet. He believed in God so much that he went wherever the Lord told him to go. Sometimes it was places he didn't want to be. Other times it was places he didn't understand. I didn't want to be in Osito on a Friday night.

I had a chocolate star named Deidre sending me pics with her legs open, panties off. She was free for the night. But business was business. This was a run we had to make.

Now, as you might have imagined, it didn't take long for the other pages to see that I was getting special treatment from the boss. I took hour lunches that were supposed to be thirty minutes. I never buttoned the top button on my dress shirt, even though it was policy. And every once in a while, one of my girls would come through.

I made sure my broads knew the deal way before they came over to Capitol Hill. First and foremost, the invitations only went to the right ladies. I couldn't have anybody up in the office who didn't have the sense not to show up in sweatpants with her hair a mess.

Kina was probably my favorite girl. She didn't have much of an ass on her but her hips were lovely, the perfect handles to hold onto while I hit it from the back. She grew up on the block but she had worked at a bank. So she knew how to dress. She came in there one day in a pin-striped skirt and blazer, heels, and a real nice blouse. The blazer was one layer too many in the summer heat, but when she came in the office she was lookin' good, like she always did. Medscar damn near started jerkin' off the minute the girl sat her purse down. I gave him that special nod that explained what I was up to.

"I'm gonna need you to get these supplies for me," he said, making sure to sound really official. Paper-clipped to the list was a key to the supply room. Every floor of the building had one. But only supervisors and the janitor had the key. It was almost as good as booking a room at a motel, without the room service.

He gave me a big wink as I motioned for Kina to follow me out the front and down the hall. I knew he'd studied every inch of the broad, imagining what he might do if her whole world was in his hands. I locked the door behind me once we were inside the room. She lifted her skirt up, flashing the fact that there was nothing between me and her wetness. And that's where I stayed, while hell broke loose all around me.

I had a couple of the other pages making runs for me. I mean, I kept the operation small but I knew beforehand that Medscar wasn't going to be able to keep his mouth shut for too long. White boys in places like that aren't good at keeping secrets. The ones who can work over at Homeland Security, or at the CIA.

So one of these kids, Jacob, a blond-haired, blue-eyed boy from out in Reston, decided that he was gonna start selling to some of the pages in the other buildings. They had a roll call every morning that he thought was the perfect place to do business. He was in college, after all. Who doesn't get high in college? Instead of selling his usual dimes and dubs, Jacob decided to get a bigger fish on the hook. Some page he'd never seen before pulls him to the side and tells him that he wants to buy a half. The kid, seeing dollars and stars (before the bars), says he can get it. He and Rory, my other guy, had about a half between them. They did the math, but not much else.

The only way to tell that Osito was even there was the lit-up sign at the city limits. The sign was made out of Christmas lights, even though it was just after Labor Day. Beyond it were just the silhouettes of buildings and small moving shadows, most likely raccoons and possums scampering around in the middle of the night. The Monrovia mobile community was about a mile in. The entrance was a concrete apron that led to a dirt road. Gary had to put the high beams on to cut through darkness. The thick dirt road had trailers on either side of it, sleeping souls who would barely remember the sound of our engine as soon as we'd rolled past them. Jeremiah's place was past those, a supersized camper parked beyond the mobile park, right next to a forest.

We were finally there. But I was still back in the supply room.

I can still remember the warmth at the back of Kina's throat; the Snoopy painted on each fingernail looking up at me as she held me tight, her mouth moving forward and backward like a well-oiled machine. She was reminding me of my prom night, and her prom night, and the way her mouth felt just like bona fide pussy when I was inside of it.

My fingers found their way through her (obviously dyed) fire-red hair. Her eyes were closed, like a monk in meditation. I ignored the first fist that came against the door. I was so close to getting *there*. Looking at her, on her knees in front of me, made me wonder what the blowjobs might be like in heaven. I came, just as the door opened, the bullet swallowed by my baby with impeccable technique. It was like a reunion. Jacob and Rory, both in cuffs, Medscar looking like he just got caught with his dick out, and me and Kina with my . . . well, you get the picture.

Jacob and Rory had apparently walked their entire stash right up to an undercover Capitol Hill cop. Of course, they couldn't even get in the squad car without putting me and Medscar's name into it. But as it turned out, the cops only came after me.

I was just another page. He was our supervisor, which gave him deniability. Two white boys selling drugs equaled someone more experienced on the next level up, which equaled me, the black dude from the wrong side of the bridge. The only card I had in my pocket was that it was my word against Jacob and Rory's. In my defense, there wasn't a second out of place on my time card. Plus, there wasn't anyone else to ID me as the top man.

So the worst thing they could do was fire me. I was pretty sad about it, mainly because I'd gotten to like being legit. I liked the check with my name printed on it every other week. But I didn't belong on Capitol Hill (or at least not at that low-ass level). They took my page jacket and my ID and told me that I couldn't come on Capitol grounds again, not even for a tour.

The train ride home was no different than on any other day. I didn't like the way I went out, but I was also looking forward to getting back to Garfield Terrace. Rico always had work there for me. No jackets and ties, no IDs and Capitol cops. There was only one thing I was really good at.

The trailer had one of those cheap locks on the door handle. You know, the kind you can do in ten seconds with some of those little screwdrivers. It was dark inside. The flickering blue light through the outer window was coming from a TV. I was about to knock when the door came open. The man standing there looked like Lil Wayne if Lil Wayne was forty, white, and had a ten-year-old for his tattoo artist. Were the five hairs at the bottom of his chin supposed to be a goatee?

"He must be Gary," the guy mumbled. "I'm Jeremiah."

"How you know *he* ain't Gary?" my driver demanded.

Jeremiah smiled enough for me to see in the dim light. "I just know," he said, welcoming us in.

The chemical smell was everywhere, like those Korean nail shops in the mall. It didn't give me a headache though. Just this dull feeling. I felt like the temperature was dropping a degree at a time. In five minutes I was going to be able to see my breath.

Jeremiah flipped on the light and we saw that we weren't alone. There was a pair of teenaged kids, a girl with dark rumpled hair (and a pair of double Ds) and a white boy with a blond buzz cut and a tattoo of Optimus Prime on his left forearm. They continued to snore like there wasn't a bright light and three people standing over them.

On the other side of the room, a woman old enough to be somebody's great-grandma was asleep in a green recliner that looked older than she was. There was a double-barrel shotgun propped up against the wall behind her, the barrels pointing at the floor.

"So how you wanna do this?" Jeremiah asked.

"We only got a two-seater," Gary shouted. Jeremiah and I both gave him that *Don't wake up the kids* look. Then again, it wasn't like it mattered.

"Where you got it at?" I asked.

"It's back here in the bathroom, brother."

"I ain't your brother," Gary yelled.

Jeremiah chuckled as we started to follow him. "I wasn't talkin' to you, big boy."

There were about five feet between us and the bathroom. I was holding a .380, my favorite piece: light and compact, but accurate as hell. I put my fingers around the grip. 11.85 ounces. Less than a pound.

The tub inside of the bathroom was small. It was the only detail I could make out before the action. Jeremiah's eyes met mine over Gary's shoulder. The stiff-neck movement that was supposed to be a nod was all I needed. There was a single shot before Gary fell forward, his corpse tumbling directly into the tub, as we'd planned. The other players came in from the living room. The old woman and the MTV kids had given the best performances of their criminal careers.

Gary would have said that we deserved "one of those gold things they give for actin'." Comments like those would make it hard for me to actually miss him.

I told you about my cousin Meechie and all that he meant to me. I told you what I went through when that asshole gunned him down in front of the strip club over that broad with more stretch marks than a bag of rubber bands. I just didn't mention that Gary was the one who did the gunning. I volunteered to do the business; Rico and I came up with the plan.

Jeremiah and his crew had gotten on Rico's payroll making D.C. bodies disappear out in the country. The drug shit was just a bonus for them. Those Pentecostal sellouts who gave us the info were Meechie and my cousins. They'd even sponsored us back in the day to keep us out of juvie for a summer or two. They knew DCPD would never think to go body-searching way out in Osito.

Everything I've told you is true, even the meth. Rico is the bank for one of the biggest meth holds in the area. But he knows better than to bring that white-boy shit any closer to the city than it needs to be. I ended up getting back into business with Medscar. But this time he was smart enough to run it all through the boys in the mailroom. My old boss, out of appreciation, pays for my golf lessons at the course uptown.

They say that God has a reason for everything. Maybe that's why I lost that job on the Hill two days before Gary got Meechie. Gary had been my muscle on and off for years. He would have walked anywhere I told him to.

"Anybody else you need to vanish, playboy?" Jeremiah asked, pouring bleach into the bucket of cleanser next to the toilet.

"I'll be in touch," I said.

"What's next?" the ancient woman asked as she leaned

against the wall outside of the bathroom, leaning on that shotgun as her cane.

"I'll let you know the next time I'm through," I said as I started past them. No goodbyes. No last words. It was done.

I could see my breath hanging in the air as I walked through the living room and out the front door. The moon was big and brown in the sky. This was the kind of night where all kinds of things come out of the woods, and out of me. They chase each other in the shadows, a game of chess played up above and down below. The moves almost always come from somewhere else. We're just here on this rock to make the moves.

Devri Richmond

JOSEPH MATTSON is the author of *Eat Hell* (Narrow Books) and *Empty the Sun* (A Barnacle Book), a novel with soundtrack by Drag City recording artist Six Organs of Admittance. His work has appeared in *Slake, Rattling Wall, Pearl, Ambit,* and more. Mattson was also the literary editor of *Two Letters Collection of Art and Writing Vol. 2* (Narrow Books). His novel, *Courting the Jaguar,* is forthcoming in 2012, and he was awarded a 2011 City of Los Angeles Artist Fellowship for his novel-in-progress, *Hexico.* Mattson lives in Los Angeles.

amp is the first word
in amphetamine
by joseph mattson

I was awakened at six a.m. after a long night of serious drink chasing down seven days of too much speed. Anvil head, brain ready to splatter, body wrought with ache and despair. Wanting nothing more than some shut-eye, against the ghost-white face of an unforgiving, barbaric narco-crash, I was brought back to the shock of life by a telephone call from an LAPD detective looking for my best friend.

"No," I croaked into the receiver.

"Hello?"

"Yes, hello, yes."

"Is this William O'Sullivan?" His tone had the seriousness of a doctor with very bad news.

"This is he."

"This is Detective Roy Mendoza of the Los Angeles Police Department."

I looked at the clock, the numbers blurry and hopeless. I began to sift through the bitter fog of my consciousness, trying to piece together any broken frames from the grim cinema that had been the past week.

"My lawyer's name is . . ." I said by instinct, but gravity stopped the sentence as I fell headfirst into the closet door, catching the corner of my right eye socket on the knob.

"I'm looking for Jim Grace," he said.

"Jim Grace?" He and I had parted just hours before. But

Grace would take a bullet before doling out my telephone number to the police. My paramount amigo—a true brute hero, rare and holy in the order of what is sacred. Sacred in the sordid world of those who walked our line.

"He's not here," I said.

"I figured. It's just that I can't . . . get through . . . to him."

The way he said it—*get through*—made me nervous. I noticed blood draining from the spot on the side of my face that took the doorknob. "He's not . . . here," I said, adding my own emphasis to see what kind of level Detective Roy Mendoza was on. I'd vicariously become a seasoned veteran in playing blue-boys and criminals, cops and fuck-ups—mostly in the shadow of Jim Grace.

"We tried his phone, but it's a dead end. Perhaps we have the number wrong."

"Look, Jim Grace and I share a mutual distaste for the telephone." I scrounged the floor like a suckerfish, looking for something to compress the wound, the red now rolling down my neck and soaking into my white A-shirt, my face already swollen from the indulgences in modern chemistry, unable to sort out the pain.

"It's in his and your best interest to get back to me. May I give you a few numbers, in the event that you see him?"

"All right, Detective Mendoza, give me the numbers."

"Call me Dozer."

"Dozer. Yeah."

I took off the shirt and clamped it against my eye, stumbling like a drunken, bucking mule through the house until I found a roll of duct tape. I tore off a long piece and wrapped it around my head to hold the makeshift bandage in place. Then I crawled back to bed.

"He's just pissed because I have a pair of his wife's panties."

"What?"

"Yeah. Long story. Another time. Help me with this," Jim Grace said, wrangling a huge yellow tent, trying to stuff it into a little nylon bag. "I'm thinking about taking a trip."

"Good God, you didn't lay a cop's wife?"

"Shit no. Although she is quite a dish. But I hate that bitch. His wife ruined my life."

"Jesus . . ." I mumbled.

"Forget it. I don't have time, nor do I want to explain. Dozer— fuck. He lives perpetually in the past. It's just sad. Two percent?" he asked, handing me a quart bottle of milk.

"Thanks." I grabbed the thing.

"Coat the stomach."

"Grease," I swallowed, "the wheel. Where do you keep them?"

"Keep what?"

"Them. The underwear."

"Underwear?" Grace asked, as if there had been no mention of women's underthings.

"Mrs. Dozer's panties."

"Oh, those. In the freezer."

"Freezer? Why for?"

"Why what? Why not?"

"Keeping a cop's wife's dandies in the freezer is rather creepy."

"You got a better idea how to preserve them?"

"Preserve . . . ?"

"What happened to your face?" Jim Grace asked, as if he'd just noticed it.

"Roy Dozer beat the shit out of me trying to get your phone number," I said. "Why do you need to preserve them?"

Grace lost color in his face, then it returned to its regular bluish flush. "He went to your house?"

I didn't like the way it sounded, in on the kill, same as the cop. Or was I just paranoid, askance from becoming a consistent dope-huffer? Jim Grace was possibly the only person I trusted in this old, bad world. "No, he didn't come to my house. I got coldcocked by the closet doorknob."

"Oh. Put some steak on that thing."

The flashing thought of a cool, thick cow shank slapped against my head, the iron scent of bovine blood and juices sopping my cheeks, dripping slowly down my face, made me feel chilly comfort in addition to horrible nausea.

"Are you coming with me? Jeez, these things. They come in these little yellow bags and once you take them out it is damn near impossible to get them back in." Jim Grace started punching hell into the tent, shoving his foot in, trying his damnedest to make it fit. "You want a Tecate?"

"Yes. What's it for, anyway?"

"Limes are in the fridge."

"What's the tent for?" I asked.

"Pico-Union."

"Pico-Union? You turning vagrant or something? What do you need a tent for to go buy speed?"

"Man, how deep in are you?" he asked.

"How deep in are *you*?"

"Deep? This is just in case," he said.

"Just in case what? In case we wander into the imaginary gnome forest behind the Food 4 Less, or decide to make a nice little home under the freeway overpass?"

"You smartass. It's to throw them off. You never know when the eye is out."

"Well, it's not like we're going to buy crack," I said.

"Man, fighting with doorknobs really fucks up your brain.

You're not thinking right at all. We have to expect that they are always looking. We have to be safe, and we need to blend in."

"Blend in? How are we blending in lugging around some huge tent in the middle of the day down in some poor-ass neighborhood with barely any grass to even pitch the stupid thing?"

"That, my friend, is exactly how we blend in. If we were hauling a tent trying to score, say, near the Arroyo hills or Griffith Park or Runyon, we'd be done for. There are reasons to have a tent around those places and we'd be worked over like two-dollar strumpets. But they aren't looking for anybody camping down by Pico-Union. There is no reason for it, precisely why we'll blend in. The obvious becomes the unobvious."

He had me. Drug rationale. Still, it was a little extravagant.

"Still," I said, "it is a little extravagant."

"Bah. Stay here if you want. I'm going to do this thing."

Don't go to Pico-Union.

Not because of the general odds of being caught in gang-war crossfire, or because it's one of the poorest neighborhoods in Los Angeles, policed by the notoriously corrupt Rampart Division, beset by crime and hopelessness, but because the best shit is down there, and by best, I mean worst. The kind of wicked stuff that simulates ecstatic invincibility to its most superlative, supernova echelon—while swiftly as a calculating eagle it grips in its icy talons your heart, your skull, still pumping, pumping and gritting the amp dance, and carries them off for the final sacrifice. Harv holds there. He's a rich mother, playing both sides of the border, he knows the game. He deals two floors subterranean in a squalid slipshod tenement built into a small slope, keeping south of the radar, and also has an estate in the Hollywood Hills, a mile above Franklin. But hell. If you're going to go get drugs, then really go get your drugs. Have some guts about it. Forget the Hollywood Hills. Go to Pico-Union.

Here, you don't have to deal with the crummy debutante princesses hanging around Harv's Hills house, the ones who mistake speed for even more ego and pageantry than they were already bequeathed from their knotty-assholed, smug Black Beauty–gulping Industry parents before them. The cycle, it just does not end. Not only those godforsaken women who drape themselves ridiculously all over the place, but worse, their Chauncey boyfriends who can't even hold their drink, let alone their amphetamine. The only thing worse than people who call the stuff "spizz"—naïve fools who can't come to terms with what they're doing and try to sugarcoat it as if it were kiddy candy, when it is exactly what it is: speed—are the inane, rich parasites who try so hard to be "down" by snorting with the proletarians, when what they really should be spending their easy money and family handouts on is holy pharmaceutically clean Dexedrine and Methedrine, or just go the other way and score some pure pressed opium, or, if they must go up, unadulterated Bolivian cocaine at the very least. Leave me and my drug of choice in peace. For my money—if I had any—I'd stick with the program.

Harv must've been up in the Hills, and Nettles, his skeleton wife, wasn't keeping shop down at Pico-Union, which meant she probably found out that Harv was banging some Westside Debbie back at the ranch. None of his "lieutenants" were there either. Nobody answered. Normally, *someone* is always there.

By this time we'd caught the urge and were facing irate collapse, due to expectation.

"What now?"

"I have to piss," Jim Grace hissed, and stormed off behind the tenement.

I leaned against the building, nauseated by the idea of going up into the Hills, when I heard a fiery "Hallelujah!" burst from the urination.

"Look at this," Grace said, returning. "Perfect."

"Your fly's down."

"Thanks. Okay, so check this out . . ."

Jim Grace had found a nice baggied chunk of ice in his customized underwear—a secret pocket sewn beneath the hangar for his testicles and padded against ball sweat with maxi pads—that he'd forgotten about. We sliced and crushed it even, two fat crystal caterpillars the size of joints, and snorted them behind a dumpster in a trash-ridden alley adjacent to Union. Instantly, my heart jammed itself up into my throat, my eyes blew wide. All dials and switches cranked. The raspy throat of the city screamed like ancient iron daggers against my eardrums and somehow it was sexy, invigorating, a mountainous delight. Compound wizards rewiring the brain to the tune of Armageddon. EVERYTHING GOES UP. I could hear a cricket jerking itself ten miles away. I was locked in.

It was a sun-destroyed four p.m. when we made for the bus. We walked dozens of blocks in swift minutes, the deltas of our chests soaked in long, wide Vs.

"We need your wheels."

"Wheels, yes. And MUSIC. WE NEED MUSIC, NOW!" I yelped.

"NOT SO LOUD," Grace said, loudly.

"Yes, you're right, push the catheter in . . ."

"Catheter?"

"Never mind. We need to get to the number 4 bus if we want the car."

"We can't take the bus all the way," Grace said.

"Into the Hills?"

"Yeah, that was all I had, for sure. We got lucky. I haven't changed my underwear is all. Shit, I'd have washed that chunk later this evening. Lucky, damn lucky."

"Let's get the car," I said.

We made it to the car in good enough time, just before the bus ride from downtown to Hollywood, to my house, might have made my cranium explode. There were bad vibes squaring us from all sides: plump brown mamas hauling bags of groceries and the tender elderly clutching lotto tickets—entirely evil in our peculiar state. Grace and I beyond tense, our innards gnashing at the walls of our skin, probably looking to our fellow passengers like two deranged deviant gimps who'd worked each other into a spastic, primordial lust fury and couldn't wait for some serious fornicating in the privacy of our own home. Or in the tent, perhaps, which Jim was clutching like a bomb whose lit fuse was about to expire. It didn't help that we were constantly whispering gibberish into each other's ears.

After about an hour I located the keys—I'd hidden them from myself during the bad run the week prior—and we were doing fifty on Franklin, feverish for the turnoff up into La-La Land.

"There it is!" Grace screamed over the wail of Neil Young's "Cortez the Killer" spun up to earsplitting decibels.

"I know."

"Man, fuck Cortez!" Grace howled, slapping his knees.

"Look," I said, pointing out the windows at thick chaparral climbing up the rise, houses disappearing into the shadows of oak and rocky crags. "Old Mexico."

"Fuck Spain! Fuck the United States! Goddamn goldbrickers! This is Mexico! Glorious Mexico!" Grace cried, now a hardwired demon full of fast rage.

"You're not Mexican," I said. I leaned into the left turn

going at least 45 mph. After a good fifteen-minute bounce up the mountain we reached the gate and were buzzed in.

"Better leave the tent in the car," I said.

"Right," Jim Grace agreed.

"Gents," Harv greeted us as we walked up the three-hundred-yard stretch from parking to the house. There were about ten cars in the lot, meaning the place was going to be a scene.

"Harv, *que pasa*," Grace said, extending his hand. I simply nodded, keeping my clenched fists in my pockets.

"Come on in. *Mi casa su casa* and all that."

We went into the den—the business room—and as we passed the kitchen I caught a glimpse of Nettles slunk against the stove smoking nothing but two inches of ash from a beaten cigarette. She had a lake of purple around her right eye. I reached up and patted my own bruised orbital plate. When we passed the sliding glass that opened into the courtyard we saw a half-naked blond girl prancing around the pool in a fried haze. She looked no older than sixteen.

"That's Tabby," Harv said. "Her and Nettles are getting . . . acclimated."

In the den Harv measured up two very generous sixties, even though I was just along for the ride; not buying, necessarily, but knowing that Grace would part me off a kind freebie.

"Don't worry about it for now," Harv said. "Two for one today, and you'll make it up to me later."

A loaded deal to be sure. Regardless, Grace and I quickly pocketed our bounties when we heard a gang of intriguing cheers and whistles explode from the clubhouse out beyond the pool. Harv eyed us cautiously, then fixed a stern, secure gaze on us that warned: *You shall not fuck with me.*

"You boys want to come out back and 'tend the ceremony?

It's totally cracked."

My throat clenched *no*, but the ill-fated notion sank back down to my gut unspoken. I had a bad feeling. I'd only been up to Harv's Hills house a handful of times, and the place didn't sit right. It always felt appropriate to leave. I'd never seen anything too strange going on outside of meth heaven and hell and their according crimes in general, mostly just a bunch of paroxysmal, self-entitled eccentric turds jettisoning their brains toward sweet oblivion; rather, it was an aura of badness, and all I wanted to do now was go home and read a thick nineteenth-century Russian novel front to back, or masturbate for four or five hours, maybe.

"Ceremony?" Grace asked.

"Yeah. The New Church of Zoom," Harv shrugged. "It's not my thing—pretty fucked-up, really—but they pay me too much to refuse."

We leaned into Harv's taster plate and each took a hefty snort. Somewhere deep down inside not wanting anything more to do with any of this, I still couldn't refuse.

"Well, okay," Grace said.

Never coming here again, I swore, *this is the end*, when Harv slid the clubhouse door aside.

"This is Jesus. He died for our—your—sins."

In the middle of the clubhouse stood a meticulously constructed seven-foot crucifix with a beautiful, sleek, powerfully built, but atrociously dead brown-and-white pit bull terrier nailed to it, flies swarming around the bloody spikes driven through its spread front paws and its bundled hind quarters. A male, his eyes expired shuddered in incomprehension. A dozen people were cajoling in a circle, swathed in sweat, caught in the frenzied, possessed grip of fanatical religious conviction. I recognized one of them as an acclaimed actor who'd been in the papers on drug charges, pornography scandal, and spousal abuse. To the right of the sacrificed dog was a much smaller cross with a fanged marmot crudely driven into it, caught sneering in its death. To the left, an empty cross the same size. On a table next to it sat a tray of pulverized methamphetamine, a giant syringe, the necessary means to fire, and a Bible. There were tufts of hair stuck to the bloody rig.

"You're just in time. I guess Judas is next," Harv said, and nodded toward a cage where a handsome white domestic shorthair cat lay apprehensively licking its paw. The dancing freaks of the New Church of Zoom paid us no attention at all.

"Judas wasn't crucified," Jim Grace said. "He killed himself."

My heart sputtered and my gut folded. I have never been one to stomach the slaughter of innocents. I gave Grace a piercing leer, a silent command that it was time to go. He looked pallid, confused, knocked silly from the scene. Before either of us could fully comprehend the massive severity of it: "Now isn't this a surprise," someone cooed from behind, just outside the clubhouse door. I recognized the voice but I couldn't place it. Grace and I turned around and found a thick, sculpted bulldog of a man walking firmly toward us.

"Shit," Grace mumbled.

"What?" I whispered.

"Nothing," Grace said. "Nothing."

The zealots continued, praising the Lord and singing "Blessed All Ye Faithful."

"What the fuck is going on?" I gasped.

The man offered his hand. "Roy Mendoza. Dozer."

It immediately struck me that Detective Dozer was doing absolutely nothing to curb the sacrifice—felony animal cruelty to the highest degree—nor making any attempt to bust Harv or anybody else on enormous drug offenses.

"You've got to be kidding me," I said. I turned to go.

"Give me a minute, Will, please," Grace said.

"Ah, William O'Sullivan," Dozer said.

"You here on a call for domestic aggravated assault?" I asked Dozer, regarding Nettles. Harv hissed a clicked tongue at me and spat on the ground.

"Let's have a seat," Dozer said.

Jim Grace, Dozer, and I sat at a picnic table in the area between the clubhouse and the pool. Dozer faced the New Church of Zoom, and Grace and I faced the house, yet I couldn't help turning my head back to look. The congregation clamored further with song. The detective remained unfazed, and Harv retreated into the angry womb of his manor.

"I haven't heard from you."

"Look, Roy, it's done, man. You can't keep living in the past, right? You've got to move on. I can't do anything more for you. I've gotten on with my life," Jim Grace said.

"Yeah, getting along well, aren't you," Dozer mocked. They talked as old friends gone sour long ago, presently uncertain of what it all amounted to.

"She's gone, man. Gone for good. How many years has it been? Five? Seven? You've got to give up the ghost," Jim Grace said.

"What the hell is going on?" I burst in.

Jim turned, his face wrung with guilt and sympathy, not for Dozer, but for me. "Shit, Will, I'm sorry. I didn't know he was going to be here."

"Just damn good timing," Dozer chimed.

"Roy—Detective Dozer—was on my case, hard, years ago, when I was a driver. Until he discovered his wife was a lesbian. He found her in bed with Cammy. Strange turn of events."

Cammy—Camille—was Jim Grace's ex-wife. He'd talked to me about her from time to time, how he had not known much true happiness since, and about getting into using afterward, but never exactly why she left. At the time he was a high-paid wheeler for the entertainment industry, escorting celebrities to the most exclusive dealers in town, when heroin was making its comeback in the '90s and speed was mostly for maintenance, and Grace himself had not yet partaken in either.

"They're still together. They divorced us both," Dozer said, his face old and worthless. "Back when I was full of piss and fire," he waved his hand, "and actually cared about all of this. A real star trooper."

I rubbed my temples and dreamed of simpler times, times that I had mistaken for complex, before my own downfall into this exciting, mesmerizing, and delicious and nefarious, dire, and abusive world. I'd been living disenchanted beyond my means for too long, so I thought, just wanting certain kicks—some sort of adjuvant freedom from the pain of life, I guess. But the fee, it seemed, had suddenly grown too large. You cannot blame it on the drug, only the people.

"Speaking of piss," I said, bewildered, disgusted, "excuse me."

I got up from the picnic table, glanced once more at the horrendous scene in the clubhouse, and stormed into the mansion. I went into the bathroom, pulled myself out, but nothing came. I zipped up, flushed the unsoiled toilet, and scrambled through the medicine cabinet for some downers. There were none. I shut the cabinet and looked in the mirror. Alien, a phantom, as if I could no longer place who I was. I produced the sack, crushed the biggest dose I'd ever considered, withdrew a single from my wallet, rolled it tight, and sucked the line dry. I didn't know what else to do. Moreover, at this point I was full of distortion, blasting like a roaring, gnashing, hot-blooded ice comet through outer space. My throbbing, beaten eye could have easily popped with stroke against the mirror. A. Am. Amp.

I walked out of the bathroom and passed Nettles. I paused, turned, and headed into the kitchen.

"What do you make of this shit?" I asked, chewing on my lips, my brain swelling to the palpable limit within the gripping palm of my skull.

"Mind your own business."

"Jesus, Net, you should cook yourself up a sandwich or something. You look like hell. Get strong, don't let the bastard hit you no more."

"I'm getting the fuck out of here," she said quietly. "And I'm taking it all with me."

"Me too. But first I'm going to cook you something to eat."

I feigned rifling through the cupboards for food, secretly contemplating the options of my exit, until I found a large cast-iron skillet that must've weighed ten pounds.

"If I don't ever see you again, for chrissakes, Net, stick up for yourself. You don't need to deal with all this just to get some good crank."

"Why you ain't got no woman, Will?"

"Hell if I know," I said. I walked past her and out toward the pool, the skillet firm in my hand.

Dozer went out like a lit match under tap water. I stood over him panting, having clocked him from behind with all of my might. I dropped the frying pan and scrambled through his clothes until I found what I was looking for. Jim Grace eyeballed the piece.

"What are you doing?"

"Did you give him my phone number?"

"No way. He's a cop, man, it takes him two minutes to figure that stuff out."

"What kind of deal do you have with him, you a selective narc or something?"

"Hell no," Jim Grace shot back, offended by the question. "Can't you tell he doesn't give a shit about the law anymore? He didn't even know we were coming. He was up here doing his own kind of business with Harv."

I almost pointed the thing at him, my best friend. Catching myself, I lowered it. I reached in my pocket for the car keys.

"Go start the car, Jim."

"Dozer just wants the panties."

"Go start the car."

He refused to take the keys. "Be calm, be calm."

"They're killing fucking animals in there!"

"It's none of our business," he said. "I don't agree with it. It's wrong. It's terrible, but . . ."

Jim Grace was holding out because this was sanctuary: a place to connect—any bad, otherwise intolerable sin washed away in the name of screwing-it-on, in the name of assured supply, in the name of, well, addiction, I suppose, or at least undeniable enchantment. The same things that had made me tolerate it all up until now as well. The dose I jammed in the toilet shifted into twentieth gear. The blood in my veins was going for the record, racing like a rocket car across a desert salt flat, reckless and proud, screaming for something official. I turned my back on Jim Grace and stomped toward the clubhouse.

I raised the gun and shot three times into the ceiling. Everyone quivered, turned, stood vacillating before me while drywall and stucco from the bullet holes blanketed the room in softly falling snow. I said nothing, but went over to the cage, opened it, and grabbed the cat by the scruff of its neck and held it close to my chest. Back to the door, I turned and piloted the barrel in a straight line across every one of them. They all stared at me blankly in disbelief—the same look Grace and I had on our own faces when we stumbled upon their terrible ritual— as if I were the one in the wrong. The semifamous, Academy Award–nominated actor moved to speak, but thought better of it. I held fast, my finger microscopically humping the trigger, but I did not bring fire on them. Instead, I honed in on the crucified dog and let a single shot go into its chest, rotated slightly, and too symbolically gave the marmot an honorable death. Then I walked out.

When I returned to the picnic table Grace was shaking. The gun had given him a fever. In the distance, next to the pool, Nettles had Tabby by the hair in one fist, and was burying the young girl's face with the other.

"You coming, Jim?"

"I'm Mexican. By marriage. My uncle. I have a right to care, you know." Grace nodded his head about, regarding the landscape. He had slipped into asylum, unable to deal with the matter at hand.

"Sure," I said. "Old Mexico."

Dozer came to, groaning, the big man curling into a bamboozled little ball.

"Never call my house again," I said. The detective didn't answer. His eyes darted about.

I walked toward the mansion, the cat's claws digging into my shoulder, my ribs. I felt my leg cover in warm wetness. I met Harv coming through the doorway, his face twisted in shock. He saw the gun and moved out of the way. The unmistakable waft of feline ammonia rose from my hip and raided my nostrils.

"What the fuck is going on out here?"

"This is my cat now," I said.

Harv hesitated. He could see it in my eyes: I had gone off to a place where diplomacy was incontrovertible. "Take good care of him," he finally replied.

"His name is Raskolnikov."

"Fine."

"Raskolnikov, you got it? Not Judas, never Judas." I motioned to go, but paused and faced the feared, respected, worshipped pusher. "No more Church of Zoom, Harv. I swear to fucking God, no more. Understand?"

Harv grudgingly nodded his head in false affirmation, with stark ballooning eyeballs full of guaranteed revenge.

"Will," Jim Grace bayed, catching up. "Give me the keys. I'll drive."

I bent sideways, nodding to my front right pocket, not letting go of the cat or the gun. Grace shoved his hand in and fished through my crotch. The episode on the bus flashed in my head. "We're queer," I said. I started laughing, then tears took over, followed by a screaming slideshow in my mind of everything that had just happened—and in the same beat I became quiet, feeling in that moment the terror of cavernous sadness. My eyes dried hard and plateaued on a crux so severe that I was now beyond weeping. We walked down the path.

"How did you get those panties?" I asked.

"I . . ." Grace stammered, struggling not to rush ahead.

"How long have you kept those underwear in your freezer?"

Grace opened the car doors, and the cat, who I'd just named Raskolnikov perhaps for the redemption of us all, trembled on, wheezing against the saturated folds of my sticky shirt. I waited patiently for an answer from Grace, as if our lives weren't in danger; as if there was no reason for concern of the weaponized mob making their way down the path; as if everything up the hill had disappeared; as if we were simply high on a gorgeous meth run; as if the earth itself had frozen and two tight bros had all the time in the world.

M. Abrahams

JAMES FRANCO is an acclaimed actor, director, artist, and writer. His film appearances include *127 Hours, Howl, Milk,* and *Pineapple Express.* On television, he starred in the critically acclaimed series *Freaks and Geeks.* Franco has written and directed several short films, and his visual art was featured at Clocktower Gallery in New York. The author of *Palo Alto: Stories,* his writing has appeared in *Esquire,* the *Wall Street Journal,* and *McSweeney's.* Franco has an MFA in creative writing from Brooklyn College, an MFA in fiction writing from Columbia University, and is enrolled in the PhD program in literature at Yale.

CRYSTAL METH

In my dream I am in Olympic National Park, it is dawn. Moss-draped, shadow-drenched, tortured tree trunks twist upward, reaching for rare sunlight.

I'd never given much thought to how I would die.

Suddenly, in this dream, every creature in the forest is deadly silent. Neither bird, beast, nor insect makes a noise. A predator is near.

Then, in the distance, a tiny snick. I run, fast.

Trees whip past, I dodge branches. I'm chasing something. It's exhilarating. Terrifying. Finally, up ahead, through the whir, the first glimpse of my prey: a deer.

417

JAMES FRANCO: I was asked to write this thing for this magazine about crystal meth and the dangers of it. I didn't know what to write. Then I had this idea: I would write this thing that was like *Twilight* but then wasn't. I mean, I would appropriate the story of *Twilight* but call it *Crystal Meth* and not change anything, and maybe with the new title it would feel different when people read it.

I realized that I couldn't go to the book as a source because the books have been eclipsed by

It's running for its life. It darts through the forest maze. It sprints, but I gain. Beyond the deer, I can see the forest's edge, white sunlight glowing against the trees. The deer races for the light. I'm just behind it, about to emerge from the shadowy darkness. The deer leaps into the light in a high arc, it hovers against the white glare of the sun. Then, bam!

It's white and only white all around.

Dying in the place of someone I love seems like a good way to go.

In Arizona, the sunlight. I have alabaster skin, I'm vulnerable. I'm an introverted, imperfect beauty.

I can't bring myself to regret the decision to leave.

Before I left Arizona, I dug up a tiny barrel cactus and put it in a clay pot.

Oh, poor little cactus.

Poor little me.

"Bye, Bella!"

The three tanned, athletic, blond girls from my old school waved as they left their

the films; at least the characters have.

You can never think of Bella Swan without thinking of Kristen Stewart, and you'll always think of Rob Pattinson as Edward Cullen, so I turned to the script, which was easy enough to find online, replete with notes f the writer to change thi such as the buck in the oper dream to a deer. I thought if I changed the format to pr took out the scene headi and put it into past tense, I wc get something new. It woul

McMansion and hopped into a convertible Mercedes. Their flawless, bought-and-paid-for beauty contrasted with my natural pale-ness.

"Good luck at your new school!"

"Don't forget to write."

"We'll miss you."

I waved back, sweetly, but halfheartedly.

"Have a good . . ."

As I stepped off the curb, I tripped. When I stood, they were gone.

"Life."

Clearly they were not close friends. I have a grown-up demeanor and innate intelligence and their kind is not for me.

Rene, my mom, came out of our house. She's in her mid-thirties. Our house was low-rent for the ritzy neighborhood. Rene is eclectic, scattered, anxious, more like my best friend than my parent. She thrust her cell phone at me.

"It won't work again, baby."

"You put it on hold."

"I did?"

be the book, and it wouldn't be the script: it would be a spare and equally bad middle ground that told the same story. I kept thinking about the scene in the biology classroom where Edward gets upset because Bella smells so good he wants to kill her. This, I thought, surely this will work, this is addiction, but not just addiction, it is flirting with death, this is the love that kills.

It was difficult to see how I would parse out the desires of the characters and parallel them to crystal meth addiction

"Look. You also called Mexico."

Rene pushed me playfully.

We laughed.

"I'll figure it out. You gotta be able to reach me and Phil on the road. I love saying it out loud, me and Phil on the road—woah, on the road."

"Very romantic."

Phil came out. He's good looking with an athlete's body. He held my three suitcases.

"If you call crappy motels, backwater towns, and ballpark hot dogs romantic."

He put his Phoenix Desert Dogs baseball hat on Rene's head and kissed her. Phil's love for Rene is reassuring. Phil headed to the old station wagon to load the luggage, while Rene slipped her arm through mine, clinging to me as we walked to the car.

"Now, you know if you change your mind, I'll race back here from wherever the game is." But her face was strained and I knew what a great sacrifice coming back would be. I forced a smile.

"I won't change my mind, Mom."

because I was starting with Bella as the focalizing character and switching to Edward when the addiction element came into play. Then the editor suggested I add some actual parallels between vampires and tweakers: never sleep, paleness, sensitive to sunlight, selective ⟨ one sole hunger, the burder living forever.

But I suppose she gets as addicted to him, in her ⟨ way. I mean, he is all she th about. And then other thi happen. He drives cars re

"You might. You've always hated Forks."

"It's not about Forks, it's about Dad. I mean, two weeks a year, we barely know each other."

Rene looked worried.

"Mom, I want to go. I'll be fine."

As she hugged me, I realized I was full of dread, doubt, and regret. I tried to keep the façade up as I climbed into the backseat of the car.

I listened to my iPod, earbuds in my ears, as I got a last glimpse of the sparkling malls, chic shoppers, and manicured cactus gardens.

I said goodbye to the McMansions and goodbye to the scorched landscape baking under the hot sun.

Washington State: nothing but deep, dark, green forests for miles. Lake Crescent. Over it all hangs the mist from the ever-present cloudy gray sky. Everything is wet and green and drenched in shade.

The thing about Charlie is that he's a cop.

fast, people get killed, and she almost gets raped, and they can't have sex because he is afraid that he will kill her, and blood is always on his mind, and teenagers get killed and kidnapped, and they hide out in hotel rooms from other murder-ous teenagers, and she is with a hundred-year-old man and she is underage, and then they go to the prom.

It seemed like ALL teenage emotions were there, all wrapped up in a fantastical premise, and they—Stephanie

He's taciturn and introverted like me. He drove me in his cruiser down a wet two-lane highway. Trees, drenched and heavy-leaved on both sides. Silence.

"Your hair's longer."

"I cut it since last time I saw you."

"How's—"

"Good . . . it grew out again."

Silence.

"Your mom?"

More silence.

THE CITY OF FORKS WELCOMES YOU. Pop. 3532. Logging town. Wood-carvings in the storefronts. Timber Museum's sign: two loggers sawing a stump. Police station: a small wooden building across from city hall, also wooden.

The old house. Two-story, a woodshed full of firewood. A small boat in the garage. Fishing gear, an old buoy. Getting out of the car, I thought: home.

Carried in the bags. The house, not stylish. Only new thing: flat-screen TV. Comfortable, lived-in. Fishing memorabilia;

Meyers, the filmmakers, and the actors—were getting away with it because it wasn't real, it was just vampires and shit.

Well, I was going to change all that. I was going to show how close meth addiction is to *Twilight*. But then something happened. My manager's part Dalton, was hit over the hea New Year's Eve. He was in front yard, it was nine at nig nice neighborhood in the Va out in the Tarzana area, he walking to his car to go get s more champagne for his gue photos of Charlie fishing with Indians. Hand-made cards to "Daddy" and photos of me. Me, age seven, in a tutu, sitting stubbornly on the ground.

"I put Grandpa's old desk in your room. And I cleared some shelves in the bathroom."

"That's right. One bathroom."

A photo: a much younger Charlie and Rene, on vacation, beaming with love.

"I'll just put these up in your room—"

"I can do it—" We both reached for the bags, bumped one another. I let Charlie carry them upstairs.

An antique rolltop desk was sitting in the corner. The room was filled with my child-hood remnants, which had seen better days. I unpacked my CD case and loneliness finally overwhelmed me. I sat heavily on the edge of the bed, tears threatening ...

Then we hear a HONK outside. Bella runs across the hall and looks out the window to see—11. OUTSIDE—A FADED RED TRUCK, CIRCA 1960, pulls up ...   11.

when he dropped his keys. When he bent over he felt something smash into the back of his head. He fell forward and then stood. No one was around. He quickly called 911 (nine-one-one).

"I think I've been hit by a meteor."

It took the ambulance only three minutes to arrive, despite the meteor comment. They found him sitting on the lawn. His wife and his son, Peter, ran out when they heard the siren. Peter was the good son, not the older son in jail for possession of

Fuck shit fuck

EXT. CHARLIE'S HOUSE—DAY

Bella exits to find Charlie greeting the driver, JACOB BLACK, 16, Quileute Indian, amiable, with long black hair, and hints of childish roundness in his face. Charlie and Jacob help Jacob's father, BILLY BLACK (from the photos), into a wheelchair.

CHARLIE: Bella, you remember Billy Bla . . .

. . . zona. Give it up for the rain. And he shakes his wet baseball cap onto Bella's head.

BELLA: xxxxxxxxxxxxxxxxxxxxxxxxxxxxxxxx

She heads toward her seat, brushing off her hair. But she freezes when she sees— Edward. Terrific.

Bella straightens, girding herself. Then strides to the table, and confidently drops her books down, ready to address him. But he looks up at her—   Hello.

EDWARD: Hello.

Bella stops. Stunned. He is direct, precise, as if every word is an effort for him.

marijuana with the intent to sell and possession of an unregistered firearm. That was Sam, the bad son, the son who got some Mexican gang shit tattooed on his boyish Jewish face.

"Please," Dalton had said in the visiting room. "Please just don't get the tattoo on your f you'll get out and you'll get this, you can get a job, but d get the tattoo."

The kid was out and he crazy and this is what it come to: His life was fucked he blamed his father. He trie

EDWARD: I didn't have a chance to introduce myself last week. My name is Edward Cullen.

She's too shocked he's talking to her to answer.

EDWARD (prompting): xxxxxxxxxxxxxxxxxxx xxxxxxxxxxxxxxxxxxxxxxxxxxxxxxxxxxx

time . . . as the SUV PEELS out, WIPING THE FRAME—

107EXT. HIGHWAY, PACIFIC NORTH-WEST—DAWN107

The sun begins to rise on the empty road as a sleek, BLACK MERCEDES SEDAN with tinted windows BLASTS through frame—

108INT. MERCEDES—SAME   108

Jasper driv lic in the passenger seat. Bella is in the back, her eyes red from crying. She talks on her cell phone –

BELLA: Mom, it's me again. You must have let your phone die. Anyway, I'm not in Forks anymore but I'm okay. I'll explain when you call . . .

kill his father.

If the ambulance had come two minutes later Dalton would have died. They put part of his skull in his abdomen to preserve it. They cut open his forehead to relieve the pressure because the brain had been pushed forward.

There was a hole in the back of his head. The police were investigating.

Then I learned that Sam wasn't out. He'd be in jail for eighteen more months.

THE
END

Designed by James Franco and Nicole Poor

PART III
METHODOLOGY

Anne Windisbar

JESS WALTER is the author of five novels, most recently *The Financial Lives of the Poets* (2009), *The Zero*, a 2006 National Book Award finalist, and *Citizen Vince*, winner of the 2005 Edgar Award for Best Novel. His books have been translated into twenty-two languages, and his short fiction, essays, and journalism have appeared in *Playboy*, *McSweeney's*, *ESPN The Magazine*, *Details*, the *Washington Post*, the *Los Angeles Times*, and many others. He lives in Spokane, Washington.

wheelbarrow kings
by jess walter

'm hungry as fuck.

Mitch knows a guy getting rid of a TV. A big-screen supposed to work great. Mitch says he watched UFC on it.

That don't make sense I say. A guy just giving away a big-screen.

Mitch says the guy has two TVs.

Mitch talks a lot of shit so I won't be surprised if there ain't no TV.

Fish and chips is what I really want. I got twelve dollars which would be plenty for fish and chips. So hungry.

Mitch says it's a heavy-ass TV and we'll need a wheelbarrow for sure.

I ask where the fuck are we supposed to get a wheelbarrow. Like I just carry a wheelbarrow around. Sometimes Mitch.

He says we'll pawn that TV for two hundred easy. Then I could spend my twelve bucks on fish and chips or steak or whatever the fuck I want.

Mitch's sister lives up on the south hill. He says she's got a wheelbarrow. She and her husband garden and shit. I met his sister one time. She seemed cool.

I started loving fish and chips when we had it at middle school. I never had it before that. I used to think chips were the different kind of fries with ridges like we had at school. But it can be any fries.

If we do get two hundred bucks for that TV me and Mitch

are gonna gear up over at Kittlestedt's. On Kittlestedt's icy shit. Get on a big old spark. None of that scungy east side peanut butter we been bulbing for a month now. Not after we sell that TV. No more twelve-buck quarters for us.

We gonna amp up on a couple of fat bags Mitch says.

I'm hungry as fuck I say to Mitch.

We gonna eat for days after we sell that TV he says.

He wants to take a bus up the south hill to borrow his sister's wheelbarrow. Mitch has a bus pass. I got that twelve dollars but no way I want to spend a buck twenty-five on the bus. Because you can't even get that east side shit for under twelve. Twelve is the cheapest I ever seen. Anywhere.

You comin' Mitch asks.

If I do spend some of my money on the bus least I could eat then. Fish and chips. Or even just get a tacquito at Circle K and some Sun Chips. I like them Sun Chips too. But I ain't buying food unless we sell that TV.

Mitch's bus pass is expired. He wants me to pay for both of us on the bus. Fuck that I say. We get off. The bus drives away.

And I think of something. How the fuck are we gonna get that wheelbarrow all the way downtown from his sister's house anyway. It's like two miles. And we'd have to take the wheelbarrow back. Uphill.

Yeah that's true Mitch says.

I known that fucker two years. First time he ever said I was right.

First time you ever been right Mitch says.

Fuck I'm hungry.

You keep saying that. Fucking buy some food then Mitch says.

But he knows I can't. I need my twelve bucks. He's just fucking jealous 'cause he ain't even got enough for a bump.

There's a coffee place downtown where I know this girl. I went to school with her. We walk down there. Keep our eyes open for wheelbarrows. You see wheelbarrows at construction sites sometimes it seems like. But when you need one you sure as fuck don't. I don't think there is a wheelbarrow in all of downtown Spokane.

The coffee shop has outside tables either side of the door. There's two guys in suits and sunglasses drinking iced coffee. They're eating scones. Them fucking scones look great. I'm hungry as shit. The business guys give me a look. Inside the coffee shop I lick my lips to get the salt.

The girl I know ain't working. Sometimes she gives me the day-old pastry. She'll say what happened to you Daryl. And I'll say what happened to you. I forget her name. She's kind of fat now. She wasn't fat in middle school. She was pretty hot I think. But she's fat now.

But that's not what I mean when I say what happened to you. About her being fat. I'm just fucking around. And I did know her name before. I just don't know it now.

Anyways it don't matter because she ain't working. Some guy is working instead. With a goatee. I ask him is the girl who works here around. He makes a face like what girl or maybe he just thinks Mitch and me stink. And he looks at the stain on my T-shirt. I was having a hot dog at the Circle K a few days ago and I was with Todo and that fucker waits until you take a bite of something and then he says the funniest shit. He could be a stand-up comedian Todo. I forget what he said exactly but the ketchup squirted on my shirt. And then it left this stain.

Mitch flops down in a booth.

The goatee guy watches Mitch pick at his face. You have to order something if you're gonna stay here the coffee guy says.

They got these cinnamon rolls must be half frosting. Fuck me I am so fucking hungry. The goatee guy looks at me like I'm a fucking jerk-spazz.

That girl—I have to start over. And then her name comes. Marci! Marci said come in and she'd give me something from the day-olds. Marci. I can't stop blinking.

Marci's not here.

Can you check. Can you check if she left me something from the day-olds.

I am so fucking hungry.

A couple ladies with shopping bags come in.

The goatee dude rubs his head. He leans forward like he's telling me a secret. If I give you tweakers a scone will you get the fuck out of here.

Give us each one.

They got a day-old basket next to the register. The dude takes two scones and gives them to me. One is a triangle. That's the one I want.

Come on Mitch I say.

We go outside. It's funny. Them two business dudes are sitting there eating scones. And Mitch and me are eating scones. Only we didn't pay for ours. Who's the fucking smart guy now.

Only that scone ain't too good. It don't taste like nothing. Not like that cinnamon roll would've. Or like fish and chips. More like wood chips.

Fuck me. I'm even hungrier now.

Mitch and me decide to just walk to the dude with the TV's house. Maybe he's got a wheelbarrow Mitch says.

It's over the river in a big house I never seen before. A covered front porch with a fridge out front. There's like ten people hanging at the house but it ain't a party. Mitch says the dude is strictly into weed but there's a smoked lightbulb on the front porch. I think maybe we'll get hooked up here. But the dude with the TV is all business.

He's eating a Hot Pocket while he talks to us. Fuck me I want that Hot Pocket. So fucking hungry.

You fucking stink this dude says to Mitch.

Yeah I'm gonna go home and get cleaned up after we sell that TV Mitch says.

What's wrong with this guy he asks.

He's just fucking hungry Mitch says.

The dude's got a brand-new TV in the living room. Two little kids are on the PS2. They're playing *Call of Duty*. I'm good on that game I say but they don't look up. The TV is pretty big. How big is that TV I ask.

Fifty-five inch the dude says. He says that's his new TV. The Double Nickel he calls it. The Sammy Hagar.

The picture is too sharp though. It's like sharper than your eyes. That would freak me out. Life ain't that real. On *Call of Duty* I see shit I never knew was there.

The other TV is on the back porch. It ain't even plugged in. It's an old-school projector TV. I worried Mitch was full of shit. But here it is just like he said. This TV is the biggest TV I ever seen. I don't even know how big. The thing's probably five feet tall and five feet wide. Probably three feet thick. It's fucking huge. Like a room. Mitch is right we're gonna need a fucking wheelbarrow.

You want it it's yours says the dude who lives here.

You know anyone who has a wheelbarrow around here Mitch asks the dude.

He looks at Mitch like get your own fucking wheelbarrow.

There's an alley behind the dude's house so Mitch and me go walking along there looking for a wheelbarrow.

I am so fucking hungry. For a while in middle school we got

free lunch. But then my mom worked at the air force base and we got off free lunch. She used to make me cold lunch but whenever there was fish and chips I'd buy my own school lunch. That's how much I liked it. And chili. I liked the chili fine but I really liked them cinnamon rolls. It's funny they always had cinnamon rolls and chili in middle school. I don't know why. They just did.

Fuck. I am so hungry.

I'm gonna kick your ass you don't stop saying that Mitch says.

You can't kick my ass.

A ten-year-old girl could kick your fucking jittery ass.

That girl's six-year-old sister could kick your picker ass.

That girl's newborn baby sister could kick your smelly ass.

That girl's kitten could kick your ass.

That girl's kitten's fleas could kick your ass.

Sometimes Mitch cracks me up. He ain't no Todo but sometimes.

We walk down that alley. There's a kid's Big Wheel. There's a turned-over grocery cart but it's got busted wheels.

And that's when I see it. Hey Mitch look. No shit. Next to a fall-down garage in back of this house. Leaning up against it. It ain't even rusted. A goddamn almost brand-new wheelbarrow. You hear that saying My Lucky Day and I guess sometimes.

There's a little chain-link fence with bent poles. I climb it easy. Grab that wheelbarrow. I wheel it up and heft it over the fence to Mitch. We push that thing back down the alley. We're practically running.

We fucking feel like kings.

I get one-fifty and you get fifty Mitch says. Out of the blue like that.

That's bullshit. I went and got the wheelbarrow.

I knew where the TV was he says.

Don't be a dick Mitch. We both gotta push that thing to the pawn.

One-twenty and eighty.

Don't be a dick.

One-ten ninety.

Fine.

I'm so fucking starving. The TV dude is eating some pretzels out of a bag when we come back. He's standing in his backyard watching his matted dog scoot around on his itchy ass on the dirt. He's laughing like it was a TV show.

The TV dude looks up and sees us. He's surprised we found a wheelbarrow.

How come you don't grow grass back here Mitch asks. That would look better. I can hear in Mitch's voice he thinks we're big shits for getting a wheelbarrow so fast.

I don't suppose you got another one of them Hot Pockets I ask the TV dude.

Nah man. He offers me some pretzels and I take a handful. But they don't taste like nothing. Just the salt.

We leave the wheelbarrow at the bottom of the stairs by the porch and go get on that TV. We can't barely budge it. That fucking TV is the heaviest fucking thing I ever lifted. I can't get under it and once we get it up we drop it.

Be fucking careful Mitch says.

You fucking be careful. You was pushing instead of lifting.

The TV dude just stands there eating his pretzels. Smiling at us. Like he did with the dog with the itchy ass.

Mitch spits on his hands. You got anything else you want to get rid of Mitch asks.

Get the fuck out of here. You guys smell like ass.

We pick it up again. We can't get a hold on it. It's all tippy. But that two hundred bucks is out there so we muscle it down the steps. It don't go in the wheelbarrow very well. Kind of sits on top on the rim. And it weighs so much it flattens the wheel. Fucking brand-new wheelbarrow and the wheel goes almost totally flat.

Fuck Mitch says. You got a pump man.

Get the fuck out of here the TV dude says. Fuckin' chalkers.

So we push it down the alley and then down the street. I'm on the front of the TV keeping it steady. Mitch is holding the wood handles of the wheelbarrow and pushing. We go really slow like that. A few feet for a minute and then we got to stop. It would be easier if the wheel had more air. But it still wouldn't be easy. I'm sweating. The sweat keeps getting in my eyes.

Fuck Mitch says.

I know I say.

I'm balancing that TV and walking backward. One time Mitch trips a little and the TV starts to go over and I just get in front of it. I just keep it from going over. Motherfucker watch what you're doing I say.

Sorry Mitch says. I tripped. He gets on the TV too and we get it balanced again.

It's six blocks to the pawn. It probably takes us ten minutes to go a block. Some kids are riding bikes like sharks around us. They stop to watch. One of them is eating a sandwich.

Mitch has to stop to wipe his sweat and breathe. I'm crazy fucking hungry.

What kind of sandwich is that I ask the little kid. It looks like cheese but not with the cheese melted just slices of cheese on white bread.

Fuck off tweaker the kid says. And he rides away on his bike eating that cheese sandwich. Or whatever kind of sandwich it is.

I swear if I wasn't on this TV I would pull that kid off his fucking bike and beat his ass. We didn't talk to older guys like that when I was a kid.

The next block goes a little faster. I think of that girl at the coffee shop and I wonder if she gives me the day-olds so I'll leave like the goatee guy did. But I don't think so. I think she likes to talk to me.

She gave me a cinnamon roll one time. That's how I know they're so good there. Remember these in middle school I asked her but she didn't remember the cinnamon rolls. Anyways that cinnamon roll was sure better than them dry scones. I wonder why them businessmen would eat scones when they could afford cinnamon rolls or even oat bars or muffins. I wonder why the fuck they make scones in the first place.

Why the fuck you think they make scones at all I ask Mitch.

Great mystery Mitch says.

Sometimes he is as funny as Todo.

The third block goes even slower. Mitch's arms are shaking. Red splotchy covered with sweat. And I feel dizzy from all the walking backward. You gotta switch me Mitch says.

So I push for a few blocks and Mitch steadies. Only I don't trust his steadying so I push more carefully than he did. It yanks your arms out of their sockets pushing that wheelbarrow. And even though it's a pretty new wheelbarrow I get a sliver from the wood handles.

Fuck me I say. I got a sliver.

I got like a hundred.

You got a hundred slivers.

I said LIKE a hundred.

We get four blocks. Only two to go. We stop at this yard and take turns steadying while the other guy rests in the grass until this old guy comes out and yells get the fuck off my yard. I'm gonna call the cops.

Fucking call 'em then Mitch says.

Where'd you steal that TV the old guy says. He's waving

something at us.

Fuck you Mitch says.

But for some reason I don't want the guy to think we stole it. We got it from a guy I say. And the wheelbarrow. Even though we didn't get that from a guy but stole it.

We start going again.

And I think of something. The old guy had a remote control. I say that to Mitch. You see that. I just thought of it. He was waving something at us and it was a fucking remote control.

Yeah Mitch says and we both laugh. Fucking people Mitch says.

Like a sword I say. He carries that remote around.

People spend their whole lives in front of that fucking box says Mitch. He says it like we got the life or something.

We're a few houses away from Monroe. The busy street with the pawn.

There's a Hawaiian grill place on Monroe just down from the pawn. They got this chicken and rice but it's at least five bucks. That sounds even better than fish and chips. That would leave me with just seven bucks though. Can't get no bump for seven bucks.

I think I'm gonna fucking starve to death Mitch. I'm dying here.

We're almost there he says.

Fucking kings.

By the time we get to the last block the whole tire has gone flat on the wheelbarrow. Now I'm just pushing on the steel rim. It's like pushing a fucking house uphill.

Pull motherfucker.

I am.

We can barely get it up on the sidewalk and then there's a curb cut and we can barely get up the other side of that. My hands are red raw. I been pushing the last three blocks. I should get half I say.

Fine Mitch says.

At the pawn I stay outside and steady the TV while Mitch goes inside. Some dude is coming out as Mitch goes in. He just bought a circular saw. He laughs at me. That's the funniest thing I ever saw he says. Fucking tweaker standing with a giant old TV on a wheelbarrow. And he takes out his phone and takes a picture of me.

I don't care. I just smile for the picture. 'Cause we made it. Fuck the TV dude and the little kid with the sandwich and that old guy with the remote and this guy with the camera phone. My big problem now is whether to have fish and chips or that Hawaiian chicken and rice.

The pawn guy comes out with a big-ass grin on his face. He stares at that TV like he can't believe we pushed it all the way there. It is pretty fucking cool now that I think about it. All the shit we went through. Fucking day this was.

How far did you guys push this thing.

A mile Mitch says.

This kind of pisses me off. It's enough what we done without making up some story. Six blocks I say.

No shit. And he shakes his head like we come from the North Pole or something.

It works great Mitch says. I just watched UFC on it this morning.

That pawn dude has the biggest grin on. Follow me he says.

I don't want to leave it here I say. It might fall.

The pawn dude helps us lean it against the wall of the store.

Then he takes us inside to where there's ten TVs hanging up. Most of them are flat and big like that TV dude's new double nickel. They're all plugged in. They all work good. Them new

TVs are like two hundred bucks is all.

You guys see any big-console projection-screen TVs in here. We say we don't.

No transistor radios or VHS players either. You guys are like five years late. I couldn't GIVE that fucking dinosaur away. I couldn't give it away if it came with a free car and a blowjob. Now get it the fuck out of my store.

In front of the pawn Mitch and I got nothing to say. We just stare at each other. Mitch looks sorry. He probably thinks I blame him. But I don't. Fuck he didn't know. It was a good try. A lot of things are like that. Good tries. I just wish I wasn't so fucking hungry. And I wish I had enough for Mitch's bump too and for some fish and chips. But I don't. I just got the twelve bucks. Mitch knows. He looks like he's gonna die. Pale as shit.

I tell you what. We look back. The pawn dude is standing there. He's been watching us. I'll give you ten bucks for the wheelbarrow.

Fifteen Mitch says.

It's got a flat fucking tire the guy says. But he smiles. Like he's watching that dog rub its ass. Okay he says. Fifteen.

You gotta take the TV too I say.

What am I the fucking United Way here the pawn guy says. Fine. Take it round back and put it in the alley. So we lift it again off the wheelbarrow. It's like needles in my back every step we take with that fucking TV. My face is pressed against the black console which is a thousand degrees from the sun. My hands are so sweaty I'm sure I'm gonna drop it. But we make it to the alley where we leave it with a bunch of other garbage. Wire. Old shopping carts. An axle.

The guy gives Mitch fifteen bucks. You guys know I'm doing you a favor he says. I'm not gonna get fifteen bucks for that wheelbarrow. You know that right.

Yeah we say.

Good he says. Then since I'm doing you a favor you can do me one. Next time you cat shit–smelling motherfuckers get some idea to steal something and pawn it you go to a different fucking store, right. Go to Double Eagle over on Division. Fuckin' chalkers the pawn dude says.

Mitch goes to give me half of the fifteen but I say that's okay. We each got twelve bucks now. Plus three left over. We ain't making it to Kittlestedt's but that's okay. We'll go over to the east side where a fucker can still be king for twelve.

And that leaves us three bucks to eat on. It ain't enough for no fucking fish and chips. But we got enough for the Circle K.

Kings.

Mitch gets a pepperoni stick. I get a ninety-nine-cent big bag of Sun Chips. And we split a Dr. Pepper. The clerk wrinkles his nose but fuck him.

Then Mitch and me start walking toward the east side. I wish I would have thought to ask that coffee shop guy when that girl works again. The one who I went to middle school with. Fuck me. I think I forgot her name again.

I can't even taste the fucking Sun Chips. It's like they got no taste at all.

Then Mitch starts telling the whole story. Remember that free scone you got us.

Like I wasn't even there. Yeah I say.

And you saw that fucking wheelbarrow like you blew out your birthday candles and wished for it.

I laugh at that. Yeah.

And we come back and that fucking dog is scooting on his ass.

And even though I was there for all of it I laugh at every fucking thing he tells me about our day. We walk and Mitch tells the whole fucking story again. I think he's gonna tell that story forever. And I didn't laugh once when we were doing that shit. But now it all seems so fucking funny I can't hardly stand it.

I guess remembering is better than living.

And what about that dude waving his remote control Mitch says.

Yeah what the fuck was that.

Maybe he was a fucking Jedi knight Mitch says and we gotta stop walking we're laughing so hard. Fucking Ben Kenobi I say. And we both bend over laughing. And fuck me it's nice to be out walking. To have twelve bucks in your pocket and some tasteless Sun Chips in your belly. We walk and we laugh. All the way over to the east side.

BETH LISICK is the author of four books, including the *New York Times* best seller *Everybody into the Pool.* She is also an actor, filmmaker, and the cofounder of San Francisco's Porchlight Storytelling Series.

tips 'n' things by elayne
by beth lisick

12/20, 7:36 a.m. Audio Recording #1
The appetizers are going to be easy-peasy because all I have to do is do what I did last year, except be a little bit more on top of things during the actual party, and then we'll see how blown away everyone is. That, and the addition of the hot pots, is really going to take it to a new level. Fondue, anyone? Who says you have to call the Tasteful Affair catering truck just to have a holiday open house? You know who you are. Just because you have money doesn't mean you can do it better by hiring someone. Fuck you, Tammy, and the horse you rode in on whose name is Jacob Martinson, a baloney of a realtor.

Are you still with me? Why, hello, listeners. Let's start over. First let me say that doing this recording was Jim's idea. I'm one of those people who always gets asked, *How do you do it?* My friends literally stand there with their hands on their hips, just shaking their heads, laughing, saying, *How do you do it all so effortlessly, Elayne? And with such verve and zest and appeal and aplomb?* And, you know, there I am with all my balls in the air and I'm wheeling around on my unicycle, blindfolded, saying, *What? What are you talking about? I'm just being me!* So Jim says, *Honey, just strap the recorder on while you're getting ready for the party as a kind of experiment. It'll be interesting,* he says. *A testament, of sorts.* Our oral histories are more important than ever. So this is for anyone who wants to know how I do it all, or maybe even for you, Sasha, if my entertaining gene ever kicks in and you decide you want to take my advice for a change. For the record, I have not seen Sasha since last night at six when she went over to her friend's house to supposedly study for the SATs. Ho ho ho, says Santa to the child. Naughty or nice, babygirl? Just answer me that one. Naughty or nice.

Okay, moving on to the official business. My day. First things first, when the feet hit the floor, is doing my tape. Before coffee or grapefruit or brushing the fuzz from my tongue, I get my exercise. I'm going to turn the recorder off while I pop my routine in the VCR and start sweating. Jim says this thing is voice-activated, that during the boring parts it'll go off, but I don't trust it yet. For the record, I do the tape five times a week, not just when I have an event. That, plus a daily walk with Galileo the Wondermutt, and my backside looks as good as it did the day I graduated from the conservatory. Goodbye.

12/20, 8:25 a.m. Audio Recording #2

Mi, mi, mi, mi! I'm baaaaaaaack. And a little winded, as you can tell. I never had asthma or anything, but sometimes I think all those backstage cigarettes I sucked down in my twenties are coming back to haunt me. I may have subpar lung capacity, but can you do this? If you stick a stock of liquor in your locker, it is slick to put a lock upon your stock, or some joker who is quicker's gonna trick you of your liquor if you fail to lock your liquor with a lock. Ha! That, my friends, was my favorite tongue twister from ye olde thespian days. I got a million of 'em! You need unique New York. Hoo. Let me catch my . . . [*sound of Elayne's breathing here, a wheeze is detected*]. Oh, brother. And don't smoke, everybody. Oh, great. Now what am I doing? A public service announcement? Next thing you know, I'll be telling you how to perform the Heimlich, which actually did save my life one time, but that's a story for another day. And it's definitely rated R for raunchy because I was nude. Excuse me! Let's get down to it.

Oh, there's Jim turning off the shower. Jim! Now, on the invitations I said the party was from four p.m. to eleven p.m. in order to give everybody a window in which they could attend. Even the Tagmeyers, who are always booked-up, are coming. Last year, we didn't start till six and I really felt that for some of the older folks in the neighborhood it would be nice to get things started while it's still light outside. Make some hay.

I don't know what I did before the island. Seriously. My hand before God, as I stand here in the kitchen, before we remodeled I didn't have this gorgeous island with the Corian countertop to sit and have my coffee at every morning. It's so smooth and durable. I could run my palm across it all day long. That, and the new automatic espresso machine that tamps the grounds down and has a self-frother, really make my mornings feel like they are straight out of a TV commercial. Or a TV show even. A program.

Oh, here comes Jim! Big Jim. Give me a kiss, honey. Big man go to work and win bread for family. I love you, big man! Jim, say hi to the recorder.

Uh, hello recorder.

I'm doing the thing you said. Breaking down my party-day schedule for people who want to be in the know.

Oh great, honey. I've always said you were a magician.

Tell the good people what a magician I am!

This woman is a magician!

I am. I feel great. I feel super-great.

Okay. I'm working a half and then I'll go to the deli on my way home and pick up the stuff.

And the special mustard.

And the special mustard.

Honey, do you ever breathe in and feel like someone put

your oxygen on ice?

Hmm?

Nothing. Just get out of here, you big galoot. There he goes. That was my prince, my number one fan.

Okay, next thing we're going to do is get out the old stone tablet and chisel our list of all the dishes that are going to be part of the big holiday smorgasbord. Here we go. Fondue. Check. Potato torta. Deviled eggs. Classic. Spare ribs and dip. Black bean dip. Side of tortilla strips with those. Peanut and dill dips with roasted veggies. Having roasted veggies as opposed to raw is so much classier, I think. Focaccia and tapenade. Crab and artichoke dip, which is so cheesy and good. Dates and Parmesan. Jumbo shrimp—gotta love that oxymoron—and cocktail sauce. Mini quiches. Throw 'em in the oven. Easy. Curried phyllo triangles. Always a winner. Nuts. Mediterranean meatballs. Baked brie with pear and cranberry preserves. Salmon with my special orange miso sauce.

There. Mouth watering yet? And we haven't even gotten to the dessert buffet. Hold onto your hips! I've made chocolate truffles and Rice Krispies treats and cookies with broken candy cane pieces on top, and of course we have Linzer torte. And Jeannette is bringing the strudel when she comes over. Now, I'm going to put this list up on the fridge, so I can easily refer to it. There's a tip for you. And let's go pull my dress out of the guest room closet and take the plastic off to air it out. Size four, fits better than ever. Red satin. Satin Doll. The Lady in Red. I heard a terrible story on the radio about how toxic dry-cleaning is, but I have to say, there are certain stains that definitely need to be removed by chemicals. And get your mind out of the gutter on that one because I am referring to a thick, creamy white substance called . . . Miracle Whip. What do you think of Dijonaisse? I don't like it, thank you for asking.

You know what? This is actually fun, talking to nobody and everybody all at once. It makes me feel free somehow. A creative outlet for a gal who's always liked to let it all hang out. There's been a little lull since closing night of *The Dinner Party*. I don't know how many of you saw me reprise my role as Yvonne. That was a blast, as anything by Neil Simon always is, but it's good to have a project like this to keep my juices flowing before the next audition. Rick says they're talking about doing Durang's *Beyond Therapy* in the fall. Total laugh riot! We shall see, we shall see.

Next thing we're going to do is hop in the Cube and take care of a few last-minute errands. I love that car. Why not be fun? Now, there are certain things that you have to do on the day of the party. Flowers, for one. I'm sure I'll end up receiving a few bouquets from my minions, but it's good to lay down a floral foundation, so to speak. I can see here as I pull away that Mr. Paco did an amazing job on the yard yesterday. He is not your typical blow-and-go gardener, so if anyone wants a referral, I'll get you in touch with my man Paco and his sons. I hate this speed bump.

Oh, just go. GO! Jesus fuck, could you learn the rules of the road? The zipper effect! Learn it! Never any parking down here anymore. My turn, my turn! Oh, those trees are cute. They put little packages underneath them. What? Are you kidding me? Kip's is supposed to be open by now and it's not. All right, people of the planet, who exactly has the spare time to sit in the car for ten minutes while this woman diddles around in the back heating up her oatmeal packet in the microwave or whatever she's doing while there are customers here? I'll be right back.

12/20, 10:06 a.m. Audio Recording #3
Done and done. Tuberoses are sent from heaven. I thought she

was going to try and overcharge me like she did last time, but apparently I made an impression. Now off to get the ice. Uh-oh. Phone call!

Sasha! I have you on the Bluetooth!

What time do I have to be home?

Well, hello, wonderful daughter. Good morning and hello. The party starts at five, but you should come home early to get pretty and help me out. And you have your appointment at 2:30.

I don't know what you're talking about.

Your weekly appointment.

Oh. I'm not going.

Of course you are. I'm out and about, so I could pick you up right now if you want, okay? Hello? Hello? Can you hear me? Sasha? Oy! Sasha!

Fifty shekels and a crêpe suzette to anyone who can solve this teenage epidemic of attention deficit and nihilism running roughshod through our society right now. At least when we were young, we used to care about something. Green means go, Lexus. Pick it up!

New topic. Kids . . . This is my radio announcer's voice, by the way, back when I did voice-over. Kids, have you ever been to a party that ran out of ice? Major bummer! Or how about when the hostess uses oniony ice from her funky old ice cube trays? Boo! Hiss! We definitely don't want that, so make sure to stop by Silver Liquor and pick up three ten-pound bags of ice for your party. You'll be glad you did!

The last thing we have to do—oh there's Linda Hakido. Linda! Linda! You're coming, right? Don't forget your dancing shoes!

You should have seen her husband last year. A real party animal.

All right, we need to stop and get a couple more cans of

crabmeat because now I'm remembering how fast that dip went last year. Come with me into the singular oasis that is Food Town. You think it's going to be a crap store from the outside, but they carry almost everything I ever need except for my brand of tampons.

12/20, 10:42 a.m. Audio Recording #4

Mohammed! I need more crab in the can! I'm having my big shindig tonight and the natives are restless. And hungry! [*Mumbling*] Well, yes. Yes, you are cordially invited, Mohammed. Of course you are. [*Mumbling*] Oh, I thought you were serious! Okay, then. Happy holidays.

Whew, sheesh. He had me going there for a minute. He did. Not that I wouldn't have him in my house, but I barely know him. We're already packed to the rafters with real friends, which might be a good topic for a separate installment. Who to invite and why? Inquiring minds. Let's get Jim on the horn.

Jim Whiting, manservant!

Stop it! I just want you to remember the dark mustard.

I'm remembering the dark mustard!

Great. I've already got the flowers and the ice and more crabmeat and I'm heading back, pronto.

You're not getting wound up, are you?

No, except for Sasha who's pulling a disappearing act.

Okay, remember to stay calm and everything's going to be fine.

Ciao, honey.

Ciao.

12/20, Noon. Audio Recording #5

Home again, home again, jiggity jig. I'll put the ice in the garage freezer and get the flowers in their vases and get on to the rest of the food prep while I have my smoothie. First I get all the veggie chopping out of the way, then I grate the cheeses and get the eggs boiling. I know you can't see me right now, but I feel as if I'm moving like a panther. Can you see me, God? Am I moving like a panther? Like, right now, as I go from cupboard to fridge to microwave to pantry to chopping block. What kind of cat am I? I want answers, and here are the meatballs nestled in their Tupperware right where I left them.

[*The stereo plays Van Morrison's greatest hits while chopping and various other kitchen noises are heard. Elayne sings along, most exuberantly to "Brown Eyed Girl," which she replays three times in a row, getting louder and more into it each time. A muffled sound that could be crying is briefly heard. Elayne blows her nose.*]

Some people find food prep boring, but I find it meditative. Let's go make sure all the chafing dishes and serving platters are where I need them and then I'm going to talk to you all about something very important. Are you ready? Galileo, you're a good doggie. So handsome. Okay. Here goes: I always feared the Taj Mahal would look like a giant biscuit box! I repeat, I always feared the Taj Mahal would look like a giant biscuit box! That's the genius of Christopher Durang, and if I don't get the part of Prudence, some little fagalag is going to be strung up by his balls. Of course we know I'm talking about Walker, who is one of my closest friends, even though he has no tact. Watch him take over the piano from Jim tonight. Just you wait!

Living room? Spectacular. There is not a mote of dust to be found after yesterday's white tornado, and I've got my bar stocked with everything you could imagine, plus I am doing a special seasonal drink. There are even a couple Santa hats there in a basket because I thought it would be cute for people to wear them when they take turns behind the bar.

Now, we shower. Don't look, recording device! I'm going to expose myself.

12/20, 3:13 p.m. Audio Recording #6

Oh, that's better. Lying down for just a minute to gather my strength. Oh, forget about it. I've got things to do.

Slide into this hot little number. Like a glove, I tell you. I'm doing my hair in a messy bun. There was a gal in the Rush Street Players who used to do this style and I think we've got similarly shaped heads and it just works. You want something loose and casual when you are rocking a dress this sexy, that's for certain. To pantyhose or not to pantyhose? That is the question!

Oh boy. This is important. One of the last things I do after I reward myself with a pre-party vodka is step outside the front door. Then I walk in as if I am a guest in my own home. Let's do it together.

Hmmm. What do we see? Where is my eye drawn? For instance, look at Sasha's ponytail holder sitting right next to little Kris Kringle. That's not very tidy, is it? Or look how the poinsettias are just slightly off-center on the mantle. I tell you, so much of this is in the eye. I'm not sure that it can be taught, the way that I see, but hopefully you're getting something out of this. I know I am! There's Jim opening the garage. Jim! How's the deli tray look?

It smells great in here!

How are my cold cuts looking? I'm about to fire up the hot pots and get the fondue going. I decided I am like some kind of cat. A wildcat!

Are you okay? Your cheeks are flushed.

Don't let Walker kick you off the piano so quickly this year!

I'm going to take a shower.

I'm in the middle of my recording.

So call me crazy for this next one, but I feel like the bathroom is a very important place to be thorough. Think about it: a fabulous open house in a charming and well-appointed home at the height of the frenetic holiday season. It's the kind of home you pass when you're out for your evening constitutional and think, *I wonder who lives there. That sure does look like a warm and inviting place to live. Some very creative, lovely people must be inside right now doing something interesting.* And suddenly, you're there! In the middle of the whirl and swirl of guests and chatter and activity and carols around the baby grand and then, boom, you've got to tinkle and/or check your lipstick. When you do, I want you to say hello to your own little sanctuary.

I like a scented candle. I like to play with lighting. I like to do my towels two ways. Plush, vibrant terry ones, of course, but also a high-quality disposable for those who would rather take that route. I'm not judging. The main goal is to make everyone feel comfortable. Now, how do I put this delicately? Because I'm taking this warts-and-all approach, let's get past the bullshit. I want to point out that it is advisable to take a quick peek inside the medicine cabinet and get a gander. Whether you'd like to admit it or not, some people, and I'm not going to call them cretins— though I'm sure Tammy Two-Tone, who gets that special name because of her horrible hairstyle—are bound to check out what's cooking inside the cupboards. Generally, the only things I relocate to my dresser drawers are Jim's fungal powder and any prescription medications that may be around. Am I right? You don't want every Tom, Dick, and Harry, and TAMMY, knowing who's on what for why.

Did you hear that? I think it was a knock at the door. Here we go scurrying down the hall, slipping into the red patent-leather pumps on the way there. Goodbye! This has been fun! Showtime!

12/20, 4:02 p.m. Audio Recording #7

Oops. My bad. I thought I heard something. No guests yet, but I am going to turn you off anyway because I still have to make the mix for the pomtinis. So perfect that pomegranate juice is red this time of year. That doesn't make sense, but you know what I mean. I couldn't resist. This is amazing. This is my night.

Rose Bunch

ROSE BUNCH'S fiction and nonfiction has appeared in *Tin House, New Letters, Gulf Coast, River Styx, Fugue,* the *Greensboro Review,* and *PMS poemmemoirstory.* Winner of a 2010 *New Letters* Dorothy Churchill Cappon Prize for the Essay, a Pushcart Prize nominee, and third-prize winner of the *Playboy* Fiction Contest, she received her MFA from the University of Montana and a PhD from Florida State University. As a Fulbright Full Grant Scholar to Indonesia, she spent the 2010/11 academic year living in Bali, and is now completing a novel set in her homeland, the Arkansas Ozarks.

pissing in perpetuity
by rose bunch

I never saw the coons that ate my koi. At least, I never saw them do the eating. What I saw Sunday morning as I lay belly-flat on the mossy river stones surrounding the hole me and John dug, lined with black tarp from Lowe's, was empty, clear water. The only movement a rippling from my water feature: a serene, concrete woman constantly pouring from an urn cradled against her naked breast. I nicknamed her "Lola" because she had a mannish jaw. "It sounds like someone taking a perpetual piss in our backyard," John said when I first plugged Lola in. I got up, poked around, and saw the coons had left behind tail bits—a fin here, a scale or two there. I imagined them washing their nimble, little hands in the empty pool at my feet. Lip-licking satisfied.

"Goddamnit," I said, and felt myself welling up a little bit, about to squirt like Lola. I named the fish after two of my favorite dead uncles, which was shortsighted of me if Winfred and Ransom had to be buried all over again should the aeration pump break down or coons come for blood. I fingered the golden flakes of their remnants and sprinkled them back into the water. A partial sea burial.

I now saw Butterball next door, watching me, pissing in my general direction. A stream of urine shooting from a small pink knob of flesh pinched between his fingers. He had lost a ton of weight in the past few months, but his frame still looked built to hang meat on, lanky and misshapen even for a teenager, with hunks of clinging lard deposits. He removed a cigarette slowly from his lips, ashed, and shook his dick, eyeballing me from behind reflective Bassmaster shades.

This was a hill trick I knew from childhood: don't stand and stare, but don't be the one to look away too quick either. A glancing square-off. From inside the old stone house behind him I could hear the keening wails of his younger brother, a six-year-old. Their mother's car was gone again, and when she was away the boys often spent too much time in their yard, worn bald by a chained dog, staring at ours. The six-year-old played in the dirt and a growing junk pile, while the former fat kid paced back and forth talking on his cell phone and smoking cigarettes, out of reach of the skinny Rottweiler pressing full chain for affection. He flicked the butts toward our house, and I had to police the yard to pick up the ones that made it across the border. I washed my hands immediately, because they had grazed what he had suckled.

I wondered what they ate when the mother was gone for long, up to several days by my count. What the inside of that house must have looked like, the darkness and stink of it. Some days I thought I could literally smell a stink coming off it, and I wondered what they did inside there, what poison they might have taken or produced.

"They seem too stupid and disorganized to be cooking," John would say whenever I brought this up. "Taking, but not cooking."

"You think it takes real smarts to cook meth?" I would say back. And we would watch on the news the ugliness unfolding night after night in the hills surrounding us, the broken and blank-eyed faces in mug shots and wailing, filthy children taken by child protective services.

My mother used to bring me to the homes of the needy families when I was a kid. We delivered donated clothes or canned goods from the church to people up in the remote hollows who squirreled their lives into whatever passed for a house. Velveteen couches and cigarette-charred La-Z-Boys, collections of Avon perfume bottles on every surface, plastic flapping on windows. They were grateful for the canned peas, the used coats, the fresh pears from our tree.

Old, isolated communities in these Ozark hills were once sustained on this type of charity. They were just poor, either by bad luck or accident, but that wasn't a crime. Lots of people were poor then. It didn't mean they had to be assholes too.

Three months ago, Butterball and family had moved into the house that the realtor claimed was condemned when he sold us our land. The houses we could afford in town were all on small lots in cow pastures out by the interstate. No sidewalks or trees. No privacy from your neighbors who were close enough to piss on. No charm either in any of them advertised as such, their gold-flecked linoleum and taupe-carpeted floors felt as dull and cheap as the interior of a shoebox. We constructed our own charm then. Here in Wesley, Butterball and family were the only neighbors close enough to holler at, and the next home over was a bunch of Guatemalans in an old trailer who worked the chicken trade and kept to themselves. I'd suspected the Guatemalans of dealing because of the traffic coming and going at the trailer, but when I called the sheriff's office a tired-sounding woman said, "Honey, they'll see if they can get around to it." Later I thought maybe all the traffic was partly because there were so many of them living there, but nobody ever came out to check. I called the sheriff again and the same woman said: "No telling what they're up to, we got so much of that we can't keep up. Whatever it is, they'll probably stick to themselves." If they weren't going to do anything I was glad nobody had pulled up in a squad car mentioning drug-trafficking complaints from the nosy white lady up the road. Still, I watched them closely looking for signs. The men, and a few women, drove past packed in an old Dodge every morning and night, a steady rotation of shifts at the poultry-gutting plant in Lowell where they all worked.

"This'll be paved in no time," the realtor had said, looking at our curve in the road, rocking back and forth, sucking on something leftover in his teeth from lunch. "You got yourself a real deal here.

Everything is shifting."

Our view to the right was open fields and distant construction of gigantic homes in a subdivision, The Vineyard. There, the stones on the homes were imported, rounded and gray, like something in New England. To the left, a potpourri of crankheads, Butterball and family's old river stone house, slumped on one side as if burdened, and past it the Guatemalan village's single crusty trailer and a dried-out hillside striped with silver commercial chicken houses. I'd dreamt of living out somewhere far away from the chicken farms I'd grown up around.

"All that'll be coming down soon," the realtor had said. He had waved his hand at what was disagreeable, including the stone house.

Butterball's mother hadn't invited me inside the two times I'd gone over. Each time, I had stepped around a hole in the porch, something growling, menacing and low beneath my feet. The first visit was to introduce myself and bring a chess pie, my grandmother's recipe, and the second to ask her to tell her youngest boy to quit slinging gravel at our roof. I'd never seen him do it, but I noticed a small chip or two in a window I blamed on him. Both times she kept the door tight to her shoulder and responded roughly the same to the greeting as the complaint. "Huh," she said. "Yeah, okay." I never got the pie plate back, and didn't want to ask for it either. Anticipating this, I had used a shitty one that had a big chip in it. Sometimes I wished the sinking pile of rocks would burn to the ground to improve our view, and the family with it. I don't have an endless supply of Christian charity and goodwill like my mother.

Turkey buzzards circled in the sky, spiraling down lazily into something rotten, probably improperly discarded carcasses cleaned off of commercial henhouse floors, waiting to be burned or turned into the litter dumps. The August heat was cranking up, the scent of chicken manure shifting with the warming breeze off fertilized fields. Inside our French Country Model #809 home (inspired by the elegant but simple lifestyle of Provence, it had said on the plans), I could hear shrill whistles and crashing, wonky noises of morning cartoons. John banged on something in the garage. I brushed the remaining scales from my fingers and walked around to the opening.

"Coons ate the fish," I said. My voice lifted and cracked the way our daughter's did when she announced a new disappointment in life.

John, bent over a riding lawnmower, looked up from under his armpit. "What?" he said, like I had asked him what he wanted on a sandwich rather than announced a tragedy.

"They just took 'em," I said. I felt the heat of a tear slide from one eye, then another, and was immediately ashamed. John stood up, his hand cradling a socket wrench, and looked at me. He politely ignored my weeping over missing fish—he taught middle school biology and was accustomed to random outbursts of emotion.

"You sure?" he asked.

"Yes, I'm fucking sure!" I said, wiping my face. I hated it when he questioned me, like I had gone stupid since I became a stay-at-home mom. I had a graphic design degree from a softball scholarship at Arkansas Tech I was going to put to real use as soon as our daughter started kindergarten. "I know their ways."

"Their ways?" he said, and laughed. He pulled a piece of material from his back pocket and twisted the oily wrench in it. I saw it was one of the fancy napkins my aunt had given us for our wedding. She said it came from India. I kept these in my grandmother's antique buffet and used them only twice a year, at Thanksgiving and Christmas dinner. John looked down at the napkin in his hand and shoved it back in his pocket. I got gut-sick and sadder right there, felt the hate building in my neck where it liked to live, and turned and went into the kitchen.

Our kitchen was designed "family friendly" with a mud/

laundry room off the garage and an open bar looking out into the living room that made me feel like a fry cook. It seemed like a good plan originally, but now I saw it was designed to trap me in one area for labor. Alexis, seeing me in the work zone, yelled that she wanted more Cocoa Puffs. "Now!" she said. Being a mother wasn't as fulfilling as advertised, not that I didn't experience a raw ache in my guts when she genuinely hurt herself or was feverish, or melt at her sudden affections. Not that I wouldn't defend her to the death from a rabid, koi-thieving coon attack. But whenever I was bored and numb from demands, her tears just another task to be addressed, I experienced a flagging doubt that I was contributing anything all that much by being there all the time. I looked at the side of her ponytailed head, her eyes glowing from reflected TV, mouth slack, and tried to remember the last time she was sweet.

John came into the kitchen, gave me a peck on the head, and grabbed his keys. "We'll get more, bigger ones, and they'll eat the coons if they come back. I gotta go pick up some things in town." Sometimes I had a hard time figuring if he possessed boundless optimism, or he simply didn't give a shit. Either way I could admire it, and I felt the tension in my neck lessen slightly. Alexis ran to him and whined that she wanted to go too, but John did a little dance, whirled her around, blew fart noises into her tubby belly, and said, "Not today, punkin'." He was an expert at waltzing in, both denying and delighting Alexis at the same time, with no ill consequences. After he left she lightly kicked the back door before turning her dissatisfaction back to me.

"Cocoa Puffs!" she said. She put her hands on her hips and made the pouty face her grandparents encouraged and photographed. We didn't live far from where me and John had grown up in Huntsville, so our parents had full access to their five-year-old granddaughter. They claimed we continued some kind of family legacy by building in that same narrow stretch of valley. Ancestors had banded together in one section of hills and fought off whatever discomfort and outlaws to build a life that lasted generations. I wondered what beauty they had imagined here, versus what they found. At times this gave us comfort. Other times we felt like failures for not making it outside the valley. My parents had a photograph of Alexis on the mantel amongst the stern great-great-grandparents who had named each bluff, each hollow surrounding us. They wore overalls and severe black dresses as if they were ready to work in the fields or be buried. In her photo, Alexis wore a pink tutu and T-shirt that said *Princess* (something they had never encouraged me to be), in that exact pose she now struck before me. I hated that fucking picture.

"You already had your breakfast," I said. And then listened to the many reasons why the first breakfast was insufficient and more sugar was necessary to survive. "Nope," I said. "Not open for discussion. Why don't you go outside and play?"

Alexis made indistinct noises, words stretched into whine, and stomped back into the living room for more cartoons. We'd purchased a slide, tire swing, monkey climber combo jungle gym and put small, rounded landscaping pebbles beneath it. "What are them fucking rocks for?" my father had asked. "For safety," I said. "From what?" he said. Wasps built nests in the tire swing that I was obliged to hose out every week in case Alexis learned to appreciate it, and the crossbeams gave the crows a place to perch and pick at the cornbread I threw out for songbirds. Next door I heard the rumblings of Butterball's rusty Z28, a car that didn't look like it had the capacity for movement, the catalytic converter removed for added annoyance. He slung a spray of gravel with his dramatic exit.

Within ten minutes after Butterball's departure the littlest one from next door was on the porch, pretending to look at my decorative ferns. Sometimes when his brother abandoned him, the boy showed up. I didn't encourage it. His mother was none too friendly the few times she had come over to get him, smoking and tapping her foot, scratching herself and ashing on my porch like I had inconvenienced her instead of the other way around. I don't know why people act like if you have one kid it's okay to dump strange ones on you like stray kittens. All kittens are cute. Not all kids are. When his older brother would fetch him he'd linger too long, adjusting his crotch and making statements that merited no response: *You like fish* or *I seen you was planting flowers.* No one ever bothered to apologize for abandoning the child to my care without notice.

There was a faint scratching noise at the door. I opened it and stared down at the kid, who, rather than make eye contact, broke off a fern leaf and looked past me into the house like he had forgotten something in there. He was puffy, like his brother used to be, and barefoot.

"Where's your mama?" I asked.

He shrugged and stuck the edge of the fern leaf in his mouth.

"Come on in," I said. The kid walked into the house with the halting uncertainty of a stray cat, but nosed his way straight for the kitchen. "Gimme that," I said. I took the sodden fern leaf away from him and threw it in the trash. He tiptoed along the countertop until he saw the Cocoa Puffs. "Want some?" I asked.

His head did a slight tilt forward and back, and then he stared at his dirty feet while I poured out a bowl. Alexis heard the sound of sugar nuggets hitting porcelain and came trotting into the kitchen. She drew back when she and the kid made eye contact and hid halfway behind the door jamb. I didn't care much for her going anywhere near that house or those boys, and had told her so many times.

"I want some too," she said.

They settled in with their bowls, far apart in separate corners of the den, and watched cartoon animals beating the shit out of each other again and again. Almost two hours later, after I guiltily looked at curtains online, and one altercation over the boy touching Alexis's coloring books on the coffee table, John came back toting bags from both Home Depot and Lowe's. He also had a bucket containing three koi, bigger than the last.

"Too big for coons to wrestle," he said. He spotted the kid in the living room and nodded toward him, raising his eyebrows.

"Yup," I said.

"We should call somebody," he said.

"Yes, but you'll be asking for trouble."

John stared at the kids in the living room, considering the balance between trouble and civic responsibility. He reached into a sack on the counter, tossed me a beer, and walked to the French doors opening onto our backyard where Lola streamed away. "Pissing in perpetuity," he said.

I didn't hear the mother return, but noted Butterball wasn't back when she rang my doorbell. She picked at a scab on the side of her head with her pinky. "He here?" she said, smoke sliding out of her tired face as if she was too weary to exhale. I opened the door wider where she could see the boy in the living room. He looked up from a coloring book, like he'd been caught, and started to scoot over toward us.

"He's too little to be left alone like he is," I said. "You need to see to it that there's someone looking out for him when you leave."

"You got a pretty room here," the mother said. "Like out of a magazine." She said this as if it were an accusation rather than a compliment. She poked her scratching pinky at a dark chocolate loveseat sitting by a front window, lined with striped pillows in varying pale blues. I'd gotten it at T.J. Maxx. It looked to be waiting for a lady to relax there and read poetry in the soft light, or gaze out at the passing chicken trucks and Guatemalans and contemplate the sanctity of her home. I'd never sat in it since I'd put it there.

"If his brother can't see to him then he needs good day care," I said.

The mother sighed and tapped ash onto my porch, then looked dully at her spent cigarette and flicked it into my azaleas. She craned her neck to see what was taking the kid so long. He was gathering the pictures I had forced Alexis to allow him to color in her *Sea Friends* book, a scribbled squid and great white shark, both in orange. "That's real good," I'd said in that bullshit way everyone praises children now. He had stopped coloring, wiggled slightly, and ducked his head, pleased but uncertain what the correct response to praise was. It made me feel shitty that I didn't mean it.

"Well, come on," she said to the boy, and lit another.

Neither of them looked at me as they turned from the porch; the boy dragged his feet as if afflicted. I watched them walk back to their askew house, her hand gripping the back of his neck, smoke trailing from behind her frizzy head. The dog barked at them, high-pitched and insistent, until the woman said something sharp and low to make it shut up. Butterball was now back and standing in the yard, gazing in the general direction of Lola, love-struck, scratching his dick. A small garbage fire burned at the edge of our borders, stinking of plastic and chemicals.

I stuck my head into the garage. John was back at his lawnmower, but with a new pack of utility rags open beside him. "Call whoever you need to call," I said.

The gravel started hitting the top of the roof again later that afternoon. First a single plunk, followed by a rattling drop into my flower bed, something I could have mistaken as a pine cone. Then a buckshot rain shower. I ran outside to yell at the kid, a single stone still making its rattling way to the azaleas below, but there was no one there. The dog lay limp from the heat in a burrowed-out hole, halfway under the foundation of the house. John offered to go talk to them, but I figured him making a call Monday morning was enough.

By Wednesday the new fish were dead. I found their swelling

bodies, iridescent gold and white, floating sideways under the indifferent gaze of Lola. On Monday, with the help of Alexis, we had named them after Disney princesses. The sharp scent of bleach was apparent. I called John at work, and he told me to just calm down until he got home.

"And then what?" I said. "After I'm all calm and you're here, then what?"

I called the sheriff's office and got the same tired woman I had spoken to before about the Guatemalans. "Honey, we'll try and send somebody out to look at it," she said. I went to the pond and turned Lola off. There was something about her pouring that didn't seem right while the bodies were still there, bobbing lightly, floating only for John to witness. I took photographs of the fish for evidence before burial, digging a big hole over near the neighbor's yard by their burn pile. The skinny Rottweiler about to strangle itself to get at me, barking hoarse. A darkness could be seen behind one of the windows. No one came outside. The dog twisted and strained against the chain, its barks no more than raspy air.

"Want one, shithead?" I said, real sweet and soft, and threw him Ariel first. The fish body, rigid, smelling of chemicals, landed with a thunk in front of the startled animal. The dog leaped back, withdrawing closer to the crumbling foundation of the house. "How about Belle then?" I said. "Sink your teeth into that." I could hear the muted sounds of Alexis calling for me, louder as she stepped out on the back patio. I reached for Cinderella's stiff body and paused to look at the delicate beauty of her scales up close. As the dog crept toward the two fish, gaining interest, the back screen door of the stone house flung open. The mother came tottering out, followed by Butterball and the kid.

"What are you doing?" she said.

Butterball didn't have his usual reflective shades on, and without concealment his eyes appeared small with dark circles, his face more childlike. He looked more like a scared, misshapen old boy than a misshapen young man. Little brother hovered behind older brother's sagging jeans. I held Cinderella and saw them standing there as uncertain as creatures disturbed under a rock and began to feel ashamed for all of us. The kid reached up to touch his brother's ass, at which the teenager snapped a hand back to slap him away, like he was waving away a fart. "Yeah," Butterball said. He stepped forward.

"Giving your dog old fish," I said. "But if you got a reason he shouldn't eat it . . ."

"Fuck you and your fish," the mother said. She kicked at either Ariel or Belle and knocked off her flip-flop. "Keep your goddamned fish to yourself and mind your own fucking business."

Alexis called for me again. I turned around to see her edging closer. She was wearing the pink tutu outfit her grandparents had given her. I hadn't yet told her the princesses were all dead. I chucked Cinderella in the hole and turned away.

"Stay away from my house," I said. I picked Alexis up and held her to me, walking quickly toward our home. I didn't look back at the neighbors, but heard muttered curses and the thump of what turned out to be Ariel, or maybe Belle, falling close behind us. Alexis didn't ask about the fish, as if fish-throwing was a given around here. She put a knuckle up to her mouth and gnawed lightly on it, like she used to when she was a baby, squinting back over my shoulder with an expression I didn't quite recognize, neither fearful nor sad, as if thoughtfully plotting some dark revenge. "How about some Cocoa Puffs?" I said.

John lectured me briefly about engaging with the enemy when he got home. "Stay the fuck away from them. Especially when I'm not here. What if they had done something more than throw a fish?"

"They did do something more!" I said. "They killed them, to start with."

"Guess they heard from child services."

Alexis liked to draw wiggly figures she called fish princesses. One blobby, gold and pink creation she gave to John to hang on the refrigerator. The Fish Princess was wearing a tutu.

"Jesus Christ," I said, and tore it down before dinner.

A policeman came to take a dead fish report the next morning. When I saw the squad car in the drive, I felt a momentary chill inside, the way I always feel around cops. Like I should run up into the woods and hide further in the hills even if I haven't done anything wrong. The biggest sons of bitches I ever knew from high school had become policemen. Bastards with badges. He had a country-cop saunter, a walk that said he could give a shit, was even vaguely amused, as he came up to the front door. I led him through the house to the backyard. He smiled and winked at Alexis, who stared back at him, unmoved.

"You say it was bleach?" he asked. "Can't really smell it." The officer stood a ways back to admire the fish pond. "Nice water feature."

"And then when I was trying to bury the fish, they threw one at me," I said.

"Who did?"

"The ones that did this," I said. "Over there." We walked to the edge of the yard and stood beside the freshly dug earth.

"You saw them poison the fish," he said, "and then they come over and grabbed them up?"

"Well, no, but I know it was them. Their dog wouldn't shut up so I threw one at it."

"You did?" He seemed to find this funny. "I'll need to have a word with them. Thank you, ma'am."

While the cop went next door I surveyed my yard: a struggling dogwood transplanted from my parent's farm, a dry bird bath, hand-painted mailbox, grass patchy with stray chicken feathers and dandelions, and the fish grave. I always thought I would wind up in town proper, away from the fields and scrub oak–lined fences, the burned-out remnants of trailers and chicken houses, away from people like our tweaker neighbors and cranked-up Guatemalans. I wanted a manicured, paved street with sidewalks. Real sidewalks.

Another truck of migrant laborers on their way to the chicken farms slowed down as it passed, a dry, fine dust billowing behind it. The men inside craned their necks to look at me and the squad car, and I heard the faint sound of tinny music from their radio. I stared back at the driver, who pulled in an arm that draped out the window and sped up. I watched them disappear around the curve. No one turned back around.

I went in the house and watched from the chocolate loveseat. The mother wasn't home, but Butterball stepped out on the porch and shut the door behind him. He pointed at our house a time or two. The policeman nodded, followed the line of his finger with his gaze, and nodded some more until he seemed satisfied.

"Ma'am," he said when he returned, "my best advice is to stay away from them, but this call is on record. Unfortunately, there's no way to prove anything."

"Fine," I replied, and shut the door.

I worked in the yard until John got home, Alexis beside me most of the time, to show the neighbors I wasn't going to take any more fish-killing kind of bullshit hiding out in the house. Alexis built things she called forts with sticks in the grass. "For fairy princesses," she said.

That night, in the early-morning hours, John and I were awakened by stones hailing onto the roof, followed by a spray of rocks at the windows. Looking into the semidarkness I saw the ember light of the mother's cigarette. She stooped to pick up another handful of gravel. She flung once more with a limp wrist. The sharp crack of the gravel hitting the window forced me to step back. Stones dribbled onto the roof. She stood there a second more, seeing us peering out from our home like treed raccoons before she flicked one last cigarette into our yard and turned to her car. The roar of Butterball's Z28 was heard sliding around on the dirt road as he drove away, and then the coughing start of the mother's engine.

"Maybe that was their last *fuck you*," John said. "I've got one back if it wasn't."

As the morning light grew stronger, so did the glow from within the stone house. Whatever shit they hadn't taken with them absorbed the smoke, the heat, perhaps embraced its welcome release. A cleansing.

"Told you they were cooking," John said, and picked up the phone to call the fire department.

"No," I said. "Wait."

We watched the gathering flames work upon the rotten insides of the house until the first flickers emerged, exploring the fresh air outside.

"Go ahead," I said.

After John called, we saw that Alexis was sleeping through everything and went out to watch the house swollen with fire. We stood back from the growing flames, hearing small explosions and pops from within, who knows what remnants of poison released in the heat. An electrical wire flipped and sparked near the collapsing porch. Two truckloads of Guatemalans on their way to work pulled over to watch. We spoke to one another in different tongues but seemed to convey the same message as we pointed and nodded. The Guatemalans looked infinitely weary. I turned back to see our own house in its soft, orange light. The colors I'd chosen for the exterior, Lambskin and Froth, looked beautiful in the warm light of the burning house, like a sculpted cake, except for a notable absence in the backyard. Lola was gone, riding the open highway in a rusted-out Z28 with Butterball wide, wide awake, probably stroking her naked tit.

A gathering of old men from the volunteer fire department hung around drinking coffee until midmorning. Happy. House fires weren't common; you were always lucky to be rousted from your retirement to attend one. And this one was better off to let burn. Toxic. The same officer who took the dead fish report was there, but this time he took notes and seemed to find me less funny. "You'd better stay away from what's left of this mess until we can get it cleaned up," he said. We all stood with our hands on our hips, shaking our heads. John promised to bring back motion detection lights to put on the house after work, but I didn't think they would be back, as the officer agreed. "Probably running to their next rat hole," he said. By noon, everyone was gone.

Midafternoon and another truck rattles past, full of birds and slinging feathers and trailing the smell of shit and fear. Bodies are tucked into dirty white balls, giving up whatever hope can flicker in a chicken's little brain. Others, stunned, dead-eye the passing landscape, more colors, shapes, and sounds than they have ever seen inside a commercial poultry house. Trucks carting chicken-catchers follow. Brown faces, empty with exhaustion, see me standing by the azaleas, surrounded by decorative lawn ornaments, holding a fistful of dandelion roots, a little girl in a pink tutu sitting in the grass beside me playing with brightly colored ponies. I wonder if any of them are our Guatemalans from nearby. I stop and stand to watch them pass and then peer back at my house. I imagine how I would crop this scene. With the afternoon haze of airborne dust giving the sky a golden glow, the dry, yellow fields surrounding us look almost like something from a magazine. The woods beyond conceal the limestone bedrock that my ancestors struggled to scratch a living from. Our French Country #809, flowers and garden, looked a fruitful place, safe from invasion. A peaceful image of a distant land where generations upon generations drink wine and watch their children grow. If you looked at it just right, it could be something beautiful.

Noah Kalina

TAO LIN is the author of six books of fiction and poetry, including *Richard Yates*, his second novel, which was published in 2010.

51 hours
by tao lin

ack woke ~2:30 p.m. and talked to Daniel on Gmail chat. Daniel said he and Allie didn't sleep last night and were getting drugs then eating brunch to celebrate Allie getting fired from the waitressing job she got a few days ago. Jack showered and left his apartment and text-messaged Daniel that his Adderall shipment, which arrived once a month from a college professor, hadn't arrived. Daniel said he didn't know if he could stay awake for a party that night without Adderall and asked if Jack wanted to buy Adderall from his drug dealer. Jack said he would contribute twenty dollars for the 11-for-$110 deal. Daniel didn't respond. Jack went to a café and drank a large iced coffee and created what he viewed as "oxy water" by dissolving a small plastic bag of blue-yellow paste consisting of OxyContin, a little Klonopin, and a little Adderall in a Tea's Tea bottle of water. He'd made the paste, accidentally, by washing his jeans in the bathtub with those drugs in the pocket. He text-messaged Daniel that he felt like most of the OxyContin disappeared, or something, when it turned into a paste, because it didn't seem like the same amount as before it became a paste. Daniel responded with a panicked-seeming text message of two compound sentences speculating on what happened to the OxyContin. Jack grinned and responded for Daniel to stay calm and that the OxyContin was safe, in a Tea's Tea bottle. Jack went online at the library feeling a little high from the Klonopin-Adderall paste on the outside of the OxyContin packet he'd licked clean, combined with the iced coffee and an amount of OxyContin he'd licked from his fingers. A few hours later he met Frank and Daniel on the second floor of a building on the Lower East Side for the one-year anniversary of an Internet company. Jack drank half the bottle of oxy water. Daniel drank the other half. It was ~9:30 p.m. "Should we go to the other thing now?" said Frank about a gallery in Brooklyn that was showing Jack's art tonight in a group show.

"Are you okay, man?" said Frank on the train to Brooklyn.

"Yes," said Jack and focused on not moving or thinking.

"You don't look okay," said Frank while grinning at Daniel.

The train arrived and they walked five blocks to the art gallery, which was someone's apartment. Jack looked at his art on a wall. He went in the bathroom, then with Frank and Daniel to the roof. "I feel a lot better," he said and went downstairs and said hi to Laila who was holding a glass of wine and seemed sober and who introduced Jack to two people whose names he didn't try to remember. One said something nice about Jack's art and Jack made a noise while not looking at anything. Sara walked toward Jack who said, "This is Sara" and "This is Laila," and, as Sara was complimenting Laila's necklace, walked away, through a door, into a small room, and sat on a foam floor. Sara entered and sat by Jack and said Laila had said, "So, what's new?" to her, and that was when she knew it was time to walk away. Jack went to the roof and looked at Daniel and Frank seated next to each other grinning. "Jack," said Daniel. "Come here." Jack stood in front of Daniel and Frank a few seconds, then went downstairs and stood near Andrew who was talking to David about if a horse could win "best athlete of the year." Jack was aware of Laila in the distance talking to people. He went to the roof and stood by Justin and said, "Look at that kitchen," and pointed at a lower floor on another building. Justin said, "What kitchen?" and Jack moved close to the edge and almost fell off the roof. He asked if Justin would have felt responsible if he had died. He went downstairs and said, "Hey, I'm leaving, just wanted to say bye," to Laila, who was sitting on the floor, and they hugged. Laila seemed incoherent and unable to stand.

Jack stood by Daniel and Andrew in the hallway.

"I used Adderall for the first time the other day," said Andrew.

"Oh, sweet," said Jack. "Did you like it?"

"Yeah. I didn't think it would work."

"How many milligrams did you use?"

"Forty," said Andrew.

"Jesus," said Jack.

"I used twenty and it wasn't working so I used another twenty."

"Nice," said Jack.

Laila was walking toward them holding an unlit cigarette dangling between two fingers, barely maneuvering the hallway. "I already said bye to her," said Jack to Daniel. "I already said bye to her," he said to Andrew.

"I thought you were leaving," she said.

"Bye," said Jack. "I am."

A few minutes later she was moving toward him from the other direction. She moved her head toward his head and said, "I'm on 'shrooms," with unfocused eyes, and moved past him in the hallway, in the opposite direction of the exit.

About ten minutes later Daniel, Frank, Andrew, Jack got in a taxicab to Manhattan Inn. Jack ordered ribs. Daniel and Frank ordered an appetizer of chicken wings to share. Andrew said, "Why doesn't she stop dancing?" Jack looked at a woman dancing alone. Daniel and Frank ignored Andrew, whose eyes, in response, seemed to unfocus a little before refocusing elsewhere. Jack thought about saying something. He picked up his glass and drank water. Frank left to sleep. Daniel left the table to talk to other people who had come from the gallery. It was ~1:45 a.m. Andrew said he was "good friends" with his roommate, an Asian girl with an administration job in a nightclub, then left to sleep. Jack ate ribs alone at the table. "I thought you were a vegetarian," someone said to him after a few minutes.

"No, I'm eating ribs," said Jack.

"I thought you didn't eat meat," said the person.

"I eat meat," said Jack.

"Oh, I didn't hear you," said the person. "I thought you said you weren't eating meat. But you're eating ribs."

Daniel returned to the table holding a drink. "You should grow an enormous afro, without any warning, for your next author photo," he said.

Jack, an artist and a writer, laughed and paid for his food and left to sleep.

He woke ~2:30 p.m., ate three mangoes, looked at the Internet, text-messaged Daniel, slept from ~3:30 p.m. to ~8:30 p.m., e-mailed Frank he was staying in tonight. He exercised in his room and showered. His Adderall had arrived and was in the kitchen and he moved it into his room. He went to a café and drank a large iced coffee with no ice and went to the library and worked on things until ~12:30 a.m. He bought bananas, a mango, a cucumber, and walked toward his apartment. He saw a text message from Daniel that said, *come hang out, Frank bought a bunch of speed*, and walked a few blocks to a bar and into the bathroom—which had a second door, leading outside—and splashed water to his face, dried off, went through the second door to the bar's outdoor area where Daniel, Frank, Maggie were standing talking. Jack and Daniel began arguing about something while grinning. Jack said Daniel needed to "lay off the eggplant," referencing a joke they had about how Daniel had been eating eggplant as a drug and was now heavily dependent on it. Frank said his eyes were red because of cat allergies.

Daniel, Frank, Maggie, Jack stood on the sidewalk outside the bar discussing where to go to snort Frank's crystal meth. They crossed the street to Harry's apartment, went upstairs, stood in a large dark room of sofas, a TV, an open kitchen, a corner table with two computers. Dance music was playing loudly. Harry was hugging people from behind, or from the sides, while making loud noises.

"Harry seems out of control," said Jack.

"He hasn't done speed before," said Frank.

Jack peeled his mango alone in darkness at the kitchen sink and ate it, then walked elsewhere and noticed Daniel, Frank, Maggie in a bathroom with the door not fully closed. Jack pushed at the door. "It's me," he said and went inside. Maggie was sitting on the bathtub's edge. Daniel and Frank were sitting on the floor, around the toilet. "We thought you left," said Daniel.

"I wouldn't just leave," said Jack.

"It seems like you, of all people, would just leave," said Daniel, putting crystal meth on the toilet cover and crushing it with his debit card. Frank asked if Jack wanted some and Jack said, "Yes, if that's okay." Frank sneezed a little while moving his rolled-up twenty-dollar bill toward the crystal meth.

"Jesus," said Daniel. "Be careful."

"Why are you berating him?" said Jack. "It's his drugs."

"Bro," said Daniel and grinned at Jack a little.

"It's his," said Jack. "And he's sharing it with us."

They each snorted a line of crystal meth, then stood in the main room where ~fifteen people seemed to be hugging each other repeatedly while talking loudly.

"What is this?" said Jack.

"A rich person's apartment," said Daniel.

"Sweet," said Jack.

About ten minutes later Daniel, Frank, Maggie, Jack went to Legion, a bar a few blocks from Harry's apartment. Maggie went to the bathroom. Jack sat on a padded seat.

"Seems bleak," he said after a few seconds.

"What's wrong with you tonight?" asked Frank.

"There aren't any girls here for me," said Jack.

"Let's dance," said Daniel.

"I'm depressed," said Jack.

Frank and Daniel walked away. Jack looked at his phone. He stared at an area of torsos. He walked outside. He text-messaged Daniel that he was going to Khim's to *stock up on eggplant*.

In Khim's he felt energetic and calm, listening to Rilo Kiley through earphones, and put an organic beef patty, two kombuchas, organic bananas, alfalfa sprouts, arugula, some other things in his basket and paid. Walking toward Legion, Jack saw Harry approaching from the opposite direction with a troubled facial expression and sweat on his forehead and other areas of his face. Harry passed without looking at Jack. At Legion, Frank and Daniel were outside, vaguely arguing about something. Daniel went inside. Jack walked toward Frank who said he and Daniel were doing a line in the back room when a security guard came toward them and he threw the bag of crystal meth somewhere and Daniel was now inside looking for it.

"Where's Maggie?" asked Jack.

"In White Castle," said Frank.

They crossed the street to White Castle and sat with Maggie in a booth. Jack put his groceries on the table. "Chicken rings," he said about a poster on a wall. "To make chicken rings they would need to, like, mold the meat into rings, right?"

"I'm worried about Daniel," said Frank.

"He'll be in jail for, like, ten years if he gets caught," said Jack. "He said he has a warrant for his arrest in Colorado."

"Jesus," said Frank.

"It's better if Daniel goes to jail than you," said Jack. "He's in debt to like five people and needs like six hundred dollars in one week, for rent, and is unemployed and owes me seventy dollars. Whereas you have a real job and a nice apartment."

Maggie went to the bathroom.

"If Daniel goes to jail I'll remove his debt to me, I think," said Jack. "We could make a blog about him and mail him letters."

"A blog," said Frank, seeming worried. "Jesus."

"Should we go look for him? I'll go look for him," said Jack and crossed the street to Legion and walked to the back room and read a text message from Daniel that said, *come outside*. On the sidewalk Daniel, walking away from Legion ahead of Jack, said Frank had panicked and threw the bag of crystal meth under a table. "He shouldn't have done that," said Daniel. "He panicked, like a little bitch."

"He has a high-paying job," said Jack.

"Shouldn't I get some of this speed, since I was put in a position where I could've gotten in trouble?"

"If you want," said Jack. "Seems like, yeah, if you want."

Daniel stared ahead with a distracted facial expression.

"Frank and Maggie are in White Castle," said Jack. "My groceries are in White Castle. Where are we going?"

"Let's go to your room to do some of this speed," said Daniel.

They were on a street with no people or moving cars.

"It's too far," said Jack. "Just snort it off your hand."

Daniel removed a rock of crystal meth from the bag and put both his hands in his jeans pockets. Jack said, "What are you doing, isn't it just going to, like, fall through your pants?" and ripped a page from his Moleskine journal and said Daniel could use it to contain the meth. Daniel was distractedly looking in different directions.

"You should snort it off the Lincoln," said Jack.

"There isn't a Lincoln here," said Daniel.

"That seems like a Lincoln," said Jack pointing at a car.

"That's a Pontiac," said Daniel.

"You should hide between two cars to do it," said Jack.

Daniel walked between two cars and kneeled, facing away from Jack, who photographed Daniel with his cell phone and sent the photograph to his own Gmail account and to Daniel's cell phone.

"Good job," said Jack walking toward White Castle.

"You know I don't do this to friends, usually," said Daniel, looking into the distance.

"You just did it," said Jack grinning. "I mean, what do you mean?"

"I mean, do you think it's okay I did that?"

"Seems fine," said Jack.

"I was put in a dangerous situation."

"Seems fine," said Jack.

"You threw the bag onto this little shelf," said Daniel to Frank in White Castle. "I was looking on the ground for it. The bag was open so I don't know how much fell out."

In Jack's room Daniel, Frank, Jack—Maggie had left to sleep—each snorted a line of crystal meth. Daniel looked at Jack's collection of time-release Adderall and questioned Jack about why one capsule was open. Jack said it broke open in the envelope. Daniel repeatedly questioned Jack about how much of the capsule was missing, implying that the person who mailed Jack the Adderall had removed some from each capsule.

Jack spoke for ~ten minutes about having been tricked, saying things like, "I'm going to message her right now telling her I know one of these capsules only has twenty milligrams and that I want an explanation, right now," in a sarcastically outraged voice while signing into Facebook and typing the message to the person, asking Daniel if he should try to get the three books he had traded to the person, who was separate from his monthly shipment person, returned to him. At some point Jack felt unable to discern if Daniel knew he was being sarcastic, which caused Jack to increase his sarcasm, until he felt that he was saying things only to entertain himself. Daniel and Frank went into Jack's roommate's room and Jack heard the word "Fuckbuttons" and went to his roommate's room and said he had talked about Fuckbuttons last night. Daniel said Jack hadn't. Daniel said he and Frank had but Jack hadn't. "Are you sure?" said Jack.

"Where were we last night?" said Daniel.

"At . . . some . . . thing," said Jack after a few seconds.

"Is Shawn Olive your boyfriend?" said Frank to Jack's roommate.

"No," she said. "We're good friends."

Daniel, Frank, Jack went into Jack's room. There was some tense discussion about a book by Jack's friend Brandon that Jack published a year ago. Daniel seemed to be saying that the book was boring and that he didn't know why Jack published it. Daniel and Frank left and Jack cooked 70 percent of his organic beef patty and ate it with flax seeds, arugula, alfalfa sprouts, cucumber, tamari, lemon juice, olive oil. It was ~4:30 a.m. Jack ingested ~fifteen milligrams of Adderall and worked on things on his MacBook, laying stomach-down on his bed, sometimes e-mailing Daniel who was at his apartment a few blocks away and was responding within a few minutes to each e-mail. They decided not to sleep and to meet at 10 a.m. to go to the Museum of Modern Art. It was ~6:45 a.m. For the next few hours Jack sometimes stood and ingested a few milligrams of Adderall, each time noticing that the sunlight through his two large windows seemed gray. He e-mailed Daniel ~9:50 a.m. that he was naked on his bed and hadn't showered. Daniel responded that he was also naked and hadn't showered. About an hour later Jack e-mailed Daniel, *where the fuck are you*, and Daniel responded, within a minute, that he was still naked on his bed.

About thirty minutes later they met, got on the train, got off at Bedford Avenue. They walked to Rockin' Raw which wasn't open yet. It was raining a little. One of them said something about how the Museum of Modern Art would probably be extremely crowded because it was Sunday and within a few seconds both agreed that they shouldn't go there. They talked about going to LifeThyme and the garden. Jack asked if Daniel wanted to go to the bookstore. Daniel said, "Not really," but that he would go if Jack wanted. They decided to sit in a café called Verb to decide what to do next. They walked there and sat and each ingested ten milligrams of Adderall. Daniel removed a glass jar with a peanut butter label on it from his backpack and poured ~four ounces of whiskey into his iced coffee with a neutral facial expression. Jack asked what Daniel was going to do about his financial situation. Daniel said Frank had mentioned, a few days ago, hiring him to write promotional copy for Frank's band, but then didn't mention it again. Jack said he would help Daniel steal things today to sell on eBay or to thrift stores. They went in the bookstore and Daniel picked up the book that had almost exactly the same cover as Shawn Olive's book and showed it to Jack and said, "Shawn Olive." Jack said they had showed the book to each other a few nights ago and also talked about it for an amount of time. "I don't remember," said Daniel.

"It was in this store," said Jack. "Like two days ago."

They went outside and Jack pointed at an area of sidewalk and talked about how he and his ex-girlfriend had sold books sitting there. "We could do that," he said. "Let's do that, maybe." They walked aimlessly a few minutes. They walked toward Jack's apartment to get books to sell. A girl saw Daniel and stopped on her bike and said she was putting up fliers for an art fair on Berry Street and biked away. Daniel said he'd had sex with her and didn't know her name currently. Jack said her name was probably Kiki. They walked on Berry Street ~ten minutes and didn't see an art fair. They walked to East River Park. It was ~11:45 a.m. and cloudy. They decided it was time to snort the crystal meth Daniel stole from Frank last night. They walked to a somewhat isolated area of logs and cement blocks and sat and decided it would be better to snort the meth in Jack's room. They walked to Rockin' Raw and sat in the outdoor area. There were many large flies for some reason on the tables. They moved inside and Daniel went to the bathroom. Jack ordered a raw almond shake to go. They walked toward his apartment, ~fifteen blocks away, and Jack asked if Daniel snorted crystal meth in the bathroom. Daniel said he wouldn't do that without Jack and they went in a pizza place. Daniel walked toward Jack and said his debit card was either maxed out or not working from cutting so much speed.

Daniel stood in the middle of Jack's room and quietly said things about feeling "fucked" about his financial situation and also "generally." He kneeled to a table and created two lines of crystal meth. Jack asked what music Daniel wanted. Daniel didn't say anything. Jack put on "Heartbeats" by The Knife and they both laughed a little. Jack put on "Last Nite" by The Strokes and stopped it and said it was too depressing. Jack put on "Such Great Heights" by The Postal Service and stopped it and said, "What are we going to listen to?" and Daniel said to put "Such Great Heights" back on, then snorted half his line and motioned for Jack to snort his. Jack moved some of his line into Daniel's half-snorted line, saying he only wanted five dollars worth and that it would be removed from Daniel's tab. "Seems like it's going to be impossible for me not to sneeze or something," said Jack and felt some difficulty in discerning "exhale" vs. "inhale" as he moved a rolled-up page of Shawn Olive's poetry collection in his right nostril toward the crystal meth by leaning his body off the bed. He snorted some then exhaled a little and some crystal meth spilled out on the table. Jack felt calm and amused as Daniel lightly berated him. "Frank did it a lot more," said Jack. "He, like, sneezed, or something. Seems like we're improving, if you view Frank and me as one person." He quickly snorted the rest of the crystal meth, then continued snorting areas of the table, including a small spot of what seemed to be colorful dust. "Stop," said Daniel and snorted the rest of his line. Jack lay on his bed in a splayed-out manner. Daniel continued to say that he felt depressed, but in a calmer voice. Jack stood and said they should go sell books now and put books, pens, blue spray paint, pieces of paper, some other things in his backpack and rolled up a small carpet. Daniel said they would probably sell three books and should probably just go to the garden instead, to relax. "Let's just try to sell books," said Jack. "If it doesn't work we can leave or just sit there relaxing. I'll give you all the profits."

They walked ~fifteen blocks and unrolled the carpet on the sidewalk. Jack put books on the carpet and wrote prices on paper and they sat with their backs against a wall. A British man picked up a book, looked at it a few seconds, said "I'll take it," gave Jack two dollars while looking in his wallet for a five-dollar bill. Daniel sincerely praised Jack's writing to the British man for a few minutes. The British man thanked them and walked away. Daniel said the British man had said "getting in on" in a hesitating manner, like he wasn't sure if he was getting the idiom right, and that Daniel had looked at Jack when he said that. Jack said he didn't notice. "He only gave me two dollars," he said. "Seems like a scam." An overweight, fashionable, shy-seeming girl bought two books without removing her large headphones or speaking. Four black male teenagers appeared. One, who seemed much more interested than the others, asked if he could read some of a book and then read some of it and laughed and said, "I'll take it."

"Sweet," said Jack.

"Do you like Adderall?" said Daniel.

"What is it?" said the teenager.

Daniel described it in a few sentences.

"So, it's like Ecstasy?" asked the teenager.

"Sort of," said Daniel. "Without the euphoria."

"Are you in?" said the teenager.

"No," said his friend. "But I'll watch you do it."

The teenager bought two Adderall.

Nick McDonnell appeared on a bike and introduced himself to Jack and said they had met before. Jack said, "I remember," and said something about KGB Bar. Nick McDonnell bought two books and said he looked forward to reading them. Jack asked him about his McSweeney's book. Jack said, "You know Mike Tonas, right?"

Nick McDonnell said he wished Mike would return from Portland.

"He's there permanently?" asked Jack.

"I think so," said Nick McDonnell.

Jack said he would move to Portland.

Daniel said, "You would?"

Jack said, "I don't know."

Nick McDonnell said he had a reading at The Half-King the next night, then rode his bike diagonally across Bedford Avenue.

"Do you know that person?" asked Jack.

"No," said Daniel. "Who is that bro?"

"He's rich," said Jack. "I liked his first novel. It was published when he was seventeen, I think. His father was the editor of *Rolling Stone* or something. His novel was blurbed by Hunter S. Thompson, Bret Easton Ellis, and Joan Didion and was just made into a movie by Joel Schumacher or someone. In the book the main character is a white person in high school who sells drugs. We should go to his reading. Tomorrow night."

They sat without talking ~twenty minutes.

"Should I use more Adderall," asked Jack.

"You're better to be around when you're on Adderall," said Daniel.

"What do you mean?" said Jack.

"You're really quiet without Adderall."

Jack went to Verb and ingested ten milligrams of Adderall, stood in line for the bathroom, peed, washed his face. He ran to where he and Daniel were selling books. The sky was mostly gray. There was some orange, red, purple in the distance. It was ~5:30 p.m. An Asian girl with a cell phone to her right ear approached and slowed a little and passed. She reappeared a few minutes later without a cell phone and said she knew who Jack was, from her coworkers. Jack said something about Adderall. "Are you guys cops?" she asked. "Because I'm waiting here to buy pot from someone. But I'm not sure about him." Daniel asked whom and she showed Daniel the drug dealer's business card. She bought two books and went to an ATM and returned and paid for three Adderall. She asked if Daniel or Jack had a driver's license, to move her friend's car from Crown Heights to the Graham L train stop for money. They talked about that a few minutes without concluding anything and it was quiet a few seconds and she removed a magazine from her bag and said she was translating an article from Mandarin and asked if Jack was good at translating. Jack said he couldn't read Mandarin. Daniel asked where she was from and after a few minutes she began talking about her boyfriend who went to India after college, then returned to America and died, a few years ago. Jack heard her say something about how her boyfriend's funeral had become a party—that, for some reason Jack didn't hear, it had been the same as a party—except everyone was wearing black.

PART IV
MEDICINE

MEGAN ABBOTT is the Edgar-winning author of the novels *The End of Everything*, *Bury Me Deep*, *Queenpin*, *The Song Is You*, and *Die a Little*. Her work has appeared in *Wall Street Noir*, *Phoenix Noir*, *Detroit Noir*, *Queens Noir*, *Between the Dark and the Daylight: And 27 More Best Crime & Mystery Stories of the Year*, *Storyglossia*, *Los Angeles Times Magazine*, and *The Believer*. She is also the author of a nonfiction book, *The Street Was Mine: White Masculinity in Hardboiled Fiction and Film Noir*, and the editor of *A Hell of a Woman*, an anthology of female crime fiction. She lives in Queens, New York.

everything i want
by megan abbott

for Courtney Love

You destroyed them, didn't you, doc?" one of the government men said, his arms deep in the drawers of the doctor's battered old filing cabinets. "All your records."

They wouldn't believe him when he said there was nothing to destroy. That he'd never kept files on any of his patients. He didn't need to keep records, to document any of it. Hundreds of patients over fourteen years of practice conducted in the second-floor office of the old Reefy Building, so much care woven into its fraying rugs, so many tears sunk deep into the heart pine floors. He could tell you everything about any of them.

"At a certain point," he said, "I could just look at them and know."

He remembered a motion picture he saw once, years ago, when he still indulged in leisure on an errant Sunday. A man sees what life would be like if he had never existed, his town a ruin, his family shorn, the world transformed into a nest of teeming vice. We would all like to believe we matter so much, he thought. That we are holding back the dam. But in his case, he knew it to be true. All those lonely souls who had darkened his office doorstep, who waited for him in the morning and lurked under the hallway sconces at night, who telephoned him at all hours, their voices keening in his ear.

If he had never arrived in town, they would still be shadow-living, tucked behind drawing room drapes, hiding under their office desks, crying into pocket squares on the bus ride home.

Life is hard. The world is punishing. These are the things he knew. In the face of such fermenting loss, the inconstant racket that is the only respite from sinking despair, why shouldn't he give them some joy?

He would always remember it, that icy December morning when he first hammered the *C. Tremblay, MD* sign on his office front door. Balanced on the window sill, his transistor radio crackled with news of Albert Schweitzer receiving the Noble Peace Prize. A man in Oslo recounted a story about how young Albert, traveling on a river in Africa, experienced an Important Moment. Gazing on the rays of the sun shimmering on the water, the abundant beauty of tropical forest, wild beasts at rest on the river banks, it was as though an "iron door had yielded, the path in the thicket had become visible." Suddenly, a phrase came to him: *Ehrfurcht vor dem Leben.* Reverence for life.

"It is the youth of today who will follow the path indicated by Albert Schweitzer," the radio man was saying as Dr. Tremblay brushed the sawdust from the door face. *"All through his long life he has been true to his own youth and he has shown us that a man's life and his dream can become one."*

The doctor stood back and observed his handiwork, the porcelain enamel sign gleaming. Until that moment, he had never once felt he belonged anywhere. From that day forward he devoted himself to all those who sought his care, working harder and harder as the years passed.

For the last four years he had seldom left those careworn 250 square feet.

Who knew, after all, when Mrs. Neel would need to be lifted

from deepest summer sorrows by the sight of the incandescent bulb glowing in his window nigh on two a.m.? Who knew when Mr. Cass, once nearly three hundred pounds and could not pick up his toddling daughter off the floor, might ask for help to fight the sound of his long-dead mother's voice telling him to clean his plate, clean all the plates?

No, he needed to be there, and so he spent his nights nestled on his tucker-leathered davenport, wrapped in an afghan lovingly knitted by Mary Floss, the proprietress of the BRE-Z Laun-Der-Rite and a woman with more than her share of dooming sorrows: two sons lost in Brittany and Kursk and a bleary husband consumed by reckless habits far worse than her own, which the doctor didn't consider a habit but a salve, a balm, a protection from the glaring sight of her mottled hands. Days spent, hands in lye, packing bachelor bundles in stiff blue paper, and the only pleasure to be had was the time with her knees clenched tight between his own, the blooming syringe settling deep in her arm, and her eyes flickering to high heaven.

Oh, Mary Floss, you deserve that, and so much more.

He was born fifty-two years ago to a sad-faced woman with no husband and a physician father with a long dark coat for whom she made meals and played the piano every evening. Within an hour of his birth, his grandfather took him from his mother's weakened arms, removed him from the house, and delivered him to one of the hospital nurses, a woman whose own infant girl had died in the crib of inanition many months before. Her breasts were still full, which she understood as a strong portent. Taking the newborn to her grieving chest, she determined to raise him as her own.

In her fruit cellar, the nurse kept a steady store of liniments, balms, demulcents, vitae, physics, and medical and homemade compounds gathered from her workplace and conjured through her own ministrations. Such is the way he learned the secrets of the body, the mind, and the heart. As he grew older and showed the facility and, she said, a native kindness, she taught him to understand the mystical properties of medicines, the ways that chemistry and the natural world and modernistic technology can all work in harmony. And that medicine is at once art, science, and magic.

One day, the nurse took him by the hand into her dark bedroom and, touching her lower belly with a trembling hand, she said that of all the things she had taught him, this he must remember most: when you have something eating you from the inside, whether it be of mind, body, or spirit—because these things are one—then you truly and at last understand what pain means and how it must be stopped. For herself, she halted it—or held it at bay—by means of the milky glass of ergot and morphine that she kept on her bedside table. And she halted it more and more as her body grew smaller and her eyes sunken. When he was thirteen, the nurse died, her body found by him in the fruit cellar in a state of undress, her hand still curled around that milky glass. Her face was both ruined and serene.

From this point forward, he made his own way. His grandfather arranged, via his lawyer, to give him sufficient funds to continue his schooling in a private young men's academy 250 miles upriver. Eventually, he ended up at a small medical college, but these details were not important to him, even as they were happening. The only thing that he recalled from those years was that he worked very hard and lived as if almost in a dream. All that mattered was that one day he would have his own practice and meet the needs of all his patients as they sought meaning and value in their lives.

This mission came to him during his first Important Moment,

which occurred when he spent three days with a young girl in Marfa, Texas, a girl with green ribbons twisted through long braids. He met her at a roller rink where she always held one leg aloft behind her. For seven years, she had worn a cast from the base of her neck to her knees and elbows, she told him, and now had one built-up shoe to accommodate the right leg shriveled still. When she skated, it was as if the cast had never been there at all, and her body was beautiful, weightless.

The last night, she took him out into a large field astride the Chinati Mountains. When dusk fell, mysterious orbs of light appeared on the horizon then rose in the sky dancing wild tangos with each other in great pulses of blue, yellow, and a kind of phosphorescent green. As he gazed in wonder, hand in hers tightly, knuckles burning, the girl told him these lights had saved her father during a terrible blizzard, lighting his way to the shelter of a cave.

Then, holding tight to his arm, the girl took off her long boot and showed him her withered leg, luminescent under the ghostly lights.

He touched her leg with trembling hands and she looked up at the sky and said, Do you know what these lights signify? And she asked it again and again until she started crying. Her face white from the gloomy lights, he at last knew beauty and magic and wanted to cure her and everyone else.

For seven years, he worked in the orthopedic ward at a hospital in Darke County, and then four years in the army. But it was not until hanging his sign on the door of the second-floor office of the Reefy Building that he felt his life had become his own. At last, he could minister to his patients in his way, in the intimate confines of that place, behind the beveled-glass door, seated on his examination table, their legs dangling, so vulnerable. And the comfort they felt the minute they looked into his eyes and saw only kindness, relief, release.

One, a jaundiced fellow with a pencil mustache, came to him weekly, nattily dressed and smelling of Violet Mints that nudged from the top of his smooth breast pocket. Before the doctor, he had been stricken by such dolor he could not rise from bed and thus had lost his job. Now, he ran the Imperial dining room at the country club and never, ever stopped smiling.

Another, why, before the doctor, he was in dire straits. Mr. Alfred Matheson. The owner of the sprawling emporium on Chess Street, but something had come undone after his beloved daughter moved to California to experience new things. Since then, Mr. Matheson had begun spending evenings at Watson's Bar, drinking and playing the same mournful Irish ballads over and over on the juke box and not letting anyone else put coins in. Long after the commuter trains had stopped rolling into the station across the street with late-returning men in rumpled suits and red Strouss' bags, he would sit under the fairy lights and speak to all who would listen, saying dark things about how the Atomic Age, like man himself, was born in suffering.

Privately, Dr. Tremblay could not disagree.

"Did you see him?" whispered the clerks at Mr. Matheson's store, the ones who spent their days dipping their dirty hands in the undergarments bins and strolling the bright aisles as if kings. "He is not sound." They would talk about how he laughed for no reason and sometimes cried into his desk blotter, shoulders heaving. And the way he licked his lips and moaned when Dinah Shore came on the radio, because, he said, Dinah hails from Winchester, Tennessee, and had polio as a child, as did his sister.

But they could not see what the doctor could. They lacked the glowing eye in the center of his forehead which no one could see but his patients. The one that said: All I need is to be tended to. That is all I need.

And the doctor did. For Albert Matheson, a steady supply of blue pills, each one shaped lovingly like a heart, and twice-weekly injections customized for his particular and exceptional (they were all exceptional) circumstances. When needed, twice a day.

"You told them you were giving them rejuvenators, regulators, revivifiers," the government man said. "But what we found were various mixes of vitamins, enzymes, procaine hydrochloride, dextroamphetamine amobarbital, methamphetamine, and . . . human placenta."

"I gave them life," the doctor replied.

Without him, he knew what many would do. There was one young woman who, before the doctor arrived in town, had relied on the proprietor of an exotic notions store on Tamm Street to provide her with a hobo bindle filled with morphine-soaked raisins she could suck on all day. Another, a crater-faced young man, consumed by misery of a variety too dark to penetrate, would surely return to his prior acts of desperation, sneaking, in the blue-dark of night, to Acme Farms to steal amphetamines from the jobby throats of chickens, who produce eggs with sumptuous rapidity so dosed. Who but the doctor could look at this nervous young man and know all there was to know for what his inner being cried? Who knew what was needed to salve the wounds of a life spent feeling Other?

What would become of Eleanor Lang, a housewife with four children under five and a husband who spent six days a week traveling for Pan Am? Without the doctor's cross-marked wonders doled out in strict tidy rows she would surely have finally done the thing she threatened to do many times before. Twice, this tiny woman nigh on five feet tall had taken a hand drill and once a Bakelite phone handle and once more an awl pick and vowed to stop the train bearing down on the center of her skull. With the doctor gone, the only thing to stop Eleanor Lang would be the experimental surgery her husband kept reading about in *The Rotarian*. No better than the hand drill, the awl.

"Conspiracy to violate federal drug laws relating to stimulant drug. Willfully, knowingly, unlawfully selling, delivering, and disposing of a stimulant drug, namely 22.1 grams of amphetamine sulfate on the following dates—"

"I never sold them," Dr. Tremblay said. "I never sold anything."

"You didn't charge for your services?" the government man said snidely. "You're just the old charity ward, eh?"

"Young man, if you think I did this for pecuniary gain," the doctor replied, his eyes grave—so grave and portentous that even the government man straightened and drew down his propped leg from the desk—"then I deeply misunderstood you. It is rare, but it does occur. Because when I looked at you, past the brute ignorance of your generation and type, I thought I saw something else. Something deeper. Perhaps I was wrong."

Yes, at times even he could not forestall all horrors. A patient who comes only once leaves his office, returns home, and assaults his lady friend with a telephone. A young woman triples her prescribed dose and takes a meat fork to her roommate, then to herself. A knot-browed young man calls at all hours to tell the doctor his skin is radioactive, that his dead mother watches him through a periscope, that his father, long dead, has poisoned the city reservoir, and that we, all of us, are drinking toxins every day. Troubled souls who did not trust enough in him and whose damage is too ancient for him to undo. But are these aberrations to be laid at his creased-leather feet?

As much as he told himself otherwise, he did in fact know he couldn't cure every heart he held in his aging hands. He couldn't even rightly reckon with all the mysteries of the heart. The dark chambers invisible even to my physician's-eyed scalpel. But he had tried.

The one they called to testify—why, watching Mrs. Moses-Pittock nearly brought him to acrid tears. A very wealthy woman, age sixty-two, with the daintiest of ways, and a thick coil of gleaming pearls that looped five times around her neck like an Egyptian snake charmer. For three years she had been coming several times a week for shots, sliding her alligator wallet from her handbag, a handbag soft as curling caramel, and giving him bills crisp from the New Century Merchants Bank, which her father founded a hundred years ago. The newspapers said that he had injected her in the throat, as if she were a horse. Why would he do that? There was no need. It was a beautiful act, seated across from one another, his knees locked against hers, hers locked together.

She would speak to him only once the medicine was in the syringe. And then she was transformed, even before he pulled the plunger.

His grip on her stemlike elbow. The needle and its blooming rescue.

The blood floating like a pink balloon.

Then she would let her moon-shaped fingertips touch his lab coat, her eyelashes fluttering, the faint sound of her filigreed rings clicking against each other.

In court, she had made her grand way to the witness stand, Chez Ninon wool suit the color of a very bright olive, pilgrim pumps tapping the oak planks, and so seeming without trouble in all God's green world. But the doctor knew. He knew about her son's wayward life in Greenwich Village, and about her own private abuses to keep her body slim as the pea shoot her husband had married, abuses he had ceased. And he knew the thing that happened twenty years before, when she accepted that ride from her husband's business partner and the thing he did to her, her mouth pressed shut by his hand, in his gleaming roadster. He knew her suffering, and how to stop it.

After an hour or more of courtroom politenesses, of delicacy, and Mrs. Pittock's sweet-faced resistance, the prosecutor mopped his forehead with frustration. "Mrs. Pittock," the prosecutor said, "do you understand that these were narcotics? That he was putting your health at risk?"

"He has always been so kind," she said from the witness stand. "One August day, I was feeling so unwell I couldn't leave my bed. He walked the four miles to my home to deliver my medications. He has no car, you know. It was nearly 102 degrees. When I asked, *Aren't you warm?* he said, *Such luxuries I can't allow myself.*"

Listening in court, the doctor remembered walking under the barrel-arch ornamental plaster ceiling, tending to her in her damask-walled sitting room, her face white with woe. It was not a world the doctor knew. The doctor knew his aluminum percolator and the prickling static of his RCA.

"He made me feel like a princess," she said.

But it was not Mrs. Moses-Pittock with whom the government men were interested. The doctor knew this. The doctor knew that it had all begun with the scientist.

"I have a voice in me that speaks," the scientist told the doctor. "He says that I am a monster. He speaks to me late at night and at other times too. When I hear him, I cannot move. I cannot rise from bed. I cannot go to my office. I cannot perform my duties. I am no longer a man."

His name was Warren Tibbs of Tibbs Square, the tree-lined common down on the central boulevard. He was a college physics professor, age forty-six but looked ten years older. He had four children, a wife with true yellow hair and a dimple in one corner, and a house that had been his father's and grandfather's, stately and American in all ways. All this, the sparkling sterling silver service and Hepplewhite chairs and a big brass front door that shone in the sun. But the sorrow in his eyes was five fathoms deep and Dr. Tremblay knew he must help him. His problem was not his heart condition, for which he took digitalis and quinidine daily.

For ten years, Warren confided to the doctor, he had been an important researcher at the Argonne National Laboratory just outside of Chicago, but the stresses of the job depleted him and he had retreated to his hometown. Warren told the doctor this while laying on the oriental carpet in his den, looking up at the doctor through hands laced across his eyes. The truth was, Warren added, his superiors felt his behavior had become erratic and his security clearances were rescinded. For which he was, he admitted, glad.

"Maybe," Warren said, his face in his hands now, "you have read of the Argonne Laboratory in the newspapers."

The doctor said he had.

"Did you know that radium used to be used to make a luminous paint?" he asked. "They used it for those clocks with the numerals that glow in the dark."

The doctor did indeed know this. Had read about it in the medical journals. He knew that the girls who worked in those clock factories painting those radium dials had all died of bone and brain cancer. It was their dentists who had discovered it.

"Every day, countless times, they wetted the tip of the brush with their tongues so they might get nice, clean numerals on the dials," Warren Tibbs told him. "Some of them had fun with it and decorated their fingers and eyelids. One painted a Cheshire Cat grin on her face to surprise her beau. At night, walking from the factory, they all gave off this lambent glow. They must have looked quite lovely, those girls."

The doctor opened his bag.

"My mother used to have one of those alarm clocks," Warren added. "Isn't that something?"

And so the doctor's treatments began.

It was two months later that Warren Tibbs summoned Dr. Tremblay to his own home. "I have things to show you," he said. "You will be amazed."

The doctor walked the mile and a half out to the Tibbs home half in wonder. Two months and the only contact had been through the physics department secretary, who called weekly and then twice weekly for the professor's prescriptions. That day, Warren Tibbs himself opened the front doors, his shirt sleeves rolled up, his smile wide, and his face flushed and vibrant.

"Dr. Tremblay, I have always wanted to do something significant," Warren Tibbs said. "Many think I already have. They are wrong." He was not wearing any socks or shoes, and the doctor noted that the brightness in his face had an intensity that worried him. "I wanted to make my mark, wanted my life to have meaning," Warren Tibbs continued, his whole body nearly shaking with energy, "and now you have made it possible."

And then Warren Tibbs opened the doors to his study. On the leather-banked walls were ten, twenty, thirty canvases, bright paintings thick with roiling swirls of oil, brilliant vermillion, scarlet, gold, and when the doctor peered closer, he saw within the swirls dainty, flickering images of what appeared to be girl sprites or elves dancing, slipping on the tiniest of feet along the swoop and whorl of each throbbing helix.

Paint spattered all over the floors and curtains and dappled Warren Tibbs's trouser cuffs and, the doctor now noticed, streaked up one of his arms. It was in his hair.

"You do not even know yet," Warren Tibbs said, voice scratchy as if he had recently been screaming. He slapped his head against the light plate on the wall and the entire room fell to darkness.

The doctor was transfixed. The sprites, the elves, they glowed with an unearthly power, a searing green luminescence radiating off every canvas and like nothing he had ever seen before. And yet he had. Long ago, in Marfa, Texas. These glowing monuments to all that is mysterious and unreachable and unknown.

Standing there in the dark, looking at these paintings, the doctor immediately knew their power, and they spoke to him, and it was like the voice from the buried center of his own buried heart. Warren Tibbs turned to him, so close the doctor could smell the rotting of his teeth. He felt Warren's hand take his, and the two men stood for some time.

It was that day, the day of the paintings, their light, that Dr. Tremblay saw what was to occur. Walking out, he saw Warren Tibbs's six-year-old daughter dancing pirouettes on the front lawn, waving one of her father's paint brushes like a magic wand. He knew he must do something.

He decided he would perform a courageous act.

Is the spirit capable of achieving what we in our distress must expect of it? That is what Albert Schweitzer asked, and Dr. Tremblay knew the answer.

"Dr. Feelgood," the government man said with a sneer. "You made Warren Tibbs feel so good he stopped taking his heart medication and died."

"That is not how I see it," he replied.

"You must have noted the strain on his heart."

The doctor did not say anything.

"You stopped his heart, Dr. Tremblay."

"His heart had stopped long ago, young man. I merely stopped the thunder in his head."

The night before the jury's verdict, Dr. Tremblay woke with a start. He realized he had been in the midst of a stunningly vivid dream in which before him passed all his patients, eyes bright and glittering, smiling at him, thanking him, hurling their hands out, unknotting their knotted fists, opening their arms to him. Until the last one appeared. Walter Tibbs, of course, and when he smiled there were no teeth inside, only an orbular glow that hummed, like a tuning fork. But as he moved closer, the doctor saw that Warren's mouth was open not in a smile but in terror. As if the light inside was choking him, swallowing him whole.

Shaking in his bedclothes, huddled on his office couch, and the thought came to him: It happened because I was too greedy for love. It was all I wanted.

"Dr. Tremblay," Mrs. Moses-Pittock pleaded as they led him out of the courtroom after the verdict, "you can't leave us. Who will take care of us? Who will take care of me?"

He touched her netted glove with two shaking fingers, looked into her watery gray eyes. "I trust you understand that our hearts can take us all to dark and ill-timed places."

James Greer

JAMES GREER is the author of two novels: *The Failure* (Akashic, 2010); and *Artificial Light* (Little House on the Bowery/Akashic, 2006), which won a California Book Award for Best Debut Novel. He is also the author of the nonfiction book *Guided By Voices: A Brief History* (BlackCat/ Grove, 2005), a biography about a band for which he once played bass guitar.

the speed of things
by james greer

part 1: ego in arcadia

othing would make me happier than to tell you, up front, that everything works out fine in the end. Can't do that, I'm afraid. Not because things don't work out fine in the end, but because I don't know how the end ends. The end hasn't happened yet (as far as I can tell). The end may never happen. Things are moving so quickly these days that the end may come and go and I might not notice. Have to allow for that possibility. Have to allow for every possibility. Facts are engrams. Engrams are hypothetical. Thus: Every. Possible. Outcome.

As for the body lying on the floor a few feet away from where I sit, at my desk: I can talk about that. I can give you a definitive answer with respect to the body. Yes, the blood pooling near her head and, less obviously, the little splatters on and around her bare feet: aftereffects of her transition from life to death by means of a series of bullets discharged from a handgun at close range. I should probably make this much (all right, fine) clear: I did not shoot the gun. She didn't shoot the gun. I have no idea who shot the gun. Not sure it matters. The gun got shot, right? A shot gun is not necessarily a shotgun, would be one conclusion you could draw from the

Cannot let this incident interfere with my work schedule. I am extremely busy. I'm on seven different deadlines. Which when you think about it, as I am sometimes given to do (think about it), presents a sort of ironie du sort. (Now I'm just playing word games.) But serious. The line drawn outside a prison beyond which prisoners were liable to be shot. From that idea to this: how? Is there any sense in which missing a deadline corresponds to going further than allowed and therefore liable to be shot and killed? Perhaps going further than allowed, yes, that much one can grant, but everything after therefore is a damned lie.

En attendant, everything is killing me. Not just the seven different deadlines but the expectations. People who know me, who have made the mistake of not shutting up (for good) the minute we met, have a series of expectations that seem to grow, perversely, in accord with my ability to disappoint each and every one. You have to say "each and every" in that sentence for the rhythm, not the meaning. The meaning can go to hell, along with all the people who expect things from me. I know my limits. I know when I've reached my limits. Hey, guess what? I've reached my limits. I might be, well, actually I am, let's not kid ourselves, he said, of at least superhuman intelligence and—did you see that? Her arm just twitched. That was disconcerting—supernal intuition, but even such a one has limits. I see everything, I understand everything, and this happens at both the conscious and all twelve subconscious levels simultaneously. You'd reasonably expect a man with such abilities to be sotted with power, joy-drunk, unintimidated by intimations of mortality. To some extent that is actual factual. To some extent just silly. I have to draw the. It's a question of. Guess. Guess not. Huh.

In the motion picture *Meet John Doe* starring that one guy and that girl and directed by what's-his-name (1939), movement is both created and just happens. Think on this: w/r/t film and music, all forms of dissemination heretofore have involved circular objects, spinning. No matter how far back you looky-loo. Revolvers each and every one, but no more, no more, no more, no more. I don't "these days" know the shape of the medium. Does anyone? Is there a shape? I have seen certain media represented as a waveform, but I suspect that waveform is merely a visual translation of a shapeless batch of numbers. Thing I need to know, has art become math or has math become art, (and) is there a meaningful distinction?

A John Doe club forms for the purpose of improving relations between and among neighbors. That's all. To be a better neighbor. Not really sure how such a thing, even if fueled by a despicable despot, takes root and flowers. Where I live, there are only seven or ten people grouped in ten or seven tin houses, then nothing interesting for many kilometers. An island afloat in the middle of a great city. Everyone is related either by marriage or blood, and everyone keeps to himself. Family members do not talk to family members. No one talks to anyone. Where I live is spectral silent except for noises made by elements and animals. Where I live is nowhere.

The potential when you harness the separate units of a great number of John Doe clubs toward some end other than neighborly. In and out of doors. Well, that's just frightening. If you agree raise your hand. No, other hand. Theoretically I am writing a history of the Federal Reserve Bank. I say theoretically because I don't believe the Federal Reserve Bank exists, evidence to the contrary notwithstanding. You could, I suppose, say with some accuracy that I'm writing a history of nothing. The History of Nothing. Written in Nowhere. Written By. (Hope is in the hand that hits you.)

I have been contracted. Contacted? After a while you forget the smaller differences. This is a known side effect, according to the materials accompanying my prescription of PROVIGIL. I thank, I praise, I grant every, no, each and every day. One hundred milligrams in the morning is my prescriptive dose. I'm not good at following instructions. Too proud or something.

Nine is the number of the muses, so nine hundred milligrams in the morning suits my symmetry. Many people say: *Where would I be without coffee?* and for coffee you can substitute other stimulants or depressants or ampersands. But where would I be without coffee? Added to nine muses of PROVIGIL you can accomplish worlds. You can eliminate sleep from your diet. How super, my love!

$C_{15}H_{15}NO_2S$

Walking through tall pines, trunks pasted with greeny moss, forest floor covered in a mass of needles and cones and deciduous leaves, brown or yellow according to their last request, Aunt Panne was over-brimmed with holy spirit of trees. Praying as she walked, slowly, for soul of dead girl lying on the floor next to desk of Writer. Dead girl or possibly not-dead girl, id est dying girl. Lovely deep blue of her lips.

Mossy ruins of a water mill. Heavyset old man with dropsical jowls and comically large glasses sat on a rotting tree limb chewing a reed.

"I am Aunt Panne."

"I am Paul Volcker, twelfth chairman of the Federal Reserve, 1979–1987. I grew up in Teaneck, New Jersey."

"What brings you to the forest, Paul Volcker?"

"I'm waiting for Writer to remember me."

"There's a plaque here by the ruin of the millstone. I can't read it."

"Because it's in Gallic. The gist of the inscription is that these ruins are symbolic of a larger wreck."

"Well, that makes sense. Did you know the dead or dying girl?"

"Not personally. Only what you read in papers. When there used to be papers. Newspapers, I mean. Les journaux."

"It wasn't all that long ago."

"No, it wasn't. You're right."

"By larger wreck you mean the design?"

"Yes."

"I've been wondering lately if the seeming incoherence of the design isn't contained, somehow, within an even larger design whose outlines we can't see. And that maybe this imperceptible scheme makes perfect sense."

"I don't engage with poetry." Paul Volcker stopped chewing his reed and fished in his jacket pocket for a small notebook.

"*Meet John Doe*," he read aloud from the notebook.

"And then what?" asked Aunt Panne.

"That's all I have so far."

"It's a good start."

Aunt Panne left Paul Volcker sitting by the remains of the mill and continued through the forest, following a path that was no path. She knew that Paul Volcker was worried about the farmers driving their tractors down C Street NW to blockade the Eccles Building, but he would never admit it, not to her, anyway. Maybe he wouldn't admit it to anyone, anymore. Maybe the reason he wouldn't admit it is related to the reason he was sitting on the rotting tree limb by the old water mill.

Was there even a trace of whatever water source once drove the mill? As she moved farther and farther away, Aunt Panne's memory similarly receded. She could no longer picture Paul Volcker's face. She could no longer in any detail picture the mossy ruin of the mill. It was entirely possible, she admitted to herself as she trudged up a gentle slope slick with mud from a recent rain, that she had imagined the whole interval. The words *lacuna* and *caesura* flitted through her brain, for a moment, and then disappeared.

Okay, but if you allow one example do you have to allow them all? Do you admit the unreality of experience generally if one experience turns out to be illusion? The brain is capable of many things when its circuits are working, even more when overloaded with catecholamines and hypothalamic histamines. The synaptic terminals release these oracles into the floodstream and you start to see things: Is it the future? Is it the past? Is it a kind of present that would otherwise be invisible to our seven dulled senses? Or is it, as most would have you think, a fantasy, the product of a disordered mind. Consciousness infected with chemicals, perception out of step with consensus. When you apply reason to the problem, you kill the problem. You derive a solution. Aunt Panne mistrusted solutions. She would rather beggar the question by withholding logic, and thus arrive at the edge of the forest rather than, say, a small clearing or a mossy ruin.

Approaching the ecotone she could see cows grazing in the meadow.

part 2: rule bretagne

Snow came in bunches to Bon Repos, on the border of the Forêt de Quénécan. The companions of the abbey were put to work sweeping the courtyard early on the morning of December 19 in the Year of Our Lord. The blinking lights of the snowplows had moved far enough away from the courtyard that you could no longer hear the susurrus of their heavy tires, nor the scrape of metal against. This has been the coldest winter of our lives. In the memory of our lives. There has been a record chute of snow. The cars are corked for miles, and hours, on the autoroutes. On the radio you are warned to bring a thermos of some hot liquid and *"perhaps something to eat"* before you set out in your car. What kind of a person would set out in his car under such perturburant circumstances? What kind of person says "set out in his car"? The wrecked bulkheads massed along the shore, covered in fresh snow, no longer move, but boy they sure do work. How do you cut the GPS tag from under your skin? You use a stolen knife. You ask the girl to use the knife because you can't do it yourself. That's how the girl ended up dead, on your floor, in your room, because she removed the GPS tag. It's starting to come back now, but in fragments. In packets.

Everybody's got a past. Everybody stinks of time. But the photography is so pure that you don't mind. The rhythm of the shots, and the rhythm within the shots, matches with exquisite rigor the languid movements of the actors inside the frame. Only the music jars. The music is ridiculous, overstated, too much. "Tonight the gates of Mercy will open." That's what the music wants to say. The clarinets. I see a crowd of black hats, everyone playing the clarinet. There's nothing wrong with the clarinet in principle. With any woodwind.

New rule: no one speaks. Not for any reason. Words have only ever caused problems. I can think of no exceptions. Everything will be communicated in images, only. No intertitles, subtitles, supertitles, titles, title cards. The moving image versus the static (photo) is obviously superior. An image that moves offers a more complete set of the infinite fractions of solitude, according to N. The history of cinema is the history of the image. Without words. The paradox of using words to describe things that. Text is text is text. This is not a text. In the event of an actual text, you would have been directed by the appropriate emergency services to destroy all evidence of yourself. I do not feel pain. Thunder and lightning ask my approval. What some call prayer is easily misused, but I command the seas.

I have no reason to doubt. I have no reason to believe. I got no reason, I prefer no reason at all. Crows gather on every street corner. Talking about something I can't quite. What's the point of so many crows? Crown, crow, cow. Unusually, you can do that in Russian too.

Phil Esposito was the consensus pick in the living room for the trivia question, *Which Buckthorn had been the fastest to score fifty goals in one season?* Writer didn't wait to hear the answer. If not Esposito, who? Cashman? Bucyk? What difference does it make? They were all fucking great. Ten seconds later his father actually said, "I have seen some terrible calls in my life, but that one takes the cake," concerning a potentially dodgy hooking call on Buckthorn player Sad Strawbo. The answer to a more pertinent question was soon thereafter provided by Sabater Pi and his caliginous table of incantatory engrams. Without the help of Sabater Pi, one finds it unlikely that anything would ever get done by anyone. A study of helicopter pilots suggested that 600 milligrams of PROVIGIL given in three doses can be used to keep pilots alert and maintain their accuracy at predeprivation levels for forty hours without sleep. Another study of fighter pilots showed that PROVIGIL given in three divided 100-milligram doses sustained the flight-control accuracy of sleep-deprived F-117 pilots to within about twenty-seven percent of baseline levels for thirty-seven hours, without any considerable side effects.

The exact mechanism of action of PROVIGIL is unclear, although numerous studies have shown it to increase the levels of various monoamines, namely: dopamine in the striatum and nucleus accumbens; noradrenaline in the hypothalamus and ventrolateral preoptic nucleus; and serotonin in the amygdala and frontal cortex. While the coadministration of a dopamine antagonist is known to decrease the stimulant effect of amphetamine, it does not entirely negate the wakefulness-promoting actions of PROVIGIL. This is not by any means the whole story.

Sabater Pi stands over his engrams and mutters incantations. These incantations are the stuff of ice creams, through which the world learns its manners. Without Sabater Pi's engrams, the world would have no memory. He decides which to keep and which to discard. It's a very important job. It might be the only important job. Sabater Pi had just decided that the engram of the dead girl in Writer's room must at all costs be kept. Could not for any reason be removed. He walked to a corner of his office, sat down at a comically small desk, and began typing.

Writer was startled by the sudden whir and clunk of the fax machine on the floor by his feet. He remembered that the Icelandic magician Flute Guðmundsdottir had once told him that her magic was meant to represent or emulate the sound of the modern world, its electronic machinery in constant motion, humming and buzzing and belling in the background even when no one was listening. This had never made any sense to Writer. He had tried to discuss the issue with Bragi Ólafsson, an Icelandic novelist who had once helped out in Sykurmolarnir, which was the name of a circus act in which Flute had also participated, doing—something. But Writer's attempt to reach Ólafsson through his American publisher had been unsuccessful, and so with some reluctance he had dropped the matter. Throughout his conversation with Flute, she had licked her lips repeatedly, small pink tongue darting out of her mouth to moisten this or that small section of unglossed upper or lower lip. It was a reflexive action. She wasn't aware she was doing that, he remembered thinking. But also a familiar one. People who are nervous, or who take any form of stimulant, even coffee, are prone to this reflex. The stimulant produces a sensation of dryness in the mouth and lips that no amount of water can remedy. There would be no reason, Writer reasoned, for Flute to be nervous in his company, in room 59 of the Chateau Marmont in Los Angeles, California. She was drinking from a deep glass of still water. It was exactly noon o'clock.

The sound of the modern world scared the wits right out of Writer (whose real name was Thomas Early). The sound of the modern world was linked inextricably to the speed of the modern world. The latter was very, very fast, and getting faster. At—what's the usual phrase—an "exponential rate." One moment we're all prosperous and happy, seals basking on the warm rocks of midday sun off the coast of Maine in summer. The next we're falling, endlessly, down a hole that used to be a floor but is no longer a floor. The banking system had run out of money, as Thomas Early understood the situation, and so everyone had run out of money, and even though everyone had run out of money years and years ago, for some reason this now actually mattered. Hence the panicky tumble down the black hole of the future, end over end, bottom over top, will-ye nill-ye, and God help us if we ever reach any kind of definite denouement, because a back-of-the-envelope calculation indicates that an abrupt halt would result in a gelatinous mess.

The best we can hope for, then, in the current situation, is to keep falling. Even though it seems as if we're falling faster and faster, we're actually falling at the same speed. The speed of a falling object does not depend on its mass. That you are a (much) fatter person than me does not mean you will fall faster. We all started at the same height, from the same point, and Galileo has proved that we will all be crushed to death simultaneously.

We are aware of our many misdeeds, our failings, our

weaknesses, our fears, our shame. We do not know how to exculpate ourselves. (Having no religion to rely on.) We do not know whether to exculpate ourselves, having no moral or philosophical base from which to extrude the principle of sin. Because we were brought up short. We were all brought up short in a long, tall world.

The dead girl's mistake was indulging her appetite for existence. We all make the same mistake, and the mistake is always fatal. An eighty-three-year-old woman is in a coma after having been attacked at the Mairie de Clichy métro station by a fourteen-year-old Romanian kid. A former journalist was killed by his seventeen-year-old son because the son was unhappy with the five hundred euros per month his father was giving him as an allowance. A man found two thousand euros, cash, in the street. He turned it over to the police. A judge ruled that the two thousand euros does not belong to the man, and is instead being kept by the court until the real owner of the money can be determined. The man declared himself in an interview to be "disappointed" by the court's ruling. "Honesty doesn't pay," he said.

Potter's Field ain't such a faraway stare when you've one foot in the quick. An argument between scholars, already tenuous, becomes untenably ephemeral within minutes if you put it in (a cloud). Unsearchable, unfindable, irretrievable. Lost. The most common side effect of speed is the acceleration of loss.

The fax from Sabater Pi was very short. It read, in full: *The dead or dying girl is you.*

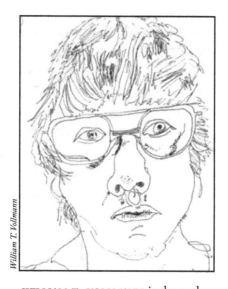

William T. Vollmann

WILLIAM T. VOLLMANN is the author of twenty books, including *Europe Central*, winner of the National Book Award; *Riding Toward Everywhere*, an examination of the train-hopping hobo lifestyle; and *Imperial*, a panoramic look at one of the poorest areas in America. He has also won the Whiting Writers' Award, the PEN Center USA Literary Award for Fiction, a Shiva Naipaul Memorial Prize, and the Strauss Living Award from the American Academy of Arts and Letters. His journalism and fiction have been published in the *New Yorker*, *Esquire*, *Spin*, and *Granta*. Vollmann lives in Sacramento, California.

no matter how beautifully it stings
by william t. vollmann

Note to the Reader: The following passages have to do with speedy substances, which, like any loyal American, I know only in the most theoretical sense. —WTV

Her face was already smoother when he looked in the mirror. He thought it was the estrogen but Rosa said it was only autosuggestion. (He had a dream that he was walking with Rosa and everyone humiliated him; Rosa said it was because they could see, thanks to the crimson collar of the sweater he wore beneath his jacket, that he was a woman.) Often now he felt as lovely-pure as this transparent meth crystal now partially crumbled to glassy sand within the multiple-folded scrap of newspaper. He broke it in half. He inhaled. The septum of his nose ached. His nostrils watered. Then he began to feel the happy lively feeling; he was alive again, "in the moment" as we Californians say. His nipples itched.

Do you want any, darling?

No, thank you, said Rosa, doing her mascara.

His penis hardened delightfully. He saw everything better; he could practically count the revolutions of the fan blades on the ceiling; oh, he surely could have had he wanted to.

While Rosa glossed her lips, he had another sniff.

Rosa offered to do his makeup, but tonight he did not care to honor his inner feminine in any outer way; better to remain a double agent. So while Rosa combed out her Isabel wig he laid happily spreadeagled on the bed, with another shot of whiskey in his hand, playing with the gray hairs on his nipples, his penis hard like never before.

One was supposed to leave the room key at the office, but he put it in his pocket. They went downstairs to the rental car. Rosa was the driver and he the navigator. It was just dusk as they rolled out of Santa Monica past the motels on Ocean and the cool beads of traffic. The sting of crystal was delicious in his nostrils. It was going to keep him excited for all of the thousand miles down Santa Monica Boulevard to the Western girls and the blond California girls with net purses. His powers of perception may safely be defined as godlike, although I grant that later he could not always remember his observations. In traffic behind taxis he saw into every car, reading the emotions of all parties even when only the backs of their heads offered themselves to his discernment. As for Dolores, she spotted a man on a bench; she could have counted every hair on his hands. Two couples crossed the street, and to her this was unique and even important. A man and a woman were kissing. Dolores got hot, and slid her big hand up Rosa's skirt. But then as they crossed Fourth he was enraged rather than titillated to find a man put his hand on a brunette's hips when *he* wanted to do it. Then the illuminated freeway became an intergalactic ride, and these were the constellations:

PSYCHIC READING BY EVE

Del's Saloon

OPEN LATE

Colby Avenue

Feminine Touch Makeovers

LEGEND OF THE SEEKER

Dolores Restaurant

and the 405 freeway where the world was darkened by red lights. Rosa seemed a trifle disappointed in him, so he put on lipstick.

SMOKING DEATHS THIS YEAR
Afrodita Flowers
Selby Avenue

(the meth shining loyally in his being, the lights calm)

LOS ANGELES – TEMPLE
Casa Isabel Wedding Gowns
Come Unto Me Katholic Shoppe
Gentlemen's Club
PROSTHETIC HEAVEN
GRANITE MONUMENTS
EYES BY HANNA
Hair by Rosa
Dr. S. R. Yemadjian, Fashion—Liposuctions
A. A. Liquors
A. A. A. Deli & Liquor
AAAAH! Female Rejuvenation
Little Friends Preschool
Little Sweeties Massage
BIG JOHN'S MARITAL AIDS
Ron's Kickass Butt Burgers
CARNICERIA — DIVORCE
Dignity Plus Discount Cremations
Esmerelda's Lingerie
Hollywood Wonder Caverns
Grinning Cave Virtual Thrill Adventures

Young Forever Breast Reduction
Buy One, Get One Free
Avenue of the Stars

and high dark towers whose rectangular windows were usually yellow but sometimes silver gathered them in like the arms of a harbor or moonbase, the red blear of the Beverly Hilton promising them that their night could be as dirty, fun, or sinister as they cared to make it; and then it grew extremely dark on Wilshire Boulevard. This long grayish-white rectangular building over there against the dirty dark cubes, what would that have meant to anyone whose gaze had not been so enhanced by meth? And what did it mean? *He* knew, but what he knew he never told me, so I cannot put it into this book. His eyesight was getting keener by the instant. His best friend Luke used to have 20-10 vision, although now that was going away. Now he understood what it must have been like for Luke, this confidence and competence; and already they were crossing Rodeo Drive. Los Angeles was flat and white and cool.

He experienced a glowing feeling, deviled warm and deviled dark, but no, neither dark nor cool—perfectly at ease, with a faintly bitter taste in his mouth, his lipstick greasy—

CITY OF WEST HOLLYWOOD
Almost Everyday People
Tell Us Your Story
BEST BURGER IN TOWN
Movie Star Styling Palace
Ereshkigal Middle Eastern Delights
TANGO GRILL

(not to mention the glowing massage parlor on La Cienega,

then Love Connection, Love Correction, Tasty Donuts, Crescent Heights Boulevard, Hollywood Electric Vacuum and Sewing, Paris House Nude Adults Only, Fat Burger—and then the velvet grid)

La Brea Avenue
$1 CHINESE EXPRESS
Adult Books
CALIFORNIA SURPLUS MART
El Centro Mini Mart
TRANS MAGIC
Gold Diggers Entertainment

—and on Western a police car screamed by—

Tropical Fish and Birds
DR. SKIN

I want to go to Dr. Skin, he thought; but what if he's creepy, and instead of improving my skin into womanly smoothness he skins me alive or turns me into a tattooed mummy?

They parked and went to a bar which had been recommended by an expert drinker named Mr. Joseph Mattson. It was called the Black Hole, and indeed it was a narrow, lightless place, deserving of the dark fumigation recommended by the fifteenth-century *Book of Buried Pearls* for those who wish to find the invisible pathway beneath the white mountain north of the Great Pyramid of Giza; here refined gold awaits the seeker who has escaped Dr. Skin. The little Japanese barmaid wore bigger breasts than Dolores. On the hot black stinking sticky walls, dancing girls had been painted in phosphorescently artificial hues. They could have been ancient terra-cotta Sirens from whose flesh the pigment was flaking. The black picnic tables were empty, but four men sat drinking quietly at the bar. It was almost Halloween. He sat down beside Rosa, gazing at a plastic jack-o'-lantern while they drank beer in plastic cups. Rosa laughingly said: I wonder why it is that the toilet seat is always up in the women's room? Around midnight the T-girls began to swish in; he especially liked the long-haired girl in the snappy dress shaking her hair, acned rough face. On the black man's lap, the white legs of two capering girls opened and closed, speaking to him like lips whose tongues were hiding. There was a curtain like a pair of nylon stockings, and it kept wavering and the busiest T-girl kept wavering through it in and out of the street, from which came another T-girl in a black skirt who took her by the hand and they went into the ladies' room. Not all of them were tall; some little young ones reminded him of black ducks swimming and pecking in the green water. There was a woman whose eyes were so white in the darkness; Rosa also loved her, so that when they gazed at her together his heart became as blue and pure as her eyeliner. Rosa, seeing how shy he felt, rose and entered this woman's golden screaming glow; she whispered into her ear, and the woman smiled, at which he began to glow at once, staring into her eyes. The woman accepted Rosa's hand. They approached him.

What's your name? she asked him.

Dolores, he replied. And yours?

Luz María Salcido.

Do you like the Black Hole?

Better than picking grapes all day in Coachella.

Soon they were in the woman's apartment, playing with her cosmetics.

Just as a line or two of meth on the second day, no matter how beautifully it stings the nasal passages or even how well one has just slept, is never as thrillingly joyous as on the first—nasal secretions run down into the throat, bitter rather than salty; and the feeling with which one is presently gifted is no high, merely a sort of weary steadfastness, as if consciousness has squared its shoulders; then slowly, slowly, one comes to feel a trifle better, more wide awake, but impurely so, lacking well being—so Dolores, who had now become a woman to the best of her capabilities, now began to take herself for granted, feeling sometimes almost bored with her lips, anus, and nipples: I'm a woman, and who cares? Do I particularly care about my downstairs neighbor Adelina? Are whatever pieties her wrinkled old brain produces any more or less of a miracle than the fact that between her legs rides a dried-up gray-haired slit? Who am I to be impressed by her, myself, or anything? What I live is merely life, nothing better. Anyway, I don't dislike Adelina; I'm even fond of myself; my life is quite fine in that way. What do I wish for? Is nothing better than sexual ecstasy, or self-love, or the love of others? Is boredom my failure or simply a requirement for not dying? I'm *sweating* with boredom! I don't feel good. I must be getting old; I'm hot and achy. No, it must be the hormones, or perhaps some disease.

By degrees her customers had become peculiarly ungrateful, even insulting at times. But then she discovered something nearly as good as Concentrax, and possibly even better. They called it *the green angel*. It was a little pill, you see, a darling little pill, and whenever she took two, or at most three, then no matter whom she was with and whatever she did, she screamingly enjoyed herself. Sometimes *the green angel* even focused her mind so that she could remember any number of ways of being a woman, for instance a certain young girl, so shy, a whispering face-averter, who in the time when Dolores was still a man would gallop upon his face so freely, and just before she came would always whisper *fuck!*

A man was sodomizing Dolores, and she loved it. Oh, how she loved it with the deep joy and purity of desire fulfilled, the animal present triumphing over the deathly future . . . Wiggling her bottom for him, leaning on her elbows, she covered her eyes with both hands as if she felt extremely reserved, then suddenly drew her hands away, wiggled her bottom as rapidly as she could, and whispered *fuck!* The man was enchanted.

But soon afterward her big male hands began stinking of sweat; her aging face went red and ugly; she felt as if contaminated liquefied fat were oozing out of the bags under her eyes, her febrile forehead salty wet, her tongue and glottis tasting like metal. She blew her nose, and there were flecks of blood in the mucus. She grew more hot and nauseous by the instant. These unpleasant sensations seemed to have come from nowhere, but don't they always? When she lay down, the granules of the popcorn ceiling refused to stop enlarging themselves. She closed her eyes, but her eyelids hurt her aching eyeballs, which sweated and sweltered in that too-hot darkness. Her face seemed to feel better when she locked it into a grimace. Why was that? She couldn't think. When would this go away? It was the third day since she had last inhaled a line of crystal. The sweat on the backs of her hands and between her fingers afflicted her almost intolerably. It felt gummy and corrosive at the same time. She wished to lie perfectly still on her back in a cool dim room. With considerable fortitude she managed to take a shower. Then she put on a clean loose dress and lay down. Instantly she could smell the stench of her armpits, which she had cleaned many times with a bar of stinging soap. The sweat on her upper lip stung almost intolerably. Sores broke out on her tongue. Twin crescent zones of hideous sweat erupted beneath her eyebrows, whose fine, almost imperceptible hairs exuded foulness. Her heart was beating very rapidly. The hairs on the backs of her arms began to sting. In her breastbone, a wide hot oval of tenderness now manifested itself, not entirely unpleasantly. Dolores lay as motionless as she could, waiting for these symptoms to pass. Now it was the backs of her wrists which felt the hottest and wettest. The insides of her elbows stung numbly. Her dress clung to her flesh like the burning poison shirt of Nessus. Her back ached. Each bone within her fingers threatened to shatter. She wanted to wipe away the sweat on her upper lip, but feared that the side of her hand might adhere there. She would have used yesterday's panties, which lay on the floor beside her, but although she could see them, she could not reach them. How hot it was here, how impure! She could not escape from feculence.

The next day the withdrawal afflicted her only in throbbing nauseating wavelets, and the day after that she was perfect. Now she knew how to manage crystal: once a week would be best. For the other times there were Concentraxes, powder-trains of cocaine snuffed up through twenty-peso bills, crack rocks, tequila, beer, whiskey, and, of course, *the green angel*. The trick was to parcel out these various vitamins and staples, so that no single one could bite too deep. When all else failed, and certainly when anything succeeded, there remained orgasm itself.

Thanks to this superbly practical insight, Dolores soon found herself quite rich in pleasures and hours. All day she rested or played with herself; all night, so it seemed, she expressed her womanhood by taking in the penises of this world, whose friends, clients, and encounters all became stacked up upon each other. Sometimes she wondered whether this was what she had made all her prior sacrifices for, but the sensations of the Femerol still thrilled her sometimes in her spectacular nipples, *the green angel* was good to her, and many of her sexual encounters gave her great joy. She said goodbye to this man and that; sometimes she wished to find a woman to love and live with forever as she should have done with Rosa, but how could she expect to see anyone like Rosa again? In a lesbian bar in Tijuana the women had been far from kind to her, and in Xalapa there might be no such place; not even Ana María had known of one. So happily Dolores let herself be carried down the weeks and months. Surely there would come another purpose, or at least a new adventure. Descending the stairs to greet her neighbor Adelina, she smiled at the world, smoothed her hair, straightened her dress, and hurried off to buy just a little more crystal. She was already itching to get her sweet breasts sucked.

THE
HEROIN
CHRONICLES

EDITED BY **JERRY STAHL**

The Heroin Chronicles is also available as an ebook:

www.amzn.to/1fHUICN (Kindle)
www.bit.ly/15O46z3 (epub)

CONTENTS

introduction
modes of desperation
by jerry stahl

> *It has not been in the pursuit of pleasure that I have periled life*
> *and reputation and reason. It has been the desperate attempt to*
> *escape from torturing memories, from a sense of insupportable*
> *loneliness and a dread of some strange impending doom.*
> —Edgar Allan Poe

Somewhere, a long time ago, I wrote: *All my heroes were junkies.* (Hey, you pick your cliché and you run with it. That's half of life.) So let's march 'em out. The Junkie All-Stars: Miles Davis, Lenny Bruce, Keith Richards, Billie Holliday, William S. Burroughs, even Dylan, there for a while. (Not to mention Cliff Edwards, otherwise known as Ukulele Ike, the voice of Jiminy Cricket and a lifelong addict. Junkies have all the best stories. But we'll get to that.)

Of course, Rush Limbaugh seems to have also colonized his hefty keister onto the Heavyweight Fiend list, but that's these days. (And we're not going to hoist up Herman Goering, another fat-ass fascist, and drag him around the track.) Oxycontin, known to newshounds, aficionados, and Justified fans as Hillbilly Heroin, is so much easier to acquire and imbibe than the old-fashioned nonprescription variety.

But don't get me wrong, I'm not judging Rush. A man's got to do what a man's got to do. And there is no finer cure to self-hate than determined, euphoria-inducing opiate use.

Culturally speaking—shout out to Rush again!—opiate consumption now packs all the glamour of the buttock boil that kept the right-wing rant-meister out of Vietnam. For which, perhaps, Drug Czar R. Gil Kerlikowske could issue a gold medal for yeoman service in the name of addiction prevention. And I say this with respect. Growing up, if some right-wing pork roast had morphed into our national dope fiend, I would have found another line of work and become an alcoholic. Everybody knows the difference between them: An alcoholic will steal your wallet in a blackout and apologize when he finds out. A junkie will steal it and help you look for it. Call it a matter of style, or a mode of desperation. Nothing wrong with *Lost Weekend* or *Arthur* or *Days of Wine and Roses*, but give me *Panic in Needle Park*, *Man with the Golden Arm*, and *Requiem for a Dream* any day.

Ply Mother Theresa with appletinis for three days straight and she'll crawl out the other end with dry mouth and a hangover. Shoot her up for three days and by Day Four the saint of Calcutta will be strung out like a lab monkey, ready to blow the mailman for dime-bag money. Being a junkie is not a lifestyle choice—it's an imperative of molecular chemistry.

Still, Keith, Miles, and Lenny made it look pretty cool. (Even if, one learns the hard way, Lou Reed and Bird aren't on hand to tamp your forehead with a wet towel when you're kicking. By which point it's pretty clear that heroin, at the proverbial end of the day, is about as glam as puking on your oatmeal.)

It may have been some twenty years since I've stuck a needle in my neck, but it's not like everything above it has healed up nicely. Shooting dope isn't what made me a crazy, pissed-off, outsider sleazeball and one-man crippling fear machine. Heroin just gave me an excuse. But that's me. If the short stories you are about to read in this collection are about nothing else, they're about actions—occasionally hell-driven, occasionally hilarious, uniformly desperation-and-delusion-fueled actions—the kind made by those in the grip of constant gnawing need. The entire anthology, on some level, can be viewed as an eclectic and festive encyclopedia of bad behavior.

But it's the need that makes the junkie a junkie. Even when it's not mentioned in any given story, it's there, like the weather, and it's always about to storm. Once the craving goes, the habit dissipates, but the dynamic—the Algebra of Need, as William S. Burroughs put it—remains in place. Junkies are like veterans, or bikers, or cancer survivors, or ex-cons. (Speaking just as a member of Team Dope Fiend, I don't trust anybody who hasn't been to hell. I may like you, I may even respect you, but, when the balls hit the griddle, I'd prefer somebody get my back who's had experience in my little neck of it. See, I know a guy, did a dime in Quentin. Been out twenty-three years. But even now—even now—according to his wife, he still wears prison sandals in the shower. Can't get wet barefoot. Once they've walked the yard, some men look over their shoulders their whole lives. Dope fiends, metaphorically or physically, live with their own brand of residual psychic baggage.)

When you're a junkie, you need junk to live. Everything's all on the line, all the time. Here's the thing: people know they're going to die—but junkies know what it feels like. They've kicked. Which hurts worse than death. But they know they're going to run out. It's a mind-set. No matter how big the pile on the table— junkies already see it gone. Junkies live under the Syringe of Damocles. Junkies exist as the anti-Nietzsches. Whatever doesn't kill you makes you need more dope.

Which doesn't make fiends unique—it makes them human. Just more so. Junkies feel too much. And need a lot to make them not feel.

Every writer you're about to read has been to places the "normal" human may not have been. And lived to talk about it. They haven't died for your sins. But they've felt like shit, in a variety of fascinating ways. And by the time you finish this fiction anthology, you will understand, from their pain, from their degradation, from their death-adjacent joy and skin-clawing, delirious three-a.m.-in-the-middle-of-the-day lows, the wisdom that comes from the nonstop drama and scarring comedy of living every second of your life in a race against the ticking clock of your own cells, a clock whose alarm is the sweaty, skin-scorching revelation that if you don't get what you need in three minutes your skin is going to burn and your bowels loosen, and whatever claim you had on dignity, self-respect, or power is going to drip down your leg and into your sock like the shaming wet shit of green-as-boiled-frog cold-turkey diarrhea.

Unlike serial killers or traditional torturers, junkies spend most of their time savaging themselves. That everyone they know and love in the world is often destroyed in the process is just a side issue. C.A.D. Collateral Addict Damage. *And yet.*

From this festive and inelegant hell, these junkie writers—some ex, some not-so-ex, but a good editor never tells—have returned with a kind of sclerosed wisdom. Their burning lives may lie scattered behind them like the remains of a plane crash in an open field, but the flames will, I guarantee, illuminate the lives of any and all who read it, whether addicted to dope, Jim Beam, gun shows, bus station sex, Mars bars, Texas Hold'em, telenovellas, fame or—thank you, Jesus, Lord of Weird Redemption—great fucking writing.

Jerry Stahl
Los Angeles, CA
September 2012

PART I
REALITY BLURS

Ferry Chung Photography

TONY O'NEILL is the author of the novels *Sick City, Down and Out on Murder Mile*, and *Digging the Vein*, as well as several books of poetry and nonfiction. He does not blog or have a Facebook page. He misses the days when drug dealers had pagers. For more information, visit www.tonyo-neill.net.

fragments of joe
by tony o'neill

My name is Joe, and I am an addict."

"*Hi, Joe.*"

They were in a small church basement in East Hollywood. The Wednesday-morning "Happy Hour" AA meeting was in full swing. Joe sat among a small group of ex-junkies, drunks, speed freaks, and crackheads, yet still looked like the sickest person in the room. A defeated-looking junkie in his late forties, Joe's face was patterned with deep creases and fresh sores. His eyes trembled in their sockets like two furtive crackheads hiding in a by-the-hour motel room.

At the back of the room was a woman called Tania, anxiously chewing a hangnail, watching the man who addressed the group. This was the second time she had noticed Joe at one of her regular meetings. Last week he was standing by the coffee urn at the Narcotics Anonymous near Hollywood and Highland, stuffing his pockets with stale cookies. And here he was today, addressing the group in a barely audible monotone, looking even worse than he had then.

Tania glanced around the room. She guessed she was the only person under thirty here, although sometimes with dope fiends you couldn't tell. This meeting attracted the old-timers, old fucks with years of sobriety under their belts who circled the newcomers like sharks around chum. She wasn't really sure why she had come here. She had already decided that this meeting would be her last. One last hour of her life just to be sure that this sobriety thing wasn't for her, and then she could return to the dealers at Bonnie Brae and 6th with a clean conscience and forty bucks in her pocket.

"Ahem," Joe said, "I don't feel good today. I relapsed again . . . a little while ago, you know? And it really took it out of me. I mean physically, it just took it out of me. Thing is, I'm finding it hard to even get the . . . *focus*, you know, the focus to begin the whole process again . . . to begin working on my recovery. I . . . I'm a heroin addict, as I'm sure some of you know." He gave a forced, self-effacing smile that didn't suit his face. "I had six months clean under my belt, but . . . right now I know I'm gonna struggle to even make it to the end of the day without using. I wasn't even planning on going to this meeting. I came here in a kind of *trance*, really. I dunno what else to do."

Tania wiped her nose with the back of her hand. Fuck, shit, piss. The meeting was a mistake. It's not as if her disillusionment with sobriety was a recent development. She'd been clean—and miserable as hell about it—for a good seven months now. The miracle they promised her never arrived. After the painful detox, expensive inpatient treatment, and her stint in that crummy sober living house, nothing was *better*. Everything was still shit. Every time she dragged her reluctant ass to a meeting, the stories of drug-induced degradation she heard just served to remind her of what she had given up. When someone like Joe came in, fresh from a relapse, she didn't feel *bad* for them. She secretly wished she had been getting high *with* them. Their sorry-ass apologies to the group just made the urge stronger.

Sober living had been a joke. Twenty-nine years old and forced to share a room with some dumb teenage methhead moron from Orange County, with perky tits and bad teeth. The bitch talked so much that Tania could only wonder what the hell she must have been like when she was doing crank. No, she'd decided as she'd hurriedly packed her bags last Sunday, I'm too old for this shit. Too smart. Something will come along.

". . . But I'm thankful to be here," Joe was saying. "And I'm going to keep trying . . . Thanks."

"Thanks, Joe."

Later they all stood, held hands, and said the serenity prayer. Years after her first meeting, Tania still felt the same indignation about the religious trappings of the program that she'd felt then. She didn't believe in God any more than she believed in redemption. They were stupid concepts, the kind of ideas that don't stand up to rational scrutiny. Plenty of people had told her to *fake it till you make it*. It was another of those irritating mantras that AA's true believers traded like baseball cards. But faking was never Tania's style.

Afterward, everybody broke into little groups to drink coffee, talk, and bullshit. Everyone except Joe. He headed straight for the door before anyone could try to intercept him. He was halfway down the block before Tania managed to catch up with him.

"Joe? Hey, *Joe!*"

He had the furtive gait of a shoplifter trying to walk away from the store as quickly—but nonchalantly—as possible. She thought for a moment that he was going to ignore her and simply keep walking. She called his name even louder this time. He paused.

"It's just like the song," she said, catching up to him.

Joe looked confused. "Song?"

"Hey Joe." Tania extended her hand. "I'm Tania."

"Oh, right. *That* song." After an awkward pause he finally took her hand and gave it a limp shake. "I'm . . ."

"You're Joe. I know." Tania removed her sunglasses. "D'you wanna go somewhere? I mean, with me?"

"Ah. Erm . . . well, I don't have time for coffee right now. Thing is, I'm on my way to see someone, you know?"

Coffee. Another in a long fucking line of AA clichés. When someone seems like they're in trouble, on the verge of a relapse or a crisis of faith, someone else always drags them out for coffee and a pep talk. Tania had been through that routine more times than she could count.

"I don't *want* a coffee. Just wanna kill some time. Who you meeting?"

Despite her taste for narcotics and the lifestyle it had often forced her into, Tania still had a face. Six months away from the needle had given her a veneer of health. There was color in her cheeks, her breasts were filling out again as she put on a little sobriety weight. She wore a long-sleeved T-shirt despite the heat, with a picture of Marc Bolan emblazoned across it. Her hair was dyed black, with some blond poking through at the roots. Joe had not talked to a woman in what seemed like a lifetime. He felt like a tongue-tied teenage boy.

"I'm just meeting . . . he's just a friend of mine. No one special."

"Can he get something for me?"

"What do you mean?"

"You know."

"Yeah, maybe. Well . . . yeah."

"Then I wanna see your friend too. You wanna kill some time together, or what?"

"Uh-hum."

"Is that all right?"

"Look, Tania, I'm broke. I mean, I've only got enough bread to get straight with, you know."

"I'm not asking for a freebie. Just some company, that's all. Is that okay?"

Joe shrugged. "Yeah, I guess."

* * *

They drove downtown together in Joe's battered Honda. His

connection operated out of a loft space near Pershing Square. They found an empty meter, and he brought her to a steel door sandwiched between a grimy-looking fried chicken joint and a store that sold Santería artifacts. Joe rang the buzzer and a voice crackled, *"Yeah?"*

"It's Joe, lemme in."

"Who'ssat with jou?"

"Friend of mine. She's cool."

The door buzzed open.

The damp concrete stairwell reeked of piss and bleach. When they almost reached the top they saw people lined up in front of them. They took their place behind two young punk girls in leather jackets and Dr. Martens, sniffling dejectedly. After a minute or two a sallow man wearing a Nike T-shirt and baseball cap clumped up the stairs and joined the line. They stood there, silently waiting for the line to move, with the cool detached manner of people waiting for a bathroom stall to open up. The guy behind them, who had a thick Russian accent, gave Joe a nudge and tried to make conversation.

"Fuck, man. I'm sick, yeah?"

Joe ignored him. Tania glanced over her shoulder and made eye contact. The guy pressed on.

"I get twenty-dollar balloon this morning. Won't even get me straight. I think his stuff getting worse, no?" The Russian wiped his runny nose with the back of his hand.

"Then why d'you come back here?" Tania asked.

"He . . . this man . . . is the only dealer I have!"

Tania glanced at Joe, who rolled his eyes and rested his head against the cool plaster.

They'd pooled their money. Eighty bucks. Two balloons of dope, and the rest for rock. Enough to take the edge off the day. The door at the top of the stairs opened and a small, skinny Latino kid—no more than twelve or thirteen years old—emerged with a nervous-looking man in a business suit, who hurried down the stairs. The kid peered down the line, then took the punk girls' money. They followed him up the stairs and through the door. Joe and Tania took a few steps forward; she felt her guts churning in anticipation. It was really going to happen. Standing in the pissy stairwell, Joe seemed more solid, healthier, somehow more *real* than before. Now that he was in his natural element, it seemed to Tania that he had taken on an extra dimension. That craggy face could almost be taken for handsome, in a damaged kind of way. The minutes dragged by. The door opened, and the punks scurried down the stairs, chipmunk-faced, the drugs stashed in their cheeks. The kid now approached Joe, who handed him the bills and they followed him up.

"Whatchoo need?"

"Cuarenta negro, cuarenta blanco."

"Sí."

"It's good stuff?"

"What *good*? Is always good, jou know that."

"The same stuff as yesterday?"

"Yeah, man." They were at the door now. "Why jou askit this?"

Joe nodded faintly in the Russian's direction. "Guy down there said the chiva was malo. Said he didn't even get high from the stuff you sold him this morning."

The kid looked visibly agitated, and muttered under his breath in Spanish. "He crazy. Mess up in the head. Always ask for credit. Get mad when we say no, jou know? Makit *trouble*."

"So it's the same as last time?"

"Sí. Is the same."

"A'right. Cool."

The kid opened the door. The room beyond was a huge,

desolate loft space. The only furnishings were a TV with an Xbox attached, a leather couch, and a coffee table. The windows were covered with black sheets. A bald man-mountain wearing a Lakers top sat with his back to them, engrossed in a game of *Grand Theft Auto*, a gun casually poking out of the waistband of his shorts. Two other guys, dressed in chinos and button-down check shirts, on the couch. One bald with a wispy mustache. The other with long, straggly hair and a goatee. On the table was a shoebox full of money. Next to it two handguns, a weighing scale, and a copy of *Trump: How to Get Rich*. The guy with the goatee was expertly wrapping preweighed lumps of tar heroin in wax paper, stuffing them into tiny black balloons, and tying them off. The young kid handed the money to the mustache. He counted it and put it into the shoebox without a word. They talked among themselves in Spanish without looking at Joe and Tania as they handed the kid the drugs. The kid passed the stuff to Joe, and he popped it in his mouth.

The kid led them back to the door, pulled back the deadbolt, turned a handle, and wrenched it open. There was a sudden rush of activity. It took Tania a moment to realize what was happening. The Russian, snot still streaming down his nose, had barged in and grabbed the kid by the shirt, pressing a pistol against his head.

"Getouttathefuckingway!" he screamed.

Joe grabbed Tania and dragged her to the side. They huddled for safety against a wall while the Russian marched the kid back into the room and started barking orders.

"Everybody up! This is a fucking robbery! On your feet. You, fatso! Toss over the gun or I blow his head off. No bullshit!"

The big guy stopped playing the Xbox, and slowly reached around and pulled the gun out of his waistband. Without turning around he gently placed it on the ground, sliding it across the floor a little. Then he rotated on his ass to face the Russian. The other two were sitting there with looks of outraged disbelief on their faces.

"Kick the gun over, fatso! And you two—on your feet or I shoot him. Hands in the air, quick, quick!"

From her vantage, Tania could see the Russian clearly. His hand was trembling. He was dope sick and desperate. By contrast, the dealers were cool as hell. Even the kid with the gun pressed against his temple seemed nonplussed. They all moved with a kind of insect calm, slowly doing whatever the Russian instructed. Waiting for the right opportunity to pounce. Tania sensed that the Russian was too nervous, too desperate to pull this off. She closed her eyes.

"Okay, everyone against the wall."

They lined up silently. They stood there, palms up, watching the guy closely as if committing every aspect of his face to memory.

"Jou really focked up," the goatee muttered.

"Shut up! Fucking beaner!"

"Jou robbing 18th Street, homie." The goatee shook his head sadly. "They gonna cut off jou balls."

"One more fucking word outta you and I'll kill him, and then I'll kill you. Yeah?"

The goatee shrugged.

The Russian glanced toward Joe and Tania, still huddling together next to the door. "You on the floor. You, bitch!"

Tania looked up.

"Listen. You need to get up slowly, no sudden movements. I want you to go over to the table and pick up the dope. Put it all in the shoebox with the money. Close it up and bring it over to me. Don't fuck around."

Joe squeezed her hand and whispered, "It's okay. Just be cool."

Tania did as she was told. She brought the box over, stopping a good three feet away from the Russian. She realized she needed to piss badly and a mad urge to laugh came over her. She watched the Russian's hand trembling wildly, the muzzle of the gun twitching against the young kid's temple.

"Now what?" she whispered.

"Put the box down and slide it over."

She did this. The box lay just in front of the Russian and the kid he was holding hostage.

"Now go. Back over there."

Tania scurried to Joe, crouched down with him again. As they huddled Joe could feel her trembling. He whispered, "It's gonna be okay." Somehow she believed him.

The Russian sniffed, more and more snot dripping down his face. "Okay, that's good. This is what's going to happen. Me and my friend here are going to go down the stairs. If anyone even peeks their head out of the door before I'm on the street, I shoot him. I'm not bullshiting, in Russia I've kill *many* men in cold blood. I'm no fucking joke. Asshole," he said, poking the gun harder against the kid's temple. "We bend down together. On three. You pick up the box, and we get out of here. Yes?"

The kid remained silent. His young face may as well have been carved in stone.

"Okay. This is one . . . two . . . and . . . and . . ."

A look of confusion came over the Russian's face. His nose and mouth twitched wildly, as if he were having some kind of facial spasm. "Ah," he bleated. He sniffed as more goop dripped from his nose. "Ah!" he said again. He wrinkled his nose wildly. "*Ahhh* . . ."

The Russian sneezed. The sound of it—and the almost instantaneous bang as the gun went off—echoed around the loft. The kid flew sideways, the contents of his skull exploded from the side of his face. When Tania opened her eyes again, the Russian was just standing there, his face slick with blood, holding the gun with a look of terrified confusion. He stared at the murder weapon as if seeing it in his hand for the first time. He peered down at the kid. He was laying with half his face blown off, in a rapidly expanding pool of blood.

"Shit!" the Russian screamed at his hand, as if it had betrayed him. "SHIT!" He looked up. The three dealers were already advancing on him. He turned the trembling gun on them. Screamed, "Back off!" They stopped advancing.

"Jou a fockin' dead man," the biggest of them said. "Jou shot my focking cousin. You fockin' dead man."

The Russian kept the gun on them, glancing down to the bloody shoebox, then over to the door, as if weighing his options. Tania thought he might be crazy enough to try and grab the box and outrun the dealers. Suddenly the Russian's hand stopped shaking and a strange calm seemed to settle over him.

"No," he said, firmly. "*You're* a fucking dead man."

He opened fire, setting off a series of deafening cracks as bullets flew around the room. One caught the big man in the chest, another hit the mustache in the groin, a third blasted the goatee in the stomach. All three hit the ground. The two who were still alive were screaming and cursing in Spanish. The Russian stood over them and used his last two bullets to put them out of their misery. He tucked the gun in his waistband and went over to the table. He grabbed the dealers' guns and then retrieved the bloodstained shoebox. Almost as an afterthought he paused on his way out and told Joe and Tania to get on their feet. They did not get up. The Russian looked at them with a curious expression on his face.

"We didn't see nothing, man," Joe said. "Look, we just wanna get the fuck outta here and go get high, that's all. We ain't going to the fucking cops or telling anyone we were here. Okay?"

The Russian nodded slowly. Then he pulled one of the dealers' guns and fired four times. The first two bullets hit Joe in the stomach. The third hit Tania in the chest. The fourth went wild, ricocheting around the room. He fired again, but there was the click of an empty chamber. Joe and Tania lay over each other, a pile of tangled limbs and hot, fresh blood. With that, the Russian fled down the stairs.

"I'm sorry," Tania said.

"What're you sorry about?"

"Peeing. I peed in my fuckin' pants, can't you smell it? It's probably on your upholstery. I'm so . . . *ugh*."

"Don't sweat it."

They were in Joe's car, heading back to Hollywood. Smoking cigarettes with still-trembling fingers. It wasn't shock or fear that made their hands shake. Instead it was something that felt like the aftermath of a particularly strong orgasm.

"What the fuck do you think just happened?"

Joe looked over to Tania. She stared off into space, but didn't answer. She just carried on smoking, and looking down impassively at the gaping, bloody hole in her shirt. She shook her head slowly.

"I mean," Joe said in a voice that was a mixture of horror and wonder, "I mean just *look* at me!"

She looked over and her eyes widened, as if she were seeing the devastation for the first time. With one hand still on the wheel, Joe lifted his bloody shirt. His stomach was ripped open, his jeans soaked with deep black blood. Something that looked like a purple, flayed snake lolled obscenely out of the moist hole. It lay glistening on his lap. She shook her head dreamily.

"Tania . . . did we *die*?"

Tania half closed her eyes and let her head rest lazily against the passenger window, as they turned down Wilcox Avenue.

"I don't know. All I know is that it felt . . ." She drifted off, a wan smile playing on her lips.

"Amazing?" Joe whispered.

"Yeah. It felt fucking *amazing.*"

As soon as they made it back to her room at the Gilbert Hotel, they got high. It was a run-down box with threadbare brown carpeting and a broken television bolted to the wall. When they stumbled in past the front desk, Joe holding his guts in with his forearm, the old Bangladeshi man behind the Plexiglas window with the NO GUESTS NO EXCEPTIONS sign pasted to it didn't look up from his newspaper.

Tania locked the door behind them while Joe busily cooked up a bag of dope in a bottle cap. He took off his shirt and wrapped it around his abdomen as a temporary fix.

"Got any vitamin C?"

"Yeah, think so."

"Lemme see a pill."

She threw over a bright orange pill from the bottle in the bathroom. Joe examined it for a moment, and nodded. He clumsily crushed half the pill into powder against the bedside cabinet, then sprinkled it into the heroin. He dropped a healthy chunk of crack into the dark brown goop and heated it again. Tania watched him curiously.

"You need an acid to break down the rock. Otherwise you can shoot it. You got a spike?"

Tania shook her head.

"I got a fresh one. You can go first if you want. You ain't got hep or nuthin', do you?"

"No." She glanced down at her T-shirt, which was plastered to her body with drying blood. "But I guess it wouldn't matter at this point, would it?"

"Guess not."

She watched him rip open the syringe and draw some of the caramel-colored mixture into it through a cigarette filter.

"Jesus, Joe. Be careful . . . I haven't had a fix in over a year . . ."

"You worried you're gonna OD or something? Like you said, probably wouldn't matter at this point, Tania."

Joe offered to hit Tania. After she got her fix, she watched him shoot up with all the practiced efficiency of an old-timer. While it felt pretty good, Tania couldn't help but think that the speedball was somehow disappointing. Shooting dope seemed pretty anticlimactic after experiencing death in all of its terrible, wonderful glory. It reminded Tania of when she had smoked crack for the first time. How alien the idea that she could ever just *snort* coke again suddenly seemed. It was instantly rendered pointless, a monstrous waste of drugs.

As Joe and Tania lay in the aftermath of their speedballs in that squalid Hollywood hotel room, they each realized intuitively that something about them had been changed forever. There was no going back to the old ways now.

Four days later, Joe lay on the floor of his apartment on Normandie and Franklin. He was puking yellow goo into a bowl that was already full to the brim with foul-smelling bile. He was shaking violently. His guts were hastily held together with layer upon layer of CVS bandages and duct tape, and each time he retched he became paranoid that they would rip apart and his insides would come spilling out again. The phone rang. He looked at the digital clock glowing on the cable box. It was two thirty a.m. He crawled over and retrieved the handset.

"Um," he mumbled. "Eh. Hello?"

"Joe? Oh God, Joe, is that you?"

"Yeah . . . I'm here, Tania."

"Joe!" She sounded like she was crying. "I'm sick! I'm fucking sick. I don't understand it. It started last night. It's getting worse . . . I bought a bottle of fucking methadone . . . drank the lot . . .

nothing *helps . . .*"

He listened as she vomited violently. He tried his best to sound comforting, shushing her gently until her convulsions seemed to recede.

"I know . . . I know . . . I shot some dope two hours ago, didn't do a thing. I can't get this sickness to go . . . I've never been this sick . . . Never . . ."

They listened to each other groan and sigh over the phone for a while. Their pain seemed to eventually give away to an exhausted surrender to the futility and horror of it all.

"Joe. I'm coming over. I need to get well."

"Okay." He gave her directions, in between retches. "Hurry, okay?"

"Okay."

Forty-five minutes later she stumbled out of a cab and staggered toward the apartment building. Finding Joe's door, she pounded frantically until he yanked it open. He was stooped over, like a little old man. The apartment was dark, and smelled of sickness and rotting meat. She couldn't tell if the smell was from Joe's apartment, or if it was rising from her own fetid wound. They embraced painfully.

"How're we gonna do this?" she gasped in his sweat-drenched mop of hair.

"The bathroom . . ."

Tania let her heavy coat fall to the floor, exposing a David Bowie shirt soaked crimson. She staggered after Joe. The fluorescent lights momentarily burned her eyes. He was standing there, pointing to the bathtub. It was full of water. An extension chord snaked in from the living room. An ancient twelve-inch black-and-white TV sat on the toilet's lid.

"This'll be the easiest way. The quickest. And it won't make a mess like the fucking bullets did."

"Yeah. I guess that's smart."

As if to emphasize the point Tania pulled off her T-shirt. Right between her tits, in the space where the bullet had gone in, was a wad of surgical cotton the size of a fist. It was stuffed into the wound and stained a gruesome shade of brown. It was clumsily held in place with peeling duct tape.

"I'm still scared," she said.

"I know."

"I mean, what if we don't come back this time? Or what if we do, but it doesn't *fix* us?"

Joe shrugged. "Could it be any worse than feeling like this?"

"No. I guess not."

Joe and Tania undressed silently. There was no embarrassment. There is nothing two people can share that is more intimate than death. They folded their clothes into neat piles and placed them by the sink, grimly focused on the task at hand. Tania went in first. Joe held her hand as she climbed into the lukewarm water. She sat at one end of the tub with her knees pressed tightly together. The water began to turn pink. Joe gingerly eased himself into the tub after her.

His bandages soaked through quickly. The bathwater steadily deepened from pink into a murky scarlet.

"Does it hurt?" Tania had a look of almost motherly concern on her face.

"Not the wound. Everything else hurts, but not the fucking wound."

"Fucking same thing here."

Joe reached over and flicked the TV on. A repeat of *Entertainment Tonight* was playing. Mark Steines was talking about Lindsay Lohan.

"Turn it down, Joe. If this doesn't work I don't want this shit to be the last thing I hear."

Joe muted the channel.

"Here we go."

Joe picked up the TV and

Dropped

It

In

The

Tub

There was a flash of intense white, a strobelike flicker, and then nothing. Lights instantly went out all over the apartment building.

And then it was over.

Joe came out of it first. The house was shrouded in darkness. The air smelled funny. In the dark, he could see the television floating in the water between them. The water was brown and fetid. They had shat themselves at the moment of death. It didn't matter. Tania started to stir, lifting her chin from her chest. Joe smiled a slow, satisfied smile.

"How do you feel?"

Tania let out a long, ecstatic sigh. "Fucking *fantastic*. You got a cigarette?"

There was a faint smell of cooking meat in the air. Joe placed a hand on his hair and it felt brittle, singed. But the unbelievable relief that he felt was better than anything he had ever experienced in his entire life. As they both sat there in a tub full of electrified water and shit, coasting on their high, they started to slowly nod off into a gentle dream state.

* * *

"My name is Joe, and I'm an addict."

"*Hi, Joe.*"

"I'm finding it impossible to quit. I've had three relapses in as many weeks. I know they say to *keep coming back* but . . . I'm sick right now. It's been two days since my last relapse. I'm here because it's all I can think to do . . ."

As Joe talked, Tania sat next to him, watching. She didn't tell him, but this morning as he lay passed out on Valium, she'd silently crept into the bathroom and looked at herself in the mirror. Withdrawal sweat was soaking every inch of her stick-thin body. Her tits looked a cup-size smaller. She reminded herself of those awful pictures of Nazi concentration camp survivors. The hole in her chest wasn't healing. In fact, it was starting to smell worse and no matter what she stuffed in there—cotton, old newspapers—the stench still leaked out from under her clothes. She had even tried an air freshener inside the rotting cavern, but that uneasy mixture of decay and potpourri was somehow worse.

What use was this if the body couldn't heal itself afterward? She had been shitting blood for four days since the last reckless, desperate fix. She had gulped down a bottle of drain cleaner in a moment of feverish madness. This morning, with the sickness back worse than ever, she *had* to do something about it. Joe was insisting that they detox and she'd initially agreed, and now he was watching her for signs of weakness. It was like being back in that fucking sober living house. Back to the cycle of meetings, prayers, and self-denial. She couldn't stand it. Joe could stick out his attempt at doing it cold turkey if that's what he really wanted. After all, she rationalized, how could she help him with his own detox if she was incapacitated by sickness? If she could just stay well enough to help him, then maybe he stood a better chance of actually making it. *Then* she would detox. Her mind made up, this morning she had a fix without telling Joe. She carefully slid the kitchen knife up into the hole in her chest, and stabbed around in there until she hit paydirt. When she came to on the bathroom floor, she finally felt human again.

Joe's words of pain and sickness washed over her as she sat in the AA meeting later that day. Even the old-timers, the lifelong drinkers with red noses and rotted teeth and dead livers, looked at this bedraggled pair with a mixture of pity and concealed disgust.

". . . And that's it. I'm going to keep going. I'm going to try and break my addiction this time. Thanks for listening."

"Thanks, Joe."

"Keep coming back!"

"One day at a time!"

Afterward they walked back toward the Hollywood and Western Metro. The car had been towed, after being illegally parked for two days.

"I feel like shit," Joe said. "I want to die."

Tania summoned up her best "sick" face. "Yeah. Me too."

"You lying fucking *bitch*. You're high as a fucking kite. Don't give me that shit."

"I'm not high! Honestly, Joe!"

She reached out to him, but he shrugged her away. He moved ahead of her, down into the station. She caught up to him as he hissed, "Don't try and bullshit me, all right? I can see it all over your damn face. You were nodding out in that fucking meeting."

Down on the platform, Tania stood next to Joe feeling like a chastised kid. She felt guilty, ashamed of her lies. On the display it said the next train to Pershing Square would arrive in one minute. She looked over at Joe. He was ashen. A droplet of sweat was forming on his nose. Even though the platform was pretty crowded, the people gave the two of them the wide berth usually reserved for the dangerously insane, or the stinking homeless. Black wind gusted through the tunnel as a train approached.

"Tania?" Joe said in a quiet voice.

"Yeah?"

"I'm sorry."

And then Joe was gone. He stepped forward, straight off the platform. For a moment it looked like he was suspended in the air. He looks like Wile E. Coyote, Tania thought for a shell-shocked moment, before Joe tumbled forward, then vanished completely as the train whooshed past her.

Thhhhhuuuuudddddddddd!

The impact carried Joe away. The scream of brakes and the yells of shocked commuters echoed around the station as Joe flew off in a hail of blood. Tania felt it hit her in the face, like some obscene custard-pie gag. Joe's insides splashed across the face of a screaming woman next to her with the impact of an open-handed slap. The woman fell to the floor screaming, covered in gore.

People were running around in confusion. The train came to a stop halfway into the tunnel, with Joe's mangled corpse caught in the wheels, ripped into meaty fragments across the track, shredded and starting to cook in the hot crevices of the brake levers. In the mayhem, nobody noticed a silent, decaying woman silently make her way off of the platform.

She considered following Joe into the path of an oncoming train in the weeks that followed. As the sickness worsened, Tania found that the quickest, easiest way to do it was asphyxiation. The biggest problem was that when she held the plastic bag tight over her head, and the heat started to build as she instinctively gasped for breath, the urge to tear the bag off was almost unbearable. It took several attempts before she was able to see it through for the first time. After that, Tania was a pro. Once you rode out those two or three minutes of panic, death came on slow and easy, like sliding into a warm bath. Instead of rotting wounds or a bleeding anus, she was left with a red face—the result of the blood vessels constantly erupting under her skin. But she looked no worse, she supposed, than many of the alcoholics she had met at the meetings.

But still, she did consider doing what Joe did. Maybe it would be easier to just cease to *be*, once and for all. The rush was becoming less and less, and the withdrawal symptoms seemed to intensify with each passing week. The past few months she had become a ghost, a shell, something that existed only in the shadows.

A month or so later, something happened that made her change her mind about following Joe. She was visiting the quiet section of Griffith Park where she'd spread Joe's ashes. She was just sitting there, watching the sky as the golden hour began to fade. The place was silent, peaceful. The noise and heat of the city may as well have been a million miles away. It was in this fleeting moment that she thought she heard it, an almost subliminal noise carried softly to her in the breeze.

Tania . . .
Taaania . . .
Pleasssee . . .
Pleasse . . .
Just one more fix . . .
And then I'll quit . . .
For goood . . .

The tears came then, as she finally understood the true extent of Joe's hell. She imagined him reduced by a crematorium's violent heat to a billion little ashes, countless tiny fragments of carbon, dumped out of an urn and left to flit around in the careless breeze. She imagined Joe clinging to the underside of plants and trees, lost in discarded beer cans, and stuck in piles of fresh dog shit. And all of those infinitesimal specks of what he once was still burning with that terrible sickness, that unimaginable yearning, a billion fragments of Joe still futilely screaming out for the relief of a fix he could never have again.

Tania stood stiffly, and addressed the breeze: "Goodbye, Joe. I'm sorry. I can't help you anymore. I've got my own habit to feed."

And then she was gone. As the sun sank behind the hills, the park fell into miserable, pensive silence once more.

SOPHIA LANGDON grew up in Tampa, Florida, and moved to New York City in 2003. She is a writer of short fiction and a poet. She is currently working on a short story collection titled *What's Normal About Love?* and two books of poetry, *Love Letters to My Master* and *Is This How the World Turns Out*. She can be seen performing selections of her poetry at various venues throughout New York City.

hot for the shot
by sophia langdon

liza stepped with light protracted steps to the bathroom two feet away from their bed, and headed toward the stash she had been hiding: her old cottons. She looked back at him as she closed the door. He was asleep. She was thankful for that. She didn't want him to be awake, his eyes searching for her next move, looking for what he could get.

She did everything with awareness of every creak, every footfall. She didn't want to share. There wouldn't be enough. She reached into the medicine cabinet, took one tampon from the back row of many, pulled it from the cardboard applicator, and emptied the hardened pelts of cotton hidden behind it into her hand. The faucet clacked and chattered. She stood unmoving for a moment, listening. Then let the dribbling of water fill a white top from a water bottle. She added the cotton stones, watching them soften and bloom. It would be a shot of mostly cool water in her veins. She began the extraction, hoping for gold. Hoping whatever made it into the syringe would take the edge off, get her a little well—it wouldn't. She would once again be the victim of her exaggerated memory.

Eliza settled onto the rim of the tub, her legs straight, locked against the door. The syringe in her mouth held in place by lip and teeth, she wrapped her hand tight around her upper arm, pumping her fist, searching for a welcome spot in the crook of her arm. She stuck the needle in, a little blood came swirling out, the edge got fuzzy. But it didn't disappear. She got up from her perch and began to clean up: syringe flushed with water and back in the cup with their toothbrushes, he would know, but she would at least make an effort.

Eliza caught her reflection in the mirror and held her own gaze. Her eyes maintained a permanent shade of fading pink, sharp high cheekbones held up her taut, hollow, brown skin. Her face littered with black spots. Souvenirs from scratching and picking, God knows what else.

"I don't look so bad. Nothing makeup can't hide." The mistake of her words hit her before she had time to find solace in her own sophism. She pulled back her long, black, thick hair—still strong. She let it fall down her back. Something to flick and play with, she thought, something for the johns to hold onto. She smiled, and too many black spaces where once there were teeth smiled back. "Fuck, I'm too young." She gripped the side of the sink, then let go, walking carelessly out of the bathroom.

His eyes glazed with sleep, yet questioning, met her. His gaze traveled the distance between where he sat at the edge of the bed, to the dribble of blood rolling down her arm. "What about me? Where's my fucking breakfast? I'd like to wake up, roll over, and get high too."

"Fuck you, Eli."

Eliza walked to the faux kitchen—a counter, a sink, a hot plate—and began to wash dishes; an assortment of kept takeout food containers, a seemingly endless supply of spoons, and a pot. Their apartment was the first in a row of the shiniest-little-shit-holes along Fifth Avenue in Ybor City, Tampa Bay. Eli's vocation of dishwasher had kept them in deluxe digs for a while, before he managed to get fired from almost every restaurant on the ten-mile stretch of the Seventh Avenue strip. Now they worked together selling themselves, usually Eliza's self, whatever it took to maintain their habits and the lifestyle.

"Roll over and get high is all you ever do, you fuck," Eliza mumbled.

"What!"

"I didn't say anything."

Eli stumbled around, checking the empty dope bags and gum wrappers that littered the apartment floor, wanting a miracle of found glory.

Eliza finished up in the kitchen. She put on her self-styled lime-green and fluorescent-pink floral-print mini-muumuu, slipped on her white platform flip-flops, and headed for the door. "I'll be right back."

"Where are you going?"

"To Brett's."

Brett was their sixty-plus-year-old neighbor. He was rumored to be a plumber, but they had never seen him head out to a job in the two years they had known him or the three they had lived on shiny-shit-hole row. Five feet and scarcely an inch more, Brett was just tall enough to not be a midget. His face, and his disposition, gave you the sense that someone had started punching him when he was three, and just kept on hitting. Brett was always good for pills after a blowjob or a quick fuck. And this morning he was the only hope for her and bright-eyed Eli making it through the day's obligations. Obligations that wouldn't be met without chemical motivation, obligations necessary to get funding for things owed, and things hoped for, from Moses, their drug dealer—referred to as PRDD (Puerto Rican Drug Dealer) or the Biblical Bringer, depending on the day and their level of admiration for what he had to offer. Right now, all they had was her pussy, her mouth, and a pill-popping plumber to ensure they wouldn't be shivering on a street corner.

Eliza muttered as she walked to Brett's. "It will be quick. It always is." When she arrived she made small talk filled with innuendo: "Haven't had my morning pounding. Eli's wet as a noodle, scouring the place for something."

"Uhuh."

"God knows what he figures he'll find. All I can think about is how I woke up with a need to be filled that's still as empty as the bags he keeps checking through."

"Uhuh."

She stopped chattering long enough to grab them both beers from the fridge. She sat on Brett's lap, rubbing his cock through his pants, her mouth pressed to his ear. "You willing to help my greedy little cunt?"

"You're too much." A half-cocked grin on his face, Brett pulled her close and ran his tongue across her lips, parted them with it, and began to kiss her. He was gentle, in that way that lonely discarded men always are.

Eliza unzipped his pants. Brett sucked in, his breath caught up by his need to fuck, to believe that she wanted him. She spat on her hand, lifted her dress, and stuck her lubricated fingers into her pussy. His hands followed hers. Fingers shoving into her well-trained holes. She moaned, and told him how badly she needed him to fuck her. He stood up and she laid on the dingy, cracked linoleum floor. She could feel the dirt rubbing into her skin. Her body called him down, no more need for words as she watched him remove his pants. Brett was short and the engagement would be shorter, but he was hung; God's obscene joke to make a man equipped but inadequate. The initial entry pleased her, made her gasp even, but it was sure to leave her wanting more. Two minutes tops. He got up and went to the bathroom. He always had to take a shit after sex. She didn't try or care to analyze it. The closing of the door was like a starter's pistol. She moved quickly, making her way back to his room.

His shelves didn't contain knickknacks, or clothes, or books, just rows and rows of pill bottles with various names of patients and doctors. It was a fucking pharmacy, a pill junkie's dream, an endless row of tiny tubs in varying states. She filled the deep pockets of her muumuu with Oxycontin, Vicodin, Percocet, Adderall, random barbiturates, and uppers whose names she'd never remember. She left while Brett was still launching shit rockets into the toilet.

As she walked to the 7-Eleven a block away, Eliza wondered if Brett knew that she was ripping him off. Maybe he went to the bathroom so she wouldn't have to beg, knowing his own fiendish propensities wouldn't allow him to simply give her the pills. It was the sort of silly romantic notion she always tried to believe—soft, false truths.

The guy behind the counter was the little brother of a friend from high school. A remainder from when she was headed toward success, he still reacted to her as if she were the key to hallway royalty. She wondered, did he want to fuck her or did he just feel a need to be polite, respecting what she used to be? He let her use the bathroom, he pretended not to notice when she was stealing, he generally gave her the run of the place.

"Tommy. How's your sister doing?" She never really stopped her forward motion to the bathroom.

Eliza filled her cupped hands with water and slurped it into her mouth. She pushed Vicodin and Oxycontin in between her clenched lips. She sat on the toilet and removed the cache of drugs from her pockets, picked out Oxys, Vicodins, Percocets, wrapped them up and tucked her package between the lips of her snatch. She patted the bulge between her legs. "Rainy-day stash." She flushed the toilet, a silly pretense, a game of making believe the store clerk didn't know.

She walked back to the apartment, the edge gone, her world a blurry sort of perfection. Occasionally patting her twat as she went, making sure her stash was still in place.

"Hey, baby, I got some pills: Vikes, Percocet, various randoms."

"You didn't get no Oxy?"

"No, the bottle was empty."

"Maybe he hid them when he heard your ass at the door. Did you come this time before your lover hopped off?"

"Fuck you."

Eliza emptied the contents of her pockets onto the coffee table, and grabbed her outfit for the day: denim miniskirt, white vintage Victorian top with cutoff sleeves and intricate folds running from the shoulders down the breast. She headed for the bathroom and counted five before doing anything. Eli busted in. She looked up from the water running into the showerless tub.

"What?"

He rolled his eyes. "Hand me my kit."

Eliza pulled the suburban-douche-bag leather kit, a junkie status symbol, out of the medicine cabinet and handed it to him. She closed the door, retrieved the package from her panties. She separated out the Vikes, Percocet, Adderall, set them on the flat edge of the sink, splashed water in the tub to feign activity, sat for a moment waiting for him to enter again. Feeling safe now, she began refilling her hollowed-out tampon with the booty of Oxycontin, and wedged it into its space at the back of the box. The other pills went into her skirt pocket. When she exited the bathroom, her eyes were surprised by the two lonely Vicodin waiting for her on the coffee table. She looked from the pills to Eli.

"Baby, you know you don't need as much as me to get high. Don't worry, I didn't do them all, I put some away for us."

"Uhuh." This motherfucker, she thought, he'll never be high enough, shoot your life into his arm and he'll still be searching for the next. She stepped in front of the floor-length mirror next to their bed. Eli went into the bathroom. She visualized him checking the medicine cabinet, hoping she'd covered her trail. Her eyes caught the clock: it had somehow become twelve thirty and they had to be in Lutz by two. They'd be late for the shoot.

She grabbed the phone. The lady who answered introduced herself as Ann-Marie. "Hi, this is Eliza, your two o'clock. We're running a little late."

"If you can't make it by three, forget shooting today."

"No worries, we'll definitely be there before three."

Eliza hung up the phone and watched the not so freshly washed Eli as he pulled on her old tattered Diesel jeans, the denim tight around his stick-thin legs, which seemed to take up most of his six-two frame, and a black cowboy shirt meant for a child, the sleeves too short. He was checking himself out, mussing his hair to a tumbled perfection, fashion choices being assessed from the tips of his pointy black shoes to the last well-managed strand of hair. He was handsome. Piercing blue eyes jumped out from the paleness of his skin at a stark juxtaposition to his jet-black hair, eyebrowless face, and perfect, full, pouty, fuck-and-suck lips. She didn't dare to say it, didn't want to give him the satisfaction of hearing it.

"Hurry up."

He grabbed her by the waist, stood her in front of him, pulling her hair back and kissing her neck. "Damn, we look good together baby." He lifted her short denim skirt, simultaneously pulling the fabric of her panties into the crack of her ass. He turned her around to look at the perfect roundness gripped in his hands. The curve of her back met the meaty suppleness of it. He lifted and held it, squeezing. She stood on the tips of her baby blue Chucks. He could feel his cock getting hard and he passed his fingers along the wetness of her cunt. She shivered just a little.

"Baby, you want me to fuck you?"

She pulled away. "We'll be late."

"Okay." He smacked her ass as she walked away from him.

Eliza grabbed her purse and the car keys off the nightstand. She stopped at the door, fanned a little air into her panties, and walked out. All the pills hit her as the sunshine seeped into her skin. She pulled her hair up into a loose chignon mimic of a bun with a black twisty-tie, before getting into the white mini–station wagon and turning the air-conditioning on full blast to fight the Florida heat. She watched the apartment door Eli had just rushed back through to get the directions their connection had given them. He waved the paper around as he came out.

Eli threw himself into the driver's seat.

"You okay to drive?" she asked.

She knew she wasn't. The pills were in control. She handed Eli the keys. They headed up Seventh toward Martin Luther King Boulevard, took that to the toll road, and got on. The car was gliding down the expressway when there was a loud boom. They looked around for a moment before realizing it was the sound of them hitting the railing along the side of the highway. Eliza snapped out of her stupor as the car screeched and scraped along the rail. Eli, his foot pushing the brake to floor, was trying to pull away and regain control. The car came to an abrupt stop. He looked over at her, his eyes stretched wide with fear and surprise.

"What the fuck! I thought you were okay to drive!"

"I am. I sorta fell asleep." He smirked, and they both started to laugh.

The little white, and now steel-gray, station wagon was banged up good. The driver's-side door wouldn't open. Eliza got out and took a look. Eli peered inquisitively at her through the windshield before sliding across the seat and getting out of the car, the air-conditioning blasting, the radio blaring, the engine still running. They stood stupefied glancing back and forth between the car and each other, shook their heads, and shrugged before walking around to get back in. Eli slid behind the wheel. Eliza got in after him, slammed the door, and looked at the time on the dashboard clock.

"Come on. Let's get out of here. It's already fucking three

thirty. We can't miss this."

Eli smiled, revved the engine, and absentmindedly tweaked the key in the ignition making the car squeal. Knowing that neither of them would pass even the suggestion of a sobriety test, they took off, looking back to make sure no one had been called to check on their welfare. Forty minutes later they were pulling up at a ranch-style house with an immaculate yard, the peek of a screened-in pool enclosure beyond the rooftop.

"You sure this is it?" asked Eli.

"I'm as sure as your bad-sorta-fell-asleep driving."

They both laughed, high, and a little nervous, as they approached the door. Eliza rang the bell and they both stood back toward the edge of the stoop. She held her hands together in front of her like a schoolgirl. Eli had one arm around her shoulder, the other behind his back. They waited.

A woman they assumed was Ann-Marie answered the door. She did not at all fit the image of the people they had become used to working for. She was blond with loosely curled hair. She wore thick blue-framed glasses that called attention to what was already a prominent nose, sharp and pointy. Her short, tanned athletic legs, the green of her veins shining through the skin, holding up her petit, frumpy frame, gave off a soccer-mom vibe. Eliza wondered what Eli was thinking, and for a moment she imagined they were both expecting two chubby little kids to come running out from behind Ann-Marie, chasing out the smell of baked cookies.

The woman stuck out her hand to greet them. They reached for it at the same time. The woman grabbed Eli's, and then Eliza's.

"Hi, I'm Ann-Marie, nice to meet you. Come on in." She led them to the kitchen. "Would either of you like a drink? There's juice, milk, sodas, beer, gin, rum, or vodka. We want you to be comfortable."

Eli and Eliza replied in unison: "Just water." They all laughed, and relaxed a bit. They sat for a time in the kitchen chattering on as if they were at an afternoon barbecue with friends. Then Roy came in and the conversation stopped. The camera in his hand served as a reminder of why they were there.

"Hey, kids. You ready to get started?" asked Roy.

"As ready as we'll ever be," said Eli.

Ann-Marie stood behind Eliza, her hands on Eliza's shoulders. "Okay, darhlin, you follow me to the back room."

Eli wasn't letting go of Eliza's hand. He squeezed it. "Hey, guys, could we have a minute?"

Ann-Marie smiled. "Of course, you can just step out on the back porch for a little privacy, and perhaps a cigarette. You kids sure you wouldn't like a drink?"

Eli acquiesced and took a beer. Eliza followed his lead and asked for vodka and soda. Drinks in hand, they went to the front room. Eliza could see Ann-Marie and Roy in her periphery, Roy shaking his head. Ann-Marie had her fingers to her lips, her head tilted slightly to the side, signaling, Eliza believed, for her husband to give his temper tantrum a rest, and let them have a moment.

"Baby, you wanna leave?"

"No, I just don't want to fuck Roy."

"Come on, Eli. Jacob would've told us if it was that kind of situation. He's never led us in blind before."

"I know."

"So shake it off. Let's get in there and get our money. Baby, it's four hundred apiece."

"Baby, you got any more pills?" It came out slurred, a sign of sufficient escape from reality. Eliza dug into her pocket and handed him two hits of Adderall; it was time to get up.

"Where'd you get that?"

"Seriously? Just fucking take it." She slipped one into her

mouth too, and washed it down with the vodka.

"You kids all right in there?" asked Ann-Marie.

They walked back into the kitchen, glanced at one another, and then headed off. Eliza, following Ann-Marie, looked back to see Eli as he stepped into the shadow of Roy and headed off toward the garage. She hoped Jacob hadn't left anything out.

Eliza walked into a pink pastel bedroom perfect for a twelve-year-old girl with a serious frills and teddy bear jones.

"Okay, doll, get naked," said Ann-Marie.

Eliza pulled a sea foam–green teddy out of her purse; she loved the way the color looked on her skin, and held it up. "Sure you wouldn't like me to start in something?"

Ann-Marie stared at the garment. "No, just naked and masturbating are all we'll need for this scene. It would be great if you could incorporate the teddy bears. There'll be no need to talk. You understand, right?"

Eliza put her lingerie away; this was about sex and not about her. The camera didn't need her memorable, just wet and ready. She got on the bed, tried to take herself to the moment when she and Eli were leaving the apartment, when fucking seemed like a natural reaction, but the thought of him was a reminder of how she got here. It stirred anger, not ecstasy. She felt empty. The deeper she dug, the harder she rubbed her clit, the harder she jammed her fingers into her pussy, the more she writhed, the tighter she squeezed her nipples, the less she felt. It went on like that, finger fucking, licking, and performing with teddy bears licking her ass for what felt like forever.

Ann-Marie's voice broke the tension of her heavy breathing. "Do you think you can come now? I know I could. Like a little help?"

Eliza looked from the camera into the willing, wanting eyes of the pornographer soccer-mom. She pressed into her clit, arched her back as she laid into the stuffed animals, moaning and screaming.

She faked her orgasm.

"That was fantastic. You can have a smoke, grab another drink, get dressed or not, and go to the porch. We'll start the next scene in a minute."

Eliza put on her shoes, nothing else, and walked into the kitchen. Eli was tied up in the center of the large kitchen table. His hands and legs were trussed up behind him with rough blond-colored rope, silver duct tape over his mouth, and a red bandanna covering his eyes. Roy smiling and directing him: "Move around more, really struggle."

Eliza grabbed a cigarette from a pack on the counter, walked outside, and lit up. She stared out at the pool. It reminded her of home, her parents' house. She wanted to dive in. Swimming always made her feel free no matter what had happened to her inside their house. Underwater she was silent, and safe. The tap on the glass door startled her.

"You ready to go again?" said Ann-Marie.

Eliza nodded her head to indicate yes, crushed her cigarette in the ashtray, and followed Ann-Marie back into the house. She always seemed to be following someone into something she'd rather be walking away from. The day went on, one room to the next, Ann-Marie leading the way to singular sex with vibrators, fingers, and remote-controlled fuck machines. The length and girth of which had convinced Eliza that the in-and-out friction, the intense pounding of her now swollen vagina, was sure to decommission her ovaries or—at the very least—provide her with the gift of a yeast infection.

Eliza and Eli saw each other one more time, both tired, him marked with red welts, during a naked cigarette break by the pool. A forty-five-minute eternity later, they left the house together, the sky now inhabited by the moon. They walked slowly, quietly back to the end of the drive eight hundred dollars heavier, and got into the car. In that silence, they quietly breathed their day in and out, Eli peering back over his shoulder every few minutes. Perhaps, Eliza thought, his furtive backward glances were to see if A & R, seeing them stationed there at the end of their drive, would be coming to ask them to do just one more scene. At the thought of it, she started the car and headed toward the highway. One hand on the steering wheel, the other digging for a cigarette in her purse.

"So, should I call Moses?"

Eli grabbed the mobile phone out of the glove compartment and dialed, smiling, revitalized at the thought of what they were moving toward.

"Hey, Moses, where are . . . ? We can be there in twenty . . . What do you mean, don't rush? You out . . . ? Oh, okay, we'll wait in the parking lot . . . What? Okay, okay."

"What'd he say?"

"He has to re-up. He doesn't want to see our faces any sooner than an hour from now. Fucker freaked out when I said we'd wait in the parking lot."

Eliza fumbled for a CD, looking between the CD case and the road. She shoved in the silver disk with *SONIC* written across it. The sound of Kim's sultry moan of a voice opening up Sonic Youth's "Teen Age Riot" filled the car:

> *Hey, you're really it*
> *You're it. No I mean it, you're it*
> *Say it, don't spray it*
> *Spirit desire (face me)*
> *Spirit desire (don't displace me) . . .*

Eliza turned the volume down before Thurston's voice could come crashing in. "Fuck it. He's going to find a reason to yell at us either way. We'll park at the edge of his lot and call the minute that obnoxious black, gold-trimmed Lexus pulls in. Don't look at me like a scared little kitten. I won't let Moses smack you up."

Eli smirked, settled back into his seat, and focused his gaze out the window. No doubt counting his chickens before they'd hatched, little dancing eggs of dope doing the conga in his head. His four hundred already spent.

Eliza killed the headlights as they pulled into the parking lot. They stationed themselves in a spot at the edge near the street, and she rolled down their windows. The night was warm and sticky, with no sign of a breeze swooping in to save them. She and Eli commenced chain-smoking cigarettes, their growing pile of butts at either side of the car—a definite trail to their destruction. They waited, occasionally remarking on something unrelated, like the fantasy that they'd get food before they booted up. Eliza called the bringer for the third time. No sign of the black car.

He finally answered. "My guy's not here yet. You two fucks better not be outside. Stop muthafuckin' ringin' me. I'll find you when it's time." The click of the phone slammed into her eardrums.

The heavily adorned Lexus—big black wheels sticking out too large for the body, soft yellow LED lights flickering inside the metallic spinning gold rims—rolled into the parking lot forty-five minutes later, Spoon's "Jonathon Fisk" pumping out of the windows in disjointed fits with reverberating bass:

> *Maybe you're locked away*
> *Maybe we'll meet again some better day some better life*
> *Jonathon Fisk speaks with his fists*
> *Can't let me walk home on my own*
> *And just like a knife down on my life . . .*

The unlikely choice of music stopped abruptly. Eliza and Eli looked at each other holding back laughter, before ducking down in their seats, thinking the inhabitants of the car might have seen them. When no sound of footsteps materialized, they sat up just in time to see Moses strolling over to the black Lexus. The lights on the car dead, the inhabitants were now just three shadows, slapping hands and making small talk. The exchange must have been going on down low, in between the front and back seats. Moses got out of the car walking backward, waving and smiling. The moment the back end of the Lexus bumped up and over the curb, he was walking toward them.

"Fuck," punctuated Eli's last meandering sentence about ninety-nine-cent burritos at Taco Bell. They froze, their fingers twitching, legs mindlessly shaking at the sight of him, their savior; his lithe cocoa-brown shape walking toward their car, seemingly gliding in slow motion, his steady approach bringing the guarantee of having to patiently sit through a flow of venomous words to get what they wanted.

He didn't speak, just got in the backseat. They forced smiles to their faces, and handed him money too soon and without any finesse, as they attempted to exchange pleasantries: *How's your wife Sheila?* His wife-girlfriend in prison on a five-year drug traffic charge he had happily let her swallow after shoving his drugs in her purse. Their questions flowed out jumbled and too close together.

Moses shook his head and let out what they presumed was a laugh. "Fucking junkies." He never answered their questions, just handed them their bundles of powder and pocketed their money. "I shouldn't sell you shit. You've been fucking sitting here the whole time, even though I told you idiots to wait somewhere else."

They played dumb; their silence was an agreed-upon sign of respect—never wanting to upset him to the point that he might make his threats real.

"Next time you get nothing. Anyway, this shit is good so be careful." The biblical bringer had spoken. He got out, slammed the door, and walked away.

"Where should we go?" Eliza asked.

"Anything with a bathroom or a parking lot."

"Let's go to Wendy's."

"Hawkeye Wendy's? Where that guy chased us out last time?"

"It's not like they posted our pictures on the fucking window."

They pulled into Wendy's, parked by the door, and headed with purpose to the back of the restaurant, checking behind them before entering the handicap bathroom.

"Hand me a bag and my spoon."

They looked at each other one more time, dueling syringes clasped between lips and teeth, the first part of the ritual complete. Needle in, blood out.

Calm. Then, her ears ringing, she dove into nothingness, didn't try to hold on. The first slap across her face was like a cool paper towel, the second shook her back into the moment. With Eli's face looming over her, his lips shaped into some sort of scream, she waited for sound to come back.

"Fuck! I thought you were dead."

"You crying?"

"Fuck off."

"That's the best shit we ever got from him."

They smiled collusively, Eliza cradled in Eli's arms. He wiped a dribble of spit from the corner of her mouth. She went to the sink to look at herself in the mirror, wash her face.

"I need a hit, baby. You're dying shit blew my high."

"Let's go back now before he runs out."

"I'll be quick."

"You take too long, I'll leave your cockroach ass."

Eli smacked her ass, then watched her smile disappear through the closing crack in the door.

Eliza was still listening to the phone ring when he came

out walking on air. Fuck me if he isn't beautiful—her thought punctuated by Eli clutching his stomach and puking on the hood of the car. "Jesus Christ, Eli."

"This ain't fuckin' Eli," came the voice on the phone. "You know whose number you callin', bitch?"

"Sorry, sorry, it's me, Eliza. Is it all right if we come by?"

"You just left."

"Yeah."

"Don't get fresh. Yeah, come up." The phone went dead.

She pulled into the bringer's, and moved toward his place solo. She knocked on the door. The mess that greeted her was a mirror reflection.

"Fucking come in."

She walked in, Eli on her heels. "What the fuck!"

He smiled. "What, baby, you thought I was gonna sit in the car and leave you to your own devices?"

A calm, subdued PRDD slumped himself onto the couch.

"Hey, is it okay if I smoke?" The cigarette was already in her mouth, the match already headed for its end.

"Guess so."

Eli and Eliza sat on the maroon, gold-trimmed love seat, PRDD remained slumped on his matching couch. The place looked like a rent-a-center model home. An uncut pile of dope winked at them from atop a large mirror covering the coffee table; the mirror's edges a no-fly zone, its passenger too precious for the floor.

"We wanna get two hundred."

"Put the money on the counter. Get me a Ziploc."

Eli started to stumble to his feet, his hand reaching out to use the mirror for leverage.

"Sit down before you do something stupid."

Eliza, sure footed, headed to the kitchen, put the money on the breakfast nook. The idea grabbed her just as her fingers reached for the baggies.

"Hey, Moses, can I grab a beer? "

"What, I'm your hostess now? Just bring the fuckin' bags."

"All right."

"Nah, just kidding, bring me one too."

She unhesitatingly dropped two bars of Xanax into his beer.

"Thanks. Wanna line, chickie?"

"Nah, not unless you're gonna let me put that line in my arm."

"Whatever."

Eli's hand moved like lightning to his back pocket. She rolled it over in her head; one shot and both these cunts will be out. She took nothing and stirred it into her spoon, preparing to shoot ice-cold water in her veins.

"Baby, hold me."

Eliza grabbed the top of Eli's arm. He went in for a spot. PRDD's head sank toward the scattered two-foot line waiting for him. Eli was out. She'd deal with him later, right now she needed him out of the way for this to work. She sat back and waited. She watched the bringer's head resting on the back of the couch, mind gone. Then he came to, swallowed down half the beer.

"Moses, can we talk in the bedroom?"

"What?"

She smiled; nudged her head toward her drooling, dope-blessed seatmate.

"Oh yeah, yeah."

She grabbed the bringer by the arm, led him to his bedroom. He pushed her up against the door, roughed up her tits. She moaned, and she passed her hands along his limp cock. They moved toward the bed. He plopped onto the corner, hard mattress protruding from between his legs, his head sagging down. She waited a few seconds, then pushed him back, started to unzip his pants. There was no need to take the charade any further; he was out.

She raced to the front room, grabbed a freezer bag, shoveled the drugs in, ran to the bathroom, took the lid off the tank, and seized the double-wide freezer bag of cash floating there. She roused Eli. "Come on, baby. Let's bounce."

"Where's the bringer?"

"Sleeping."

Eli didn't notice the extra baggage she was toting. She shuffled him down the stairs and into the car, not looking back once. They'd have to leave to wherever now, or they'd be dead by tomorrow. One stop. They needed to go to the apartment to get clothes, a quick in-and-out.

The car came to a screeching halt, half on the street, half on the walkway. "Wait here. I'll grab our things. Be right back."

"Where's our stash, baby?"

"Not now. We gotta leave."

"Why?"

"Don't ask."

"Come on, baby. I need it."

"Okay, let's go."

She'd miss him when he was gone. He was so beautiful. She watched him stumble into the bathroom with a ridiculous scoop of drugs in his paw; ritual. The door closed.

"I'll be waiting in the car when you're done."

Eliza walked out, got in the car, and headed for the highway.

At least he'd be high when the bringer came. She'd be high, too, in a couple of hours. On some beach figuring out what was next. Fuck, maybe rehab was in her future. There had to be something beyond this, there had to be a better way to live. She turned up DNA's "Not Moving" and let it screech through her speakers as she laughed and cried over the memory of the men she had just left behind; the looks that would be etched onto their faces when they finally came to.

Monika Manowska

NATHAN LARSON is best known as an award-winning film music composer, having created the scores for over thirty movies, including *Boys Don't Cry*, *Dirty Pretty Things*, and *Margin Call*. In the 1990s, he was lead guitarist for the influential prog-punk outfit Shudder to Think. He is the author of the novel *The Dewey Decimal System* and its sequel *The Nervous System*. Larson lives in Harlem, New York City, with his wife and son.

dos mac + the jones
by nathan larson

os Mac, accomplished urban planner and the mind behind some heavy-duty military technology, is draining his first cup of coffee as he notes an ancient but absolutely unmistakable tug in his groin and stomach.

Dos gives it a second. Player, please, he thinks. But there it is, that heat in his gut. If you've felt it once you couldn't possibly misdiagnose it.

Sets down his brown MTA mug on the metal gurney that now supports his piecemeal bachelor's kitchenette. "Motherfucker," says Dos into the stale air of his cavernous live/work laboratory.

How long had it been? Three years plus, but Dos knows this is irrelevant. The Jones is an eternal flame. The Jones is terminal. The Jones rides shotgun in your lizard brain toward the infinite night, its soft tendrils tickling your prostate. Into the grave, perhaps beyond.

Dos rocks an off-off-white Puma tracksuit, flip flops. Clothes he fled his apartment in, over six months ago, when they blew up the bridge nearby. Everything is outsized, he is shrinking, drying up. The loose flesh of a once stocky man hangs off him like a shitty suit. His hair is untended, or natural, or "nappy," shooting skyward from his scalp in a salt-and-pepper afro. He places his hand on his cheek, calculates the length of his beard to be just shy of a centimeter. A yellowed plastic breathing apparatus hangs loose around his neck, from which a thin tube dangles freely.

Dos Mac is not the name he was born with.

"Motherfucker," the man repeats. For there is no doubt as to what he must do.

He envisions his "day" with growing horror and annoyance. Plans for further microscopic tweaking of the 3-D model of the reconstructed subway system (which, admittedly, he has been tweaking for weeks on end) are now fucked. He would need his oxygen tank and hand cart. He would need . . .

Problems present themselves to the man, with respect to securing some heroin. Dos Mac has no idea what day or time it could possibly be. And more to the point: he has no idea where to look in New York City, his hometown rendered alien to him after the "attacks" of February 14, the island of Manhattan a decimated void, now in an endless state of rebuilding, seemingly leading nowhere, one massive semi-abandoned construction site. He has no clue as to who would have the good stuff on hand. Or if shaking some loose is even a remote possibility.

He shuffles sideways, turns a bit. Blinks at the wall of computer monitors, stacked willy-nilly, closed-circuit cameras showing Times Square, barren save a tractor, a couple NYPD vans, and a loose grouping of soldiers in black ninja suits. Another screen shows the corner of Hester and Broome, and forty feet east of that, yet another camera is trained on the sidewalk outside his front door, which is virtually traffic free.

The fluorescent light over the right-hand side of the rear of the gigantic room flickers. Once that goes, simply getting a bulb for the shit will be a serious, likely a very dangerous, task. And suddenly he has the fucking stones to fancy he can saunter out, pick up some smack, and be back before lunch? Dos Mac is kidding no one.

His regular NA posse would be disgusted with him. His sponsor would wobble his head at the staggering waste of it all. All that work. The breakthroughs and milestones, the weepy mea culpas and poker chips, all for naught.

But there is no more NA. Finito. No more meetings. The "rooms" sitting silent and derelict, or buried under rubble and ash. Either way, that crutch is history.

As addicts go, Dos had been more than highly functional. In this and in all things, the Mac excelled. Some labeled him an overachiever, perhaps attempting to compensate for his bleak roots in the housing projects of Brownsville, Brooklyn. Dos found this insulting, simplistic. Everybody's got their scene. His scene was that he was black and poor in America, but damn, haven't we done away with the stereotypes and all that bullshit? Apparently not.

At what point do you stop being a prodigy? When you hit eighteen? At twelve? When is it no longer charming? At what juncture do you become just another annoying brain clogging the coffee shops and microbreweries near MIT?

The thing with Dos and the smack was never an issue of health or well-being. Nor did anybody aware of his habit do more than whine at him for being fucking lazy. Or for not sharing. Most of his trashy ex-boyfriends, with their nonstop waxing and bulimia, most of these trifling faggots he wouldn't wish on his most hated enemy.

No, the issue was money. As in, he spent it all on drugs and therefore had none. That was what got him, eventually.

At the absolute height of his game, Dos floated untouchable through space and time, his habit and his career tracking parallel, neither affecting the other in the slightest. He had a long good run: as a youngster Dos had fast-tracked it through Brooklyn Tech. By night, he mainlined and freebased it through as much junk as his body could handle. Somehow his sense of how much was too much was very finely honed, and Dos Mac made sure to stay on the right side of that line.

For all his scag consumption, Dos had always been a bit of a health nut, with an emphasis on the nut. No alcohol, no over-the-counter painkillers . . . plus, a strictly meat-, gluten-, and dairy-free diet. Even in these current conditions. And trust, this regime is not easy to maintain in the best of circumstances. Try keeping it up in a husk of a town like this one.

After his creation of the missile guidance system (originally conceived as an attempt to increase efficiency in the NYC subway), and Mac's subsequent courtship by the government, his stint in naval intelligence made maintaining his smack hobby a touch trickier. The pop drug-testing, the security screening. He's positive that brass willfully ignored some serious red flags. And although folks can get used to anything, it wasn't exactly comfortable, smuggling clean urine around the academy grounds, plastic test tube shoved up his ass.

Yeah, it was trickier in the navy; that is, until he got deployed to the Motherland. That depopulated hole, where the poppy fields grow wild and unchecked. Manna, in unending supply. Dos even toyed with the notion of investing in the thriving export operation, whose participants and actors were countless within the ranks of the military and private contractors. It seemed safe enough, but in the end, Dos, content in his role as a user, wanted only to get high and play with his models. He was no businessman and certainly not an enthusiastic risk-taker.

Now Dos Mac catches himself itching his arm, in anticipation. For a dude of extreme caution and calculation, what he's contemplating would have to count as one of the most reckless acts he's ever undertaken.

He'll have to go Out.

It's just that way, that's just the way it is. Damn.

How long, how long since he's been outside? He glances at his monitors again, anxiously, as if they might hold some crucial information. Weeks? A month? If anything has changed it will have been for the worse, that much is for sure. Fucked up as it all is.

Tells himself: one last time. It's been a stressful year, to say the least. Isn't a man entitled to a little relaxation, having survived what some might describe as an apocalypse? And having bounced back in fine style to boot . . .

Even so, he'll have to go Out.

Where will he even begin? It's sure to have all been shaken up. Have to start locally, hope it's easier than anticipated. Maybe he'll luck out. He'd never bought in Chinatown, but seeing as everything else has been turned on its head, Dos sees no reason why the drug market will be any different. Then he'll turn to spots he knew well and see what that might render.

He'll need goods to barter with. That's the way folks do now.

Dos dusts off a largish nylon sports bag, which bears the faded word *Modell's*. Tosses his desk drawers, not knowing what he's looking for. What do people need anymore?

Keys to the big locker—beside the hydroponic lighting, useless now as the plants have been dry and lifeless for ages (how did he allow that to happen?), here is his stock of premium items with which to barter: his seitan jerky, a couple cases of Fiji water, four Zippos, lighter fluid, several packs of rechargeable batteries, and the main event, a pair of Motorola Talkabout two-way radios. Dumps a sampling of everything into the bag, then pauses at the radios. This would be blowing his wad. Other than his generator, without which he would quickly find himself dead, these radios are the most valuable objects he has. The computer shit, the cameras, they'd be useless to most people. In giving up the radios he'd be severely limiting his options, in the likely event his generator fails.

At the moment, however, anything that might bring him closer to drugs must be put into play.

Extreme times, extreme measures, says the Jones, from behind his inner ear. It's the voice of his former sponsor, Charles Morgan, for reasons Dos doesn't care to explore, a voice island-tinged, disciplinarian, prone to faux-profundity and platitudes, probably to lay down cover for the workings of a simple mind.

Dos takes a long, truly loving gander at his lab, his cell, his womb, his asylum. The amount of sweat and effort he's put into making it safe, making it a proper workshop. February 14 was a blessing in this way; he'd never felt as secure anywhere else. So much of him is here. His plans, his model of the perfect subway system, with its flat-zero carbon footprint, a version of the jammie he'd set up in Washington, D.C., writ large . . .

If you love something, set it free, says the Jones, which apparently is going to persist uttering goofy clichés that don't even apply to the situation at hand.

Regardless, Dos figures, making a final scan of his improvised safe house, he has little choice but to set out, because sometimes a brother simply has got to get high.

That smack won't be coming to him. He'll have to go to the smack. He tosses the radios in with the rest of his crap, and shoulders the bag.

Outside.

The air, the air crackles and pops with toxins, chemicals, fumes. The air is visible, a permanent fog. It's gotten much worse, worse than even a month or two back. Dos sucks at his oxygen, glad for the mask. Behind his chunky glasses his eyes burn, tear up. Would def not want to wipe at them with his bare hands; he learned that lesson early on.

On the corner of Chrystie and Delancey he squats, blinking rapidly. Feeling that inner drug-tug in his stomach. Thinking, can't believe I'm actually doing this.

Thinking, goddamn, peep all this. It's *all* Chinese now.

It was nearly all Chinese prior to 2/14 anyway, but given their resilience, economic superiority, and their steady access to bodies/cheap labor, they seem to be doubly thriving in this new environment. Dos is well aware that the Chinese have been awarded a fair number of Reconstruction contracts. And with that seems to have come a new energy, a new confidence. A palpable sense of Chinese superiority cuts through the nasty fog. What limited bustle can be observed seems purposeful, competent.

Glances that Dos has had at evil-looking Chinese military units leave him humbled. Wouldn't want to come to those dudes' attention. So, in this sense, the impression that he is completely invisible is a positive thing.

There's a trickle of rickshaws, electric vans, and sporadic drifts of workers on foot. Nobody loiters or appears remotely shady, with the exception of himself, reckons Dos; so he wouldn't dare approach any of these folks. No uniform, no proper ID . . . Where are the hustlers, the freaks, the lesser criminals? It's a rhetorical question. If he understood the Chinese even a little, such human debris would not be exactly welcome.

Oh snap. With discomfort, Dos recalls the Chinese government's posture of zero tolerance regarding narcotics. Given that these various neighborhoods have been all but handed over to the dominant group's rule of law, this area is looking less and less score-friendly.

Rising to his feet, ridiculous in his gas mask and flip flops, Dos Mac figures he'll have to press on. Head north, into Christ knows what.

Stepping around an open manhole, he trudges up Chrystie, dragging his oxygen tank behind him, clanking and top heavy on its rickety cart.

Ludlow between Houston and Stanton.

Third Street at Avenue C.

Avenue B between 7th and 6th Streets.

The "laundry" on 7th Street between B and C.

Nothing but blank spaces, in some cases the entire façade having been cemented over if not removed wholesale.

Near the former site of the "laundry," a work crew crouches, uniform gray coveralls, silently engaged in some kind of mah-jongg–like game. Dos Mac is positively ignored. Which is a good thing.

Dos realizing he's reaching as far back as the late 1980s, which is fucking sad, and that by the second address his wanderings have become nothing more than a masturbatory nostalgia jag. The Jones doesn't mind. It seems to only intensify the thirst, as the muscle/body memory is as strong as the perfume of a former lover. He digs on it, digs the internal heat.

Dos doubles down on this, his righteous mission to score. He's strong enough to make it this far? Motherfucker, he's strong enough to complete this simple task. The tug in his sphincter is, if anything, amplified as he moves through this neighborhood.

Does a nigger have to go uptown? Never comfortable around the dealers in Harlem . . . not that he expected to find anybody still hustling. What's going on uptown? Maybe, just maybe, an abandoned lab, somebody looking to unload weight for which there is no longer a market . . . but Dos knows he's just pipe-dreaming. Anything worth anything has been stolen, swapped, or sold.

Here, just look at his sorry ass. Dos Mac should be a subject for derision, should be attracting gawkers despite the thin population. But not so; not a solitary soul registers his movements. Dos makes no attempt at stealth, but he gets the sense that he's resonating ghostly, shadelike.

Besides appearing pathetic, and besides the fact that he's

aware that a low profile is what will keep him standing, Dos Mac starts to question his own solidity; is he simply being snubbed, or has he somehow slipped into another dimension of being? Some sort of high-level physics at play here? Is he less real than the tire on the flatbed pickup that slows to collect the group of men, not pausing as they chase the vehicle and haul themselves up and onto the back of the truck, disappearing into the dirty fog?

Even the past has long split the scene, nothing is remotely recognizable, and all is brutally clean. Near silent as well, with the exception of far-off construction sites to the north and south. To all appearances virtually every structure has been carved out, shaved, scrubbed free of any former identity, and converted to serve some new and strictly functional purpose, or no purpose at all.

As Dos approaches 11th Street between A and B to find the entire block of former tenements razed, and an ad hoc shanty town in its place, he gets his first fleeting view of what might possibly be children and females. He takes a tentative step onto 11th Street. Chinese army tents, some semipermanent-looking, hard-plastic structures. The lingering smell of cooking animal meat, causing his mouth to immediately fill with saliva. He reminds himself, suddenly ashamed and slightly nauseous, of his principles regarding matters dietary.

The hood of old is gone, figures Dos. Which suggests he bring this swing down memory lane to a close. Operate in the now. The surface of the city he once knew is forever altered, and Dos Mac has to accept this fact, move forward accordingly. Or perish.

By the time Dos reaches what was at one time known as Union Square, he has to admit that he had no idea that Chinatown had exploded so comprehensively.

All Chinese.

With the exception of a small but intense Ukrainian/Eastern

European enclave Dos stumbled through as he moved west, at about Second Avenue and 9th Street. Vehicles and buildings with Cyrillic lettering could still be observed. The old buildings less molested than further east. Knots of white dudes tracked his passage, chattering rapidly amongst themselves, hair cut close, veins protruding. No women, no women at all. Bemuscled goons with tattooed necks and hands displayed shoulder-holstered Glocks over their wifebeaters and polo shirts. Another trio of thugs, leaning out of a small truck, wanted to be very sure Dos clocked their hypermodern automatic rifles. All of which radiated some Aryan Nation shit for Dos, who put his head down and scurried on . . . As much as his mission calls for improvisation, he wasn't about to start up a conversation with these killers, despite the fact that they appeared rather likely to be in possession of narcotics. And all the more likely to start taking shots at him just out of boredom, or to audition their fancy weaponry.

Otherwise? The Chinese, goddamn, those fuckers have the lock on like every little thing.

Those Eastern European yahoos were way far from welcoming, but it was the first and only time on the journey thus far that anyone appeared to actually notice him. To see him, to see him and let be known he has been seen.

Hunkered down at the intersection of 15th Street and Union Square East, Dos sees it. In this new paradigm, there is no space for a drug like heroin. Oh, he can dig it. Any substance that might render the user vulnerable is less than useless. Allow your attention to flag here, you're extending an invitation to be looted, hollowed out, and stripped for parts like an abandoned car.

No, manic clarity is called for, and not the chemically induced kind of clarity . . . Watching an industrial crane lift crates off the back of a semi in the middle of the former park, flanked by gasmasked gunmen in Port Authority uniforms.

This is meth-amp territory, if anything. Good for physical labor.

But a substance which, at least in Dos Mac's estimation, is the narcotic equivalent of a panic attack.

Dos seeks to escape this colorless nightmare, if only for a matter of hours. Not gonna hassle anybody. This is all he's looking to get done. Merely a short hiatus in the daily grind. Tomorrow morning? He'll be back at his desk, primed to do God's work, hankerings sated and silenced.

"That's it, man," he whispers, itching at his beard. "That's all I'm doing, taking time out. To look after me."

Well shit: his goal is certainly not to make himself all the more viciously present in the manner of the coked and methed up.

Look left, right, and sideways. Downtown is a fucking bust.

No. Dos will have to continue north. North is where the major Reconstructions sites are, and that's where dealers will orbit should there be any.

Friendless, there's no one, figures Dos. I need a gun.

The thought takes him from behind, and comes complete with a plan. The thought stops him cold.

A hospital. Why had he not thought of this from the jump?

Get a gun, get to a hospital, jack the staff for whatever's on hand in the opiate family. Do it fast and easy, nobody need get hurt. Forget digging up a bag; that format would seem to be extinct.

Get a gun. Tougher than it might seem, given the prevalence of guns. Helpless as he is, Dos will have to ask somebody nice, who in turn will have to give him a weapon of his own free will. It won't be the Chinese, or the Ukrainians.

Unbidden, the Jones pontificates: *That which kills you only makes you s—*

"Shut the fuck up," says Dos out loud. "Trying to think."

No. If I want to get a gun with only a moderate amount of risk, only one man springs to mind. And a serious wild card of a motherfucker at that.

The Librarian. Damn. I gotta see the Librarian.

* * *

Approached from the west, past the gigantic flame pits of Bryant Park, the New York Public Library remains almost eerily intact.

Mac makes his way around the corner of 42nd Street and pauses within sight of the famous twin marble lions. He is exhausted. At this point he's so far north, there's no way he'll make it back downtown without running out of oxygen. He's not positive if this will make any difference, but it's a huge risk.

Nobody around. Pauses to listen . . . Beyond the general hubbub of the fires and the clanging due east, which Dos assumes to be construction at Grand Central, the streets are barren.

Up the exterior stairs, his oxygen tank lighter and lighter, bouncing along behind him . . . he tries the main doors, finds them open. Dos steps inside and takes a moment, his weak peepers calibrating to the gloom.

The Librarian, he didn't want to think about how he knew this cat. Sure, he wasn't a bad guy, but damn. Goes without saying, this is not a dude you want to sneak up on unannounced.

On the other hand, Dos would hate to wake the man up. That could be an even darker scenario.

The lesser of two. Mac clears his throat.

"Librarian!" he calls, voice cracked and arid. Bounces off the vaulted ceiling. "Librarian! Dos Mac here! I'm unarmed, brother, I come in peace!" Trying to keep his tone light. You never know how the Librarian will come at you.

Dos gets no response.

There's two conflicting knots in his intestines; one is related to fear, and one is all junk-lust. It's the latter that pushes him upward.

Nothing ventured, drones the Jones, and Dos shuts it down. Jesus, what bullshit.

Calls: "Coming upstairs!"

Tough to see much on the stairwell, so Dos takes it slow and easy. Hefts the near-empty tank so as to make less noise. His flip flops feeling insubstantial and wrong against the cold stone.

One flight, and Dos takes a moment. Out of shape, breathing ragged. What the fuck does he think he's doing? I mean, honestly? Despite his military credentials, he is an engineer, a technician, a brain. The brother at the party who faded into the background, the dude who spoke too quiet or too loud, his movements subtly wrong, nervous, the kid who could never bust anything smooth. The guy you didn't notice till he, inevitably, knocked something over. Dos always liked to say he was a lover, not a fighter, but he wasn't much of either really.

Abort, reckons the Mac. Fuck this. Takes a step backward, reversing himself down the stairs. Cut your losses, son. Feels vastly relieved, having made this decision.

Crack.

A flip-flopped foot has found some kind of shell, crushing it under his weight. Not like the Librarian, thinks Dos idly, to leave garbage lying around . . . the Librarian, who to put it mildly is a bit of a neat freak . . .

Wham, and Dos's head hits a stair, as his legs are cut out from under him. The cart and tank go tumbling, and he finds himself facedown in a frighteningly professional choke-hold.

Smells: latex, baby powder . . . alco-gel. No doubt.

"Hey, Librarian," he manages, panic percolating, hold it together now . . . "It's Dos, brother, it's Dos Mac here . . ."

Overhead lights come on with a deep clunk, and Dos is released. He sucks open air, his mouthpiece knocked aside, and is grateful for it. Pushes himself up to a sitting position.

The Librarian hangs over Dos, blocking the light like a shadow puppet. Sharp angles, that signature hat.

"Well I'll be goddamned."

It's a rusty sound, that voice, dried syrup, tinted with cigarettes and filtered by the surgical face mask the Librarian wears.

"Mister. Dos. Mac," he says, separating the words.

"That's me, son," answers Dos, hoping he sounds calmer than he feels.

Librarian saying, "Gotta ask you first. Have you been in contact with any livestock, any individual who might possibly be carrying a communicable disease, shit along those lines?"

Dos shakes his head negative.

The Librarian extends a rubber-gloved hand. "Okay then. My second question then: what's a downtown nigger like yourself doing up here in the nosebleed section?"

Dos accepts the man's paw, and is hauled to his feet.

Mask dangling from its chinstrap, the Librarian is frowning at the spine of a blue hardbound volume. He taps it and looks up at the stack in front of him, which is a couple of feet higher than the top of his hat, leaning crazy. Says, "You're not for real." Says, "Thought Dos Mac, the gentleman, is all about peace . . ."

Dos raises a shoulder, thinking this was most def a mistake. The Librarian could be working for anybody and everybody. He had thought the man was strictly on muscle jobs for the city, but he could very easily be doing the odd Chinese gig, in which case . . . but this was paranoia.

Librarian saying, "Intelligent motherfucker like you? I don't need to point out—huh, do I?—that the mere presence of a firearm in the home exponentially increases the chances of . . ." He falters, distracted by some tiny aspect of the book's binding. He shakes his head rapidly, pops a pill of some kind. As he turns to Dos, he is shifting his mask back into place over his mouth and nose. "I'm not putting a judgment thing on you, man. No sir. Everybody gotta look out for their own . . ."

Dos ducks his head, murmuring his agreement.

"I mean, shit," continues the Librarian, stripping off his gloves and producing a four-ounce bottle of hand sanitizer. "I don't even wanna know what you need it for. Just, let's leave it there." Squirt. Rubs his hands vigorously, grabs a new pair of gloves.

Feeling the compulsion to give him something, Dos is aware of himself saying, ". . . Folks know I got computers, com units, and whatnot down at my place, word is I better watch my back should people get ideas . . ." Thinking, if this man can't smell a bullshitter . . .

The Librarian, adjusting his glove, lifts a hand and sets an index finger against his masked lips.

"Yo. Hush, Mac, I got you. I don't wanna know about it and that's my word. Wanna just plant this seed, though, an alternative approach, check it. Rather than bringing some heavy gun energy into your castle. I talk to the DA, we set up a man or two down at your joint, discretion for sure . . . 'Scuse me, is that a no?"

Dos has been shaking his afro. Says, "Don't want to put you all out. Just, just the loaner, and I'm straight."

The Librarian scans him. Curious. His eyes glaze a touch, and snap to a point just over Dos's left shoulder.

Spooked, Dos throws a glance behind him. Books, space, darkness. Returns his attention to the Librarian, who is in fugue mode.

"Crop sprayer."

Dos swallows. "Don't follow, my man . . ."

"We used to do it like that in the sandbox. You know about that? Helicopter, nerve gas, just blanket spots, neighborhoods. You could do it with drones. Insurgents hiding out, yeah, you get them but this, this shit kills everything, so you get . . . you get everybody else too. Regardless . . ."

Dos knows about this practice but doesn't see the relevance. "What's that got to do with—"

"Chinese, Russians, Saudis, all doing it to each other on the island. Knock out the competition and all that. Say to themselves, damn, it'd be nice to have that Brooklyn Bridge contract those other folks got and all, something sweet, meaty. Chrysler Building, whatever. Do a flyover, spray 'em, then before their crew can get more live bodies in there, you take the site. That's the realness. You haven't seen this?"

The Librarian seems to want to have a conversation about this subject, Dos is thinking it's fucked up to be talking to somebody when you can't see their mouth. He can only say, "I don't get out much, man. Doesn't surprise me, I've just never seen it, I don't go anywhere. Keep my head down."

The Librarian is nodding, looking at him. Out of nowhere he drops an explosive laugh, loud in this huge space even through the surgical mask, which morphs into a dry coughing fit.

"Head down, yeah," says the man, recovering. "Well, brother, that can only be a good thing. All I'm trying to say is, watch for low-flying helicopters, and you spot one? Run. See, the way I figure it . . . and mind you, I try to stick with this plan myself . . . if you don't appear aligned with one crew or the other, you're less likely to get targeted. Word to the worldly wise. You dig?"

Dos is nodding.

"Yeah," the Librarian is looking around like he's misplaced something, "yeah, just keep your head down like you're doing, you'll be all right, baby. For all I know? You and me are the last . . . *educated* black men on this island. I need you around, Mac, need somebody I can talk to. So, hey, if you tell me you got people trying to creep up on you, you want to be able to defend yourself in your own *home*, I hear you and am happy to be of service . . . You know what's a motherfucking shame and a travesty is the fact that a man has to . . ."

He disappears behind a pile of books, into the semidarkness. Continues talking quietly but Mac can't make out specifics.

This motherfucker, thinks Dos, this motherfucker is insane. I can make a break for the exit, should this go south. Throw my bag at him and move. In fact . . .

Dos takes two steps toward the doorway and the Librarian is in front of him, mask down again. Smiling crookedly. Eyes black, with greenish shards, whites bloodshot. He points his chin at a gun, flat on both gloved palms. Shrugs.

"This here," he says with a chuckle, placing one hand over the pistol, "is a CZ-99 semiauto. Fifteen-round mag. Not so different than what y'all must've been issued. Point and shoot. Easy like that."

Hands Dos the gun, butt first.

"I appreciate this, I really do, man," says Dos. The weapon has been gaffer taped, light but solid; Dos thinking, I really do hate guns. I jockeyed a desk, *I sat it out*, there's a reason why I walked the path I did. Even so. Unzips his bag and places the pistol, gingerly, inside.

"This is a loan; heard me, you'll get it back."

Waving this away, Librarian says, "Hell, I borrowed it myself. And I reckon the previous owner ain't exactly gonna miss it, nah mean?" Winks at Dos, then snaps his be-gloved fingers. "Reminds me." He digs in a jacket pocket and fishes out a laminated card. "You're gonna want one of these, kid."

It's one of those city-issued jobs, featuring only a barcode and the words, *JUSTICE DEPARTMENT, PROPERTY OF THE STATE OF NEW YORK.*

Seen these before. Carried by protected scavengers/freelancers, like the Librarian here. Who says now: "Take it. For real."

Dos is pretty positive he's already had his DNA replicated,

somewhat standard government stuff, etc., etc. Hell. If he looked hard enough he'd find a clone of himself swanning around. So he's not about to get all precious about his genetic code; otherwise he wouldn't handle such an object.

Plus, he's anxious to bounce. So as it is, he accepts the card, sliding it into his sweat jacket pocket. "Thanks, brother. Again, I owe you large."

The Librarian bats this sentiment out of the air.

Silence descends on them like a saturated blanket. Dos nods and makes to move for the stairs—

The Librarian intercepts him, wagging his skull, still wearing that shattered smile, snatches Dos's upper arm, hands like talons, a dead man's hands, thinks Dos.

"Snipers," whispers the Librarian. "Snipers everywhere, Mac. What's more . . ."

Comes closer, Dos smells sweat, cigarettes, stomach acid, and a faint undercurrent of urine. We all probably smell something like that, he reckons, weird I can't smell myself.

The Librarian speaks, quieter still, out of the side of his mouth: "Don't know about cameras but this bitch is bugged. Can't speak freely. Walk directly out the front and do it quick fast. I'll straighten it all out with the boss, though, not to worry. Jah bless, Mac, you're my brother."

Dos gets a stinging slap on the shoulder, probably meant to be friendly, but he's already turning, and without a backward glance he speed walks out of there, dragging his tank and cart. His bag feeling far heavier already.

Parked under a nonworking streetlight on the northwest corner of First Avenue and 33rd Street, Dos Mac is lightheaded, his chest tight. His balls ache, his mouth is dry. The Jones has him. His oxygen tank, dead weight, lies abandoned somewhere near Herald

Square.

His choice of the former NYU Medical Center is based on the fact that he knew where it was—next to what very little remains of an older hospital, once called Bellevue, which has apparently been entirely demolished. Good fucking riddance, mulls Dos, who'd had the misfortune of being consigned to that institution years and years ago now, in the meaningless past.

Gets lucky in the sense that NYU is still up and running. No question, a private military-industrial joint now. Point of fact: the spot is jumping, here in the pumpkin dusk, UN, army, NYPD, unmarked vehicles coming and going. Dos even spots an old-school ambulance, lights on, no siren. Stenciling on its side reads, *CORNELL/NEW YORK HO*. Everything's worn, mismatched.

Choppers sail past every couple minutes, visible only by their floodlights overhead. An open pickup truck rolls by, packed with Chinese men shoulder to shoulder.

All things in moderation, rambles the Jones in his inner ear. *Old dog, new tricks . . .*

He can smell the proximity of the pharmaceuticals. They vibrate, rattle him on a cellular level. Drug radar erect, drug meter pinned. There are drugs and they lie within reach. He's come this far to be warmed by their honey-sweet light, and yet he finds himself afraid. For if he cannot get to them, he will freeze to death, from the inside.

Scratches at his beard, rough. If Dos didn't know better, he'd tell you he is suffering withdrawal symptoms. Impossible. Doesn't fucking make sense, but there it is. It hurts, Dos is beat, and longs to have this done with, to float into the delicious embrace of the medicine, one fucking way or another.

A bird in the hand, says the Jones, and his stomach quivers. Unzips the bag, unsteady on his haunches, withdraws the gun, trying to decide how and where to carry the damn thing, settling on the shallow pocket of his sweat jacket, which barely covers the weapon and necessitates that he hold it by the butt.

Pulls the hood on the jacket up over his unkempt hair.

Observes the sorry details of his position, this parody. An unlit New York City alcove, a weaponized junkie in a hooded tracksuit, resolute, ill intent, eyes on the prize. Not exactly a novel picture. Ghetto stuff, unbefitting a learned man like Dos Mac.

Funny I managed to avoid such a situation until this very moment. All that focus and energy wresting free of the near-inescapable, gravitational field of a black hole like Brownsville. Shit. What heights I've known. Relatively speaking. And yet here I am.

Corrects himself immediately; of course, I am not a lost user, not anymore, don't be a fucking clown . . . I am, simply, an adult human, having a crazy day, indulging a craving, and am I not entitled to a little break, some misbehavior, as disciplined as I am, as hard as I apply myself to my work?

Scrolls through the available options for the umpteenth time. In terms of approach, they're pretty limited. Not much to do but waltz right in there and get as scary as possible.

Dos figures if there's a move to make he'd better make it before he passes out. The traffic has abated to the point where it's just gotta be done.

Plenty of time for analysis and/or shame, logics Dos, after I secure some drugs.

It's just me, thinks Dos, stepping into the street, abandoning his bag. Bearing witness to my own debasement.

Hands jammed into his insubstantial pockets, eyes on a Humvee and an NYPD Volt, both of which seem to be unmanned. Dos heads straight across First Avenue, aiming himself at the hospital's main entrance. He doesn't feel scary.

The gun is half in and half out of his jacket, Dos thinking

he might be rushing events, contemplates turning around, the borrowed pistol continuing to slip, Dos scrabbling at the thing, feeling the duct tape, the rubber grip, his fingers seeking a more solid purchase, sliding through the trigger guard . . .

Doesn't so much hear the burst as register the abrupt absence of sound, followed swiftly by a numbness in his left hip. He is then aware that there has been a gunshot of some kind, pivots slightly uptown as the Librarian's disembodied mug floats on by, sniggering, mumbling, *Snipers.* Of course, thinks Dos, of course, and he turns again to face the hospital, peripheral vision gone, scanning the rooftops and balconies for some sign of . . .

Trying to work out why he would be targeted, trying to understand the intent of the handful of soldiers and cops emerging from the hospital entry, apparently headed his way, apparently shouting things he cannot quite hear. Dos brings his left hand out of his pocket and notes with detached interest that it is warm and wet with blood, tucks in his chin to discover yet more blood, an alarming quantity of blood, and it occurs to him that someone must have been quite severely hurt, and if this is the case it might make his mission to score that much more difficult.

This is as far as he gets before that thought bubble pops, and Dos Mac wilts sideways, collapsing to the pocked tar of First Avenue.

" . . . Anywhere from thirty and fifty, gunshot wound to the hip . . ."

Dos is ripped out of a fairly neutral stupor by excruciating shards of pain in his side, faintly detects his body lifted and borne aloft, the pain abates momentarily, only to come crashing back as he is dropped on a hard surface. His bladder empties into his pants, hand wrenched awkwardly back, a metallic ratchet . . . his eyes are open and he is looking at his left wrist, secured to a bar with a pair of handcuffs, the attached hand apparently having been dunked in cartoon-red paint.

"Flip him," instructs a female voice from somewhere in this overly lit room, and the agony that accompanies this action causes him to pass out again, though it's his impression that he comes to within seconds. On his side, cool air caressing an ass cheek . . .

". . . in and out," the female is saying.

"Self-inflicted," chimes in somebody else.

"Obviously," says the lady. Irritated. "But we can't do civi's. You rolled him in here? Now roll him back out."

". . . ID says he's Class A."

"This fucking guy?"

"Gotta confirm it but that's what he was carrying."

The lady sighs audibly. "All right, then. But I want security."

"Of course."

"It is what it is, let's clean him up."

The room starts getting shifted around, a uniformed guy materializes all up in Dos's grill speaking far too loud, as if to a retarded child: "Sir, do you know why you're here?"

Vision clearing by drips and drabs, Dos registers the faux-concerned, acne-scarred face of a white soldier. Not finding this worth deep study, he rotates his head, taking in a standard hospital room, several folks attending to the business of prepping for surgery, an Asian girl in Winnie the Pooh scrubs leaning over him, hooking a heavy plastic sack to an overhead rung . . . a bag of liquid . . . a bag of . . .

A bag of morphine.

"Sir, *do you know why you're here?*" repeats the soldier, sounding further and further away.

Dos saying, "I surely do, son. I surely do."

And like a cadaverous Buddha, Dos Mac smiles with his whole body. Extends his right arm.

Novelist, journalist, and screenwriter, JERRY STAHL is the author of six books, including *Permanent Midnight*, *Pain Killers*, and *I, Fatty*. Most recently, he wrote the HBO film, *Hemingway & Gellhorn*.

possible side effects
by jerry stahl

Bad Penny, She Always Turns Up. That was one of my most popular campaigns, back when the porn business was referred to as Adult Films, not "triple-X content." Not that I'm a porn guy. I'm not. Anymore. I'm the kind of writer you don't hear about. The guy who always wanted to be a writer—who read the backs of cereal boxes as a kid—dreamed of being Ernest Hemingway, then grew up and wrote the backs of boxes. You don't think about the people who write the side effect copy for Abilify or Olestra ads . . . It's not as easy as you think. You need to decide whether anal leakage goes best before or after suicidal thoughts and dry mouth . . . I take a ribbing from some of the guys (and gals) at the office—which, I have to admit, gets to me. They know I've been working on a novel, but it's been awhile. I guess I should also admit that the heroin helps with some of the shame I feel about writing this stuff. Or life in general. I'm not, like, a junkie-junkie. I use it, I don't let it use me. And I'm not going to lie, it helps. It's like, suddenly you have a mommy who loves you. You just have to keep paying her.

Not that life is bad—I'm making a living, and not a bad one, considering; when I got my MFA I thought for sure all I had to do was start writing stories and things would just kind of take care of themselves. I realize now that it probably wasn't smart to use my "craft" to make my living. "Don't use the same muscle you write fiction with to pay the rent," my professor and thesis advisor, Jo Bergy, advised. Of course I ignored her. I wanted to be a writer!

In New York! But gradually, as the years passed, the bar for what counted as writing got a little lower while the pay, occasionally, got a lot higher. Why is that? Why should I be paid more for vibrator copy than my searching and personal novella about growing up the son of a blind rabbi and his kleptomaniac adulteress wife in Signet, Ohio? Sure, I placed a few "chunks" of the book as short stories in the beginning. That's what made me think I could do it. Though why I thought the three free copies from *Party Ball* magazine, or the two hundred I got from *Prose for Shmoes*, out of Portland, was going to make a dent in my living expenses, I don't know. I had some encouraging correspondence from *The Believer*. But ultimately they ended up printing the letter of protest I wrote when they rejected my twenty-first submission. Again, the drugs helped. I feel a terrific sense of shame about my whole life situation. I see other people my age making big money doing memoirs, getting screenplay deals based on tweets, and here I am bouncing around from porn dog to New Media Guy to Uh-Oh Boy—industry lingo for Side Effects Specialists, a.k.a. Sessies.

And yes, just thinking about this, the knife-in-the-chest regret I feel at chances blown, assignments fucked up, books unwritten or written badly . . . public scenes (more than once involving kneewalking, twice on a plane) when I was, you know, more high than I thought I was, it all twists me up. On smack, sometimes, you feel so perfect, you just assume everything you do is perfect, too. And when you remember, and the remorse kicks in, it's like a razor-legged tarantula crawling upside down in your heart, cursing you in dirty Serbian for being a lame-ass dope fiend who blew every chance he ever had and ended up in the world of incontinence-wear and catheters. (Referred to, just between us girls, as "dump-lockers" and "caths.") Well, do a little heroin, and you can remember the good things. On smack, everything feels good. I would gladly slit my own throat, attend the funeral, and dig my own grave, if I could do it all on decent dope—and not have to actually cop it. As William Burroughs said, it's not the heroin that'll kill you, it's the lifestyle.

But we were talking about the good things! Reasons for me to like y-o-*me*.

Like, not to brag, it was my idea to refer to the discharge from the rectal area as "anal leakage," rather than actual "intestinal discharge." Which, technically (if not linguistically) speaking, are two different things. My thinking was—and I said this to Cliff and Chandra, the husband-wife team who took over the agency—my thinking was, bad as "anal leakage" is, at least it's vaguely familiar. Tires leak, faucets leak, it's round-the-house stuff, and we all have anuses. (Ani?) But discharge is never good. Try and think of one situation involving "discharge" from your body that is not kind of horrible. Perhaps, hearing about my life and "career," you think *they* sound pretty horrible. Or maybe you're thinking to yourself: okay, he has some problems, he's had a bumpy career path, but he doesn't seem like a heroin guy.

Exactly! It's no big deal! Everybody has their little rituals. Miles Dreek, the other Sessie, walks in with his raspberry cruller and chai tea every morning. When I come in, I have my own stations of the cross. I go to the men's room, cook up a shot in my favorite stall, grab coffee in my ironic Dilbert mug, and amble back to my cubicle where the latest batch of American maladies awaits. Today, for example, is Embarrassing Flaky Patches Day. I watch the moving drama the clients have already filmed, showing a nice white lady with other nice white people in a nice restaurant, and listen to her VO: *It was a weekend to relax with friends and family. But even here, there was no escaping it. It's called moderate to severe chronic plaque psoriasis. Once again, I had to deal with these embarrassing, flaky, painful red patches. It was time for a serious talk with my dermatologist.*

Here's where I roll up my sleeves. (Well, at least one of them—haha!) From a list of heinous side effects I start cobbling together the Authoritative-but-Friendly PSE (possible side effects) list. *HUMIRA can lower your ability to fight infections, including tuberculosis. Serious, sometimes fatal, events can occur, such as lymphoma or other types of cancer, blood, liver, and nervous system problems, serious allergic reactions, and new or worsening heart failure.*

I had me at cancer! Seriously. I don't care if bloody images of Satan bubble up on my flesh, I'd have to do heroin just to stop worrying about the lymphoma and heart failure I might get for taking this shit to get rid of them. But that's me. That's the dirty little secret of TV medicine spots. The people who write them wouldn't go near the stuff.

Of course, people will tell you heroin is bad. But let me tell you my experience. If you take it for a reason, and you just happen to have a reason every day, then it's not exactly addictive behavior. It's more like medicine. Or a special survival tool. For example, there may be a thought that crops up in your head. (We're only as sick as our secrets!) Like how, lately, I have this thing, whenever I see a pregnant woman, especially if she's, you know, exotically dimpled, or has a really great ass, where I just sort of see her in stirrups, giving birth, her sweaty thighs wide open, the doctor and nurses with their masks on, the doctor reaching in, up to the wrists. It's better if it's a female doctor, I don't know why; I'm not proud of any of this. Once there's the actual pulling out of some bloody placenta-covered screamer, I'm gone. But still I think about—this is really not cool, really not something I want to *think* I'm thinking about—but nonetheless, what I think about, almost against my will, is how her vaginal walls—for which the Brits have a singularly disgusting word—will just be gaping. I remember it from when my ex-wife gave birth to our son Mickey. (She left me, years ago; last I heard she was running a preschool for upscale biters. Which is a syndrome now; Squibb R&D has some meds in development. But never mind. Kids' drugs take a little longer for the FDA to rubber stamp.) Anyway, I just picture the gape. As riveting as Animal Planet footage of boas dislocating their jaws to swallow an entire baby boar. (The same arousal, it goes without saying, does not apply during a caesarean; I'm not an animal.) But still . . . when my thoughts—how can I put this?—veer in this direction, some nonwholesome wouldn't-want-to-have-my-mind-read-in-front-of-a-room-full-of-friends-or-strangers direction, I need something to get rid of the thoughts. I need the heroin.

Worse than fantasies are memories. Which may, arguably, qualify as disguised fantasy. Didn't George Bernard Shaw say, "The only thing more painful than recollecting the things I did as a child are recalling things I did as an adult"? Or was that Cher?

I actually started writing in rehab. (My first one. I've been in eleven. Three in Arizona.) And it was awful. The writing, I mean. We were supposed to paint a portrait of ourselves in words. I still remember my first sentence. *I AM TAPIOCA TRAPPED IN ARMOR!* Followed by: *Little Lloyd* (that's my name; well, *Lloyd*, not Little Lloyd.) "Little Lloyd" has cowered continually, long into adulthood, at the memory of deeds perpetrated on his young unprotected self, scenes of unspeakable humiliation. Which—can somebody tell me why? Freudians? Melanie Kleiners? Anybody?—barge into my psyche at the most inopportune moments. Imagine a big-screen TV that turns on by itself and blasts Shame Porn to all your neighbors at four in the morning. Like, say, I'll be at a job interview, talking to some wing-tipped toad named Gromes about my special abilities recounting the consequences of ingesting Malvesta, a prescription adult onset acne pill (glandular swelling, discomfort in the forehead, bad breath, strange or disturbing dreams), when I am suddenly overcome with memories of my mother paddling around the house with her hands cupped under her large blue-veined breasts, blaring Dean Martin. *When the moon hits your eye like a big pizza pie, that's amore!* She's high-kicking while our mailman, a long-faced Greek with a nervous twitch, peers in the window. And Mom knows he's there. I'm three and a half, and waiting to get taken to kindergarten. Mom's supposed to drive me, but instead, she starts screaming, over the music: *Why don't you play?* Why don't I play? It makes me anxious. Should the mailman be looking in the window? Where is his other hand? What happened to his bag? Ahhhhhh . . . Not even four, and I already need a fix.

Well, that's it. After the *That's Amore* flashback, I'm cooked. Forget the job interview. I'm like Biff in *Death of a Salesman*, grabbing a fountain pen and running out of the office. Except I run straight to the bathroom and pull a syringe from my boot. Minutes later, before the needle is out—AHHHH, YESS-S-S-S-S-S-S, *thank you, Jesus!*—The Mommy-Tits-Amore-Mailman image furs and softens at the edges. Until—MMMMM, lemme just dab off this little kiss of blood—what began as horror morphs into suffused light, savaged memory softened by euphoria into benevolence, to some slightly disquieting, distant image . . . Mom is no longer doing a dirty can-can in the living room, entertaining a twitchy peeper in government issue . . . Now—*I love you, Ma, I really love you*—now her legs are simply floating up and down. My mind has been tucked into bed. A loving hand brushes my troubled little brow . . . Heroin's the cool-fingered loving caretaker I never had. I mean, everything's all right now . . . As if my memory's parked in the very last row of a flickering drive-in, with fog rolling in over all the cars up front . . . So even though I know what's on the screen, and I know it's bad—*Is that a knife going into Janet Leigh?*—it . . . just . . . does . . . not . . . matter. It's still nice. Really nice. Provided, that is, I don't pass out in the men's room, and they end up calling paramedics, and I wake up chained to the hospital bed. *Again.* In California they can arrest for you for tracks. Those fascists!

And now—oh God, no! *No!* Here comes another memory. STOP, PLEASE! Why does my own brain hate me? I'm picking my son up at preschool, and I'm early, and I've just copped, so I go in the boy's bathroom. And—NO NO NO NO—I come to—you never wake up on heroin, you just come to—to screams of, *Daddy, what's wrong!* See my little boy in his SpongBob SquarePants hat, his mouth a giant O. He's screaming, screaming, and—what's this?—my ratty jeans are already at my ankles and there's a needle in my arm and my boy's teachers and the principal of the preschool are hovering over me, like a circle of disapproving angels on the ceiling of the Sistine Chapel and—

And I hear myself, with my child looking on, like it's some kind of *Aw shucks* normal thing, saying, *Hey, could you guys just let me, y'know . . . Just give me a second here?* And in front of all of them, in front of my sweet, quivering-chinned son, I push down that plunger. And suddenly, everything's fine. Everything's awful, but everything's fine . . . My little boy's horrified coffee-brown eyes glisten with tears. *Goodbye little Mickey, goodbye . . .* My wife will get a call from Family Services. I'll be leaving now. In cuffs. I manage a little wave to Mickey, who gives me a private little wave back. In spite of everything. I'm still his daddy. For years afterward, I have to get high just to think about what I did that day to get high. But it's okay. Really. It's fine.

Heroin. Because, once you shed your dignity, everything's a little easier.

Where was I? (And yes, maybe the dope did diminish my capacity for linear thinking. So what?) When my boss moved to pharmaceuticals from "marital aids," I followed. (He insisted on the old-school term his father used: *marital aids*. Instead of the more contempo *sex toys*.) We'd been taken over by a conglomerate. I cut my teeth on Doc Johnson double dildos (for "ass-to-ass action like you've never dreamed of!") and Ben Wa Balls ("Ladies, no one has to know!"). Then it was up (or down) the ladder to men's magazines, romance mags, even a couple of *Cat Fancy* imitators. Starting in back-of-the-book "one inchers" for everything from Mighty Man trusses to Kitty Mittens to X-Ray Specs. (A big seller for more than fifty years.) When I tried the specs, and—naturally—they didn't work, my boss said, with no irony whatsoever, "We're selling a dream, Lloyd. Did you go to Catholic School?"

"Methoheeb," I told him.

"What's that, kid?"

"Half-Jewish, Half-Methodist, and my mom did a lot of speed."

"Lucky you," he said, "I was schooled by nuns. But when I put on those X-Ray Specs, I swear, I could see Sister Mary Theresa's fong-hair . . ."

Don't kid yourself, this is a serious, high-stakes business. To stay on top of the competition, you have to know what's out there. Like, just now, on the *Dylan Ratigan Show*—What great hair! Like a rockabilly gym teacher!—I caught this: *Life with Crohn's disease is a daily game of "What if . . . ?" What if I can't make it to . . .* Here the audio fades and there's a picture of a pretty middle-aged brunette looking anxiously across a tony restaurant at a ladies' room door . . . The subtext: *If you don't take this, you are going to paint your panties.*

Listen, I spent a lot of time watching daytime commercials. I had to. (Billie Holliday said she knew she was strung out when she started watching television. And she didn't even talk about *daytime!*)

Back when it was still on, I'd try to sit through *Live with Regis and Kelly* without a bang of chiba. Knock yourself out, Jimmy-Jane. I couldn't make it past Regis's rouge without a second shot. At this point he looked like somebody who'd try and touch your child on a bus to New Jersey.

Is it any accident that so much of contempo TV ad content concerns . . . *accidents?* This is the prevailing mood. Look at the economy. Things are so bad, you don't need to have Crohn's disease to lose control. But worse than pants-shitting is public pants-shitting. Americans like to think of themselves as mud-holders. You don't see the Greatest Generation diapering up, do you? (Well, not only recently, anyway.)

Junkies may be obsessed with bathooms, but America's got them beat. So many cable-advertised products involve human waste, you imagine the audience sitting at home, eating no-fat potato chips on a pile of their own secretions. As *Ad Week* put it on a recent cover, "American Business Is in the Toilet."

Right now, the real big gun in the Bodily Function sweepstakes is Depends. Go ahead and laugh. These guys are genius. Why? I'll tell you. *Because they make the Bad Thing okay.* (Just like heroin!) Listen: *Incontinence doesn't have to limit you. It all starts with finding the right fit and protection. The fact is, you can manage it so you can feel like yourself again.* (Oddly, I used to lose bowel control after I copped. May as well tell you. I'd get so excited, it just happened. So I'm no stranger to "mampers," as we say in the industry. They could ask me for a testimonial. Though, in all honesty, if it were my campaign I'd have gone with something more macho. Something, call me crazy, patriotic. *Depends. Because this is America, damnit!*)

Then again, maybe the macho thing is wrong. Maybe—I'm just spitballing here—maybe you make it more of a convenience thing. Or—wait, wait!—more *Morning in America*-ish, more

Reagany. Take two: *America, we know you're busy. And you don't always have time to pull over and find somewhere convenient to do your business. With new Depends, you can go where you are—and keep on going. Depends—because you've earned it.* Subtext, of course: *We're Americans! We can shit wherever we want!*

See what I mean about dope making you more creative?

Not that I can mock. Ironically, because of my own decade-and-a-half imbibing kiestered Mexican tar, I got some kind of heinous, indestructible parasites. Souvenir of Los Angeles smackdom. For a while I had a job in downtown LA, five minutes from Pico-Union, where twelve-year-old 18th Street bangers kept the stuff in balloons in their mouths. You'd give them cash, then put the balloons in *your* mouth. If you put them in your pockets, the UCs would roll up and arrest you before the spit was dry. Keeping it in your mouth was safer. Unhygienic (parasites!), but on the plus side—visit any LA junkie pad, and there was always something festive about the little pieces of red, blue, green, and yellow balloons all over the place. Like somebody'd thrown a child's birthday party in hell, and never cleaned up.

But now—call it Narco-Karma—I have to give myself coffee enemas every day. Part of the "protocol" my homeopath, Bobbi, herself in recovery, has put me on for the Parasite Situation. Bobbi also does my colonics . . . She likes calypso music, which I find a little unsettling. Though Robert Mitchum singing "Coconut Water" while I'm buns-up and tubed is the least of my issues. Bob knew his calypso.

Like I say, part of my job is recon. And, I'm not going to lie, just thinking about that killer Crohn's copy makes me a little jealous. The subject, after all, was shame. What does some pharma-hired disease jockey know about *shame?* Did he have *my* mother? Scooping his stainy underpants out of the hamper and waggling them in *his* face, screaming she was going to hang them on the line for all his friends to see? (No, that's not why I do heroin. Or why I ended up in side effects. Whatever doesn't kill us just makes *us*.)

For one semester, I attended the School of Visual Arts in New York City. I studied advertising with Joe Sacco, whose "Stronger than Dirt" campaign, arguably, sheathed a proto–Aryan Superiority sensibility under the genial façade of Arthurian legend. (For you youngsters, the ad featured a knight riding into a dirty kitchen on a white steed.) White Power might as well have been embossed on the filth-fighter's T-shirt. See—excuse me while I scratch my nose—there's a connection, in the White American subconscious, between Aryan superiority and cleanliness. "Clean genes," as Himmler used to say. Tune into MSNBC *Lockup* some weekend, when the network trades in the faux-progressive programming for prison porn. Half the shot-callers in Quentin look like Mr. Clean: shaved head and muscles that could really hold a race-traitor down. Lots of dope in prison. But—big surprise—the fave sponsors of *Lockup* viewers, to judge by the ads, are Extenze (penis size); Uromed (urinary infection); our old friend Depends (bowel control); and Flomax (frequent peeing.) The Founding Fathers would be proud.

You think junkies don't have a conscience? All the snappy patter I've cranked out, and you know what made me really feel bad? Feel the worst? Gold coin copy. People are so dumb when they buy gold—a hedge against the collapse of world markets!—they think it matters if it comes in a commemorative coin. A genuine recreation of an authentic 18-Something-Something mint issue Civil War coin with our nation's greatest president, Abraham Lincoln, on one side, and the thirty-three-star Union flag on the other. Worth fifty "dollar gold." *Yours for only* $9.99. The "dollar gold" was my idea. I don't even know why. I just knew it sounded more important than "dollars." Later, in the running text under the screen (known as *flash text* in the biz), I deliberately misspelled gold as *genuine multikarat pure god*. I think this was my best move. Not that I can take credit. Just one of those serendipitous bonbons you get when you type on heroin. This happened when I did too much. In an effort not to fall off my chair, I'd type with one eye closed. As if I were trying to aim my fingers, the way I aimed my car, squinting one-eyed over the wheel to stay between the white lines.

So now, now, now, now, now, what do I *do?* I mean—shut up, okay?—I did leave out a key detail. Like, how it all ended?

Okay. Let me come clean. (So to speak.) I got caught shooting up on the job. Dropped my syringe and it rolled leeward into the stall beside me, where my archrival, Miles Dreek (can a name get more Dickensian?) found it. And, long story short, ratted me out. I couldn't even plead diabetes, because the rig was full of blood, and everybody's seen enough bad junkie movies to know how the syringe fllls up with blood. (Generally, on film, in roseate slo-mo, Dawn of the Galaxy Exploding Nebulae-adjacent Scarlet, which—come on, buddy—does not happen when Gramps drops trou and Grandma slaps his leathery butt cheek and sticks in the insulin. That was my first experience of needles: Grandma spanking Grandpa and jabbing the rig in. Grandpa had it down. The second his wife of his sixty-seven years geezed him, he'd pop a butterscotch Life Saver and crunch. Hard candy! Sugar and insulin at the same time. A diabetic speedball. *These are my people!*)

But wait—I was just getting busted. At work. (People think only alcohol can give you blackouts. But heroin? Guess what, Lou Reed wannabe. Sometimes I think I'm still in one . . .)

I remember, right before the needle-dropping incident, I was just sitting there, on the toilet, with a spike in my arm. Suddenly I jerked awake, feeling like one of those warehouse-raised chickens, the kind photographed by secret camera in *Food, Inc.*, on some infernal industrial farm, feet grafted to the cage, shitting on the chicken below as the chicken above shits on them.

You don't think they should give chickens heroin? Don't think they deserve it? Well, call me visionary, if they're already pumping the poultry full of antibiotics and breast-building hormones (rendering, they say, half the chicken-eating male population of America estrogen-heavy, sterile, and sporadically man-papped), then why not lace the white meat with hard narcotics? *Chicken McJunkets!* Whatever. Give me one night and three bags and I'll Don Draper a better name . . . Or I would, if I had a place to live. Right now I have enough to stay at this hotel, the Grandee (an SRO), for a couple more weeks. After that I don't know . . . Guy behind the cage in the lobby looks liver-yellow. Doesn't talk much. But never mind, never mind . . . Me being here has nothing to do with heroin. Just bad luck. But weren't we talking about heroin chicken? Believe me, plenty of clean-living junkies would hit the drive-through—provided Mickey D's could take those other damn drugs out of his birds. Hormones, antibiotics, beak-mite repellent . . . No thanks! That stuff could kill you.

Don't worry. I won't be out of the business for long. I have a plan. A new campaign. Look: Camera pans a modest but nice house. Outside, a sweet LITTLE BOY swings on a swing. Stressed-but-pleasant-looking MOM looks on, wiping her brow. *Mommy, watch!* yells the boy. *I'm watching,* says the pretty-but-tired woman, casting glances back toward the second-floor window. In which—REVERSE—we see our GUY peering out. We push in on him. He looks down at a foreclosure notice in his hand, then back out at the scene in the yard. His face registers complicated feelings: pain, regret, sadness . . . But we know what he wants. He wants relief. The man sits down on the bed, pulls out his works, and prepares a shot. We hear, in V.O.: *When I have emotions I don't like, I take heroin* . . . CUT TO: Man and wife together, in front of the swings. The man has his arm around the woman. The boy's beaming.

Heroin. It makes everything good . . .

PART II

SURRENDER TO THE VOID

L.Z. HANSEN came to New York City in the early 1980s at seventeen years old, from London, England. She lived in the Chelsea Hotel and Hell's Kitchen before eventually settling in the East Village. Hansen has worked as a hair and makeup stylist, clothing store owner, streetwalker, speedball addict, escort, massage parlor owner, writer, and madam. She has been published in various magazines and anthologies, has spoken at colleges on her life and writing, and is working on her first novel. Hansen hosts her own monthly reading series, and enjoys life in the East Village, where she resides with her family.

going down
by l.z. hansen

Streets were hot, stinking hot. Sticky cans and discarded food collected around full garbage cans, and the flies were feasting. I felt cold. Goose bumps stood out on my arms. I noticed blood spots on the sleeve of my white long-sleeved shirt. I rolled them up just enough to hide the blood while still covering the pit of my elbow.

Sweat trickled down my back, and made me squirm.

A banged-up undercover cop car crawled past. The windows were rolled down, and two fat cops were sucking air. I slowed down and stood under a torn awning so they wouldn't see me.

One of them was the bastard who stopped me two nights ago on Rivington. On the street they called him Flash. I didn't know if it was in reference to Flash the superhero or the Queen song. I hadn't copped yet, but Flash swore he'd seen me score. He pulled me into a stairwell to pat me down. I knew he wasn't allowed, but there was nothing I could do. I was lucky he didn't plant something, and take me in. It's best to let the cops do whatever they are going to do. He felt me up, and stuck his hands down my pants. I think he wanted me to resist. The fact that I didn't pissed him off, and he told me to fuck off.

"Mama, youse looking for the good shit?" A man with one eye and one leg steadied himself against the wall. He smiled a toothless grin.

"No. Leave me alone." I said. The man's face stayed with me.

One eye, one leg, and no teeth. I wondered what else he had lost. If I had one eye I'd wear a patch. Don't see too many girls with an eye patch.

Walk down Avenue C. It's so quiet, and still daytime. The fiends weren't fiending, yet.

Houston Street. I saw a young hip-hop kid selling Road Runner by the Parkside Lounge.

Butterflies flipped in my gut as I neared the buzzing block. The seller was wearing a lot of gold, and stood out too much. I had five hundred dollars on me, which when transferred into dope, should have been enough to get me through the weekend, but it never did. It's never enough. Money had lost all meaning to me. It had become various amounts of heroin. My new currency. A hundred bucks meant a bundle; fifty, half a bundle; ten bucks, a bag; five bucks, a pack of smokes, not enough for a bag, and therefore meaningless. An annoying little piece of paper, unless accompanied by another five dollars, which had meaning, a whole bag of heroin.

A haggard street hooker stood in front of me in the dope line, and bought one bag. A nice-looking rock dude, the type I liked, pushed in front of me.

"Yo, da lady waz in front of youse," the dealer said.

Rock dude looked at me with hollow eyes and stepped back. Shame, looked like a cool guy, minus the dope.

"How many, Mama?"

"Five bundles."

"I got youse, I got youse . . ." He smiled flirtatiously. Then reached into his underwear and pulled out five bundles, tightly wrapped in rubber bands. I traded, money for heroin.

Beautiful. All's okay with the world. Now nothing could go wrong today. I felt my security blanket surround me.

"Thanks. Will you be here later?" Don't know why I said that, but I always did.

Walk quickly, quickly. Get off the block, off the block. Don't want to get stopped by the cops now. Hands deep in pockets, holding my life line.

It felt so good to have dope on me. It was the only time in my day that I could slow down, and view the world I had long ago stepped out of. The sky, the blue-blue cloudless sky, the people, feelings. I felt powerful and . . . safe at that moment. No one could touch me.

Then a large sweaty man appeared out of nowhere.

"Lady, please, you got a few dollars? I gotta get straight."

"Err . . . Hell no!" I looked at him like he was insane. I got mine, fuck him. Why would I give money away? That's bullshit. I felt guilty at being so cold and mean, but everyone for themselves, right?

I looked back, and saw him watching me. He made me nervous, and broke my momentary blissful view of the real world. I was bought back into my universe.

I saw Marilyn walking with a young, thin Hispanic male I didn't recognize.

"Marilyn!" I yelled.

Thank God, perfect timing. I could go over to her pad to get straight, instead of using the filthy bathroom at Odessa Restaurant.

"Can I use your place?" She knew what I meant.

"I was going to Tito's, you can get straight there. Got a bag for me?" she said smiling, linking arms.

Tito walked ahead, not talking. He took his T-shirt off and mopped his brow with it. He had a rough jailhouse tattoo of Jesus crying on the cross in the middle of his back.

I trusted Marilyn. She had been out on these streets her entire life, and knew everyone. Every dealer, hustler, whore, and thief. In this life of disease, Marilyn was a beam of sunshine. She was always smiling. Even though she had little to smile about. She whored on Allen Street for ten bucks a pop and told me horrific tales of her life of abuse. Her ability to forgive and forget was astounding, and unusual. She had asked me why I spoke with an accent. I told her I was from London, England. She asked where that was, and if they spoke a different language there.

We headed to 3rd Street between Avenues C and D. The south side of the street was an open lot, where a building used to be. It burned down. Now, children played on strewn rubble and junkies turned tricks on discarded mattresses.

Tito pushed open the front door to the building. The lock was broken, and the hall stunk of piss and garbage. He angrily kicked an empty can of beer down the hall. It rattled into a corner and made me jump. Did he really have to do that? Asshole.

It was dark, the lightbulb was blown. We followed him to the second floor, to the back apartment.

Graffiti, newspapers, scattered bits of broken everything were everywhere. A young man was standing in a corner stooped over, on the nod, with an unlit cigarette in one hand and a lighter in the other. He looked frozen.

"Wake up!" Tito bellowed in the man's face. The guy opened one eye, smiled a crooked grin, and went back to his dreams.

Tito banged loudly, and put his ear against the door.

It clicked open and we all filed in past Tito's mother. She said she was going out to the liquor store.

How did people live in these filthy cramped places?

A sink was overfilled with plates and flies. Two shirtless men, one younger than the other, smoked crack at the kitchen table, filling the air with a sickly sweet smell. I held my breath.

"Yo, my man, Jojo? You gotta leave, dude. My mama needs you outta here," Tito said.

"She cool, I gave her money to go get two forties. I ain't leaving right now anyways. I gotta get me some more rock," Jojo replied.

"Yo, you can't sit here all motherfuckin' day . . . You been here two days, motherfucker, give me some more money then . . . nigga."

"I already give you fifty yesterday, fifty last night, motherfucker . . . Fuck you, T."

I followed Marilyn to the bathroom, passing Jojo, who eyed me up and down, licking his shiny lips. He was dripping in sweat, and his eyes were black and crazed. He made me nervous. I had to get straight, then get out of there fast.

"Where you find the white girl? Damn, I need me some white bitch . . . She got money, T?"

"Shut the fuck up . . . hell if I know . . ."

I heard them talk back and forth about me as though I wasn't there. I locked us in the small bathroom. I'd be quick. Gotta get straight.

I took the toilet seat. Marilyn took the edge of the bathtub. We quickly set up. I could do this blindfolded.

I wondered how many times I had stuck a needle in my arm . . . in my whole life? I shoulda kept a record.

I handed Marilyn a bag. She smiled and thanked me.

"What if the world runs out of water . . . ?" Marilyn asked.

"Huh?" Marilyn often came up with these bizarre paranoid thoughts.

"What if there's no more water on the earth, then what?" she asked, drawing up from a leaking bathtub tap.

"Don't worry about it," I said, annoyed, tying my arm with a shoelace.

"I mean, if there's no water, how are we gonna get high?"

"What?" I'd gone through this with her last week. "Babe, ain't never gonna happen . . . Look at the ocean, for God's sake, there's enough water for the whole world of heroin addicts to shoot up with."

"You sure 'bout that."

"Swear."

"Ain't it salty?"

Motherfuck!

"Think of all the rivers then . . . Babe, of all the things to worry about, that isn't something you should think about . . . really!"

Thankfully, she shut up for a minute.

Marilyn skin-popped because she'd long ago lost every vein in her body. She had large gouged-out craters all over her limbs, where she'd stuck herself a billion times. Once I'd watched her try to fix in the artery in the middle of her forehead.

The dope had already hit her, and she was feeling good, and beginning to ramble. Nothing worse than a fucking dope fiend feeling good when you're still trying to find a vein.

"Motherfuck. I fucking hate this fuck shit, fuck. My life is HELL!" I spat out furiously, as I tied up my other arm.

Sweat poured off my face. I was soaking wet. So was Marilyn. Still she smiled.

I couldn't get a hit. It was hotter than the devil's bedroom, and I couldn't breath. Sweat trickled into my eyes. I wanted to cry, but was too angry.

Blood dripped onto the floor. I marveled at how perfectly round and dark the drops were.

I heard Tito arguing outside the door.

I was so frustrated at repeatedly sticking myself; my works were filled with blood, and I didn't want them to clog. I finally asked Marilyn to hit me.

She grabbed my left arm, twisted it around, and squeezed. A decent vein I'd never seen appeared. She jabbed the needle in with one hand, while holding my arm tight with the other.

"You should have been a nurse," I said, as dark blood registered.

"Shoulda coulda . . ." She smiled.

I tasted the heroin. Warmth. Comfort. Relief.

At that moment, I loved Marilyn. Love. All's okay. *I really must control my anger.*

"There ya go." She pulled the spike out, and pressed her thumb to the spot that dripped blood. Her nails were dirty.

Nice. Not bad shit for Road Runner. *Don't know why I get so pissed anyway.*

We heard a loud crash and a scuffle. Jojo was threatening to burn the place up and kill me and Marilyn. Tito was yelling to get the fuck out, but Jojo said he needed money. Something smashed against a wall.

Marilyn and I locked eyes. She motioned to get into the bathtub. We did, and closed the shower curtains, quietly. Not that this was doing any good. We couldn't disappear and they knew we were in there. I thought Marilyn believed if she closed her eyes, no one else could see her.

Adrenaline and fear ruined my high.

We waited for something.

I was wondering how I got into these situations. I began making a deal with God that if I got out of this jam, I'd think about making some changes. Stupid negotiations I'd made with my God many times before . . . but somehow He'd always listened, long after I'd given up on myself. I seemed to live in someone else's life—how did my world become so . . . abstract?

"It's Jojo. He crazy, that crack shit turns him into el diablo, he with the Kings, he OG." Marilyn put her finger to her mouth listening. "Oh shit, he wants Tito to give him more money."

"Why? Tito has money?" I asked.

"No, he ain't got shit."

I prayed that the door to the bathroom wouldn't fly open.

"What does he want?" I whispered. My mouth was dry, I needed water, badly.

"Dope, money, what else is there?" Yeah, what else is there?

I looked at the peeling ceiling . . . and the tap that was leaking down Marilyn's back . . . Who cleans this place? Soap scum ringed the tub . . . my arm still hurt.

I needed a cigarette . . . always needed something.

The door to the bathroom suddenly blew open. I was terrified. The shower curtain was torn down. Jojo's face was deranged, a vein in his forehead looked swollen and about to burst.

"Get out. Get the fuck outta the fucking room NOW!" he yelled.

"Oh no, Jojo, don't do this," Marilyn begged.

"Where the dope?" he demanded, staring at me. "I know you got it."

He grabbed me by my hair, twisted it around his hand, and stuck a kitchen carving knife under my chin. The point pressed into my jaw bone, forcing my head upward. Jojo whispered between clenched teeth. His breath stunk like monkey balls, and he spit saliva onto my cheek with each word. I squinted my eyes, breathing through my mouth. His eyes were black and manic. His lower jaw jutted from side to side in spasms. His face and shoulders were twitching and jumping. He'd obviously been up for days smoking crack.

Jojo yanked me out of the tub and pulled me into the kitchen, ordering Marilyn to walk in front of us. He referred to the younger guy as D, who was holding a gun to Tito's head.

D then put the gun in the middle of Tito's back and walked him into the back room.

Tito yelled: "Jojo, I can't believe you, man, how long I know you, motherfucker, how long I known you? Damn, nigga . . ."

"It ain't personal . . . Shut the fuck up anyways!" Jojo screeched.

I jerked my head back and the point of the knife slipped and cut me under my chin. Blood dripped onto my white shirt. I felt the wetness run down my chest.

Jojo put his face into my hair and inhaled. He whispered, "I'm gonna fuck you, white bitch . . . but first you gonna suck my dick. I gonna fuck your tight ass . . . You like my dick, you gonna like me fucking your ass . . . ain't you?"

I held my breath as he talked. His teeth were stained and crooked. He pressed my hand on his crotch, which felt limp. His heart was thumping so hard, he was racing. There was no way he was going to get a hard-on. Sweat ran down the side of his face.

"Come on, touch it, touch it . . ." He opened his zipper. I looked straight at him and yanked on his soft sweaty dick. Way too much coke.

He leaned into me and rammed his tongue into my mouth, slobbering all over my face. His tongue searching my mouth, I tried not to gag, and left my body. Then, suddenly, as though remembering what he was meant to be doing, he got up with his pants still open and screamed, "Give me the fucking dope! I know you got dope, bitch." He looked in my eyes. "We can party together . . . I can get some rock . . . Yo, you like to smoke?"

My good God, was he serious? This had gone from a possible assault/rape/robbery to a fucking date. I knew my only way out of there was to stay calm and pretend I liked him.

"Yes, I like to smoke, of course I do . . . Papi." I giggled flirtatiously. I tossed my hair back and stuck my tits out. "Here's the dope, Papi." I wanted to hold onto as much as possible. Nothing hurt worse than losing drugs. I passed him the two bundles stashed in my right boot. Maybe the dope would mellow him out a bit and he'd let us go.

He put the knife down, tore open a bag, and snorted it. Then another. Robbing us was like shooting dead fish in a barrel. What were we going to do? Yell for help? I just wanted to get the hell out of this place immediately.

I looked at Marilyn, who was standing wide-eyed and nervous. We heard Tito shouting from the back room, talking in English and half Spanish. D was asking Tito where he kept his money.

It got louder. Marilyn pleaded with Jojo to let us go. Jojo grabbed the knife that he had placed on the table and stormed into the back room, knocking over a kitchen chair.

I glanced at Marilyn, then the door, then Marilyn. Those few seconds seemed to tick in slow motion. Can we make it out of the door and down the street without them catching us?

We both leaped up and darted toward the front door, which had all sorts of bolts and locks on it. I slid the deadbolt, and pulled the door. It didn't open. I was never so terrified, my fingers trembled, Marilyn was banging me on my shoulder. I felt I was in one of those nightmares where I'm trying to run from someone, and my feet are stuck in quicksand.

"Come on . . . Mama, come on . . . hurry," she whispered.

"What the fuck do you think I'm doing?" I fumbled with two other locks, just yanking at them all. It opened! We both tripped over each other racing down the hall. Marilyn was practically on my back. I grabbed the staircase banister and flew, and I mean *flew*, down three stairs at a time . . . when we heard an extremely loud *POP* . . . from upstairs. Marilyn screamed. The gun? I couldn't believe it . . . I was running on the basic human reflex to save my life. Were they coming after us?

"Oh nooo . . . Dios mio . . . Dios mio!" Marilyn started yelling as we ran down the hall to the front door.

"Shut up, shush," I said. Two kids were sitting on the front stoop. We jumped through them onto the hot sidewalk that we had been on just twenty minutes ago.

The blistering sun, never-ending heat. I squinted my eyes to the blinding light. Marilyn says to *walk calmly, like nothing's unusual.* Whatever that means. We slowed down to a fast walk.

"What the hell . . . You know, that must have been D who fired that shot. I hope Tito's okay."

My mind was racing. I had to get some water. The thought of Jojo's tongue in my mouth makes me want to gag. I turned around to see if anyone was following us. The street's desolate, apart from an old woman rummaging through a garbage can.

We coulda got killed. I felt ill. We stopped at the corner of Avenue C to catch our breath. Two cops cars flew over potholes past us. I felt their speed as they smashed through still air.

They must be going to Tito's. Someone in the building called in the gunshot.

We stood at the light, waiting to cross. Marilyn turned around.

"They didn't stop at the building," she said as we crossed the street.

"What do you mean?" I looked around to see both cop cars turning onto Avenue D.

"No one cares," Marilyn said.

"You think anyone saw us? You think we should go to the cops?" I asked nervously.

Marilyn smiled. "Cops? Hell, no one goes to the cops." I amuse her with my naiveté. She shook her head, laughing at my panic. "We weren't there, we saw nothing . . . Whatever," she grinned.

I felt for the three fat bundles in my bra, and smiled back at her.

Yeah, whatever . . .

Michael Albo

MICHAEL ALBO is a Los Angeles–based author and journalist who has written about crime, music, and popular culture. He is a regular contributor to the *LA Weekly* and the *Los Angeles Times*. His work has also appeared in the *Chicago Tribune, Premiere* magazine, *Men's Edge* magazine, and *Sonic Boomers* music magazine. From 1993–2003, he served as the editor of *Hustler Erotic Video Guide,* which he describes as "a half-assed, porn-world version of *People* magazine."

baby, i need to see a man about a duck
by michael albo

Having the habit is an exercise in living undercover, and all afternoon my cover's been blown apart by degrees.

It was coming down evening on a hot and smoggy September day, and I wheeled a dusty white Ford Ranger pickup truck with bald tires and no air-conditioning through moderate traffic on the southbound 605 freeway. The asphalt was tinged blood-red by a sinking sun. This section of freeway carved through a surreal, heat-blasted moonscape of an alluvial fan near the confluence of the nearly dry San Gabriel and Rio Hondo rivers. I was on my way back home from Johnny Gato's ranchita in Irwindale, and I carried just enough drugs to warrant a solid felony charge. The big, white, pissed-off, gimp-legged Long Island duck that I had secured in a cardboard box was escaping its makeshift cell and it was going to be one fucked-up situation if—or, more likely, when—it broke free in the tight confines of that cab. The white head and yellow beak had already crowned. I regretted passing up Johnny Gato's offer to seal the box with duct tape and I regretted even more the decision to let the duck, that I named Quacky, ride up front.

Four hours earlier, I hadn't seen any of this developing. I was a world away in Beverly Hills with a real-life porn slut.

She called herself Eve Eden. "My real name's Eve," she drawled in that insincere way hustlers have when they're laying down the whore con, "and I used to work at this strip club back home called the Garden of Eden, so I use that for my last name." "Back home" was some dismal, bug-infested, malarial Alabama swamp, but Eve had left that all behind to make her sinuous way through the big city as a freshly minted adult-movie starlet. After two weeks in the neon-lit, subterranean depths of Greater Los Angeles, she had come around to realize that she was a lot farther from home than she could ever measure by miles. Attractive enough, but not beautiful, she wore heavy bangs and a pink eye patch to cover the results of girlhood run-in with the business end of a pellet gun. "My brother was huntin' squirrels and he accidentally shot me," she explained. "If I hold a strong magnet to my eye, I can feel the pellet move. It's trippy. It's still in there." She lifted the patch and flashed a milky orb tinted by a smear of blue that was no doubt thankful for all the things it had never seen. She said it was an embarrassment to her. "The kids at school called me Cyclops . . . or Blinky," she said. She wasn't the kind of girl who got many eye-to-eye gazes these days, not since she bought herself a pair of ridiculously enhanced breasts that jutted from her chest like a pair of twin defense missiles and were sheathed in a tight, glittery pink tube top that read, *PORN WHORE*. The pastel pink of her outfit, the patch, the matching pink-frost lipstick and nail polish, and her overly dyed and fried blond hair made her look like a serving of carnival cotton candy that had lost a few bites before being tossed on the midway for the ants that crawled in the dust.

We sat at a table in the sun-splintered dining room of Mary Kate's, a precious and overly fussy Beverly Hills parody of a workingman's chop house on Wilshire Boulevard. She drew the attention from an early lunch crowd of bankers, business squares, and locals with money. It wasn't her clothes or overt whorishness that pulled eyes, but her absolutely white-trash table manners. She was loud, and she was mightily impressed by the complimentary sourdough. "Oh . . . my . . . GOD! This is the best bread I ever ate!"

she crowed. She used a steak knife to slather a crusty piece with an ungodly amount of pale yellow churned cream and suggestively licked the blade clean. She was fascinated by my order of spaghetti all'aglio e olio. "I've never had THAT! Is that what real Eye-talians eat? Can I try some?" I handed her a fork and tablespoon so she could do the proper noodle-twirl like a civilized girl, but she reached past me with a bare hand and grabbed a big, oily handful, leaned her head back, and dropped it down her gullet like a fledgling eating worms. "That IS good!" she smiled through oil-slicked lips. In another setting, it might have been sexy.

The last thing a dope fiend needs or wants is attention. A steady stream of misdirection needs to flow to present yourself as close to normal to the always-watching world around you. I had three simple tricks: I kept a job, I wore a business suit, and I drank. The current job was running a pornographic magazine from an office in an imposing black-glass tower in the heart of Beverly Hills for a limping, moon-faced Greek millionaire. He trundled along with the aid of an ebony cane with a silver and gold lion's head for the handle. The eyes were set with diamonds. He didn't actually need the prop, but told me once that it conferred "power and respect" upon him from underlings like me. I didn't argue. He signed my checks and as long as the copy got in on time and sales didn't fall, I remained an employed and productive member of society. The job also provided an excuse to use the company expense account to entertain feature subjects like Eve, who had just shot a centerfold layout for us. Right now, though, she was turning into a lunchroom liability. Even though I was dressed in my somber navy suit, blue oxford shirt, and mirror-shined black wingtips, the other diners had shifted some of their attention from Eve onto me . . . as if I was supposed to do something about her behavior. And this is why I drank: Americans are a lot more likely to forgive a drunk than they are a dope fiend, and, usually, social mistakes can be glossed over by the simple statement, "I've had a little too much."

Until now, I'd done just fine topping off my daily doses of tar with Wild Turkey 101 served over ice or Bombay Sapphire martinis, both generally backed by freebase cocaine, a stash of which I always kept hidden above a ceiling tile in my office. Today, however, was different. When I ordered a very dry martini and the starch-shirted, whey-faced waiter brought it to our table, I gagged at the poisonous bloom of raw alcohol on my tongue. Eve, her mouth still smeared with butter and oil, and who initially declined my offer of a cocktail, said, "Give me that!" before downing the glass in one gulp. Well, it was supposed to be a thank-you lunch for doing her shoot for far below her day rate . . . as long as she was assured of being the cover girl.

"May I bring something else, sir?" whispered the waiter.

"Uh, yeah. Can you have the bartender make me a double piña colada? But make sure that he puts it in a regular tumbler and leaves off the fruit salad and paper umbrella," I said with a lot of shame. It's not a very masculine drink.

"Absolutely, sir."

"I'll have another martini," chimed Eve, then added with cartoonish lasciviousness, "and make it *diiiirrrty* this time."

She hadn't bothered to wipe her mouth and continued to help herself to my plate of spaghetti with her bare hand and it was driving me to distraction. When the waiter came back with our drinks, I gulped the frothy kiddie-cocktail so fast it gave me a headache. I registered that pineapple and coconut completely masked the taste of the rum. I also noted that my morning dose was wearing off and I'd better do something quick to maintain my equilibrium. I excused myself and made my way into the single-occupancy restroom.

Once the door was securely locked and I was alone in that tomb of green marble, black porcelain, and mirrored walls, I fished around in the pocket of my jacket and came up with a carefully folded square of tinfoil, a brass Zippo lighter, and an antique pill box that held a little black blob of tar heroin the size of three match heads. I unfolded the foil and creased it into a V and put the dope on it before I melted it just enough to make sure it stuck to the shiny surface. I took the straw that I had surreptitiously slipped from my piña colada and put it between my teeth. I held the foil under my chin with one hand and, with the other, I struck the Zippo to bring the flame under the foil. I heard a comforting hiss as the dope liquefied and burst into a cloud of smoke that boiled up the crease. I sucked through the straw. This ballet, from the time I locked the door, took about a minute. I held in the acrid smoke as long as I could and then exhaled, pleased to see that almost nothing escaped my lungs.

I ditched the foil down the toilet, tossed the straw into the wastebasket, and dropped the lighter and pill box back into my pocket. I could already feel the wave of narcotic euphoria like some sea-spawned tidal welling spread from my testicles to points north. I checked the restroom to make sure I left it like I found it. Satisfied, I turned the knob and hit the floor as an unexpected rush of nausea bubbled up. I turned in the opposite direction of our table and exited the restaurant into the afternoon sunshine that burnished the pristine Beverly Hills sidewalk. My stomach churned and before I could react, a long, arcing fountain of slightly used piña colada erupted from me and splattered wetly into the gutter in full view of passing traffic. I took out my pocket square and dabbed delicately at the corner of my mouth and dully noted that, if it doesn't stay in too long, a piña colada tastes exactly the same coming up as it does going down.

Embarrassed, I reentered the restaurant's bar and made my way to the table, and hoped none of the diners had seen my sidewalk display. I stopped, surprised, before I reached my spot.

Sitting in my chair, swathed in oversized plaid, was a homunculus the color of wrought iron. I recognized him right off as a washed-up former child actor with the improbable name of Lemuel Washington DiHarris who had once starred in a popular sitcom about the misadventures of a disadvantaged, pint-sized black child who had come to live under the care of a wealthy, white, industrialist playboy. For reasons that escaped me, the show had acquired a kitschy, nostalgic cult following in the years after its cancellation. I always thought it was paternalistic and racist, but I never watched it much. Maybe I had missed something. I did know that Lemuel's signature catch phrase, which had entered the popular lexicon, grated on me like words seldom did. And as I reached the table, he flashed a gold-toothed grin at me and said it in a thick urban patois: "You don' wan' know 'bout dat!" He laughed while pointing at me.

I hated to admit it, but he was right. I didn't want to know about it. I had no idea who was hustling who at this point, but he and Eve were getting awfully friendly with each other. Lemuel stayed in my chair but graciously invited me to join them. "Pull up a seat, homie," he said.

Eve chirped, "He's a RAPPER!" I had read somewhere that he aspired to revive his career through thug-rap and it amused me to think that this young man, who had been a child TV star and, before that, a pint-sized pitchman for a number of national products in TV commercials, could convince anyone that he was a hard-ass criminal fresh off the streets. But the proof was right in front of me. It was obvious Eve thought she had traded up from me, and there was no sense in sticking around. There would be no pink candy floss for dessert.

I leaned in close to her and said, "Baby, I need to see a man about a duck." It was a euphemism I used when going to cop dope at Johnny Gato's, since he lived on a small ranch overrun by poultry, a pig or two, and several goats. Most people just took it as a goodbye. I breathed in her whore aroma: too much perfume, gin, stale tobacco, Juicy Fruit gum, and, underneath it all, a musky, feminine funk. It made me even more pissed off at the sawed-off little runt who was twisting a gold pinky ring on his finger. I straightened up and said, "You guys enjoy yourselves. Order what you want! It's all taken care of."

"You all right, homeboy!" said Lemuel.

I nodded and made my way to the front of the restaurant where I tipped the day-shift manager fifty dollars of my own money. I was a good customer and was in there at least twice a week. I always tipped him and the staff well and made sure to introduce him to the girls I brought in. He appreciated it. "Look, man, that guy sitting at my table said he'd pay the tab today, so I'm out of here," I said, pointing at Lemuel.

"I used to watch him on TV when he was a kid," replied the manager, a chubby middle-aged guy in browline specs and a floral-print tie who was not beyond being impressed with whatever celebrities, great or small, entered his domain. "He was funny. What was that thing he used to say?"

"You don' wan' know 'bout dat!" I said, certain that Lemuel didn't want to know that he just got stuck with the check.

I didn't see this as shady or underhanded. A good junkie can always justify his actions. This was revenge, and it felt good.

I walked past the valet stand and navigated through several blocks of side streets to get to my truck. Beverly Hills parking could be pricey, but if you knew where to look, and didn't mind a little walk, you could always get a few hours for free. There were never parking concerns at Johnny Gato's, and I set my wheels east and made the afternoon drive in less than an hour, a good time for a Friday.

* * *

Johnny Gato's place wasn't much to look at from the dirt access road that led up to it. A small stucco house, built before World War II, garishly painted raspberry and turquoise with a sagging porch and lots of shade trees, it nested down in a spot between the freeway and the San Gabriel River. In the front yard, two of Johnny's kids, Junior and Angel, had hoisted and secured a bicycle frame from the limb of a live oak tree. They had chopped and lengthened the frame with steel tubing and were preparing to spray-paint it and mint another one of their two-wheeled low-rider creations. It was certain that these two preteen criminals, in their tube-socks, cutoff khakis, and starched white T-shirts with a vertical crease that cut as sharp and vicious as a Saturday-night straight-razor fight, had stolen the frame.

"*Ese*! Your truck looks like shit, eh!" Junior laughed.

"We'll wash it for ten dollars!" said Angel.

"How about I give you guys twenty and you do a good job?"

The boys were fine with that. I crossed the yard and asked, "Just go on in?"

"You always say that, dude. Yes. You don't need to knock. They're in the back," admonished Junior.

I stepped across the rickety flooring of the porch and pushed open a steel-mesh door that squealed out in protest. In the cool darkness of the immaculately kept front room, two old folks, Doña Flor and Don Frank, were watching the Spanish-language news. A woman newscaster was dressed a lot like Eve and was rattling off something in machine-gunfire Spanish.

"Buenas tardes," I offered.

Don Frank pointed at the TV and said, "Can you believe those clothes?"

"It's a crazy world," I replied.

"They're out back," said Doña Flor.

I continued through to the kitchen, which was as surgically

clean as everything else in this tiny house, and saw that Johnny Gato's wife Rose, a big old gal, was working at an ancient stove. A big pot of pinto beans simmered over one burner, and in another, a red stew bubbled. The tight little space smelled of garlic, chilis, and the fresh, citrus tang of cilantro.

"Hey! How you doing?" smiled Rose. "We got birria! One of our goats! You gotta have some."

I had learned a long time ago to never pass up anything Rose offered. Her skill as a housekeeper was surpassed only by her ability as a cook. She moved quickly and filled a bowl with the spicy goat stew, on top of which she stacked some warm corn tortillas and placed a few slices of lime on top of those. I was hungry. I'd only managed a few bites of spaghetti back in Beverly Hills before Eve started slopping her hands into it.

Johnny Gato's head popped in from the door that led to the backyard and field. "Amigo! Bring that stuff with you and eat out here," he invited. He was six feet and 350 pounds of intimidation. His last name wasn't Gato, obviously, but we all called him that because of his resemblance to a fat, mean-eyed cat. Like his kids, he wore the cholo uniform of cutoff khakis, sneakers, and starched T-shirt. His arms were covered with tattoos, acquired in various correctional facilities, that depicted variations of La Adelita, the sombrero-wearing, pistol-packing female warrior icon of the Mexican Revolution. It was a look that worked for him.

"Did you give him any of the peppers?" he asked his wife, who shot him a concerned look.

"No, no," he said, "I've seen this loco eat. He's more hardcore than the kids." Rose plopped a few small green chilis into the stew and I followed Johnny out back.

Underneath the spreading branches of a gnarled and ancient plum tree that was giving up the last of its summer bounty sat a shiftless crew playing dominoes in the late-afternoon sun. By complicated bloodlines and affiliations, we had all known each other since junior high school here in the San Gabriel Valley. Shuffling the tiles was Backyard Bob, who ran a pot-selling enterprise out of his mom's backyard and who rarely left home. Waiting for their bones were the Sorendahl brothers—Tumblin' Dan and Little Gigantor. They were sturdy brawlers and good guys to have on your side if trouble broke out, even if they were usually the cause of it. Tumblin' Dan had been laying low lately. He had earned his nickname from a series of run-ins with the law, each more serious than the last. His downward plunge had been put on hold by a recent embrace of the New Testament, but the boredom of not running wild weighed heavily on him. We all expected a spectacular fuck-up from him any day now.

His younger brother, Little Gigantor, was short, squat, and as powerfully constructed as the space-age Japanese cartoon robot that inspired his name. He was capable of amazing feats of strength and sudden violence. I had been with him on a liquor run one night when we bumped into a spindly little cholo we knew from high school named Manny Saldana. Manny was dusted and wearing a bandanna so low on his brow he needed to tilt his head back to see. He noticed us and wanted a cigarette. "Got a frajo, *ese?*" he asked, and shifted his melon back even further. Quick as a rattlesnake strike, Little Gigantor grabbed him by the collar and belt, spun like an Olympic hammer-thrower, and tossed Manny right through the plate glass window of the liquor store.

"What the fuck did you do that for?" I shouted.

"Did you see the way that punk was looking at me? Nobody challenges me."

"Dude, he didn't challenge you. He was just trying to see from under that stupid rag of his. We need to get the fuck out of here!"

"Aw, don't be such a pussy, doper. I'm getting a twelve-pack first," he said, and calmly walked into the store, bought his beer, and threatened the owner not to call the cops. It must have worked because we made it back without seeing any flashing red and blue lights.

"None of you boys eating?" I asked as I sat down at the redwood picnic table that served as headquarters for this crew.

"We were until Johnny made us try those goddamn chilis," said Tumblin' Dan.

"You guys are a bunch of jotos," assessed Johnny.

I wrapped some birria in a tortilla and dunked it into the red broth. That first bite allowed some grease to coat my tongue—my theory was that it would provide a cushion for the chili. Then I grabbed one slender green stem from the stew, shook it dry, and bit in. Nothing.

"See? That's how you eat a chili!" said Johnny, who slapped me on the back. But as he did, I could feel a warmth build quickly to a fire. I took another bite of birria. That's the trick. A little bit of grease will cut through and dissipate the effects of even the hottest chili. Of course, you still have to deal with the intestinal aftermath, but you'll be able to amaze and impress your friends.

Little Gigantor passed me a sweating bottle of Lucky lager from a cooler while Backyard Bob finished spit-sealing a huge, guppy-shaped hand-rolled joint spiced with freebase cocaine. "Coca-puffs," he cautioned as he took the first hit and passed it on. I declined because I'd be driving home with contraband. Why open the door for a screw-up? I'd never seen the inside of a jail cell and I didn't want to start now.

Johnny Gato sat down next to me and asked, "So, what do you need?"

I pushed away the bowl of birria and told him, "Two grams of the tar and an eight ball of base."

"Two-fifty," he said. Same price as always. "Jorge will take care of it. He's back with the goats. Just go tell him."

This always made me uncomfortable. Jorge was the youngest of Johnny's kids. A fifth-grader. And unlike his two wayward brothers, he was a kid who had a love for reading, science, and school. Of the three boys, I was laying odds on Jorge to be the one who lived long enough to see his twenty-first birthday.

I shuffled across the dust and patchy crabgrass of the backyard and through a chain-link fence that opened onto about two acres of dirt and gravel divided by pens made of galvanized pipe. A couple of hogs wallowed in mud inside one of them. In the other, several small goats were mobbing a little black-haired kid in overalls who scattered feed on the ground.

"Hey, Jorge!" I called.

He knew why I was there. "What do you need?"

"Two and a ball," I told him.

"Just a minute," he said, and heaved the sack of feed outside the pen where it landed near my feet. The goats followed it and stared expectantly at me with their rectangular, demonic pupils.

"Can I feed 'em?" I called after him.

"Go ahead," he said.

I took a handful of pelleted feed from the sack and held it through the rails of the pen as the goats jostled for their share. Jorge had gone off to a rusty steel shed and was in there for about five minutes. When he came out, he was followed by a small flock of quacking white ducks. He handed me a neatly wrapped package. I looked inside; the goods were there. I didn't check closely. I had done business with this family for so long, there was no need. It was always a square deal. The ducks flowed around his feet and concentrated on bullying one of their own that had a malformed foot. It was twisted inward, but its owner didn't seem to be in any pain.

"What's with these ducks?" I asked.

"They don't like that one because he's different with the bad foot," was Jorge's explanation.

"So what do you do?" I wanted to know.

"We'll cook him, probably," was his deadpan reply. "You ever had duck?"

"Yeah. Not a big fan."

"Hey, you got a garden, right?"

"I do. A small one," I answered.

"Why don't you take him home with you? They make good pets . . . and they eat snails," he tossed in, trying to sweeten the deal.

Normally, I wouldn't have acted so impulsively, but Jorge was a good kid and I felt guilty about my part in exposing him to the darker side of adult behavior, so I said, "Tell your dad to get me a box."

Jorge grabbed the duck which sat calmly in his arms as he stroked him, and we walked back to the yard. "He says he'll take the duck, but he needs a box."

First things first, I handed over the cash to Johnny Gato, who pocketed it and went around the side of the house and came back with a cardboard box. He was poking holes in the side with a folding Buck knife.

"How far you going with him?" Johnny asked.

"To Marina del Rey."

"This should be okay then. But maybe we'd better tape the box."

"Nah, we can just weave the flaps. He won't be able to get out."

"Dude, they're pretty strong," cautioned Johnny Gato. But as we put the duck into the box, it settled right in and grew still. "Maybe you're right," he said, sounding awfully unsure.

But now that I had my dope and felt it weighing down my pocket like a two-ton anchor, I wanted to get home, get high, and put the week behind me. I was antsy and needed to go.

"All right, man, I'm gone. Tell Rose thanks for the birria. You boys stay out of trouble," I said. Everybody was used to my quick exits after I copped and they barely looked up from their game of dominoes.

"Just go through the side yard," said Johnny, and slapped my back again.

I walked around the house and into the front yard. I could see that Junior and Angel hadn't washed the truck. "Dude, you didn't give us enough time to even get started!" cried Angel.

"Don't worry. You still get paid . . . but next time I'm here, you give me a wash, right?" I said, and handed them each ten dollars.

"What's in the box?" Junior asked.

"One of Jorge's ducks."

"Good luck with that," said Angel, and made a mock Catholic blessing.

Smart-ass kids, but they were entertaining.

I should have shoved the duck into the bed of the truck, but I didn't want any accidental escapes, so I placed it on the bench seat instead. I walked around to the driver's side, got in, and drove in the direction of the freeway.

Everything was cool until I popped in a Captain Beyond cassette tape as I hit the 605 on-ramp. The duck didn't dig the noise and got agitated. Even after I turned off the music, it only got wilder.

"Shut up, Quacky!" I said as I knocked on the side of his cardboard prison with my fist. That was a mistake that only made the duck more determined to get out.

Once its beak pushed through the cardboard, followed by its head, the duck saw its new surroundings and didn't like them. A tremendous ruckus kicked up as it started flapping its wings, kicking its feet, and pitching a fit. This was a dangerous situation.

I kept looking in the rearview mirror to make sure I hadn't picked up the Highway Patrol.

There was no shoulder on the 605 on which to pull off. I took the transition to the eastbound 60 toward Los Angeles as the duck managed to get one twitching wing out of the box. I knew there was a shoulder dead ahead so I eased over and stopped. The duck did not, and kept up its fury of hisses, quacks, and near convulsive efforts to escape. I set the emergency blinkers, got out, and walked around to the passenger side. As I opened the door, Quacky finally burst from the box and shot toward the first avenue of escape it saw. All I could do was get out of the way. *Well, fuck him,* I thought. He could take his gimpy webbed foot and the rest of himself down to the San Gabriel River that lay right below us.

I tried for a minute to shoo the duck over the bridge and into the river, but realized I presented a target of suspicious activity to anyone passing by. Best to let nature sort it out. I got back in the truck and merged into traffic. I looked in the side mirror and saw Quacky take a short and panicked flight right into the front grille of a Mack MH Ultra-Liner. There he stayed, pinned to the chrome like a figurehead on an old-time seagoing freighter. As the rig passed, I gave a solemn wave to poor Quacky. I muttered a quick prayer of thanks that no cops had seen me and continued my drive back home to hearth and high.

There wasn't anything else I could do . . . except to make sure to always tell young Jorge that his duck was doing just fine, strutting in the garden, eating snails, and living the waterfowl high-life.

It made the kid happy.

T. Bogosian

ERIC BOGOSIAN wrote the plays and films *subUrbia* and *Talk Radio* (in which he also starred). He often acts on stage and screen, last appearing on Broadway in Donald Margulies's *Time Stands Still*. His most recent novel is *Perforated Heart*.

godhead
by eric bogosian

A strip of white light falls across a man seated in pitch-black, holding a microphone. He speaks in a slow, deliberate voice with a New Orleans accent.

The way I see it, it's a fucked-up world, it's not going anyplace, nothing good is happening to nobody, you think about it these days and nothing good is happening to anybody and if something good is happening to anybody, it's not happening to me, it's not happening to myself.

The way I see it, there be this man, some man sitting in a chair behind a desk in a room somewhere down in Washington, D.C. See, and this man, he be sitting there, he be thinking about what we should do about crime rate, air pollution, space race . . . Whatever this guy supposed to be thinking about. And this guy, he be sitting down there and thinking, and he be thinking about what's happenin' in *my* life . . . he be deciding on food stamps, and work programs, and the welfare, and the medical aid and the hospitals, whether I be working today. Makin' all kinds a decisions for me. He be worrying about how I spen' my time! Then he lean back in his ol' leather chair, he start thinkin' about da nukular bomb. He be deciding whether I live or die today! Nobody makes those decisions for me. That's for me to decide. I decide when I want to get up in da mornin', when I want to work, when I want to play, when I want to do shit! That's my decision. I'm free. When I die,

that's up to God or somebody, not some guy sittin' in a chair.
See?

I just wanna live my life. I don't hurt nobody. I turn on the TV
set, I see the way everybody be livin'. With their swimming pools
and their cars and houses and living room with the fireplace in
the living room . . . There's a fire burnin' in the fireplace, a rug in
front of the fireplace. Lady. She be lyin' on the rug, evenin' gown
on . . . jewelry, sippin' a glass o' cognac . . . She be lookin' in the
fire, watchin' the branches burnin' up . . . thinkin' about things.
Thinkin'. Thinkin'. What's she thinkin' about?

I jus' wanna live my life. I don't ask for too much. I got my room
. . . got my bed . . . my chair, my TV set . . . my needle, my spoon,
I'm okay, see? I'm okay.

I get up in the mornin', I combs my hair, I wash my face. I go
out. I hustle me up a couple a bags a D . . . new works if I can find
it.

I take it back to my room, I take that hairwon. I cook it up good in
the spoon there . . . I fill my needle up.

Then I tie my arm [*caressing his arm*] . . . I use a necktie, it's a
pretty necktie, my daughter gave it to me . . . Tie it tight . . . pump
my arm . . . then I take the needle, I stick it up into my arm . . . find
the hit . . . blood . . .

Then I undoes the tie . . . I push down on that needle [*pause*] . . .
and I got everything any man ever had in the history of this world.
Jus' sittin' in my chair . . .

[*Voice lower*] I got love and I got blood. That's all you need. I can feel that blood all going up behind my knees, into my stomach, in my mouth I can taste it . . . Sometimes it goes back down my arm, come out the hole . . . stain my shirt . . .

I know . . . I know there's people who can't handle it. Maybe I can't handle it. Maybe I'm gonna get all strung out and fucked up . . .

. . . Even if I get all strung out and fucked up, don't make no difference to me . . . Even I get that hepatitis and the broken veins and the ulcers on my arms . . . addicted. Don't make no difference to me. I was all strung out and fucked up in the first place . . .

Life is a monkey on my back. You ride aroun' in your car, swim in your warm swimming pool. Watch the fire . . . I don't mind. I don't mind at all. Just let me have my taste. Have my peace. Jus' leave me be. Jus' leave me be.

[*Turns in toward the dark*]

Jervey Tervalon

JERVEY TERVALON is the author of
several books, including the novels
Serving Monster and *Dead Above
Ground*, and coeditor, with Gary Phillips, of *The Cocaine Chronicles*. He is
currently directing the Literature for
Life project. Literature for Life is a
new kind of forum: part literary magazine, part educational resource center,
part salon. Writers, journalists, artists,
and educators come together to ignite
young minds while celebrating the di-
versity of Los Angeles.

gift horse
by jervey tervalon

eroin didn't blow up in the neighborhood, not like red devils and weed. We held out for rock cocaine to go insane and then we burned shit up until there was nothing left to burn. But heroin did make a run at us—one fine spring the white devil drug appeared with the help of a banged-up Nova turning the corner, tires squealing as it fishtailed along Second Avenue and the fool at the wheel with the big afro flung a brown bag out the window, and then a roller took the turn *French Connection*–style, and should have caught that knucklehead in the Nova before the next corner, but he drove like a nigga who had nothing to lose but doing life.

I sat on the porch with Sidney sitting across from me with his nice-ass leather jacket on, sipping a Mickey's Big Mouth; ignoring my comic book–reading pootbutt ass like I was invisible. I knew he was waiting on my brother to make a run for weed or red devils or whatever. I wasn't surprised that he didn't have a spare word for me, and I didn't mind because I hated motherfucking Sidney. He wasn't obvious about being a dick to me except for the time he broke my finger because I made the mistake of trying to save a seat on the couch. Should have figured that he'd ignore my hand and flop down, and yeah, he broke my little finger and I knew he didn't care even with all those fake apologies to my mama. Sidney and my brother just kept watching the Rams while I had to go to the hospital to get a splint. He was my nemesis, though it wasn't much of a contest with me being fifteen. I couldn't hang with just throwing a punch at his smug face. Jude, my brother, didn't have a high opinion of me, saying I started shit and pissed people off so I shouldn't be expecting him to have my back.

The roar of the big engine of the roller drifted away and my attention turned to the brown bag at the curb. Sidney gave me a sinister grin and sauntered over to it, hiked his pressed jeans a bit, glanced about as though he was daring the police to roll up on him, and nonchalantly picked it up and returned to the porch. He examined the contents of the paper bag; about a hundred little baggies with powder inside.

"What's that?" I asked.

"What's what?"

"What's inside the baggies?"

"Nothing," he said, and walked away like he was on top of the world, and Sydney always looked like he was on top of the world.

Though I hated him, I couldn't help admiring his style. He didn't fight, or carry a gun, he never engaged in open hostility. He won a lofty position in the neighborhood because of his ability to get along with anybody who was worth anything to get along with, and his ability to make everybody trust him completely, except for me, and I didn't count. Once they trusted him, Sydney would get in on what was good, and leave the rest. He had a great talent that made everything work; he talked better than anybody and he knew everything. He knew how to sell drugs in such a way that he never seemed to be dealing, and thus, he had an understated pimp-splendor thing happening. He rode a tricked-out metallic blue chopper with an airbrushed image of a flying saucer hovering over Los Angeles on the gas tank; and this was before his heroin windfall.

Sidney's dealings were all undercover except for Leslie, the sheboonie up the street who wore curlers, slippers, and a matching bathrobe. Youngsters thought she was an ugly-ass woman until you saw her up close and you realized she was a dude who wanted to be an ugly-ass woman. He would show up at Sidney's door, which Sidney told him not to do—who really wanted a sheboonie coming to the house?—early in the morning to get some stepped-on baggies of powder, because even though I didn't know a thing about heroin, I knew that Sidney would toss in all kinds of shit to stretch it and keep that money flowing. Leslie shared her heroin with Norman Zerka, the dude who was so light-skinned that even with his lame afro, no one was sure if he was black or not. Norman took to living with Leslie because he liked that heroin high and he even left Bernadette, the woman who was supposed to be his wife, cause she couldn't afford to keep him stoned like he wanted to be. I didn't mind Norman cause he was polite, and didn't break my fingers. He always had hot shit to sell, nice bikes he would jack at UCLA from the white boys, but people who knew better wouldn't buy his magic television, like my mother did. "I can't pass up this great deal," she said, and Norman, polite as always, brought back her change for a ten, and sold her this really new-looking, all-white and shiny, tiny television that my mama placed in the kitchen so we could eat dinner and watch Alfred Hitchcock movies. But Norman wasn't really selling the hot television, he was renting it. Within a week, he sneaked in the house and stole the television back and sold it to somebody else.

Sidney, who had already been the king of the neighborhood, and now seemed to be king of the world, lived exactly like he had lived before, but with more aplomb. One sunny afternoon, he was holding court under the big pine tree. He sat there on the fire hydrant, a six-pack near his feet, with most of the fellas in the neighborhood laughing at his jokes and drinking his Heinekens.

"I don't know about you knuckleheads, but I'm going on vacation."

"Where to?" Henry-Hank, the neighborhood's handsome idiot asked.

"Amsterdam."

Everyone nodded as though they knew where and what he was talking about.

"You can smoke weed in coffee houses. Police don't fuck with you and the women are cool and don't mind taking care of you."

Who could argue with Sidney's success? He had a plan, and the funds to pull it off. I imagined myself kicking it with beautiful blond women; then I shook that nonsense out of my head. That was a mistake; suddenly they noticed me, particularly my brother. Usually, he was too high to care.

"What you doing here! Take your ass home. Hang out with Googie, somebody your own age," he said.

I shrugged and walked away, making a slow meandering circle and ending up exactly where I had been in the first place. Then, as if by instinct, the fellas uprooted themselves and ended up at my house. As long as my mother was at work, the fellas—an ever-changing number of brothers who would hold sway on the lawn or in the living room, smoking weed and watching sports, or drinking beer on the beautiful Saint Augustine grass that my dad had planted before he and my mother divorced—kicked it at our house. I listened to them argue about the Lakers and the Rams, and I even heard an argument about whether or not H.P. Lovecraft was racist. Then Henry-Hank appeared, agitated as Lassie with an urgent message.

"Sidney is passed out, facedown in the ivy in front of his house."

Weed and beer might make you mellow, but everybody was now alert and hustling to Sidney's house.

Henry-Hank was right; there was Sidney, facedown in the ivy, looking stylishly dead.

Jude squatted next to him and shook his shoulder.

"He ain't dead, he's passed out."

Jude and Lil' Dell lifted him up and walked him up the steps and knocked on the door.

Mrs. Green opened the door and for a moment was shocked, but then she looked so angry that it didn't seem she cared that her son was right there, drooling, head lolling about.

"What did you do to my boy? Did y'all get him drunk?"

Jude, never too quick on the uptake, just shook his head. "I didn't get him drunk."

"Well, he's drunk; he's even pissed on himself."

"Like I said, we didn't get him drunk."

She opened the door and Jude and Lil' Dell dragged him to the couch and tossed him on it.

Sidney wasn't much good for anything after that. Every day he was fucked up, passed out on somebody's lawn or porch, or maybe unconscious in the backseat of somebody's car. I got to wondering about heroin then, how somebody as social as Sidney would decide to leave what he was behind, and become something else altogether: a straight dope fiend. He stopped selling weed and red devils and he certainly wasn't going to be selling his stash of heroin; he was running through it like Halloween candy.

Mrs. Green came home from work one day to see all the furniture turned upside down and ripped apart; nothing was stolen as far as she knew other than the cute little television Sidney had picked up for her from Norman Zerka. But Sidney knew what had been stolen—the basis for his economic existence and his happiness—and he was right out on the street looking for it.

Sidney, possessed of super ghetto cool, walked around the neighborhood in such casual good humor that if you didn't know him you'd think he was on top of the world. And despite Sidney having been robbed of his livelihood, his mother kept him in spending money, a whole lot of spending money, because she made serious cash running the Department of Recreation and Parks for the city of Los Angeles. Sidney began buying beer for anyone who wandered onto the corner under the big tree. He let Henry-Hank have a Heineken, even Googie. I could have had one myself, but I didn't like the taste of beer and didn't want to be beholden to Sidney. All the generosity was not how I knew Sidney to be. It didn't take a genius to figure out why; he needed information.

It almost looked normal around the neighborhood with Sidney back on his throne passing the joint around like how it used to be done before the heroin descended upon Second Avenue. He just took it when the running joke got to be asking him if he had any red devils, and he'd just shrug, smile broadly, open his arms, and say, "Wish I did," or, "Red devils, me?"

A week or so later, Sidney getting ripped off was history, and he was ready to make his move. Googie told me Sidney had showed up at his window, rapping on it just loud enough not to wake his daddy. In a few minutes Googie stumbled outside buckling up his overalls.

"What it be like?" Googie asked, trying to sound hard and hiding how excited he was to have Sidney, even in his fallen state, blessing his house with his presence. Sidney sat on a wooden picnic table, near the patio, smoking a square. He offered Googie one, and Googie wanted it, knowing that he couldn't handle it, even a menthol. He reached for it and Sidney yanked it away and laughed.

"Does your daddy let you smoke now?"

"I don't know. Maybe I should ask your mama," Googie said, and headed back into the house.

"Hey, Googie, don't go away mad. I got a money-making proposition that I know you're going to like."

"What's that?"

"I want you to hang out at Leslie's house. She likes to play *Monopoly* and shit. Get into one of them games. Keep your eyes open to where Norman Zerka might have the stash. I'm sure that's the fool who ripped me off."

Whatever Googie felt before, the giddiness of making money, the pride at having Sidney cajoling him to do a favor—all of that vanished. In its place was a Fatburger, pink at the center with a runny egg on top, queasiness.

"You want me to kick it with a sheboonie?"

Sidney shrugged. "I ain't asking you to be one."

"If you think they got it, why don't you just strong arm them and get it back?"

Sidney drew on his cigarette. "Norman Zerka, no problem. Leslie might be a sheboonie, but she can straight beat the shit out of you and she's strapped and knows how to shoot. Once, Lil' Dil tried to steal her purse, and she said, *You made me jump out of my femaleness, back into my maleness, and now I'm gonna kick your ass!* And she did, beat his ass south and north. She was a paratrooper when she was living as a man. She went through jump school with Jimi Hendrix."

"Jimi who?" Googie didn't hear any of that; what he heard was what Sidney wanted him to do. It wasn't something he wanted to do—chance getting beat down by a sheboonie for the world to know. *Fuck that!* "I ain't cool with this. Get somebody else to do it," Googie said, and turned around again.

"I'll give you forty dollars."

Googie pivoted like Kareem doing an up-and-under. "Fifty, up front."

"Aw, I see you learning how to negotiate," Sidney said, and pulled two twenties and a ten off a roll and flicked them to Googie; floating weirdly, they reached his hand.

"You help me get my shit back and I'll give you twice that much."

"What? A hundred fifty?"

Sidney squinted. "Don't they teach you anything at school? You knuckleheads can't multiply."

"Shit, I can multiply. Ask me eight times eight! It's sixty-four! How about six times six? It's thirty-six!"

"What's nine times eight?" Sidney asked.

"Ninety-eight," Googie responded, with the confidence of a pathologically bad guesser.

Sidney shook his head. "Yep, your ass really knocked that out of the park."

Googie wanted to say *Fuck you,* but he felt the crisp bills in hand and instead watched Sidney walk away into the darkness of the alley.

"Naw, man, I'm not cool with that," I said.

"I'll give you five dollars."

"Your ass just said Sidney gave you fifty. I'm gonna be hanging with you at the sheboonie's house and I'm getting one-tenth of what you got for doing the same thing!"

I sipped my Strawberry Crush shaking my head, waiting for Googie to come back at me. I knew something was up since he'd knocked on my door with a drink and chili Fritos for me. I knew I should have asked why he was bringing me something, cause usually his ass would be trying to bum a quarter off of me. I sat on the porch while he stretched out on the lawn like the fellas did, looking as rakish as a fat boy can look.

"I ain't kicking it with a sheboonie. Nope. I ain't rolling with you so you can find Sidney's lost heroin. I'm going to college. I ain't doing knucklehead shit like that."

Googie snorted. "Look, if you never do anything, how's that

living? You always talking about tomorrow—what if you get hit by a car and die? Then all the shit you could have been doing, you didn't do, and what did that get you? You just missed out."

"You saying I need to kick it with a sheboonie before I die? That don't make no kind of sense."

Googie's face trembled and he looked genuinely hurt, like a huge baby about ready to cry. I knew he was going to come back pleading something ridiculous. "Aw . . . come on . . . I thought we were ace-boon-coon pardners. We go way back, don't leave me hanging, I wouldn't do that—shit, you remember when I saved your ass at that dance at Forshay?"

He finished but I knew that it wouldn't stop, that he would keep at me until I either slapped him or gave in.

"If we going to go, let's roll. I ain't going over there at night. Don't know what kind of shit goes down over there at night."

We walked the two blocks in silence. I hung back when he got to the door, hoping that no one would notice me. After he knocked, it seemed like nobody was home, which was cool. Then the door swung open so abruptly that Googie covered his head and ran. There was Leslie in an aquamarine bathrobe with matching curlers and fuzzy slippers, wearing lots of makeup on her strangely girlish face.

"Hey, Leslie."

"What are you doing here?" she asked in a voice that sounded sort of womanly and sort of mannish, but weirder than usual because she was slurring her words.

"You want to play *Monopoly*? I heard you're good. Me and Garvy like to play."

It seemed like it took a second for the words to register in Leslie's buzzing brain, but she nodded.

"Yeah, I love me some *Monopoly*, but Norman is always too fucked up for board games," Leslie said, and waved for Googie to follow. Her robe opened revealing smooth, brown, muscular legs that sent Googie into a panic. He looked about for me but I waved to him from the sidewalk.

"Where's your friend going?"

"I think his mama called him. He's chicken-shit like that," Googie said, and before I could run he was already on me, and grabbed my arm in a sweaty, iron grip and dragged me through the open door into Leslie's house. We smelled sweet, cloying incense and strange music playing, singing and shit, and trumpets.

"You don't like Billie Holiday?" Leslie asked.

"Who's he?" Googie replied.

"Sit down," Leslie said, ignoring the question, and handed Googie the game. "Do you want something to drink?"

"You got a joint?" Googie asked.

Leslie laughed. "We do not do drugs in my house." She laughed again and coughed. "You set up the board and I'll get us something to drink."

Soon as she left the room, Googie stood. "You set up the game, I'm gonna check shit out."

Googie casually searched the immaculate house—all the furniture covered in plastic with plastic runners protecting the carpets—as though the heroin would spring up and land in his hand.

"You wasting your time. Let's bail," I said, but Googie just got on his knees to look under the couch.

Leslie returned with 7UPs on a lacquered tray.

"I hope you boys are good. I hate to waste my time with rookies."

Googie snorted, "I kick much butt at *Monopoly*."

They began to play and we both saw just how sprung Leslie was for the game. She rolled dice and skipped her silver dog about the board, laughing too hard, even drooling a little. Googie glanced at me a few times and I shook my head. I had no idea of how this was going to go; how this was going to work out in his favor. All I wanted was to get the fuck out of there, especially after Leslie started getting all flirty and taking turns tickling us. Homechick wasn't going away and all she wanted to do was kick our asses at *Monopoly*, and she was. Well anyway, Googie was up fifty dollars on Sidney and that wasn't bad, but I wasn't up on Sidney, not a dime.

"I'm going to use the bathroom for a bit," she said after a while, looking kind of irritated.

"Let's bail," I said to Googie, but he shook me off and started searching again. I tried the front door but it was deadlocked. Googie returned to the table trying to figure out a plan, but soon we both noticed Leslie hadn't returned.

Finally, we got tired of waiting and found her passed out on the floor of the bathroom, needle in arm, like Sidney when he had that shit. With her robe twisted around her waist, we saw her weird-looking leather panties with rhinestones.

"Yeah, you know, freaks got to be freaky." Googie shrugged and went about the house looking for the heroin, and wondering where Norman Zerka might be. I hung by the door, but Googie called to me. He found Norman in the master bedroom, passed out across the narrow bed, with his head hanging on one side and his feet the other, pale like the sun never shined on his white ass, even if he had a big fucking 'fro, and just about naked except he wore the same leather panties as Leslie, like that bald chick with the whip on the Ohio Players cover. Googie looked over the room but didn't find anything except for empty baggies with white residue sticking to them. Sidney was shit out of luck.

"These muthafucking weirdos ran through the heroin faster than Sidney thought they would. Dope fiends," Googie said, as we shoved each other trying to climb through the bedroom window first. I won, but then Googie noticed the little white television near Norman Zerka's head. He snagged it and finished climbing through the window.

"Hey, man, that's my mama's television."

"Yeah, how it get in there?" he asked, and handed it to me.

"Norman stole it from her after selling it."

"Yeah, well, now we stole it back."

We walked home, Googie talking about what he'd tell Sidney; maybe that the dope was still there and exactly where to find it for another twenty . . . fuck that, another fifty. A nigga needed to get paid these days; times were tough in 1972.

"Yeah, but I didn't get shit except the chili Fritos you brought me."

"What's that in your hands? You got your mama's little television back. It all worked out."

Or so it seemed. A few days later, a VW Bug driven by Norman Zerka stopped in front of Googie's house as he was watering the lawn, and Leslie sprang out still in curlers, bathrobe, and slippers, and caught Googie with an overhand right and dropped him flat on his back with the hose shooting wild around him. He came over and told me this, with his eye swollen and purple, looking around like he might get clocked again.

Me, I stayed inside and watched that little white television until I heard that Leslie and Norman had left town after robbing the Security Pacific Bank on Jefferson. On the corner, I heard Sidney, who had found himself another stash of red devils and was back to dealing—though the heroin was gone for good—say that they were living like Bonnie and Clyde, robbing banks up and down the coast.

"Romantic motherfuckers," he said, while lighting another joint.

PART III
GETTING A GRIP

mbgarcia

LYDIA LUNCH is always rebelling against the hypocrisy of America's picture-perfect Hollywood image, which it exports through television, films, and commercial music. Her art has always revealed the down-and-dirty side of the all-too-real American underbelly. She is the author of *Paradoxia* and *Will Work for Drugs*, both published by Akashic Books.

ghost town
by lydia lunch

Never answer the door at five forty-five a.m. on a Sunday morning. Either somebody's too high, somebody has just died, or somebody has just arrived who wants to kill you.

I drove 2,777 miles just to get away from him. From the Hudson River to the Pacific Ocean and it still wasn't far enough away.

A low-brow dirt bike racer from Topanga Canyon who was hell bent on a cross-country creepy crawl had pulled up, swept me off my feet, threw me into the front seat of his dilapidated pickup truck, and headed west, gunning it at full speed until we hit the "Slum by the Sea": Venice, California. He said he was on a rescue mission to save me. That he had been sent east by a mutual friend who was concerned for my safety after hearing stories about hospital stays and late-night 911 calls. Great, the sociopath abducts the schizophrenic out from under the psychopath in a late-night snatch-and-grab.

Something had to give because I was at the breaking point. The burned-out buildings, uncollected garbage, broken streetlights, endless break-ins, chronic shake-downs, and general havoc wreaked on the streets of New York City's Lower East Side, circa 1979, were a cake walk next to the damage being done in my own apartment. The alcoholic pill-popping Irish construction worker who I'd been holed up with for the past few months was getting mean.

Jealous, cruel, and beautiful. An irresistible combination of mania and machismo. By day he'd play iron man. Up at the crack of six sporting boxers and a wife beater, Lucky Strike behind his left ear, throwing sandwiches in a bag, filling a thermos with black coffee and Irish whiskey, singing a silly rockabilly song, a sly smile dancing under sleepy green eyes, happy to just be alive as he kissed me goodbye and disappeared out the door. Everything hunky dory until the sun went down, the knives came out, and he stumbled back from the bar half plastered after banging steel girders together for another eight-hour stretch. The first thirty minutes were always filled with bliss. We'd kiss, fall back onto the bed, and batter our bodies into each other until one of us started bleeding. Then batter away a little more after swallowing a couple of Seconals with a back of Johnnie Walker Black.

And that, my friend, is where the trouble came in. Loverboy loved his booze more than he loved me, and in return the booze hated my fucking guts. Probably because I refused to play slave to it and only used it as a lubricant for pharmaceuticals. A treacherous combination which triggered the bitch that provoked the bastard and resulted in a fucking that felt more like fighting, and the fighting would flare up over some petty jealous bullshit usually concerning who I was or wasn't fucking while the dick was dry humping rebar over at the construction site breaking his goddamn ass, and on and on until the garbage trucks rumbled on their early-morning run and he'd pass out for two or three hours, waking up refreshed and ready to greet the day as if nothing had happened, with a "Good mornin', darlin', care for a cup of joe?" as he smiled whistling through his wolfen teeth.

If Brando did *Badlands* while stoned on barbiturates and booze . . . well . . . you get the picture. The one that played in rerun like a bad Turner Classic that our TV eyes got stuck on night after night for weeks on end.

Yeah . . . yeah, and so it went, so wrapped up in torturing the shit out of each other that the world outside our ghetto hidey-hole was a squirrel-gray cotton-candy haze that we were too fucked up to realize didn't muffle the screeching or screams forever leaching out the windows and reverberating into the street below, and if anyone was tuned in they probably could have heard us all the way to the West Coast. Our psychosis getting carried away like radio frequencies emitting toxic shock waves into the ionosphere. I needed to get the fuck out. And fast.

I spiked his drink, packed a bag, left a note, and climbed into the front seat of the grease monkey's pickup truck, which was parked on the corner of 12th Street and Avenue B where he had been waiting for me to show up for thirty-six hours so that he could "save me."

Four days later we landed in Ghost Town. A grungy biker and his nubile Las Vegas bride, a bitchy witch dressed in black casting voodoo glances at the neighboring hood rats. They probably feared the look on my face more than I feared what they hid in their waistbands. The gangbangers left me alone. But the ghosts wouldn't. They were everywhere.

Some people are afraid of ghosts and what lurks in the dark. Terrified of the possibility of the unseen violators sneaking around within its murky shadows. But true evil is arrogant by nature and doesn't always bother to hide its intentions under the cloak of night. It gathers even more power by flaunting its vigor in the unadulterated glare of a perpetual high noon.

Los Angeles. A beautifully hideous sprawl. Stretching like an ever-expanding virus of sick contagion under the relentless sun as hot Devil Winds blow down from the mountains scorching the landscape. The promise of an endless summer shattered by gunshots and sirens, helicopters and hospital beds.

In 1980, Los Angeles County reported 51,448 violent crimes, 27,987 cases of aggravated assault, and 1,011 murders. The Sunset

Strip Slayers preyed on young women, ex-lovers, and each other's twisted fantasies as they played out depraved rituals with the decapitated head of one of their victims. Welcome to Hollywood, asshole, where anything is possible.

New York City may have been bankrupt, decrepit, and suffering from the final stages of rigor mortis, but the California Dream was a waking nightmare of dead-end streets ripe with bloated corpses where bad beat poets, dope-sick singers, cracked actors, and petty criminals were all praying to a burned-out star on the sidewalk. All betting on a chance encounter which would flip the script in the lousy late-night made-for-TV movie of their wasted lives. I guess I was no different.

Everything was fucking peaches and whipped cream for the first six months of matrimonial bliss, until the lunatic who rescued me from the maniac took a bad spill on the Pacific Coast Highway and ended up in a coma with two charges of vehicular manslaughter on his rap sheet and a letter at the side of his bed which threatened eviction from our Venice crash pad. I went home and started to pack my bags.

In the same way that a shark can smell blood, a junkie's sixth sense alerts him to any possible random opportunity that may arise in which he can hustle, steal, score, or move in on and take advantage of an unsuspecting mark's benevolent disposition, a friend's temporary weakness, or an ex-girlfriend's first night alone in a near-empty house. It was five forty-five a.m. on a Sunday morning when the doorbell blasted and shattered what was left of my nerves.

Impeccable timing. The bastard always had it. Even down to the way he smoked a cigarette as I opened the door. Holding it down between thumb and index, deep drag, a small puckering sound as he pulled it away from his lips, staring straight into my eyes before he flung the butt into the wet grass. A sadistic smirk creeping in and cracking up the left side of his face. His husky whisper, hypnotic and irresistible . . . "Good mornin', darlin', spare a cup of joe for the road warrior?"

The Irish construction worker. One hundred and ninety-three days later and a distance of almost three thousand miles meant nothing to the madman convinced he could walk right in whistling Dixie and simply steal me back. Don't laugh. I let him in.

With the cunning of a snake that can sense whether or not you're about to attack it first, a schizophrenic can detect the atmospheric flux in a psychopath's gravitational force field. Something inside him had shifted slightly since I last saw him. His magnetism seemed less manic. More mesmerizing. Fucking hypnotic.

"I'm off the sauce." He grinned, head cocked, a quick wink, and one hand pulling out a small white packet of what I assumed to be coke from the inside pocket of his leather jacket.

"And on the skids," I quipped, turning toward the bedroom door, which he quickly pinned me against.

"Don't walk away from me. Not again. I'll leave. I will. Let's just smoke a cigarette, do a little line, and if you want me to leave, I'll go. Promise. I just want to look at you for another five minutes."

He slowly backed away, pulling me with him, easing me onto the couch as he got down on one knee, like a love-struck delinquent, sucking air between his teeth and whispering, "Damn . . . You are a luscious little bitch . . ." He opened the packet, spilled out some powder, rolled a note, and handed it to me with a sweet smile that concealed his deceit and treachery. I had to get the hell away from him or I'd be suckered right back in.

"I need coffee . . ." I lied. I needed to split. "I'll put some on."

I slithered off the couch, fake smile planted on my lips, and suggested he chop out a few fatties. I'd be right back. I planned on spiking him again. I still had half a dozen Seconals left over from our binge in New York. I quit that shit when I quit him. Make it strong enough and black enough and he'll never know what hit him. I'd grab a bag, write a note, and leave both the psychopath and the sociopath where they belonged. In fucking comas.

I could hear the methodical rhythm of razor on glass. A deep snotty inhalation as he cleared his throat. A quick snort followed by a soft chuckle. Why the hell was that motherfucker chuckling? It prickled the hair on the back of my neck.

I poured the coffee, emptied the red devils into the muddy brew, and prayed for deliverance while slinking over to the couch. He handed me the note, I gave him the cup. I just wanted to get this over with.

He swigged the coffee like he was chugging beer. Old habits and all that shit. I snorted a fat blast of what I thought was coke and immediately fell ass backward, landing on the bag I had been packing earlier that night and hitting my head on the edge of the table. It knocked me out.

I woke up bloody and puking. Projectile vomiting. All over the table. All over his dope. All over his boots. Down the front of my slip. Great heaving waves of gelatinous funk shooting out of my mouth and nose. Thick rich fists of sour phlegm cascading in golden arcs all over the room. I pissed myself and started to laugh. The bastard had almost killed me. I had never done heroin. He knew that. It just wasn't my trip. I wasn't looking for nirvana, a velvet womb, or a soft euphoric haze of interstellar space to melt into. I dug the shit that jacked up the irritation level. Barbs and booze. Coke or speed. LSD. Something that accelerated my already jacked-up metabolism. I wasn't interested in slowing shit down. Smoothing it out. Softening the edges. I wanted to keep the edges rough, like the one I had just hit my head against. The one that had finally banged a bit of sense into my thick nugget. Never, under any circumstances, will I ever again answer the door at five forty-five a.m. on a Sunday morning.

Deedee Cheriel

JOHN ALBERT grew up in Los Angeles. As a teenager he cofounded the seminal "death rock" band Christian Death, then played drums for a stint in Bad Religion. He has written for the *Los Angeles Times*, *LA Weekly*, *Fader*, and *Hustler*, winning national awards for sports and music writing. His essays have appeared in numerous national anthologies. The film rights to his book *Wrecking Crew*, which chronicles the true-life adventures of an amateur baseball team comprised of drug addicts, transvestites, and washed-up rock stars, have been optioned by the actor Philip Seymour Hoffman.

the monster
by john albert

I wake up to the sound of surf with sand in my mouth. After a few seconds I manage to sit up and focus on my surroundings. I'm underneath a lifeguard stand on a beach just south of the Los Angeles airport. It is dawn so I instinctively check the water. It's smooth as glass with perfectly shaped peaks rolling in. I am wearing a thrift-store suit and suede Hush Puppies. Not exactly the latest in surf wear. As I trudge toward the parking lot, a group of long-haired surfers carrying short dayglo boards approach. They get closer and recognize me.

"Danny, what's up? It's good to see you. Welcome back, dude!"

I force a smile feeling like a has-been. A week ago I turned twenty years old.

Half an hour later I'm nearby in the residential neighborhood I grew up in. It's typical Southern California suburbia: flat houses, dying lawns, and campers. I walk to my parents' front door, reach under a fern, and grab their spare key.

Inside the house is quiet. It's just past dawn and my parents are still asleep. I walk into the kitchen and pour myself a glass of milk. My old cat appears on the counter purring loudly and I scratch his head. I walk down the hallway into my old room and sit on the bed which seems surprisingly small. I remember how safe I felt as a kid and want so badly to go back in time. I don't notice my mom standing in the doorway until she speaks.

"You're home."

I nod and fight an urge to start crying.

"Do you want some breakfast?"

I say yes, but not because I'm hungry. The pills are wearing off and I am starting to feel nauseous. But eating breakfast in my parents' kitchen seems like it might somehow bring me back to a world less horrific than where I have just been. "I'm gonna wash up," I tell her. "I'll be out in a minute."

In the bathroom I glance in the mirror. My pupils are getting huge from withdrawal. I notice something dark in my hair, pick it out, and inspect it. It is congealed blood. I drop it in the toilet and the water clouds red. I immediately slide a small plastic bottle from my pocket, shake out the two remaining pills, and dump them in as well. I am done.

A day before, I'm wearing the same suit and feeling much better. I'm sitting on the fold-out bed in my small apartment with five hundred dollars on the coffee table in front of me. That afternoon, my rich young girlfriend left for the desert with a group of our friends. The plan is for me to join them later that night after scoring the necessary narcotics. Ordinarily, with cash in hand, this would take a couple of hours at the most. This afternoon the task is made far more difficult by a citywide police crackdown.

In the last month there has been a series of home invasion–style robberies in the wealthy Westside neighborhoods. Victims have been violently assaulted in their beautiful homes, sometimes even sexually, their valuables stolen. What really set the world on tilt was when the perpetrators busted into the home of world-famous actress Betty Le Mat. The grand dame is well into her seventies, her classic roles distant history, but she remains a beloved figure and cultural icon. Beyond merely robbing the regal old lady, rumors have been circulating about a particularly gruesome sexual assault involving her cherished "best actress" Oscar statuette.

In response, the entire police force is prowling the streets day and night in a collective rage, clamping down on anything remotely illegal. They are making arrests by the thousands, packing the already overflowing jails in an effort to gain information from anyone willing to talk in exchange for freedom. As a direct result, every respectable drug dealer has either been arrested or has decided to visit out-of-town relatives.

So here I am—money in hand, tapping my feet, racked with nervous twitchy energy, and working the phones. I've been calling everyone I can think of who might know where to score. So far it's been a unanimous chorus of no's accompanied by a lot of sniffling noses and junkie whining. To combat my own withdrawals I've been swallowing some codeine pills I stole from my dad's medicine cabinet last time I visited my dear parents. While not in full dry heave withdrawals, I'm not exactly comfortable either. That said, the pile of cash in front of me makes the world a more hopeful place.

My persistence pays off and I get a serious lead. A once famous singer of a now defunct hair metal band says he scored some overpriced Persian the night before. The deal was facilitated by an older record executive turned cokehead we both casually know. Without saying goodbye I hang up and make the call.

Twenty minutes later I'm getting buzzed into a large art deco apartment building just off a seedy stretch of Hollywood Boulevard. Not waiting for the elevator I scurry up several flights of stairs and arrive at a door where a shirtless tanned man in his sixties named Ron lets me into a spacious apartment. Behind him stands a far-too-thin, forty-something woman named Ann whose ravaged beauty perfectly mimics the fading grandeur of the building. The two have obviously been on a cocaine binge. Ron is sweating and talking a mile a minute about music. He used to be a big shot in the business and keeps dropping names of new bands he thinks will impress me. I really don't give a shit. This kind of chatter is strictly a coke thing and I find it annoying.

The buzzer finally rings; the connection has arrived. He's a thin Persian kid in his early twenties, dressed kind of new wave. He appears as jittery as the other two, avoiding eye contact and laughing at nothing in particular. The three seem to know one another so I hand over my cash. I will wait there while he gets the dope and brings it back. It's something I would never do on the street, but a mutual friend's apartment is another story.

He doesn't come back. Initially I tell myself he's just late like every other power-drunk dealer. I eventually persuade Ron to call him but there's no answer. To placate me Ron and his girl offer some cocaine. I know it will only exasperate my withdrawals, but I still say yes. I just need drugs. After the rush it makes things worse. No surprise. After several more hits I am crawling out of my skin and so desperate for heroin that I feel like I can kill.

"Fuck you guys!" I suddenly roar at Ron and his girlfriend. "You were in on this the whole time. *You're* fucking responsible."

"We had no idea!" Ron's girlfriend yells back, with shrill indignation. "See what happens when you get involved with junkies? Just get the fuck out of here!"

I skulk toward the door, stop, and turn back. "You're responsible" I repeat, pointing an accusatory finger at them both. "This isn't over!"

I step outside and the sun is already up. As I walk back to my car I am absolutely seething. The whole thing is made immensely worse by my increasing need for heroin. The world now appears too bright and everything looks ugly. With the cash gone my options are severely limited and I point the car once again for my parents' house. Maybe my dad has left his pain pills in their usual hiding place. Forty minutes later I walk out of their house with the remaining four pills. It should last me a few hours at best. I drive and try to think of who might still be willing to loan me some money. It's a nonexistent list. I decide to get some alcohol to take the edge off and pull into a liquor store. As I climb out I see a familiar figure leaning against the wall, lighting a cigarette, and I get an idea I will come to regret.

Troy Galt is the most frightening person I know. He is enormous, well over six-foot-five, and built like a professional football player, which is what he would have become if he hadn't gone off to war. He has a thick beard that makes him look far older than his twenty-two years and he is undeniably insane. Not the kind of crazy where he directs traffic with a potted plant on his head—the kind where he will cripple someone and then calmly wash the blood from his hands. If that isn't enough, Troy has a metal plate in his head. He took a bullet to the dome while butchering some enemy combatants in close quarters. It seems the army approved of the deed but not his methods—which reportedly involved a decapitation. He was awarded an honorable discharge and came home to wander the streets and sleep on the beaches of his previous life.

Troy and I went to school together from elementary up to high school. Even as a kid Troy wasn't exactly a pacifist and was capable of beating the shit out of anyone who challenged him. But after several years doing unspeakable things in the Special Forces, he seemed a different species

"How's it going?" I ask, climbing out of my car.

He studies me and furrows his brow. "Hey, dude," he says. "I want some heroin. You have any?"

I shake my head. "I should have a whole bunch of good dope, but some fucking dude burned me last night."

"Robbed you?"

"Listen, man, if you help me get my dope back, half of it is yours. Interested?"

He smiles weirdly like he's amused and I'm certain he's going to tell me to get lost. Unfortunately he doesn't. "I'll get your dope back," he says, and flicks his cigarette against my car.

We arrive back at the Hollywood apartment building and grab the door as a tanned actor type is walking out. He starts to object, sees Troy, and keeps moving. Upstairs, an irritated and still shirtless Ron opens the door thinking it is just me. I see concern in his eyes when Troy follows in behind me.

I calmly ask if there have been any new developments. Before he can answer his girlfriend walks into the room, her eyes wild from the cocaine.

Who the fuck is this?" she says, gesturing wildly at Troy.

"This is my friend. Half the money was his."

"Don't even try it, asshole!" she screams at me.

Ron shoots her a look to shut up. She either doesn't notice or doesn't care. "We're not scared of you and your fucking goon here," she continues. "I know people that will eat you two for fucking lunch. Get the hell out of here before I make a call."

I'm thinking of a proper response when there's a flash of movement to my side. I turn and see Ron crumpled on the floor with Troy looming over him.

"Hey!" the girl yells out, and begins to scramble for the phone. Troy picks up a floor lamp and throws it like a javelin. It hits her in the face and she drops to her knees with a groan. She brings her hands to her mouth and blood trickles out through her fingers. I am stunned by the sudden violence. Fantasies are one thing, but to actually see people hurt is something entirely different. I stand there as if in shock.

Troy studies me a beat. "Why don't you go wait in the car, dude," he says.

I nod and start for the door.

"Hey," he calls after me. I look back. "Don't you fucking drive off," he says, staring at me as a warning.

I sit in my little car with my head just spinning. I have made a serious mistake. I think about calling the police and try to envision the various outcomes. When I finally make up my mind to call, the passenger door swings open and Troy slides in. He hands me a slip of paper with a handwritten address. There is blood smeared on it.

"Are those two still alive?" I ask, my heart pounding so hard I can feel it in my ears.

Troy lights a cigarette, expressionless. I notice blood on his knuckles. "They'll live," he replies. "Let's go."

We drive west on Santa Monica Boulevard in silence. The streets are crawling with cop cars. An hour ago I would have been frightened by them. Now I have to fight the urge to flag one down. The address takes us to an expensive-looking modern apartment building a block off Westwood Boulevard in the Little Tehran neighborhood. As the two of us walk into the mirrored lobby, I decide to speak up.

"I don't want any more violence, Troy. Maybe we can just scare the dude a little. He didn't seem very tough."

Troy stares at me blankly, like a dog trying to read a novel. "Why do you hate violence so much?" he asks sincerely.

"Because it's fucking ugly," I respond.

"The world is ugly. Always has been. Go back and read your history books." He presses the elevator button and pulls a large military knife from his pant leg. "I'm going to do whatever the situation calls for."

"And what if they have a gun, then what?"

"Oh well . . ."

We exit the elevator and count door numbers till we arrive at the unit. The door has been left open slightly which seems odd. Troy just walks in. I stand there, terrified. When I don't hear anything I head in after him. I see Troy standing in a living room, fishing a butterscotch candy out of a jar. I walk in to join him and get a surge of adrenalin. There on the floor is the young heroin dealer who ripped me off. He has a very noticeable bullet wound in his stomach. His eyes are open and blinking.

"Oh shit, he's shot?!" I exclaim, my voice shaking. I have never seen someone this seriously injured in my life.

"Yep," Troy responds, sucking on the candy.

"We have to call an ambulance."

"He'll be dead before they get here," Troy explains calmly.

It suddenly occurs to me that the guy on the floor is listening to us. Before I can say anything, Troy takes a knee, leans close, and talks to him: "I'm not gonna bullshit you—we can't help you, you are gonna die here, and that's a fact. But there is something I can do for you. Tell me who killed you and stole your dope, and I promise I will make them pay for what they did."

The guy stares up at Troy and I'm not sure he understands. Then he speaks in a dry-mouthed whisper: "Nazis . . . The Snake Pit . . ."

The Snake Pit is a located across Pacific Coast Highway from Topanga State Beach at the southern end of Malibu. It is hidden away in a brush-filled canyon and only accessible by a narrow winding dirt road. There are about ten old bungalows there, nearly all of them submerged into the ground so people have to enter through the second story. It's the result of near constant flooding over several decades and has left the once sought after real estate a den of drugs and fringe dwellers. Both Troy and I have been there on different occasions, both to buy drugs. In my case it was a month ago when I spent a sketched-out night waiting for some heroin with two Nazi greaser types, one of them holding a baby.

As we drive up the coast, I ask Troy what his plan is. He pauses so long I think he's not going to answer. Then he does, kind of. "We're going to go in there and get our drugs. Then you're going to leave and I am going to fuck shit up."

I can't help but let out a short laugh. The situation seems surreal. "These guys we're going to see? These are some hardcore penitentiary peckerwoods. I'm thinking they're gonna be ready for us."

Troy smiles. "Definitely."

"I don't suppose you would consider not going?"

"We're gonna finish this."

Troy and I sit on some crumbling steps leading down to the beach across the highway from the Snake Pit. We are waiting for darkness, staring out at the waves, surfers visible in silhouette.

"You miss it?" I ask him, nodding to the surf. "You were good."

"Nah," Troy responds. "That ain't me anymore."

"It could be again."

"There ain't nothing good left in me."

"What do you mean?"

"I was never a saint, I know that. But I'm not even human anymore." He taps his forehead. "Shit is broken."

"Maybe it's just gonna take some time . . . Dude, let's just go home. We don't need to go on with this. I'll find another way to get us some dope."

"It's not about that, never was." He stands up. "Besides, I promised that dead kid I would get him some justice. If nothing else, I am a man of my word."

It is night and we are down in the Snake Pit. Troy waits behind in a tree line as I walk up to a ramshackle house and knock on a window that now serves as a door. The plan is for me to tell them I want to buy some more heroin and see who is inside. But before I am even ready, the door swings open and I am pulled inside. Someone shoves me to the ground and kicks me in the ribs. "Stay down!" a rough voice orders.

I eventually roll over and manage a glance around. There is a muscular convict type with greased-back hair and a cowboy mustache standing over me. The small room is filled with expensive goods: jewelry, high-end electronics, fur coats. And there, on a nearby table next to some used syringes and a pistol, is Betty Le Mat's gleaming Oscar. The sudden realization that I have found the guys doing the home invasions is instantly followed by the understanding that they will surely kill me.

One of the Nazi greasers I met there before walks in and looks at me. He is shirtless—the words *South Bay* tattooed across his stomach—and holding a large revolver. His eyes have a crystal meth intensity. "I remember you," he says, then nods to the others. "Take him into the bathroom and stick him. Make sure to hold him over the bathtub when he bleeds out."

South Bay starts to light a Camel nonfilter when a figure looms behind him. It is Troy. He reaches forward and moves a knife across the man's throat. A mist of blood sprays out and the guy stumbles forward. His gun goes off making a popping noise. As the other greasers scramble for their weapons, I dive behind a couch. The room erupts into complete chaos as men shout and shoot off guns.

I hear a crashing noise and one of the Nazis falls beside me on the floor and starts convulsing. With a new burst of adrenalin I stand and bolt through the house toward what I hope is a back door. I race through a kitchen area and out another makeshift door into the surrounding trees. As I move away, there is high-pitched screaming unlike anything I have ever heard.

I frantically claw my way up a hillside on my hands and knees. When I get some distance I finally look back. The house below is now on fire. There are several gunshots and then an eerie silence. I sit there gasping for breath as the house burns. I take out my cell phone and, with trembling hands, call 911. Troy never emerges. No one does. I hear sirens approaching and soon there are emergency lights descending into the darkness of the canyon.

In the ensuing days, a sanitized story of what happened is offered up to the public. News broadcasts tell of a decorated war veteran who lost his life single-handedly taking down an ultra-violent crime ring. And really, that is what happened. The rest is merely context. In my opinion Troy knew he couldn't exist in the civilized world anymore so he went out doing something he thought was noble. Beyond the fact that he had become a monster, my friend rescued the city.

And in the end he saved my life as well. I was literally scared straight by my day with Troy and have been clean since. That night I left the Snake Pit and drove south along the coast, eventually falling asleep on my local beach, curled up beneath the very same lifeguard stand I had slept under as a clear-eyed kid waiting to surf the dawn patrol. I held onto the sand with an anguished desperation, listening to the waves and willing myself back into a less horrific world.

Robin Doyno

GARY PHILLIPS has edited and con-
tributed to several Akashic Books
anthologies, including *The Cocaine
Chronicles*, which he coedited with
Jervey Tervalon. Recent work includes
The Rinse, a graphic novel about a
money launderer; the novel *The War-
lord of Willow Ridge;* and *Treacherous:
Grifters, Ruffians and Killers*, a collection of his short stories. For information, visit www.gdphillips.com.

black caesar's gold
by gary phillips

He had a dream, but it would have made Martin Luther King, Jr. shake his head woefully, Malcolm X tongue lash him severely, and Stokely Carmichael would have pimp slapped him. Frank Matthews, along with the other Frank, Lucas, and Leroy "Nicky" Barnes were, for a time, the kingpins of the heroin trade on the East Coast. Matthews, the self-styled Black Caesar, was a country boy like Lucas. But once he got to the big city, he went all in. Maybe Barnes could quote *Moby-Dick* and *King Lear*, but ascending from juvenile chicken thief in his native Durham to numbers runner in Philadelphia to becoming the first major drug lord in Harlem, Matthews had built an organization his compatriots admired and the Mob feared.

"That moulie's getting too damn big for that mink coat he struts around in," Godfather Joe Bonanno was want to observe.

For Matthews moved product like no other, a Robin Hood in the community and a terror outside of it. Unlike other smaller pushers in Harlem and beyond, he didn't rely on La Cosa Nostra to keep him supplied—as generally speaking, they controlled the pipeline. Matthews had a direct South American connection and brought in H and coke that way, cutting out the usual middleman. He invested in property under various fronts and had cash couriered overseas into tax havens.

One time in Atlanta, Matthews brought together a roomful of big swingin'-dick black and Latino drug dealers to form a combine so as to chill the growing static with the Italian mobsters. Matthews was a strategic motherfucker.

Like Barnes and Lucas, the high-flying Matthews eventually got his wings clipped and was busted by agents of the then newly constituted Drug Enforcement Administration. But different than those two, he didn't rat out his peers for a reduction of his sentence. Then again, Matthews didn't do time in the slammer, either. He liked to gamble in Vegas, these trips also a way for him to launder more of his money.

As these things happen, he had been in Vegas at the time with a beauty on his arm, losing at the craps tables but not sweating it. His plan was to soon be on his way to LA to catch Super Bowl VII between the Redskins and Dolphins. Yet unbeknownst to him, members of his South American network, along with a lieutenant, had already been arrested. The trap was closing in on him, and at McCarran Airport the DEA slapped the cuffs on Matthews and his lady friend.

"What took you so long?" he was quoted as saying jauntily.

Incredibly, his lawyer successfully argued for his bail reduction, at which point Matthews got out of jail and then disappeared. That was 1973. From Chicago to Rome, Nigeria to Atlanta, sightings of Matthews abounded. But none of them panned out. He was never found. Maybe the Mafia had him whacked or maybe Matthews had his face changed and retired to some island with a woman who liked to wear miniskirts and no underwear.

Chuck Grayson pondered Frank Matthews's fate and history as he pretended not to fawn over the too-sweet 1969 Mustang Fastback with a Boss 420 engine. Grayson had done his homework and knew less than a thousand of these particular Mustangs were produced that year. There must have been modifications to the engine compartment to accommodate the larger motor, he mused. A woman in stylish clothes and a wide-brimmed sun hat preceded him from the parking lot where several vehicles were on display.

Along with other potential buyers, they reentered the main room of Stedler and Sons Auctioneers. There was a photo of the maroon Mustang tacked to a padded board with its order in the auction noted. There were other pictures of various items pinned there as well, including vases and an ivory-inlaid cigar box said to have belonged to President Grover Cleveland.

Grayson had come to the auction house because this particular Mustang had belonged to Frank Matthews. Stedler and Sons listed the car as having belonged to Ken Schmecken, a producer and shadowy part owner of three X-rated movie theaters in the Los Angeles area. Grayson was something of a Matthews aficionado and always on the lookout for items connected to the gangster. He knew that *Schmecken*, an oblique slang term for heroin, was one of the names the drug lord had used in hiding his investments.

Because the car had value as being only one of a limited number, there were several interested parties contending for it when it came up for bid. But Grayson was something of a limited edition himself.

He was a mid-thirties African American male who'd made his money as part of a start-up online entity that got sold for a nice profit to a conglomerate controlling various commercial websites. He and his friends' site was one of the first catering to the multicultural geek crowd in all things pop culture, lifestyles, and fashion. Turned out people-of-color dweebs, a group of which Grayson was proudly a member, liked to hang together.

The car cost him more than he would have liked to pay. This was due to the woman across the room in the hat who kept upping him. But she'd dropped out when the asking price went past $25,000. One, two . . . the third strike of the gavel sounded and Grayson would soon possess the vehicle.

The Mustang was found in Altadena in the garage of a house belonging to a long-retired Department of Water and Power secretary named Deborah Keyson. She'd died of pulmonary failure, and any connection she may have had to Frank Matthews or Ken Schmecken was not known.

The auctioneers had put money into restoring the car and it had been fairly well-preserved under a tarp, the gas and fluids having been drained from it back when. Grayson had chanced upon its photo and description while sitting in his dentist's office paging through a freshly minted Stedler and Sons catalogue. He immediately recognized the name Schmecken in the brief write-up.

The paperwork done and money deposited, Grayson drove his prize away from the auction house in Glendale. He couldn't help but imagine he was Matthews at the wheel on his way to cement a nefarious deal as he drove home to Santa Monica. Along the way his phone rang and he answered, putting it on speaker and propping it in the opening of the car's built-in ashtray.

"So?" his girlfriend Mora Fleming asked.

"Scored it, sweeite."

"I knew you would."

"Yeah, well."

"Want me to bring Chinese or Indian?"

"I could go for some kung pao chicken."

She chuckled. "When do you *not* want that?"

"I want you."

"Hmmmm. See you soon."

Fleming, without her heavy boots on, was two inches taller than Grayson and outweighed his wiry frame by forty pounds— forty solid pounds. She was a bodybuilding chiropractor and gaming enthusiast. They'd met at the annual Nexus of Nerds— Comic-Con in San Diego. She'd come with a girlfriend, a fellow bodybuilder, and they'd turned the heads of fanboys and their put-upon fathers—the two of them dressed in the fantasy of scantily clad sword-wielding barbarian women.

Standing in line to get into a panel with comics superstar writer Neil Gaiman, Fleming had been impressed with Grayson's knowledge of the *S.T.A.R. Ops* game in phantom mode. That, and he managed to look at her face and not just her substantial chest.

In bed later, cuddling after making love to Fleming in his second-floor bedroom, Grayson saw through the slats of the window the light over his garage snap on. The light was motion sensitive and normally it coming on meant one of his neighbors' cats was lazing by. But the Mustang was parked in the driveway, near the garage door. He hadn't outfitted the car with an alarm yet, though he'd put a lock bar on the steering wheel.

Grayson waited for the sound of the vehicle's door being opened. He smiled, realizing he better wake up his girlfriend if there was trouble. But the light went off again and there were no more sounds of disturbance from below.

The following morning he was changing out the battery in the trunk when Fleming asked, "Why the heck is it back here?"

"They needed all the room up front to squeeze in the big block engine," Grayson explained, lifting the battery out. He figured the auction house had spent money on the car's looks but not on a more heavy-duty battery. He intended to not scrimp when it came to his new beauty. He was going to use his electric motor Leaf and go to the auto parts store to trade this battery in for a better one. There was a recessed metal shell that held the battery in its cavity. He removed the housing to inspect it for rust.

"What's this?" Fleming asked, reaching a hand into the cavity in the trunk's floorboard. She worked for a few moments undoing some tape and held aloft a plastic sandwich baggie that had been secured on the frame below the battery's shell.

The couple exchanged a look of anticipation as Fleming tore the aged baggie apart and removed a sheet of yellowed paper.

Gingerly she unfolded the stiff note and flattened it on the slope of the car's fastback. On the paper was a sentence in block lettering: *SIXTY YARDS NORTH FROM THE PANZER.*

"Panzer?" Fleming asked. "Like German for tank?"

"Precisely," Grayson said, heading for the house. "Let me check something, but I think we might have a road trip this morning."

"Yeah, where?"

"Why, a bombed-out French village, my dear."

The village had gone by various names and had been used in TV shows and movies several times. It was a World War II–era set in Canyon Country that by the late '60s had become mired in an ownership battle between its original builder and the children of one of the ex-partners. This made it difficult to rent out. But in 1970, the village was utilized illegally—that is, the producers didn't bother to pay—for a hardcore shoot called *Madam Satan of the SS.*

"You've seen this epic?" Fleming asked.

"Way before I had the pleasure of your acquaintance. In fact, there was a sequel but that one took place in a mad scientist's castle. Same woman played Madam Satan both times, Jackie Salvo."

"Uh-huh."

"Of course I only know this due to my research into the wild and varied career of Frank Matthews."

"Of course."

Grayson had recalled that under the Ken Schmecken alias, Matthews had been a producer of a porno set during World War II. He'd confirmed this in a nonfiction book he had at home about twentieth-century gangsters which featured an extensive chapter on the disappeared drug lord.

Fleming wondered aloud, "Does *heron*, to use the vernacular of the day, retain its potency over decades?"

"You figure that's what he has buried there?"

She regarded the freeway outside the rolled-down passenger window. The Mustang didn't have air-conditioning. "You think he buried money?"

"He was a careful dude, Mora. Maybe he was planning in case he had to go on the run and needed to make sure he had enough liquid assets to make a break to Mexico or the Bahamas."

She leaned over and kissed him on the cheek. "My little Scarface."

He squeezed her muscular thigh. "Better know it."

Canyon Country was in Santa Clarita, in the northwest section of LA County. In the last twenty years the area had seen the proliferation of housing subdivisions, but there were still large swaths of underpopulated nature. Using tax records and past articles he'd accessed online, Grayson had obtained the location for the place most commonly called Attack Squad Village, as the set had been used several times in the popular 1960s World War II TV show *Attack Squad.*

Once there, they parked and walked along a dusty street bordered by French-style buildings of the proper vintage, a bombed-out church, and a bar called Millie Marie's among the façades. There was another street, then behind the false front of an apartment building, in the tall weeds, they found the German tank.

"North is this way," Fleming said. Each carried shovels. Using a tape measure and allowing for human error, they marked off 180 feet from the tank. Grayson used the point of the shovel to scribe a large circle in the dirt.

Fleming nodded and got started. He began in another section inside the circle. In less than fifteen minutes they'd uncovered a coffin.

"Wow," Fleming intoned. "I didn't expect that."

"We've come this far," he said. They dug the dirt out from around the coffin and together hefted it above ground.

"Damn!" Fleming exclaimed, sweat on her brow.

"Here goes," Grayson said. He used the shovel to lift the lid and let it flop open.

"Oh shit!" Fleming rasped.

Inside the coffin were bricks of gold. Grayson picked up a bar, assessing its weight in his hand—roughly two pounds, he estimated. "How is this possible?" he wondered aloud.

"Gold is good anywhere, Chuck," Fleming observed.

"I got that, but it's illegal to own gold bars."

Hands on her hips, she said, "A drug lord isn't worried about the rules, honey."

"I know that, but what foundry would cast these for him?"

"I can answer that," a new voice said.

The two looked around to find three newcomers, two men in sport coats and slacks, flanking a slender woman in a loose top, white jeans, and heels. She wore a feathered and beaded Mardi Gras eye mask. The two men had on pedestrian ski masks. One of the men, slimmer than the other, pointed a semiauto pistol-grip shotgun at Grayson. A slight wind blew but the couple didn't notice the breeze.

"How'd you know to find us here?" Grayson asked.

The shotgun man snorted. "Like that purple car is hard to follow."

"What you need to worry about," the woman interjected, "is how you're going to pace yourself loading my goods." There was a trace of an accent in her voice.

The smile below her mask was brittle, like a robot trying to be chummy. Grayson, who figured she was the one in the wide-brimmed hat at the auction, noted a mole to the left of her plump lips. The lines on her face indicated a woman of some years, though clearly fit.

The shotgun still on Grayson, the stockier thug retrieved a white van and backed it close to the loot. He opened the rear swing doors. Resigned, Grayson and Fleming loaded the ingots into the rear cargo area. There were 124 bars.

"Now what?" Grayson said, using the heel of his hand to wipe sweat from his brow. The temperature had risen past the mid-eighties.

"Now we say bye-bye," the woman answered triumphantly.

Fleming was standing near the rear of the van, at an angle to the shotgun holder. She rushed at the man, hoping to tackle him and relieve him of his weapon. But he was a pro and wasn't rattled.

"Back that ass up, you big bitch," he said, clubbing her with the pistol-grip end of the shotgun.

Fleming went down heavy.

"Mora!" Grayson blared, rushing to aid her. The larger hood produced a stun device and jammed it against Grayson's neck. He convulsed and spittle coated his lips as he too dropped to the ground on his knees. A second jolt toppled him and he lay twitching, his muscles unresponsive to his commands. He wet himself.

"That's a cherry ride you got, bro," the one who'd shocked him said. "I'll look good driving that bad boy." The hood removed the keys from Grayson's pocket, easily knocking aside the other man's hand in his feeble attempt to stop the thug.

"Is that necessary?" the woman said.

"It's a perk, baby," the man shot back. He and the shotgunner laughed harshly. The woman said something in Spanish, and the three left in the two vehicles.

Mora Fleming moaned and rolled onto her side. She then got herself up and helped Grayson to his feet.

"That was exciting," she said dryly.

"How're you feeling?" Tenderly, he placed the flat of his hand on the side of her face.

She touched the back of her head. "Some painkillers and intravenous tequila ought to remedy the situation."

He looked beyond her. "I hate getting beat," he declared. "Not to mention, that was a serious haul of gold. And that bastard took my car."

"Maybe we should be happy to be alive, Chuck."

He had an odd smile on his face when he addressed her. It wasn't an expression she'd seen before. "Maybe they shouldn't have left me alive."

Despite him just standing there with the front of his jeans dark from urine, Fleming got nervous.

There were hardly any photos of Frank Matthews aside from booking shots. But Grayson found one of him at a club in Harlem taken by the black-owned *Amsterdam News,* as the white press at that point didn't know who he was. Using a magnifying glass, Grayson studied the picture that showed Matthews smoking a cigar, holding court with a tableful of cohorts. Because it was a close-in shot, not all the faces were distinct. He wonderd if there were other shots from the club.

Via the online records of the New York Public Library, Grayson was able to narrow his possibles to two photographers who worked for the *News* then and who might have taken the uncredited shot. One was dead, and the other, Tim "Cheaters" Pleasy, was still alive. He was seventy-six and taught an extension photography class in Sarasota. Grayson promptly got him on the phone.

"Yeah," Pleasy said after the exchange of pleasantries, his voice clear and young sounding. "Ol' Frank fancied himself the big shot all right. Passing out twenties to the kids on the streets like free lunch, buying color TVs for the senior center . . . Yeah, he was something."

Grayson let the old timer drone on some, then asked, "You remember a shot you might have taken of him at the Montreaux Club? Him at a table of people having a good time?" He described the scene in further detail.

"Naw, young man, that don't ring no bell," Cheaters Pleasy said. "I'd bet Garmes took that shot." Davis Garmes was the deceased photographer.

"Any idea where his outtakes got to? He have family? I wanted to see if he had other shots showing the faces clearly."

"You sure seem to want to go through a lot for your book," Pleasy observed.

"I might have an uncle in that shot, and I want to know for certain," he lied.

"I got you," the older man said. "I'll check on that and will get back to you. I might know where some of his old photos went."

"That would be great, Mr. Pleasy."

It didn't take the photographer long, as he and the late Garmes had stayed in touch. He was able to locate the man's photos left in the possession of an ex-wife he also knew. Garmes's photos were in various film boxes designated by years. She found two other shots Garmes had taken that night, had them scanned, and eventually they reached Grayson via e-mail.

"There she is," Grayson said to Fleming. They sat at his kitchen island. He tapped the magnifying glass against his opposite hand. "That beauty mark, mole, whatever you want to call it, gives her away. She's at the table here with Matthews."

Fleming folded her arms. "And she's the one playing Madam Satan in those two pornos he produced?"

"Yep. Jackie Salvo, but that's an alias."

Fleming frowned. "Okay, let's say you find out her real name, which isn't hard, then what?"

"Get our shit back."

She put a hand on his. "Darling, we go see action-adventure movies and read comic books. But unfortunately, I'm not Wonder Woman and you aren't the Punisher."

He winked. "But we've role-played them."

"I'm serious, Chuck. This woman ain't playing."

"We've handled guns," he countered.

"Shooting targets at a firing range isn't the same thing as blasting a human being, and you know it. We might be geekazoids but we're solid citizens, baby. We pay taxes, have businesses, homes—in other words, unless you're willing to give all that up, I say drop this."

"Let me just identify her. Just that, for my own satisfaction."

She folded her arms again, a questioning look to her. "Don't think you're slick."

"Me? Never."

Finding out the real name of a woman who starred in two X-rated cult movies from the '70s was easier than buttoning a shirt. Once he had that information, Grayson was able to document the up-and-down career of Pilar Ortega Renaud De La Fontana. She'd gained notoriety back then from the Madam Satan films and graduated to starring in a few grade-C horror and sci-fi movies. She had some TV roles too, and in the '90s hosted a cable access show where she made smart-ass remarks and one-liners throughout whatever turkey she was showing.

Naturally, there were a couple of fan clubs devoted to her among nerd-dom, and getting an address for the woman wasn't too tough either, given Grayson knew who to ask what. At a coffee shop on Olympic Boulevard, he met with a man who De La Fontana twice had imposed a restraining order against.

"It's not like I meant her any harm," said Fred Summerville, an underemployed box store clerk. He nibbled on the second Rice Krispies treat Grayson had bought him.

Grayson sized up Summerville as the type who got off on some peep action, and heaven would be sniffing De La Fontana's panties. But he said, "I feel you, man, where would these celebs be if it wasn't for us keeping their names out there?"

"Exactly," Summerville agreed happily, bits of his treat exploding from his mouth.

More commiserating included Summerville warning Grayson about a fifty-some-odd-old boyfriend of De La Fontana named Boris who'd done time for strong arm robbery. He didn't know the last name of this bruiser, but what the restraining orders couldn't do, Boris had done when he'd come into Summerville's store and calmly broken his hand.

"I stayed away after that," the former stalker stated flatly, looking down.

The $150 in cash Grayson offered elevated the man's mood and produced an address. She lived in a modest Craftsman in East Hollywood not too far from the large Kaiser medical facility on Sunset and Vermont.

On the second night of his stakeout in his Leaf, Grayson saw the Mustang arrive and a stocky man in his fifties exit the vehicle and enter the house.

Fleming was right. Grayson wasn't about to storm in there armed with an AK, a bandanna tied around his head, demanding the gold and his car back. But he'd be damned if he was going to get taken advantage of and not do something. Driving back to Santa Monica, he came up with a plan and discussed it with his girlfriend the next day in her office.

"Oh, man," she said finally. "That's a shitty idea, Chuck."

"It could work."

"Or we could spend several years in prison, if we don't get

killed. And if it's the former, I couldn't stand the thought of a booty bandit wearing out that fine ass of yours."

"Good to know," he said. "Anyway, it's not we, just me."

"Bullshit. He's my patient and you're not doing this without my help. Besides, I don't want you going to the next con talking about how I pussied out on you."

They both grinned broadly.

Grayson wanted to obtain a kilo of black tar heroin—those tense opening teasers of many a *Miami Vice* of cool crooks and sweating undercover cops flashing through his mind. He owned the complete box set on DVD. But trying to buy that kind of weight also meant making connections beyond Fleming's patient. And this meant gaining the acquaintance of certain individuals who'd cut out your intestines and sell them back to you as a scarf. So he settled for two small glassine packets with a blue devil head stenciled on them.

The patient Fleming was treating for back alignment problems was very much into holistic health and organic foods, which he gladly talked about extensively. Yet when you work on a person's body up close and personal like she did, the conversing invariably covered a lot of territory—like one's past.

Todd Jessup, the patient, had been a pharmacist who got hooked on the drugs he dispensed. He lost his license and in his descent, encountered various unsavory individuals. He'd subsequently rebuilt his life, and it took some coaxing but he came up with a few contacts from the bad old days. Thereafter, Grayson and Fleming bought the blue devil packets from a hard-ass runaway teenager working for her pusher-pimp boyfriend in the Valley. The one-time pharmacist verified the authenticity of the packets' contents.

Staging the accident came next. Boris no-last-name was

driving the Mustang back to De La Fontana's house from the Vons supermarket, blasting the Eagles on the aftermarket CD unit. Grayson almost cried as he purposely bashed his Leaf into the left front fender of the classic vehicle. Boris was out in a shot, yelling.

"The fuck is wrong with you, man? You blind or something? Hey, it's you," he said, recognizing Grayson.

"Your mama's blind, bitch," Grayson responded.

Boris rushed over and Grayson jabbed him in the face without hesitation. This earned him a left to the stomach and a right to the chin. He was younger than Boris by more than twenty years, but the other man was far more experienced with his fists.

"What, figured you'd try and get your car back, punk? Well come on."

He laughed and again hit Grayson, who rocked back; he ducked the next blow but the inevitable was upon him. A crowd gathered, cheering the combatants. By the time the motorcycle cop arrived, there was a cell phone video of Grayson getting his ass kicked up on YouTube. Though at one point, down on all fours, Grayson had managed to get ahold of his tormentor's calf and bite through his pant leg. A couple of people watching clapped at that.

As Boris Stallings had no paperwork for the Mustang, nor proof of insurance, the car was impounded and searched. Stallings was arrested for possession of heroin, planted under the floor mat on the passenger side by Mora Fleming as her boyfriend took his beatdown. The door had been locked, but when Grayson got the car he'd been given two sets of keys. She'd argued she should be the one to plow into the Mustang as she felt she could handle herself better against Stallings.

"Dammit, woman, you've already seen me piss myself. What pride do I have left?" Grayson had said.

She'd kissed him. "A man must do what he must do."

It took a week to recuperate at home from his encounter with Stallings. His face was still tender. The Santa Monica PD notified Grayson about his car once LAPD contacted them. Grayson told the police he had been in the area to shop at Skylight Books and was shocked to see the Mustang that had been jacked from him the week before. He'd lost control of the car and that's when this horrible Stallings person went wild on him.

He also saw on the news that De La Fontana had been found shotgunned to death in her house, though no ingots were mentioned. A known associate of Stallings was said to be a person of interest.

Among the online fan club there was talk that De La Fontana had family ties to one of Frank Matthews's South American financiers. It was speculated that she and Mathews had been romantically linked at one point. There was also a rumor about her being the mistress at age seventeen of a general who'd absconded with treasures from his country's coffers.

In a chat room, Grayson read the suggestion that maybe she'd done Matthews in after he ripped her off, and that she must have been on the hunt for the gold for a long time. But her killing him didn't make sense, since she would have needed him alive to reveal where the gold was hidden. Though could be she got carried away having him worked over, someone else offered, and so it went, back and forth. All this merely conjecture among her fans.

Grayson got the Mustang repaired and painted a sedate color. Now and then behind the wheel, Mora Fleming humming to an oldie on the radio beside him, he wondered whatever became of Black Caesar's gold.

ANTONIA CRANE is the only person from Humboldt County who doesn't smoke or grow weed. Her work can be found or is forthcoming in the *Rumpus, Black Clock, Slake, PANK,* the *Los Angeles Review of Books,* ZYZZYVA, and elsewhere. She wrote a memoir about her mother's illness and the sex industry, *SPENT,* and is currently seeking representation for that memoir. She teaches incarcerated teenage girls creative writing in Los Angeles. For more information, visit antoniacrane.com.

sunshine for adrienne
by antonia crane

The first man who raped her went blind. Her mom called with the news.

"That handsome football player you dated got eye cancer in both eyes," she said.

Adrienne heard chewing and the wet slurp of Nicorette gum. Her ma chewed two or three pieces at a time and when they lost flavor, she rolled the spit stones into gray balls and stuck them to the kitchen counter. The orange cat knocked them onto the floor and batted them around.

"You mean Terry?" Adrienne's asshole clenched. Ma didn't know. All the girls at St. Julian's High School swooned over Terry's tanned wide receiver chest and tennis legs. She heard something being chopped on a cutting board with a steady *whack, whack, whack.*

"He's blind as a bat. His poor mother." The chopping got faster and faster and more precise. She could slice a carrot into paper-thin pieces in less than thirty seconds. She hated cooking.

"She's a nut job, Amy!" her father hollered in the background. A cupboard door slammed shut. She heard the refrigerator door make a sucking sound as it opened.

Adrienne found her prework hit and bent spoon in the top drawer of her dresser, but no lighter. She rummaged around in another drawer where she last saw it and found ticket stubs from a show her father took her to when she graduated high school. It was the Della Davidson Dance Company's *Ten p.m. Dream*, an interpretation of *Alice in Wonderland*. They'd nibbled calamari beforehand next door. Her football-watching, beer-drinking father even sported a silky burgundy tie that matched her favorite red skirt. She'd taken her father's elbow as he led her to the front row, so close she felt the dancers' abdominal muscles vibrate and their snaky necks glisten and strain. She watched them as he watched the music pulse through her skin.

He liked to look at her pictures of birds too. She'd started drawing turkeys, doves, and chickens when she was six years old with accidental skill. Her father couldn't draw an Easter egg if there was a gun to his head. Where he lacked imagination, she swelled with it. Her talents delighted him and he bragged about her to his roofing buddies. "My daughter's a genius," he'd say while ripping off grubby tiles. He collected her bird drawings and stuck them to the refrigerator door, where they were held in place by 49er magnets.

"Her only son. Can you imagine?" Ma's voice matched the sucking thud the refrigerator door made when it closed.

The thing being chopped was gone and in its place, her father's voice: "Her loser son, still living at home at twenty-nine?" He grunted, which was the same as his laugh.

Adrienne pictured him in his stretched white gym socks with a spaghetti noodle dangling from a fork, daring Ma to slap his hand away from her butt, which he pinched when he wasn't yelling at the TV, drinking Coors Light, with their orange cat on the footstool. The skin on his hands matched his face: tanned, calloused, and flaking off from working outside in the wind, rain, and dense fog that made roofs wet and slippery. He fell off a ladder and sprained his ankle last year. It swelled like a grapefruit so he managed the office and bid jobs, and farmed out the labor to his friends.

It was at St. Julian's High School where Adrienne got sneaky.

She'd tiptoe behind him on her way upstairs to her room. She'd been meeting Terry and getting high, staying out past curfew.

"Where the hell you been?" Her father had stopped looking at her. He held the TV remote in one hand, raised like an arrow, in the other, a beer. He was a channel surfer. There had been a steadily growing gulf between them. Her curves brought popularity, lip gloss, tampons, and boys, but also self-righteousness and danger. She became reckless and reticent. He'd hear her whispering on the phone well after midnight. He'd smell alcohol on her breath. She'd become too pretty for her own good, he sensed.

"Where?" he asked. He was made of sounds: slurps, moans, burps, and coughs. Startled, the cat leaped off the footstool and ran into the kitchen. She watched a red river of varicose veins travel up his chubby calves to his thighs. She didn't have to hide her tiny-dot pupils or her droopy, rubbery skin that hung on her face. He watched the football game on TV: "Olson, you pile of shit, you throw like a girl!"

She fingered the box of Marlboros in her pocket.

"I was out buying smokes." She waved the box in the air so he could see it reflected in the TV screen.

"You're too young to smoke."

"I'm seventeen."

"It's eleven o'clock on a school night, Addy." Along with breasts, she'd sprouted a shitty new petulance. Her father disliked the distance between them. He gripped his Coors Light tighter knowing that if he didn't keep engaging with her, she would slip away and it would be too late. Perhaps it was already too late. The amount of rage he felt surprised him.

Adrienne shrugged her shoulders. She walked briskly into the kitchen where her ma buzzed around in slippers, gnashing her gum and talking on the phone aggressively like the women on *The View*.

* * *

The sun dropped into her tenderloin apartment like a dried, rancid apricot, bringing night. She spotted her lighter on the floor next to the trash. She leaned over, swiped, and shook it. It was out of fluid, but when she tried it anyway, a low flame appeared.

"Terry's not a loser. He's ill. How would you like to be blind, hmm?"

"Wow, Ma. That's awful," Adrienne said. The bathroom where she was raped was light blue with no windows. She reached for the soft brown belt on the floor, next to her Lucite stripper shoes. A gray pigeon stood on the single window ledge in her studio apartment. Her hands began to sweat.

"I'm going to bring them my famous broccoli casserole. You should come with me."

Adrienne grabbed the belt and tied it around her forearm. She pulled it taught, gripping it with her teeth. Her best wormy vein surfaced inside her left elbow. The sweat from her hands transferred onto the worn leather where there were tiny dots of blood. She pictured diced sweet yellow onions and the hard shell of orange melted cheese on top. Terry would peel the hard cheese layer off and chew it with his bleached Chiclets. He would shake Ma's hand with his tennis doubles grip.

When he asked about Adrienne, her ma would lie. She'd tell him, "She's waiting tables and taking World Religions at City College." But that was four years ago. It was the story she liked to tell the neighbors. The needle hit the vein nicely and delivered the juicy black heat from Adrienne's belly up to her neck. She levitated from her chest to the top of her head. Butterflies came to mind. She took a dull pencil and drew some on a Post-it.

"If you get on BART now, you can make it in an hour." Her ma's voice turned smoky and silver.

The chopping sound was back but softer, like a slow finger

tapping on water in a bowl. *Tap. Tap. Tap.*

"Adrienne, are you still there?" Her cheeks warmed and her eyes drifted like a plant leaning toward sunlight.

"I can't go to Oakland tonight, Ma. I have to work." The space between them stretched far and wide as the Pacific Ocean.

"Come over for dinner tomorrow night. Spend some time with your father."

Ma's breath was heavy and slow like hers. There was no more gum noise. She heard the oven door snap shut and a timer tick. She felt comfort knowing the casserole was inside and the cheese would spread like butter and the chopped broccoli would sizzle, as planned. She heard relief in her ma's mighty exhale. She exhaled too.

"I can't. I have to make rent for this shitty rat-hole apartment."

"Okay, honey. We'll see you on Sunday."

Adrienne felt elegant and weightless in her tall, thick black motorcycle boots. They were heavier than she was. She chose a fishnet top to cover the purple-red scars that lined her forearms. Her hair was pulled back in a neat, shiny bun. She hadn't washed it in days. When she was high, water felt like nails. Besides, the high rollers liked the tight bun. It read ballerina. Well groomed. Middle class. Her boyfriend Dennis liked it too. "You look like a French lingerie model," he'd said. They lived together in a dinky apartment on Hyde Street where they listened to trance techno music, counted pigeons, and slammed dope. Dennis looked at least forty, with crooked lines around his mouth and creased eyes. But he was twenty-eight, like her.

She checked her mailbox on the way out and found a red envelope from her father. She shoved it in her costume bag and walked the few blocks to Market Street Cinema, past the garbage that blew over the sidewalk and into the gutter. Fog drifted in and circled her like wet smoke. She gave a light wave to the homeless guy who always tried to sell her stolen perfume. Pigeons picked through the trash and carried off chicken bones in their beaks. Three pigeons in the trash can; three grams of dope per day.

On the floor at the MSC, she saw her regular customer, the man in the white shirt, sitting in his usual spot. He was good for a hundred bucks. He sometimes brought her a single red carnation, which she thought was cheap and sad, but she smiled and thanked him and later tossed it into the gutter on Market Street. He glanced at his watch. She climbed over the crossed legs of a guy in a stocking cap, to get to the man in the white shirt. A familiar hand touched her bare stomach as she walked by.

"Sorry."

She bent in half to lean in for a closer look. Dennis had a swollen, bruised eye that she could see, even in the dark, and he was bleeding from one corner of his mouth.

"What are you doing at my work?"

The white-shirt customer now had a thick blonde gyrating on his crotch. Timing is everything.

"I was trying to bring you . . ."

"What?"

Dennis uncrossed his legs. His fingers were long and graceful. He hid his face in his hands. Adrienne leaned in and hissed in his ear. He smelled like bleach, dirt, and night. His eyes were badly swollen.

"You are never supposed to come into my work."

"I need . . ." Adrienne peeled his hands away from his face and remembered the birthday card from her father. She had torn open the envelope and found eighty dollars. He'd written, *Hope Your Birthday is Ducky*, on top of a picture of a fluffy green duck she drew when she was about nine years old. It was her "duck phase," her father liked to remind her.

She smashed forty crisp dollars into Dennis's sweaty palm. A leggy redhead whispered to a customer next to him, then glanced in her direction. It was obvious they were arguing, and it was making customers tense. The white-shirt customer smiled at her. She smiled big. She smiled rectus. She smiled Cheshire. The vein in Dennis's neck bulged, the same way it did when he came. She moved her chest up to his bruised eyes, like she was about to dance for him.

"Get the fuck out of my work."

The white-shirt customer motioned to her to come over to him. She walked over and leaned in to kiss his cheek. Most nights, after work, Dennis took her money and met their dealer. Then they got high together and Dennis played guitar on their dingy brown sheets.

"Promise me you'll never come into my work," she said.

"Promise."

The numbers were good at the MSC. She gave five or eight handjobs a night and left with seven or eight hundred bucks, enough for six grams. If she only did her share, she and Dennis could stay blazed for a couple days. The next night, she'd come back to work and do it again. And the next day the exact same thing. Never mind the bruises on the backs of her knees. She felt light and graceful on stage. Six years of ballet as a little girl kept her toes pointed and her arms loose. And there was her techno trance music where she got lost on stage.

She had three songs to get naked. The first one was frantic and unrelenting. She walked on stage slow as caramel, traveling to the side. Back and forth. When the beat got faster, she slowed down even more, pulling her shadow across the length of the stage toward the pole. She grabbed it with one hand and slid down to the floor. She spread her thighs wide and gazed into the black space of the audience. Her chin dropped. Her eyelids closed. Her mouth went slack. Then she caught herself. That was the good thing about techno: it was a loop so she could start right where she left off. She used the pole as leverage to lift herself up to stand. The white lights could trigger a migraine, but this was no migraine. This was blindness.

She remembered Terry's megawatt smile and million-crunches abs. He snuck her into the boy's bathroom after cheerleading practice. The plan was to make out and try his dope. "'Walking on Sunshine,' Addy," he'd said.

"What?" she asked with one hand on her hip. Terry pulled her into the blue bathroom stall and removed his smooth brown belt from his plaid shorts. They dropped down past his knees. He looked slimmer than usual.

"You should've used 'Walking on Sunshine.'" He wrapped the belt around her forearm. The dope was brown and gritty, but when the fire heated it, it blackened like bubbling vinegar. Terry's arms were so veiny he didn't use the belt. He just flexed. "'Walking on Sunshine' is the best song for a cheerleading routine," he said.

He stuck the needle in her arm and it stung. The bathroom wasn't blue. It was mint-green and freezing. She shivered.

"'Walking on Sunshine' by Katrina and the Waves." The dope was a warm liquid kiss inside her skin. She nearly slipped back onto the toilet. He caught her. She laughed.

"No. We're using 'New Attitude' because it's slow enough for flips."

He turned her around to face the toilet with her back to him. He yanked on her underwear.

"Wait," she said. She snatched a condom from her makeup bag and ripped it open with her teeth. She dropped the condom. She reached down to pick it up, but there was orange piss and curly black hairs where it had landed.

The dope made her queasy. She threw up Diet Pepsi and gummy bear bile and the sweetness mixed with the piss and soap smell. She tasted dope at last: burnt vinegar and warm ash. A dark shadow moved across the bathroom. The room turned blue. She flushed the toilet and the sound was so loud, as if monsters lived in the pipes inside the walls.

Terry laughed. He didn't use spit when he put his cock in her ass. He didn't use lube. She didn't feel it or see the blood until later. Speckled lights twinkled behind her eyes. Prism zigzag light blurred the edges of the walls, of the toilet, of Terry. She saw her drool trickle from her open mouth.

"Don't."

"I don't want to get you pregnant," he said.

Her thin spit was a rainbow thread hitting the toilet water, soft and certain.

Later she'd: Bleed on toilet paper. Sit on ice. Sleep on her belly. Buy more dope from Terry. He wasn't very good at shooting her up, but Dennis could find a vein in a garbage can.

On stage at the MSC, the second song began. It was more manic and fast than the first. It was trance party music where a woman wailed about ecstasy and a little bit of you and me. Adrienne stepped out of her slinky black dress like a spider discarding its skin. Her black bra was next. She tossed it to the one man sitting up front. Her pale skin and glossed red lips and sharp cheekbones shimmered under the white lights. She stepped on her dress and tripped. She fell down onto her knees. Her black thigh-high stockings covered the tracks on the backs of her legs but they were needle sore. She slid forward and felt the hot lights pierce her neck. Her tiny swollen hands touched her small breasts. Her chest was flat as an open road; men loved that about her. She removed her black thong for the guy in the white shirt and tossed it in his direction. He removed a twenty from his pocket and set it down on the stage, where she could see it. She crawled closer to him to let him know she saw it. She removed his glasses and put them in his shirt pocket. She took his face in her fingers and wiggled it across her skin beneath her fishnet shirt. She felt his pointy nose and wet mouth brush against her nipples. She felt his slick forehead leave a greasy film on her rib cage. She loosened her bun and allowed her black hair to smack her cheeks. She watched the man's expression slide from guilt to anger, as if she'd just become his eleven-year-old niece.

"There's more where that came from," she said, tossing him her best prepubescent smile.

You should have used the song I suggested.

He said: "You should come talk to me after this song." He placed a single red carnation on the stage in front of her. She didn't look at it, but she knew it was there.

"One more song and then I'll come," she answered. Her fingers lingered on her abdomen but she wanted to scratch her arms. The itch was back.

He said: "You have the best breasts."

She stared up at the lights that opened her like a bone. She was lighter than air.

AVA STANDER is the editor of the *New York Times* best seller *Dirty Blonde*, as well as the creative director and researcher of the book *Cobain: Unseen*. Born and raised in London, England, she now lives in Los Angeles.

poppy love
by Ava Stander

I am done with heroin, but heroin is not done with me. The scars on my body may be fading, but the scars on my liver bear the evidence of my addiction. Sharing needles has infected me with hepatitis C.

The treatment I undergo for the twelve months after quitting is referred to as "chemo lite." I wake drenched in sweat with what feels like the flu times a thousand. Days and nights are spent with my head hanging over the toilet bowl, retching bile. I am a piece of hot coal lying on the cool tile floor. My skin is radioactive. My bones itch so badly it feels as though they are infested with fleas. My body's covered in wounds and scabs from scratching myself so viciously. I look like a leper. Dozens of times I think of getting loaded but I'm too stubborn to cash in the freedom I won back from the poppy.

Depression is a side effect and I catch it bad. I am unrecognizable to myself. I am reduced to a wretched, polluted amoeba unable to move from the couch. I enter suicide chat rooms online, only to be told to leave by other chatters because I am "too depressing." I plunge deeper and deeper into an abyss of desolation. All the medication and therapy in the world can't put me back together again.

It is an awful Southern Californian sunny day. The sky above me is blue, my heart is black. I have been at work for half an hour when I hear my own voice inside my head.

Drive your car off Mulholland.

I grab my purse and get into my car. Just as I escaped from the bonds of my addiction, so would I escape from this depression the past year of chemo bestowed upon me. I stop at a gas station to fill up my tank, to guarantee a fiery finish. Chain-smoking my way up the winding road of Laurel Canyon, I pass Houdini's property. I envision him immersed in a tank of water weighted down by chains, and the image won't leave my head. I drive along the serpentine twists and turns of Mulholland Drive for an hour looking for the perfect spot. I don't want to launch myself into oncoming traffic or land on anyone's house. After all, I have a conscience and don't want to hurt anyone else. I find a lookout post on a dangerous curve, with a stretch of dirt road a thousand feet long leading up to a guardrail. In it is an opening wide enough for my Honda to fit through.

I step out, into the majestic scenery of the Hollywood Hills. It is eerily quiet, as though the volume of the city had been muted. I look down and satisfy myself that the drop is sufficiently steep. I know the only way I am getting off this cliff is in a body bag.

I reverse my car to give me a good running start, but just as I reach the edge I press on the brake. I repeat this twice. My heart is punching against my rib cage. Catching my breath, fighting back tears, hands clenched around the steering wheel, I see a legal pad on the passenger seat. Should I write a goodbye note? Why bother, what I'm about to do really needs no explanation. It's a bold statement in and of itself. I'm finally going to get well. I close my eyes, put my foot on the gas, and floor it. The car takes flight, but instead of nosediving it hovers in midair for a split second, and that's when I know something has gone horribly wrong . . .

Addiction is like love. You don't know when it enters the room but you sure know when it exits. Hedonistic, idealistic, nihilistic, and above all dangerous. Have you ever been so parched that you feel like your esophagus is lined with cotton? You know that your only salvation is water, that cold, magical elixir pouring down your throat, trickling into every cell in your body. Nothing else will quench that burning need, nothing except water.

I'm not looking for God. I want to be God. I want to feel like God. Godly. My proclivity for heroin is unmatched. My affliction has been my driving force for a decade. I have traded in the glamour of Hollywood for the squalor of MacArthur Park. A neighborhood on the western edge of downtown Los Angeles, it centers around a large grassy park. Working-class Mexican and Central South American families populate the surrounding neighborhood. And then there are the undesirables. Gang members, petty criminals, ex-cons, prostitutes, pimps, the mentally sick, and the drug addicted.

I have disappeared into this milieu, only a few miles from my previous life. But the twenty-minute bus ride may as well be the distance from the earth to the moon. I left everything behind without batting an eyelash. Adapting to my surroundings. Indifferent to the consequences.

The Casa Sonora, a seedy motel a few blocks from the park that rents only to lost souls, will be the last permanent roof over my head until I get clean. My small room contains bulky, antiquated wooden furniture, carpet worn thin as cloth, and stark white walls. Cheaply framed Van Goghs that I rip out of a dime store calendar offset the funereal atmosphere.

A local gangbanger crack dealer, Spooky, sometimes stows away in my room to smoke so his homies don't find out he's getting high on his own supply. He rarely says a word. The only evidence of his presence in my room is the noise the lighter makes when he lights up. He likes that I never pester him for a hit. He is gorgeous. The ladies swoon.

On what will become my last night here, Spooky's ex-girlfriend ambushes me in the hallway. In a murderous rage, she grabs me by the throat and drags me to the banister to throw me over. I fall back into the wall and make myself as heavy as possible. When she realizes she can't lift me she unleashes punches to the back of my head, stomach, torso, and chest. I am so terrified I can't scream for help. She spits at me. I keep my head down to safeguard my face. She tries to push me down the seven flights of stairs. She tries to pry my hands open but I grip the railing with every ounce of strength I can muster and she's powerless. I don't want to die this way, murdered by someone else's hands. It is my life, mine to destroy and no one else's, and I want to live. I figure that everybody has to take a beating at some point and this is my turn. But I'll be damned if I'll let this mindless Medusa take my life. Her kicks are like a baseball bat on the side of my body. She's screaming vitriolic obscenities inches from my face. No one comes out to check on the commotion. I cling onto the railing with all the life force within me. My mouth tastes metallic. My sweat feels sticky. I look down—it's blood. Her screaming pierces my eardrums like daggers. Neither of us notice my gigantic ex-con neighbor, Cadillac, until he pulls her off me and throws her against the wall.

"You better watch yourself, bitch," she snarls, and takes off. My eyes are squeezed shut. I don't dare move. I jump at the tap on my shoulder. Cadillac asks if I need help getting back to my room. I assure him I'm okay. He treads softly back to his room as if he knows the slightest movement may cause me more pain. After an eternity, I let go of the railing. I crawl back to my room on my hands and knees, and once inside I lie down against the door and curl up in the fetal position. I fall asleep counting my bloodstained tears as they soak into the carpet. I dream of floating on waves, suspended between a starless night and the deep blue sea.

The Van Goghs frown upon me in the morning as I throw

some clothes and toiletries into my junkie luggage—a black trash bag. Miraculously, my face doesn't bear any traces of last night's homicidal attack, but the rest of me feels like I did ten rounds with Muhammad Ali. When I reach the foyer I picture myself splattered on the snow-white marble floor. My blood pouring out into the street. It sends shivers through me as though someone walked over my grave. Scoring is the first order of the day. The monster is awake and it's demanding to be fed.

I've been thrown out of every other motel in the area for nonpayment or drama. There's nowhere left to go. I'm living like a feral alley cat, in the basement of an abandoned building. I have dragged a chair and table out of the trash through the hole in the chain-link fence. The perfect setup for the day's only activities. Cooking up, shooting up, and nodding out. I can't risk being on the streets during the day. I have racked up a number of felonies and nonappearances in court, and the local cops know my face. I may as well be wearing a scarlet "A" for Addict. I'm an arrest waiting to happen. Next time I'm stopped I'm going to the pokey. And that's a hell I don't want to visit because there I would have to kick. There's no dope in jail. And that is what I fear the most.

I cop before sunrise, walking through the side streets and back alleys, passing the cardboard dwellers and sleeping bodies on the ground. After my early-morning dose of stress and anxiety, relief and gratitude pour over me once back in the safety of my living and dying room. Unwrapping the balloon takes a small forever. Who wraps these, Mexican midgets with tiny midget fingers? At long last I get the dope into the spoon. I squirt a bit of water over it and heat the mixture with my lighter to dissolve it. My needle is as dull as one of the nails used to crucify Jesus, so I sharpen it on a matchbox. The amber nectar has cooled, and I draw it into the syringe. I have to swing my arm around like a windmill to get my blood pumping. Otherwise I won't hit a vein and will end up looking like a bleeding pincushion.

I caress my arm in search of a vessel to carry me to oblivion. One pops up and my teeth clench as the needle goes in. I pull back the plunger and watch my blood blooming like flowers in the syringe.

The shades of my blood are ever-changing, depending on time of day, body temperature, and circumstances. I label the crimson and red hues each time they appear in the needle, like tubes of lipstick. *Scarlet Harlot, Better Red than Dead, Poppy Love, The Bride Wore Crimson, Devil's Magenta, Fuchsia Fox.* Mine are more romantic sounding than the names the makeup companies use. I push the plunger down, and before the needle's even out of my vein, my breathing slows and my heartbeat is barely there. I am God. I want to live forever. I don't want to die, I just want to stay high. My chin hits my chest. Let the drooling commence. A movie plays in my mind's eye, directed by David Lynch. In it I'm fronting a rhythm & blues band, wearing gold lamé pedal pushers with a matching gold jacket and nothing underneath. My tiny breasts make a cameo appearance every so often. The backing vocalists are horrified. I'm singing at 33 rpm, though I should be at 45 rpm. Swaying on my gold five-inch stilettos like a wounded bull in a bullfight, bleeding out as it struggles to stay standing. The audience below waits for me to keel over and die, or for the song to end, to put them and me out of our collective misery. I can't keep up but I carry on butchering the classic James Brown tune.

> *I feel good,*
> *I knew that I would, now*
> *I feel good,*
> *I knew that I would, now*
> *So good,*

So good,
I got you.

I feel someone's presence down here with me. I lift my two-hundred-pound head up off my chest. A silhouette stands in the doorway, backlit by the unrelenting sun.

"Girl, I would knock but you ain't got a door. Girl, you in there?" The Marilyn Monroe voice belongs to Angela, a six-foot-tall Nicaraguan ladyboy. She's stunning; black cat eyes, black shiny shoulder-length hair, cherry-red lips, and legs that put any supermodel's to shame. Angela just got out from doing three months in jail. She's still in the men's clothing the county gave her upon her release. I'm annoyed she found my hideout but I try not to show it. There aren't any steps and she has to jump down onto the dirt floor.

She glances at our surroundings and asks, "How you livin'?"

"Large."

We howl with laughter and hug.

"Preciosa, give me something to wear and some whorepaint. I need to get out of this boy drag. I'm keeping a low profile until I go into this drug program in the desert. I got bumped up their waiting list cause of the SIDA. You should come with me."

SIDA is Spanish for AIDS.

"Don't be a vibe slayer," I say, raising an eyebrow and giving her my best stink eye.

"I heard about the beating you got. You should get out of the neighborhood. This place ain't no joke. Get yourself in a program. Don't you know there's nothing but hope for us until we're six feet under?"

"Hope is for suckers, Angela. And frankly, I would rather get the shit kicked out of me again than go to rehab."

Angela keeps up a steady stream of mindless chatter. I stop

listening. The only way to get rid of her is to give her what she wants. I want to go back to nodding in solitude. My trash bag's hidden behind some rotting cardboard boxes. In exchange for clothes, she gives me a balloon. We prepare a shot. I fix first, before letting her use my rig. She has no problem hitting a vein. They're thick as ropes; they're all that's left of her masculinity. I'm jealous of her veins. The Marilyn voice has slowed to a purr. I light a cigarette for her and put it between her lips. Eyes closed, she smiles with every part of her face as if this were the kindest gesture anyone has ever made toward her. The first shot of dope's always the best after a period of abstinence. The cigarette falls onto the trash bag lying between her feet, and I pick it up and finish it in a few drags.

I come to some time later. It's dark and quiet. I could be the last surviving person on earth. All of Angela's happy horseshit about getting clean keeps echoing around inside my skull. I have to obliterate the thoughts. I have to do more dope to forget what I had to do to get the dope. I lead a vampiric existence—out of the sunlight during the day and into the moonlight at night. I only come out at neon. An existence as mediocre and mundane as the bourgeoisie and the nine-to-fivers I detest. My life's become so small you can barely see it under a microscope. Being a dope fiend is a twenty-four-hour-a-day job with no time off and no vacations. And the most dreadful thought of them all: *What am I doing?* That is the one thought I have to kill. I need to end this unwanted moment of clarity. I still have a tiny piece left of Angela's gift. I light a few candles and prepare another shot. Hitting a vein by the flickering light turns into a bloodbath. If the blood coagulates the heroin clogs up and won't go through the tiny opening of the spike. That's a waste I can't afford. A dozen holes later I'm in.

The girl's face staring back at me from my compact is suffering from malnutrition. My skin is diaphanous, I can almost see the bones in the front part of my skull. All I need now is lipstick and I'll look fabulous. It's not in my purse. Probably because its nestled in Angela's faux cleavage. She's an unrepentant thief.

Crouching in the wild overgrown weeds, I poke my head out of the hole in the fence to make sure the coast is clear. At dusk the air reeks of night-blooming jasmine intermingled with exhaust fumes and the infamous smog blanketing the City of Angels. Six to nine is family values time. A sea of bodies flows in and out of the local stores. A pulsating microorganism, the antithesis of the invading scary monsters and super freaks that come out after all the good people have turned in for the night. The hustle and bustle takes away my loneliness.

Waiting for the traffic light to turn green, I see a man and his young son struggling to get a cart up the steps of a building. I met Jose and Jesus selling homemade tamales outside a mini-mall where foot traffic is always heavy. When I was hungry I would stop by, and more often than not they would feed me for free. They were Christian; what Christians should be. Even though I politely decline Jose's numerous invitations to go to church, they are always happy to see me. Even though I am part of the problem, another neighborhood junkie, they don't judge and they don't ask questions.

Jose and I share a love of Pablo Neruda's poems. He told me he wooed his wife Maria by reciting them to her. These sporadic exchanges bring me close to them. Awakening a small desire in me to be "normal" again.

I hurry across the street to help, eager to do something for them for a change. When we get the cart into the lobby, Jose insists I come stay with his family for a couple of nights. My protestations fall on deaf ears. I follow them up the three flights of stairs and Jose opens the door into a small living room. The aroma of garlic and freshly cooked chicken fills the apartment. It feels like home. Maria, his wife, comes out of the kitchen and puts her arms around me.

"I'm so glad to meet you, those two have told me so much about you," she says, still holding me. She has an exquisite Roman nose, hazel eyes, and white skin. Her hair is pulled back off her face in a chignon. For a brief moment, I'm not a motherless daughter.

Grandma sits in front of the TV. She isn't thrilled. Maria leads me into the kitchen and sits me at the table. Grandma and Jose are arguing in Spanish about me staying. He comes into the kitchen and says, "Don't worry, she's just a frightened old woman who never leaves the house except on Sundays to go to church."

The walls in the small apartment are adorned with saints. It's been years since I've sat down at a table to have a meal. After dinner, Maria hands me of pair of sweats and suggests I take a shower. I do so and rejoin them. Above the television is an ornately framed picture of a saint holding two eyeballs on a plate. I ask Grandma who she is.

"Santa Lucia, the patron saint of the blind. Like you."

I am insulted by her remark, but I soon fall asleep on the couch watching TV. Much later I awake to Grandma covering me up with a blanket. I drift off again.

It's early dawn when the monster begins to stir. I come to. I panic, I have no idea where I am until I hear Grandma snoring gently. The monkey on my back is doing cartwheels on my spine. I feel my way to the bathroom, change back into my clothes, and slither away.

The streets are deserted. The neighborhood is still slumbering. I have an ominous feeling that something's amiss. As I walk down the sidewalk, I notice the same car go past me twice. It's a curb-crawler, circling me like a vulture. He pulls alongside me slowly. When the tinted window rolls down I see a man's face covered in third-degree burns.

"Are you workin'?"

I'm already too sick to turn a trick, and I yell at him to fuck off.

He speeds away. My veins are ravenous. The backs of my legs are being sliced by razors. In the movie *Barbarella* there's a scene where Jane Fonda is tied to a post while a gang of mechanical dollies with sharp teeth bite at her sinewy legs. Now I'm in the leading role. With every step I take my legs grow heavier from the discomfort. I hear footsteps approaching fast. I want to run but I can't. I turn around abruptly. It's a friend from the park that goes by Willie, but I call him Abdullah after the militant character played by Bill Duke in the movie *Car Wash*. He calls me Che Guevara. He says it as one word, *Cheguevara*. Our conversations are almost always political. We are a couple of park-bench revolutionaries. Abdullah needs a gallon of vodka daily.

When I get dopesick my mood turns foul. I let loose a stream of expletives at him for scaring me. Ignoring my outburst, he fills me in on what I've missed during the two days I've spent sleeping. The police did a mass sweep of the area and arrested dozens of people. The neighborhood's hot. I tell him I have to go to the park to find Angela. She'll give me something to tide me over if she has any.

"Angela was picked up this morning," he says sadly.

We reach the park, and Abdullah is right. In the aftermath of the mass arrests nothing is jumping off. Usually at this early hour there are still a few homeless crackheads left. But it's deserted, and they have all scurried off like rats to wherever it is that rats go during daytime. The powers that be have put forth a valiant effort in the war on drugs.

The only ones here are the three wise men, sitting on their usual bench from which they run their own apothecary. They sell every kind of pill imaginable. They are the only African Americans allowed to sell in the park. But they still have to pay taxes to the local gang. The leader, Mr. James, had been a sax player when the jazz clubs were in full swing. He finally kicked his forty-year habit in exchange for a methadone maintenance program. The first time I met him he said to me, "Dope is misery."

In my youthful arrogance I shot back, "Of course it is for YOU, old man."

They make room for me on the bench. Seeing that I am in good hands, Abdullah bids his farewell and leaves for the liquor store. Midway through my tale of woe they begin discussing my financial predicament amongst themselves as if I'm not even there. Finally Mr. James turns to me.

"Because you're a hustla and you always come correct, we have decided to donate the first twenty dollars we make to your cause. This is the only time we'll ever help you out, so don't be gettin' any ideas."

There is a God after all. I thank them profusely and say to Mr. James, "You are a prince among men."

He corrects me: "No, senorita, I'm a king. Now go sit over there. I'm a superstitious fool. This is our place of business and you throw the numbers off."

I do as I am told, but not before he gives me a Klonopin to tide me over. I swallow it immediately.

I lie down in the wet grass a couple hundred yards away from them. My insides are on a slow burn; within the hour they will be boiling over into my abdomen. I can feel my blood pounding against my eardrums. I shut my eyes to stop myself from continuously checking up on the wise men. When you're jonesing, a minute lasts an hour. It's still cool, the fireball in the sky hasn't covered the neighborhood. I'm grateful for the cold chills—the sun always makes me feel worse. I can't take the suspense any longer. I open my eyes to see Mr. James walking toward me. He gives me the money, I thank him again, and I'm gone.

I score behind a dumpster in an alley, half a block from my favorite Laundromat. It's the cleanest one I've ever been in.

Whenever I enter I'm overcome by the scent of detergent. It's intoxicating. And the toilet in the bathroom is pristine, bleached as white as the heavenly clouds. I have actually eaten in there. My works are hidden in the bathroom wall in a hole at ceiling level. I no longer carry paraphernalia just in case the cops stop me. With the balloon safely tucked between my upper gum and cheek, I already feel less nauseous as I begin the walk. All I can think of is the needle going into my vein. The promise of relief, sweet euphoria, waits for me in my celestial white bathroom.

Out of the corner of my eye I see a car peel out from the curb on the other side of the street. Pulling a sharp U-turn, it comes to a stop directly in front of me. I know without looking up who it is. I have to remain calm. Staring at the ground, I continue walking. I have nothing on me anyone can find. All that stands between me and getting well is this cop obstacle. I start praying to a God I don't believe in. The car door opens, obstructing my path.

"Stop right there. Drop the purse, put your arms above your head, and face the wall."

It's Mr. Undercover. He's stopped me on many occasions and is responsible for my only arrest, which got me locked up for three days. Mr. Undercover's one of those hard-boiled film noir detectives. He picks up my purse.

"Is there anything in here I can cut myself on, any needles?"

I must stick to monosyllabic responses. If I swallow the balloon I'll have to wait for hours to shit it out. And like every junkie I have a serious case of constant constipation, a side effect of opiates. He finishes his search of my purse and hands it back to me.

"Well, Miss Hype, looks like I'm going to have to let you go."

I thank him, and the balloon falls onto my tongue. He catches a glimpse of the bright yellow color.

"What's that in your mouth?"

"Chewing gum," I answer, trying to swallow it. My throat's so dry it won't go down.

"Spit it out, NOW!"

He pulls down my bottom lip. The pain's horrific. I think he's ripped it off my face. Tears shoot out of my eyes. Stifling a scream, my mouth opens up and out plops the balloon onto the ground.

"You're under arrest."

Coming down the street are Jose, Maria, Jesus, and Grandma, dressed in their Sunday best, on their way to church. They avoid looking in my direction. I know they are averting their gaze to spare me the indignity of being handcuffed in public. Still, Jesus turns and waves at me, tugging his father's hand. Jose pulls him forward.

On the drive to the station, Mr. Undercover gets chatty. I'm not in the mood to talk. I keep wishing he would give me back my dope and drive me to my Laundromat. He won't shut up. He says drugs are just a platform for politicians to get easy votes. *Dare to Keep Kids off Drugs* is a scaremongering tactic, a lame slogan on T-shirts. Narcotics should be legal. Only pregnant users should be arrested. Addicts are only killing themselves. The CIA is responsible for flooding the ghettos with cheap cocaine to fund the Contras. This is not what he signed up for. In hindsight this all makes sense—when his division makes international headlines for corruption.

When he's done with his monologue, I ask why he won't let me go if this is such a charade.

"I got a job to do, paperwork to fill out," he replies sarcastically. We finally arrive at the dreaded cop shop. I ask Mr. Undercover if I can have one last smoke. He uncuffs me, takes a cigarette out of the packet in my purse, and lights it.

"Why are you a junkie?" he asks. I envision the scene from *The Wild One* where Johnny's asked, "What are you rebelling against?" to which he replies, "What have you got?"

With a sweeping dramatic hand gesture I declare, "Because

of all this."

Without missing a beat he says, "That's just not good enough."

My Marlon Brando moment is ruined.

Sitting in the cell like a wounded animal, I recollect an argument I had with my mother in my early teens.

"It's my life to destroy," I had hissed at her.

"You can't handle freedom."

Cold turkey is taking a hold of me. The Klonopin that Mr. James gave me helps me doze off.

I'm in a holding cell inside the women's correctional facility at the Twin Towers jail in downtown Los Angeles. We call them Twisted Towers. I want to scream but I'm afraid I'll vomit. It's an infraction here in the catacombs that will get you a beatdown. There are thirty of us squashed into a sardine can made for twenty. I lie on the floor wishing that the physical pain would kill me. Wishing these feelings would kill me. I am rotting from the inside out. My guts feel like an abattoir. The symptoms of my soul sickness. The agony that stems from my heroin addiction. It's all that remains alive within me. It's all there is. I want to smash my head against the concrete floor. My skin is on fire, my every pore is being torched. My eyes are swimming in battery acid. Please, someone; please, Mr. Policeman with the gun, come in and open fire, please kill me. Put me out of my misery. For I know that even this torture I'm enduring won't stop me from going back to the poppy at the first opportunity. I'm not a victim, I'm a volunteer. I am a junkie, a bottomless pit of despair and desperation. My dreams, desires, and wishes, my hopes and ambitions all cooked up in the spoon. Lying next to me is another girl in the same shape I'm in. She reaches out to me and we hold hands.

It's five a.m. and I am on the toilet. I haven't pulled my regulation blues all the way down to my ankles, instead they rest on my thighs. I want to appear as if I'm just sitting here, because what I'm really doing is taking a shit. Even though the correctional officers are busy, they can see me. I flush immediately, so the smell doesn't linger. I wipe myself quickly. And flush again. My humiliation is palpable. It fills the tiny cell. I take a seat on the steel desk attached to the wall. A slither of bulletproof glass doubles as a window. I realize all that I have taken for granted as I gaze upon the hills.

The car plummets through trees and bushes, finally landing on a small precipice with a sonic crash. Smoke pours from the hood. I wait for the explosion that will blow me to bits, but after a couple of minutes, it fizzles out. Reality hits me. Not only am I still alive, but a fate far worse than death has befallen me. I am now carless in Los Angeles. Tears of rage lash down my face. How is it possible for one to launch oneself off a decent-size cliff and survive? The doors are jammed shut. I hurl myself out of the open window and lay sobbing on the moist ground. I want to crawl away and hide forever. It is pathetic. There is no way humanly possible of making it back up to the road. I have to call for help. I dial my friend Marie two thousand miles away in Chicago. I explain the quandary I'm in. Her words, so loving and compassionate, make me feel like an even bigger piece of shit. She is thinking logically, and calls 911. The EMTs find me almost an hour later, and strap me into a flexible stretcher, encasing my head in a contraption that prevents me from seeing anything. All I need is a ball gag and I could be the star of my own S&M movie.

The noise of the helicopter is getting closer. As it lifts me into the air, I start to spin round and round like a whirling dervish. I am pulled inside, the blinders removed, and I gaze into the face of a rather handsome medical worker. Another time, another place, I would have asked for his number. I apologize to him for wasting his time when there are others who really are sick and in need of his help. He holds my hand as I sob my way to the hospital.

Once there, I am wheeled into an emergency cubicle. The fury welling up inside me is matched in fervor only by the disappointment at having failed. A social worker informs me that I will be committed to the psychiatric unit; she asks who she can call for me. The idea of seeing those I cherish fills me with dread. She hands me a pen and paper, and reluctantly I write down some numbers. Before long, my friends start to arrive. I don't want to look at them, but my neck brace makes it impossible to turn away. The combination of painkillers and physical discomfort sends me off on a belligerent diatribe.

"I'm going to keep trying until I get it right!" I yell at them. It's cruel and spiteful. In their shoes I would've suggested a .357 Magnum for my next attempt.

My mother is the last to visit me. She is told it was an accident. I can never tell her the truth. She would be devastated to know that her only child was going to leave her all alone. She is frail and old, quietly crying over me. She was right. I can't handle freedom.

It is then, when I am faced with the anguish and sorrow I have caused to the ones I love, that I am able to take responsibility for what I have done. Responsibility is love. And I want to fall in love again. During my years in the heroin wilderness I lost my dignity, my integrity, and my self-respect. I thought that freedom meant having no ties to anyone, no possessions and no responsibility. When I was loaded there was a ten-foot wall of cotton candy between me and the world, shielding me from sadness, hopelessness, and pain. I was in my own nebula. And I didn't realize until it was too late that the sugar walls had closed in and I was trapped, a prisoner of my euphoria. Just another slave to the poppy. There is no freedom in death. I lie in the hospital bed, bound tightly by the splints and bandages, with an overwhelming rage to live.

ALSO IN THIS SERIES:

THE MARIJUANA CHRONICLES

Marijuana is the everyman drug. Teenagers surreptitiously toke on it, politicians refuse to inhale it and even your mum and dad have had a go. The Marijuana Chronicles presents tales of the weird, wonderful and just plain stoned from some of the coolest most chilled out writers around. From drug busts to recipes, this is the stoner's definitive literary bible.

Featuring brand-new stories by Joyce Carol Oates, Lee Child, Linda Yablonsky, Jonathan Santlofer, Thad Ziolkowski, Raymond Mungo, Cheryl Lu-Lien Tan, Edward M. Gómez, Philip Spitzer, Dean Haspiel, Maggie Estep, Amanda Stern, Bob Holman, Rachel Shteir, Abraham Rodriguez, Jan Heller Levi, and Josh Gilbert.

PAPERBACK AVAILABLE FROM APRIL 2014

EBOOK AVAILABLE NOW AT:

WWW.AMZN.TO/H1MBHL (KINDLE)
WWW.BIT.LY/17XMTAE (EPUB)